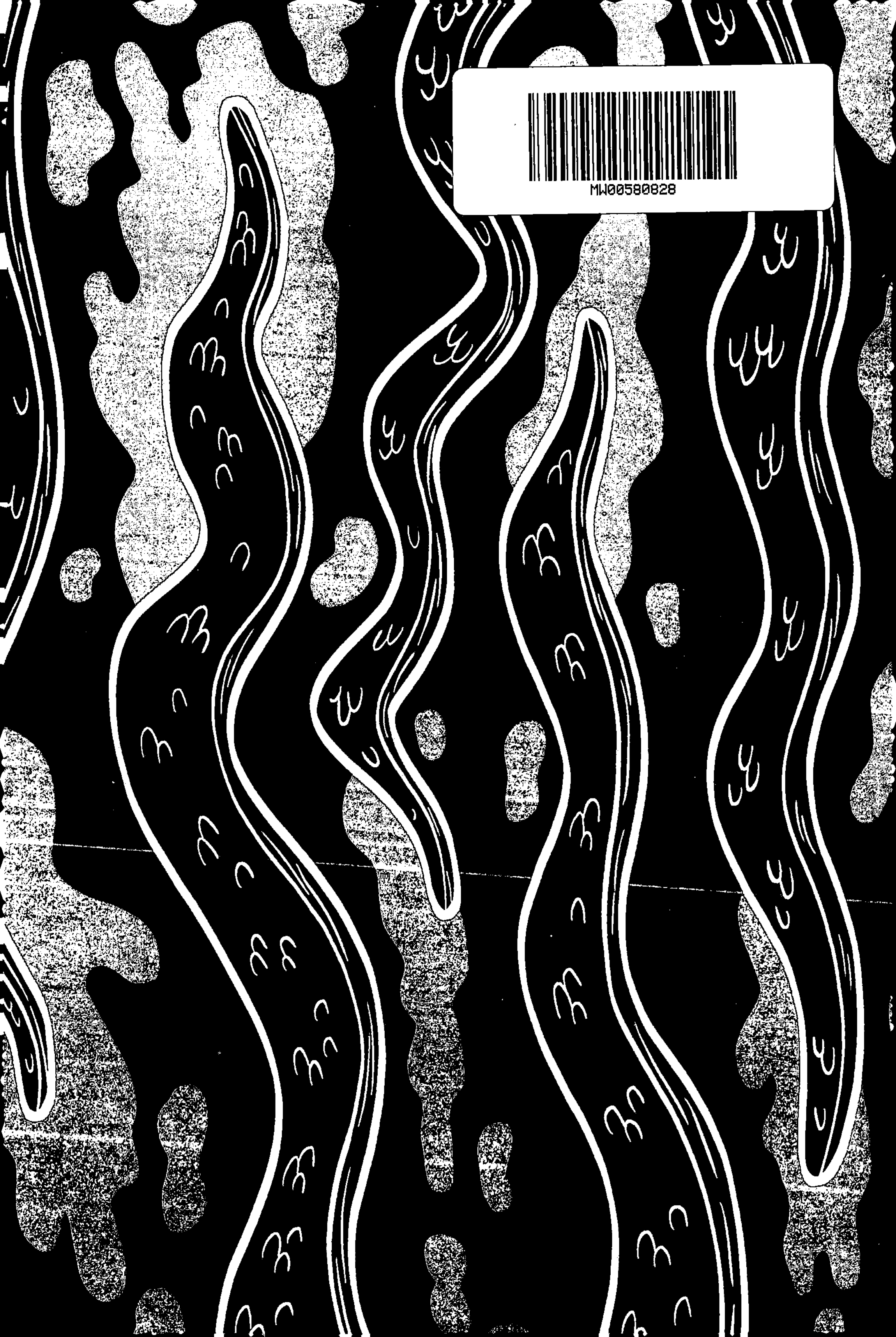

BOYS WEEKEND

BOYS WEEKEND

MATTIE LUBCHANSKY

PANTHEON BOOKS, NEW YORK

This is a work of fiction. Names, characters, places, and incidents either are the product of the author's imagination or are used fictitiously. Any resemblance to actual persons, living or dead, events, or locales is entirely coincidental.

 Published in the United States by Pantheon Books, a division of Penguin Random House LLC, New York, and distributed in Canada by Penguin Random House Canada Limited, Toronto.

Pantheon Books and colophon are registered trademarks of Penguin Random House LLC.

Library of Congress Cataloging-in-Publication Data
Names: Lubchansky, Matt, author, artist.
Title: Boys weekend / Mattie Lubchansky.
Description: First edition. New York: Pantheon Books, 2023.
Series: Pantheon graphic library
Identifiers: LCCN 2022029680 (print). LCCN 2022029681 (ebook).
ISBN 9780593316719 (hardcover). ISBN 9780593316733 (ebook).
Subjects: LCSH: Transgender people--Comic books, strips, etc.
Bachelor parties--Comic books, strips, etc. Male friendship--Comic books, strips, etc. Cults--Comic books, strips, etc. LCGFT: Horror comics.
Transgender comics. Graphic novels.
Classification: LCC PN6727.L8 B69 2023 (print) | LCC PN6727.L8 (ebook) |
DDC 741.5/973--dc23/eng/20220812
LC record available at https://lccn.loc.gov/2022029680
LC ebook record available at https://lccn.loc.gov/2022029681

www.pantheonbooks.com

Jacket illustration by Mattie Lubchansky
Cover design and illustration by Mattie Lubchansky

Printed in China
First Edition
2 4 6 8 9 7 5 3 1

To the men in my life, whom I love dearly.
What's better than this? Guys being dudes.

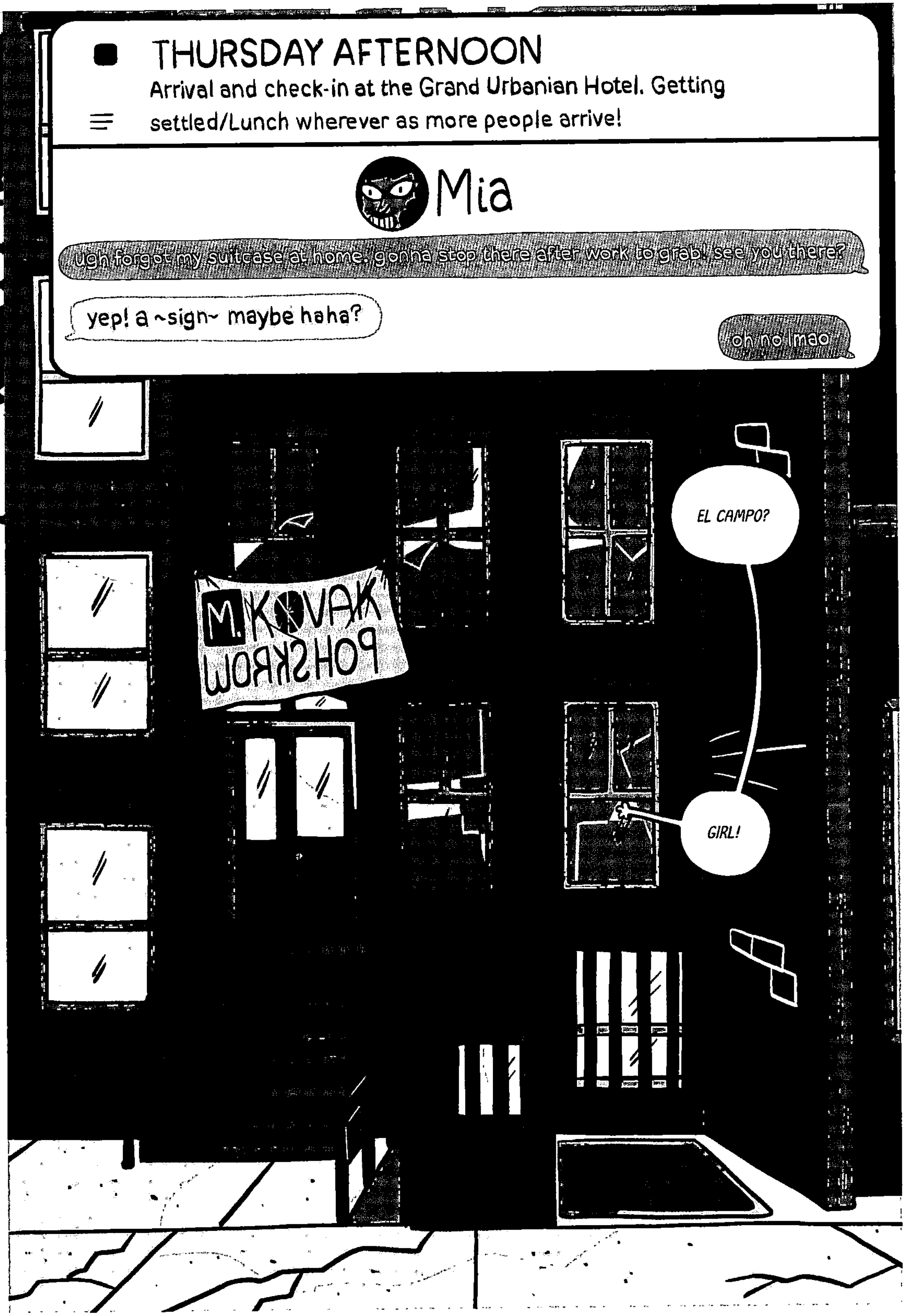
THURSDAY AFTERNOON
Arrival and check-in at the Grand Urbanian Hotel. Getting settled/Lunch wherever as more people arrive!
Mia
ugh forgot my suitcase at home. gonna stop there after work to grab! see you there?
yep! a ~sign~ maybe haha?
oh no lmao
M. KOVAK
EL CAMPO?
GIRL!

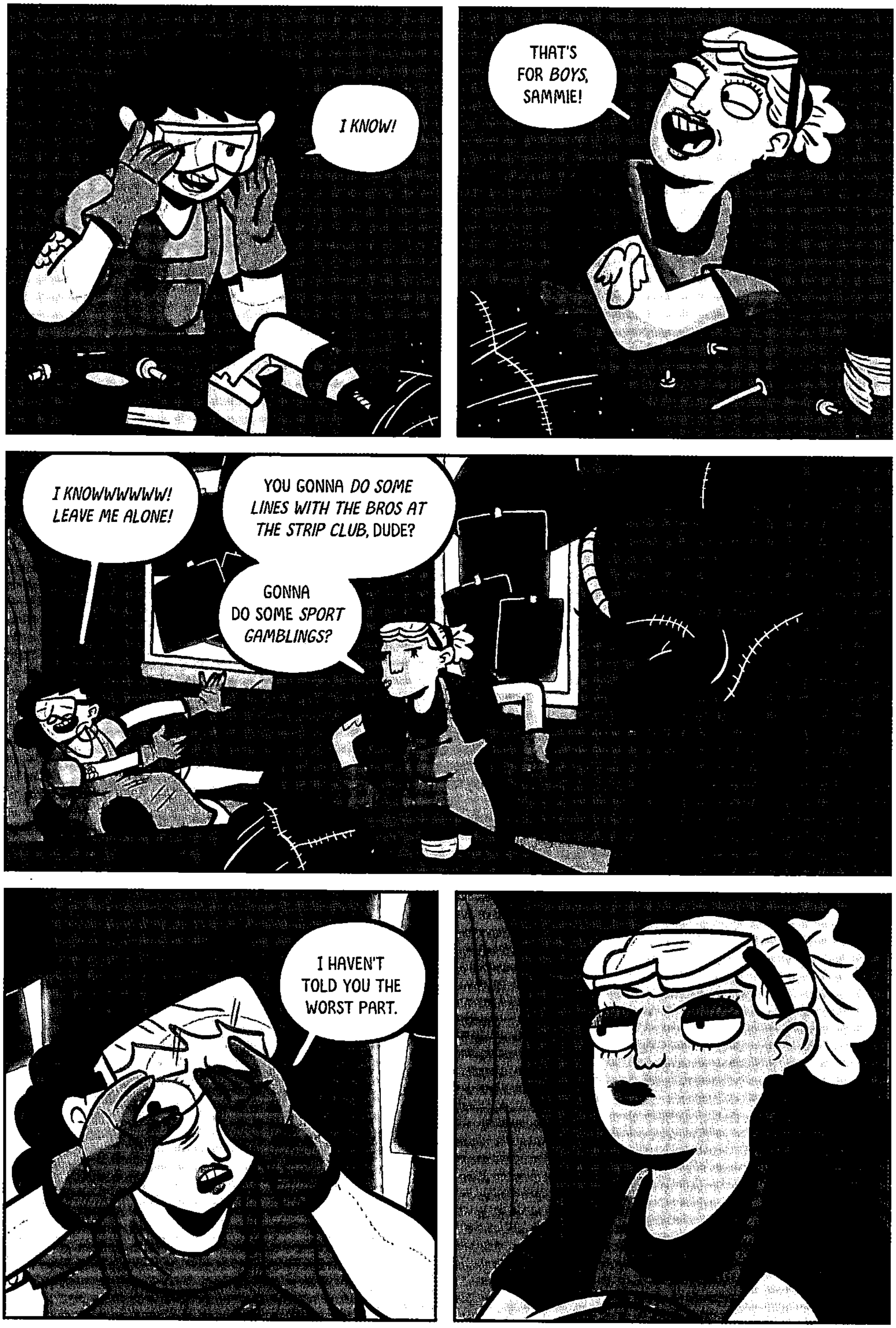
I KNOW!
THAT'S FOR BOYS, SAMMIE!
I KNOWWWWWW! LEAVE ME ALONE!
YOU GONNA DO SOME LINES WITH THE BROS AT THE STRIP CLUB, DUDE?
GONNA DO SOME SPORT GAMBLINGS?
I HAVEN'T TOLD YOU THE WORST PART.

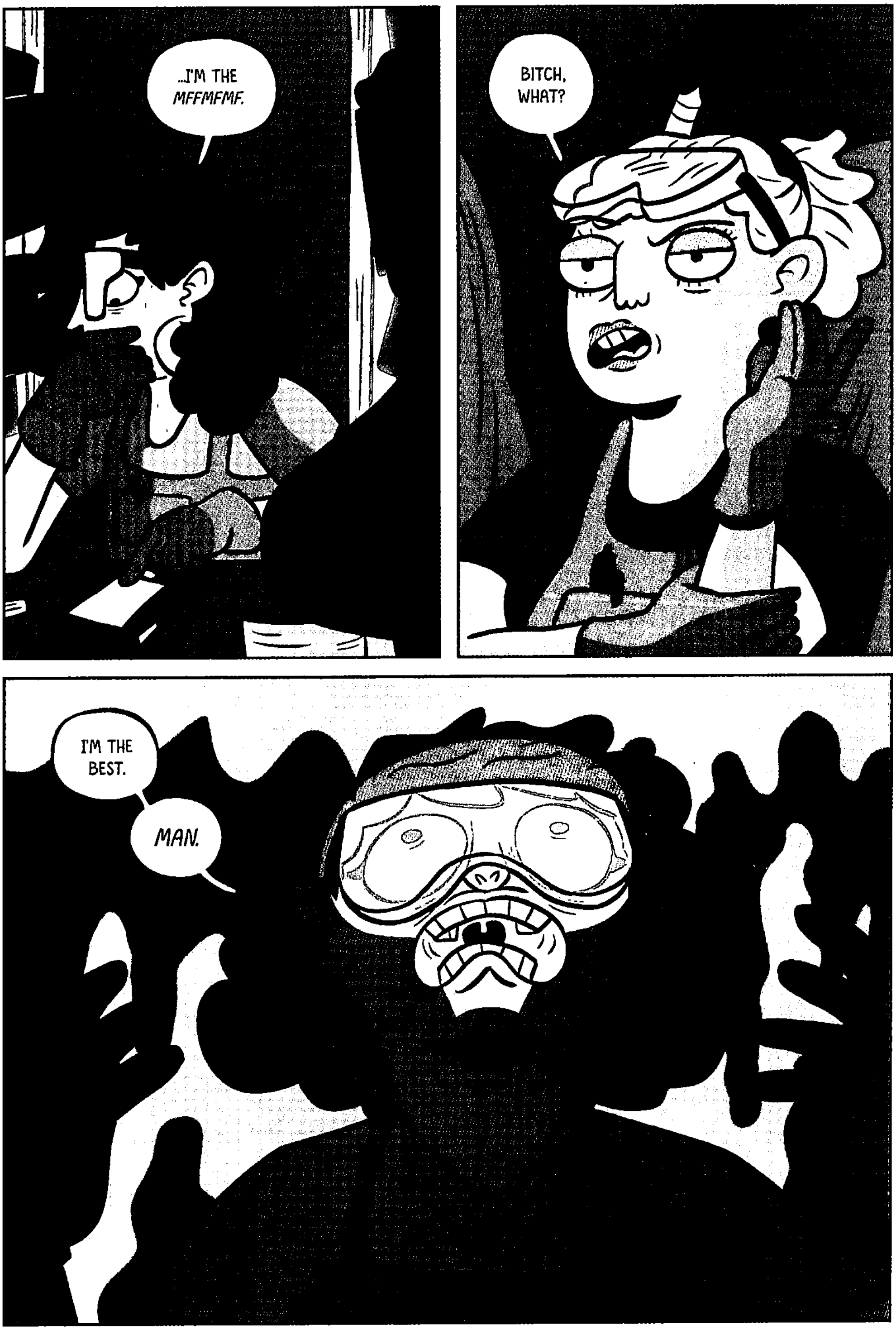

...I'M THE *MFFMFMF.*
BITCH, WHAT?
I'M THE BEST.
MAN.

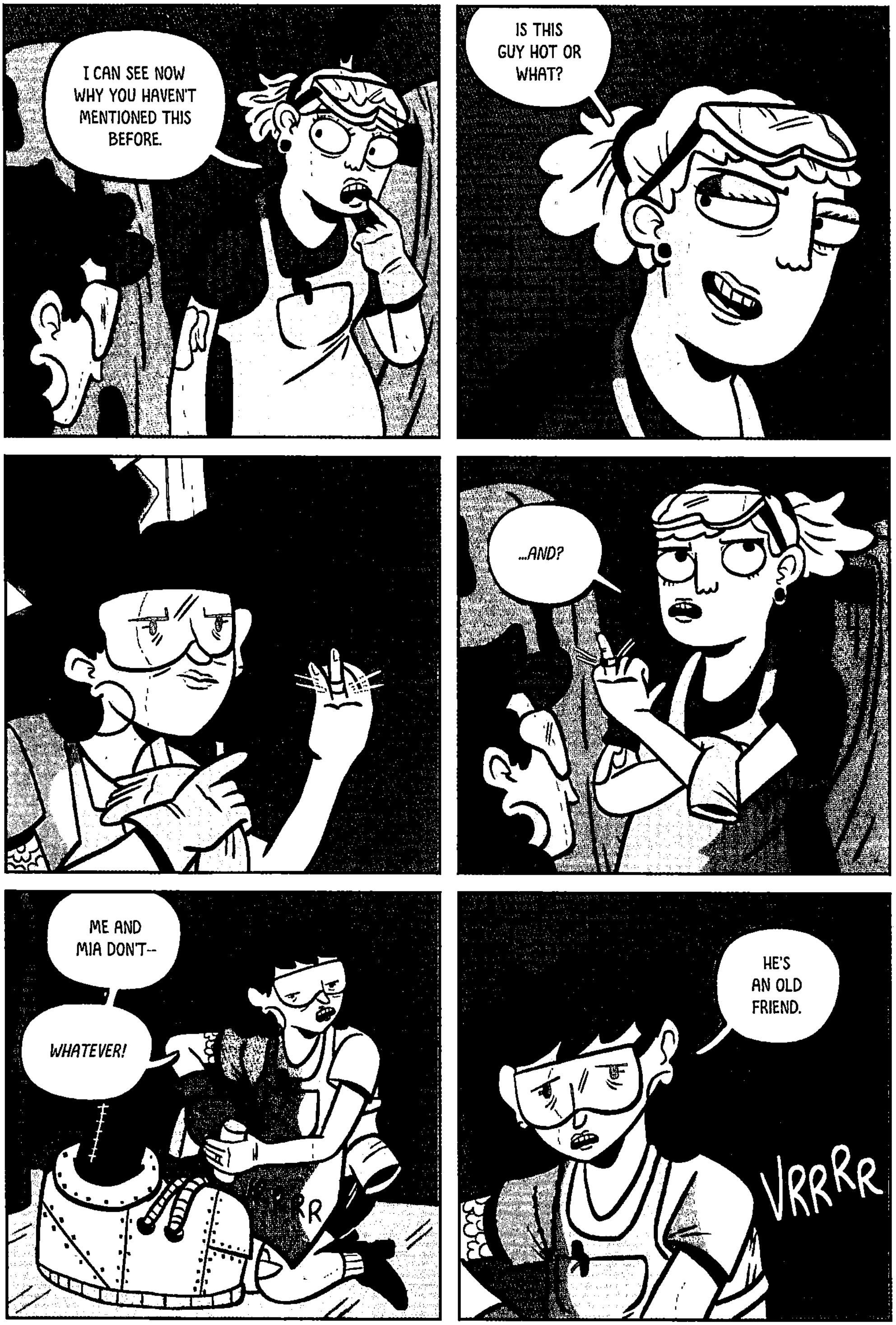
I CAN SEE NOW WHY YOU HAVEN'T MENTIONED THIS BEFORE.
IS THIS GUY HOT OR WHAT?
...AND?
ME AND MIA DON'T--
WHATEVER!
HE'S AN OLD FRIEND.
VRRRR

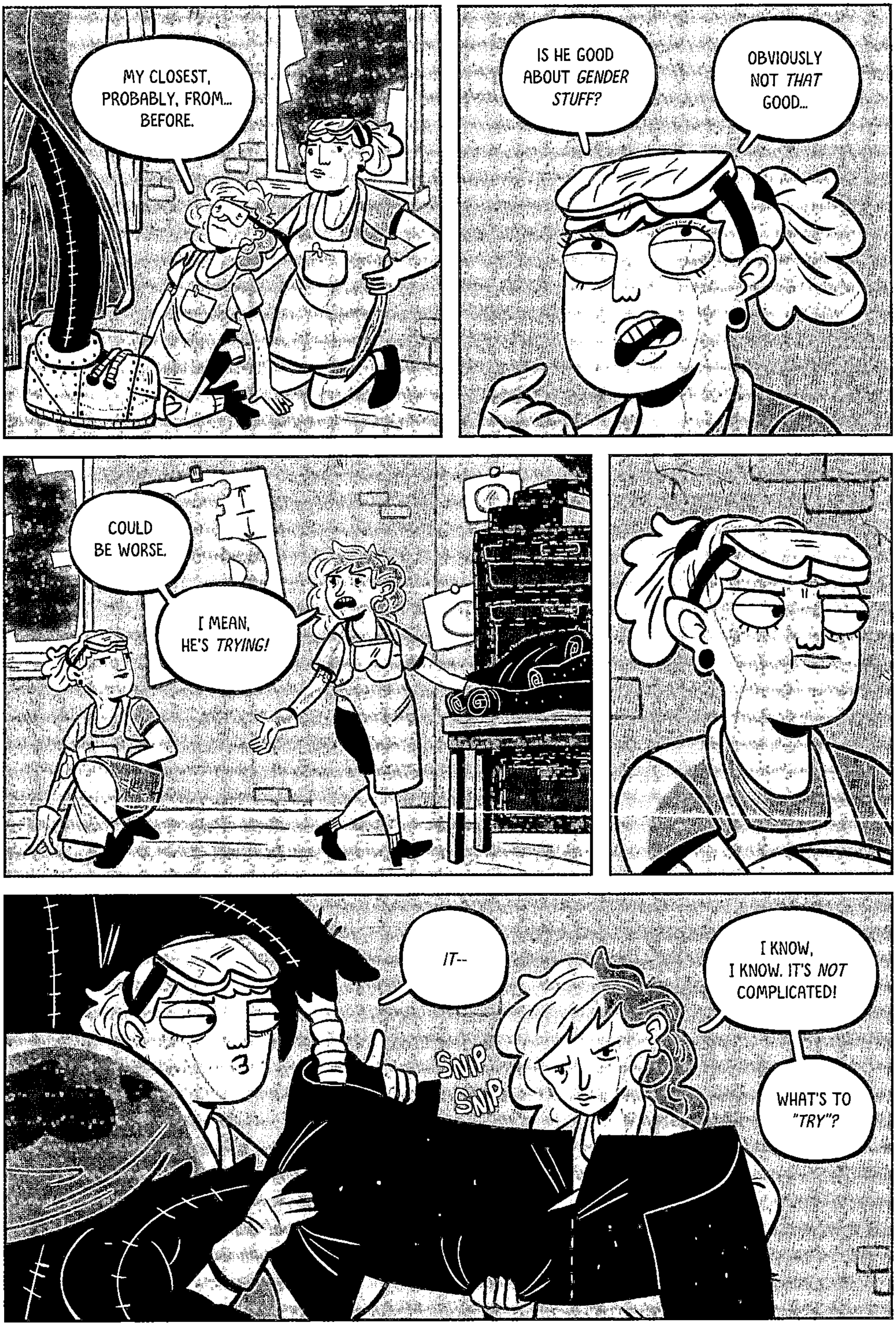
MY CLOSEST, PROBABLY, FROM... BEFORE.
IS HE GOOD ABOUT *GENDER STUFF?*
OBVIOUSLY NOT *THAT* GOOD...
COULD BE WORSE.
I MEAN, HE'S *TRYING!*
IT--
SNIP SNIP
I KNOW, I KNOW. IT'S *NOT* COMPLICATED!
WHAT'S TO *"TRY"*?

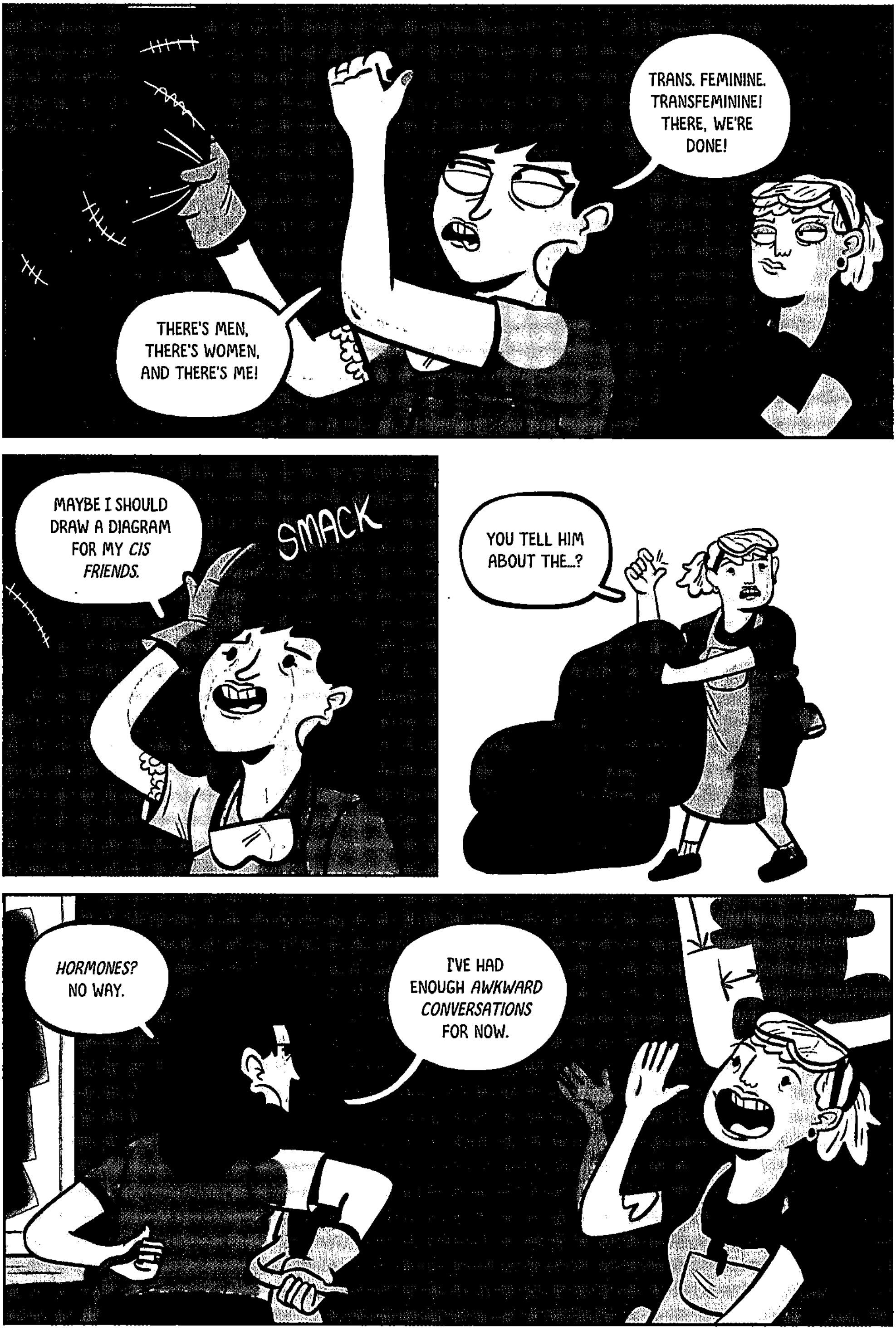
TRANS. FEMININE. TRANSFEMININE! THERE, WE'RE DONE!
THERE'S MEN, THERE'S WOMEN, AND THERE'S ME!
MAYBE I SHOULD DRAW A DIAGRAM FOR MY *CIS FRIENDS.*
SMACK
YOU TELL HIM ABOUT THE...?
HORMONES? NO WAY.
I'VE HAD ENOUGH *AWKWARD CONVERSATIONS* FOR NOW.

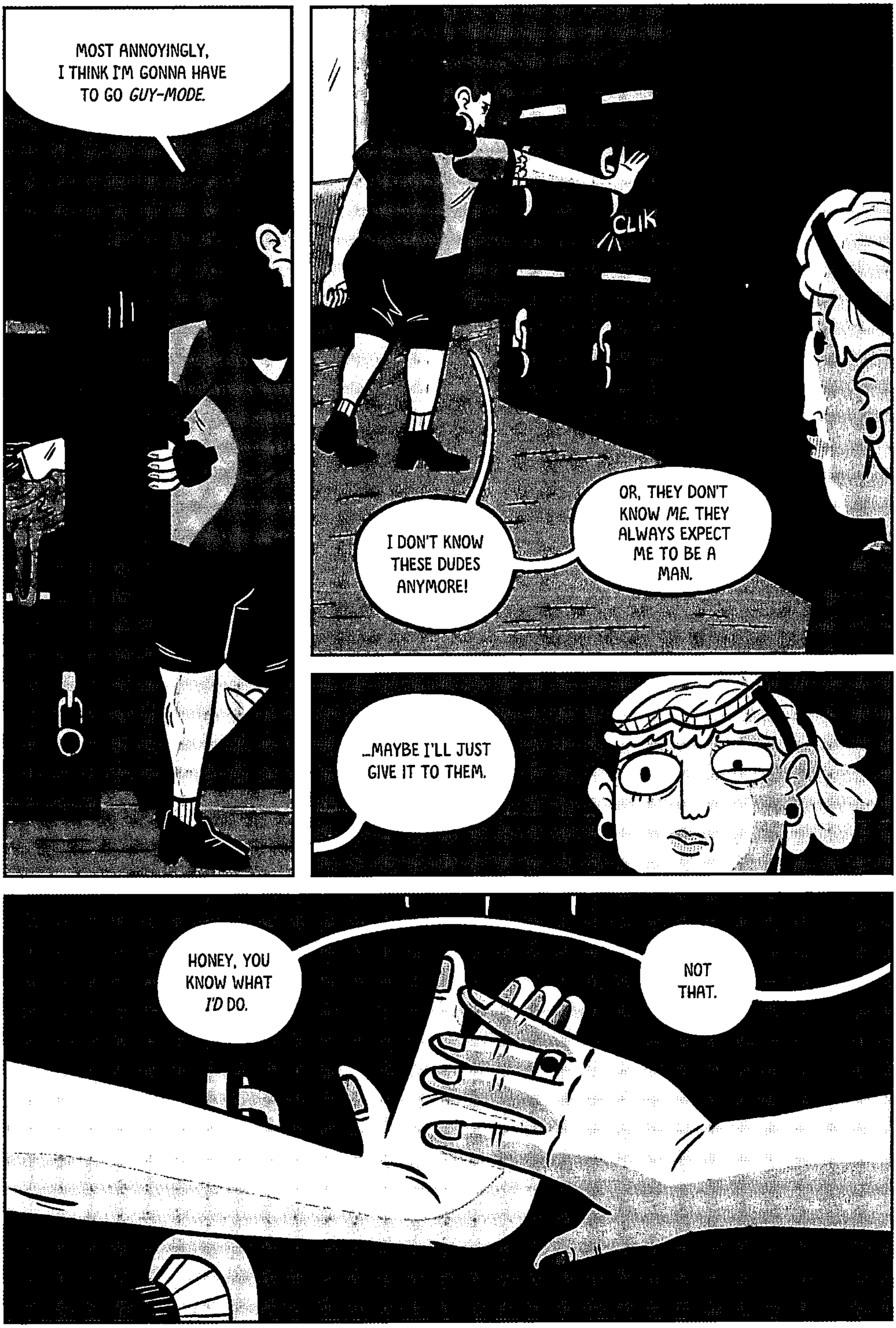
MOST ANNOYINGLY, I THINK I'M GONNA HAVE TO GO *GUY-MODE.*
CLIK
I DON'T KNOW THESE DUDES ANYMORE!
OR, THEY DON'T KNOW *ME.* THEY ALWAYS EXPECT ME TO BE A MAN.
...MAYBE I'LL JUST GIVE IT TO THEM.
HONEY, YOU KNOW WHAT *I'D* DO.
NOT THAT.

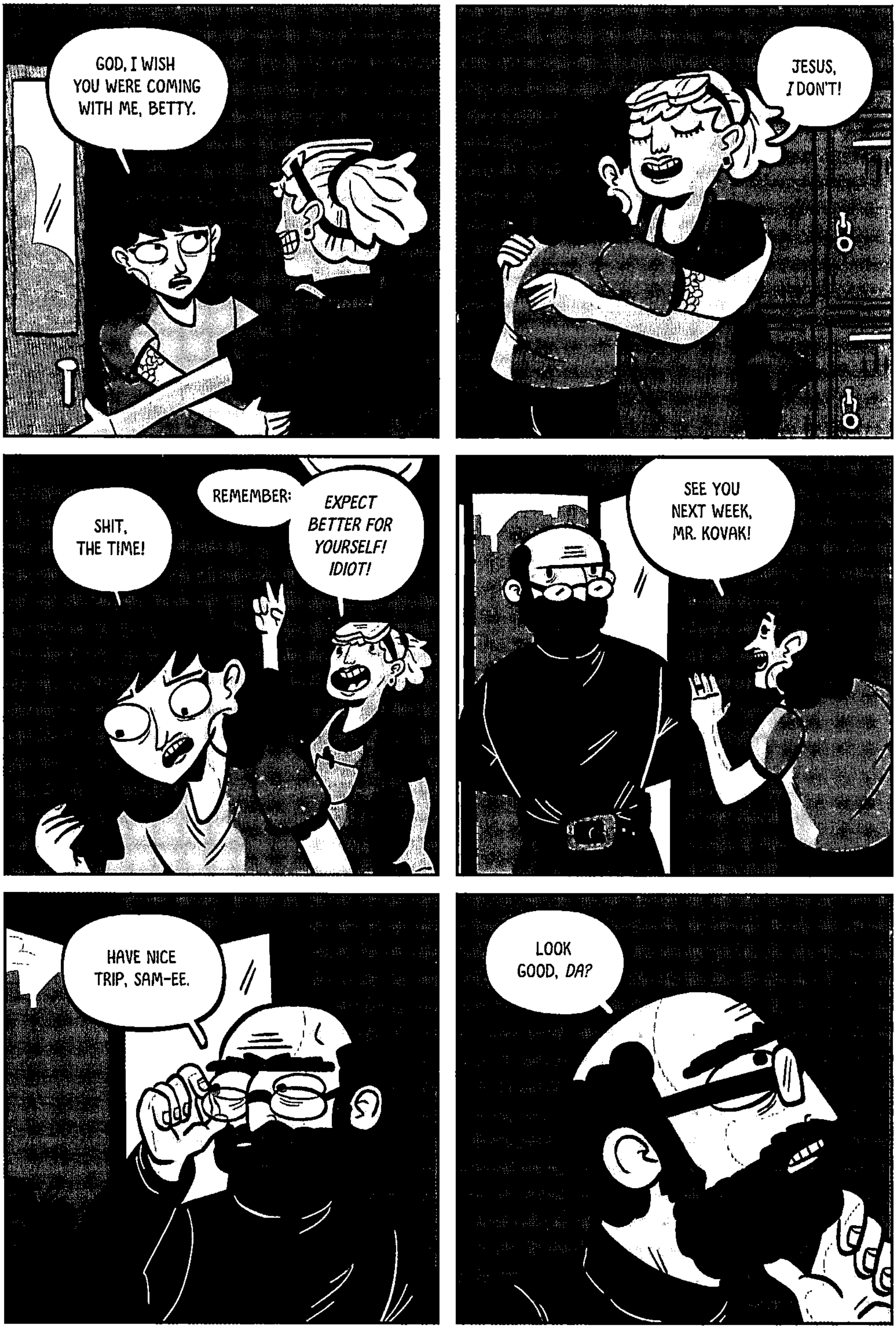
GOD, I WISH YOU WERE COMING WITH ME, BETTY.
JESUS, *I* DON'T!
SHIT, THE TIME!
REMEMBER:
EXPECT BETTER FOR YOURSELF! IDIOT!
SEE YOU NEXT WEEK, MR. KOVAK!
HAVE NICE TRIP, SAM-EE.
LOOK GOOD, *DA?*

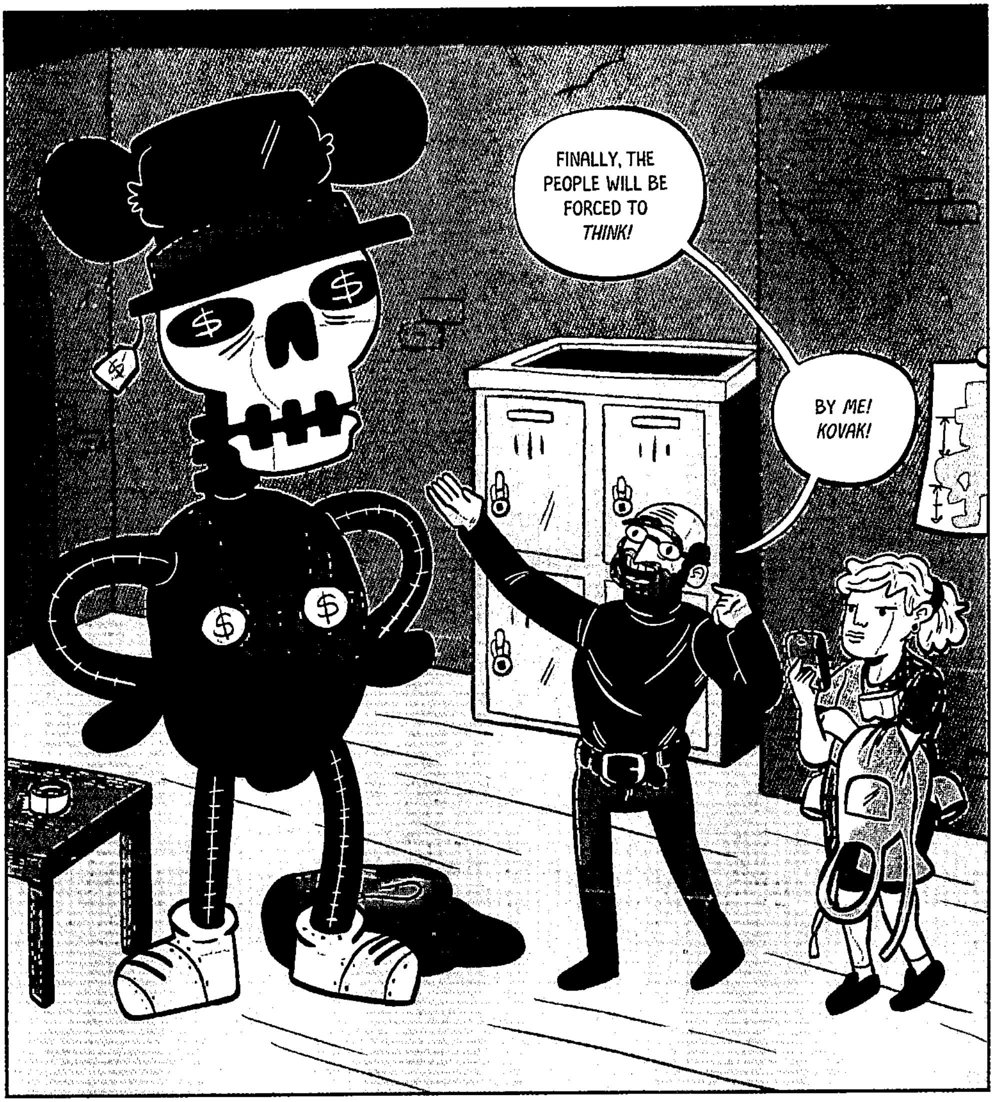
FINALLY, THE PEOPLE WILL BE FORCED TO *THINK!*
BY *ME! KOVAK!*

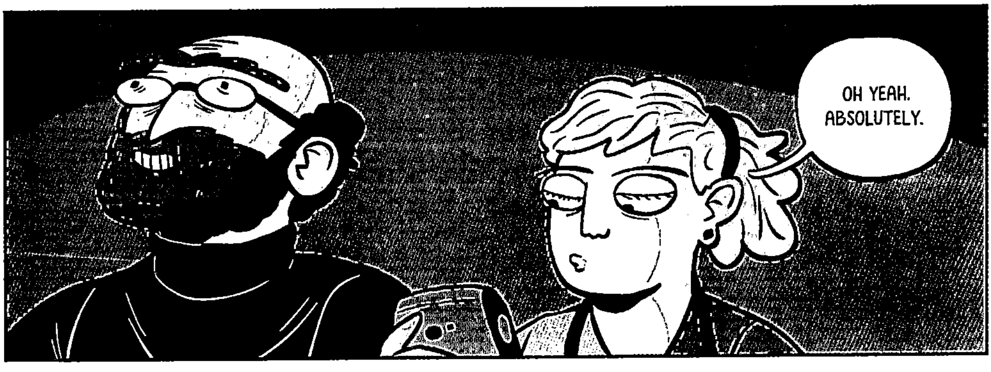
OH YEAH. ABSOLUTELY.

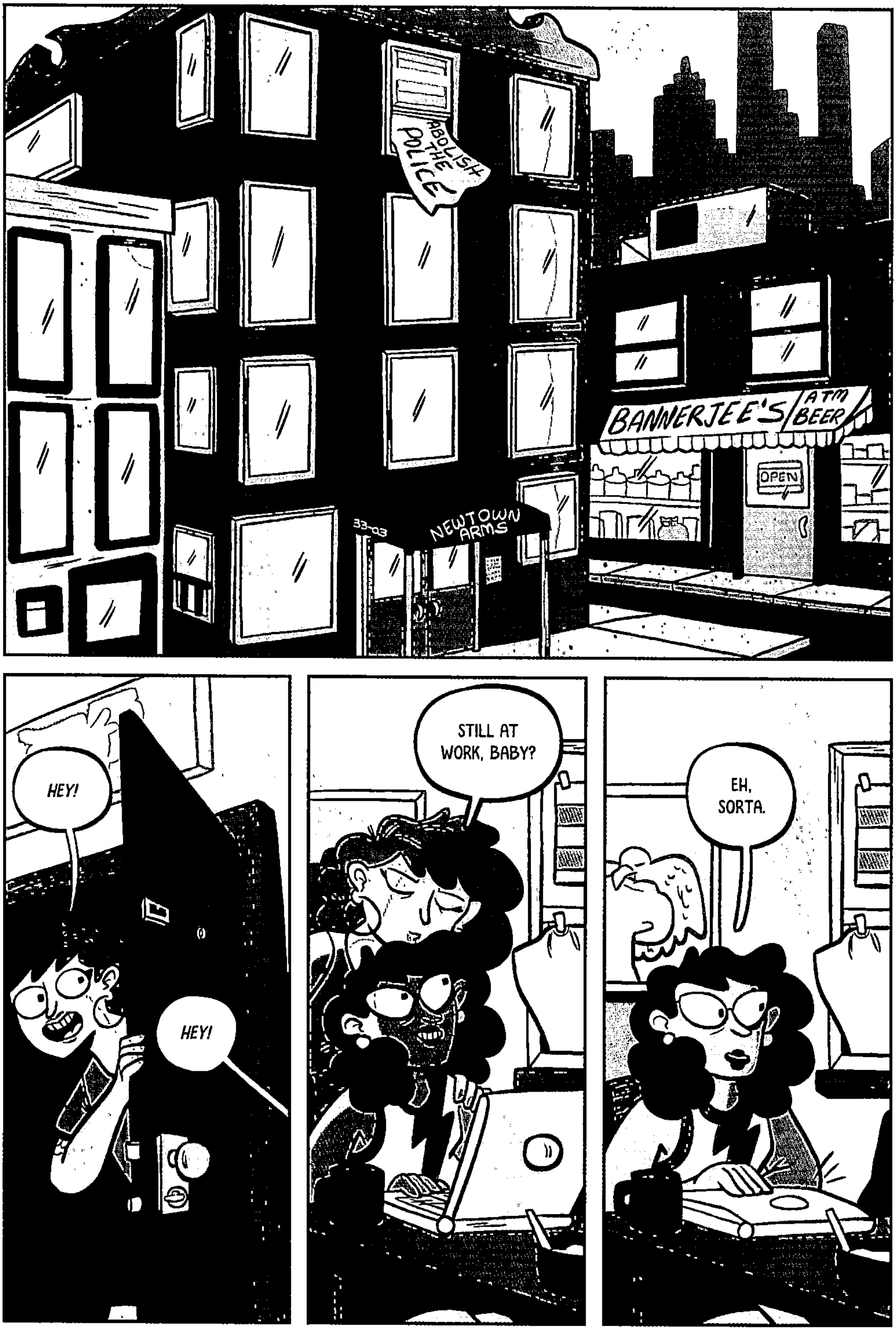
ABOLISH THE POLICE
BANNERJEE'S
ATM BEER
OPEN
33-03
NEWTOWN ARMS
HEY!
HEY!
STILL AT WORK, BABY?
EH, SORTA.

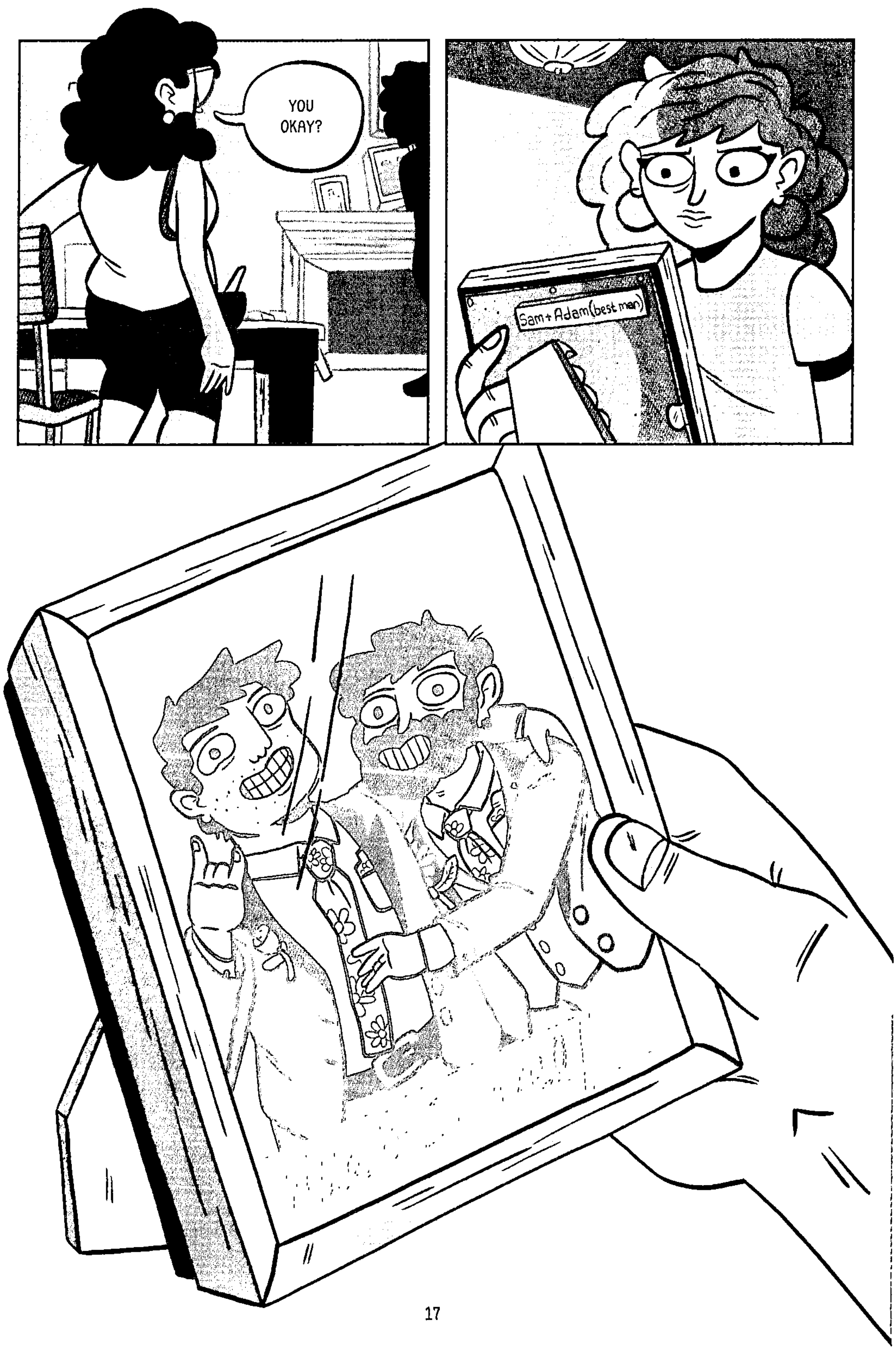
YOU OKAY?
Sam + Adam (best man)

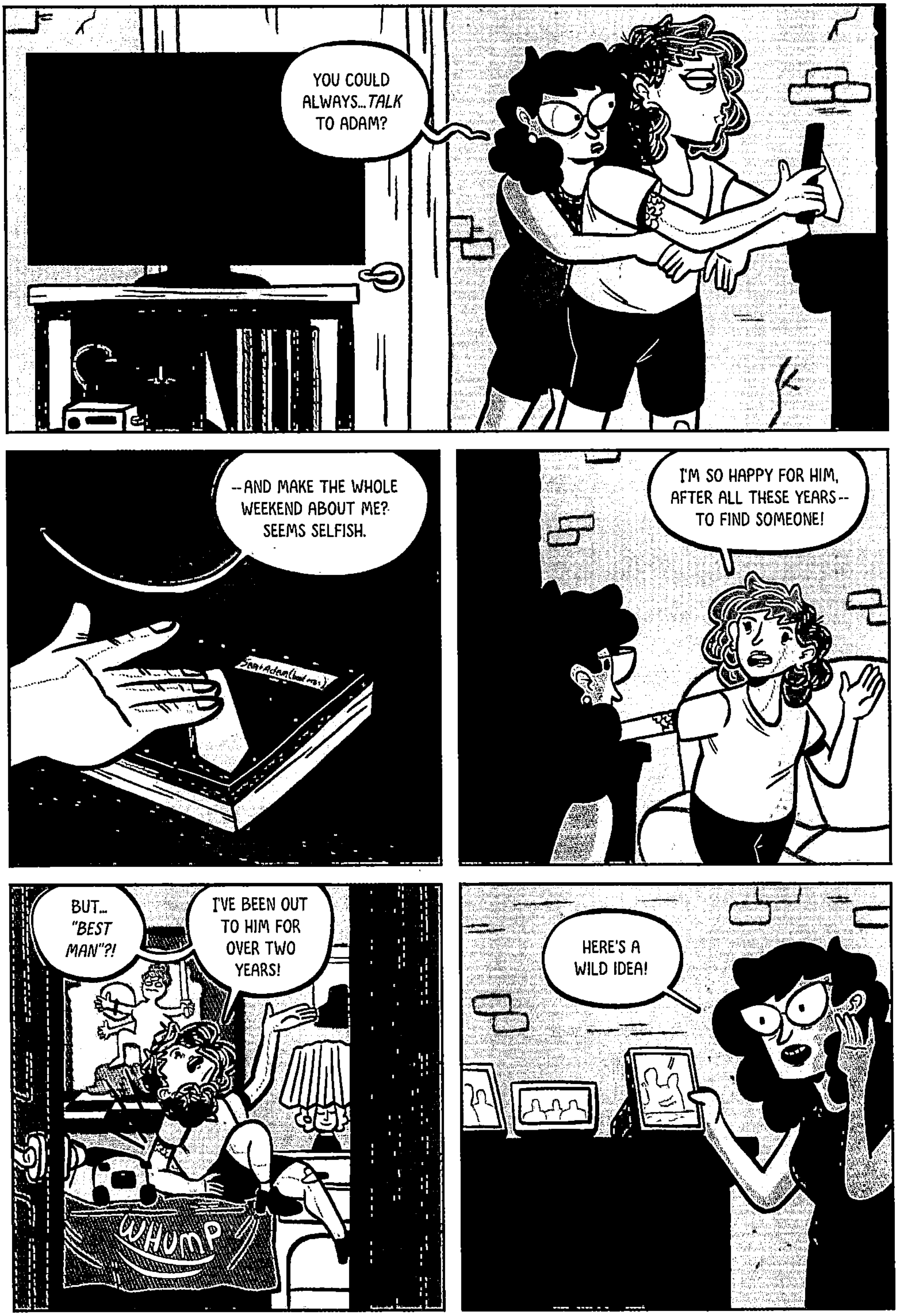
YOU COULD ALWAYS...*TALK* TO ADAM?
--AND MAKE THE WHOLE WEEKEND ABOUT ME? SEEMS SELFISH.
I'M SO HAPPY FOR HIM, AFTER ALL THESE YEARS-- TO FIND SOMEONE!
BUT... *"BEST MAN"?!*
I'VE BEEN OUT TO HIM FOR OVER TWO YEARS!
WHUMP
HERE'S A WILD IDEA!

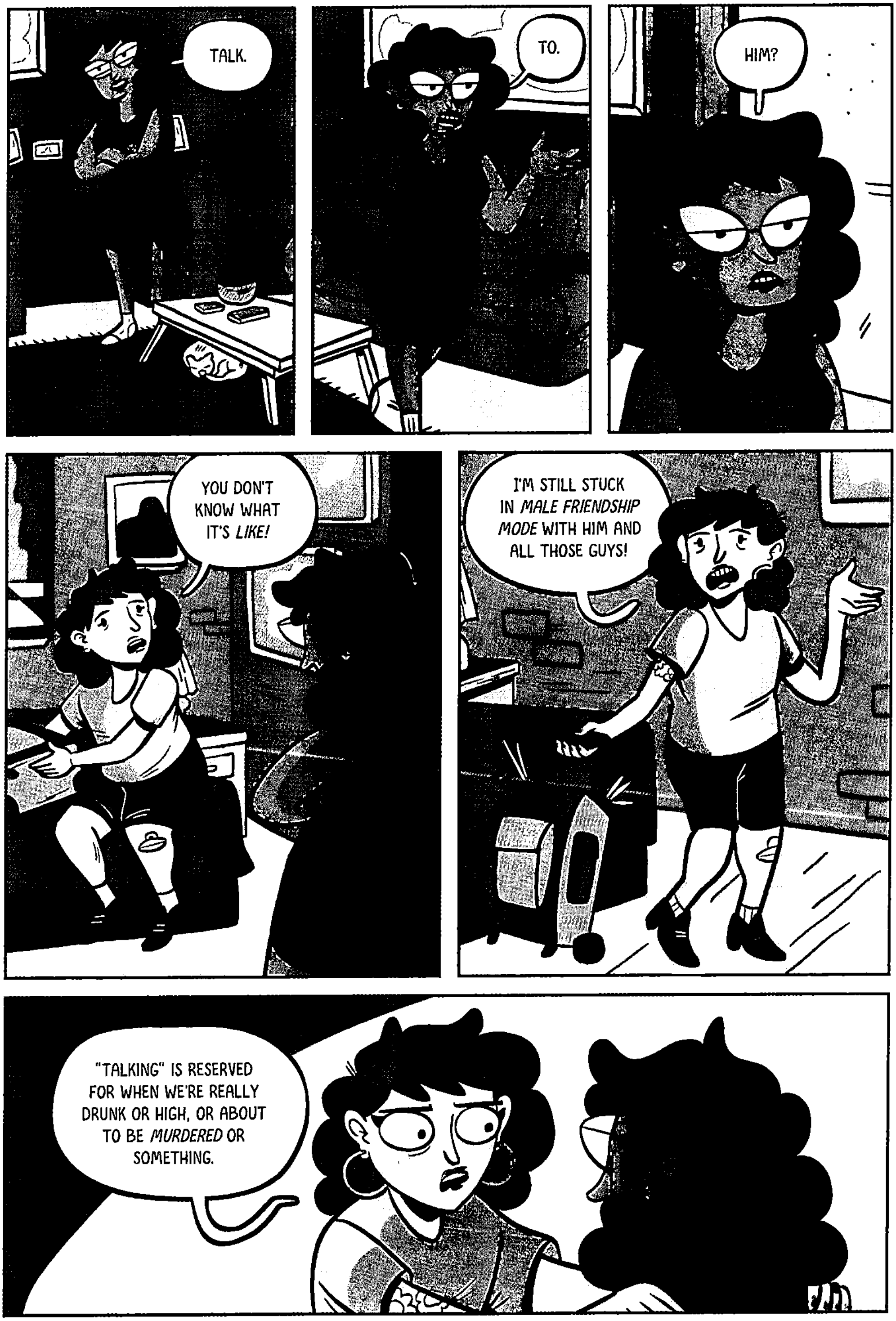
TALK.
TO.
HIM?
YOU DON'T KNOW WHAT IT'S *LIKE!*
I'M STILL STUCK IN *MALE FRIENDSHIP MODE* WITH HIM AND ALL THOSE GUYS!
"TALKING" IS RESERVED FOR WHEN WE'RE REALLY DRUNK OR HIGH, OR ABOUT TO BE *MURDERED* OR SOMETHING.

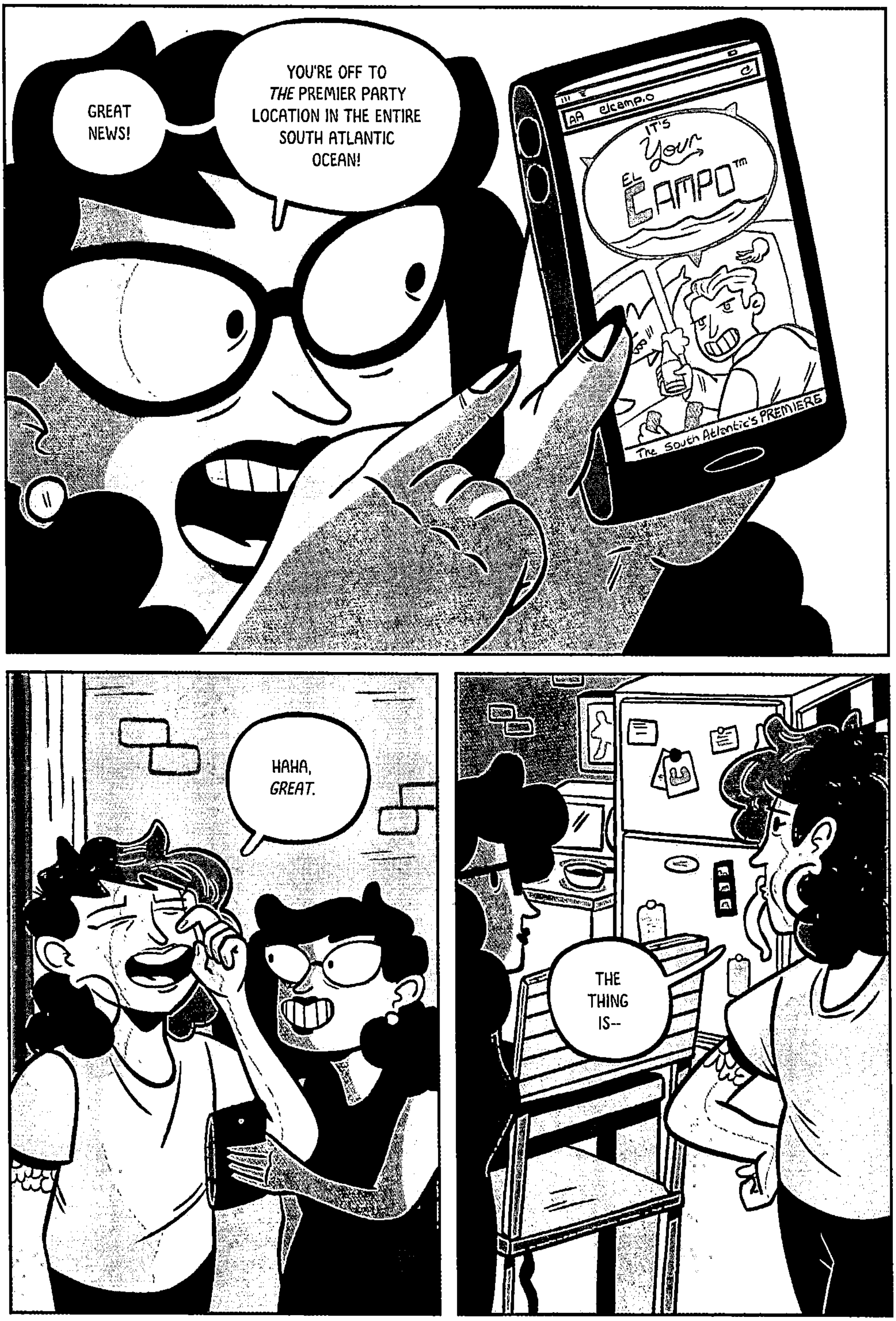
GREAT NEWS!
YOU'RE OFF TO *THE* PREMIER PARTY LOCATION IN THE ENTIRE SOUTH ATLANTIC OCEAN!
IT'S Your EL CAMPO™
The South Atlantic's PREMIERE
HAHA, *GREAT.*
THE THING IS--

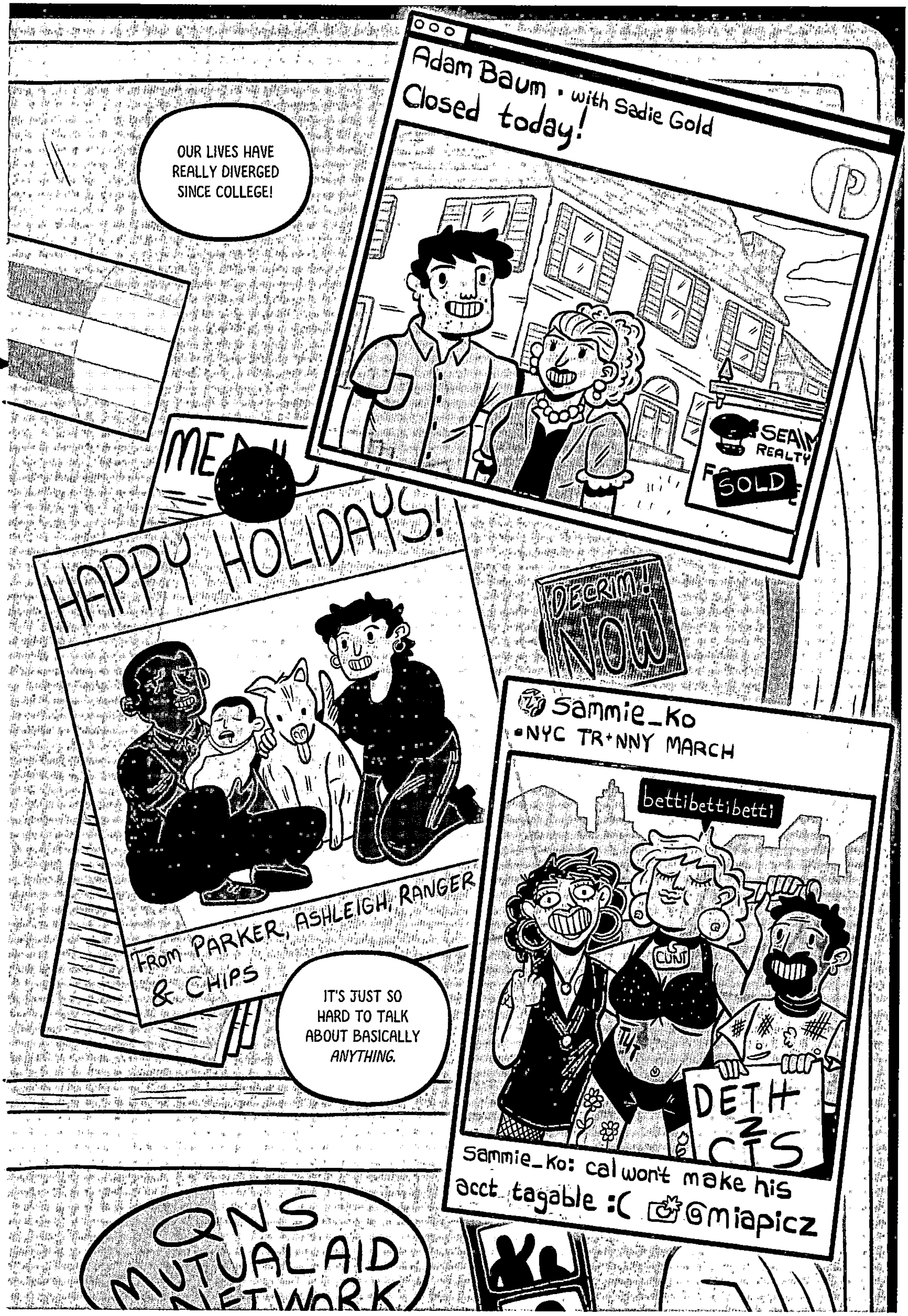
OUR LIVES HAVE REALLY DIVERGED SINCE COLLEGE!
Adam Baum • with Sadie Gold
Closed today!
SEA REALTY
SOLD
MENU
HAPPY HOLIDAYS!
FROM PARKER, ASHLEIGH, RANGER & CHIPS
DECRIM! NOW
sammie_ko
• NYC TR+NNY MARCH
bettibettibetti
CUNT
DETH 2 CIS
sammie_ko: cal won't make his acct tagable :(
@miapicz
IT'S JUST SO HARD TO TALK ABOUT BASICALLY *ANYTHING.*
QNS MUTUAL AID NETWORK

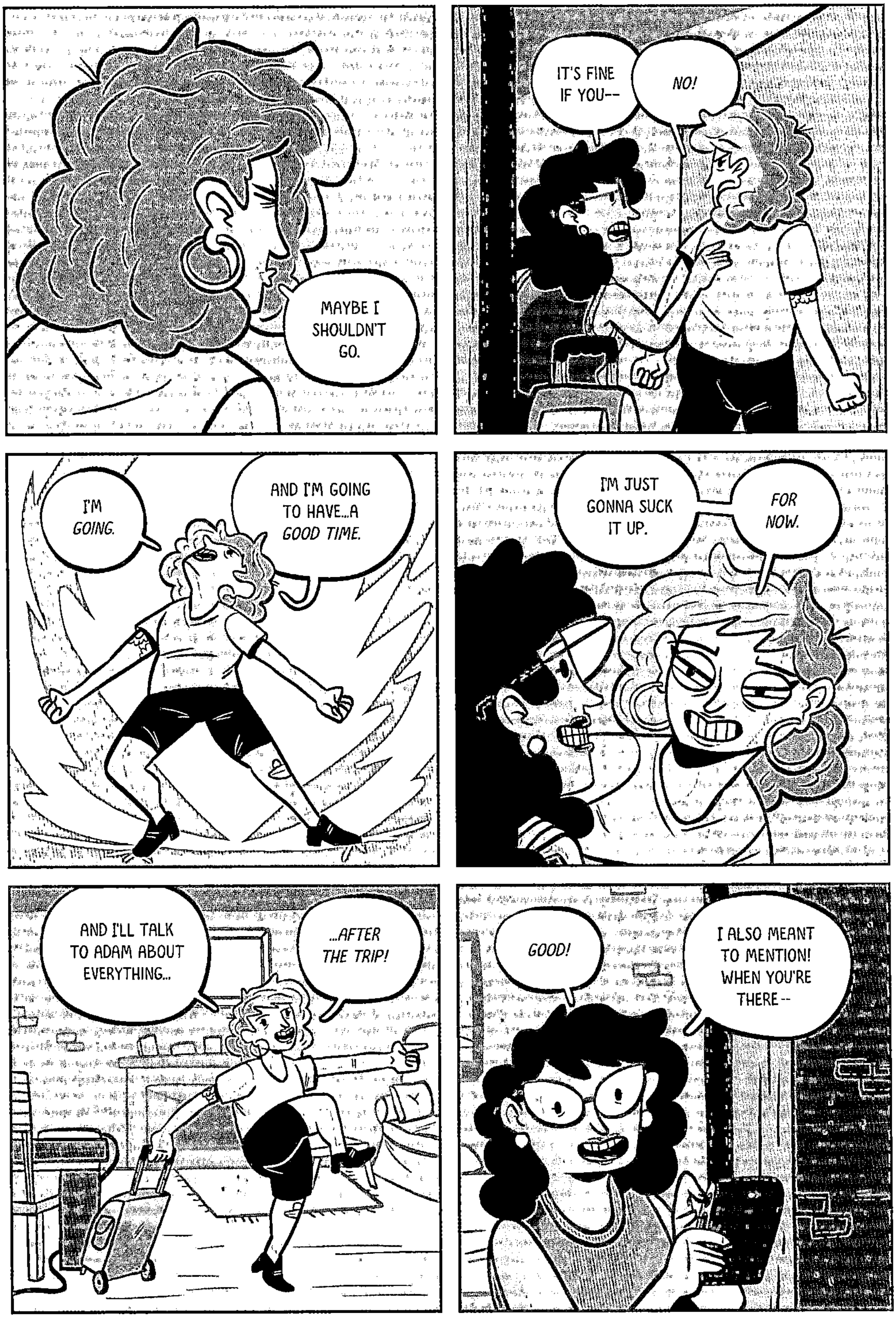
MAYBE I SHOULDN'T GO.
IT'S FINE IF YOU--
NO!
I'M GOING.
AND I'M GOING TO HAVE...A GOOD TIME.
I'M JUST GONNA SUCK IT UP.
FOR NOW.
AND I'LL TALK TO ADAM ABOUT EVERYTHING...
...AFTER THE TRIP!
GOOD!
I ALSO MEANT TO MENTION! WHEN YOU'RE THERE--

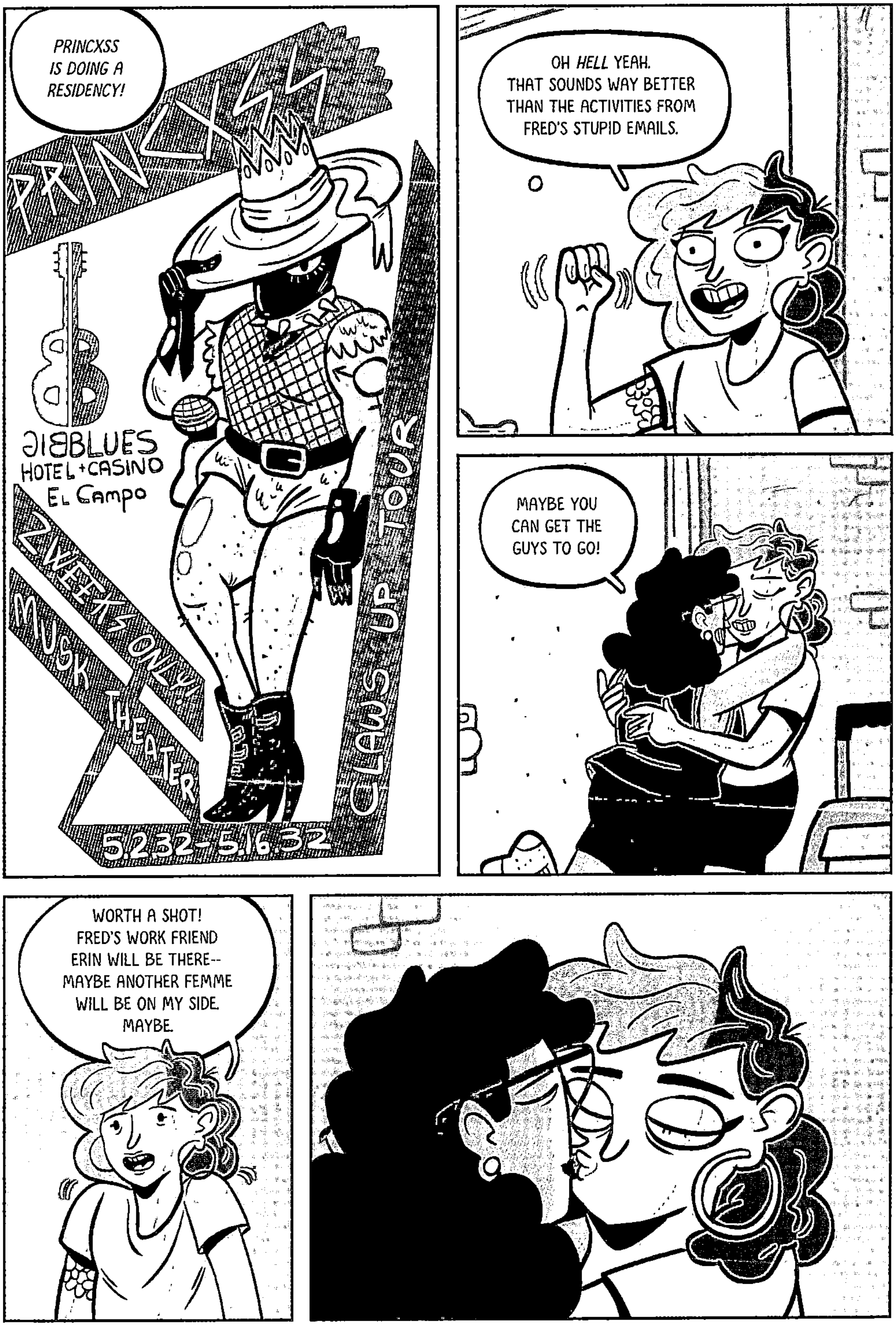
PRINCXSS IS DOING A RESIDENCY!
PRINCXSS
HOTEL+CASINO
El Campo
2 WEEKS ONLY!
MUSK THEATER
CLAWS UP TOUR
5.2.32–5.16.32
OH *HELL* YEAH. THAT SOUNDS WAY BETTER THAN THE ACTIVITIES FROM FRED'S STUPID EMAILS.
MAYBE YOU CAN GET THE GUYS TO GO!
WORTH A SHOT! FRED'S WORK FRIEND ERIN WILL BE THERE-- MAYBE ANOTHER FEMME WILL BE ON MY SIDE. MAYBE.

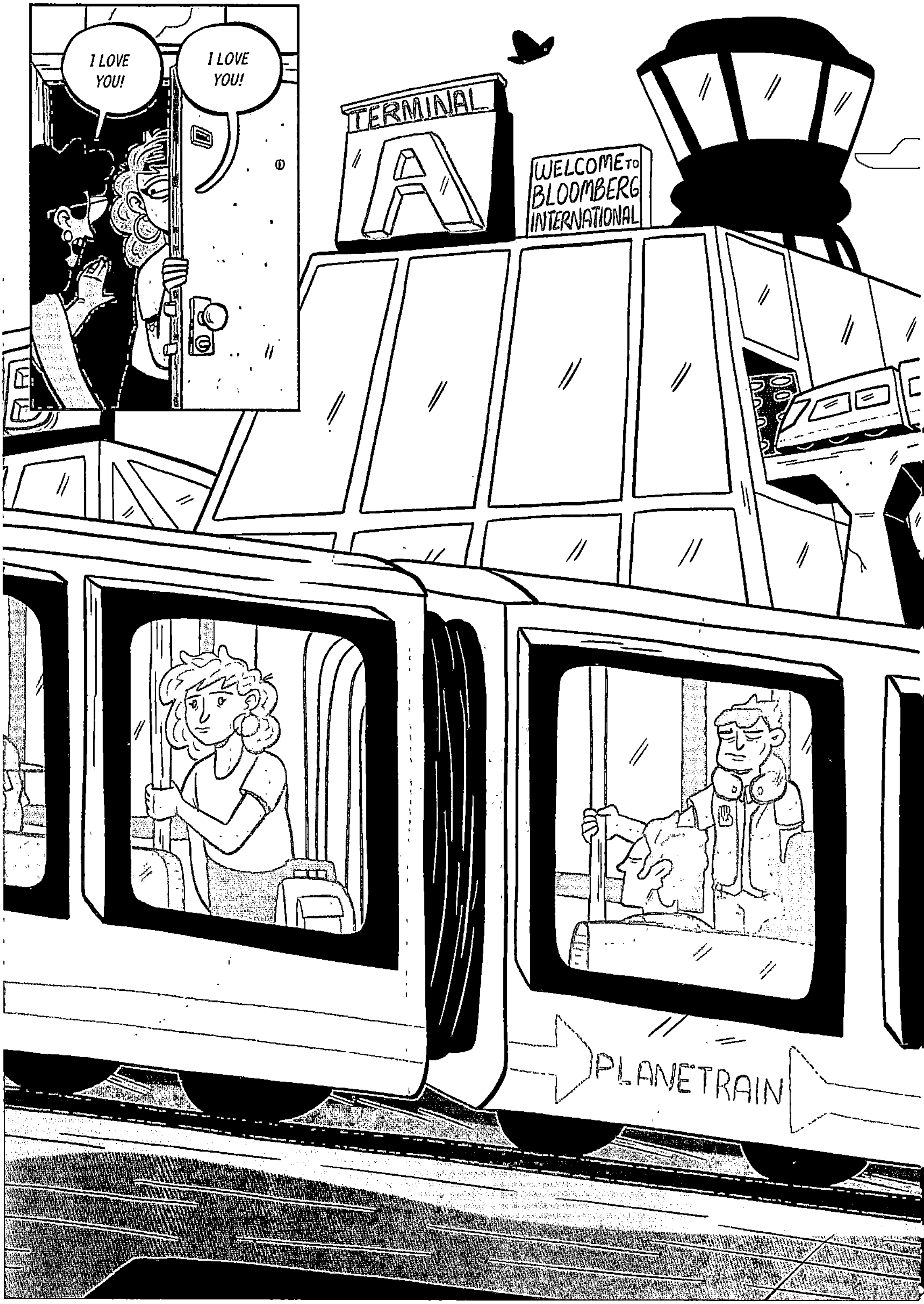
I LOVE YOU!
I LOVE YOU!
TERMINAL A
WELCOME TO BLOOMBERG INTERNATIONAL
PLANETRAIN

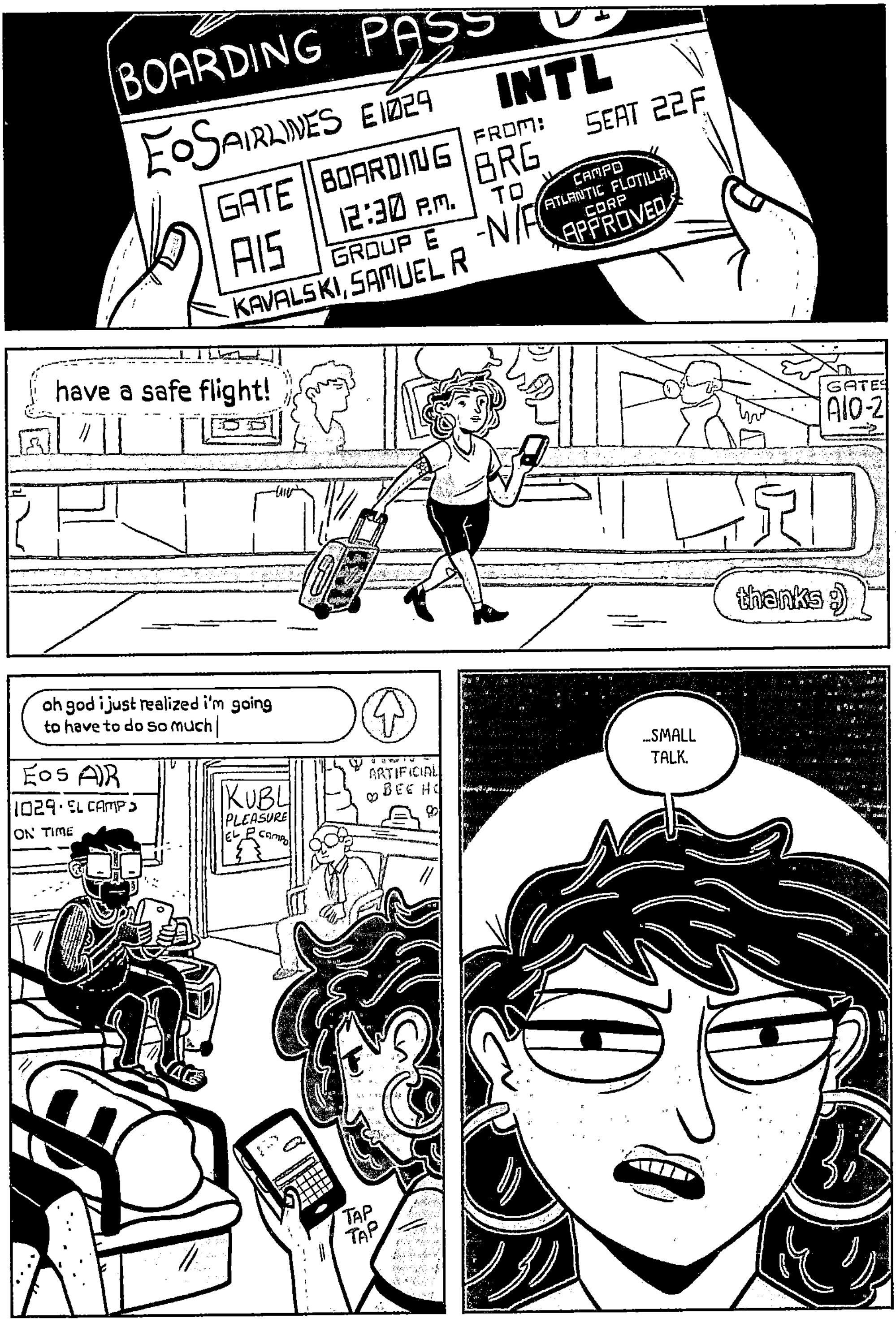
BOARDING PASS
EoS AIRLINES E1029
INTL
FROM: BRG TO N/A
SEAT 22F
GATE A15
BOARDING 12:30 P.M.
GROUP E
KAVALSKI, SAMUEL R
CAMPO ATLANTIC FLOTILLA CORP APPROVED
have a safe flight!
GATES A10-2
thanks :)
oh god i just realized i'm going to have to do so much
EOS AIR
1029 · EL CAMPO
ON TIME
KUBL PLEASURE EL CAMPO
ARTIFICIAL BEE H
TAP TAP
...SMALL TALK.

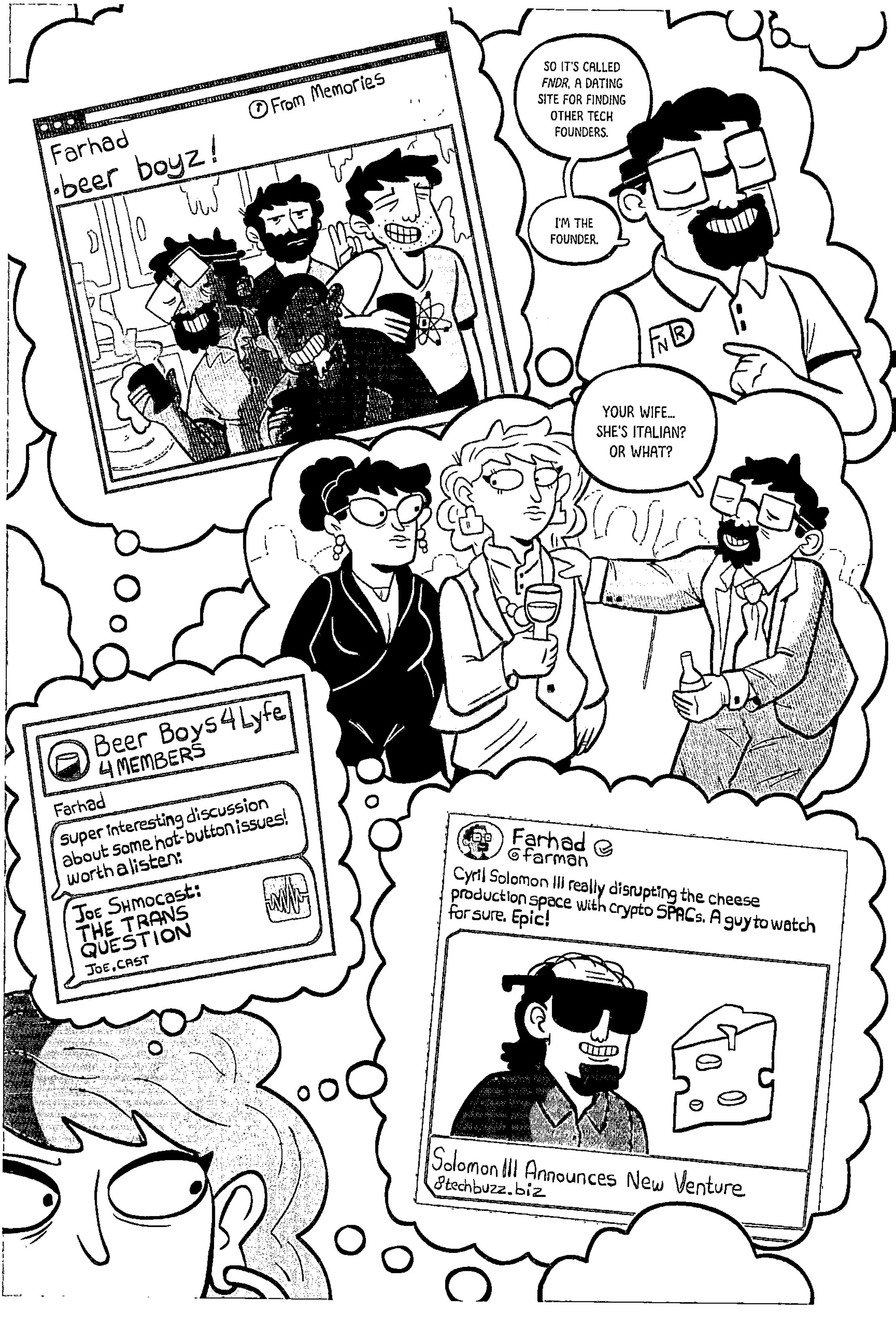
From Memories
Farhad
beer boyz!
SO IT'S CALLED FNDR, A DATING SITE FOR FINDING OTHER TECH FOUNDERS.
I'M THE FOUNDER.
FNDR
YOUR WIFE... SHE'S ITALIAN? OR WHAT?
Beer Boys 4 Lyfe
4 MEMBERS
Farhad
super interesting discussion about some hot-button issues! worth a listen:
Joe Shmocast: THE TRANS QUESTION
JOE.CAST
Farhad
@farman
Cyril Solomon III really disrupting the cheese production space with crypto SPACs. A guy to watch for sure. Epic!
Solomon III Announces New Venture
@techbuzz.biz

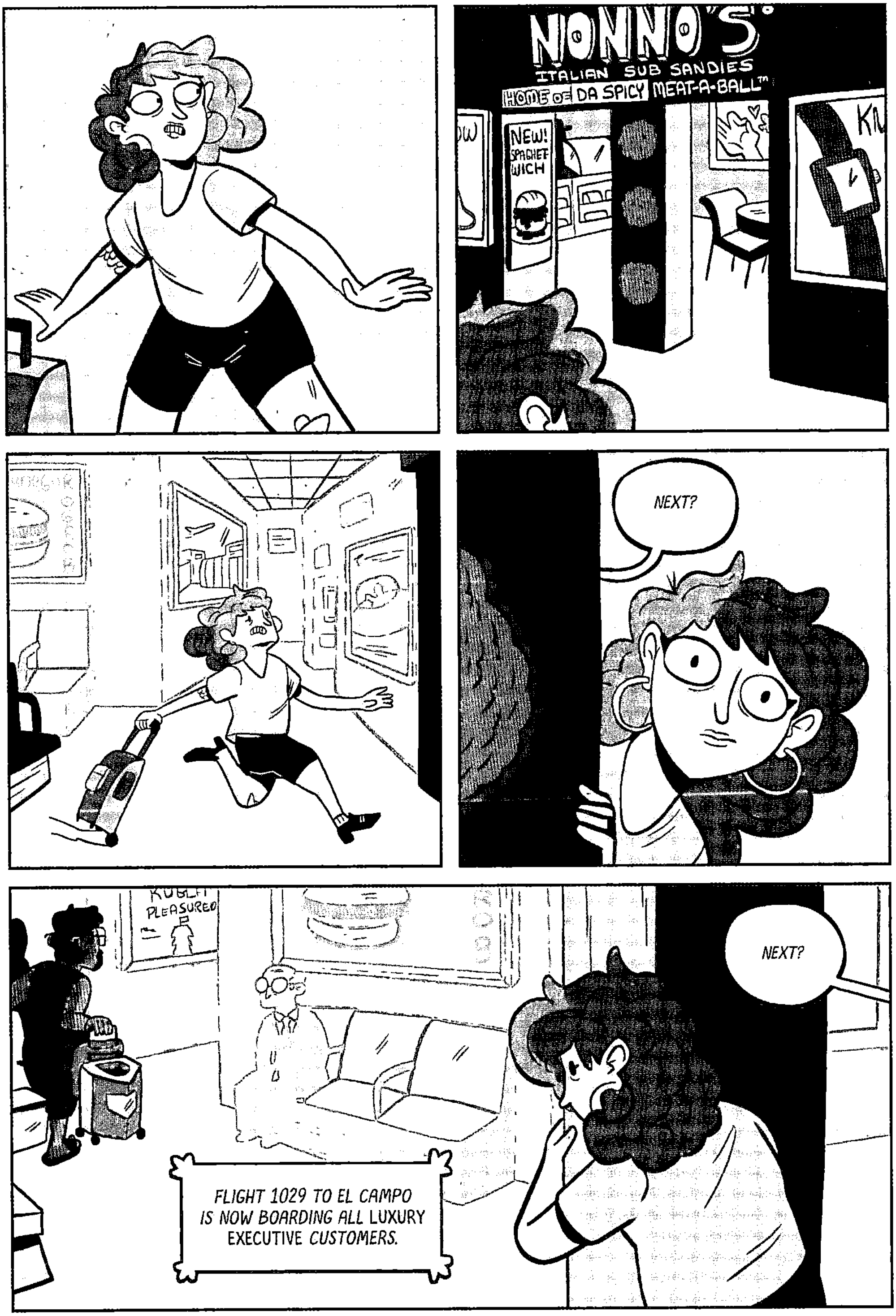
NONNO'S
ITALIAN SUB SANDIES
HOME OF DA SPICY MEAT-A-BALL™
NEW! SPAGHETT WICH
NEXT?
PLEASURED
NEXT?
FLIGHT 1029 TO EL CAMPO IS NOW BOARDING ALL LUXURY EXECUTIVE CUSTOMERS.

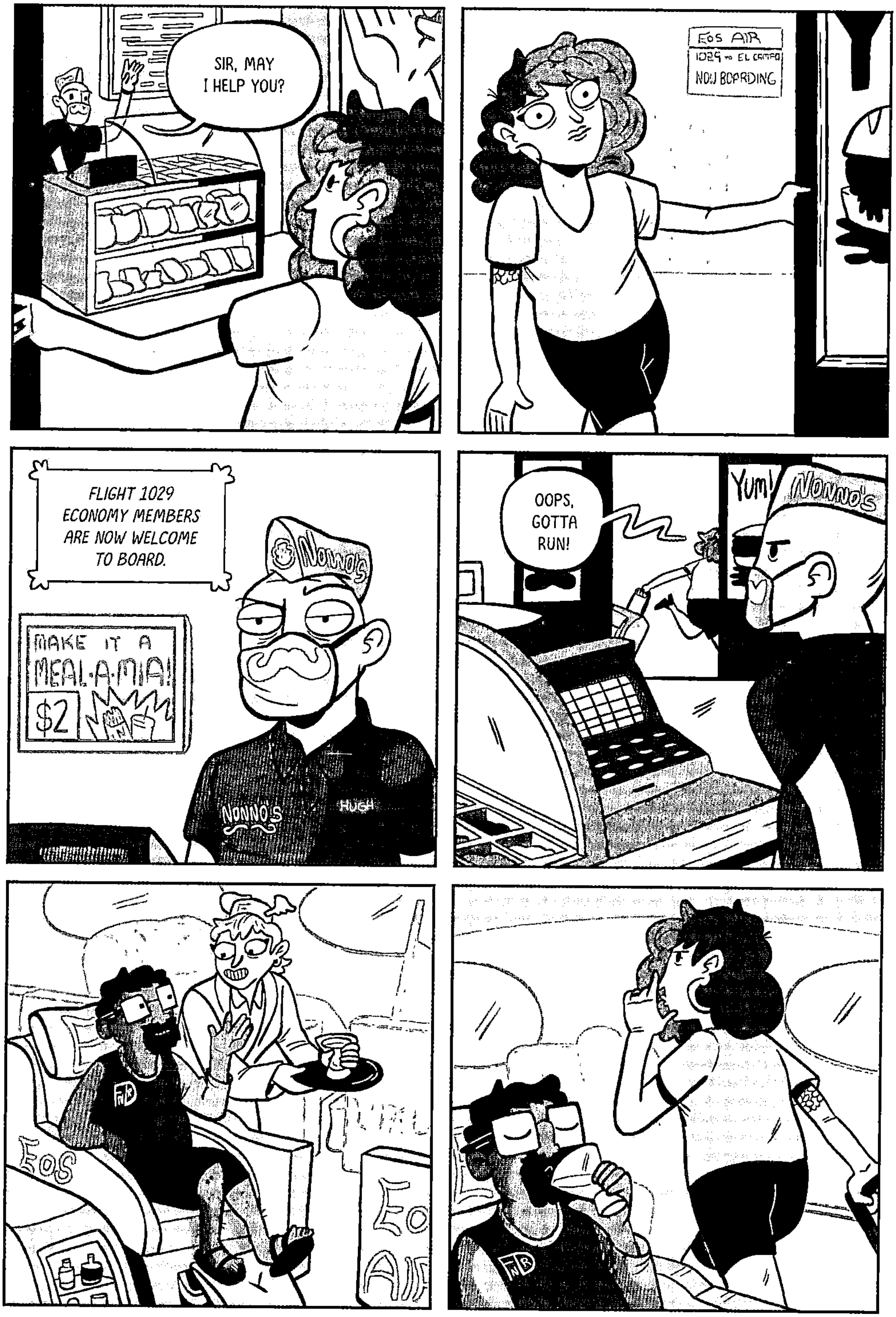
SIR, MAY I HELP YOU?
EOS AIR
NOW BOARDING
FLIGHT 1029 ECONOMY MEMBERS ARE NOW WELCOME TO BOARD.
NONNO'S
MAKE IT A MEAL-A-MIA!
$2
NONNO'S
HUGH
OOPS, GOTTA RUN!
YUM!
NONNO'S
EOS
EOS AIR

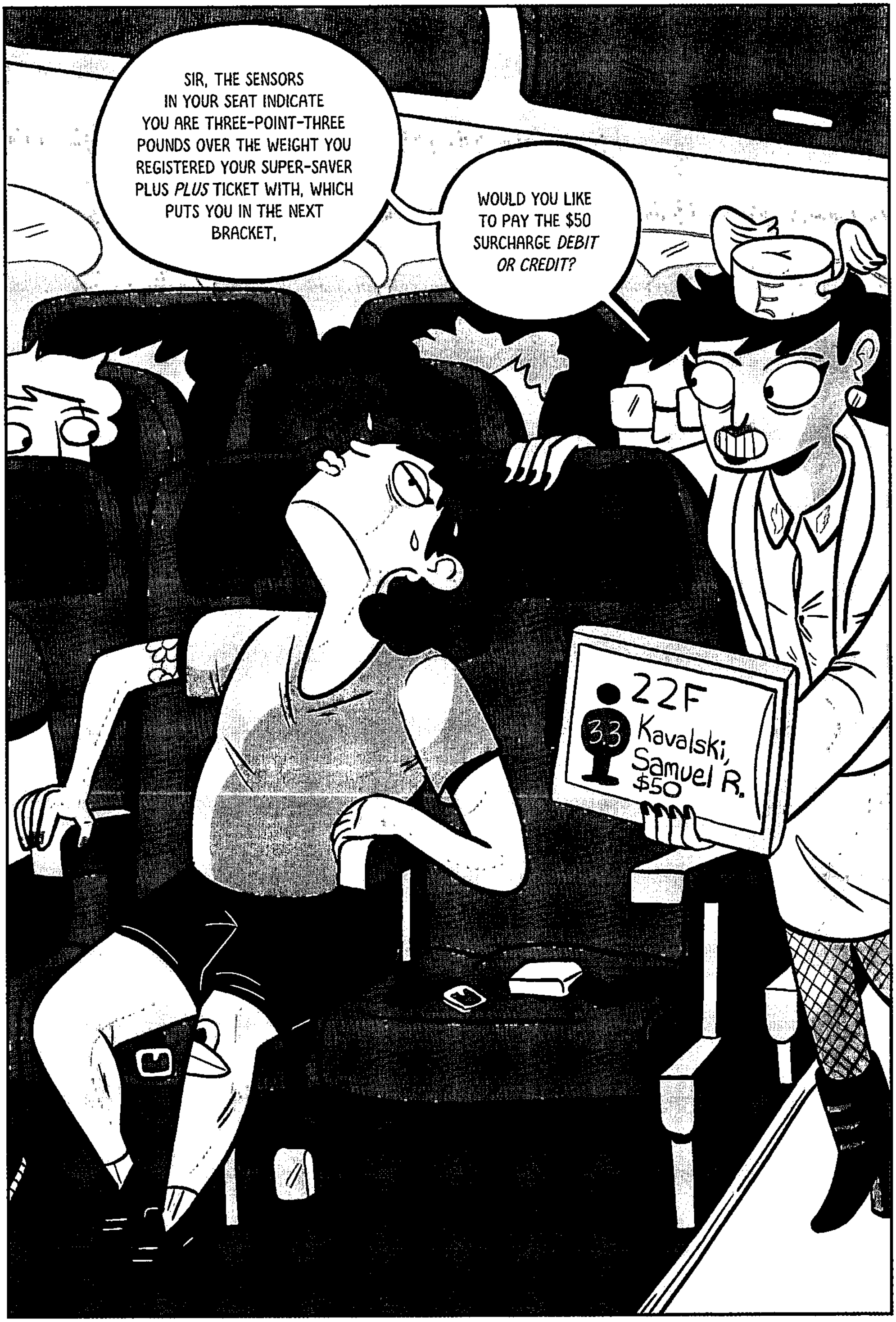
SIR, THE SENSORS IN YOUR SEAT INDICATE YOU ARE THREE-POINT-THREE POUNDS OVER THE WEIGHT YOU REGISTERED YOUR SUPER-SAVER PLUS *PLUS* TICKET WITH, WHICH PUTS YOU IN THE NEXT BRACKET.
WOULD YOU LIKE TO PAY THE $50 SURCHARGE *DEBIT OR CREDIT?*
22F
3.3
Kavalski, Samuel R.
$50

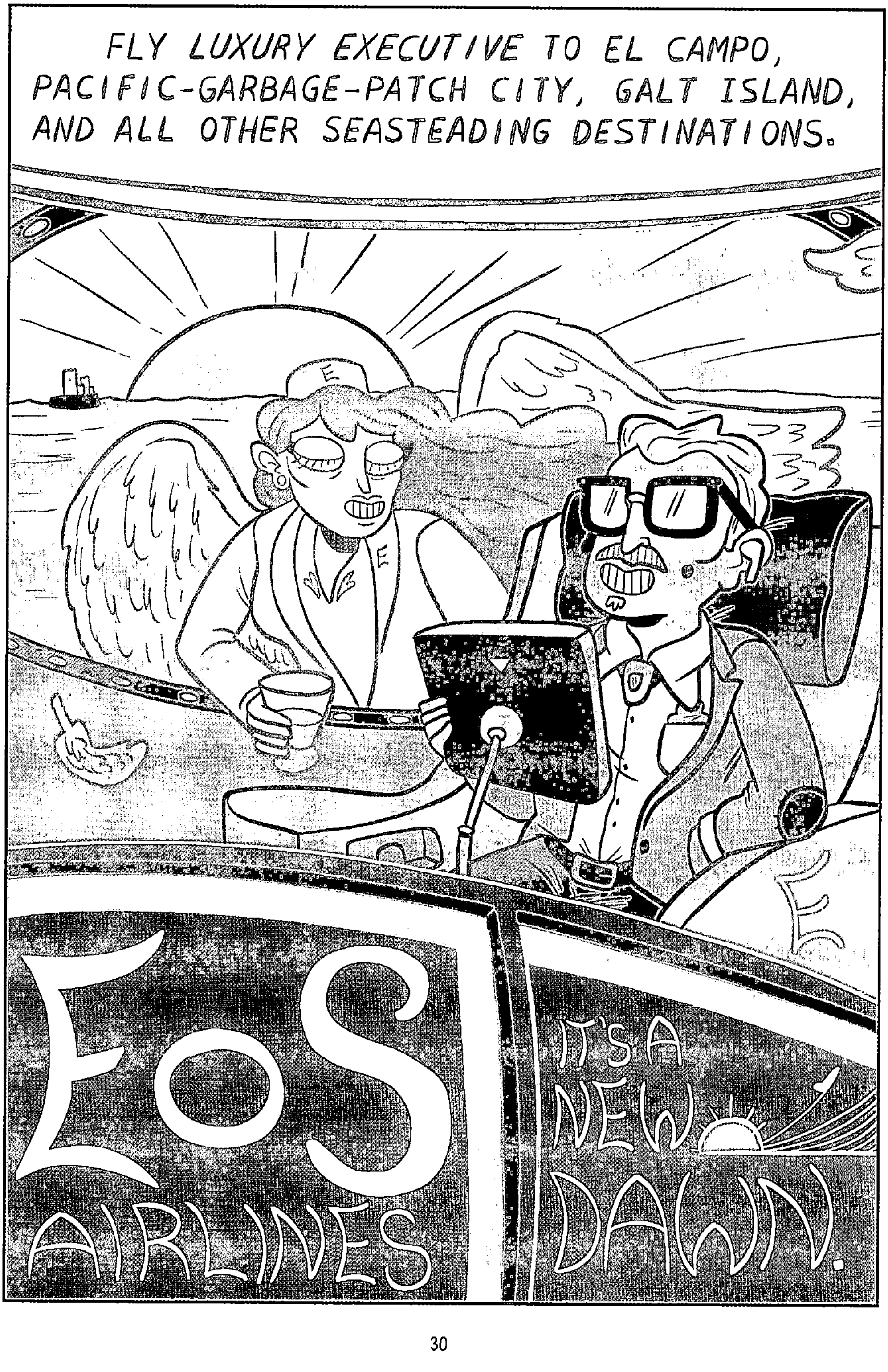
FLY LUXURY EXECUTIVE TO EL CAMPO, PACIFIC-GARBAGE-PATCH CITY, GALT ISLAND, AND ALL OTHER SEASTEADING DESTINATIONS.
EOS AIRLINES
IT'S A NEW DAWN.

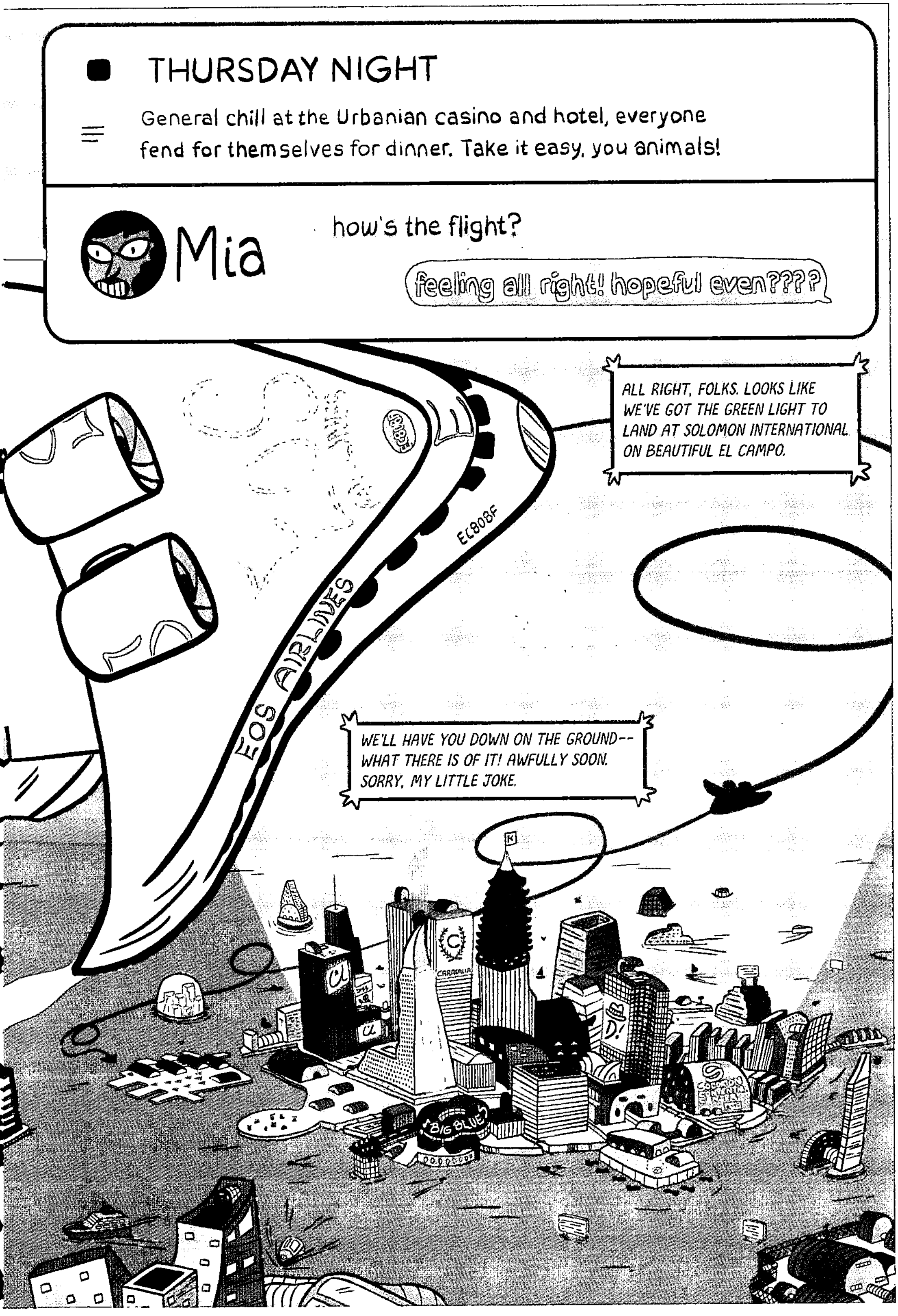
THURSDAY NIGHT
General chill at the Urbanian casino and hotel, everyone fend for themselves for dinner. Take it easy, you animals!
Mia
how's the flight?
feeling all right! hopeful even????
ALL RIGHT, FOLKS. LOOKS LIKE WE'VE GOT THE GREEN LIGHT TO LAND AT SOLOMON INTERNATIONAL ON BEAUTIFUL EL CAMPO.
EOS AIRLINES
EC808F
WE'LL HAVE YOU DOWN ON THE GROUND--WHAT THERE IS OF IT! AWFULLY SOON. SORRY, MY LITTLE JOKE.
BIG BLUES

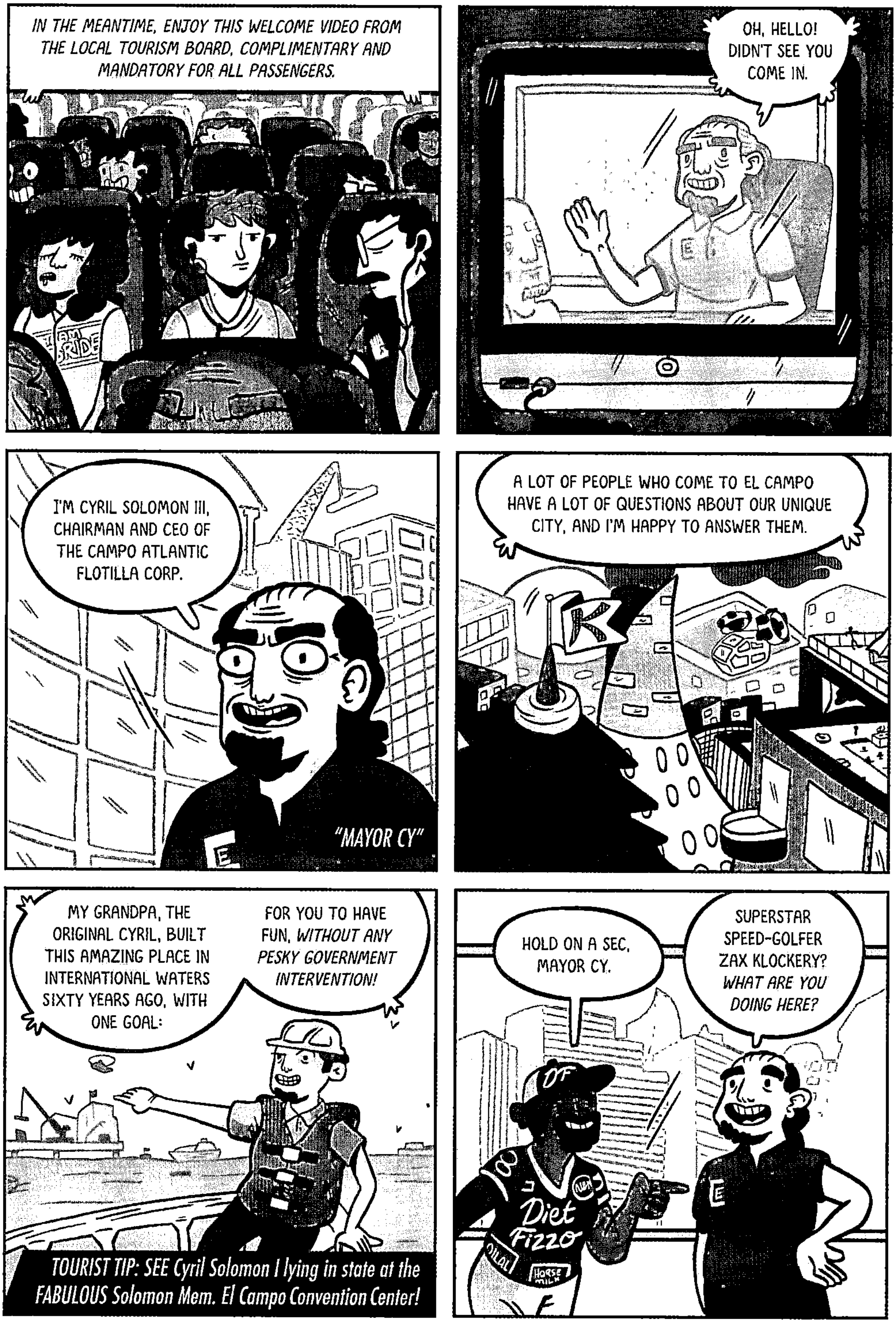
IN THE MEANTIME, ENJOY THIS WELCOME VIDEO FROM THE LOCAL TOURISM BOARD, COMPLIMENTARY AND MANDATORY FOR ALL PASSENGERS.
OH, HELLO! DIDN'T SEE YOU COME IN.
I'M CYRIL SOLOMON III, CHAIRMAN AND CEO OF THE CAMPO ATLANTIC FLOTILLA CORP.
"MAYOR CY"
A LOT OF PEOPLE WHO COME TO EL CAMPO HAVE A LOT OF QUESTIONS ABOUT OUR UNIQUE CITY, AND I'M HAPPY TO ANSWER THEM.
MY GRANDPA, THE ORIGINAL CYRIL, BUILT THIS AMAZING PLACE IN INTERNATIONAL WATERS SIXTY YEARS AGO, WITH ONE GOAL:
FOR YOU TO HAVE FUN, *WITHOUT ANY PESKY GOVERNMENT INTERVENTION!*
TOURIST TIP: SEE Cyril Solomon I lying in state at the FABULOUS Solomon Mem. El Campo Convention Center!
HOLD ON A SEC, MAYOR CY.
SUPERSTAR SPEED-GOLFER ZAX KLOCKERY? *WHAT ARE YOU DOING HERE?*
Diet Fizzo

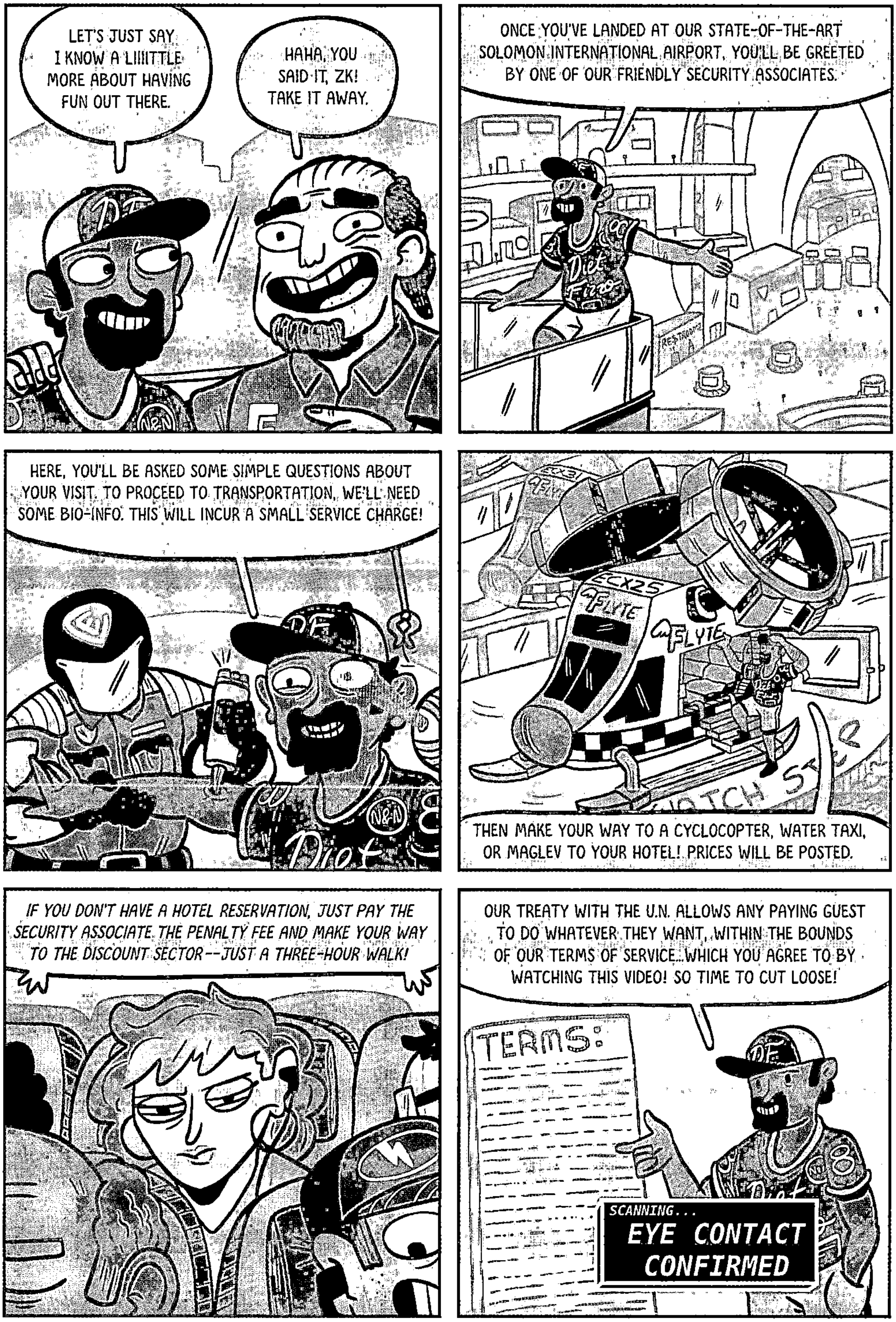
LET'S JUST SAY I KNOW A LIIIITTLE MORE ABOUT HAVING FUN OUT THERE.
HAHA, YOU SAID IT, ZK! TAKE IT AWAY.
ONCE YOU'VE LANDED AT OUR STATE-OF-THE-ART SOLOMON INTERNATIONAL AIRPORT, YOU'LL BE GREETED BY ONE OF OUR FRIENDLY SECURITY ASSOCIATES.
HERE, YOU'LL BE ASKED SOME SIMPLE QUESTIONS ABOUT YOUR VISIT. TO PROCEED TO TRANSPORTATION, WE'LL NEED SOME BIO-INFO. THIS WILL INCUR A SMALL SERVICE CHARGE!
ECX25
FLYTE
THEN MAKE YOUR WAY TO A CYCLOCOPTER, WATER TAXI, OR MAGLEV TO YOUR HOTEL! PRICES WILL BE POSTED.
IF YOU DON'T HAVE A HOTEL RESERVATION, JUST PAY THE SECURITY ASSOCIATE THE PENALTY FEE AND MAKE YOUR WAY TO THE DISCOUNT SECTOR--JUST A THREE-HOUR WALK!
OUR TREATY WITH THE U.N. ALLOWS ANY PAYING GUEST TO DO WHATEVER THEY WANT, WITHIN THE BOUNDS OF OUR TERMS OF SERVICE...WHICH YOU AGREE TO BY WATCHING THIS VIDEO! SO TIME TO CUT LOOSE!
TERMS:
SCANNING...
EYE CONTACT CONFIRMED

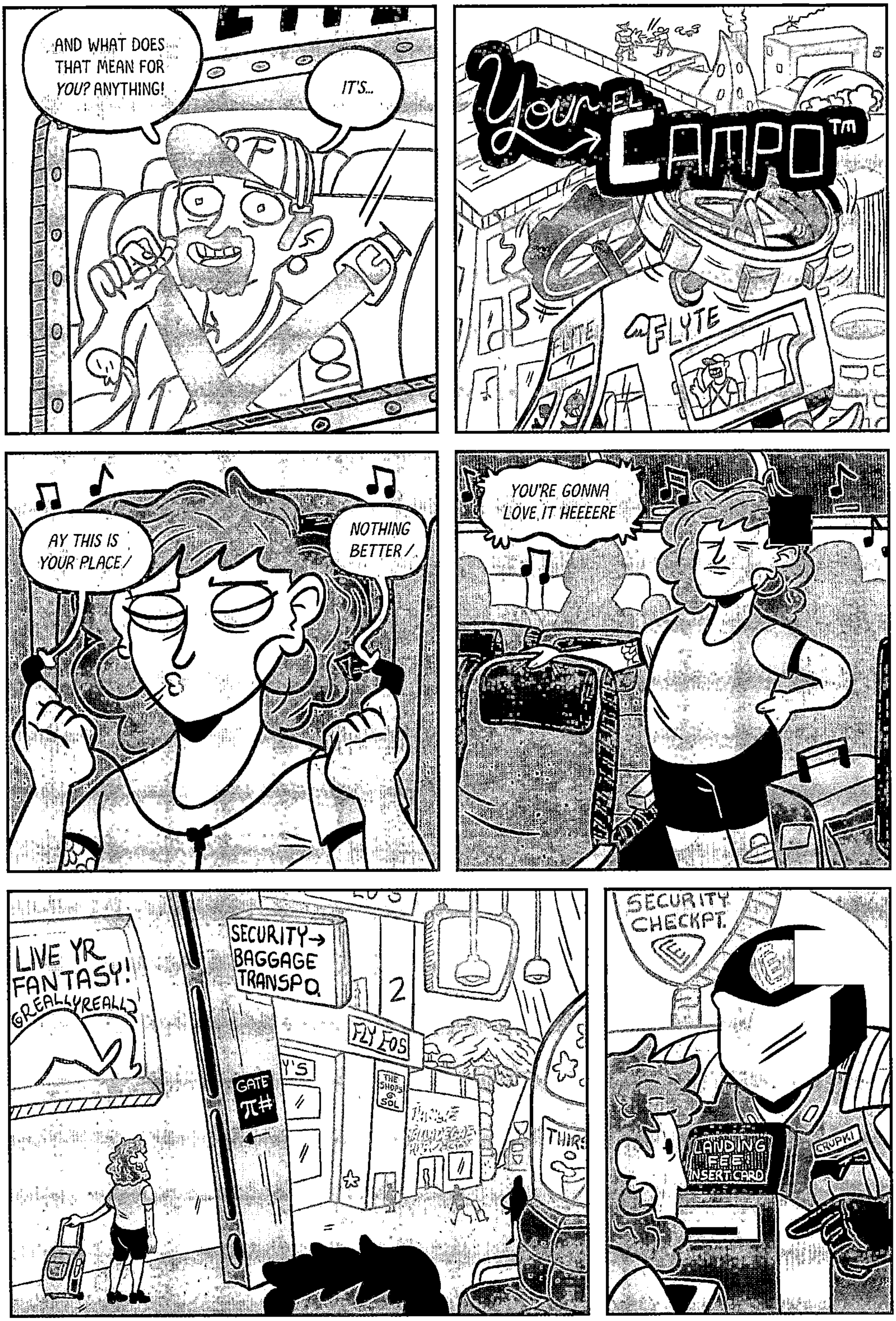
AND WHAT DOES THAT MEAN FOR *YOU?* ANYTHING!
IT'S...
Your EL CAMPO™
FLYTE
FLYTE
AY THIS IS YOUR PLACE!
NOTHING BETTER!
YOU'RE GONNA LOVE IT HEEEERE
LIVE YR FANTASY!
SECURITY→ BAGGAGE TRANSPO.
2
FLY EOS
GATE π#
THE SHOPS @ SOL
SECURITY CHECKPT.
LANDING FEE INSERT CARD
CRUPKI

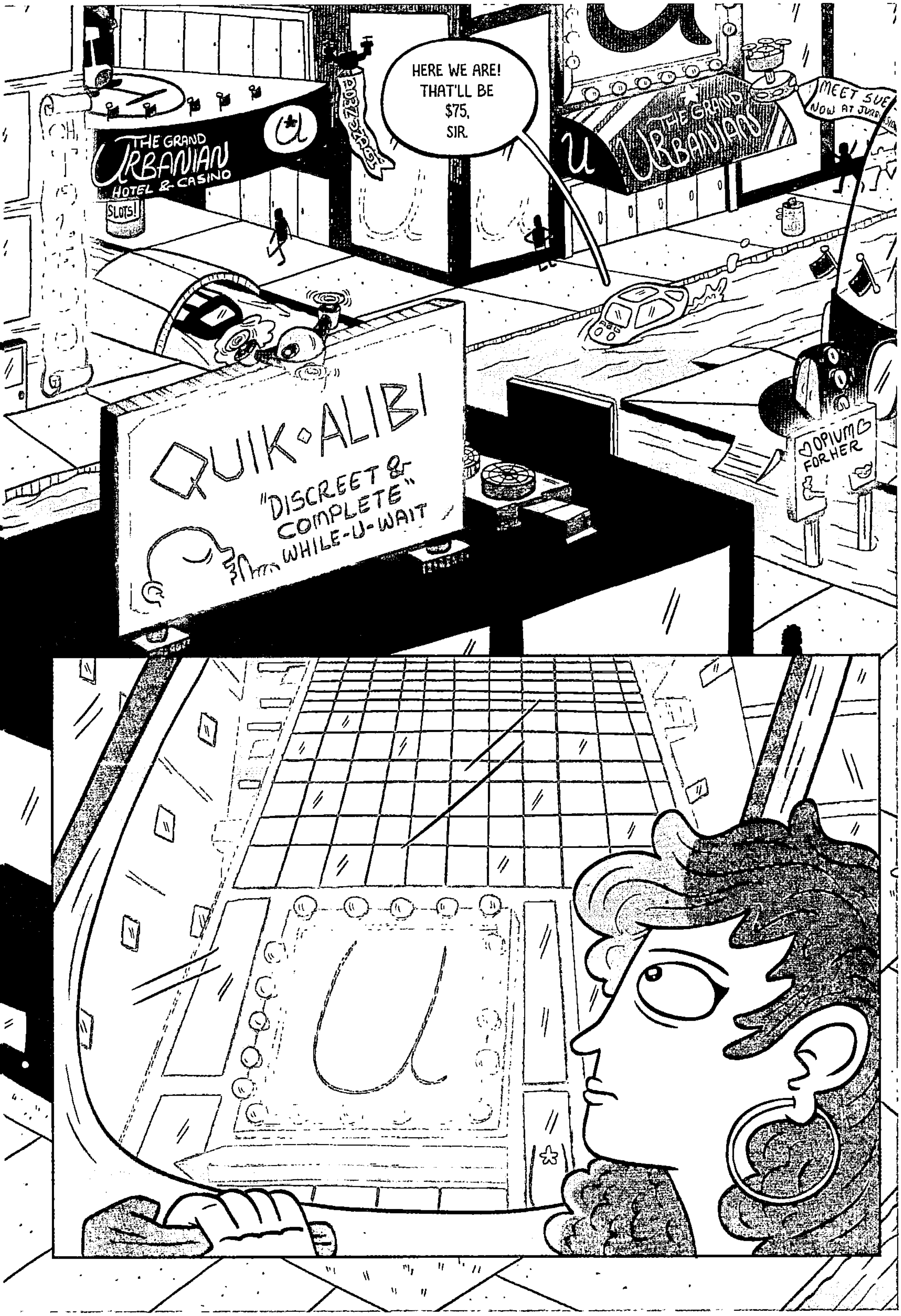
THE GRAND URBANIAN HOTEL & CASINO
SLOTS!
HERE WE ARE! THAT'LL BE $75, SIR.
THE GRAND URBANIAN
MEET SUE
NOW AT
QUIK·ALIBI
"DISCREET & COMPLETE" WHILE-U-WAIT
OPIUM FOR HER

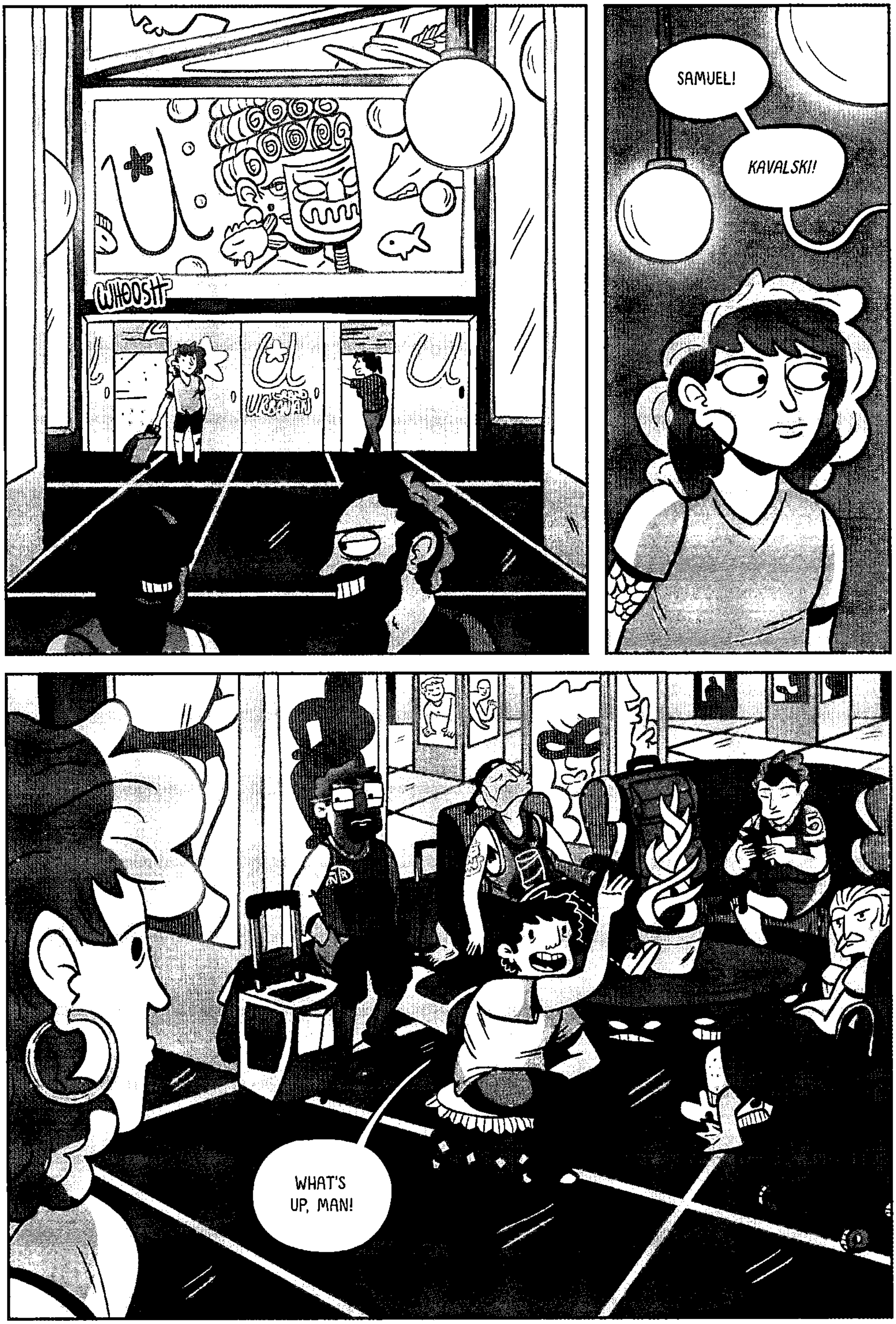
WHOOSH
SAMUEL!
KAVALSKI!
WHAT'S UP, MAN!

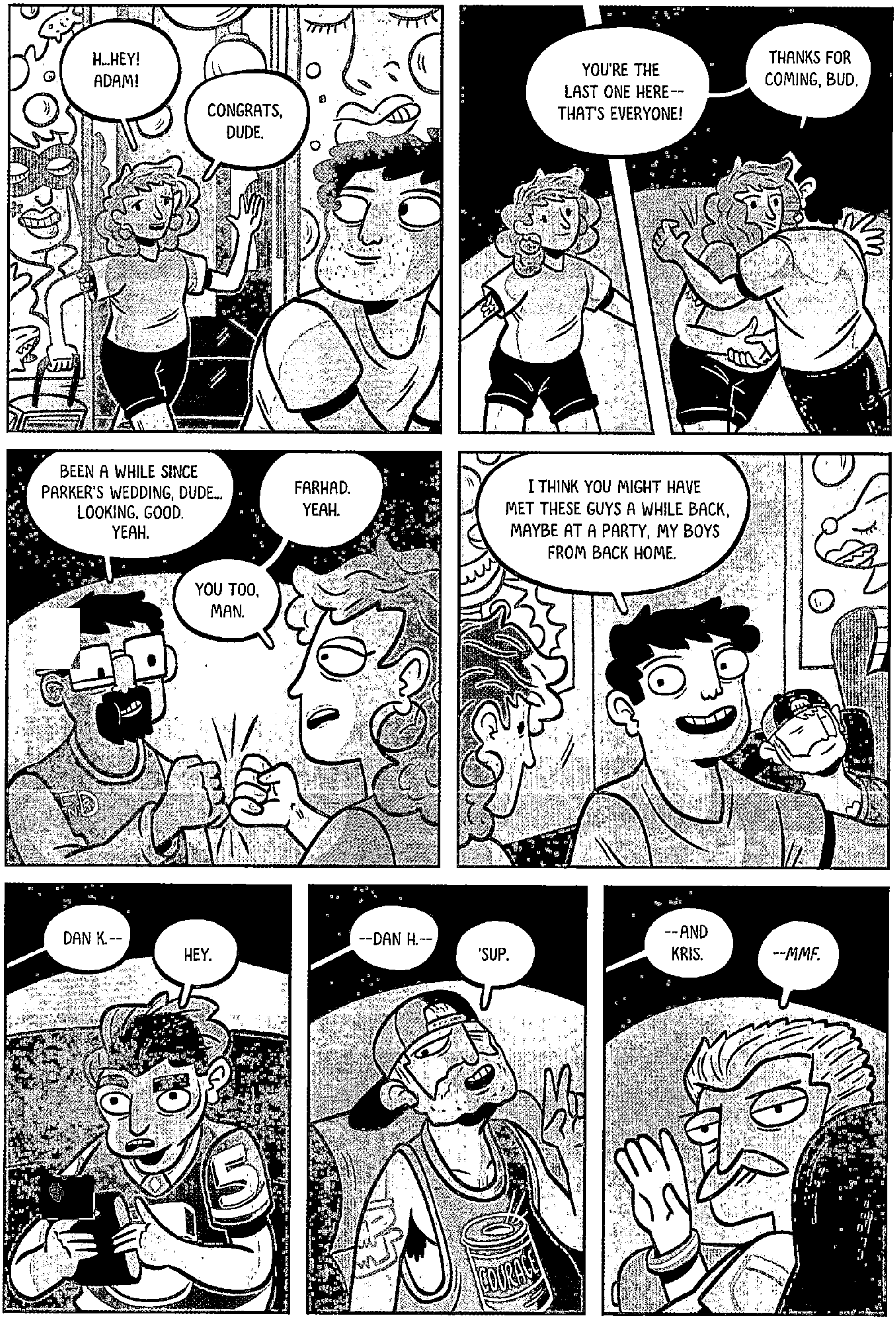
H...HEY! ADAM!
CONGRATS, DUDE.
YOU'RE THE LAST ONE HERE-- THAT'S EVERYONE!
THANKS FOR COMING, BUD.
BEEN A WHILE SINCE PARKER'S WEDDING, DUDE... LOOKING. GOOD. YEAH.
FARHAD. YEAH.
YOU TOO, MAN.
I THINK YOU MIGHT HAVE MET THESE GUYS A WHILE BACK, MAYBE AT A PARTY, MY BOYS FROM BACK HOME.
DAN K.--
HEY.
--DAN H.--
'SUP.
COURAGE
--AND KRIS.
--*MMF.*

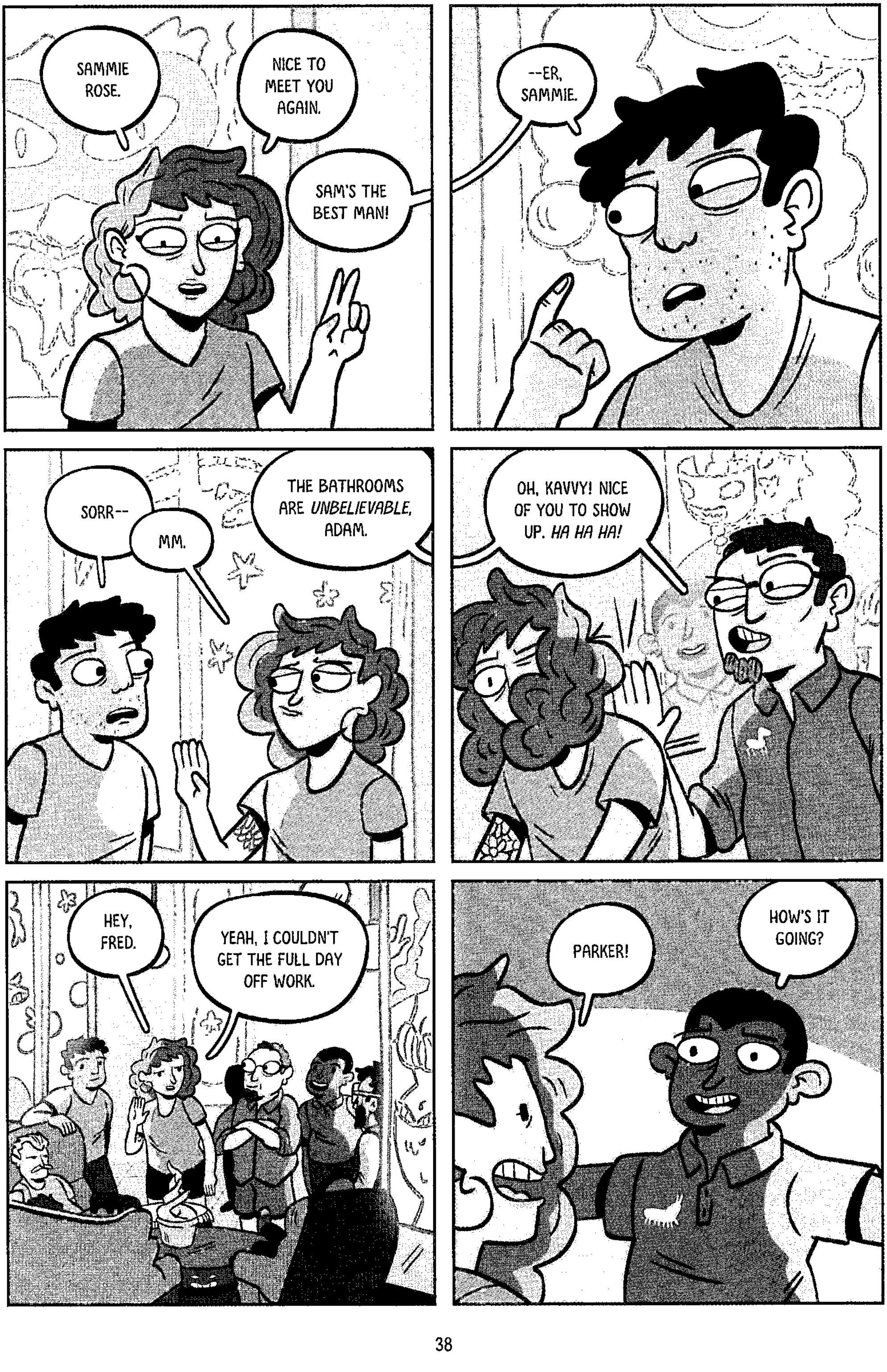
SAMMIE ROSE.
NICE TO MEET YOU AGAIN.
SAM'S THE BEST MAN!
--ER, SAMMIE.
SORR--
MM.
THE BATHROOMS ARE *UNBELIEVABLE*, ADAM.
OH, KAVVY! NICE OF YOU TO SHOW UP. *HA HA HA!*
HEY, FRED.
YEAH, I COULDN'T GET THE FULL DAY OFF WORK.
PARKER!
HOW'S IT GOING?

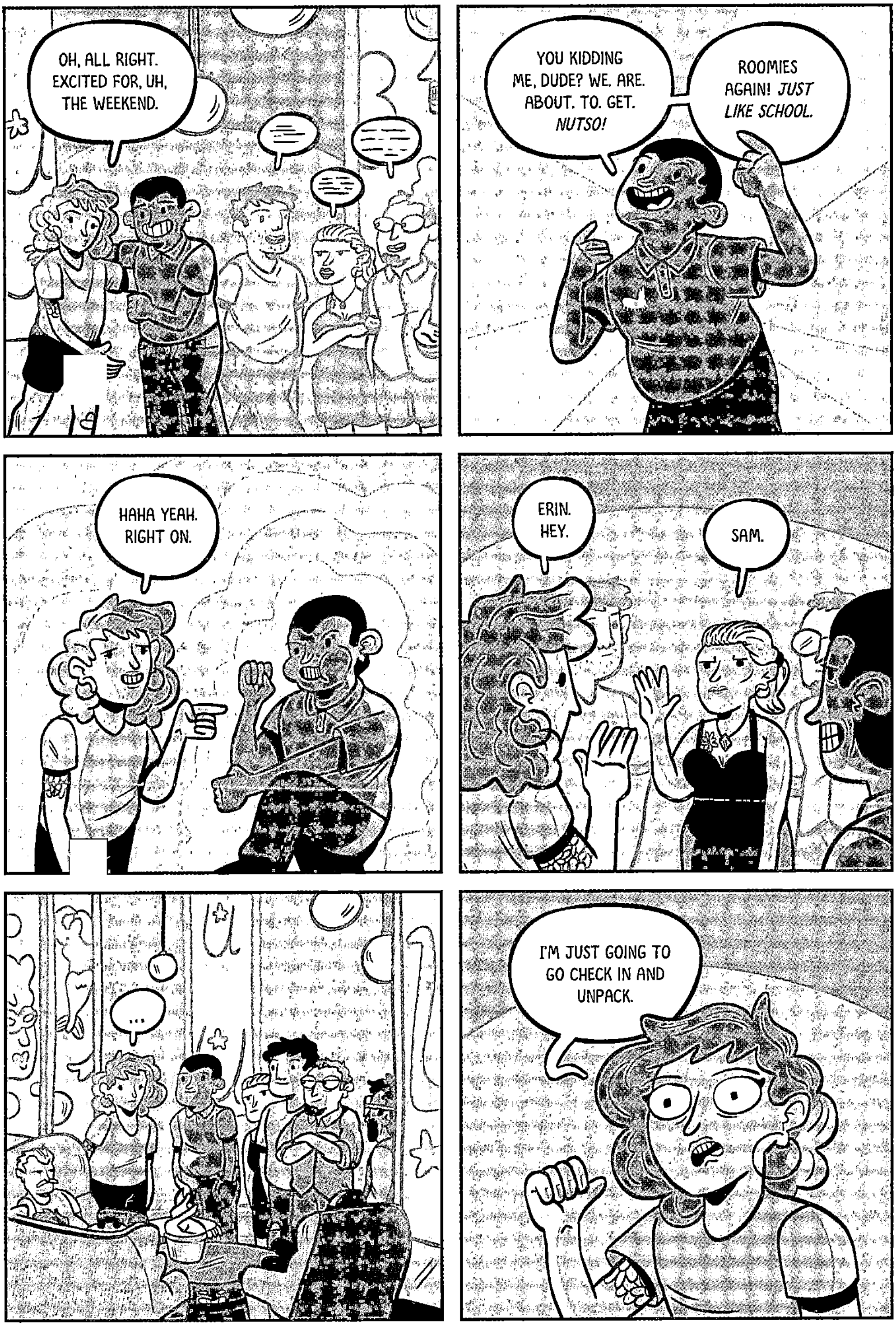
OH, ALL RIGHT. EXCITED FOR, UH, THE WEEKEND.
YOU KIDDING ME, DUDE? WE. ARE. ABOUT. TO. GET. *NUTSO!*
ROOMIES AGAIN! *JUST LIKE SCHOOL.*
HAHA YEAH. RIGHT ON.
ERIN. HEY.
SAM.
...
I'M JUST GOING TO GO CHECK IN AND UNPACK.

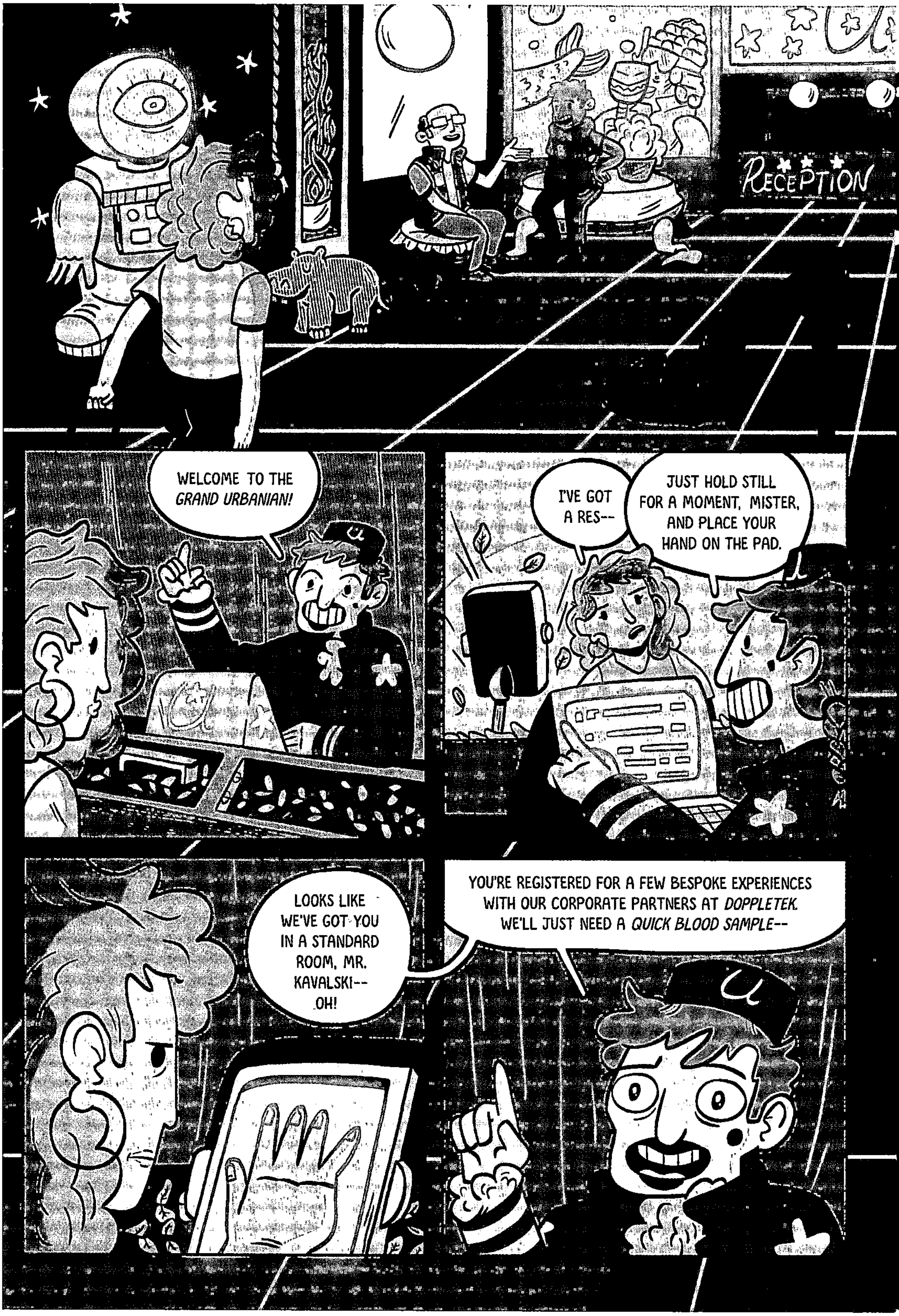
RECEPTION
WELCOME TO THE *GRAND URBANIAN!*
I'VE GOT A RES--
JUST HOLD STILL FOR A MOMENT, MISTER, AND PLACE YOUR HAND ON THE PAD.
LOOKS LIKE WE'VE GOT YOU IN A STANDARD ROOM, MR. KAVALSKI-- OH!
YOU'RE REGISTERED FOR A FEW BESPOKE EXPERIENCES WITH OUR CORPORATE PARTNERS AT *DOPPLETEK.* WE'LL JUST NEED A *QUICK BLOOD SAMPLE*--

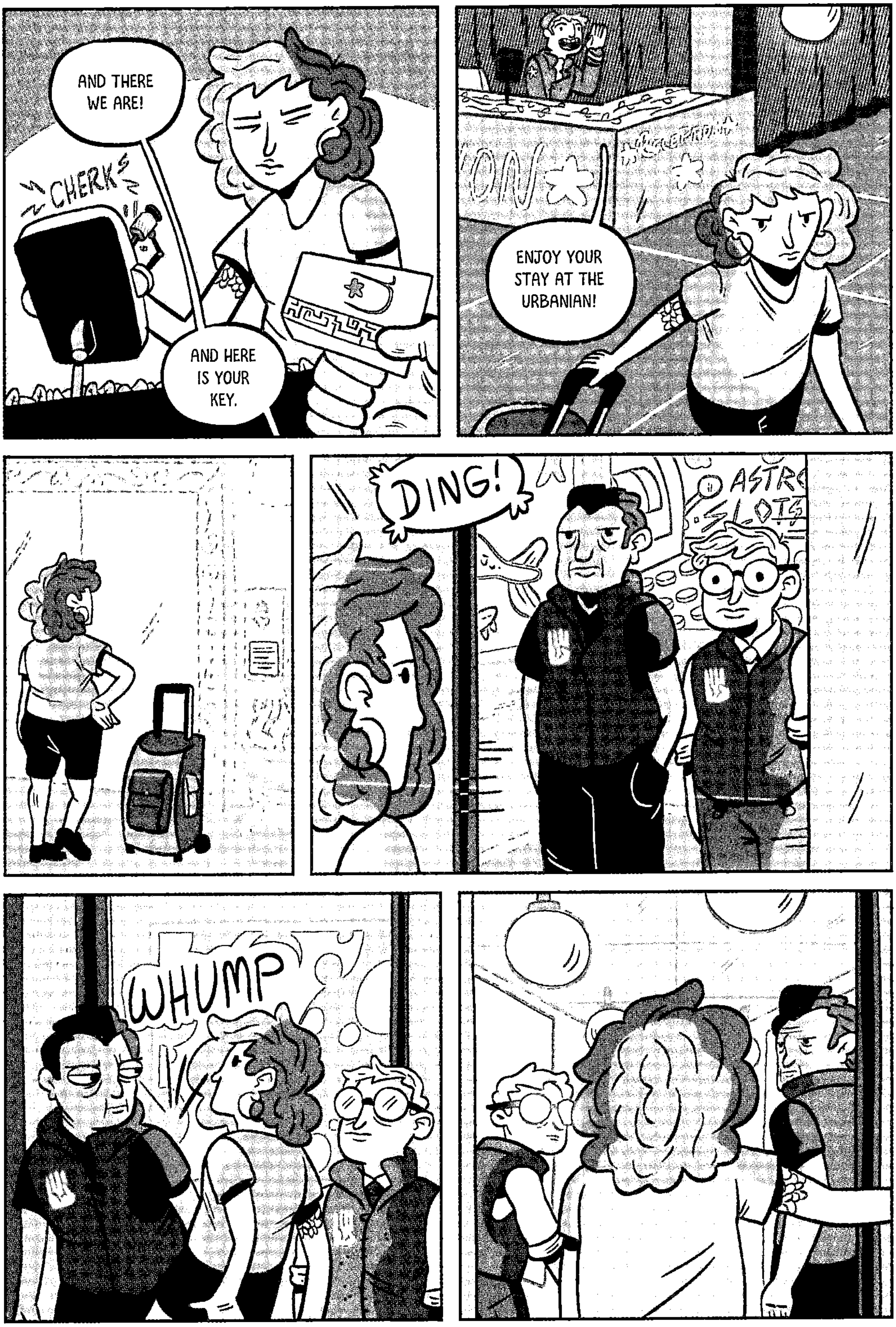
CHERK
AND THERE WE ARE!
AND HERE IS YOUR KEY.
ENJOY YOUR STAY AT THE URBANIAN!
DING!
ASTRO
WHUMP

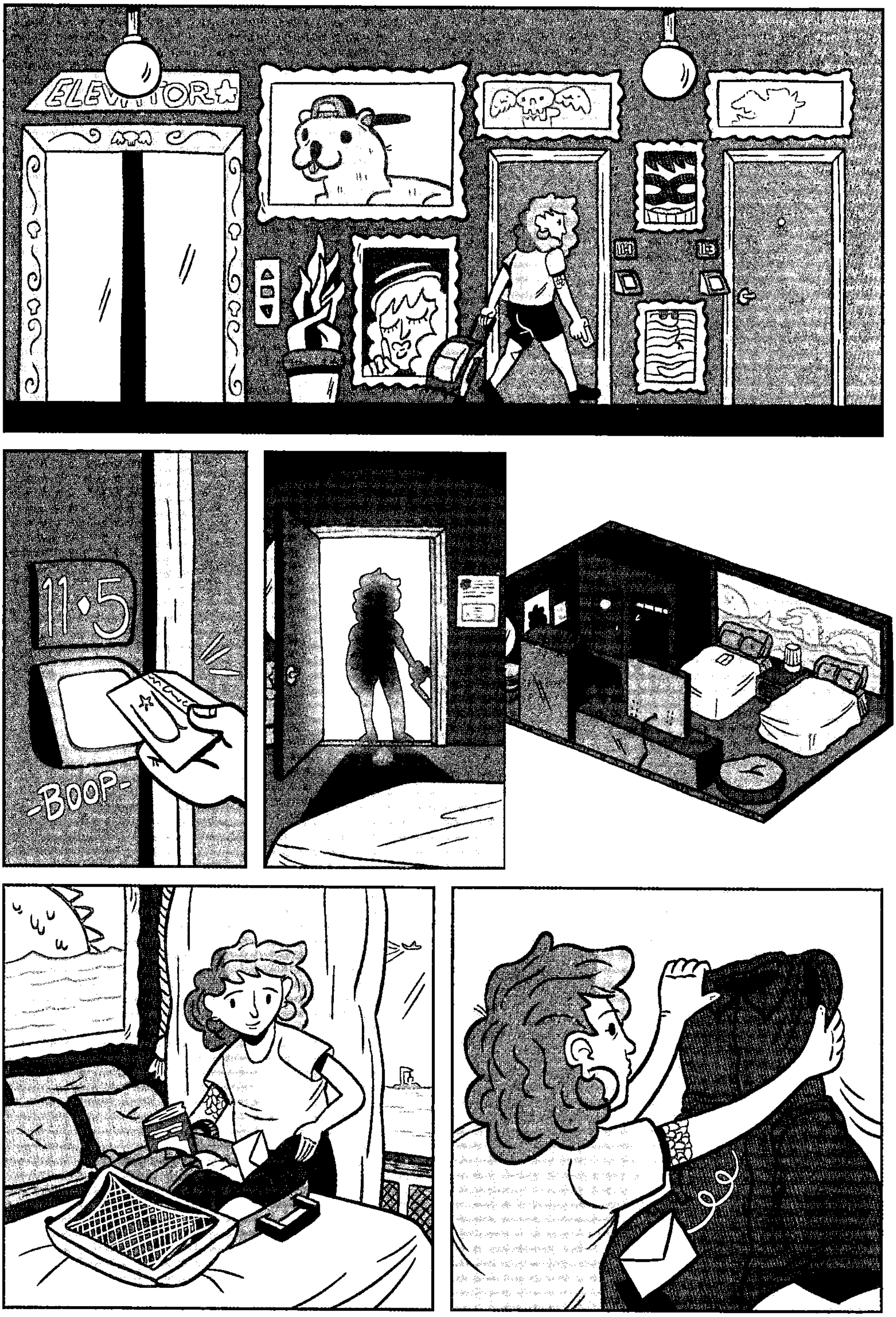
ELEV TOR
11·5
-BOOP-

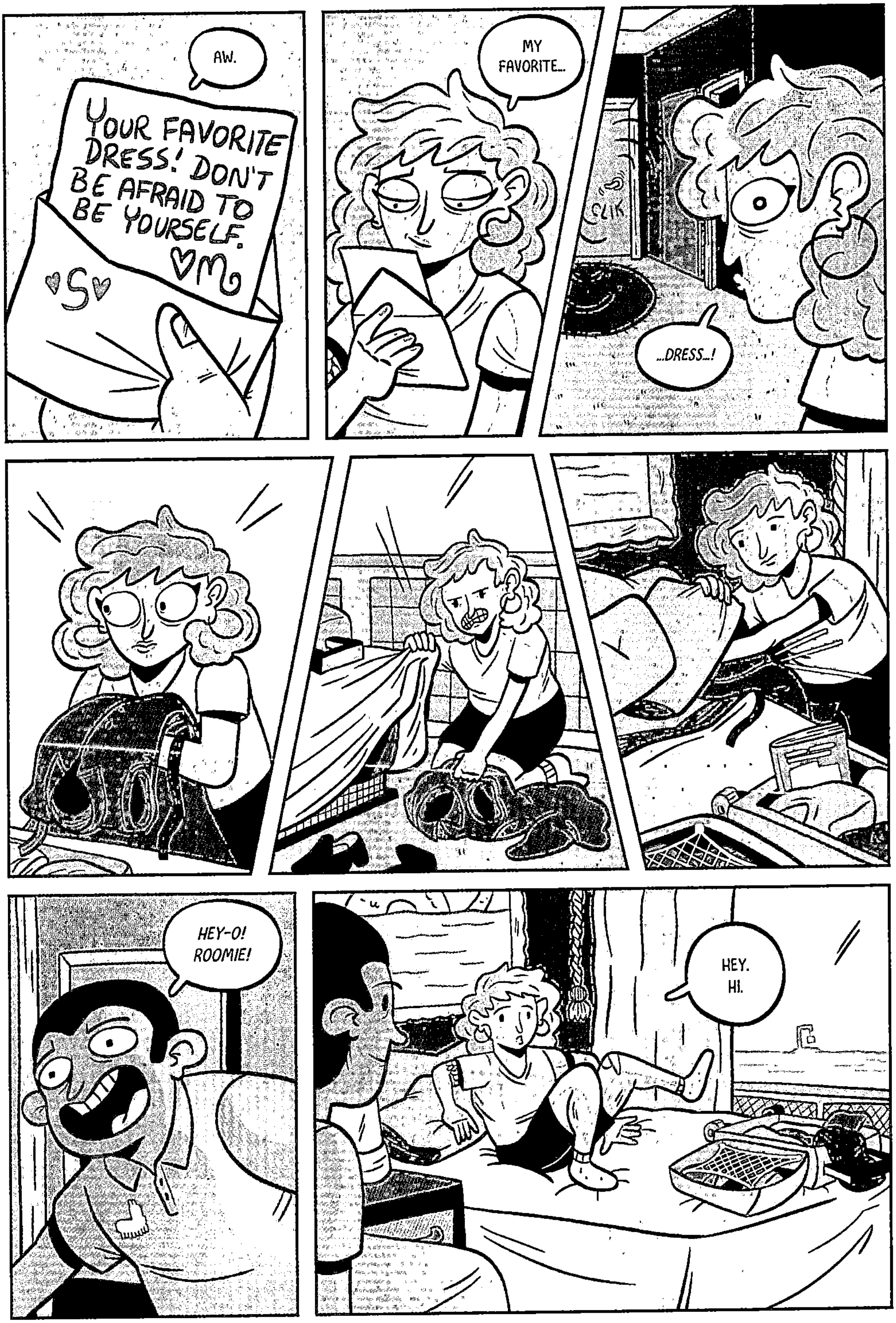
AW.
YOUR FAVORITE DRESS! DON'T BE AFRAID TO BE YOURSELF. ♥M
♥S♥
MY FAVORITE...
CLIK
...DRESS...!
HEY-O! ROOMIE!
HEY. HI.

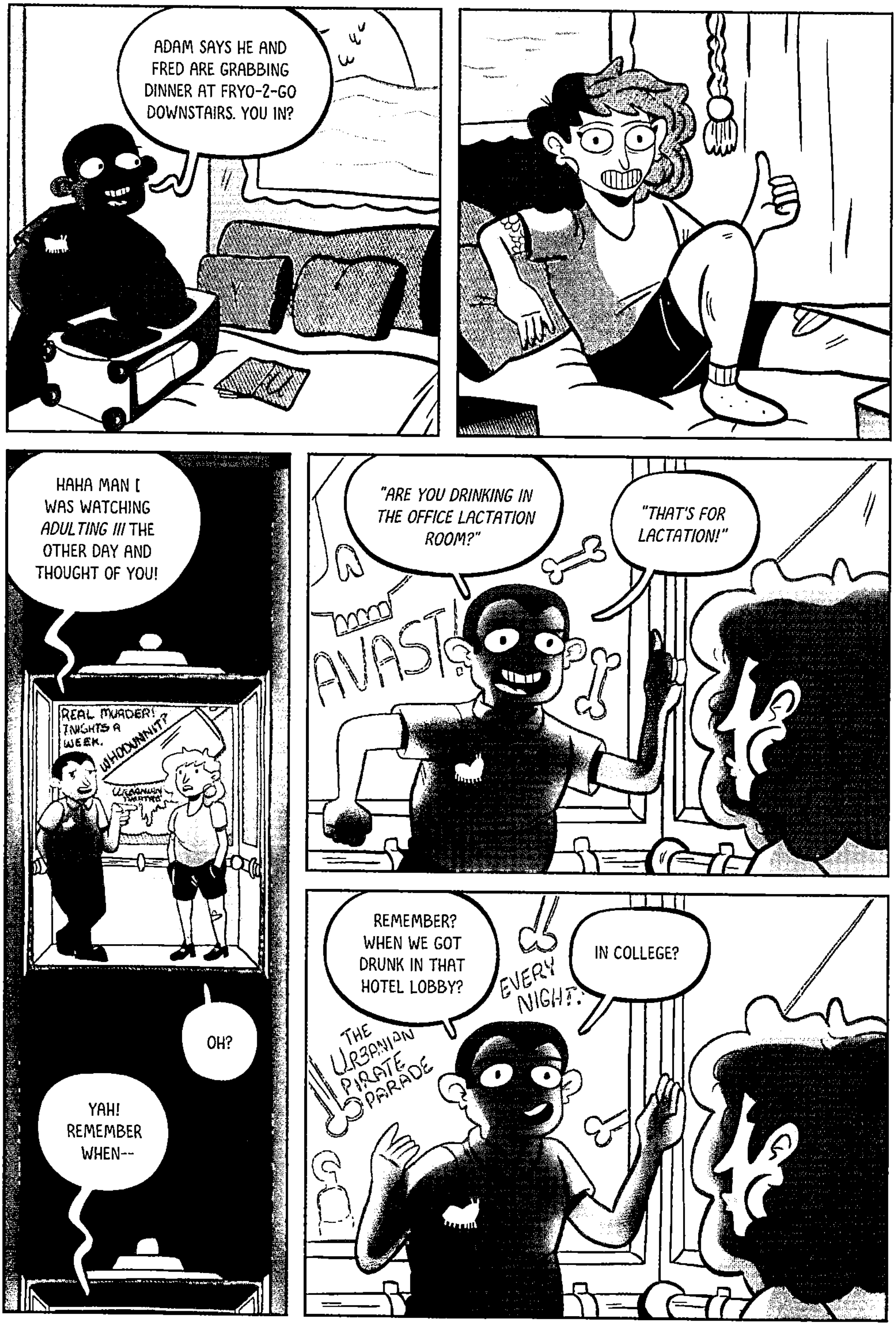
ADAM SAYS HE AND FRED ARE GRABBING DINNER AT FRYO-2-GO DOWNSTAIRS. YOU IN?
HAHA MAN I WAS WATCHING *ADULTING III* THE OTHER DAY AND THOUGHT OF YOU!
REAL MURDER! 7 NIGHTS A WEEK.
WHODUNNIT?
OH?
YAH! REMEMBER WHEN--
"ARE YOU DRINKING IN THE OFFICE LACTATION ROOM?"
"THAT'S FOR LACTATION!"
AVAST!
REMEMBER? WHEN WE GOT DRUNK IN THAT HOTEL LOBBY?
IN COLLEGE?
EVERY NIGHT!
THE URBANIAN PIRATE PARADE

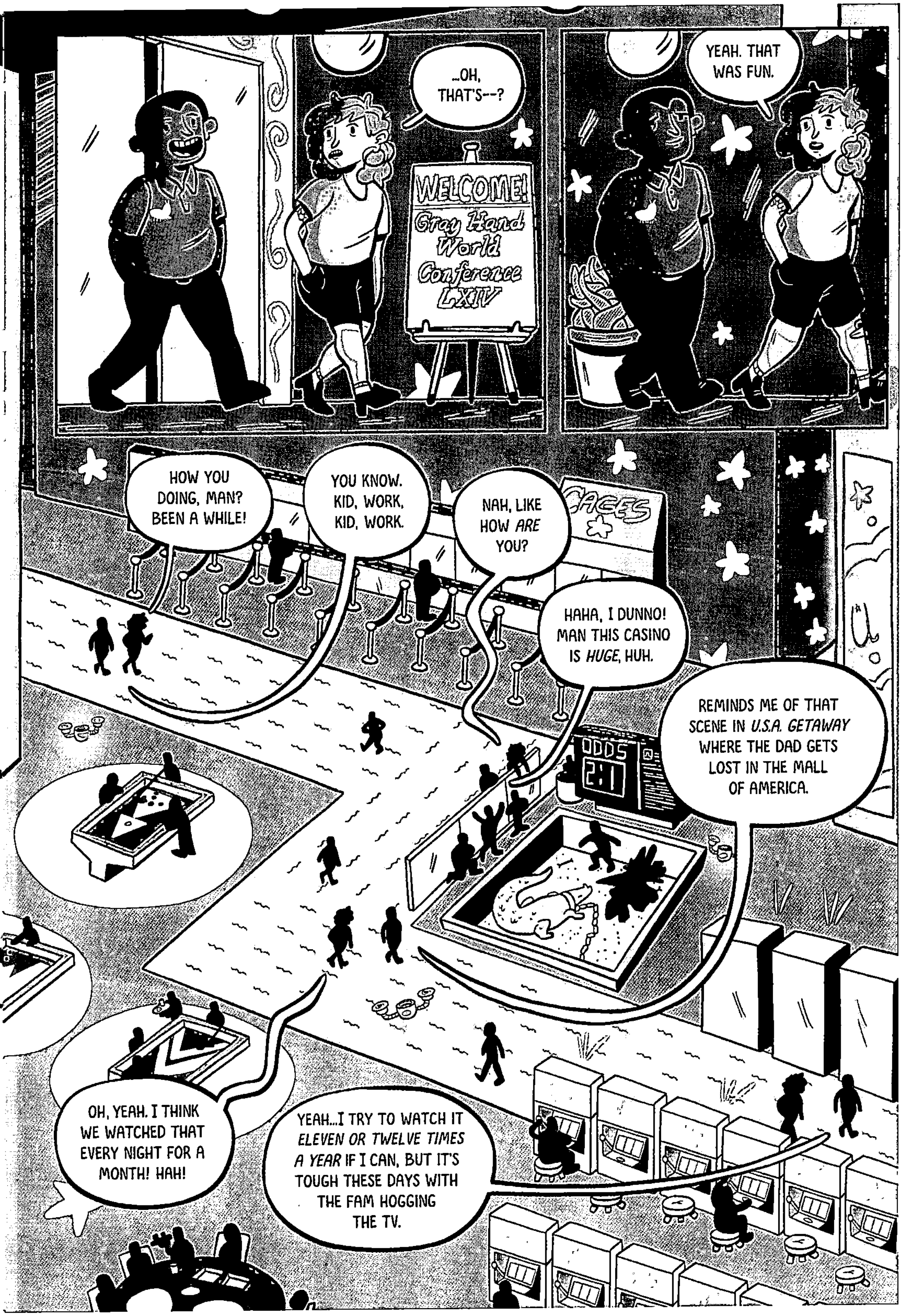
...OH, THAT'S--?
WELCOME! Gray Hand World Conference LXIV
YEAH. THAT WAS FUN.
HOW YOU DOING, MAN? BEEN A WHILE!
YOU KNOW. KID, WORK, KID, WORK.
NAH, LIKE HOW *ARE* YOU?
CAGES
HAHA, I DUNNO! MAN THIS CASINO IS *HUGE*, HUH.
ODDS 2:1
REMINDS ME OF THAT SCENE IN *U.S.A. GETAWAY* WHERE THE DAD GETS LOST IN THE MALL OF AMERICA.
OH, YEAH. I THINK WE WATCHED THAT EVERY NIGHT FOR A MONTH! HAH!
YEAH...I TRY TO WATCH IT *ELEVEN OR TWELVE TIMES A YEAR* IF I CAN, BUT IT'S TOUGH THESE DAYS WITH THE FAM HOGGING THE TV.

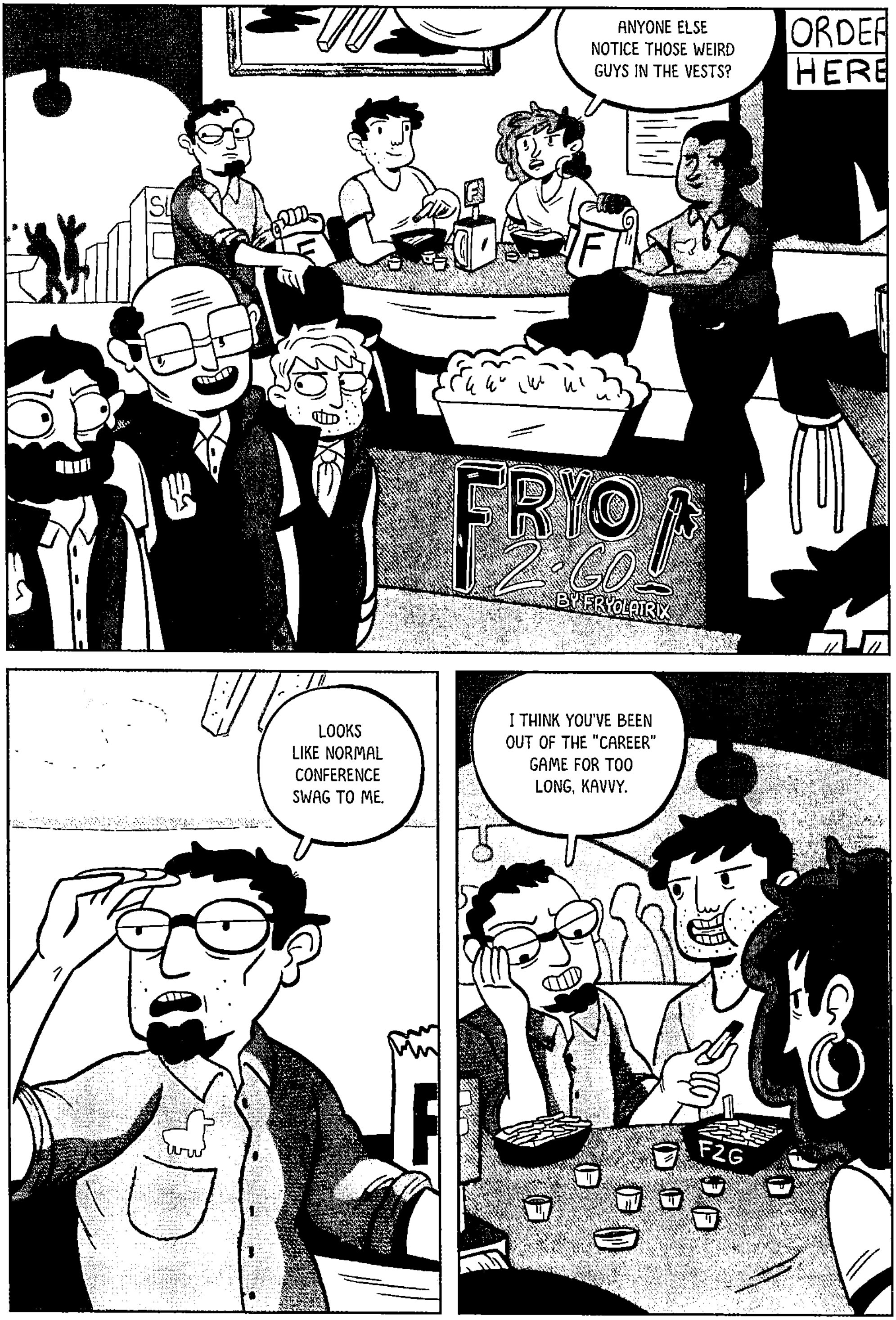
ANYONE ELSE NOTICE THOSE WEIRD GUYS IN THE VESTS?
ORDER HERE
FRYO 2-GO! BY: FRYOLATRIX
LOOKS LIKE NORMAL CONFERENCE SWAG TO ME.
I THINK YOU'VE BEEN OUT OF THE "CAREER" GAME FOR TOO LONG, KAVVY.
F2G

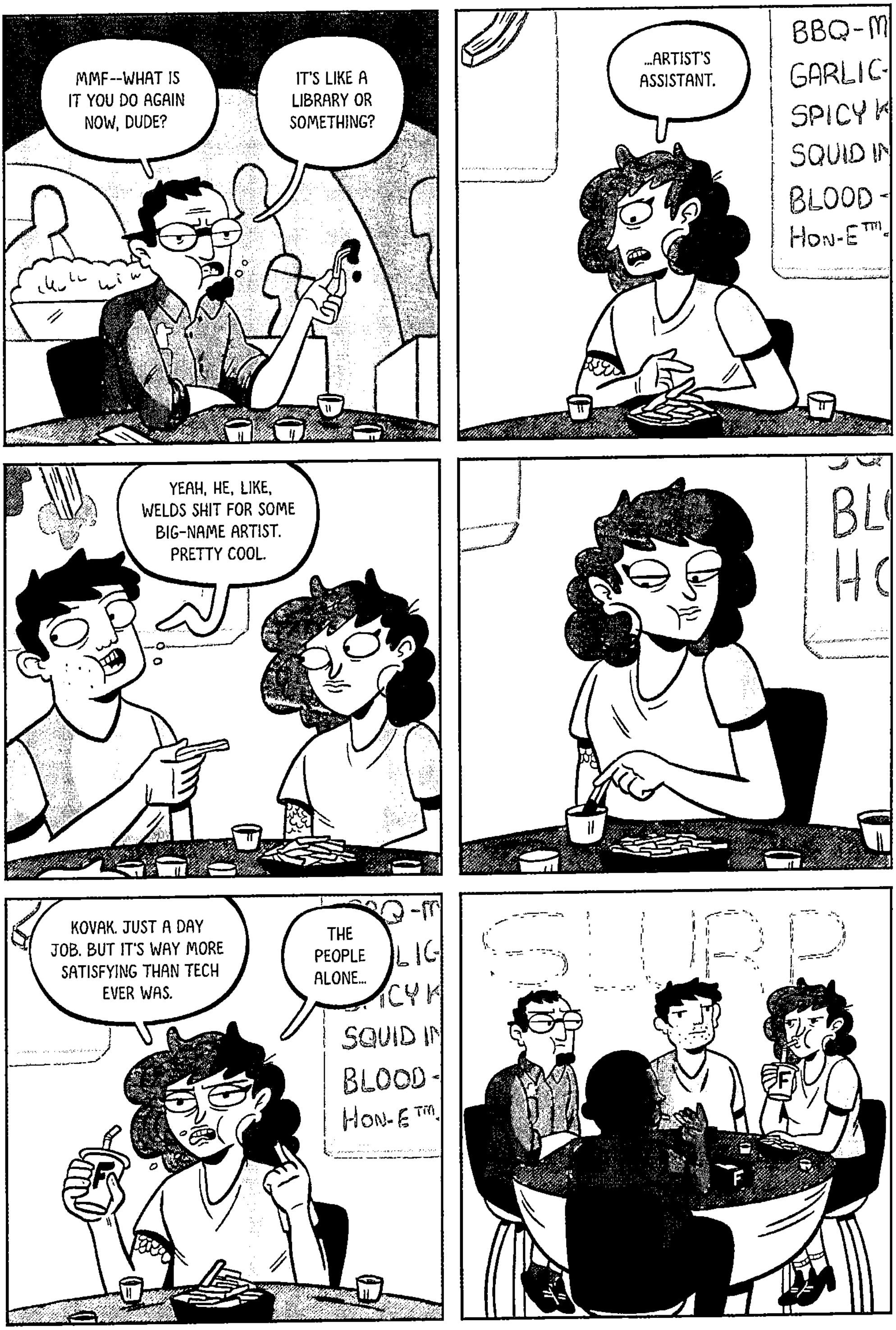
MMF--WHAT IS IT YOU DO AGAIN NOW, DUDE?
IT'S LIKE A LIBRARY OR SOMETHING?
...ARTIST'S ASSISTANT.
BBQ-M
GARLIC-
SPICY K
SQUID IN
BLOOD-
HON-E™
YEAH, HE, LIKE, WELDS SHIT FOR SOME BIG-NAME ARTIST. PRETTY COOL.
KOVAK. JUST A DAY JOB. BUT IT'S WAY MORE SATISFYING THAN TECH EVER WAS.
THE PEOPLE ALONE...
SLURP

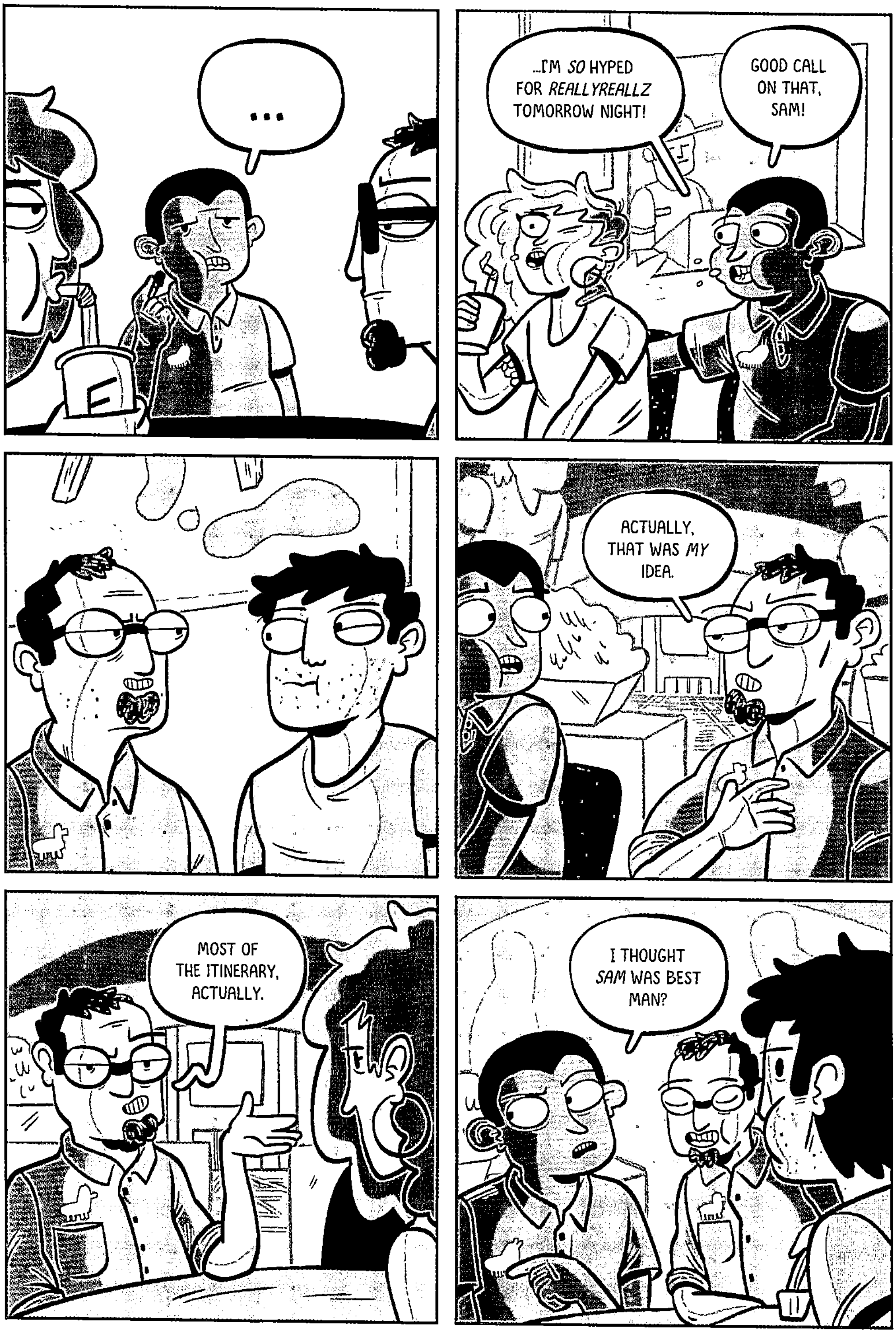
...
...I'M *SO* HYPED FOR *REALLYREALLZ* TOMORROW NIGHT!
GOOD CALL ON THAT, SAM!
ACTUALLY, THAT WAS *MY* IDEA.
MOST OF THE ITINERARY, ACTUALLY.
I THOUGHT *SAM* WAS BEST MAN?

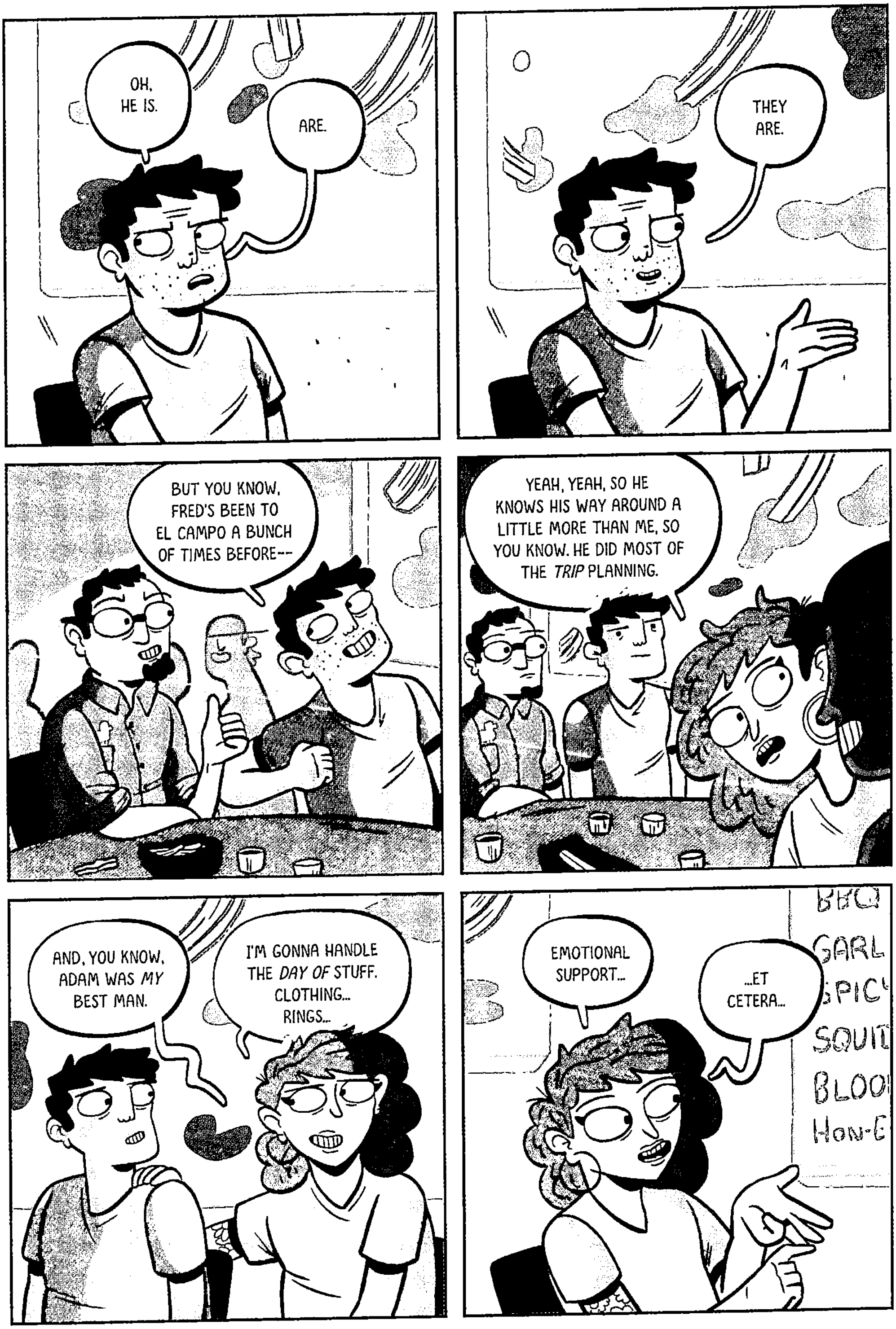
OH, HE IS.
ARE.
THEY ARE.
BUT YOU KNOW, FRED'S BEEN TO EL CAMPO A BUNCH OF TIMES BEFORE--
YEAH, YEAH, SO HE KNOWS HIS WAY AROUND A LITTLE MORE THAN ME, SO YOU KNOW. HE DID MOST OF THE *TRIP* PLANNING.
AND, YOU KNOW, ADAM WAS *MY* BEST MAN.
I'M GONNA HANDLE THE *DAY OF* STUFF. CLOTHING... RINGS...
EMOTIONAL SUPPORT...
...ET CETERA...

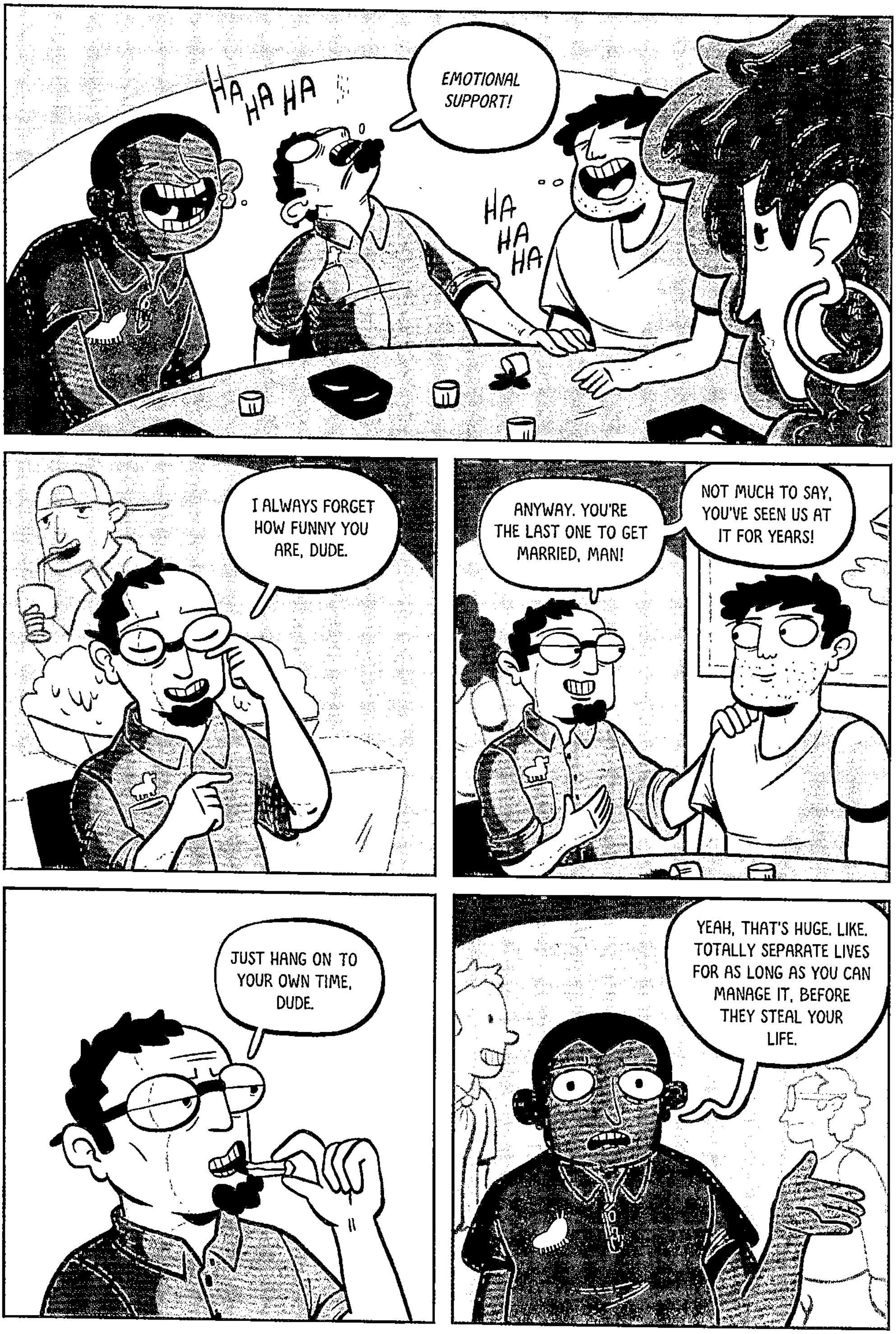
HA HA HA
EMOTIONAL SUPPORT!
HA HA HA
I ALWAYS FORGET HOW FUNNY YOU ARE, DUDE.
ANYWAY. YOU'RE THE LAST ONE TO GET MARRIED, MAN!
NOT MUCH TO SAY, YOU'VE SEEN US AT IT FOR YEARS!
JUST HANG ON TO YOUR OWN TIME, DUDE.
YEAH, THAT'S HUGE. LIKE. TOTALLY SEPARATE LIVES FOR AS LONG AS YOU CAN MANAGE IT, BEFORE THEY STEAL YOUR LIFE.

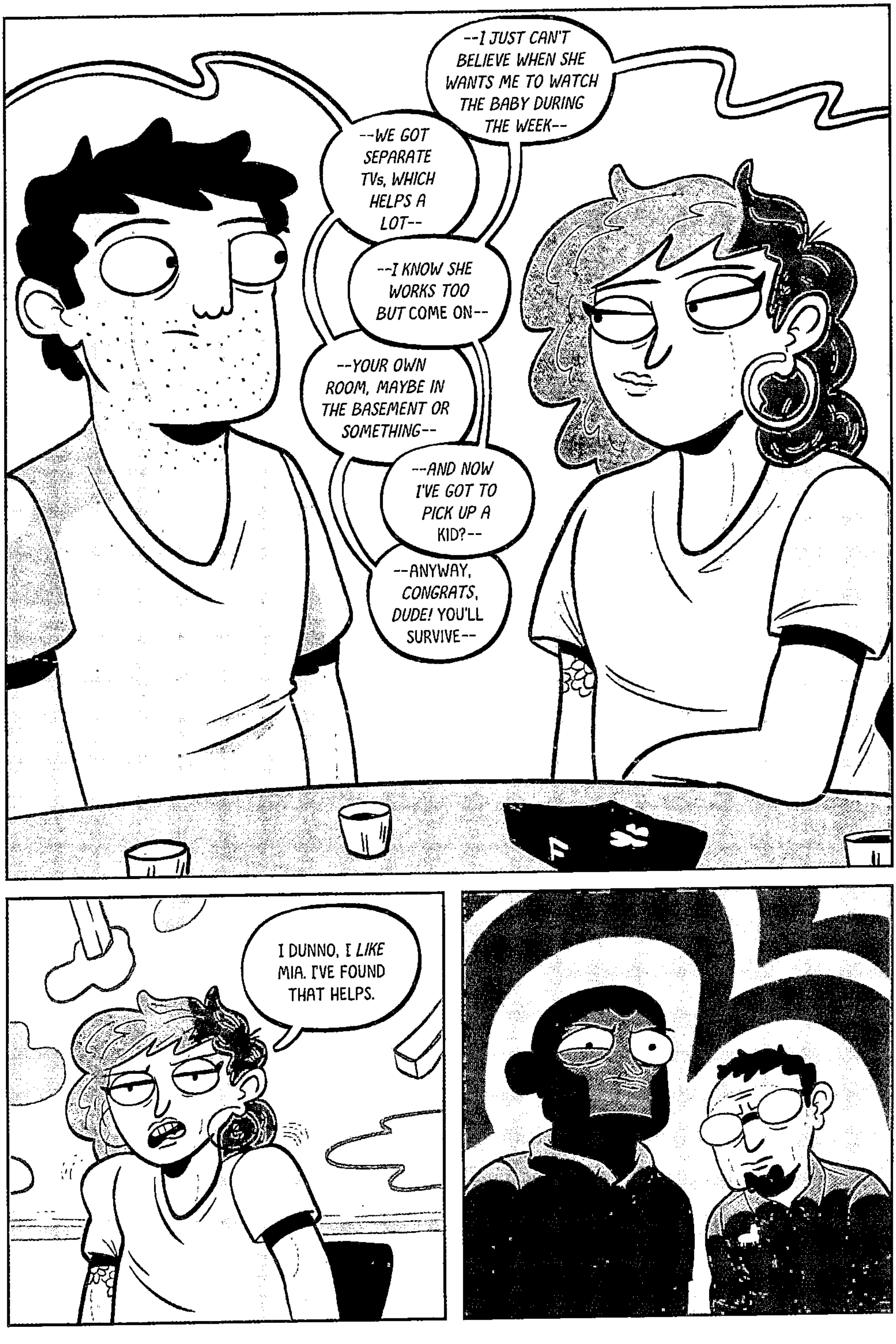
--I JUST CAN'T BELIEVE WHEN SHE WANTS ME TO WATCH THE BABY DURING THE WEEK--
--WE GOT SEPARATE TVs, WHICH HELPS A LOT--
--I KNOW SHE WORKS TOO BUT COME ON--
--YOUR OWN ROOM, MAYBE IN THE BASEMENT OR SOMETHING--
--AND NOW I'VE GOT TO PICK UP A KID?--
--ANYWAY, CONGRATS, DUDE! YOU'LL SURVIVE--
I DUNNO, I LIKE MIA. I'VE FOUND THAT HELPS.

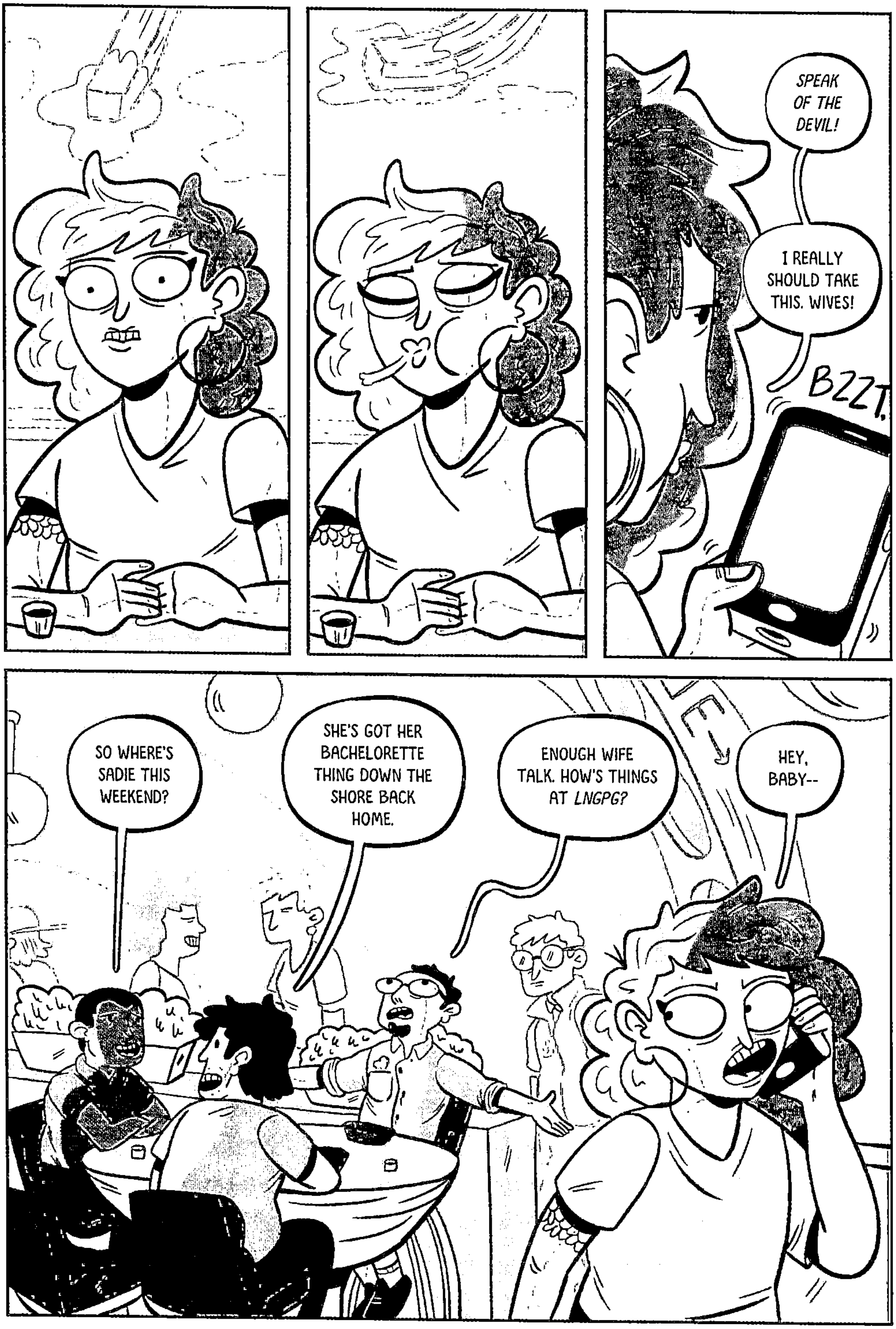
SPEAK OF THE DEVIL!
I REALLY SHOULD TAKE THIS. WIVES!
BZZT.
SO WHERE'S SADIE THIS WEEKEND?
SHE'S GOT HER BACHELORETTE THING DOWN THE SHORE BACK HOME.
ENOUGH WIFE TALK. HOW'S THINGS AT *LNGPG?*
HEY, BABY--

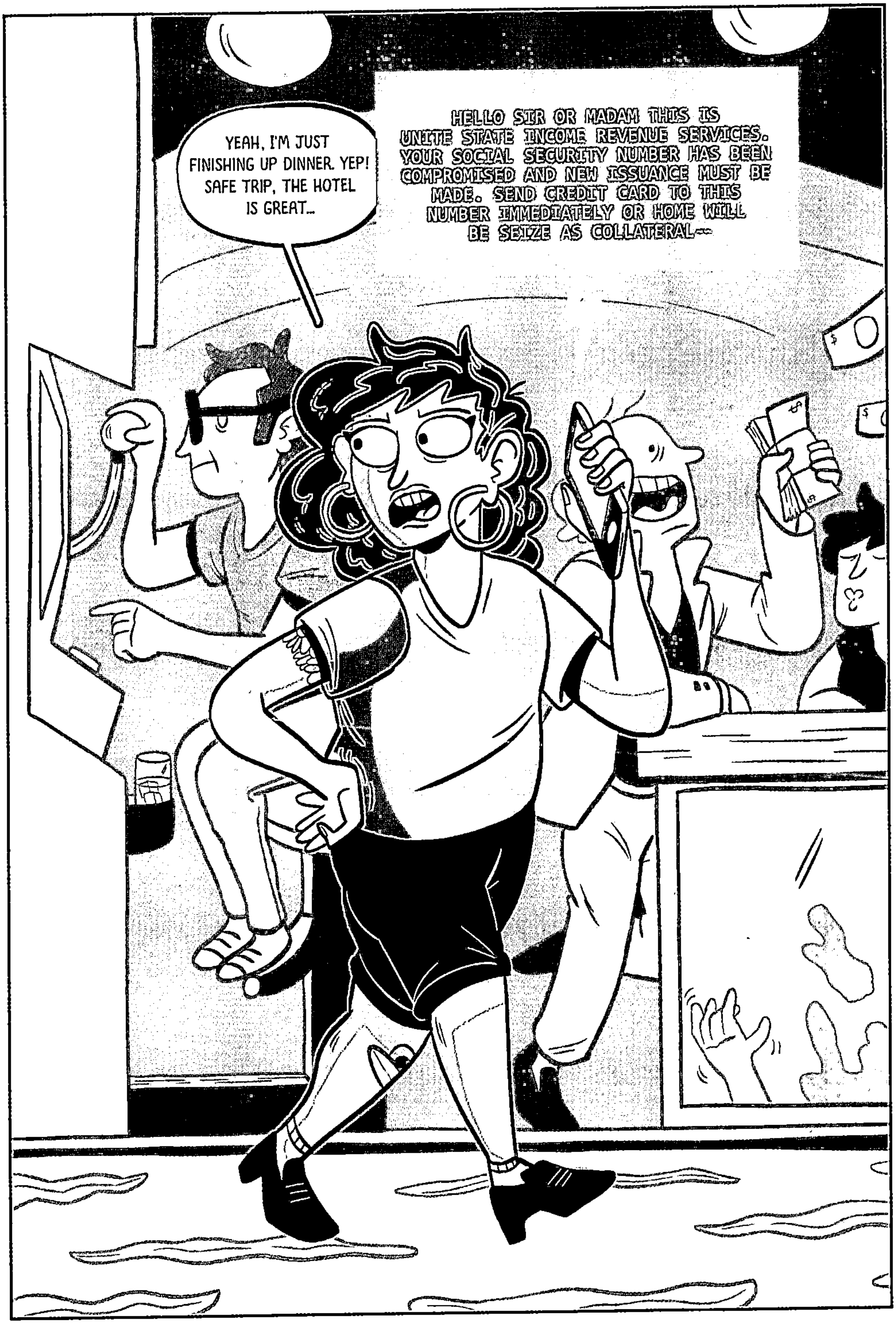
YEAH, I'M JUST FINISHING UP DINNER. YEP! SAFE TRIP, THE HOTEL IS GREAT...
HELLO SIR OR MADAM THIS IS UNITE STATE INCOME REVENUE SERVICES. YOUR SOCIAL SECURITY NUMBER HAS BEEN COMPROMISED AND NEW ISSUANCE MUST BE MADE. SEND CREDIT CARD TO THIS NUMBER IMMEDIATELY OR HOME WILL BE SEIZE AS COLLATERAL--

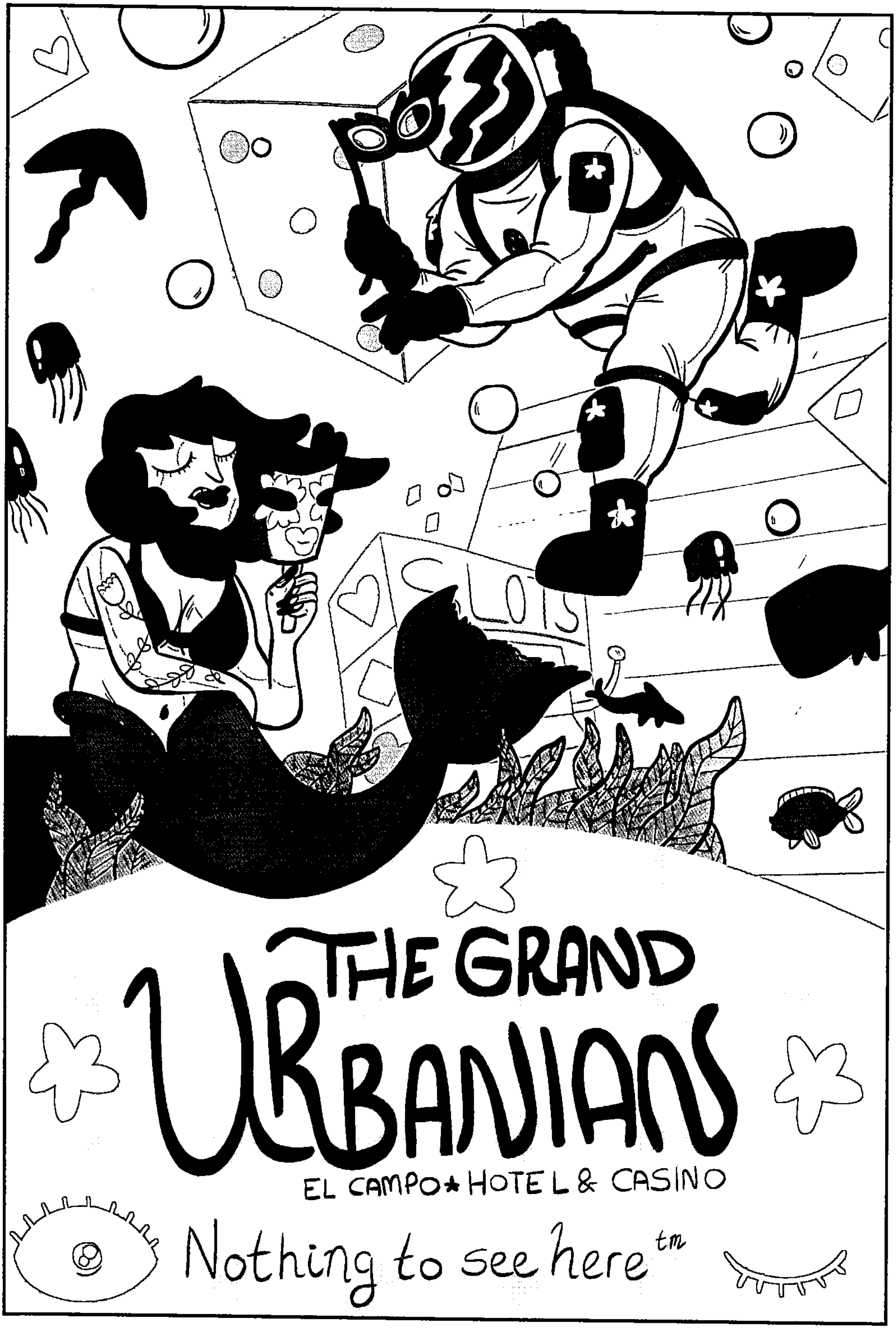
SLOTS
THE GRAND
URBANIANS
EL CAMPO★HOTEL & CASINO
Nothing to see here™

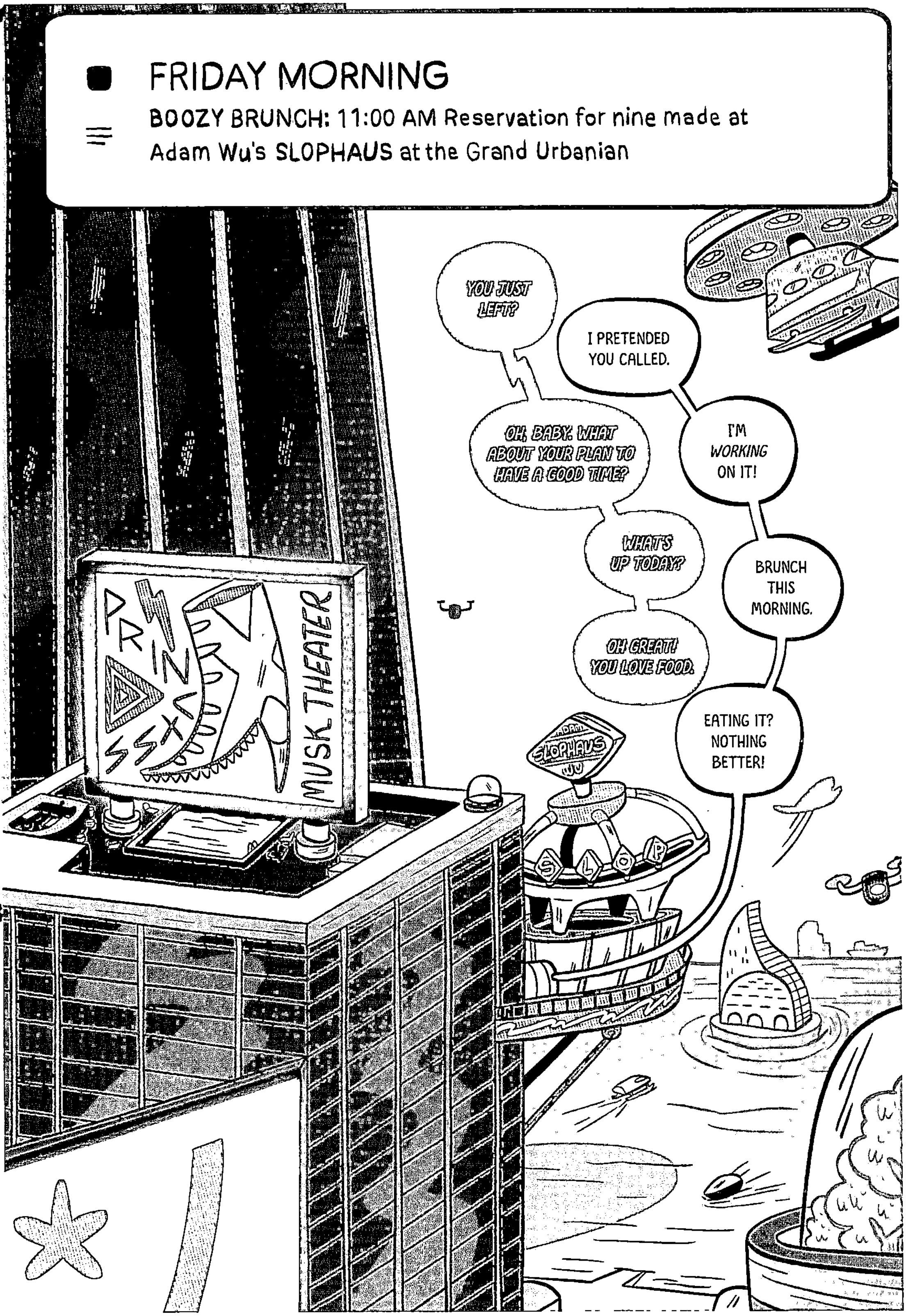
FRIDAY MORNING
BOOZY BRUNCH: 11:00 AM Reservation for nine made at Adam Wu's SLOPHAUS at the Grand Urbanian
YOU JUST LEFT?
I PRETENDED YOU CALLED.
OH, BABY. WHAT ABOUT YOUR PLAN TO HAVE A GOOD TIME?
I'M WORKING ON IT!
WHAT'S UP TODAY?
BRUNCH THIS MORNING.
OH GREAT! YOU LOVE FOOD.
EATING IT? NOTHING BETTER!
MUSK THEATER
ADAM SLOPHAUS WU
S L O P

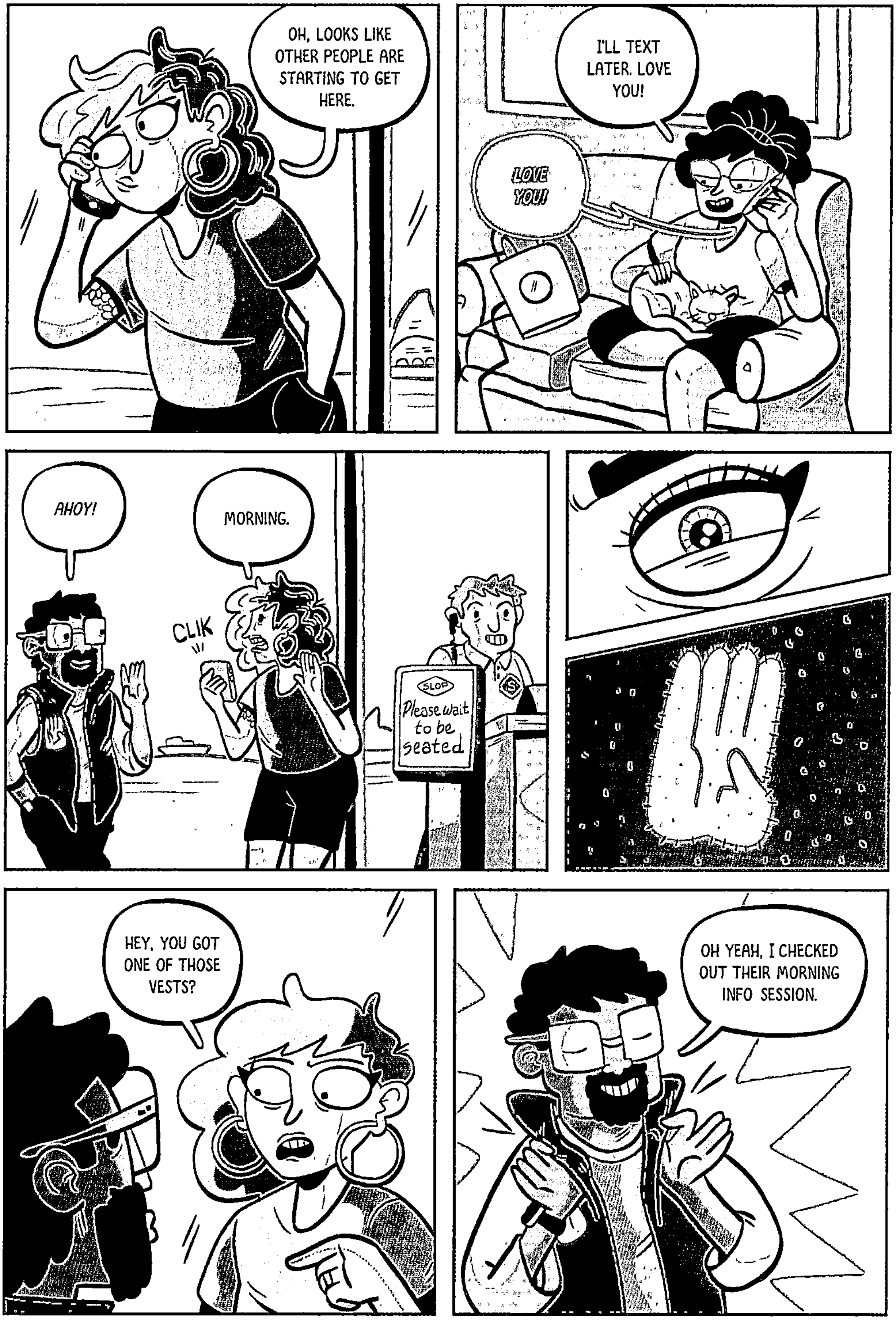
OH, LOOKS LIKE OTHER PEOPLE ARE STARTING TO GET HERE.
I'LL TEXT LATER. LOVE YOU!
LOVE YOU!
AHOY!
MORNING.
CLIK
SLOP
Please wait to be seated
HEY, YOU GOT ONE OF THOSE VESTS?
OH YEAH, I CHECKED OUT THEIR MORNING INFO SESSION.

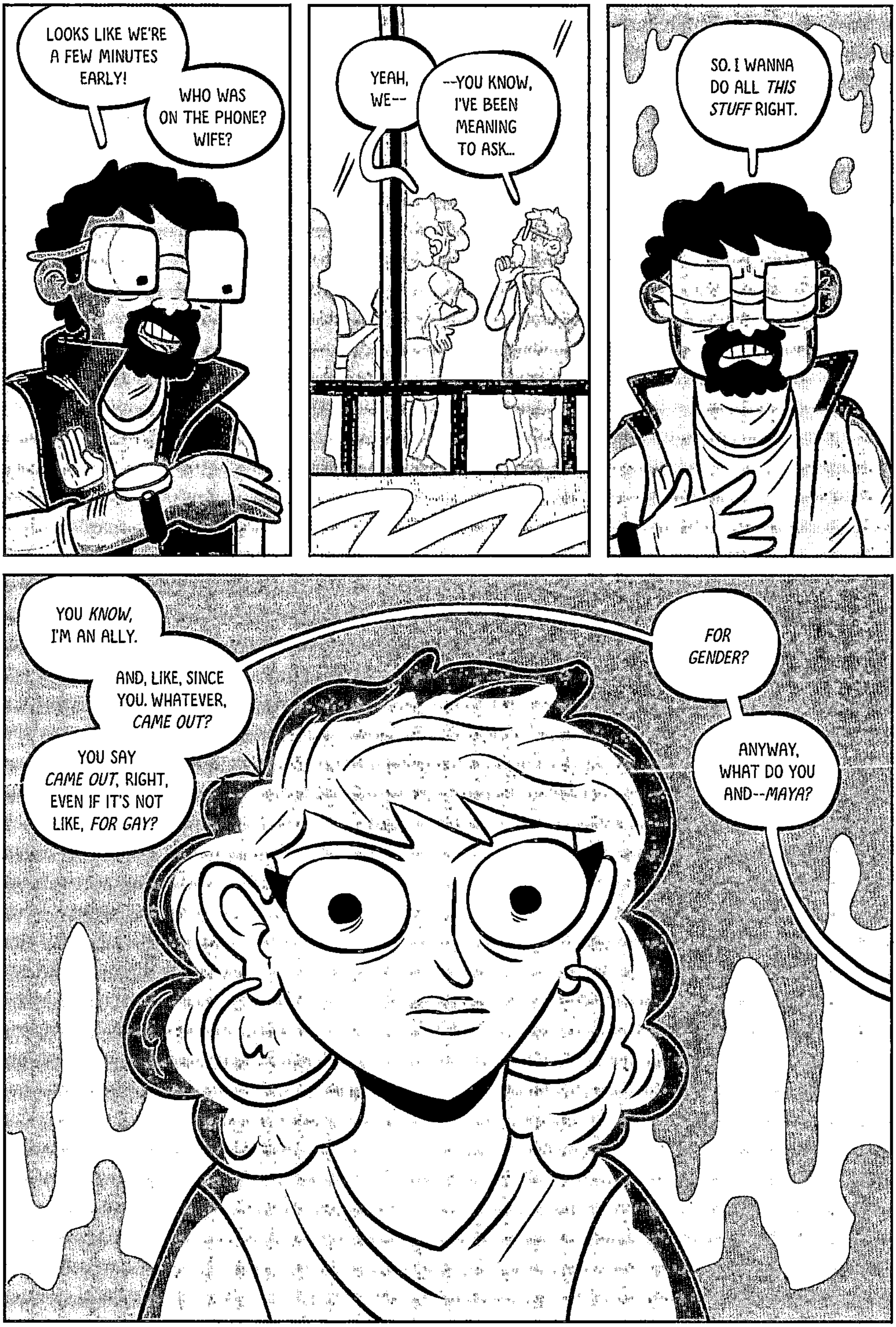
LOOKS LIKE WE'RE A FEW MINUTES EARLY!
WHO WAS ON THE PHONE? WIFE?
YEAH, WE--
--YOU KNOW, I'VE BEEN MEANING TO ASK...
SO. I WANNA DO ALL *THIS STUFF* RIGHT.
YOU *KNOW,* I'M AN ALLY.
AND, LIKE, SINCE YOU. WHATEVER, *CAME OUT?*
YOU SAY *CAME OUT*, RIGHT, EVEN IF IT'S NOT LIKE, *FOR GAY?*
FOR GENDER?
ANYWAY, WHAT DO YOU AND--*MAYA?*

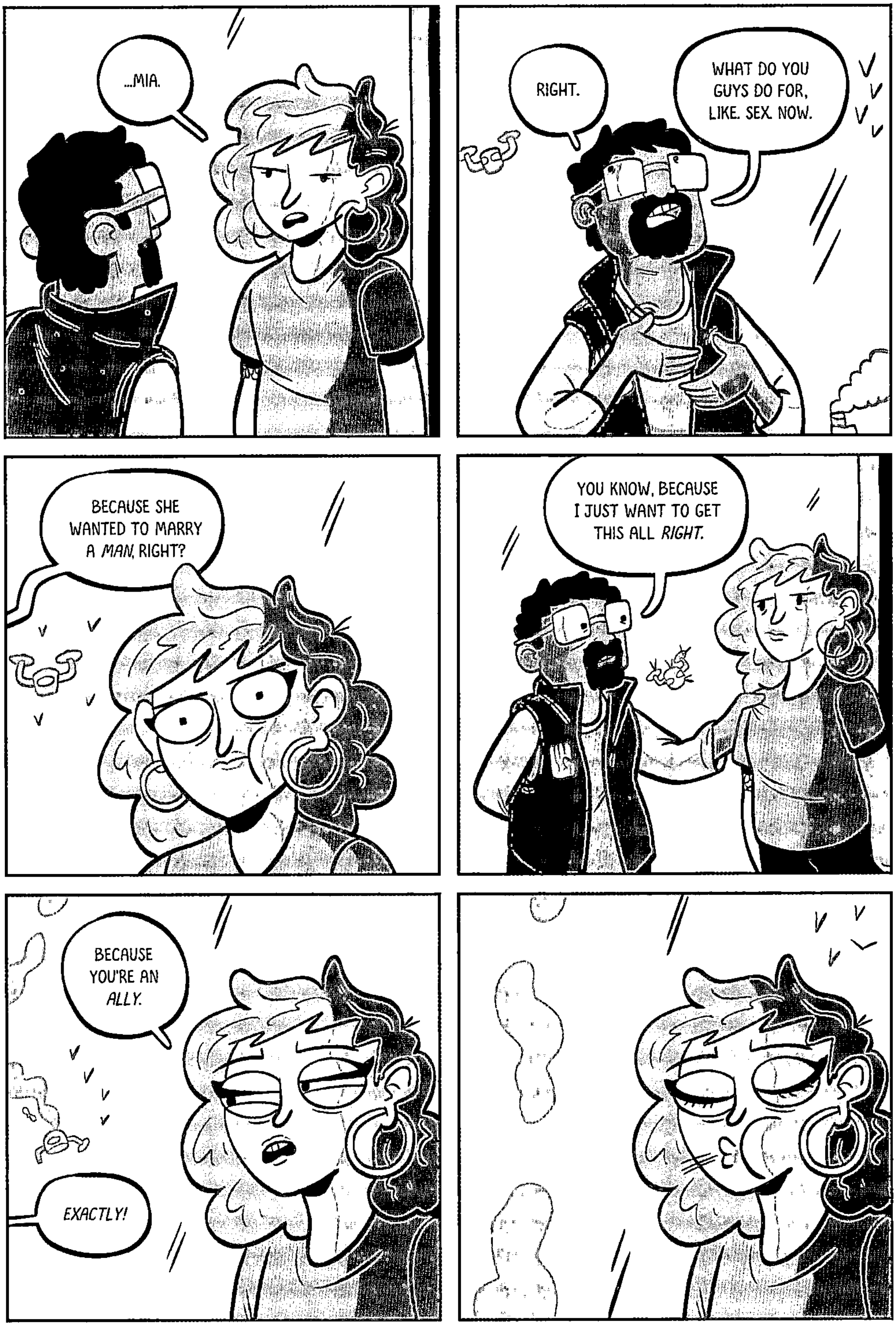
...MIA.
RIGHT.
WHAT DO YOU GUYS DO FOR, LIKE. SEX. NOW.
BECAUSE SHE WANTED TO MARRY A *MAN*, RIGHT?
YOU KNOW, BECAUSE I JUST WANT TO GET THIS ALL *RIGHT*.
BECAUSE YOU'RE AN *ALLY*.
EXACTLY!

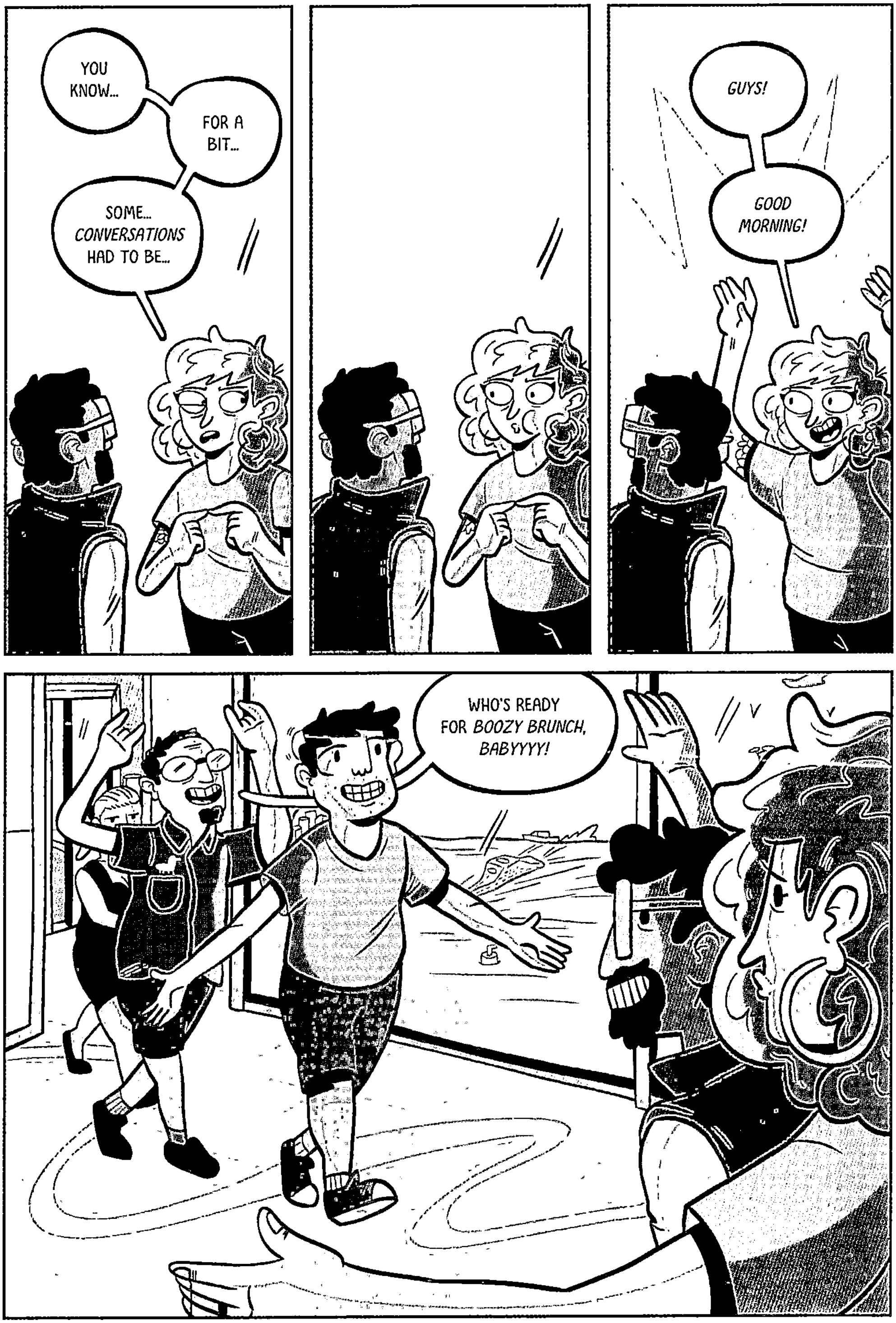
YOU KNOW...
FOR A BIT...
SOME... *CONVERSATIONS* HAD TO BE...
GUYS!
GOOD MORNING!
WHO'S READY FOR *BOOZY BRUNCH, BABYYYY!*

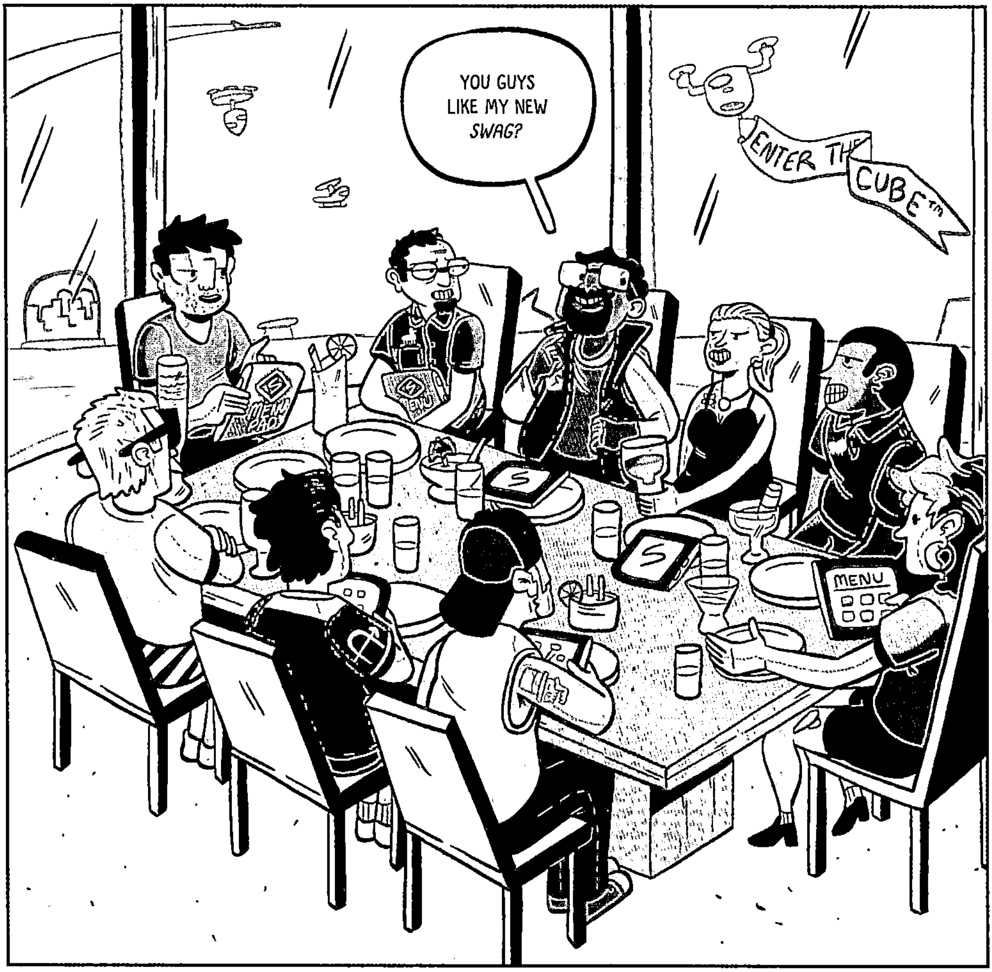
YOU GUYS LIKE MY NEW *SWAG?*
ENTER THE CUBE™
MENU PAD
MENU

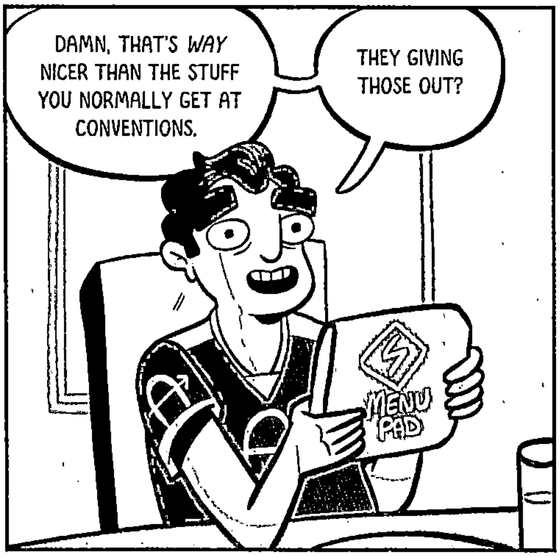
DAMN, THAT'S *WAY* NICER THAN THE STUFF YOU NORMALLY GET AT CONVENTIONS.
THEY GIVING THOSE OUT?
MENU PAD

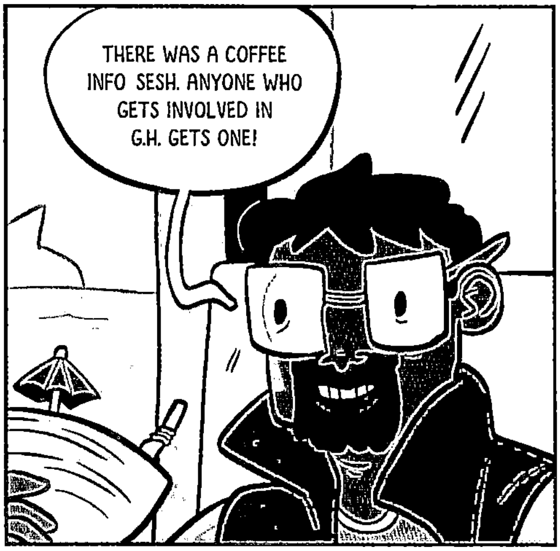
THERE WAS A COFFEE INFO SESH. ANYONE WHO GETS INVOLVED IN G.H. GETS ONE!

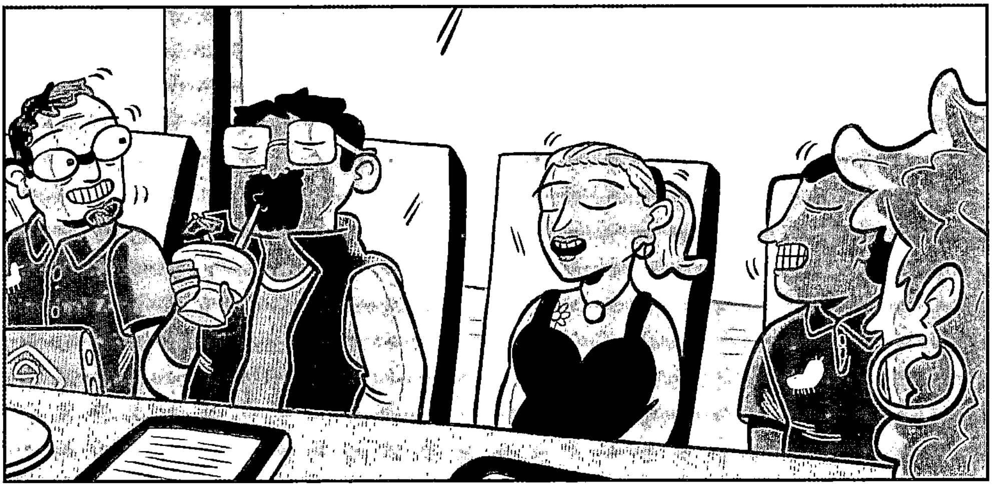

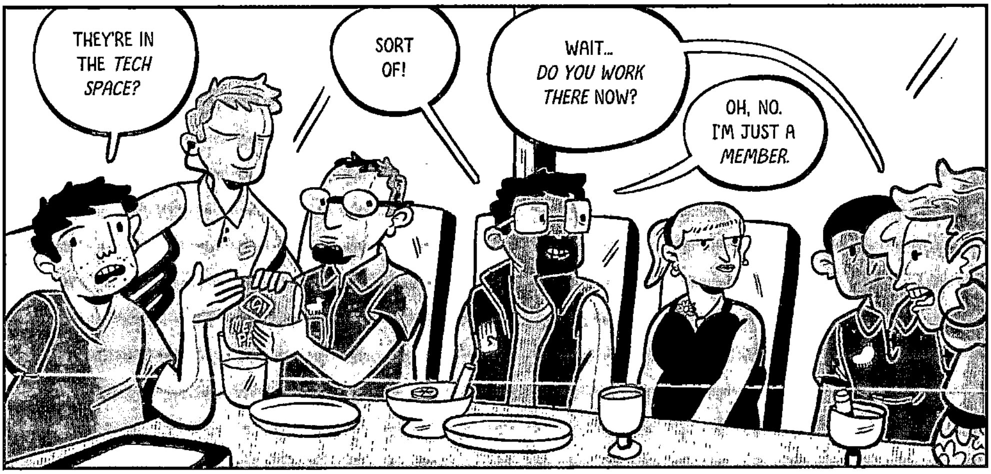
THEY'RE IN THE *TECH SPACE?*
SORT OF!
WAIT... *DO YOU WORK THERE* NOW?
OH, NO. I'M JUST A *MEMBER.*

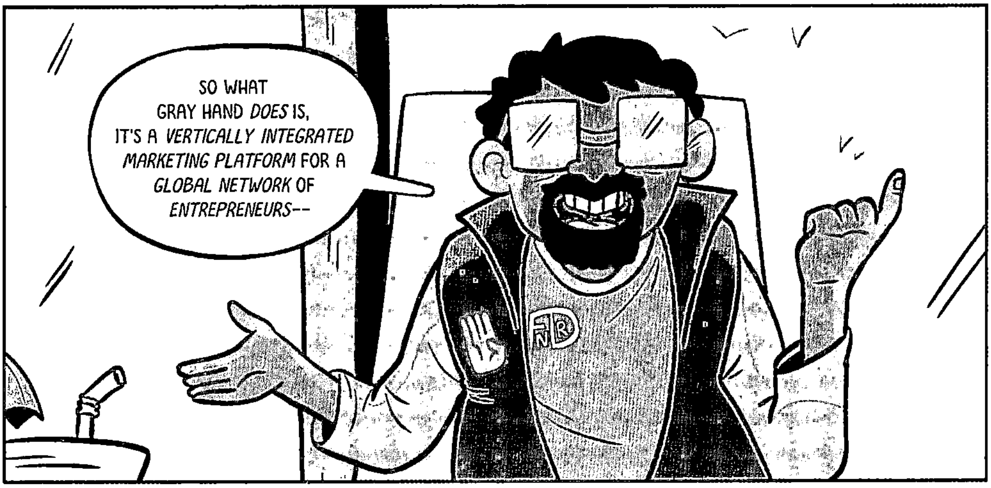
SO WHAT GRAY HAND *DOES* IS, IT'S A *VERTICALLY INTEGRATED MARKETING PLATFORM* FOR A *GLOBAL NETWORK* OF *ENTREPRENEURS*--

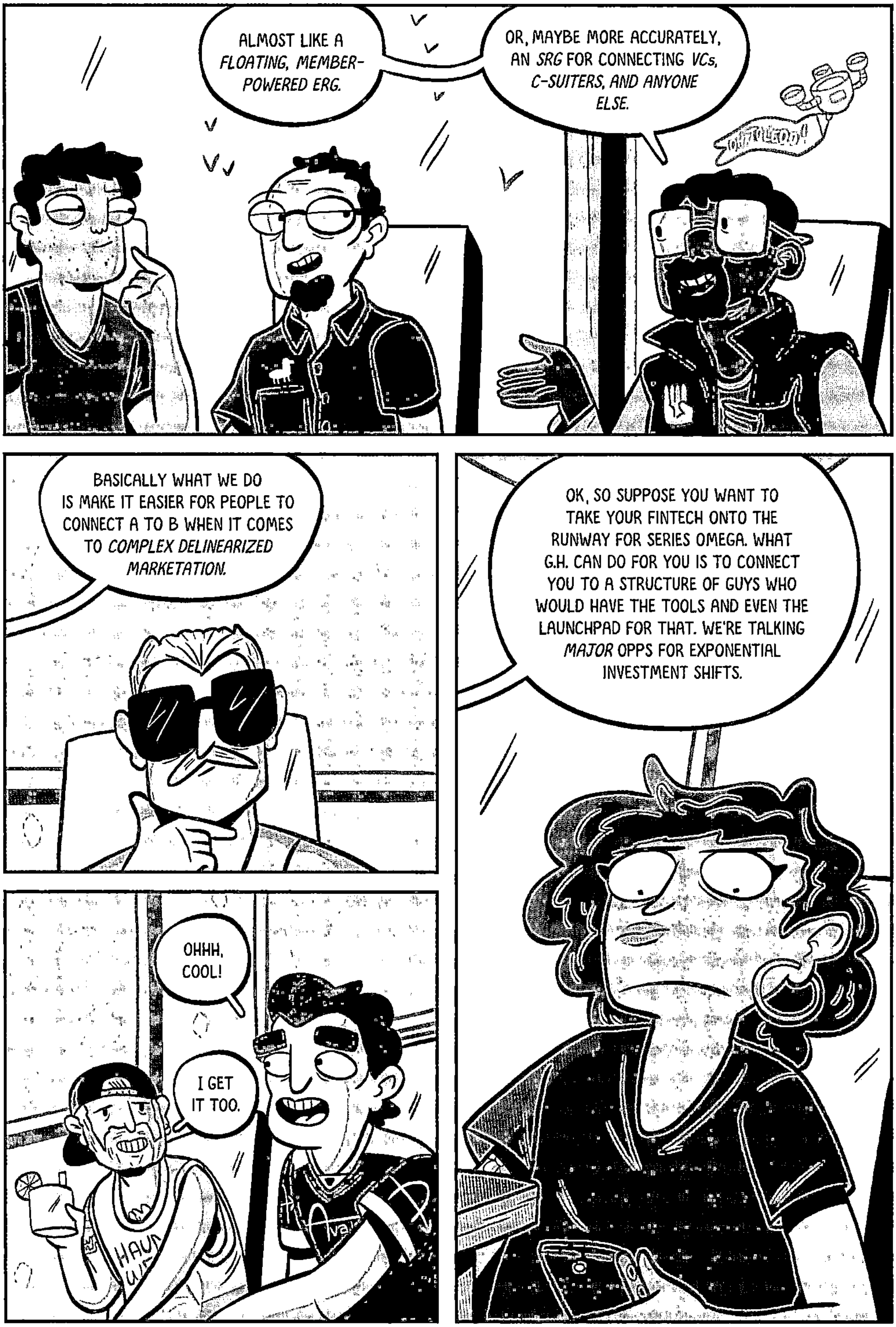
ALMOST LIKE A *FLOATING, MEMBER-POWERED ERG.*
OR, MAYBE MORE ACCURATELY, AN *SRG* FOR CONNECTING *VCs, C-SUITERS, AND ANYONE ELSE.*
BASICALLY WHAT WE DO IS MAKE IT EASIER FOR PEOPLE TO CONNECT A TO B WHEN IT COMES TO *COMPLEX DELINEARIZED MARKETATION.*
OHHH, COOL!
I GET IT TOO.
OK, SO SUPPOSE YOU WANT TO TAKE YOUR FINTECH ONTO THE RUNWAY FOR SERIES OMEGA. WHAT G.H. CAN DO FOR YOU IS TO CONNECT YOU TO A STRUCTURE OF GUYS WHO WOULD HAVE THE TOOLS AND EVEN THE LAUNCHPAD FOR THAT. WE'RE TALKING *MAJOR* OPPS FOR EXPONENTIAL INVESTMENT SHIFTS.

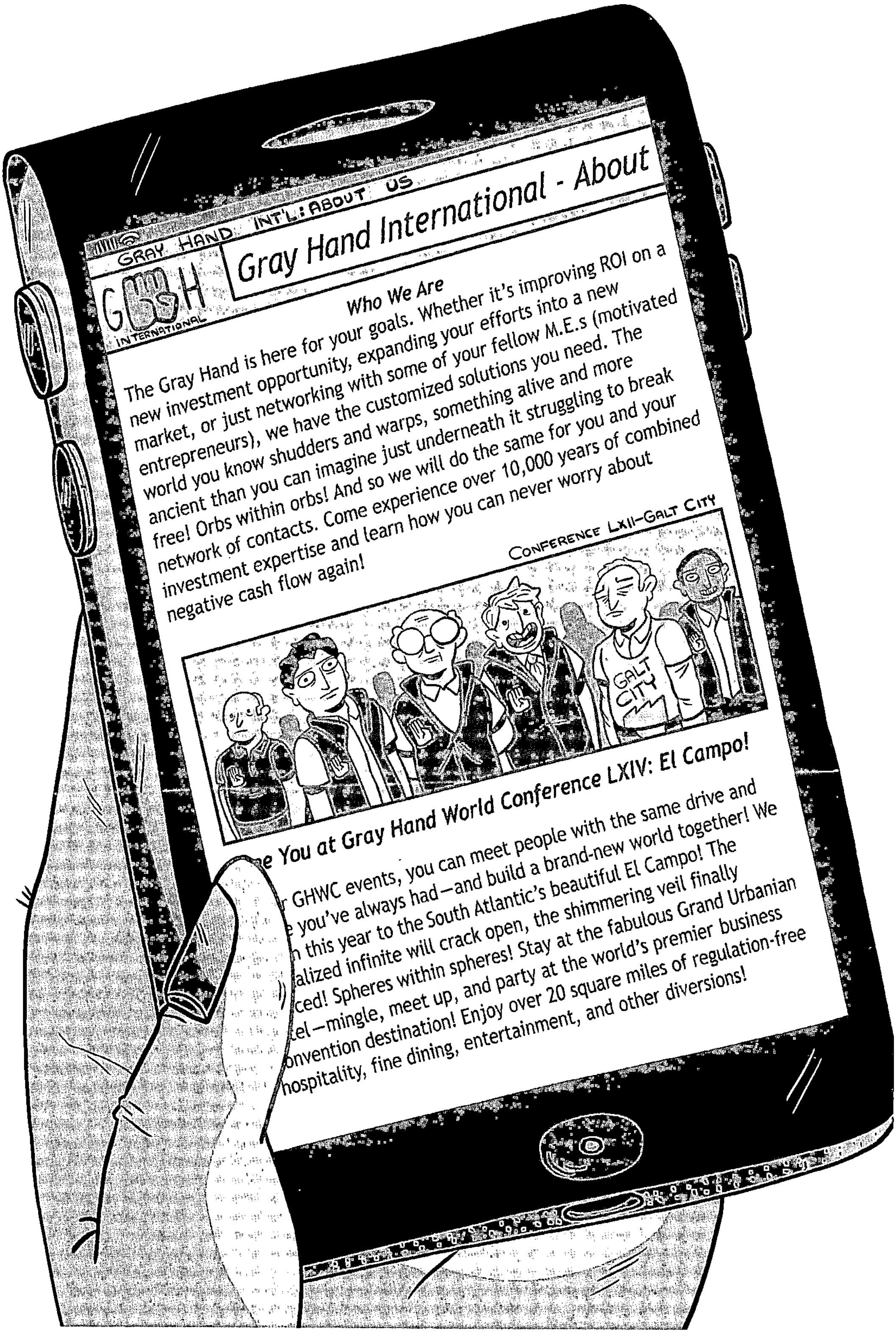
GRAY HAND INT'L: ABOUT US
Gray Hand International - About
GH INTERNATIONAL
Who We Are
The Gray Hand is here for your goals. Whether it's improving ROI on a new investment opportunity, expanding your efforts into a new market, or just networking with some of your fellow M.E.s (motivated entrepreneurs), we have the customized solutions you need. The world you know shudders and warps, something alive and more ancient than you can imagine just underneath it struggling to break free! Orbs within orbs! And so we will do the same for you and your network of contacts. Come experience over 10,000 years of combined investment expertise and learn how you can never worry about negative cash flow again!
CONFERENCE LXII–GALT CITY
GALT CITY
e You at Gray Hand World Conference LXIV: El Campo!
r GHWC events, you can meet people with the same drive and
e you've always had—and build a brand-new world together! We
n this year to the South Atlantic's beautiful El Campo! The
alized infinite will crack open, the shimmering veil finally
ced! Spheres within spheres! Stay at the fabulous Grand Urbanian
tel—mingle, meet up, and party at the world's premier business
onvention destination! Enjoy over 20 square miles of regulation-free
hospitality, fine dining, entertainment, and other diversions!

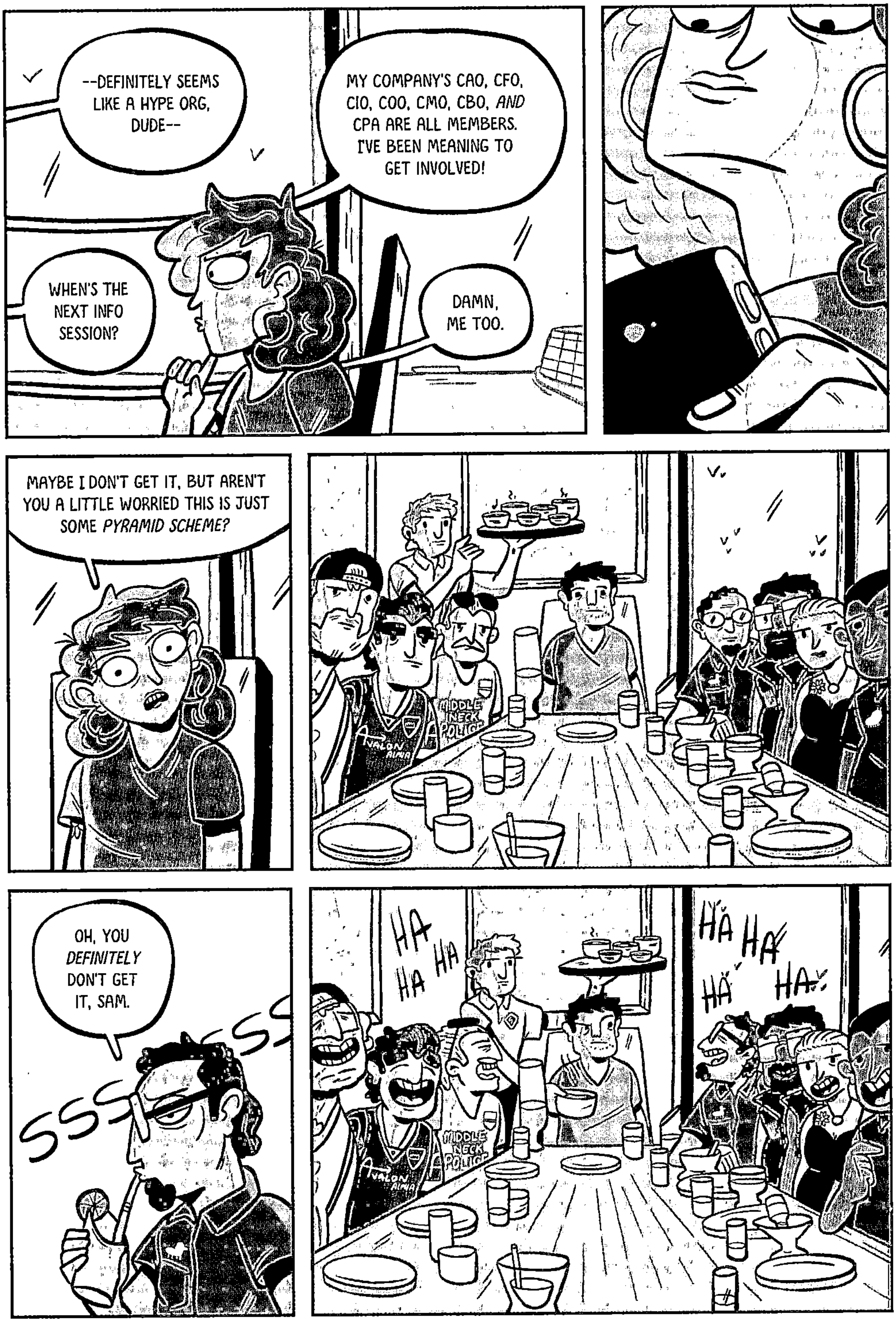

--DEFINITELY SEEMS LIKE A HYPE ORG, DUDE--
MY COMPANY'S CAO, CFO, CIO, COO, CMO, CBO, *AND* CPA ARE ALL MEMBERS. I'VE BEEN MEANING TO GET INVOLVED!
WHEN'S THE NEXT INFO SESSION?
DAMN, ME TOO.
MAYBE I DON'T GET IT, BUT AREN'T YOU A LITTLE WORRIED THIS IS JUST SOME *PYRAMID SCHEME?*
MIDDLE NECK POLICE
OH, YOU *DEFINITELY* DON'T GET IT, SAM.
SSSSSSS
HA HA HA HA
HA HA HA HA

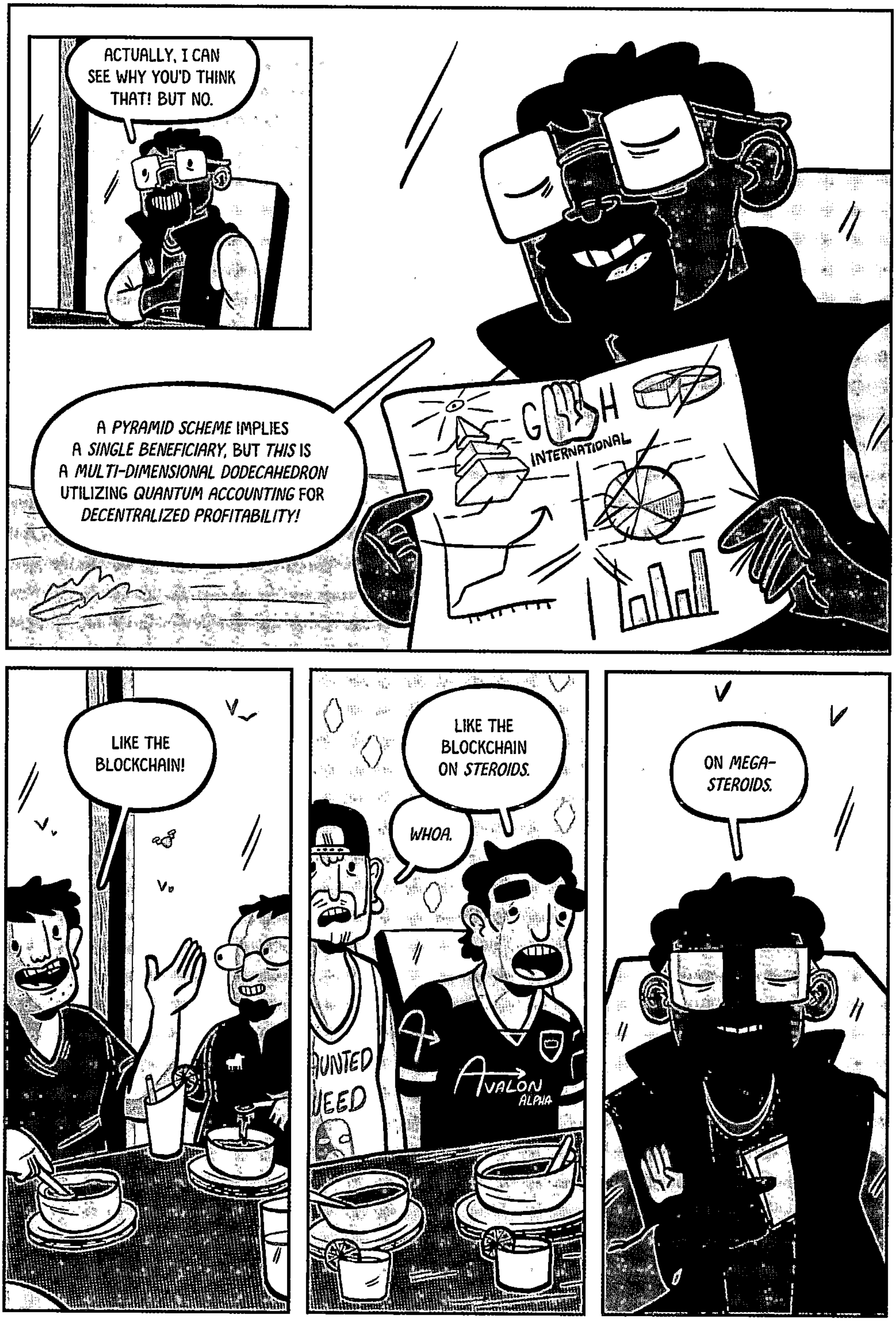
ACTUALLY, I CAN SEE WHY YOU'D THINK THAT! BUT NO.
A *PYRAMID SCHEME* IMPLIES A *SINGLE BENEFICIARY*, BUT *THIS* IS A *MULTI-DIMENSIONAL DODECAHEDRON* UTILIZING *QUANTUM ACCOUNTING* FOR *DECENTRALIZED PROFITABILITY!*
INTERNATIONAL
LIKE THE BLOCKCHAIN!
LIKE THE BLOCKCHAIN ON *STEROIDS.*
WHOA.
UNTED
EED
AVALON
ALPHA
ON *MEGA-STEROIDS.*

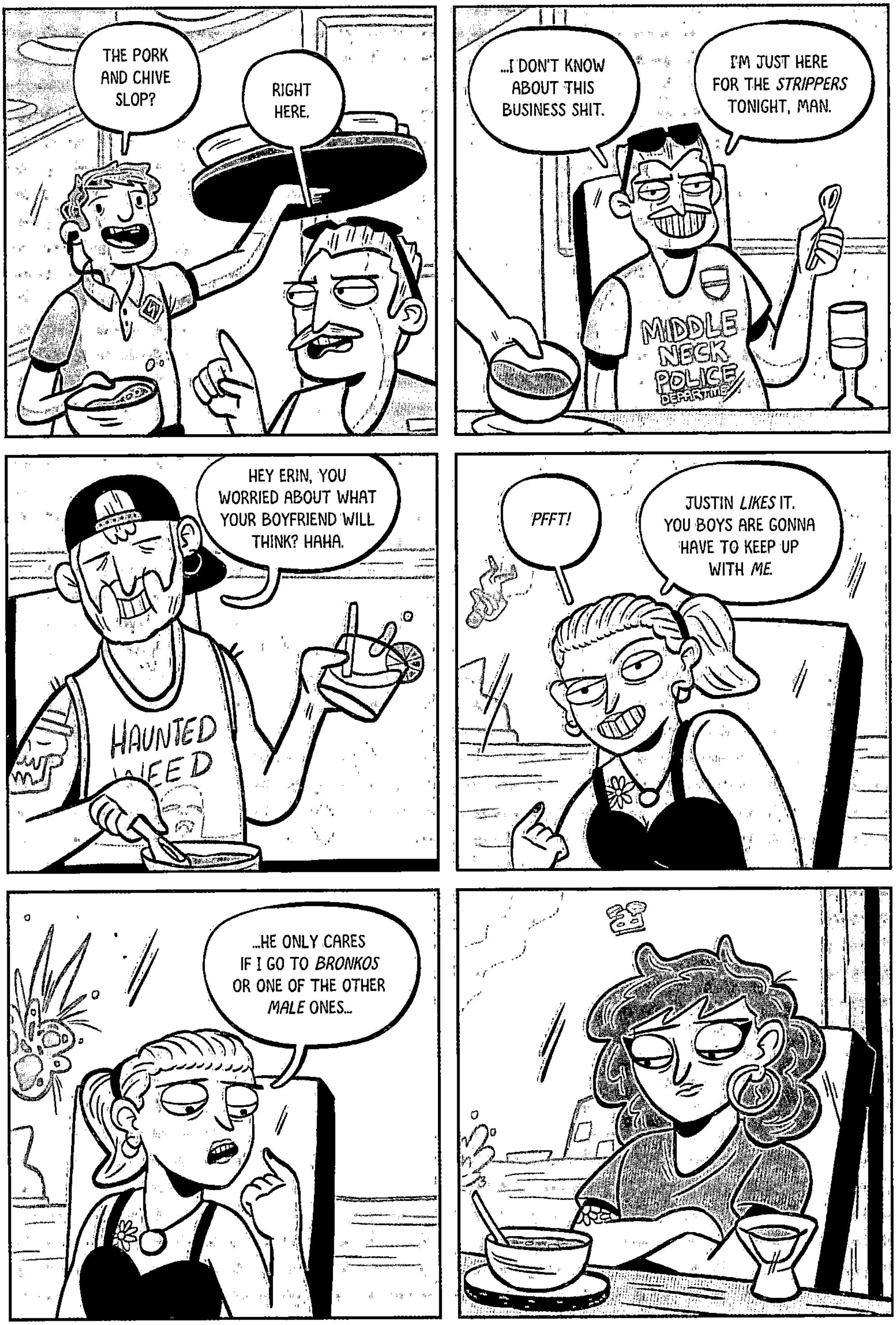
THE PORK AND CHIVE SLOP?
RIGHT HERE.
...I DON'T KNOW ABOUT THIS BUSINESS SHIT.
I'M JUST HERE FOR THE *STRIPPERS* TONIGHT, MAN.
MIDDLE NECK POLICE
HEY ERIN, YOU WORRIED ABOUT WHAT YOUR BOYFRIEND WILL THINK? HAHA.
HAUNTED
PFFT!
JUSTIN *LIKES* IT. YOU BOYS ARE GONNA HAVE TO KEEP UP WITH *ME*.
...HE ONLY CARES IF I GO TO *BRONKOS* OR ONE OF THE OTHER *MALE* ONES...

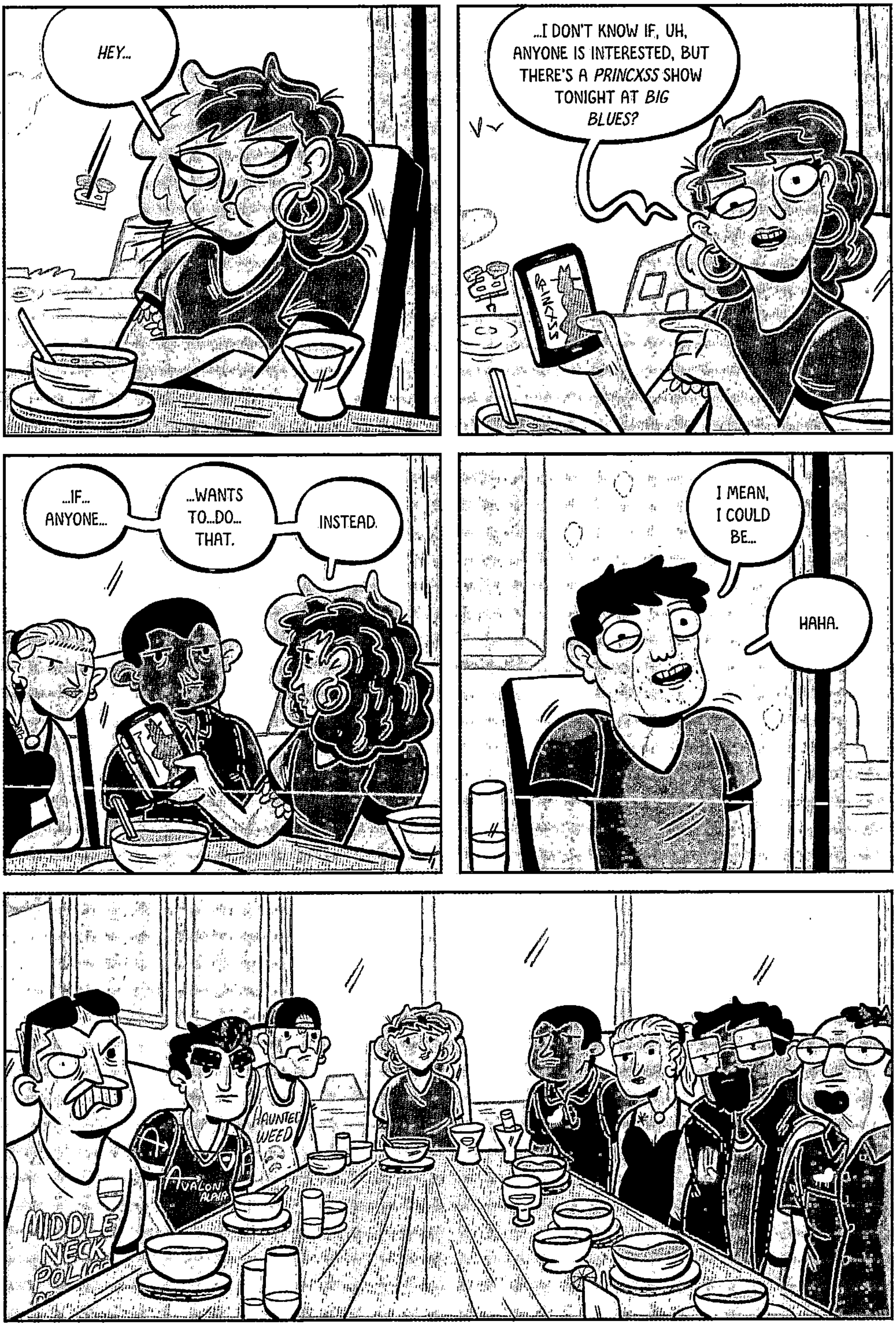
HEY...
...I DON'T KNOW IF, UH, ANYONE IS INTERESTED, BUT THERE'S A *PRINCXSS* SHOW TONIGHT AT *BIG BLUES?*
...IF... ANYONE...
...WANTS TO...DO... THAT.
INSTEAD.
I MEAN, I COULD BE...
HAHA.
MIDDLE NECK POLICE
AVALON ALPHA
HAUNTED WEED

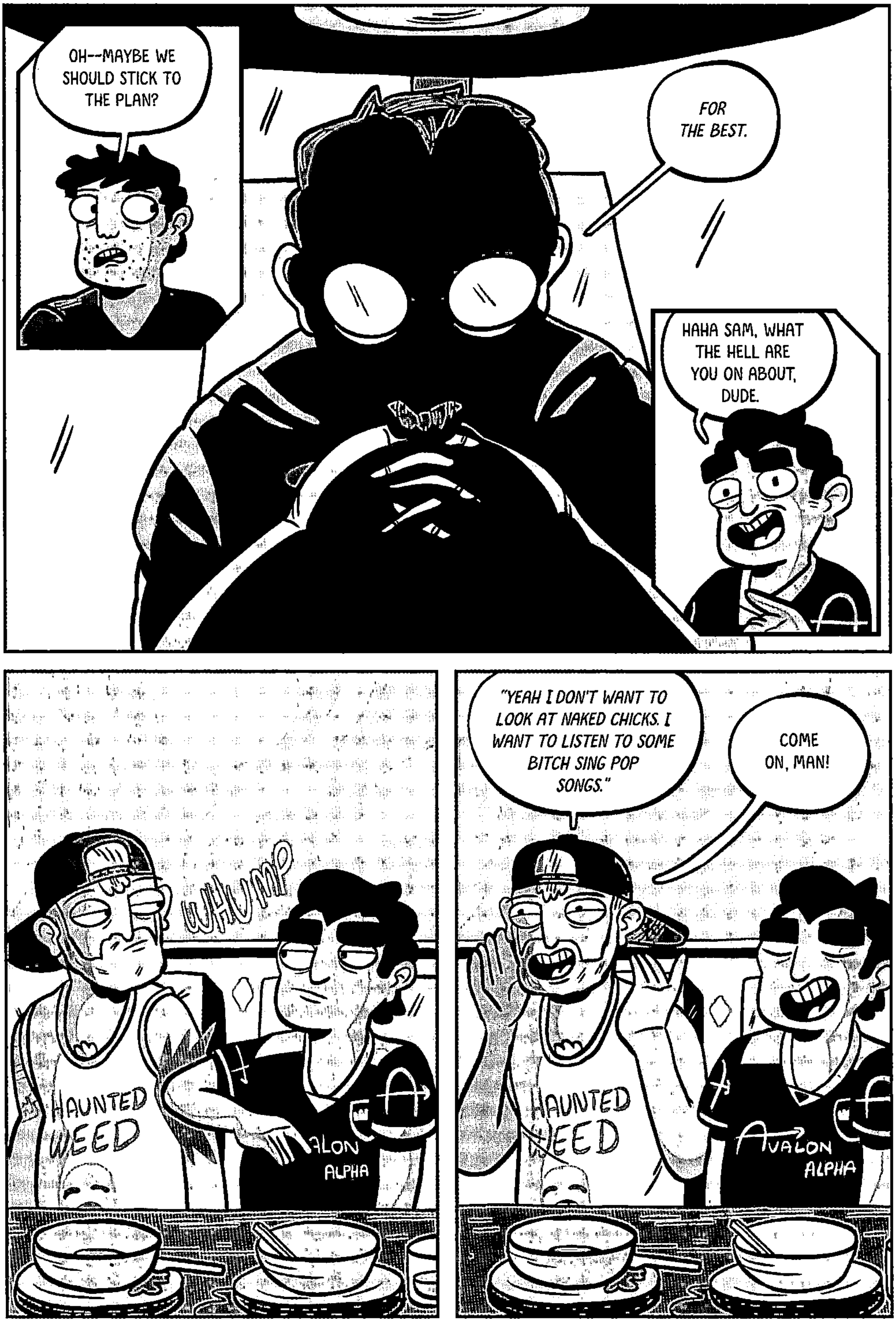
OH--MAYBE WE SHOULD STICK TO THE PLAN?
FOR THE BEST.
HAHA SAM, WHAT THE HELL ARE YOU ON ABOUT, DUDE.
WHUMP
HAUNTED WEED
AVALON ALPHA
"YEAH I DON'T WANT TO LOOK AT NAKED CHICKS. I WANT TO LISTEN TO SOME BITCH SING POP SONGS."
COME ON, MAN!
HAUNTED WEED
AVALON ALPHA

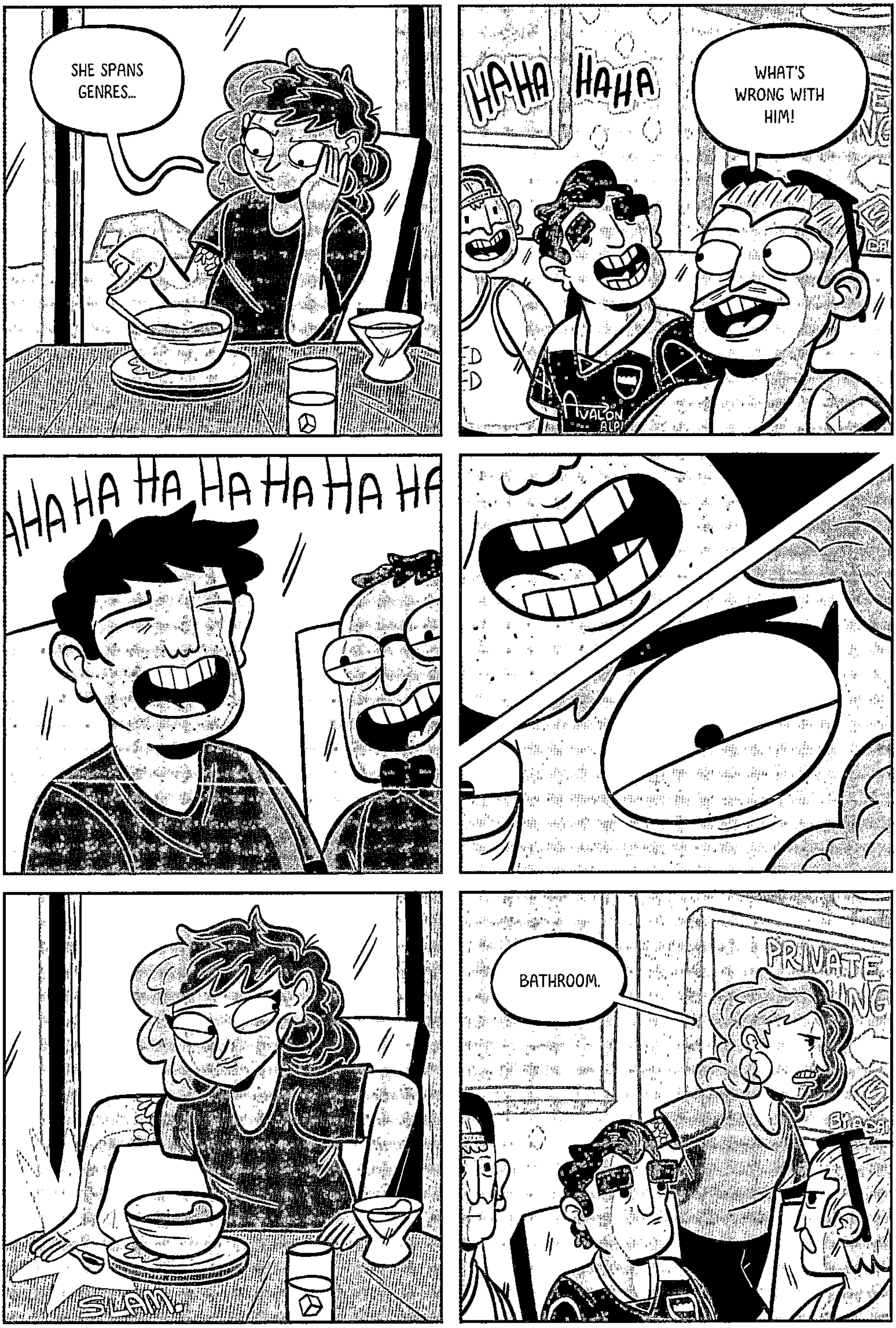
SHE SPANS GENRES...
HAHA HAHA
WHAT'S WRONG WITH HIM!
AHAHA HA HA HA HA HA HA HA
SLAM.
BATHROOM.

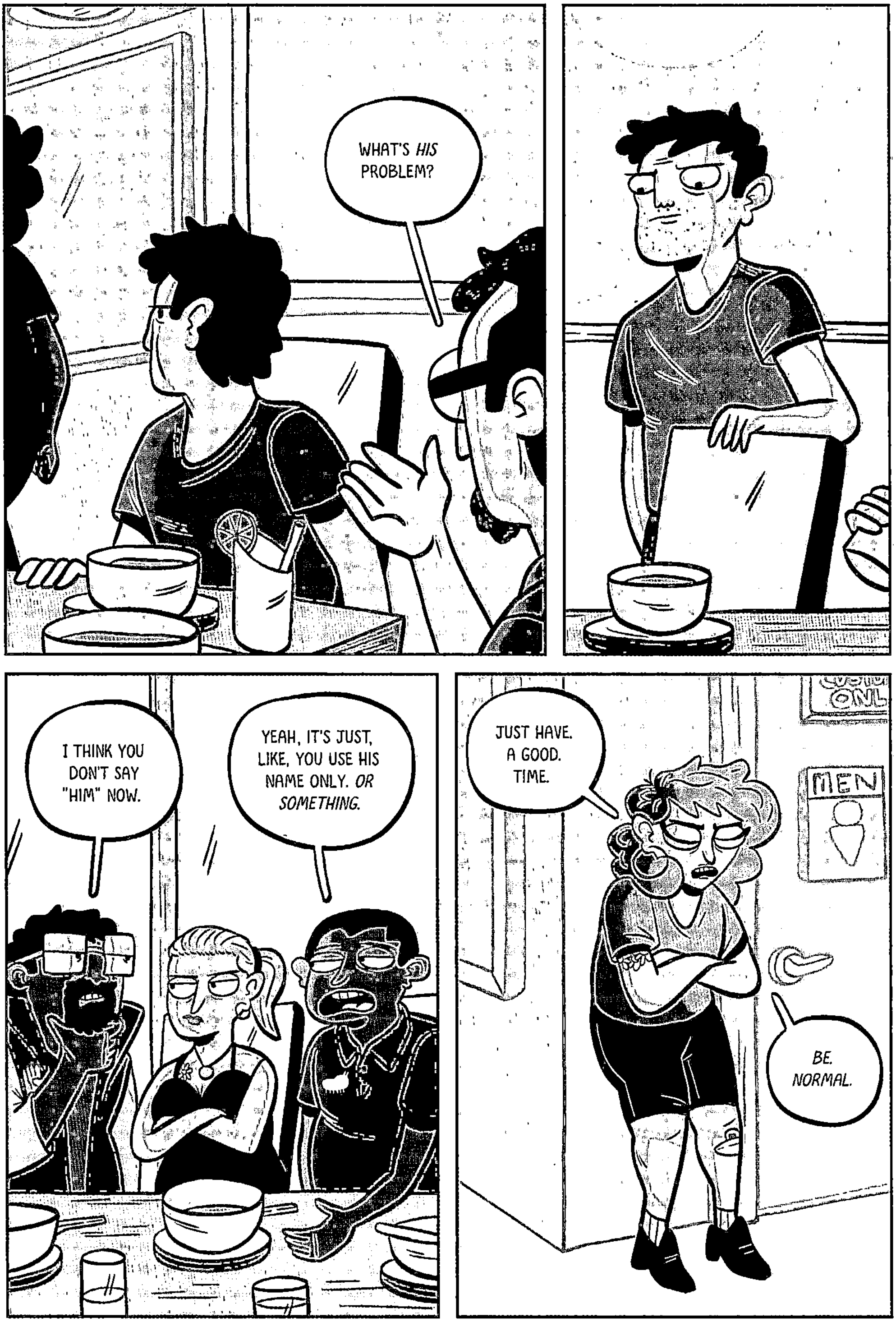
WHAT'S *HIS* PROBLEM?
I THINK YOU DON'T SAY "HIM" NOW.
YEAH, IT'S JUST, LIKE, YOU USE HIS NAME ONLY. *OR SOMETHING.*
JUST HAVE. A GOOD. TIME.
MEN
BE. NORMAL.

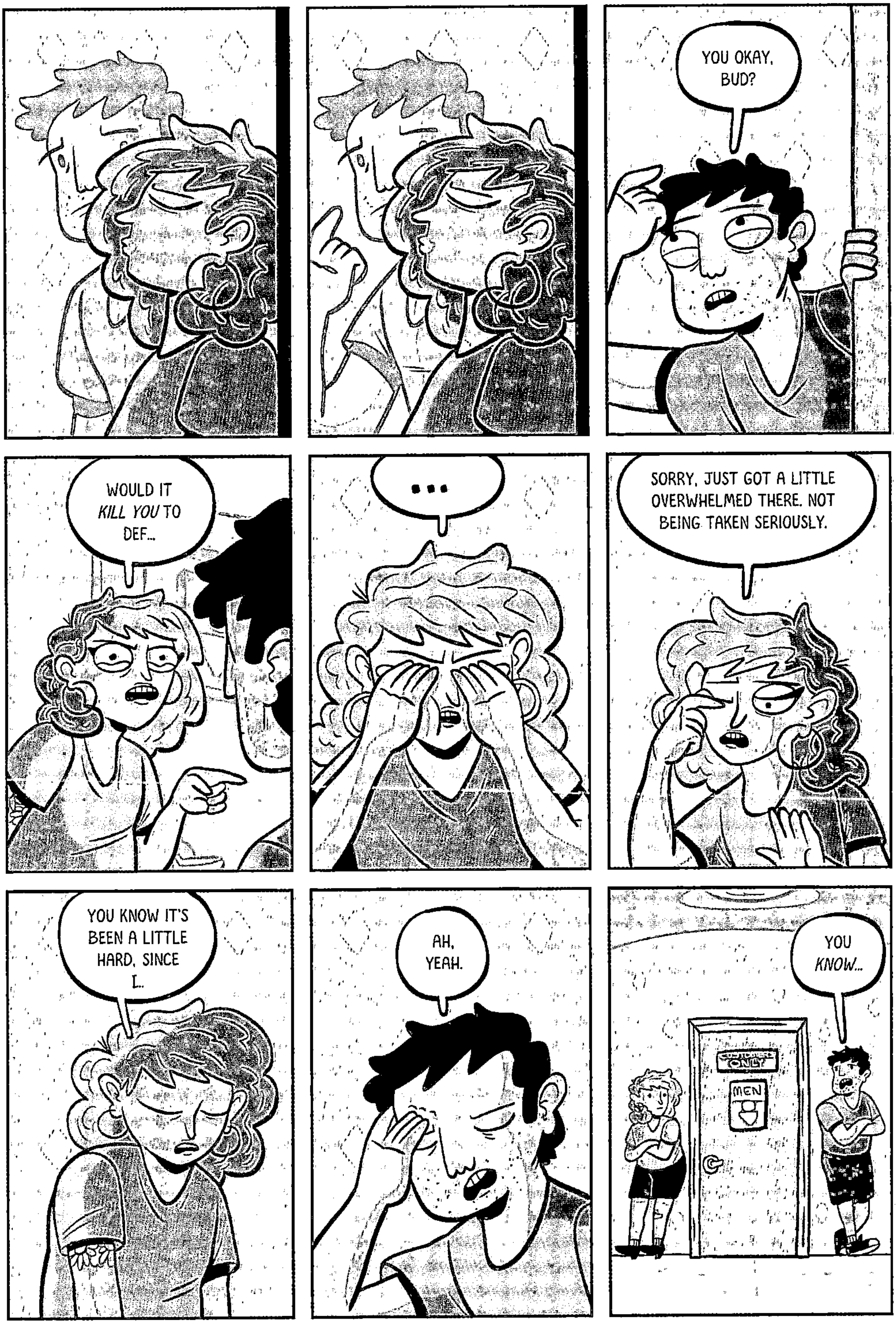
YOU OKAY, BUD?
WOULD IT *KILL YOU* TO DEF...
...
SORRY, JUST GOT A LITTLE OVERWHELMED THERE. NOT BEING TAKEN SERIOUSLY.
YOU KNOW IT'S BEEN A LITTLE HARD, SINCE I...
AH, YEAH.
MEN
YOU *KNOW*...

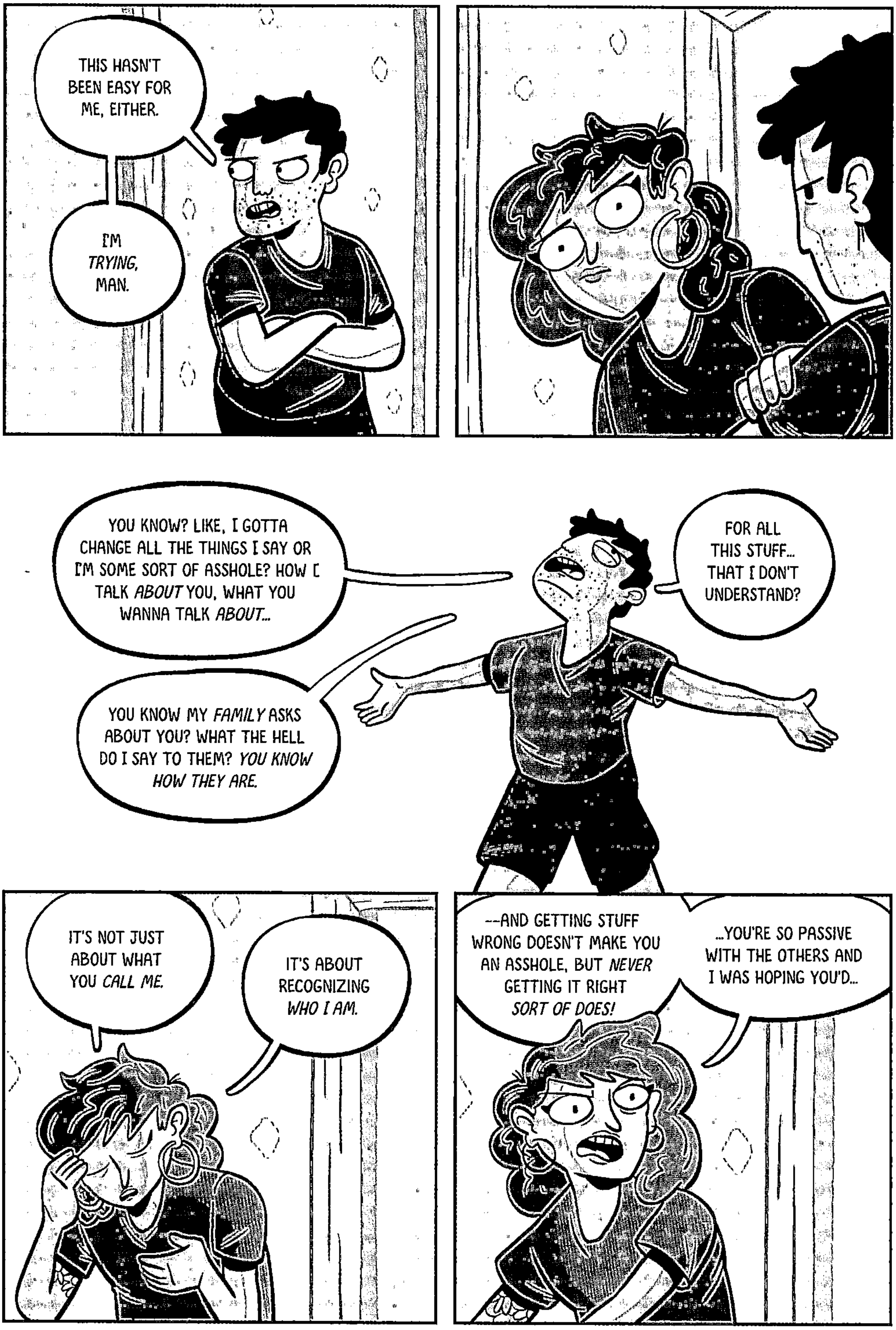
THIS HASN'T BEEN EASY FOR ME, EITHER.
I'M *TRYING,* MAN.
YOU KNOW? LIKE, I GOTTA CHANGE ALL THE THINGS I SAY OR I'M SOME SORT OF ASSHOLE? HOW I TALK *ABOUT* YOU, WHAT YOU WANNA TALK *ABOUT...*
FOR ALL THIS STUFF... THAT I DON'T UNDERSTAND?
YOU KNOW MY *FAMILY* ASKS ABOUT YOU? WHAT THE HELL DO I SAY TO THEM? *YOU KNOW HOW THEY ARE.*
IT'S NOT JUST ABOUT WHAT YOU *CALL ME.*
IT'S ABOUT RECOGNIZING *WHO I AM.*
...YOU'RE SO PASSIVE WITH THE OTHERS AND I WAS HOPING YOU'D...
--AND GETTING STUFF WRONG DOESN'T MAKE YOU AN ASSHOLE, BUT *NEVER* GETTING IT RIGHT *SORT OF DOES!*

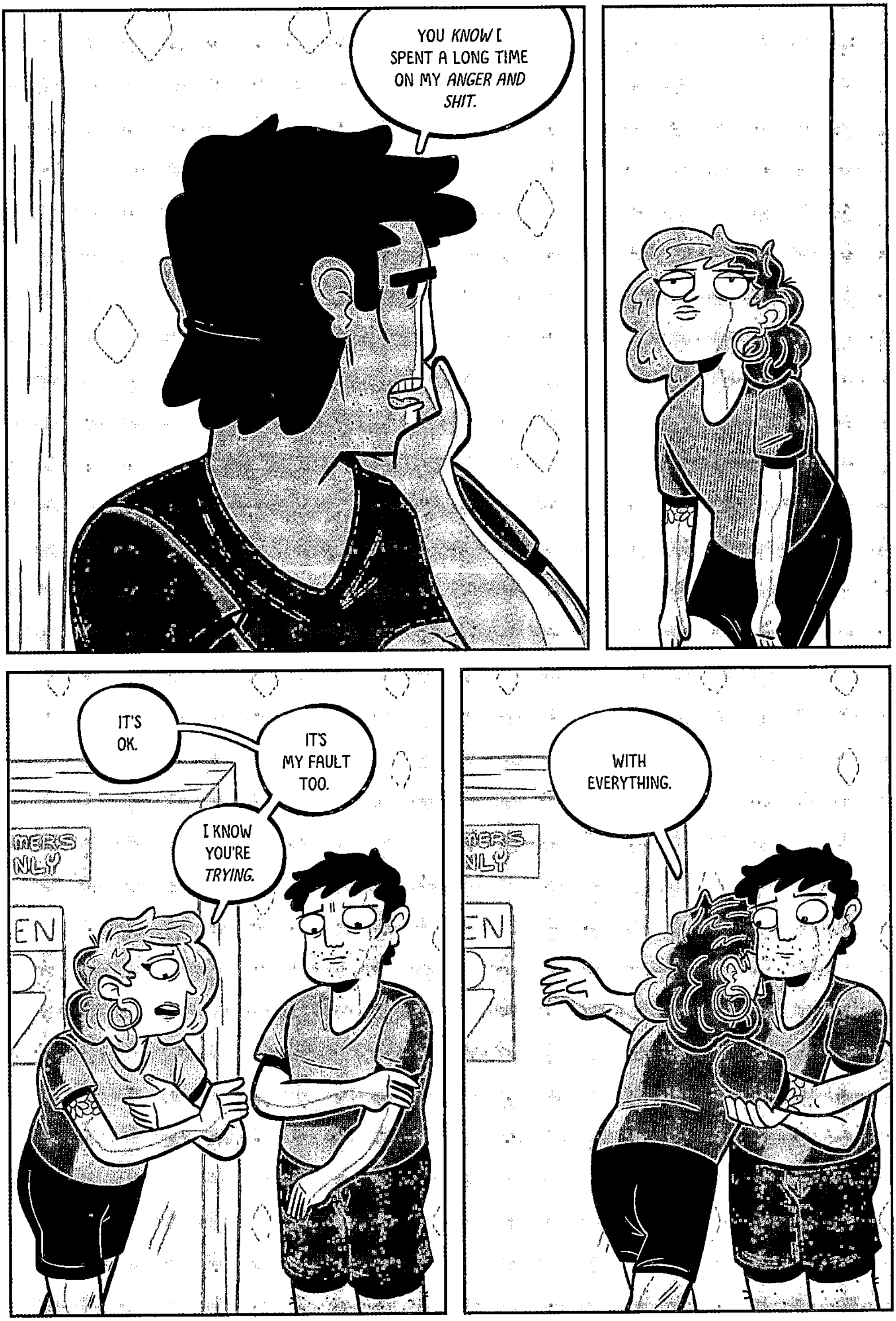
YOU *KNOW* I SPENT A LONG TIME ON MY *ANGER AND SHIT.*
IT'S OK.
IT'S MY FAULT TOO.
I KNOW YOU'RE *TRYING.*
WITH EVERYTHING.

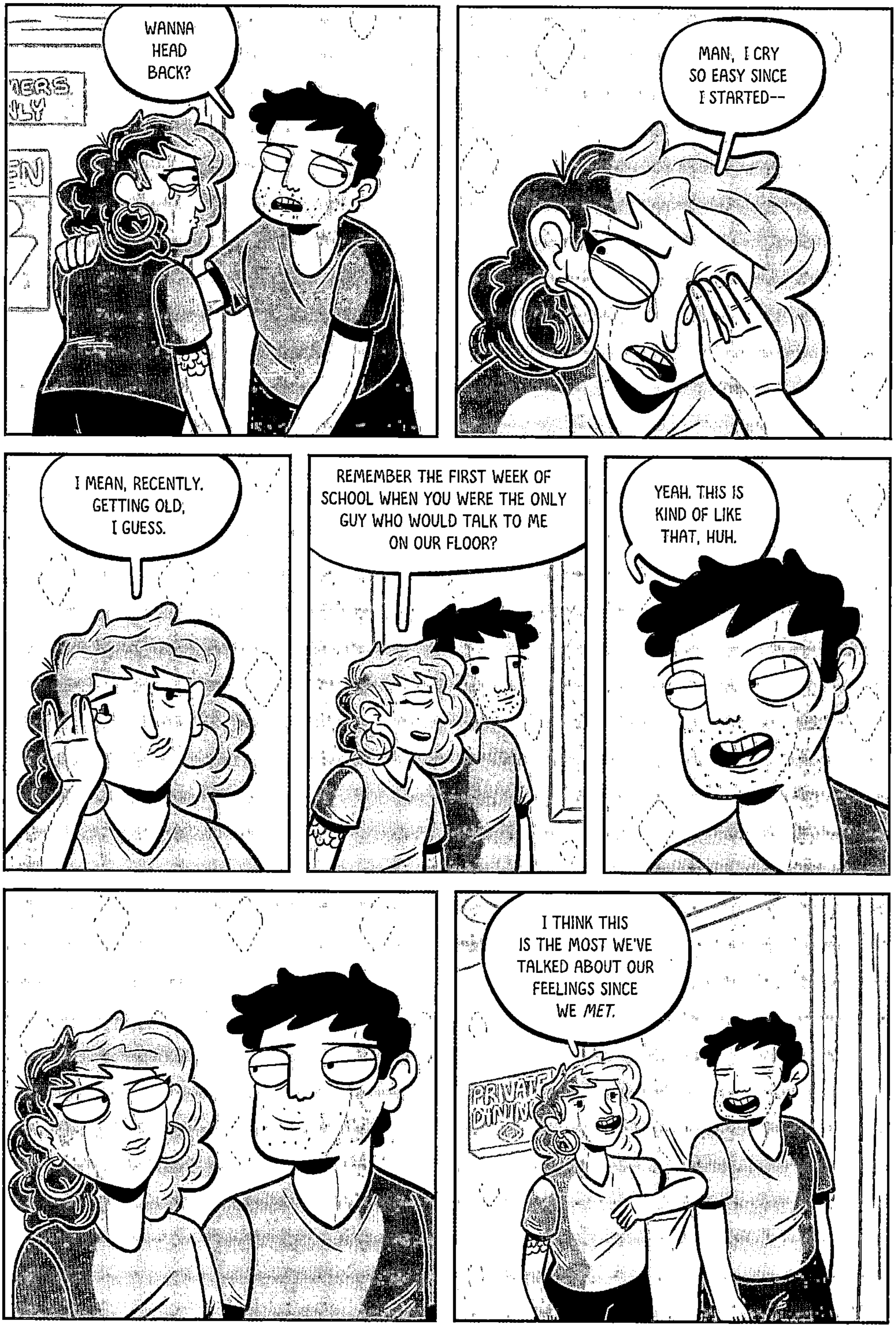
WANNA HEAD BACK?
MAN, I CRY SO EASY SINCE I STARTED--
I MEAN, RECENTLY. GETTING OLD, I GUESS.
REMEMBER THE FIRST WEEK OF SCHOOL WHEN YOU WERE THE ONLY GUY WHO WOULD TALK TO ME ON OUR FLOOR?
YEAH. THIS IS KIND OF LIKE THAT, HUH.
I THINK THIS IS THE MOST WE'VE TALKED ABOUT OUR FEELINGS SINCE WE *MET*.

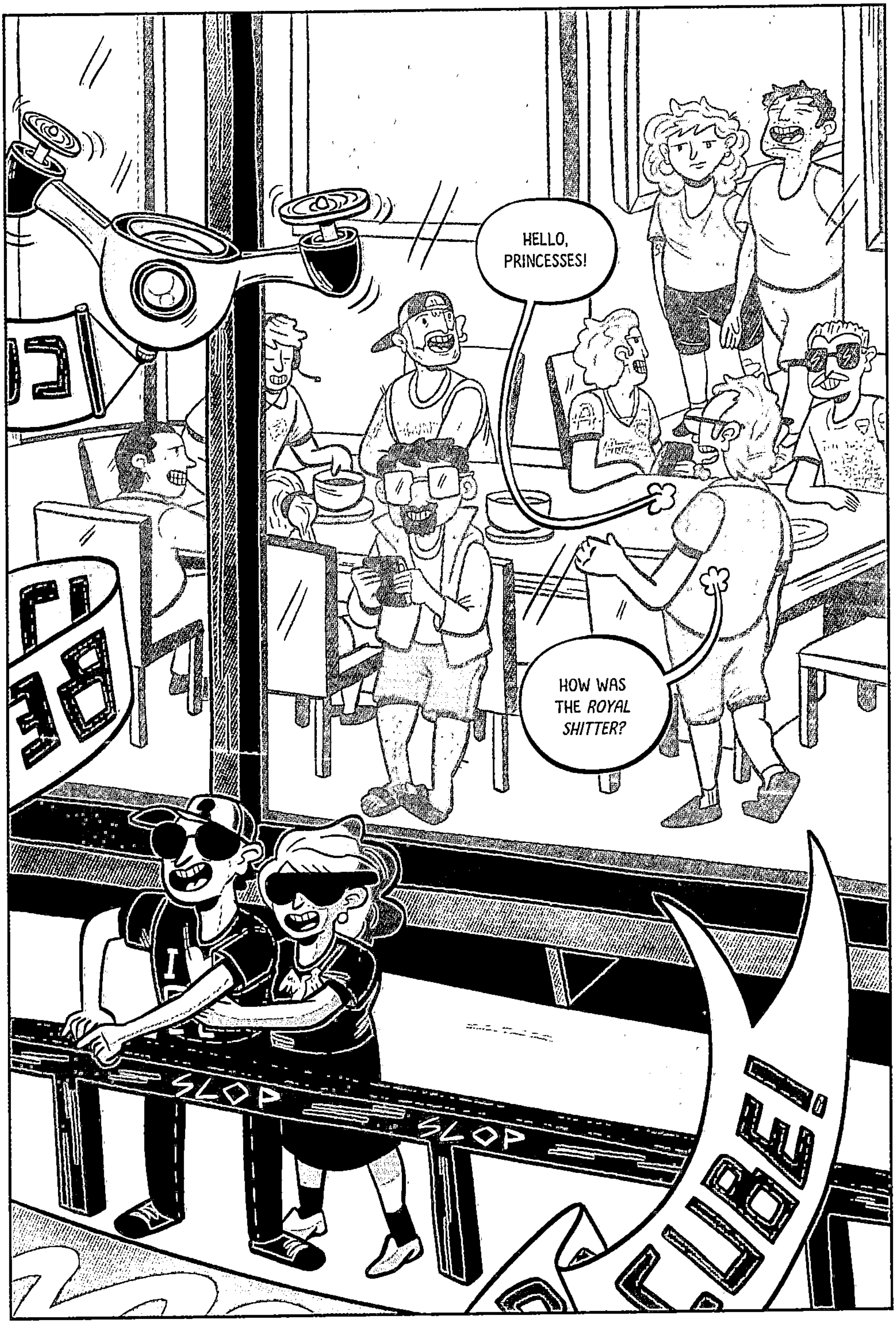
HELLO, PRINCESSES!
HOW WAS THE *ROYAL SHITTER?*
SLOP
SLOP
CUBE!

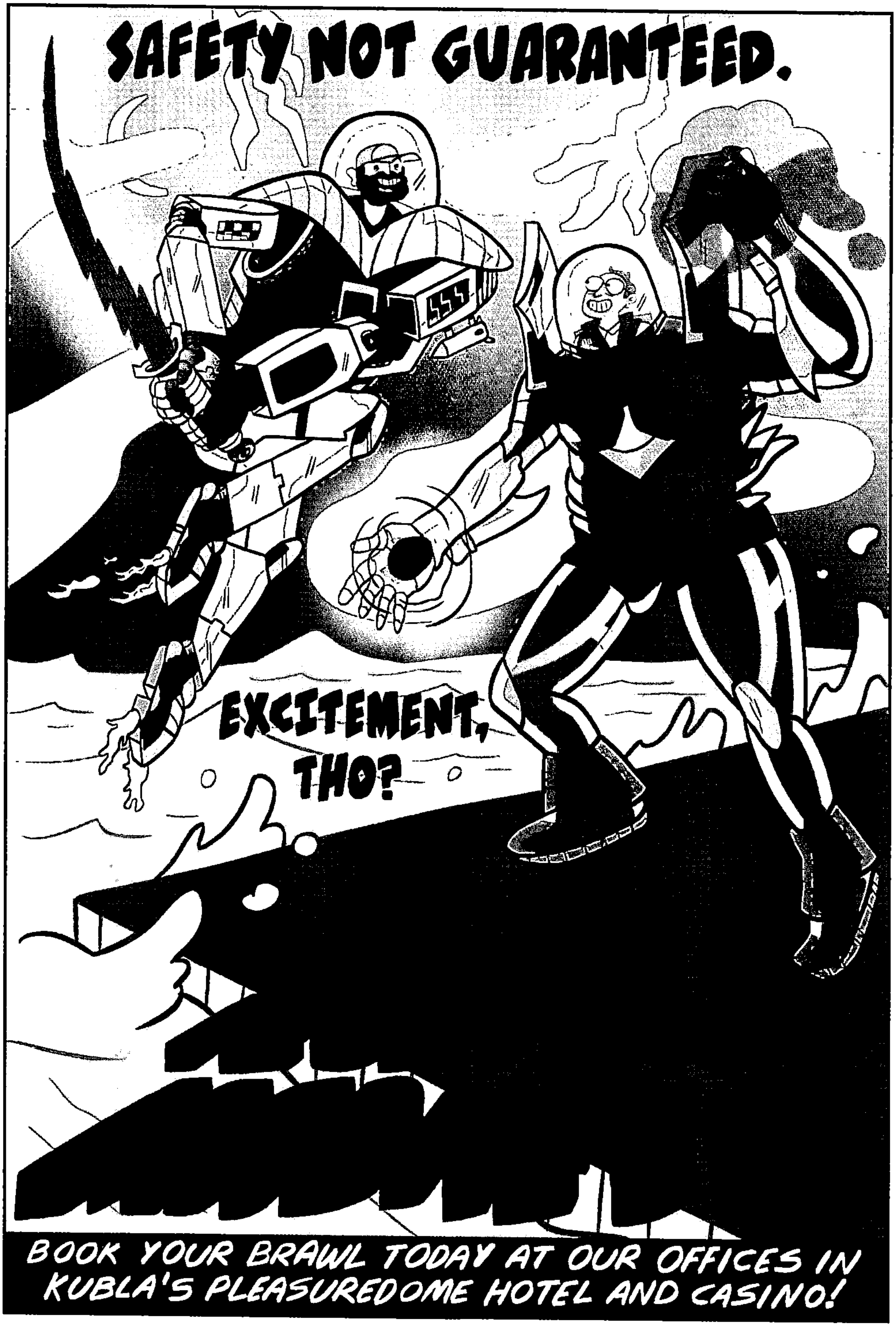
SAFETY NOT GUARANTEED.
EXCITEMENT, THO?
BOOK YOUR BRAWL TODAY AT OUR OFFICES IN KUBLA'S PLEASUREDOME HOTEL AND CASINO!

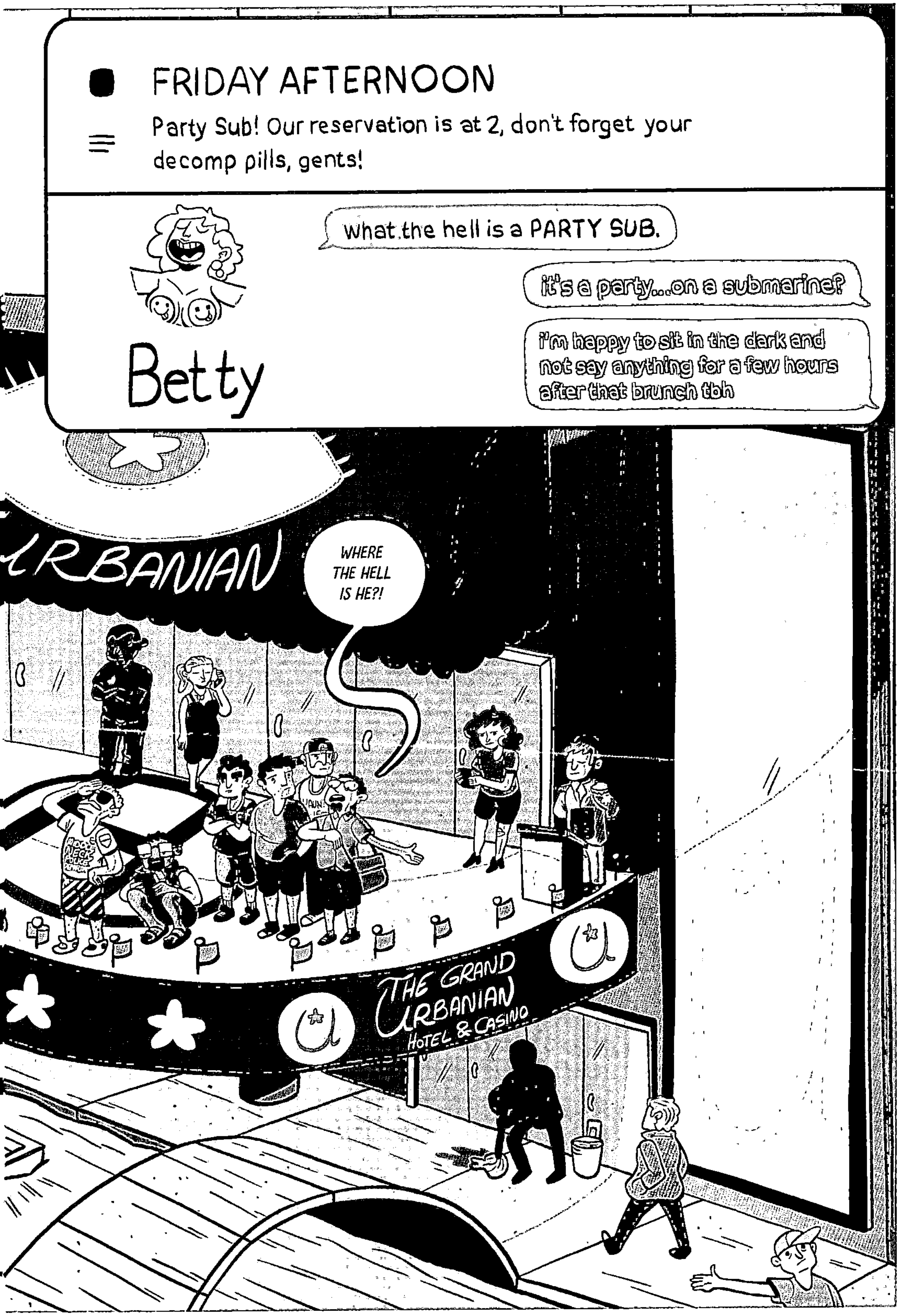
FRIDAY AFTERNOON
Party Sub! Our reservation is at 2, don't forget your decomp pills, gents!
Betty
What the hell is a PARTY SUB.
it's a party...on a submarine?
i'm happy to sit in the dark and not say anything for a few hours after that brunch tbh
URBANIAN
WHERE THE HELL IS HE?!
THE GRAND URBANIAN HOTEL & CASINO

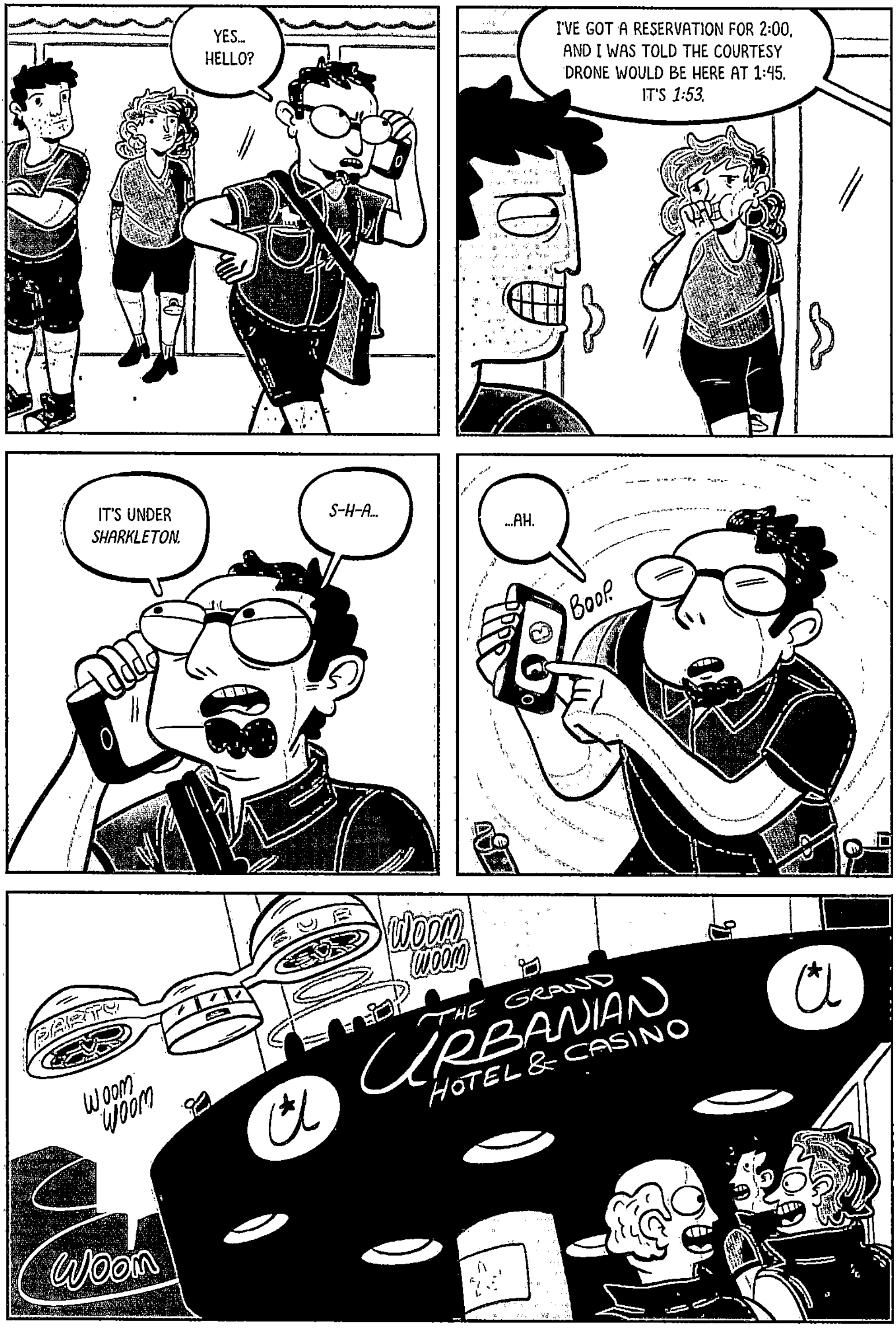
YES... HELLO?
I'VE GOT A RESERVATION FOR 2:00, AND I WAS TOLD THE COURTESY DRONE WOULD BE HERE AT 1:45. IT'S 1:53.
IT'S UNDER SHARKLETON.
S-H-A...
...AH.
BOOP
WOOM WOOM
PARTY
THE GRAND URBANIAN HOTEL & CASINO
WOOM WOOM
WOOM

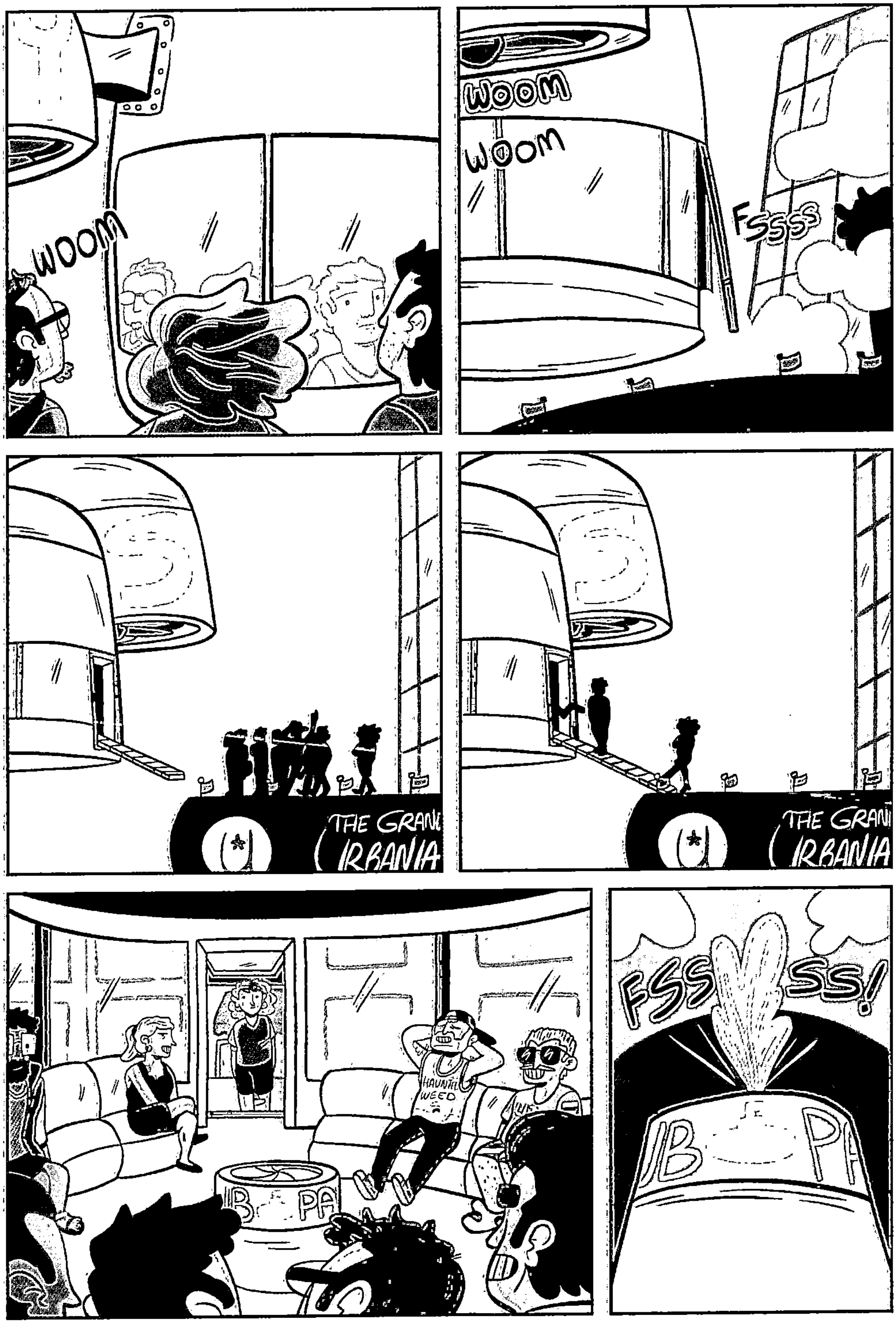
WOOM
WOOM
WOOM
FSSSS
THE GRAN
IRBANIA
THE GRAN
IRBANIA
HAUNTED WEED
FSSSSS!

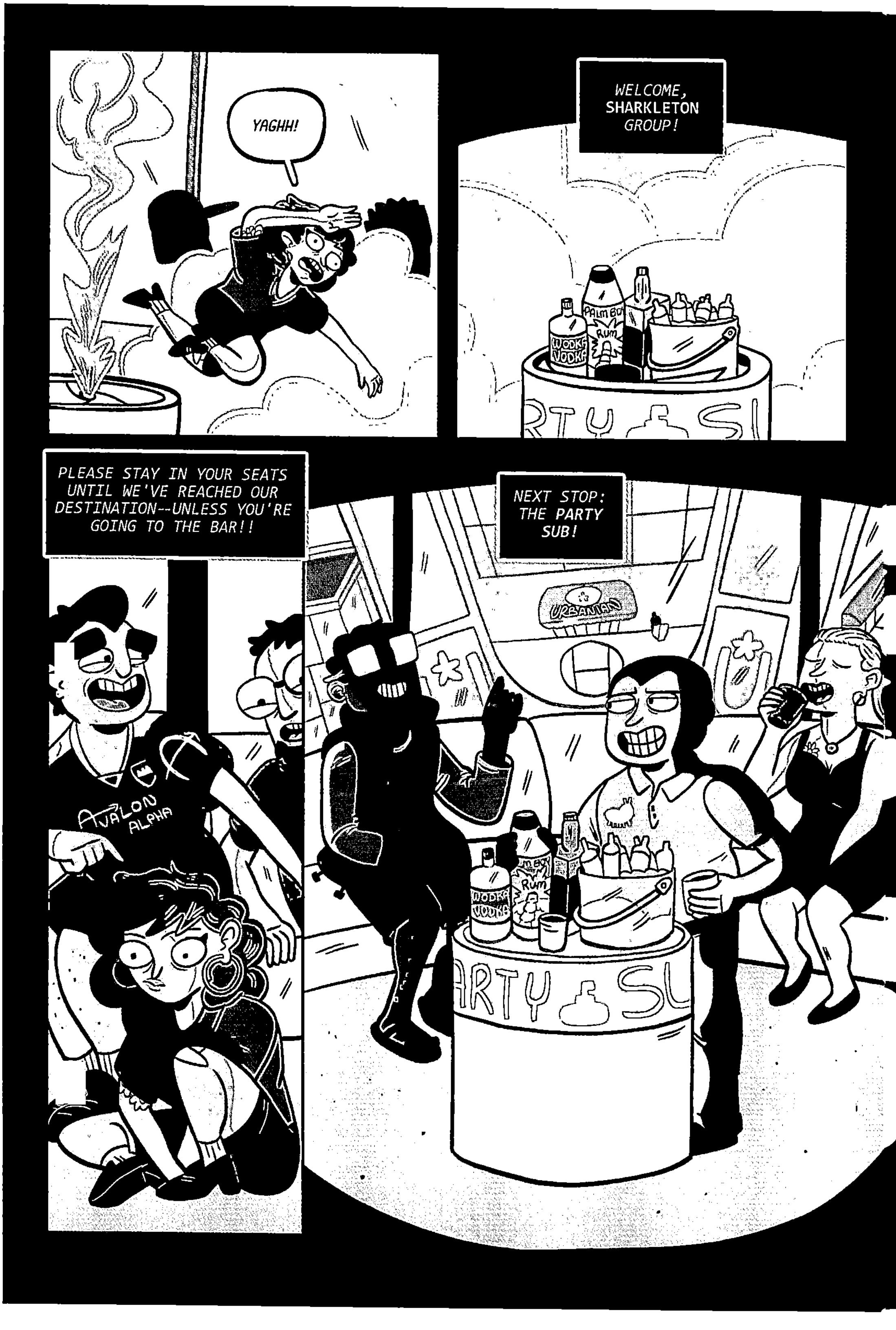
YAGHH!
WELCOME, SHARKLETON GROUP!
PALM BOY
RUM
VODKA
VODKA
PLEASE STAY IN YOUR SEATS UNTIL WE'VE REACHED OUR DESTINATION--UNLESS YOU'RE GOING TO THE BAR!!
NEXT STOP: THE PARTY SUB!
URBANIAN
AVALON ALPHA
VODKA
VODKA
RUM
ARTY SU

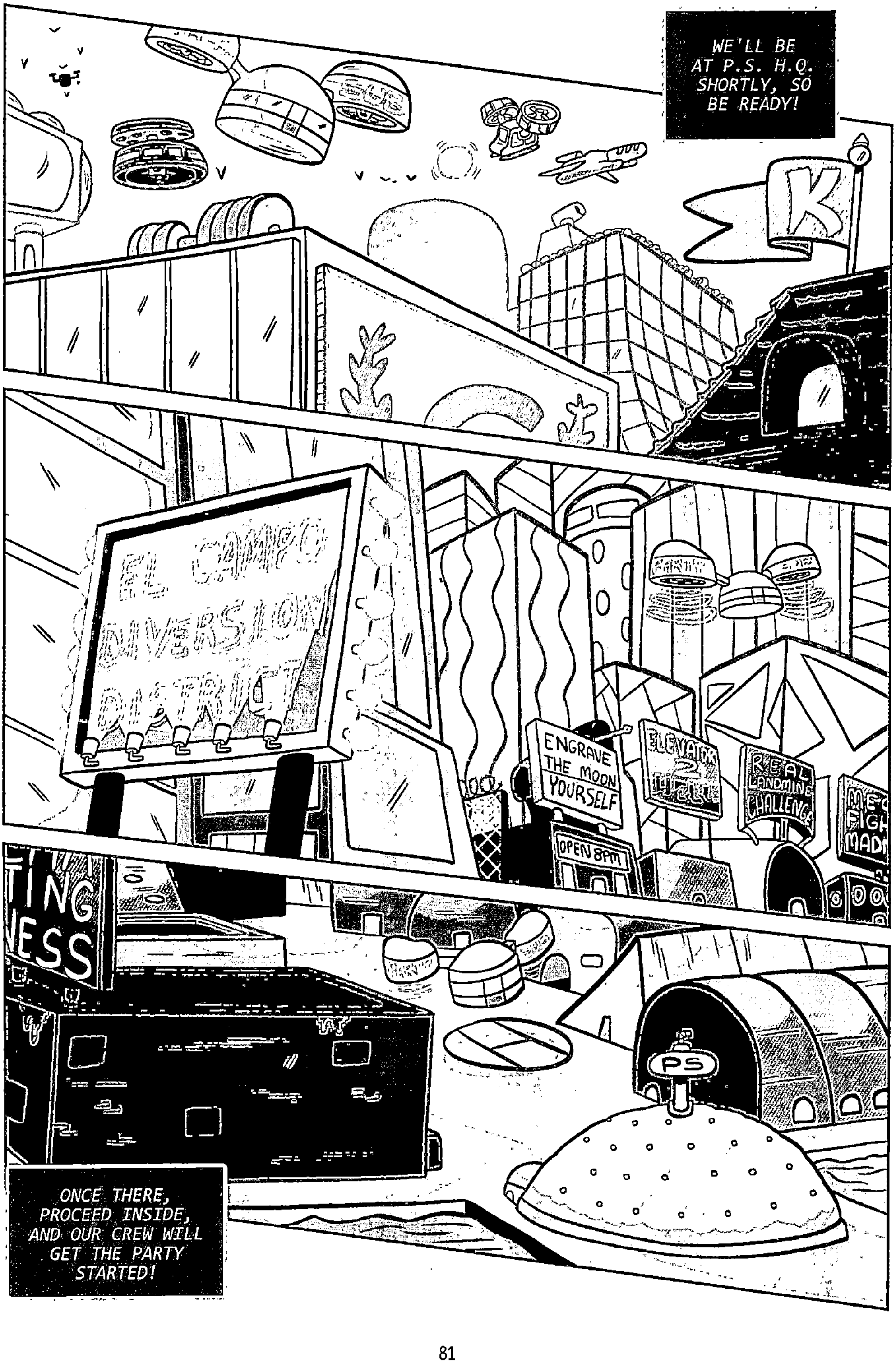
WE'LL BE AT P.S. H.Q. SHORTLY, SO BE READY!
EL CAMPO DIVERSION DISTRICT
ENGRAVE THE MOON YOURSELF
OPEN 8PM
PS
ONCE THERE, PROCEED INSIDE, AND OUR CREW WILL GET THE PARTY STARTED!

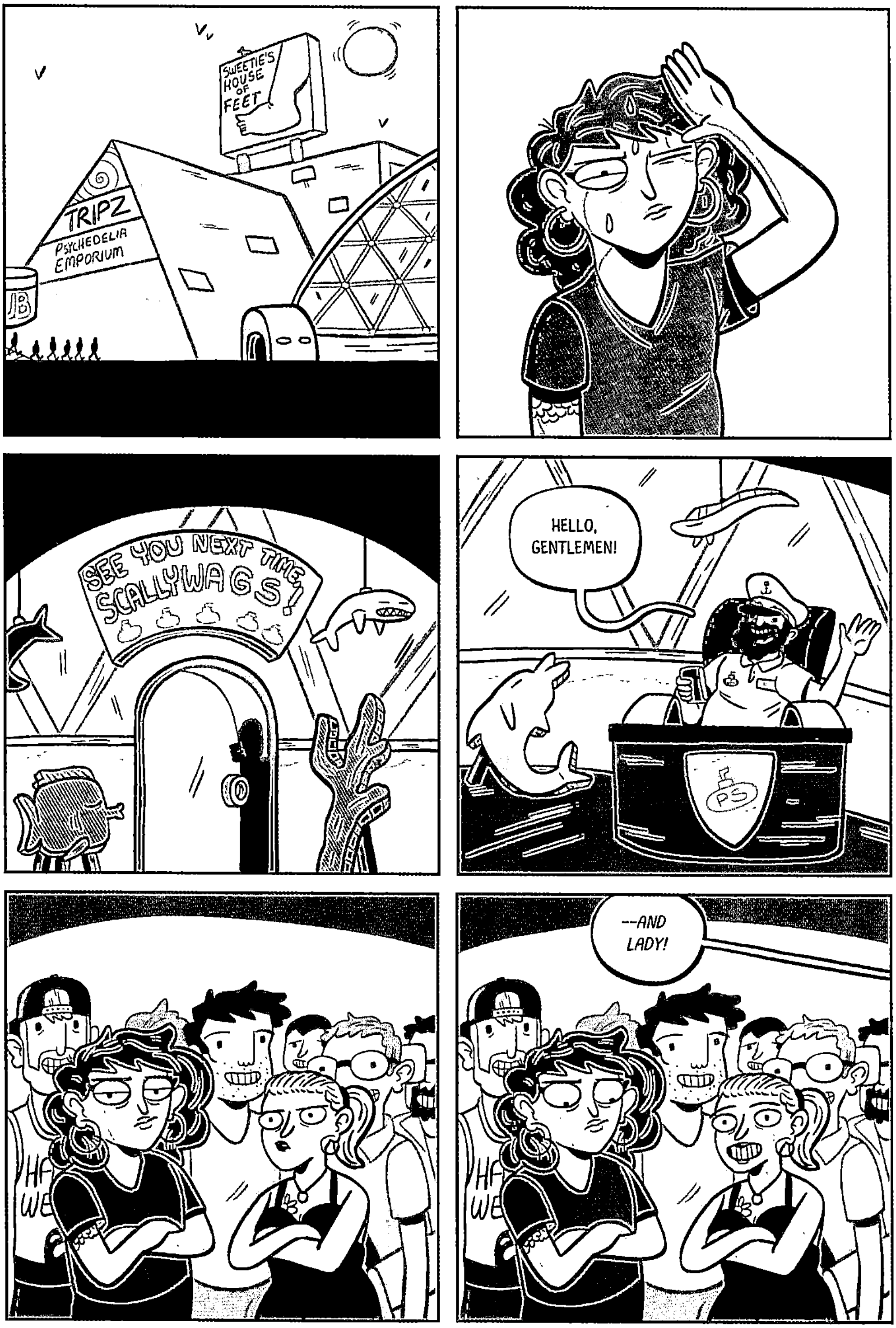

SWEETIE'S HOUSE OF FEET
TRIPZ
PSYCHEDELIA EMPORIUM
JB
SEE YOU NEXT TIME, SCALLYWAGS!
PS
HELLO, GENTLEMEN!
--AND LADY!

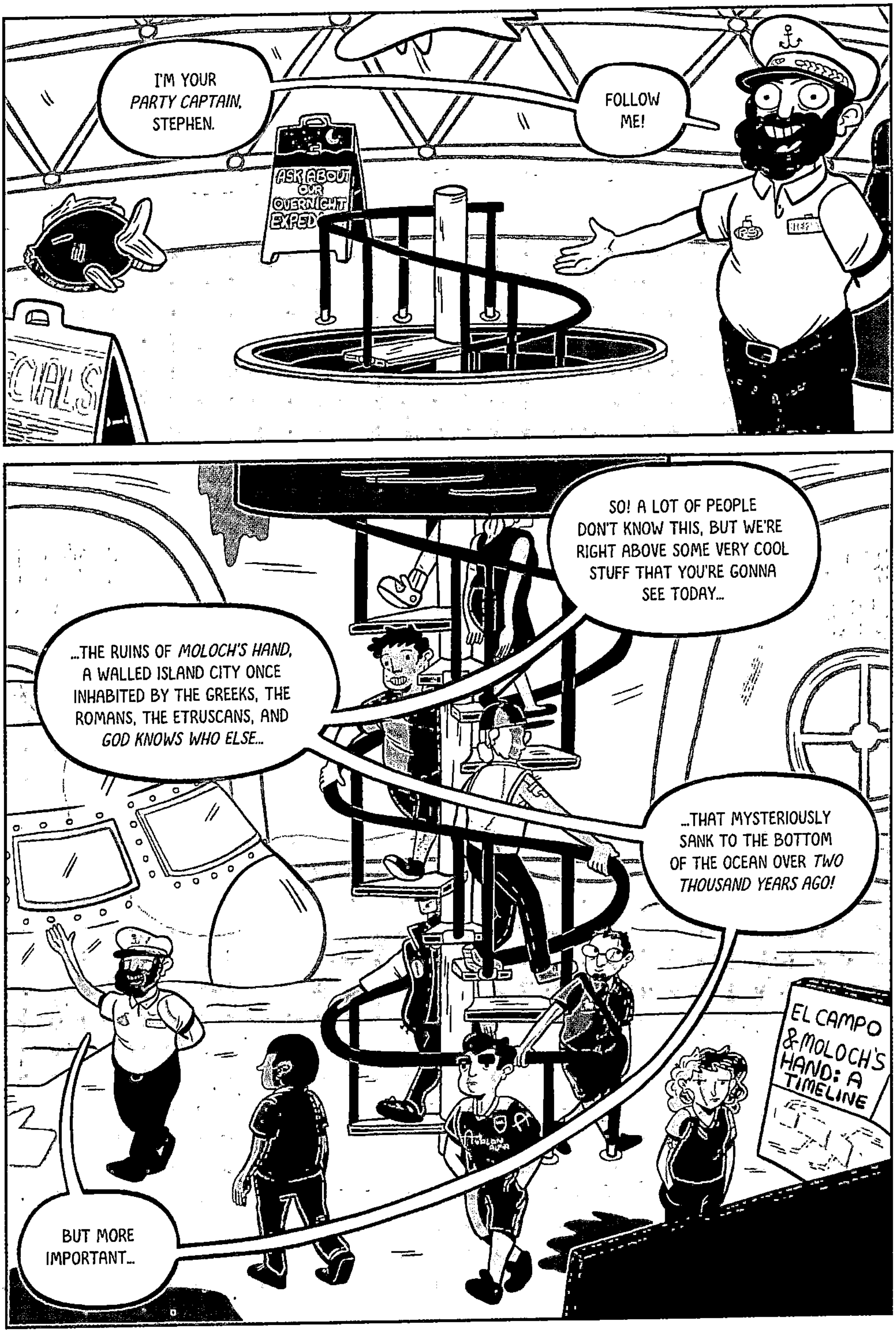
I'M YOUR *PARTY CAPTAIN,* STEPHEN.
FOLLOW ME!
ASK ABOUT OUR OVERNIGHT EXPED
CIALS
SO! A LOT OF PEOPLE DON'T KNOW THIS, BUT WE'RE RIGHT ABOVE SOME VERY COOL STUFF THAT YOU'RE GONNA SEE TODAY...
...THE RUINS OF *MOLOCH'S HAND,* A WALLED ISLAND CITY ONCE INHABITED BY THE GREEKS, THE ROMANS, THE ETRUSCANS, AND *GOD KNOWS WHO ELSE...*
...THAT MYSTERIOUSLY SANK TO THE BOTTOM OF THE OCEAN OVER *TWO THOUSAND YEARS AGO!*
EL CAMPO & MOLOCH'S HAND: A TIMELINE
BUT MORE IMPORTANT...

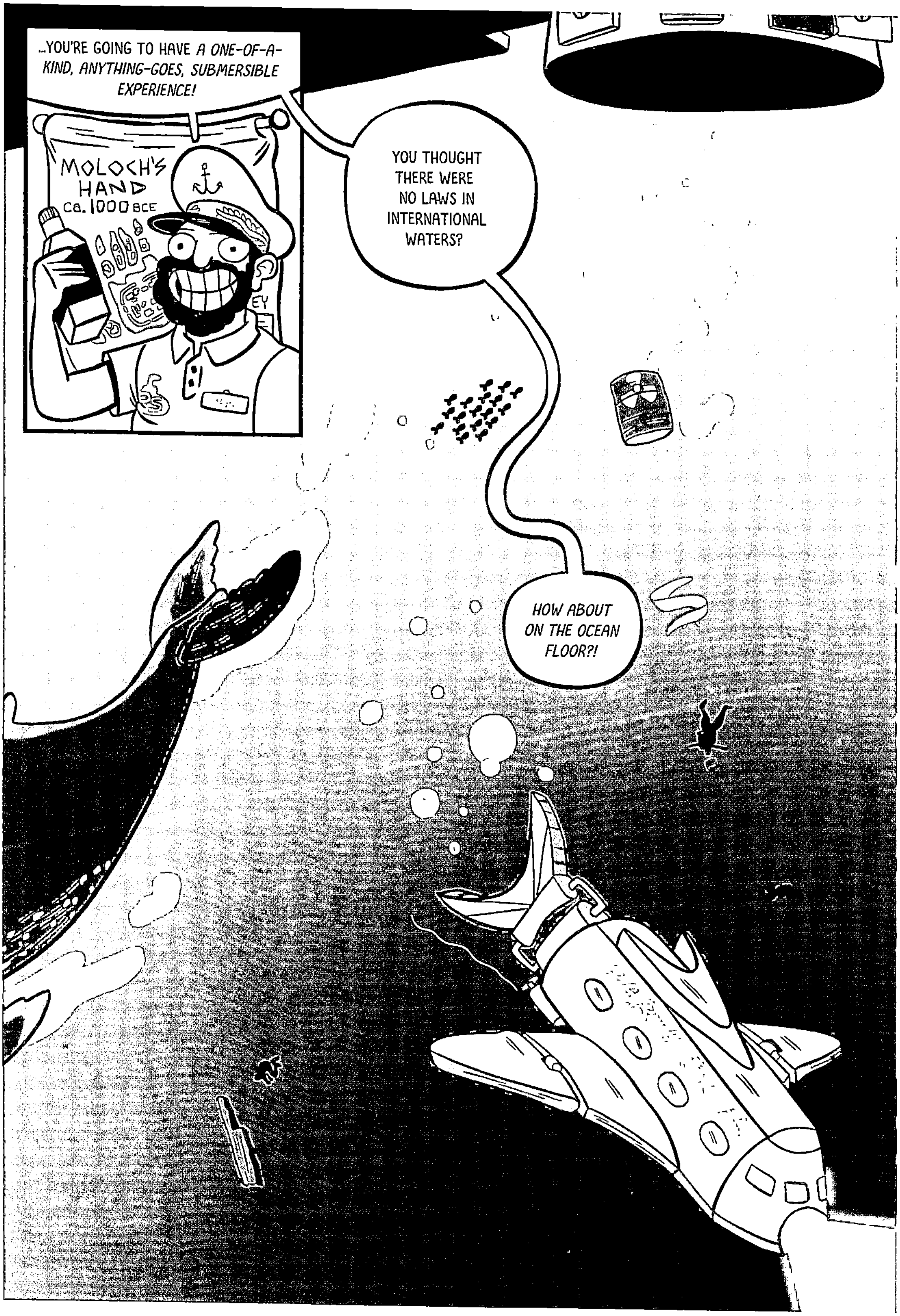
...YOU'RE GOING TO HAVE *A ONE-OF-A-KIND, ANYTHING-GOES, SUBMERSIBLE EXPERIENCE!*
MOLOCH'S HAND Ca. 1000 BCE
YOU THOUGHT THERE WERE NO LAWS IN INTERNATIONAL WATERS?
HOW ABOUT ON THE OCEAN FLOOR?!

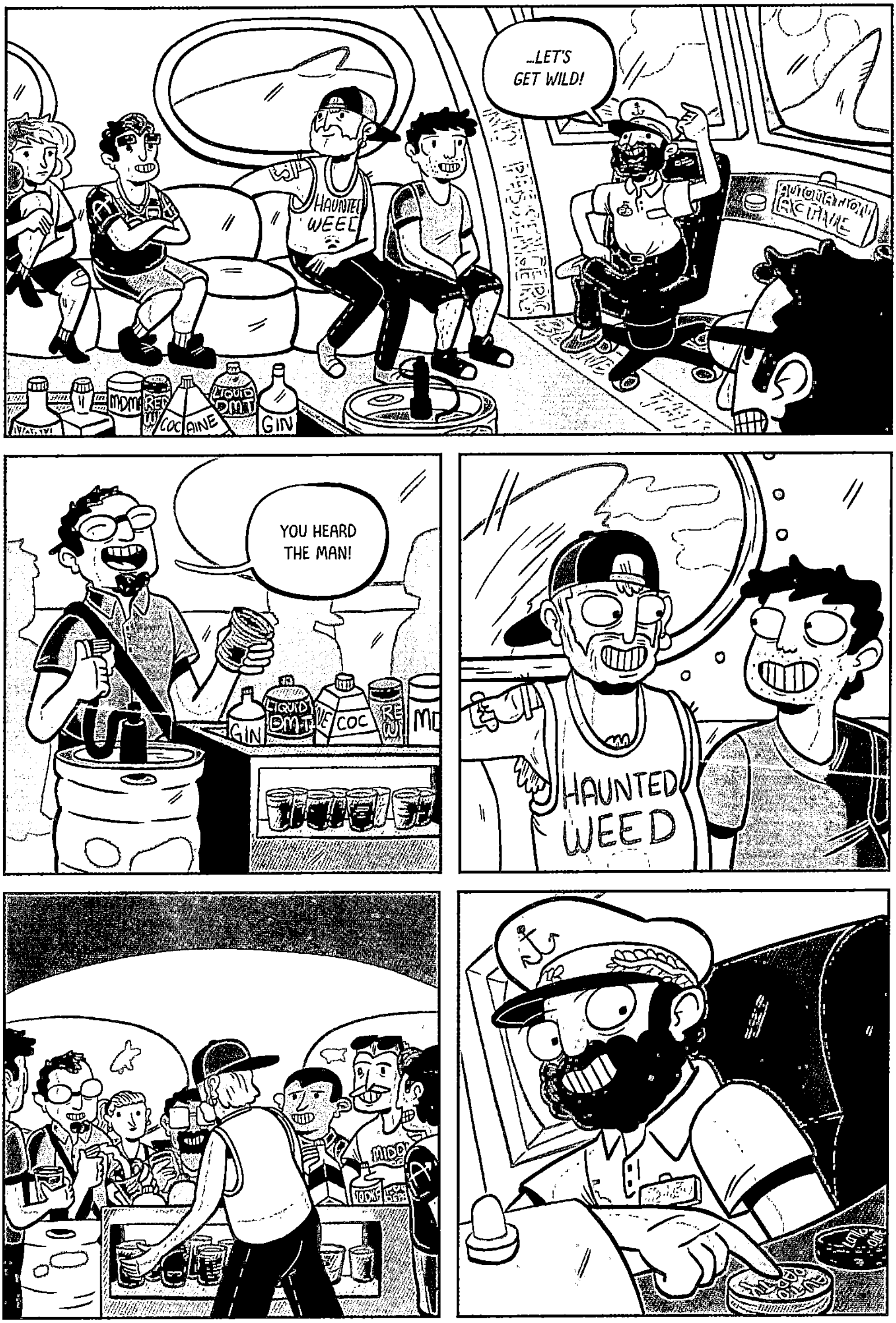
...LET'S GET WILD!
HAUNTED WEED
AUTOMATION ACTIVE
MDMA
COCAINE
LIQUID DMT
GIN
YOU HEARD THE MAN!
HAUNTED WEED

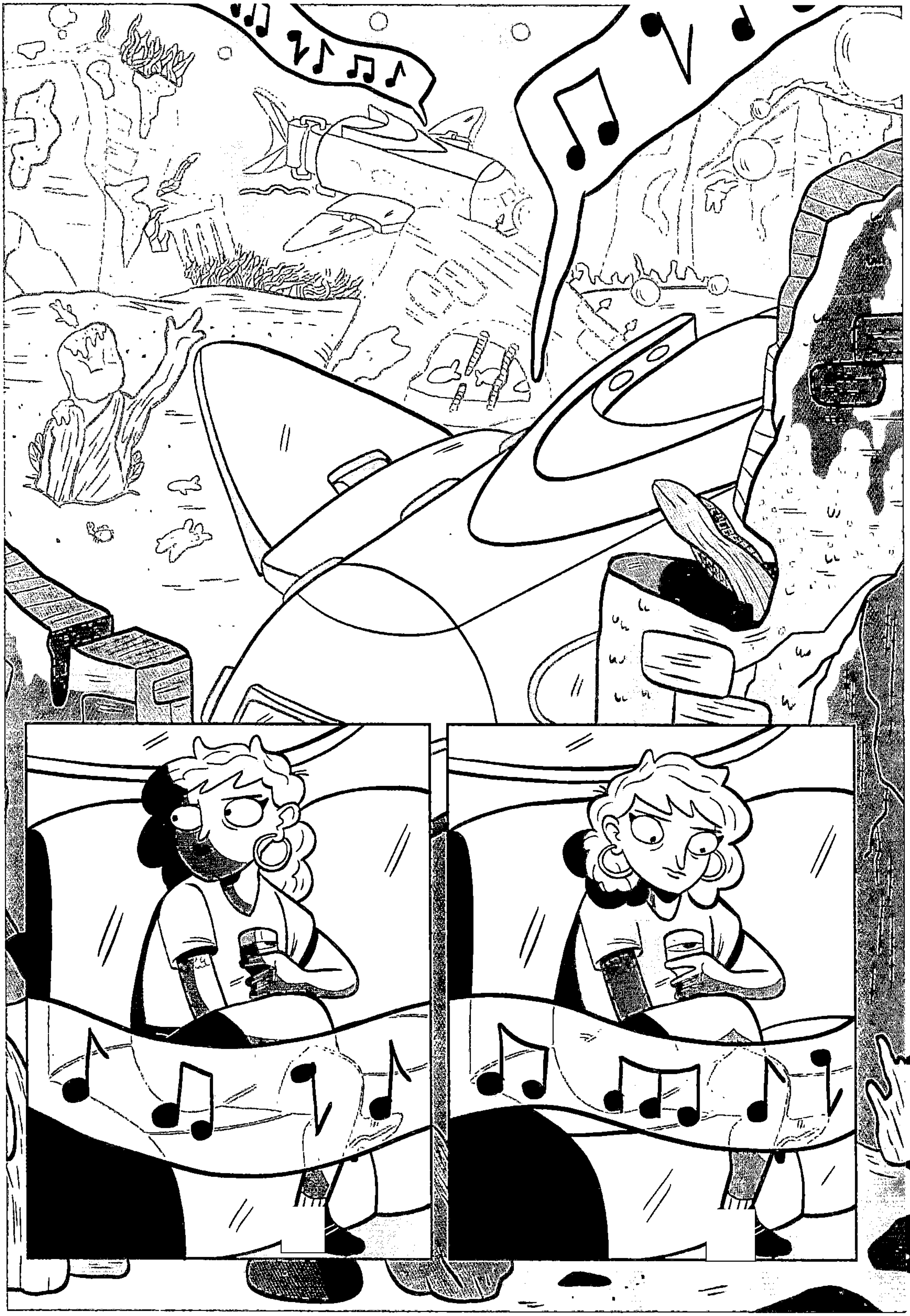

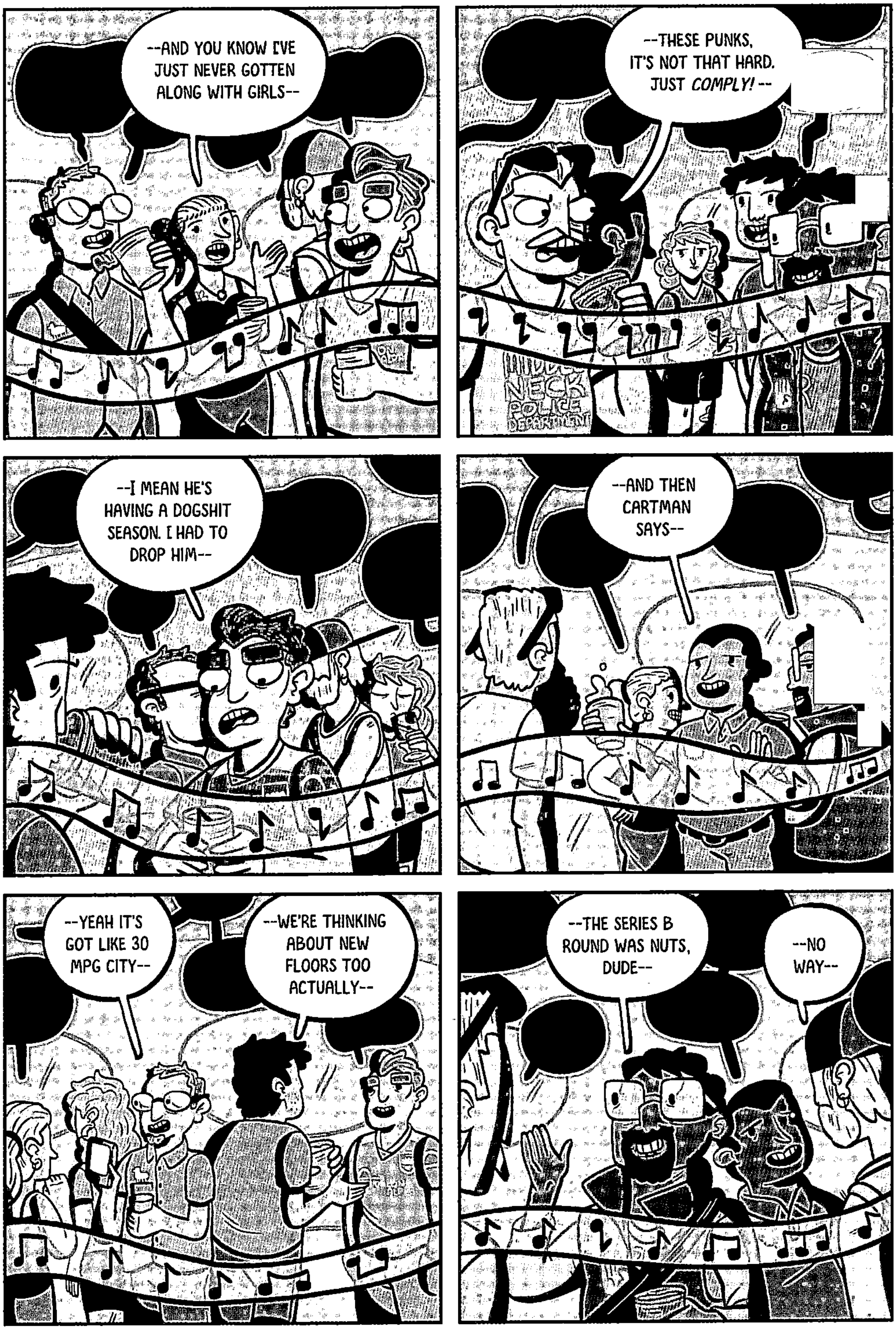

--AND YOU KNOW I'VE JUST NEVER GOTTEN ALONG WITH GIRLS--
--THESE PUNKS, IT'S NOT THAT HARD. JUST *COMPLY!*--
--I MEAN HE'S HAVING A DOGSHIT SEASON. I HAD TO DROP HIM--
--AND THEN CARTMAN SAYS--
--YEAH IT'S GOT LIKE 30 MPG CITY--
--WE'RE THINKING ABOUT NEW FLOORS TOO ACTUALLY--
--THE SERIES B ROUND WAS NUTS, DUDE--
--NO WAY--

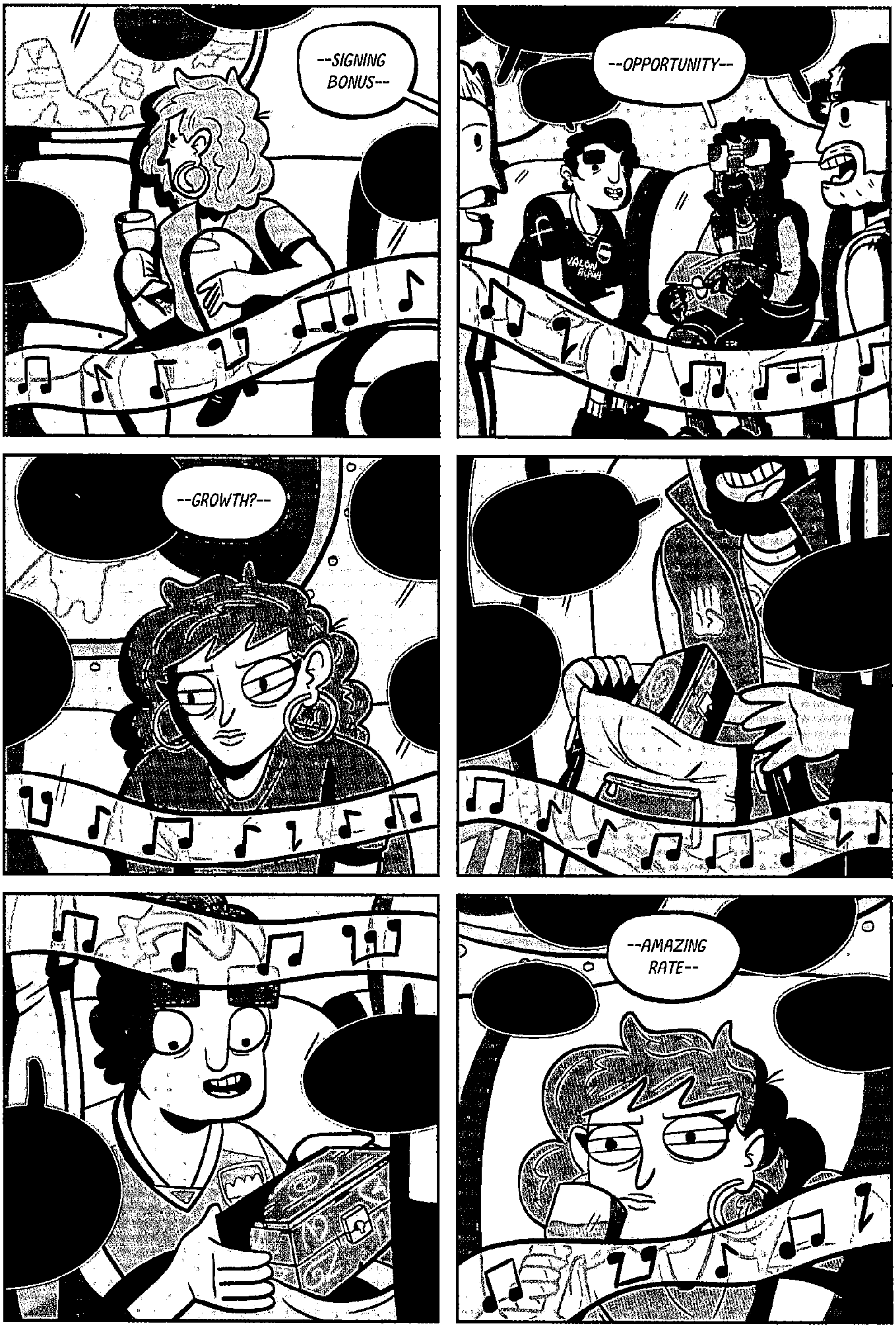
--SIGNING BONUS--
--OPPORTUNITY--
VALON
--GROWTH?--
--AMAZING RATE--

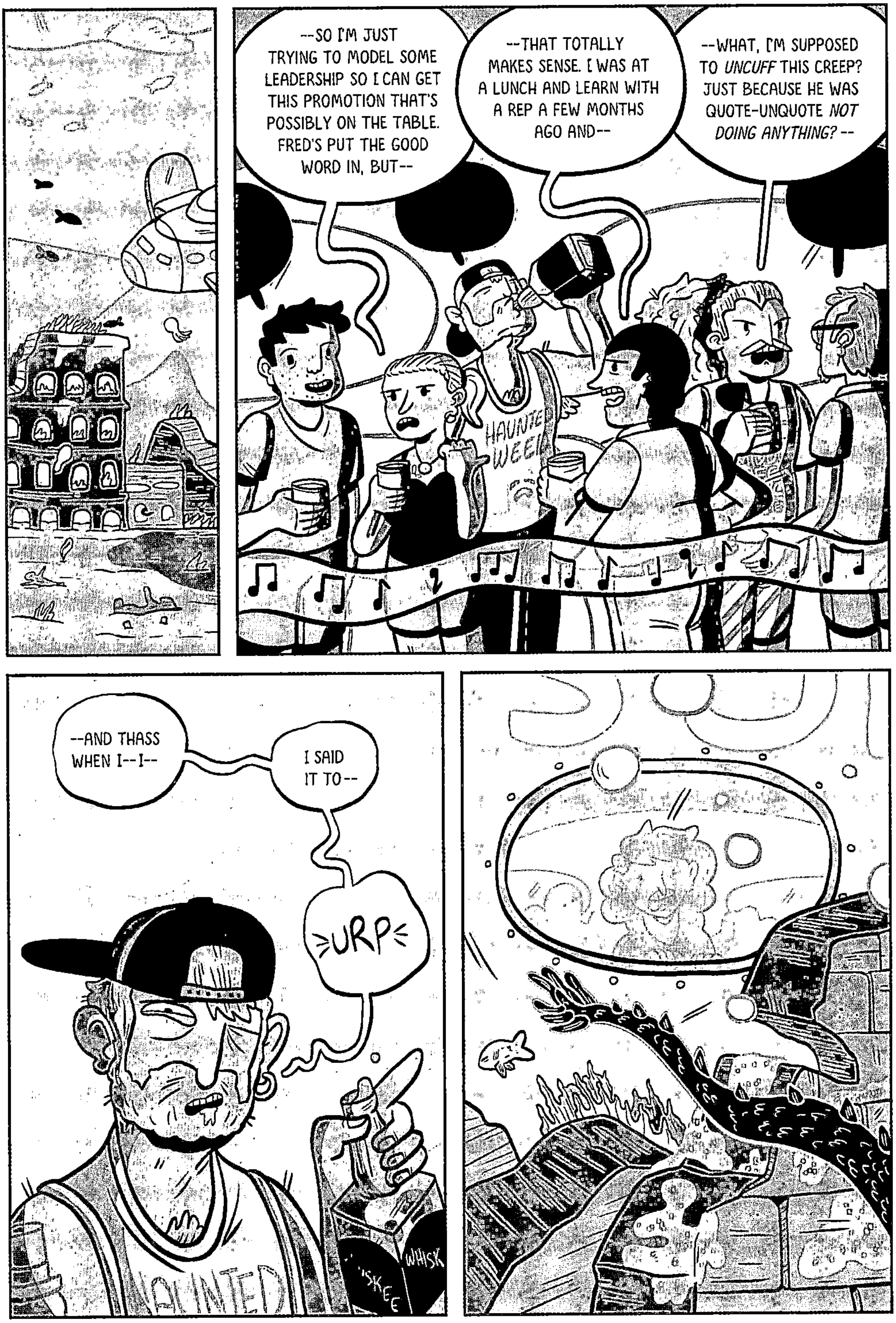
--SO I'M JUST TRYING TO MODEL SOME LEADERSHIP SO I CAN GET THIS PROMOTION THAT'S POSSIBLY ON THE TABLE. FRED'S PUT THE GOOD WORD IN, BUT--
--THAT TOTALLY MAKES SENSE. I WAS AT A LUNCH AND LEARN WITH A REP A FEW MONTHS AGO AND--
--WHAT, I'M SUPPOSED TO *UNCUFF* THIS CREEP? JUST BECAUSE HE WAS QUOTE-UNQUOTE *NOT DOING ANYTHING?* --
--AND THASS WHEN I--I--
I SAID IT TO--
URP

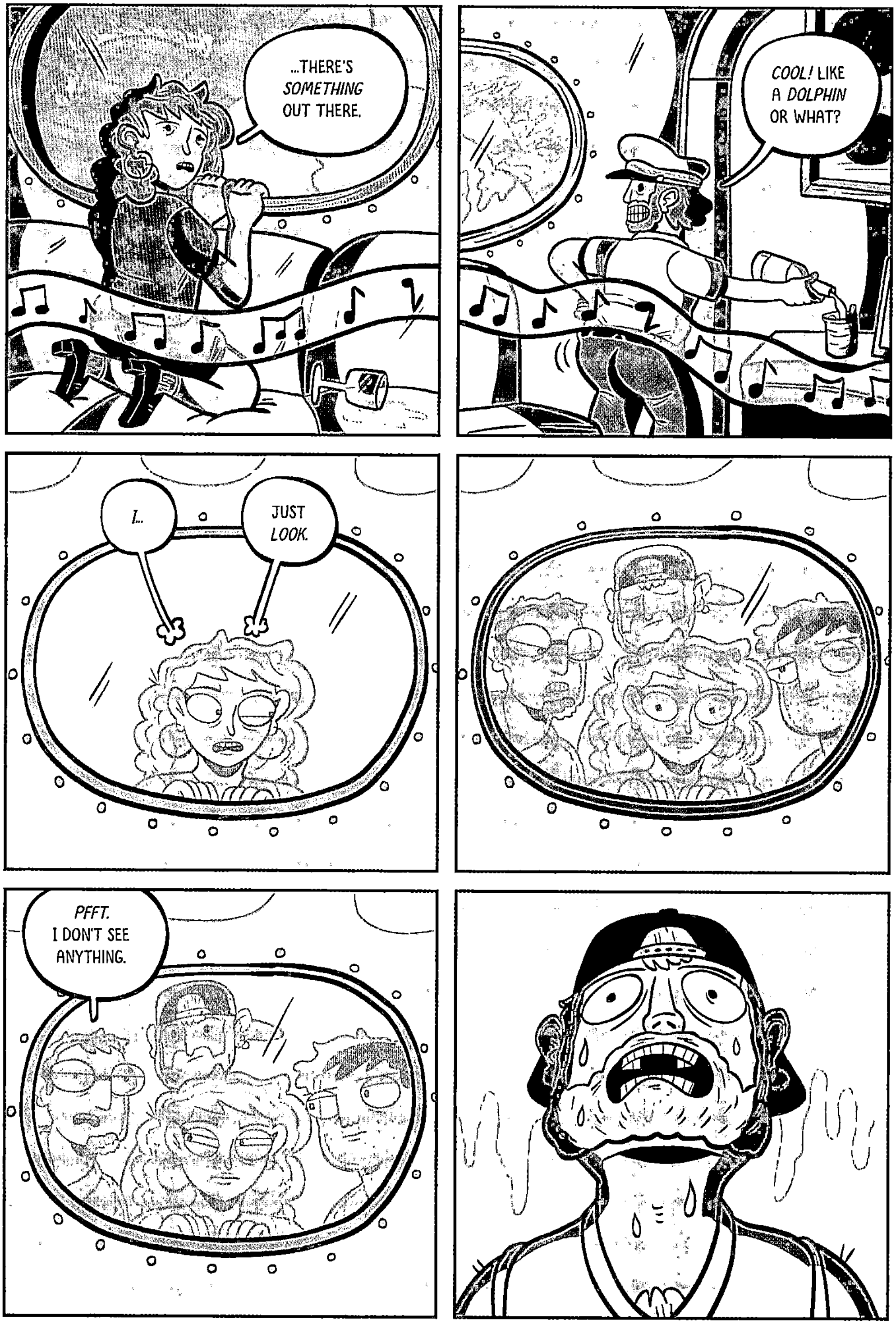
...THERE'S *SOMETHING* OUT THERE.
COOL! LIKE A *DOLPHIN* OR WHAT?
I...
JUST *LOOK.*
PFFT. I DON'T SEE ANYTHING.

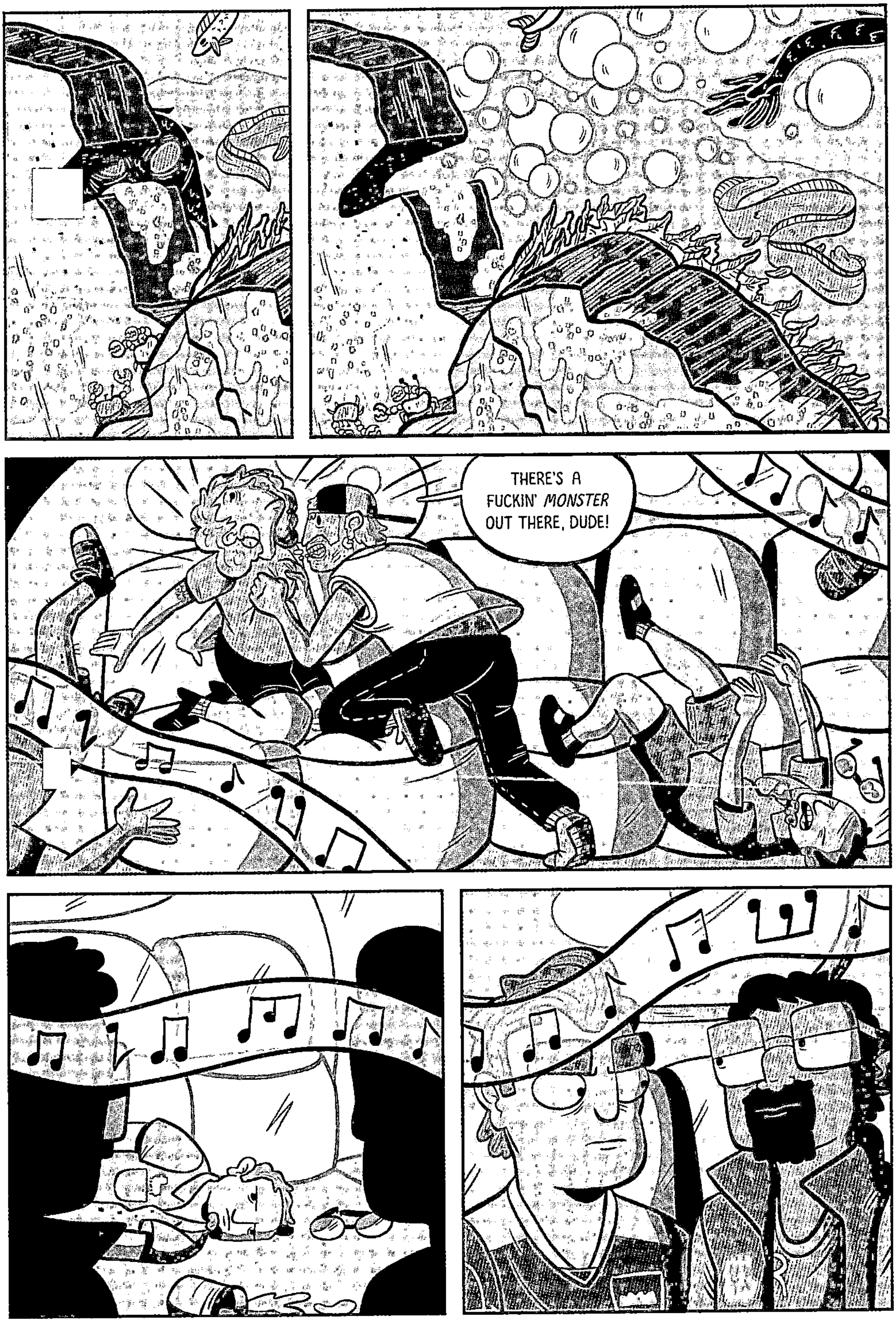
THERE'S A FUCKIN' *MONSTER* OUT THERE, DUDE!

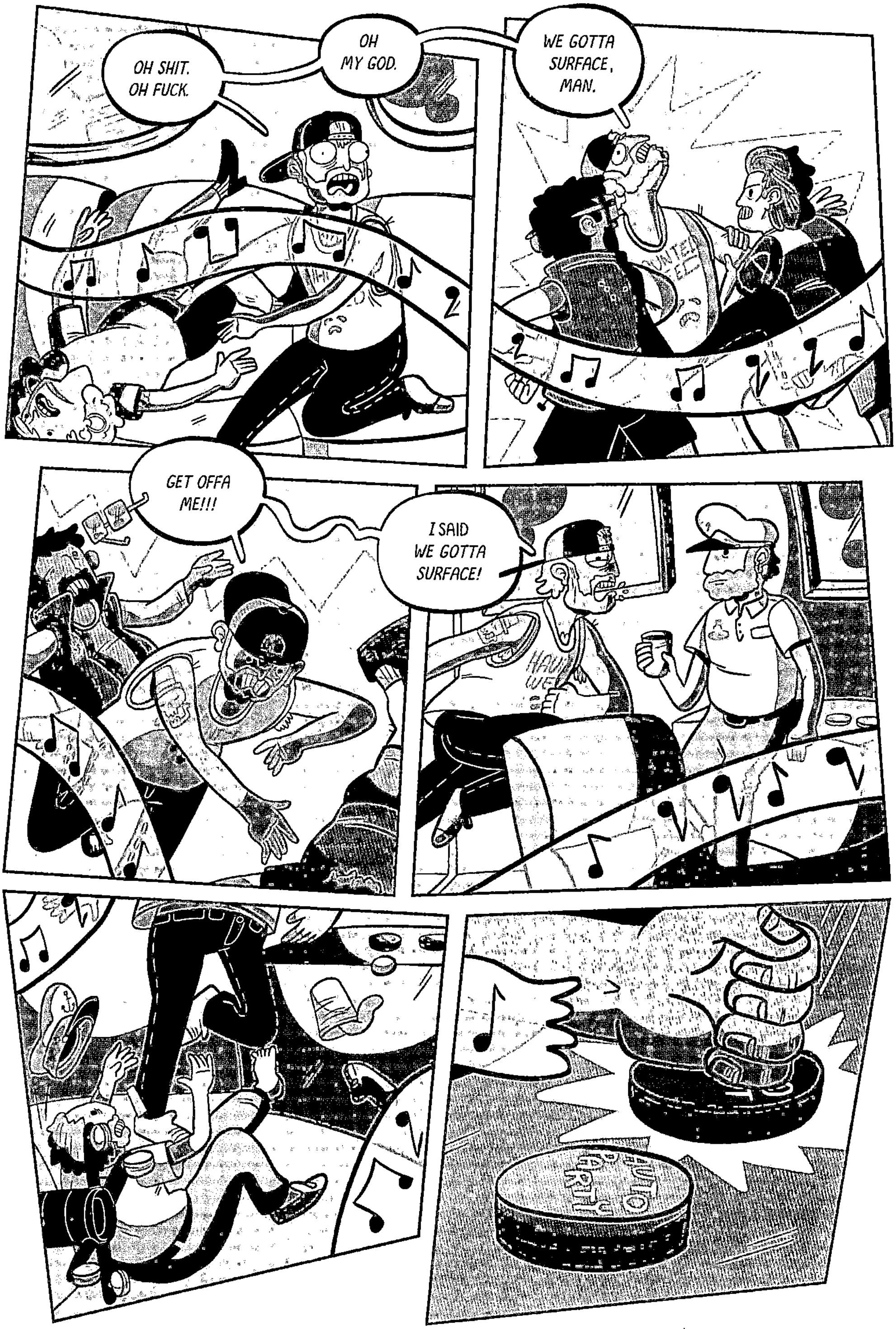
OH SHIT. OH FUCK.
OH MY GOD.
WE GOTTA SURFACE, MAN.
GET OFFA ME!!!
I SAID WE GOTTA SURFACE!
AUTO PARTY

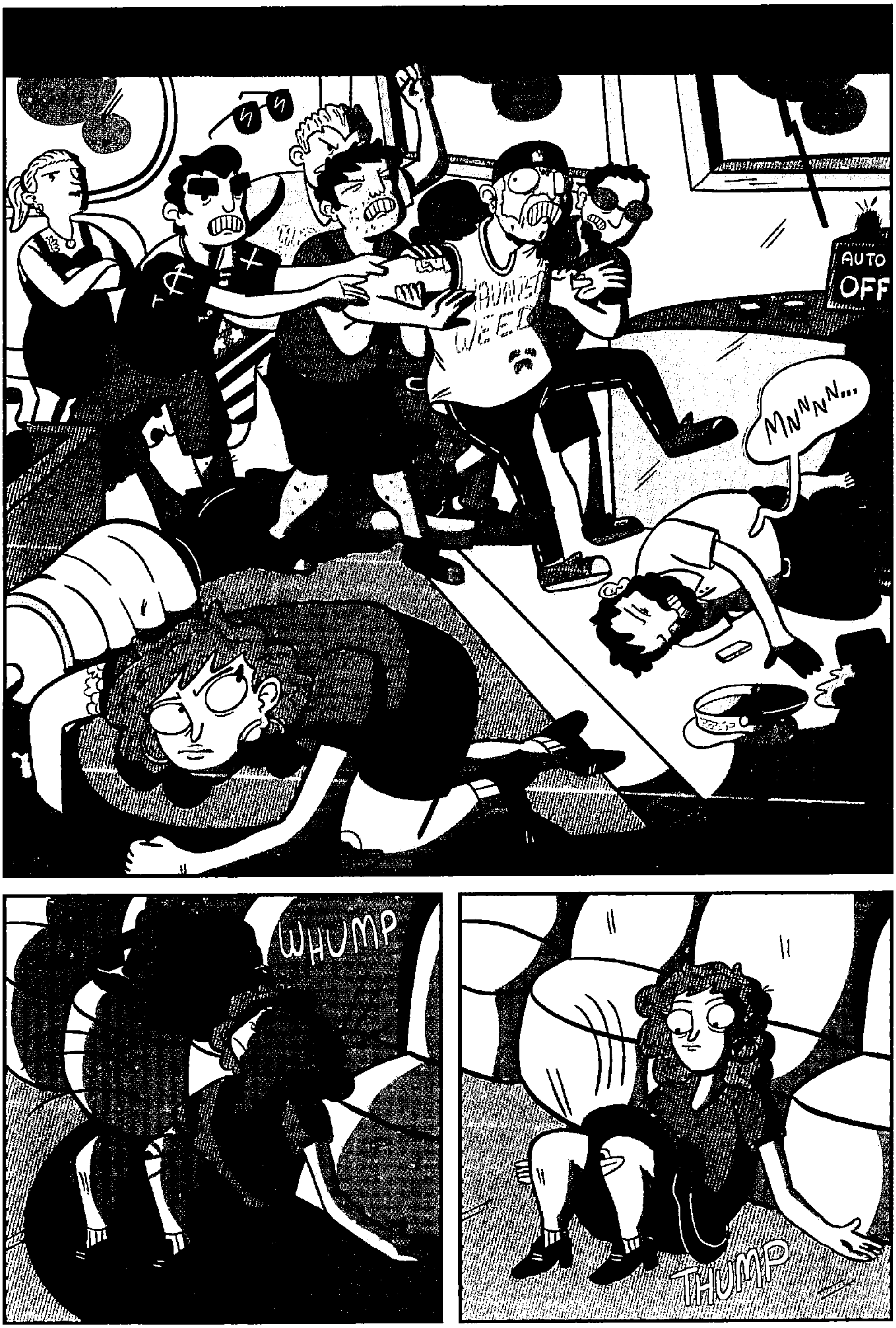
AUTO OFF
MNNNN...
WHUMP
THUMP

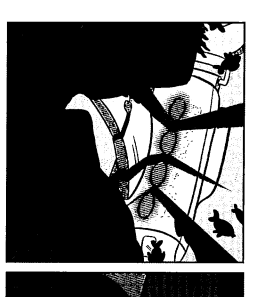

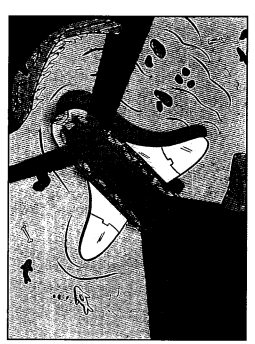

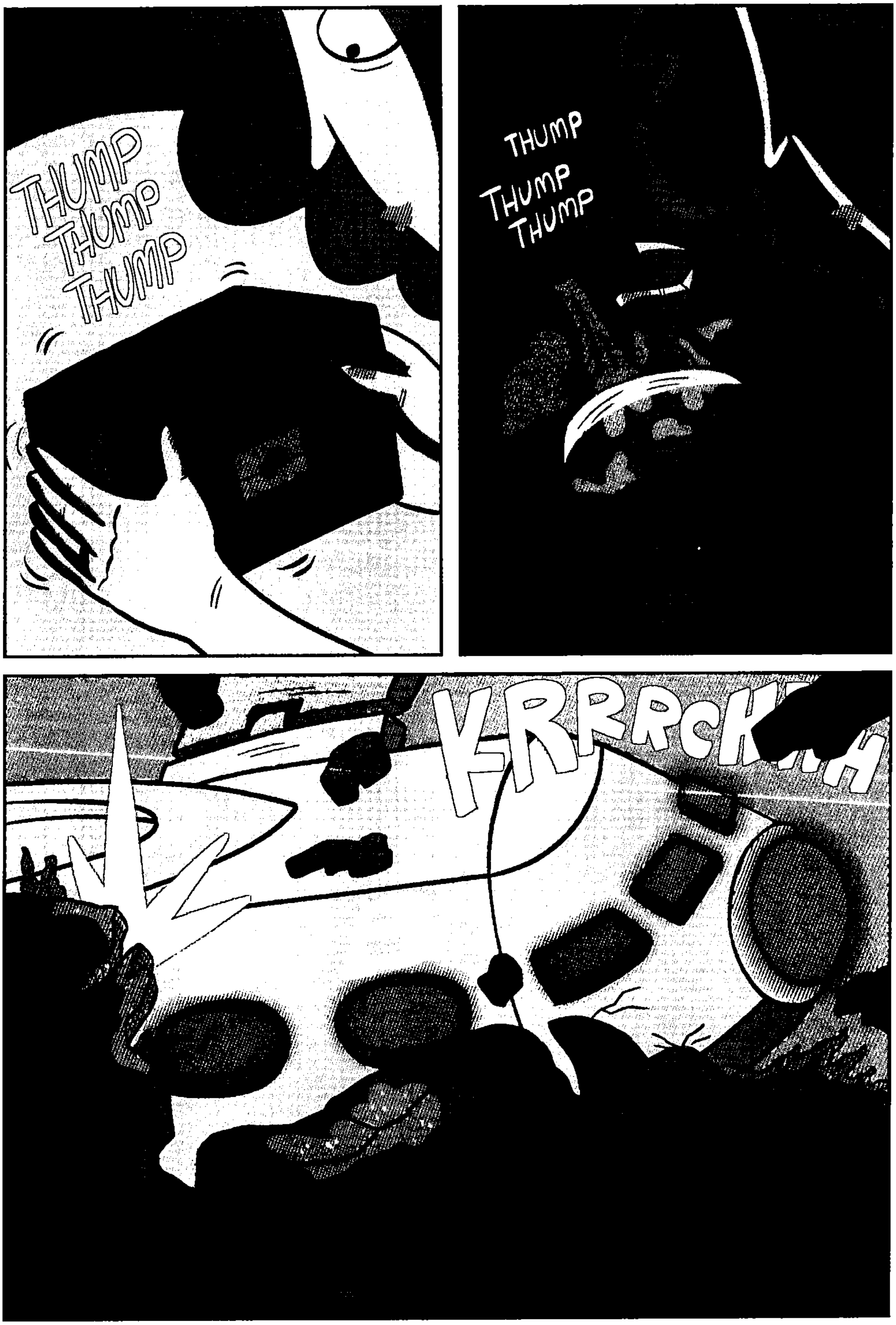
THUMP
THUMP
THUMP
THUMP
THUMP
THUMP
KRRRCKH

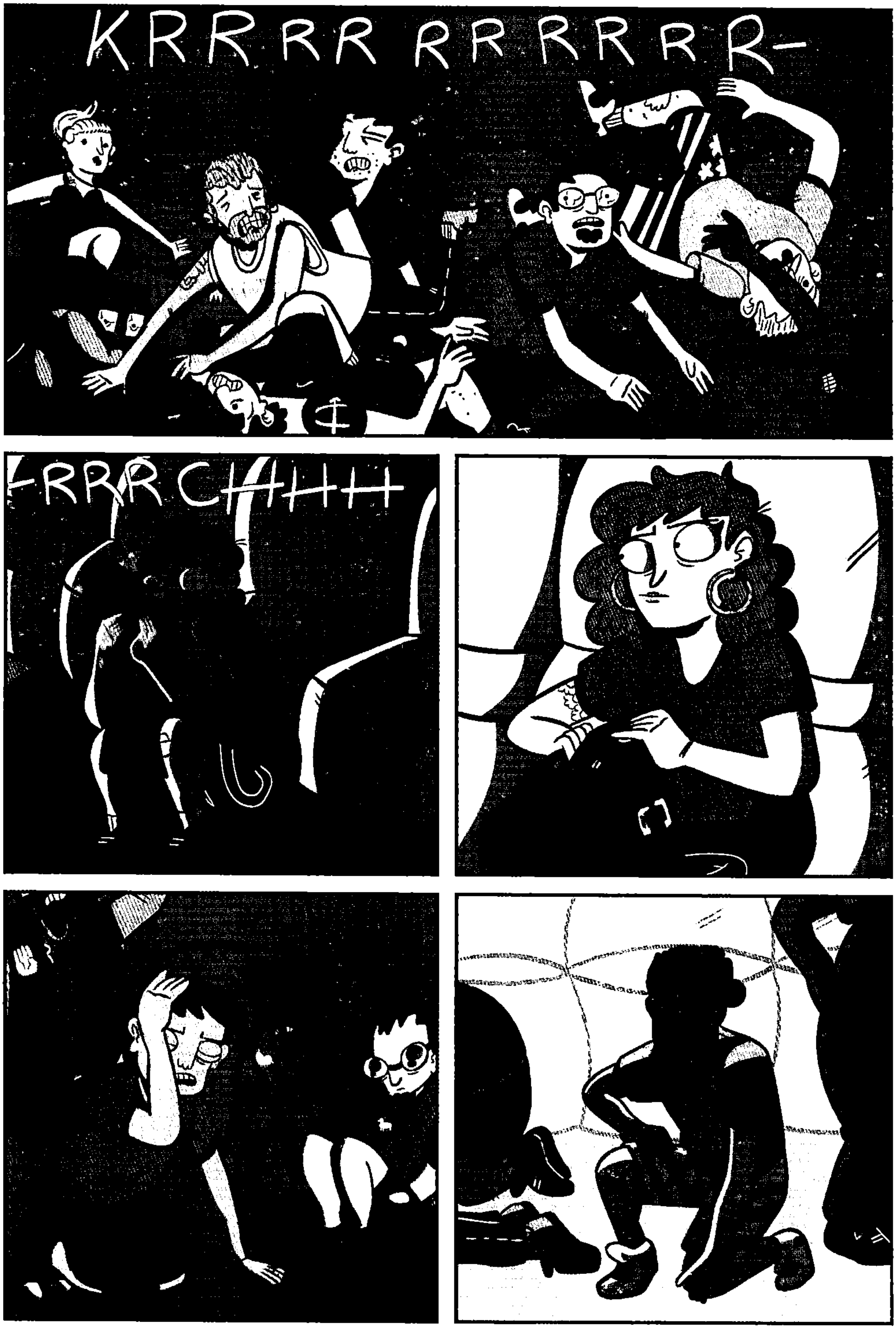
KRRRRRRRRRRR-
-RRRCHHHH

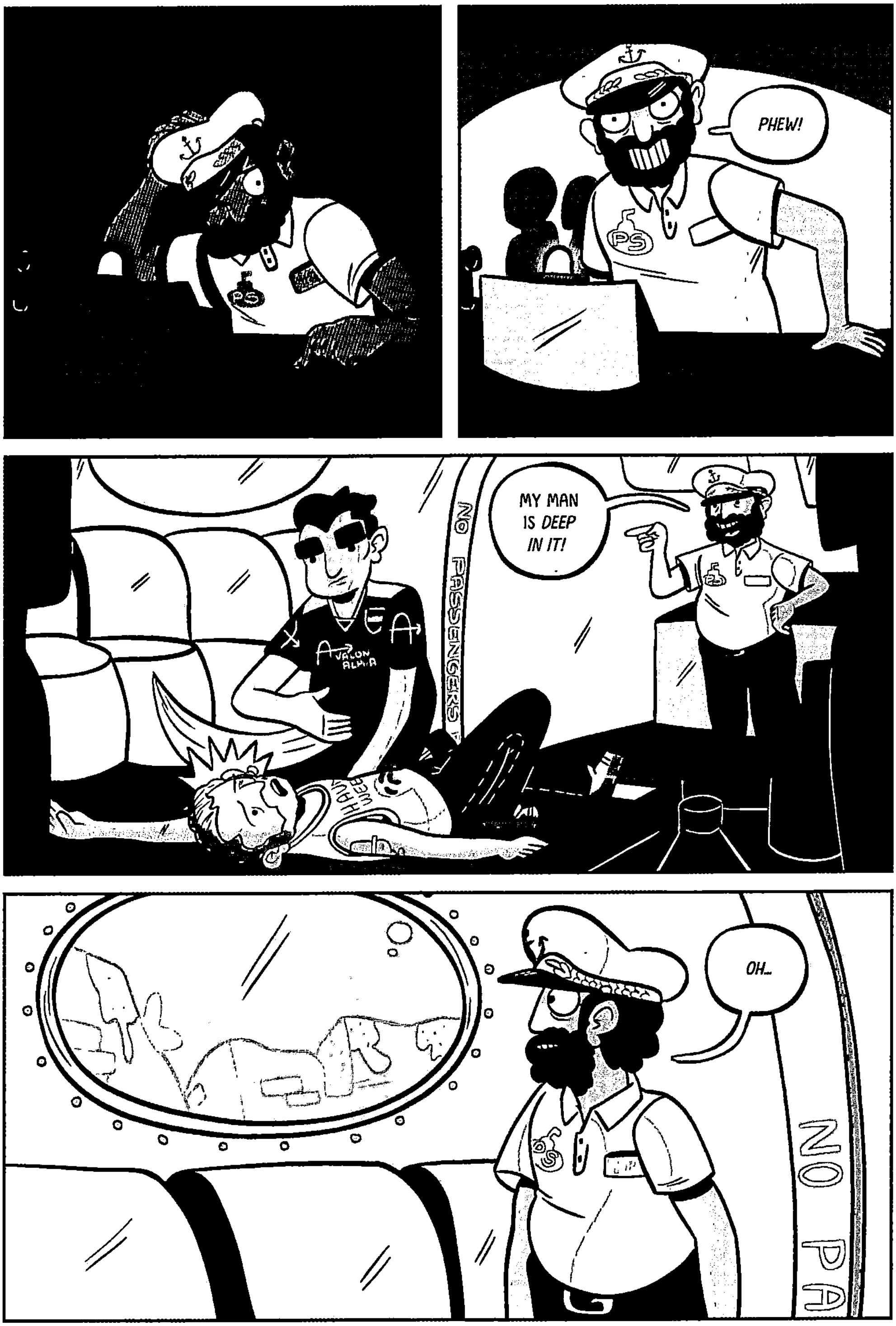
PHEW!
MY MAN IS DEEP IN IT!
AVALON ALPHA
NO PASSENGERS
OH...
NO PA

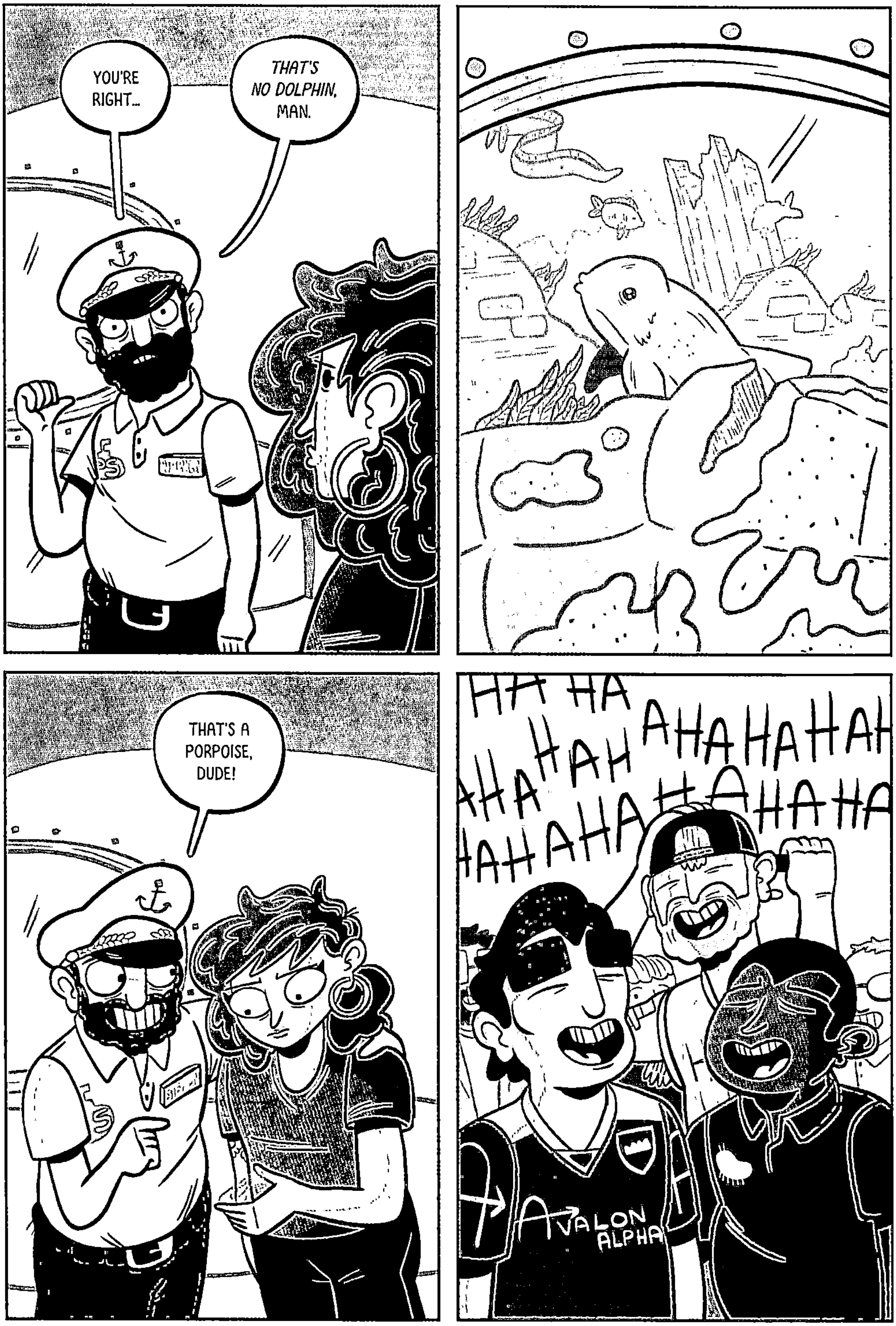

YOU'RE RIGHT...
THAT'S NO DOLPHIN, MAN.
THAT'S A PORPOISE, DUDE!
HA HA
HAH AHAHAHAH
AHAHAHAHAHAHA
AVALON ALPHA

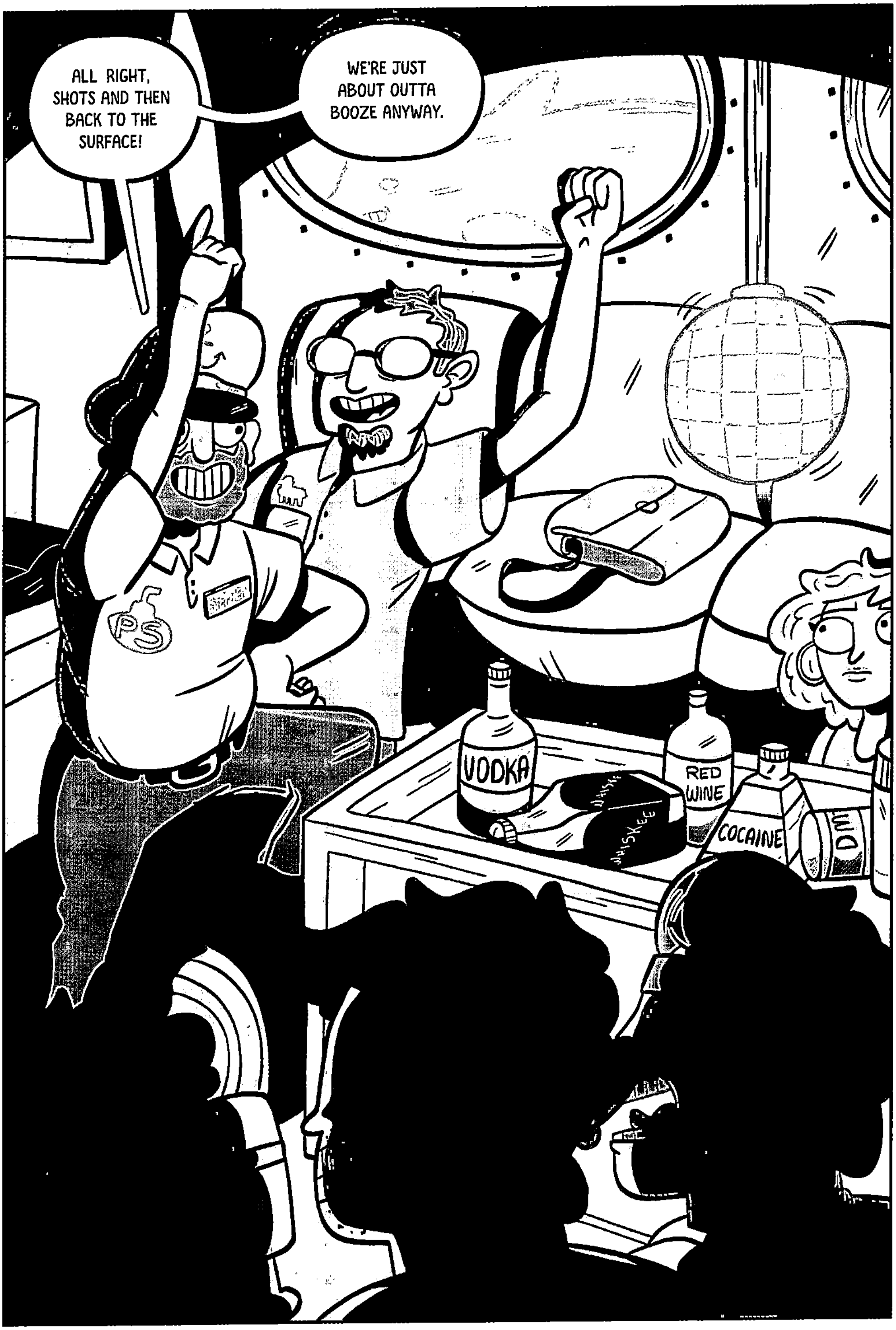
ALL RIGHT, SHOTS AND THEN BACK TO THE SURFACE!
WE'RE JUST ABOUT OUTTA BOOZE ANYWAY.
VODKA
RED WINE
WHISKEE
COCAINE

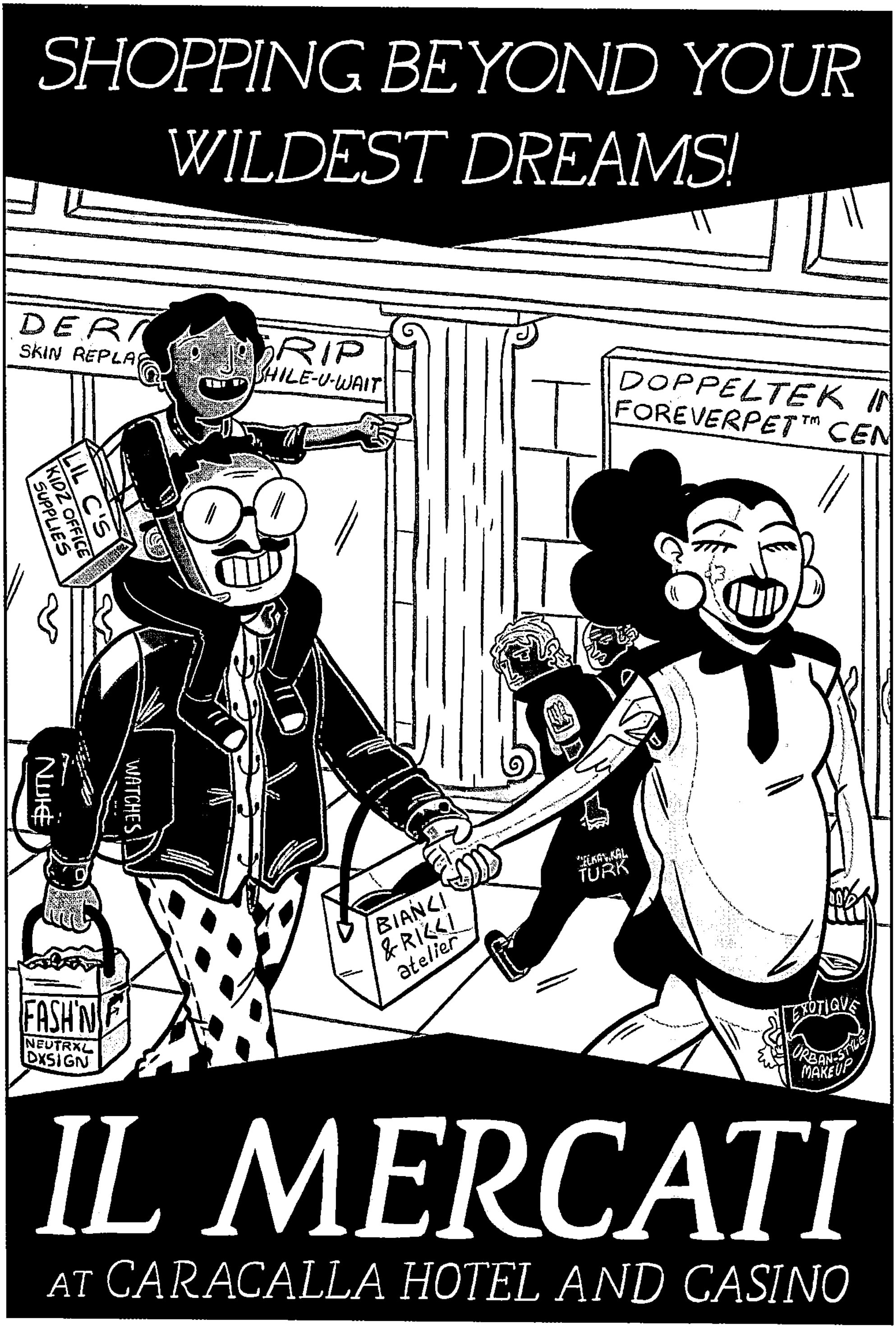
SHOPPING BEYOND YOUR WILDEST DREAMS!
SKIN REPLA
RIP
HILE-U-WAIT
DOPPELTEK IN
FOREVERPET™ CEN
LIL C'S
KIDZ OFFICE SUPPLIES
WATCHES
FASH'N
NEUTRXL DXSIGN
BIANCI & RICCI atelier
TURK
EXOTIQUE
URBAN-STYLE MAKEUP
IL MERCATI
AT CARACALLA HOTEL AND CASINO

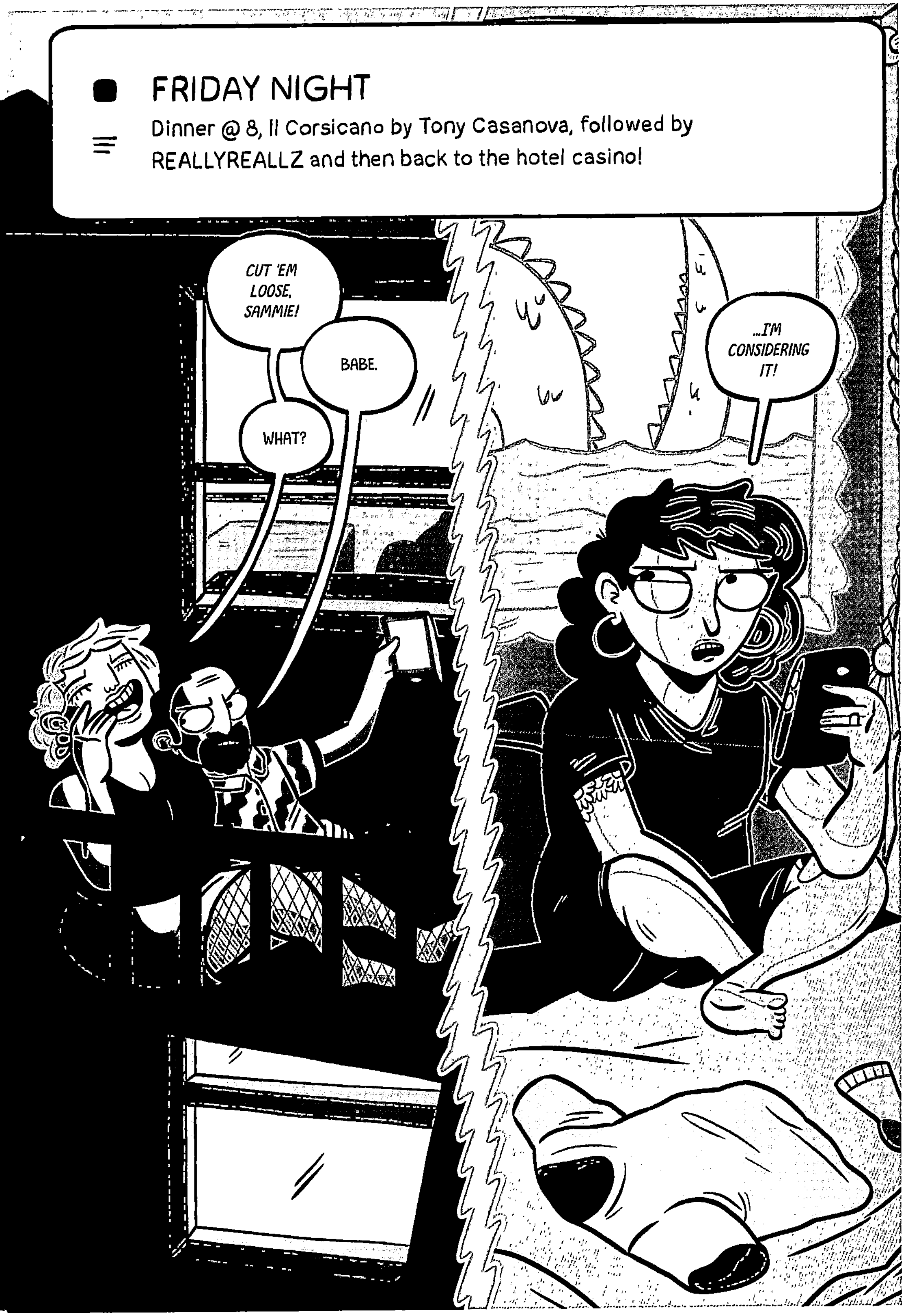
FRIDAY NIGHT
Dinner @ 8, Il Corsicano by Tony Casanova, followed by REALLYREALLZ and then back to the hotel casino!
CUT 'EM LOOSE, SAMMIE!
WHAT?
BABE.
...I'M CONSIDERING IT!

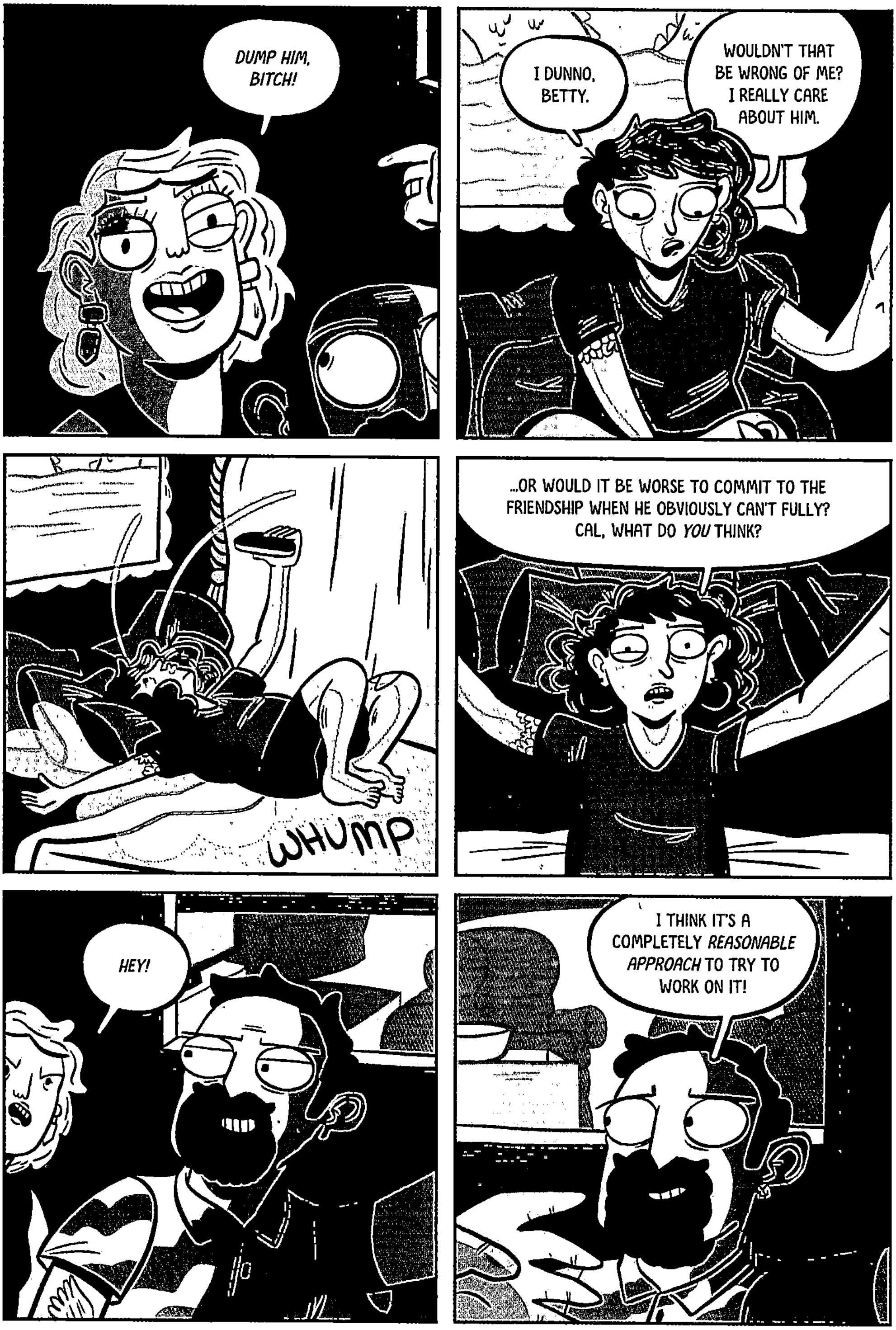

DUMP HIM, BITCH!
I DUNNO, BETTY.
WOULDN'T THAT BE WRONG OF ME? I REALLY CARE ABOUT HIM.
WHUMP
...OR WOULD IT BE WORSE TO COMMIT TO THE FRIENDSHIP WHEN HE OBVIOUSLY CAN'T FULLY? CAL, WHAT DO *YOU* THINK?
HEY!
I THINK IT'S A COMPLETELY *REASONABLE APPROACH* TO TRY TO WORK ON IT!

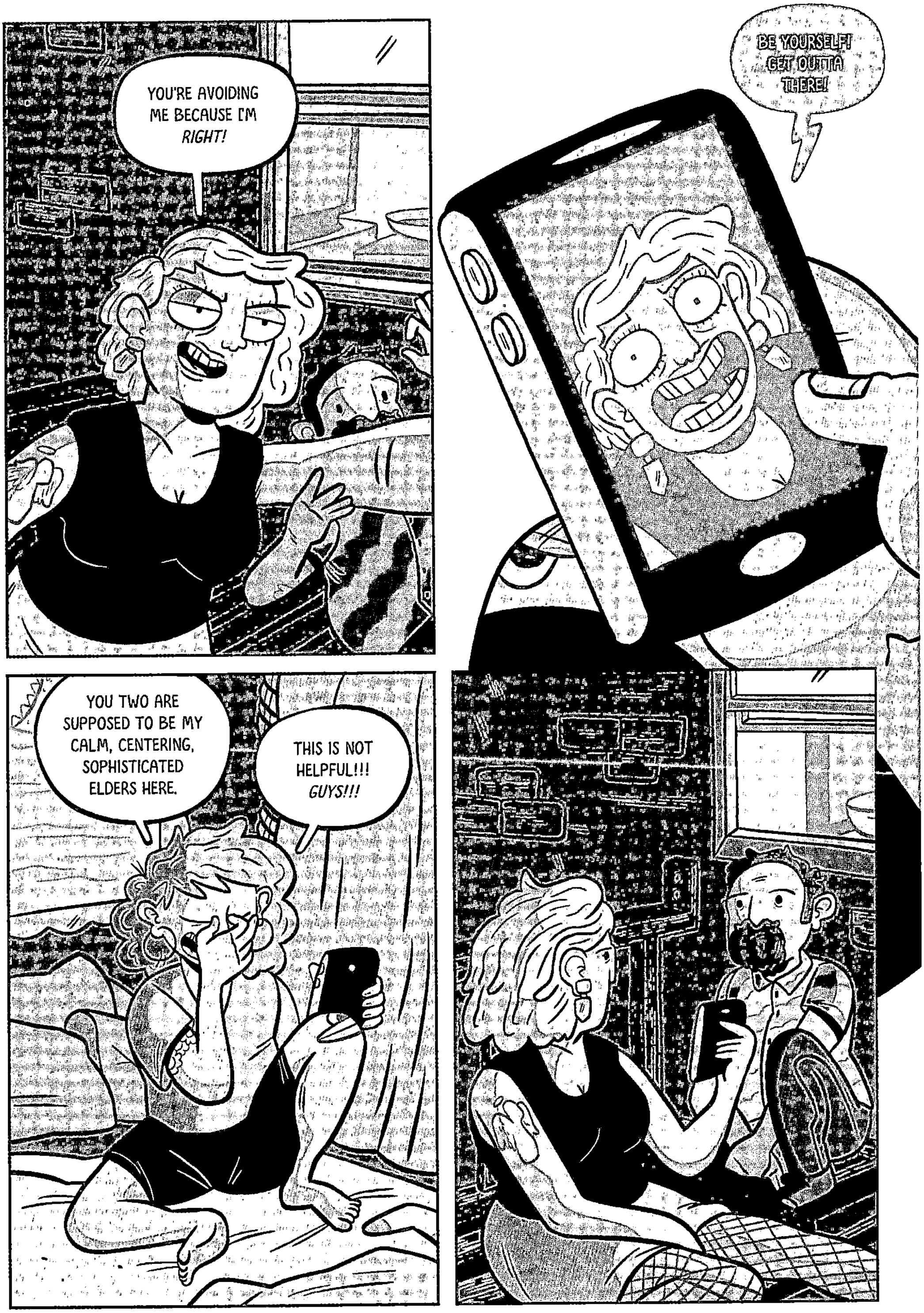
YOU'RE AVOIDING ME BECAUSE I'M *RIGHT!*
BE YOURSELF! GET OUTTA THERE!
YOU TWO ARE SUPPOSED TO BE MY CALM, CENTERING, SOPHISTICATED ELDERS HERE.
THIS IS NOT HELPFUL!!! *GUYS!!!*

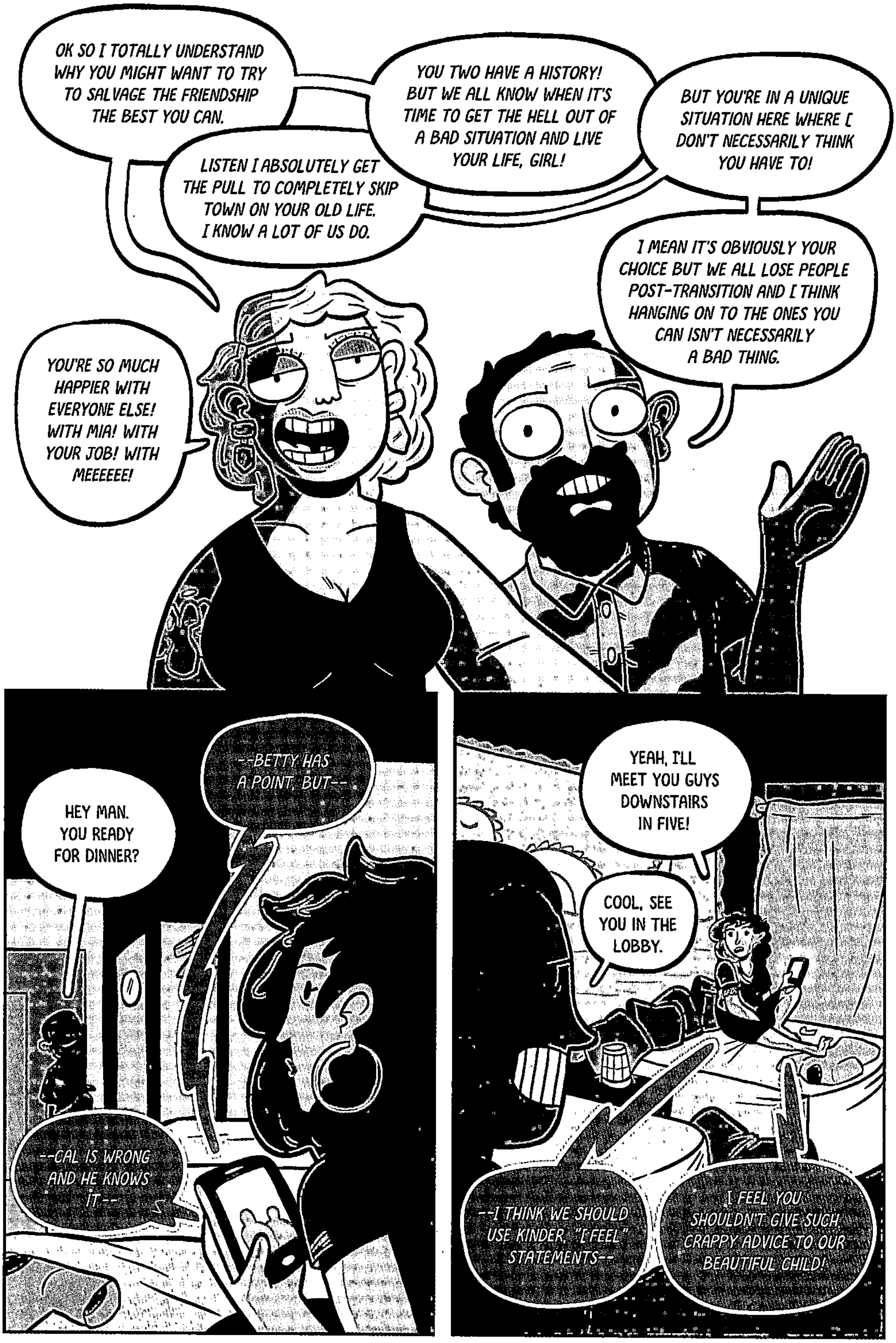
OK SO I TOTALLY UNDERSTAND WHY YOU MIGHT WANT TO TRY TO SALVAGE THE FRIENDSHIP THE BEST YOU CAN.
YOU TWO HAVE A HISTORY! BUT WE ALL KNOW WHEN IT'S TIME TO GET THE HELL OUT OF A BAD SITUATION AND LIVE YOUR LIFE, GIRL!
BUT YOU'RE IN A UNIQUE SITUATION HERE WHERE I DON'T NECESSARILY THINK YOU HAVE TO!
LISTEN I ABSOLUTELY GET THE PULL TO COMPLETELY SKIP TOWN ON YOUR OLD LIFE. I KNOW A LOT OF US DO.
I MEAN IT'S OBVIOUSLY YOUR CHOICE BUT WE ALL LOSE PEOPLE POST-TRANSITION AND I THINK HANGING ON TO THE ONES YOU CAN ISN'T NECESSARILY A BAD THING.
YOU'RE SO MUCH HAPPIER WITH EVERYONE ELSE! WITH MIA! WITH YOUR JOB! WITH MEEEEEE!
HEY MAN. YOU READY FOR DINNER?
--BETTY HAS A POINT, BUT--
--CAL IS WRONG AND HE KNOWS IT--
YEAH, I'LL MEET YOU GUYS DOWNSTAIRS IN FIVE!
COOL, SEE YOU IN THE LOBBY.
--I THINK WE SHOULD USE KINDER, "I FEEL" STATEMENTS--
I FEEL YOU SHOULDN'T GIVE SUCH CRAPPY ADVICE TO OUR BEAUTIFUL CHILD!

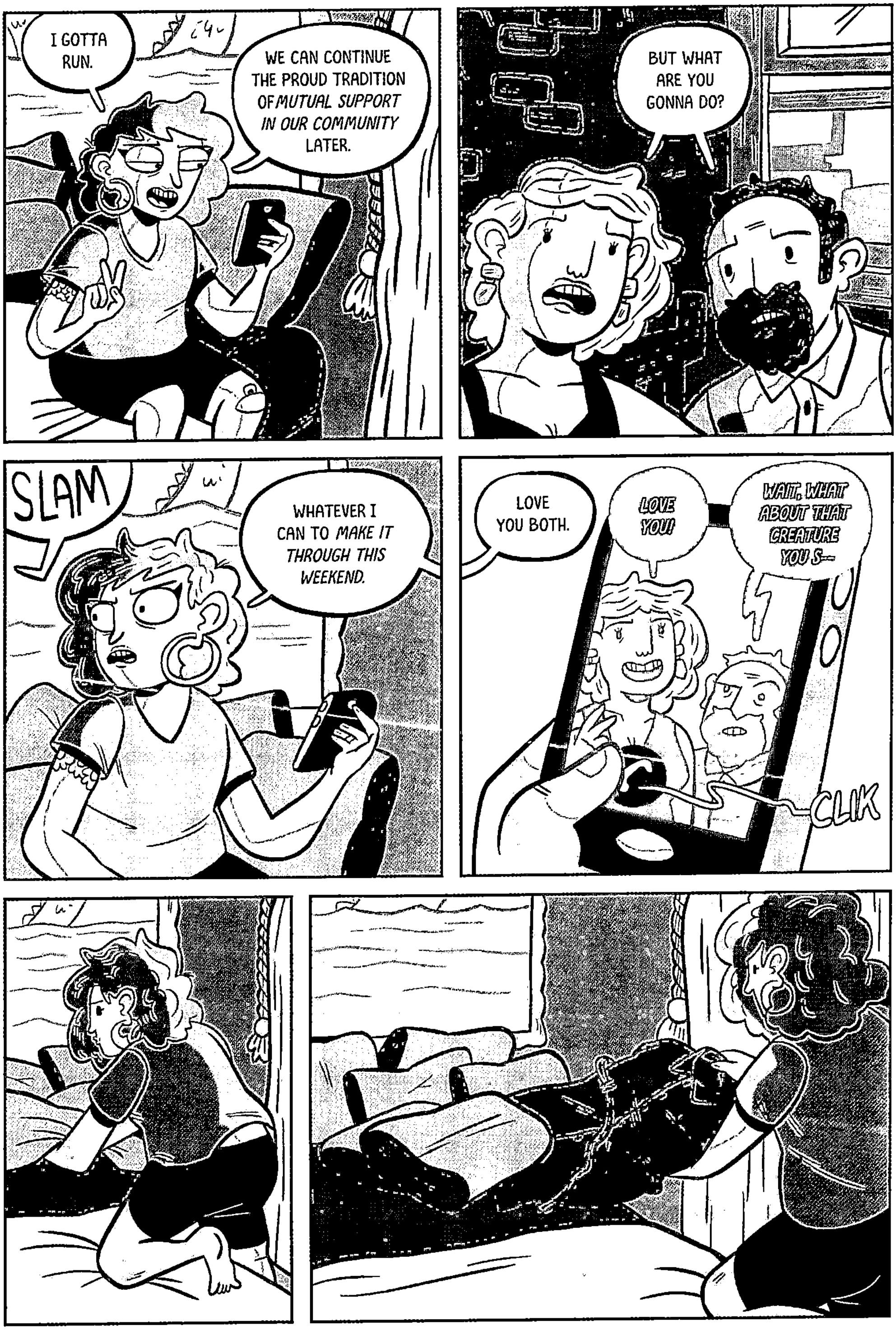
I GOTTA RUN.
WE CAN CONTINUE THE PROUD TRADITION OF *MUTUAL SUPPORT IN OUR COMMUNITY* LATER.
BUT WHAT ARE YOU GONNA DO?
SLAM
WHATEVER I CAN TO *MAKE IT THROUGH THIS WEEKEND.*
LOVE YOU BOTH.
LOVE YOU!
WAIT, WHAT ABOUT THAT CREATURE YOU S—
CLIK

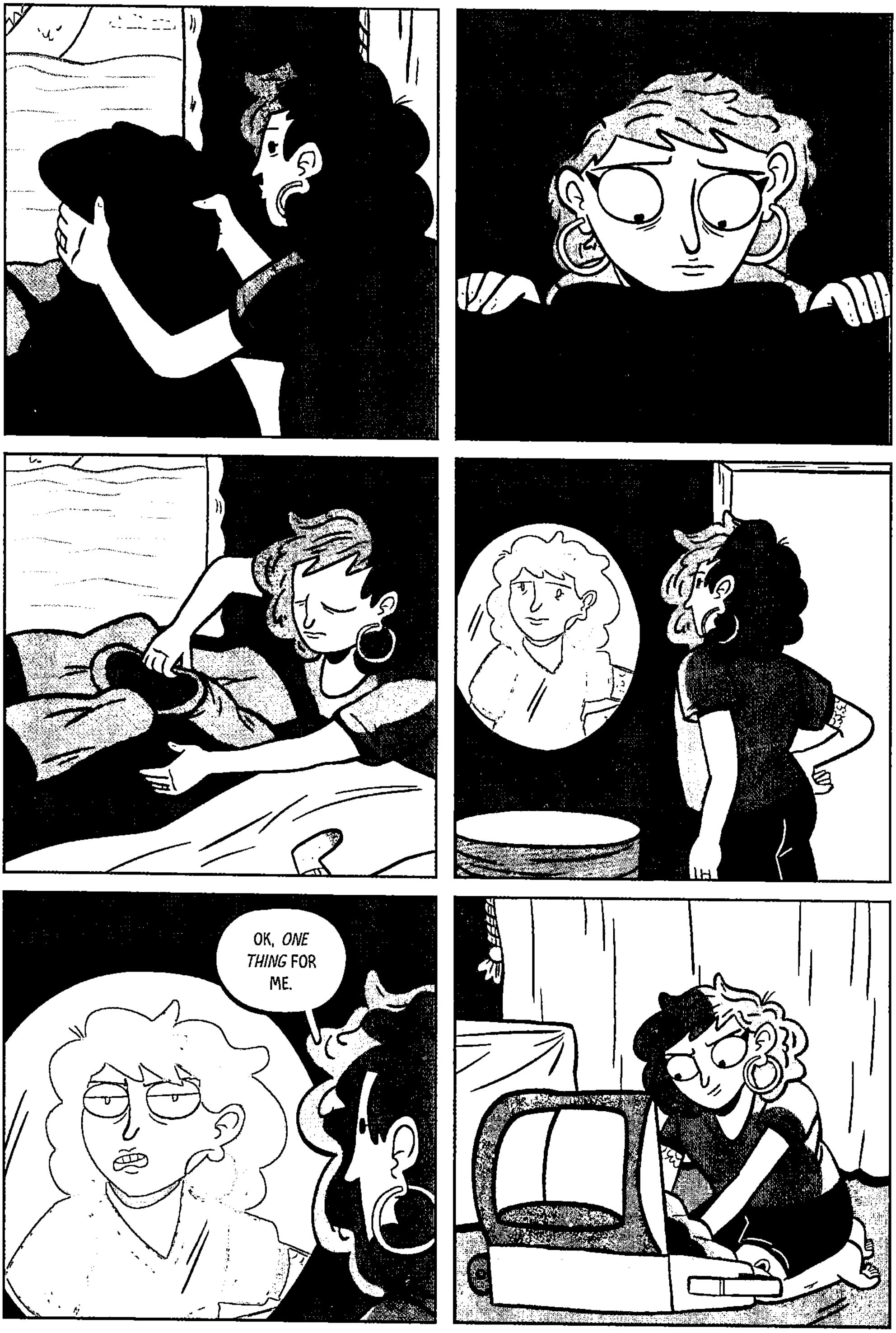
OK, *ONE THING* FOR ME.

LASHED
FUCKABLE™ MASCARA
IDE3
SHADOW

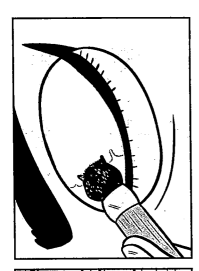

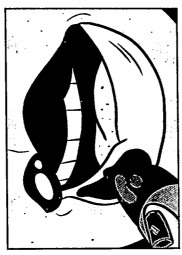

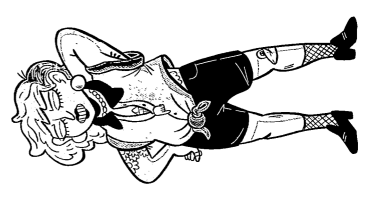

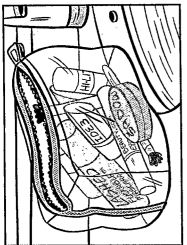

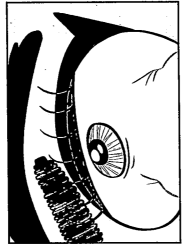

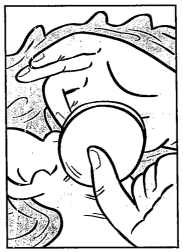

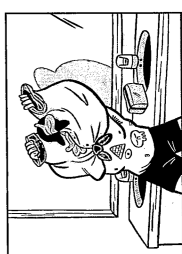

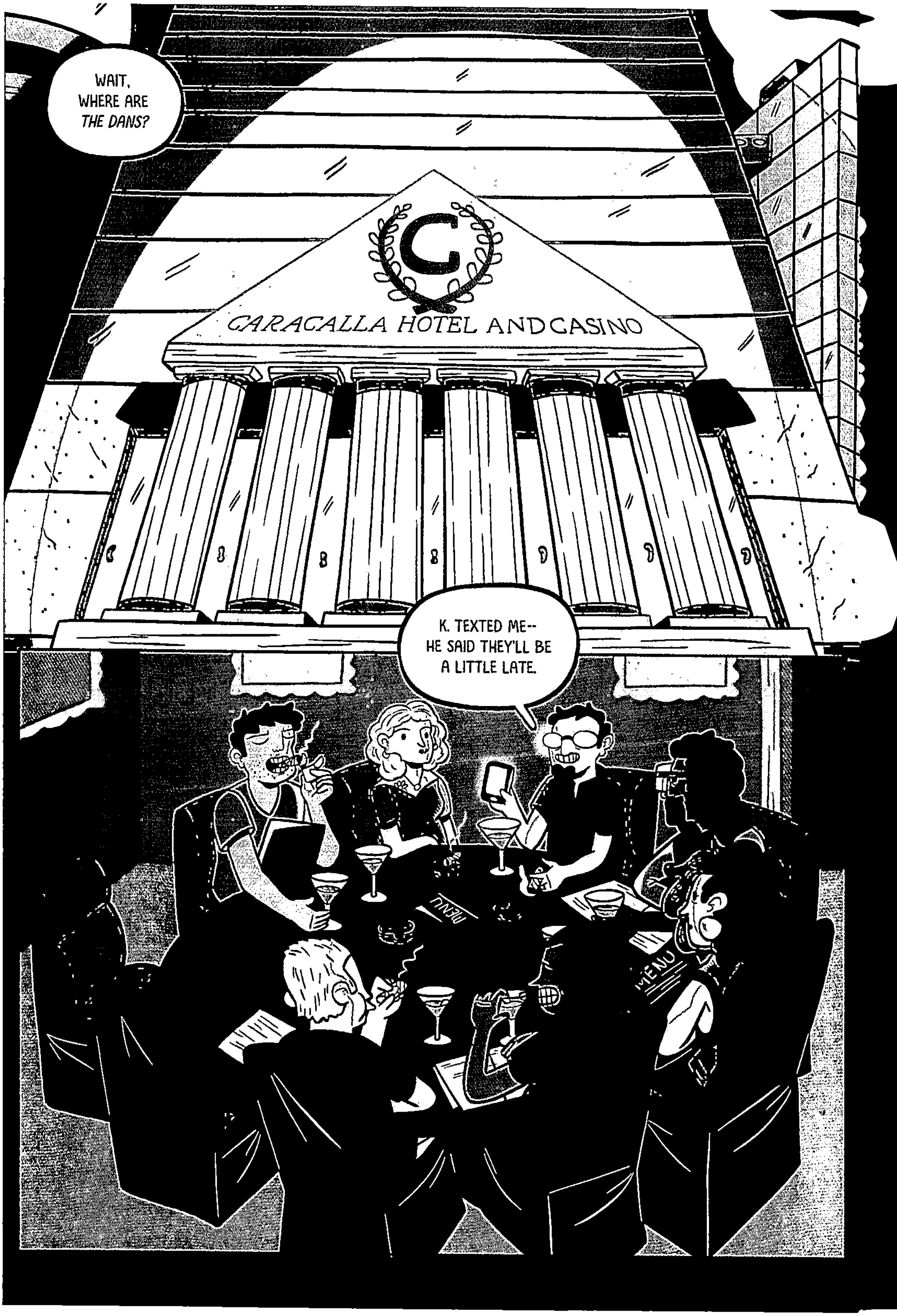
WAIT, WHERE ARE *THE DANS?*
C
CARACALLA HOTEL AND CASINO
K. TEXTED ME-- HE SAID THEY'LL BE A LITTLE LATE.
MENU
MENU

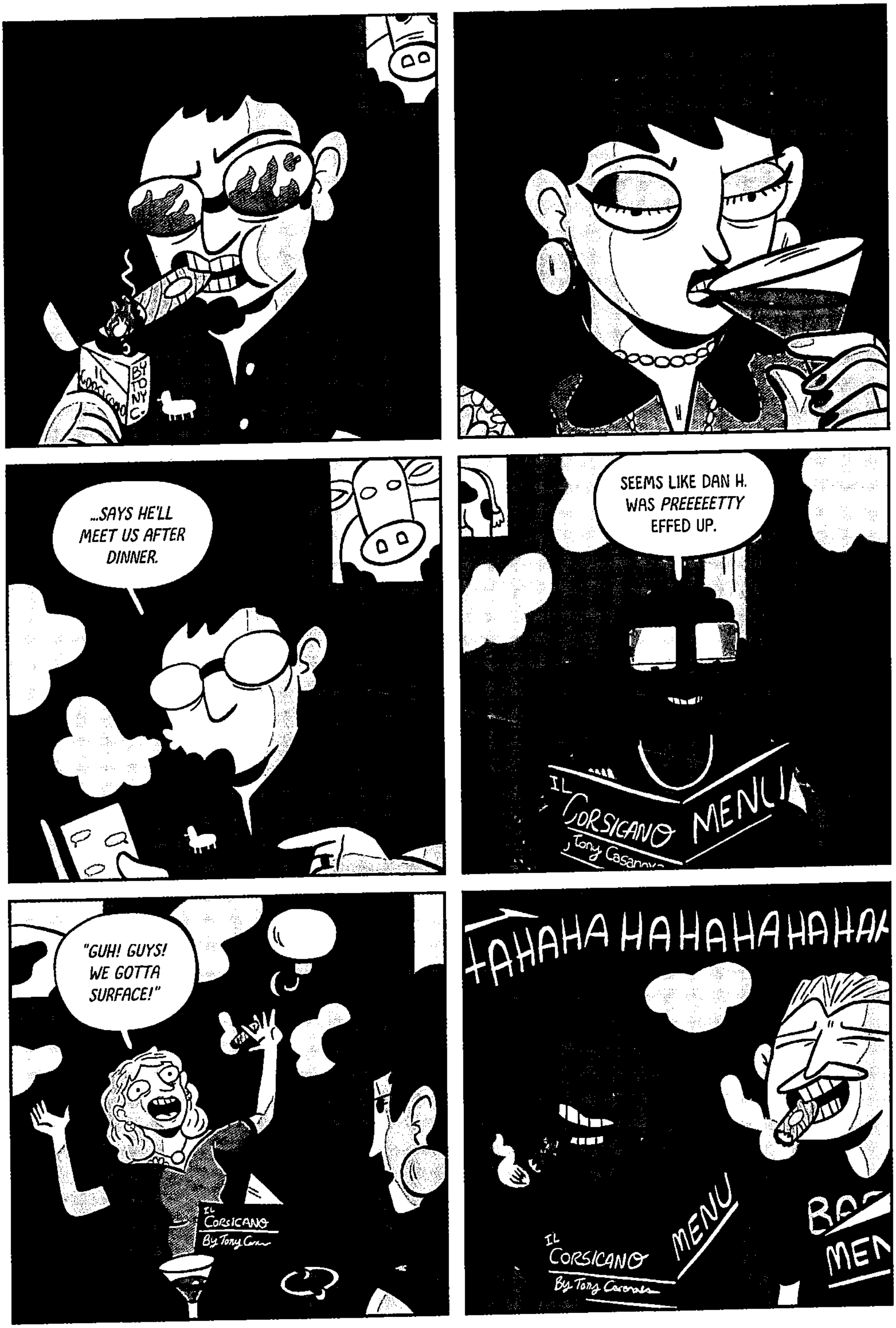
IL Corsicano
BY TONY C.
...SAYS HE'LL MEET US AFTER DINNER.
SEEMS LIKE DAN H. WAS PREEEEETTY EFFED UP.
IL CORSICANO MENU
Tony Casanova
"GUH! GUYS! WE GOTTA SURFACE!"
IL CORSICANO
HAHAHA HAHAHAHAHAHA
IL CORSICANO MENU

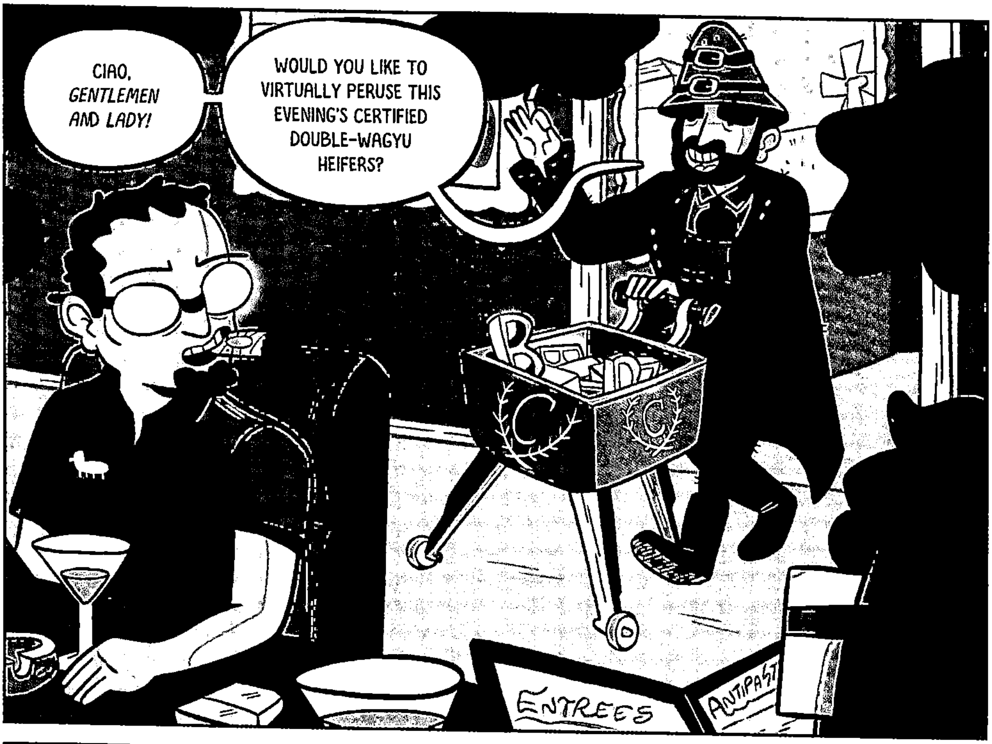
CIAO, *GENTLEMEN AND LADY!*
WOULD YOU LIKE TO VIRTUALLY PERUSE THIS EVENING'S CERTIFIED DOUBLE-WAGYU HEIFERS?
ENTREES
ANTIPASTI

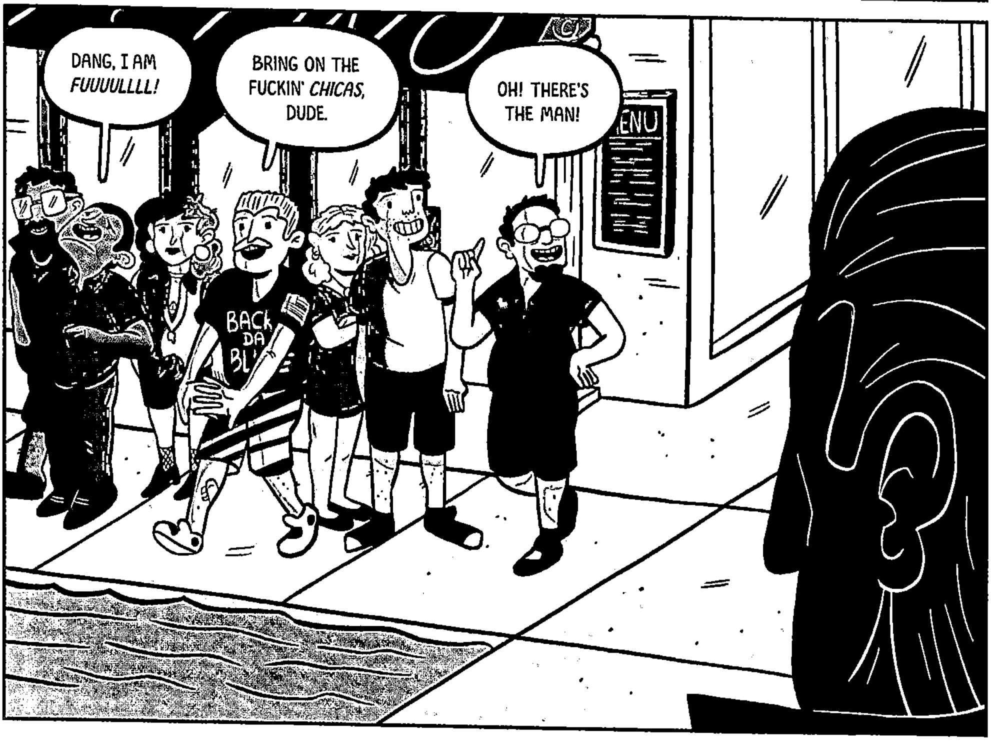
DANG, I AM *FUUUULLLL!*
BRING ON THE FUCKIN' *CHICAS,* DUDE.
OH! THERE'S THE MAN!
MENU
BACK DA BL

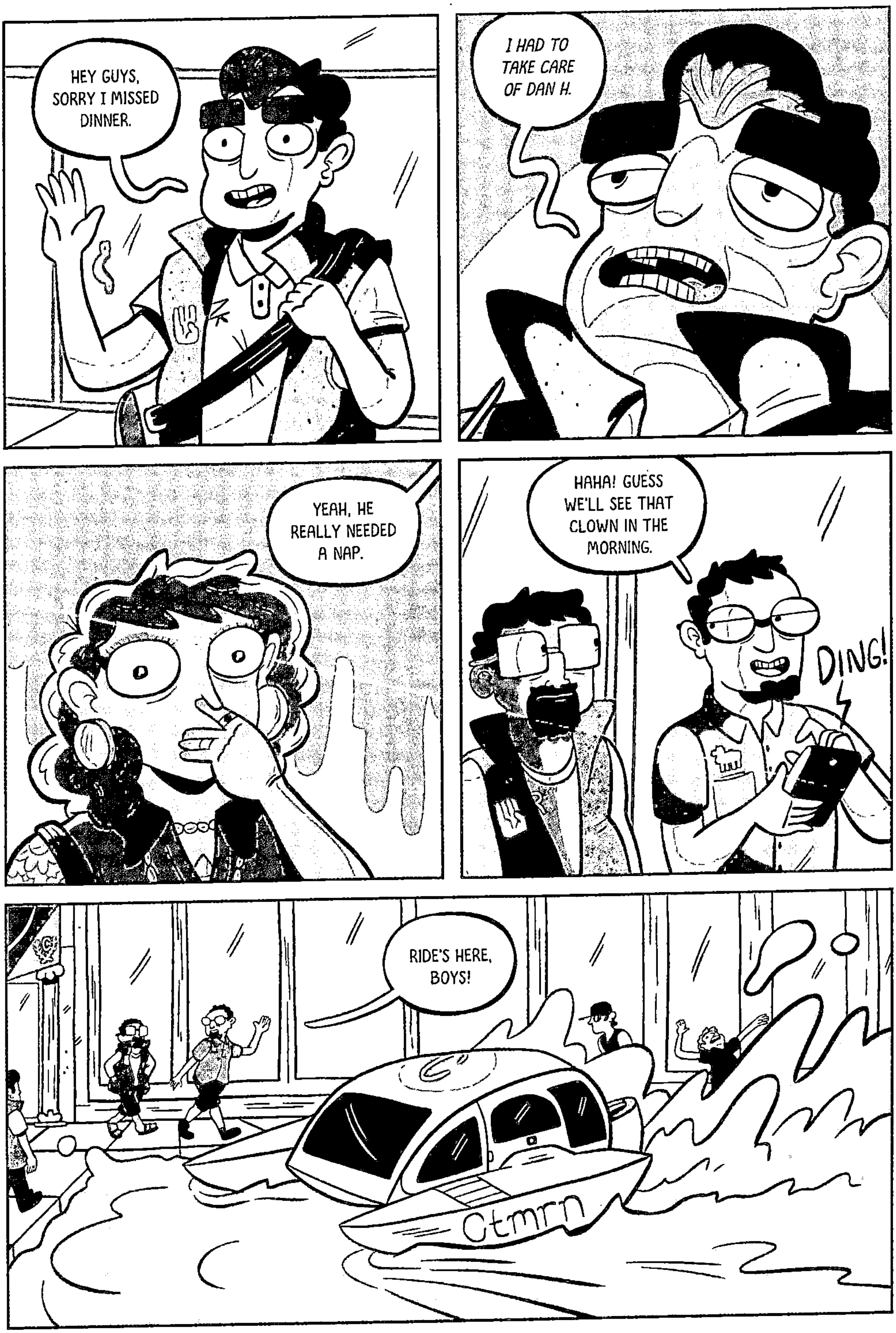
HEY GUYS, SORRY I MISSED DINNER.
I HAD TO TAKE CARE OF DAN H.
YEAH, HE REALLY NEEDED A NAP.
HAHA! GUESS WE'LL SEE THAT CLOWN IN THE MORNING.
DING!
RIDE'S HERE, BOYS!
Ctmrn

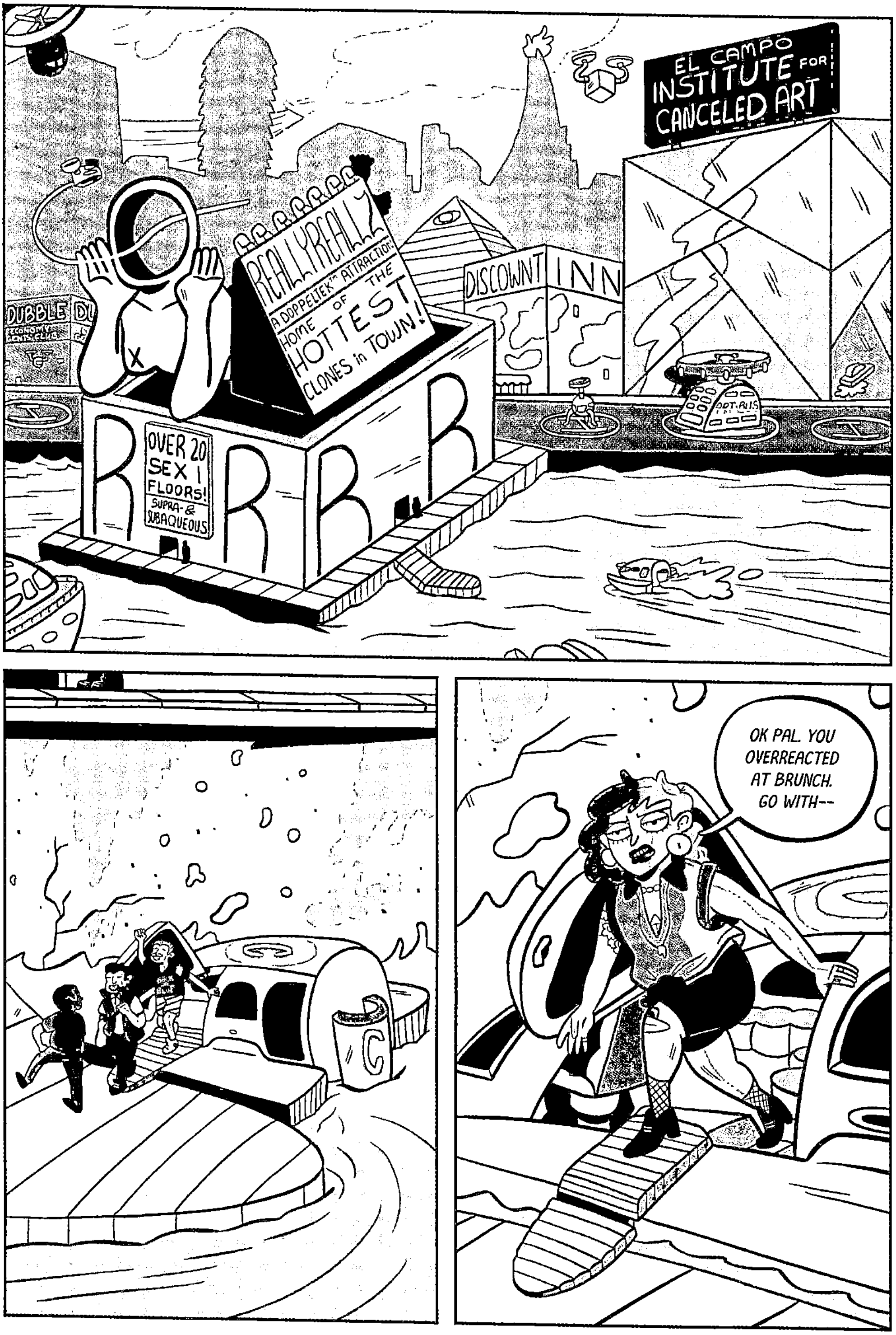
EL CAMPO INSTITUTE FOR CANCELED ART
REALLYREALLY
A DOPPELTEK™ ATTRACTION: HOME OF THE HOTTEST CLONES in TOWN!
OVER 20 SEX! FLOORS! SUPRA- & SUBAQUEOUS
DISCOWNT INN
OK PAL. YOU OVERREACTED AT BRUNCH. GO WITH--

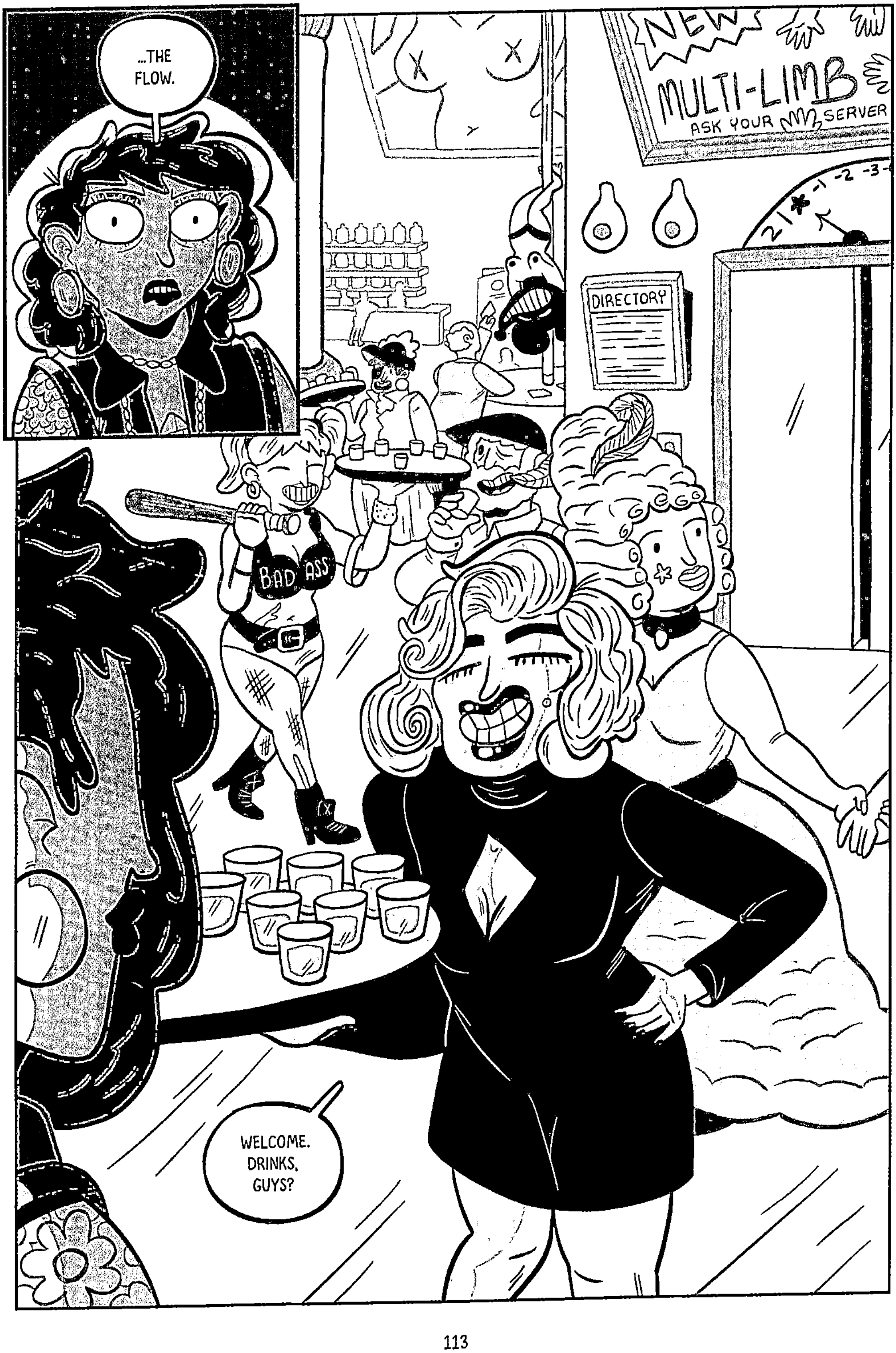
...THE FLOW.
NEW
MULTI-LIMB
ASK YOUR SERVER
DIRECTORY
BAD ASS
WELCOME. DRINKS, GUYS?

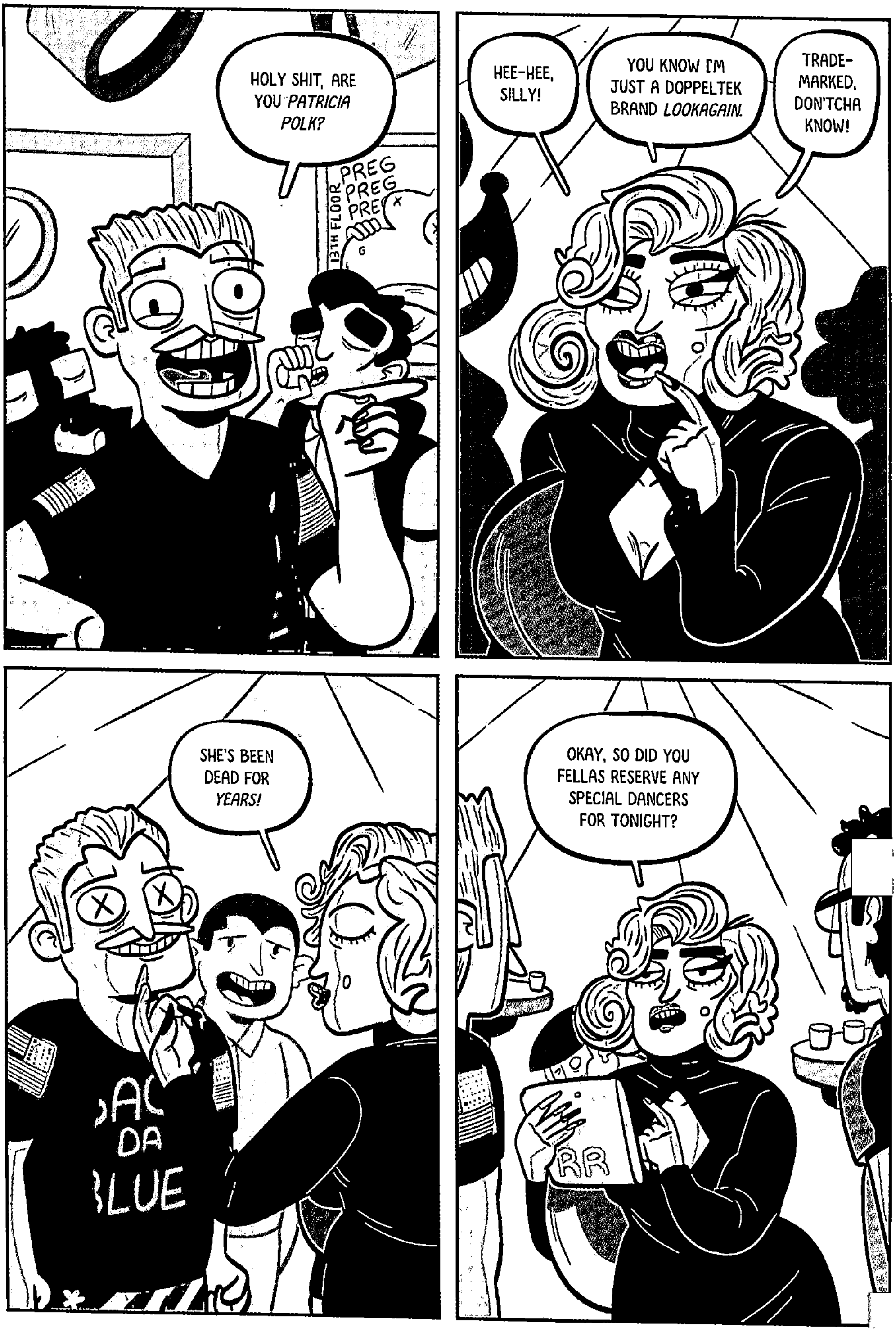
HOLY SHIT, ARE YOU *PATRICIA POLK?*
PREG PREG PREG
13TH FLOOR
HEE-HEE, SILLY!
YOU KNOW I'M JUST A DOPPELTEK BRAND *LOOKAGAIN.*
TRADE-MARKED, DON'TCHA KNOW!
SHE'S BEEN DEAD FOR *YEARS!*
DA
LUE
OKAY, SO DID YOU FELLAS RESERVE ANY SPECIAL DANCERS FOR TONIGHT?
RR

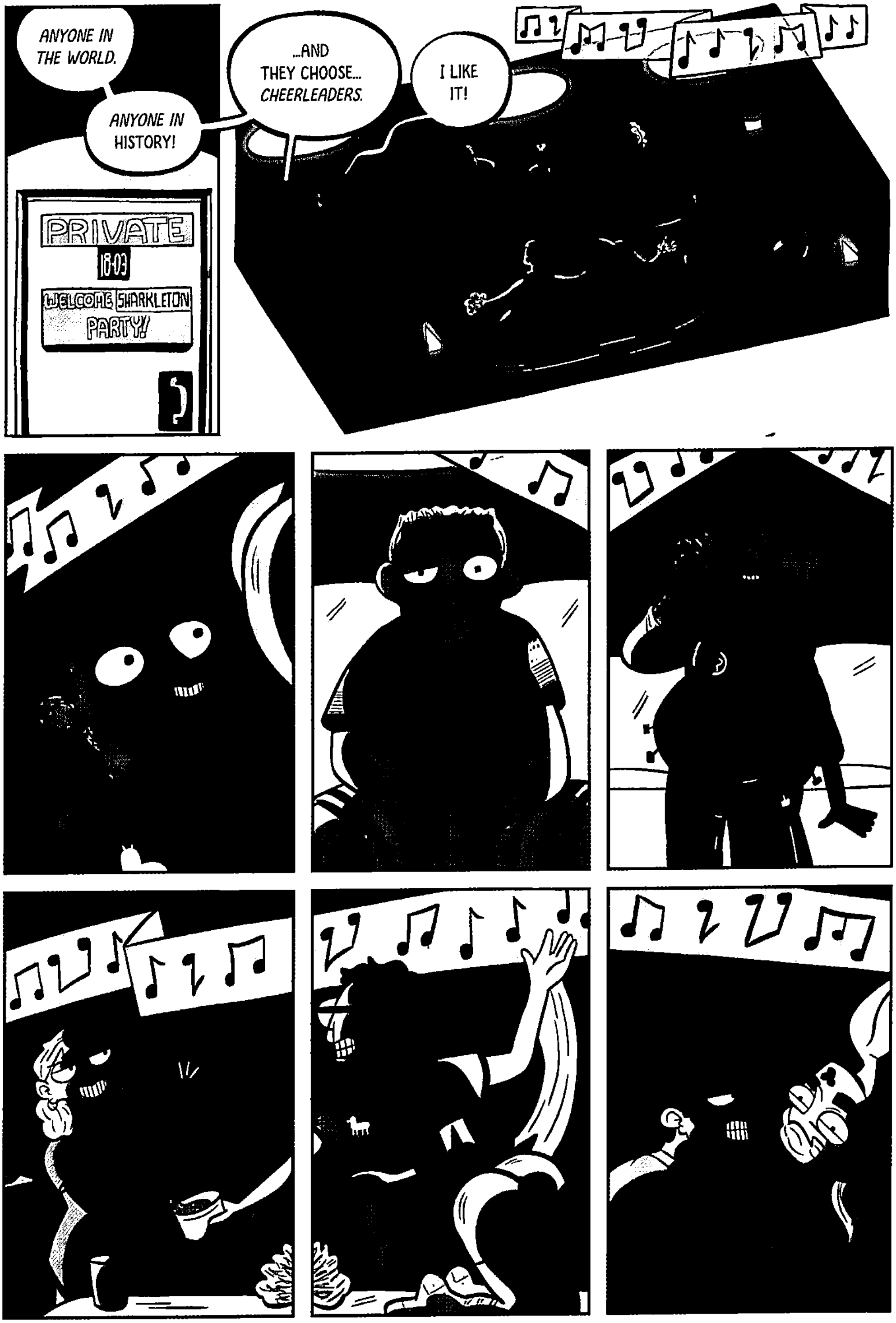
ANYONE IN THE WORLD.
ANYONE IN HISTORY!
...AND THEY CHOOSE... CHEERLEADERS.
I LIKE IT!
PRIVATE
WELCOME SHARKLETON PARTY!

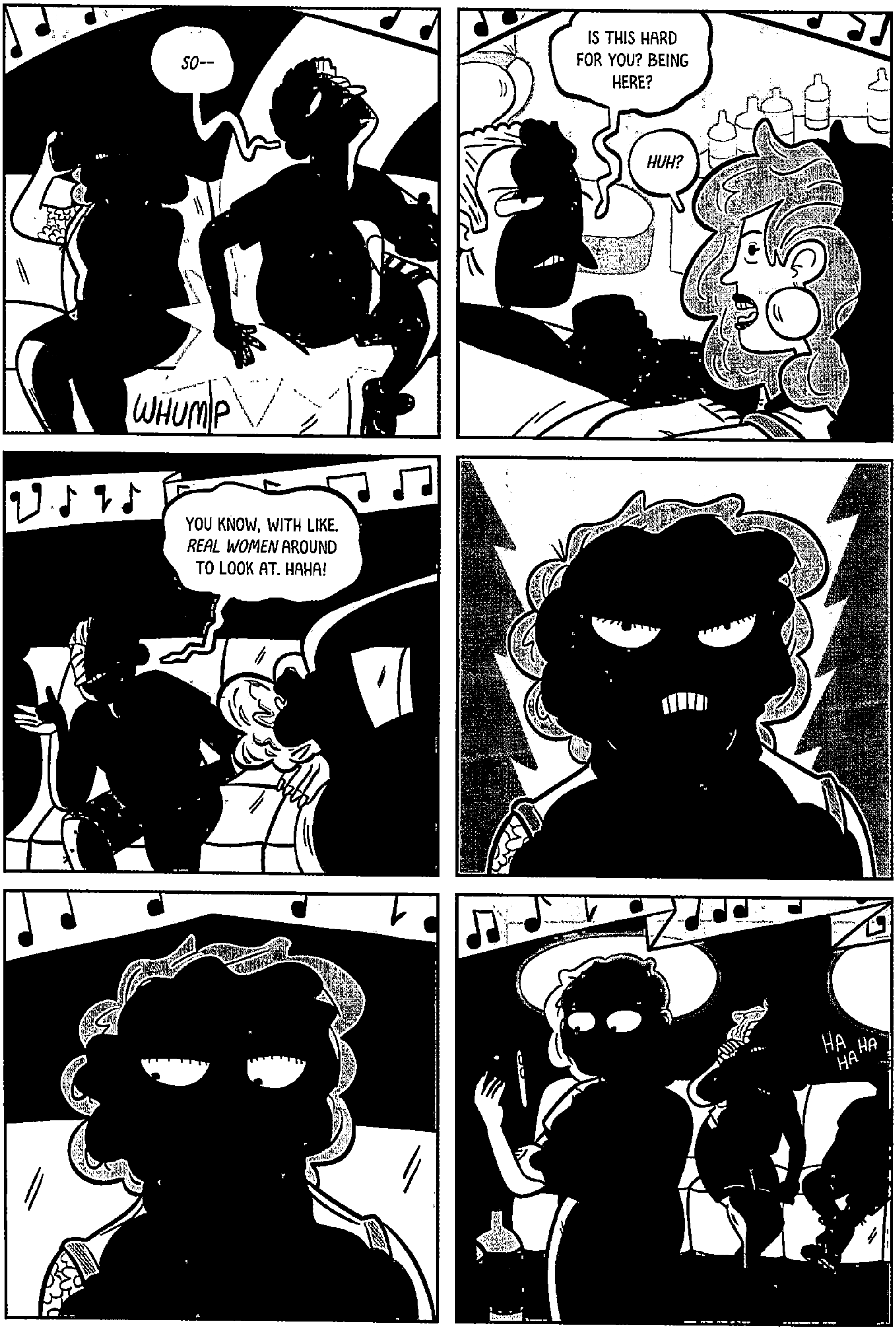
SO--
WHUMP
IS THIS HARD FOR YOU? BEING HERE?
HUH?
YOU KNOW, WITH LIKE. REAL WOMEN AROUND TO LOOK AT. HAHA!
HA HA HA

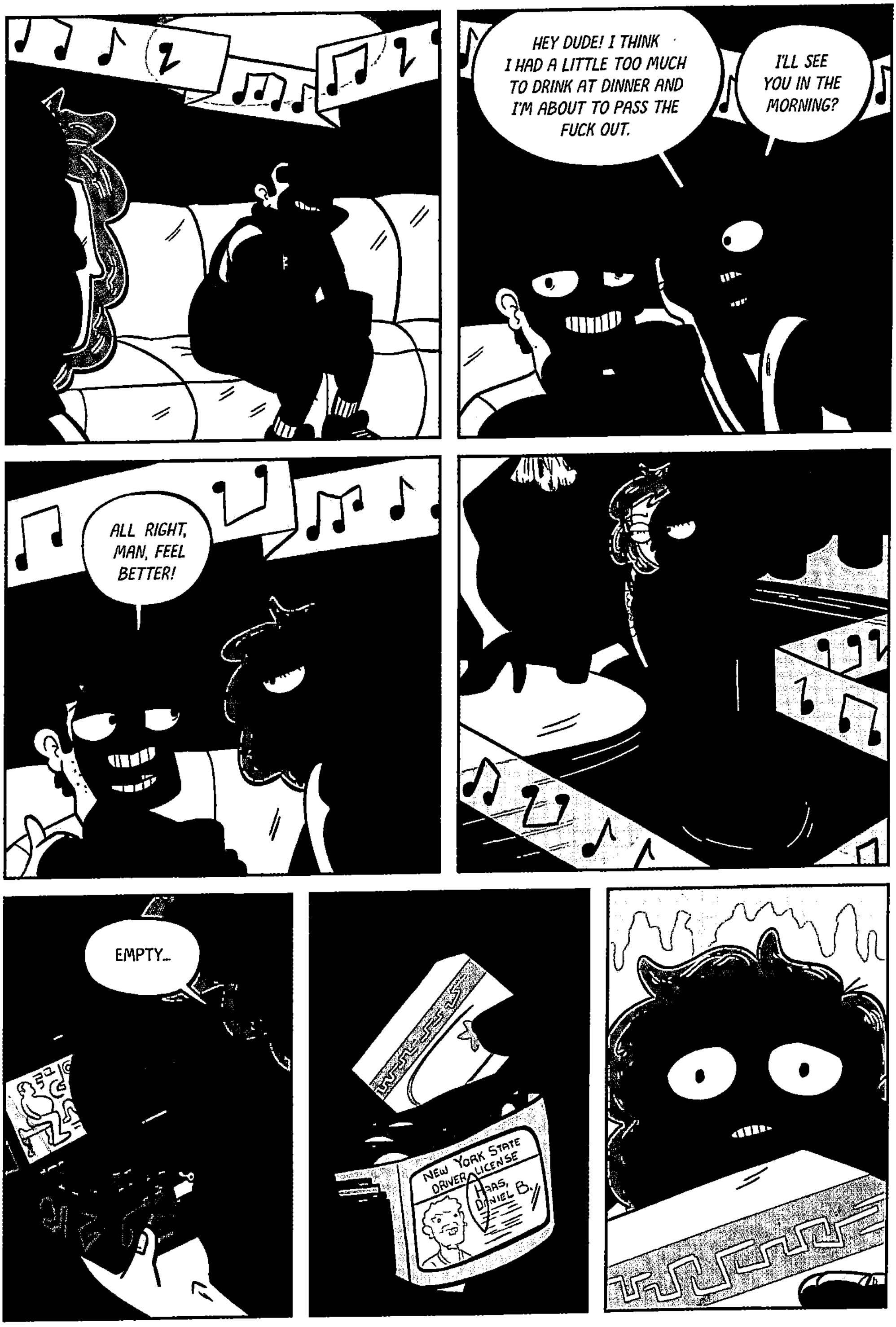
HEY DUDE! I THINK I HAD A LITTLE TOO MUCH TO DRINK AT DINNER AND I'M ABOUT TO PASS THE FUCK OUT.
I'LL SEE YOU IN THE MORNING?
ALL RIGHT, MAN, FEEL BETTER!
EMPTY...
NEW YORK STATE DRIVER LICENSE
HAAS, DANIEL B.

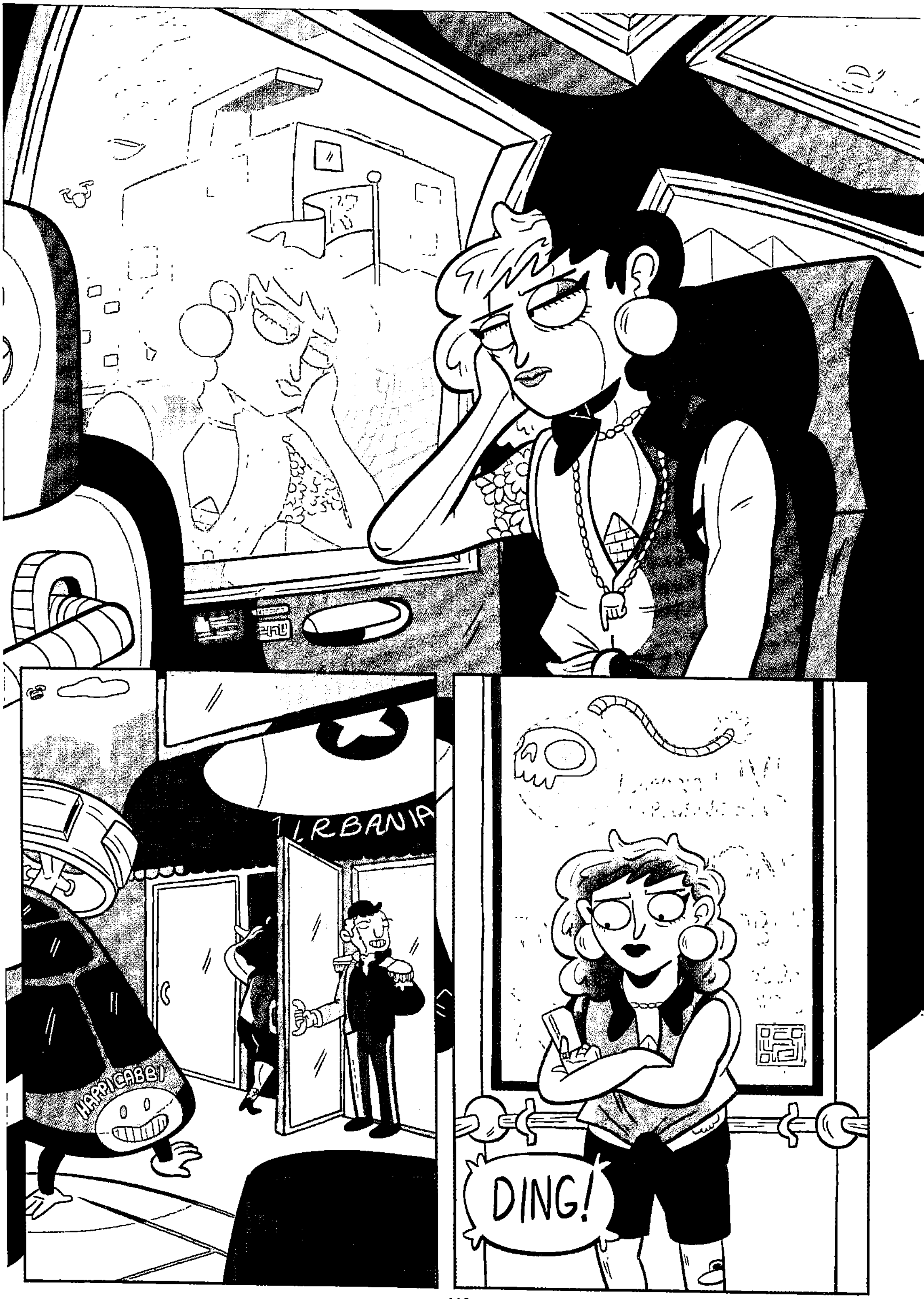

HAPPICABBI
URBANIA
DING!

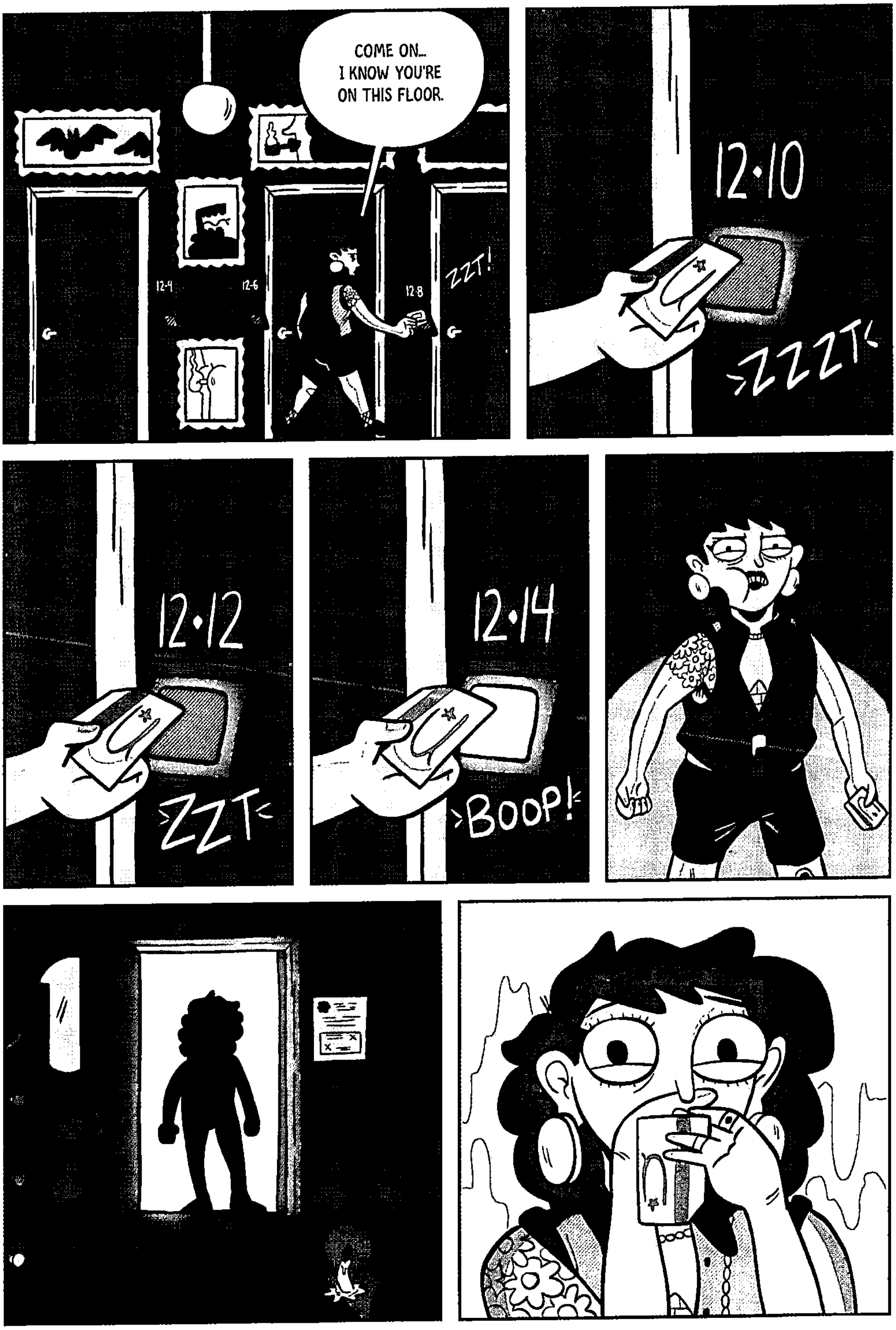

COME ON...
I KNOW YOU'RE
ON THIS FLOOR.
12-4
12-6
12-8
ZZT!
12·10
ZZZZT
12·12
ZZT
12·14
BOOP!

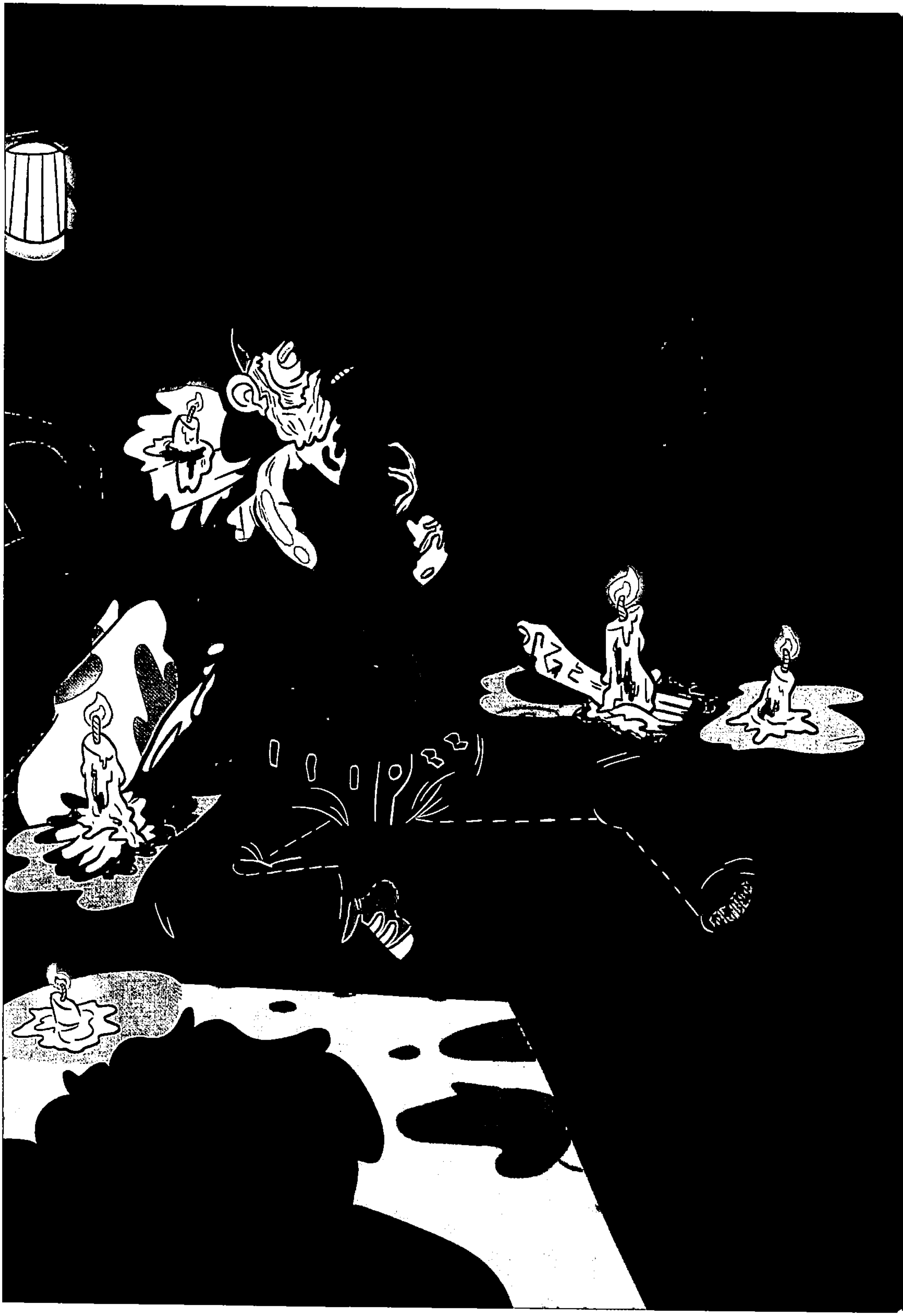

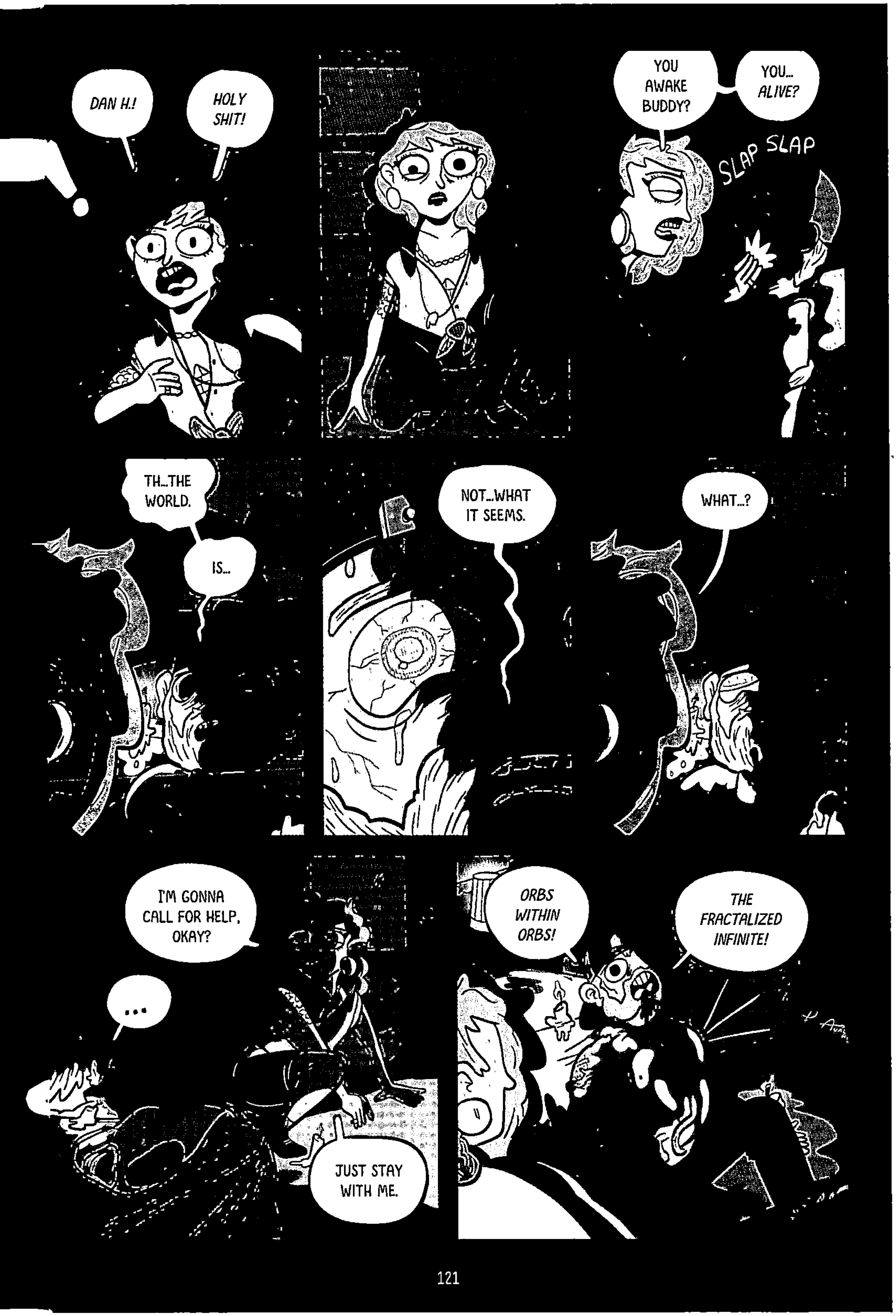
DAN H.!
HOLY SHIT!
YOU AWAKE BUDDY?
YOU... ALIVE?
SLAP SLAP
TH...THE WORLD.
IS...
NOT...WHAT IT SEEMS.
WHAT...?
I'M GONNA CALL FOR HELP, OKAY?
...
JUST STAY WITH ME.
ORBS WITHIN ORBS!
THE FRACTALIZED INFINITE!

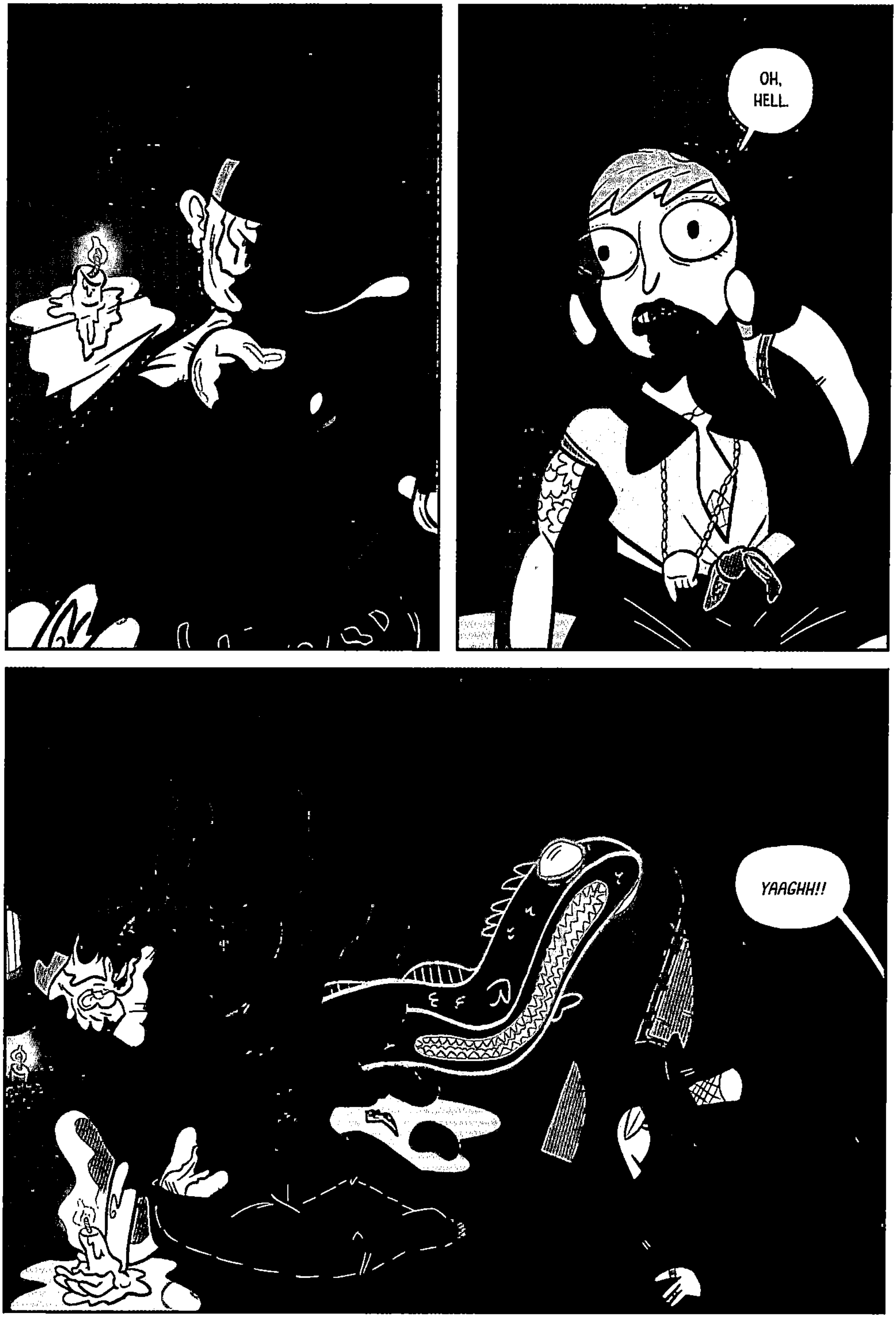
OH, HELL.
YAAGHH!!

HSSS
UHH-
NICE. CALM. YES. OKAY.
ME? I'M LEAVING NOW. GOODBYE.
WHUMP.

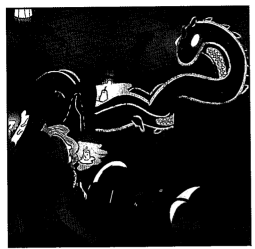

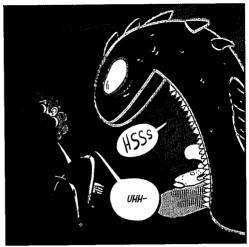

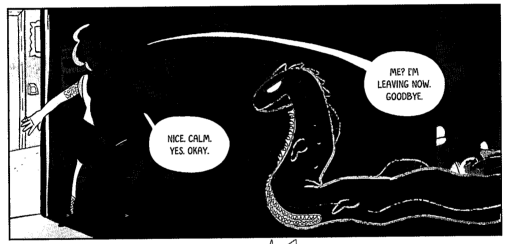

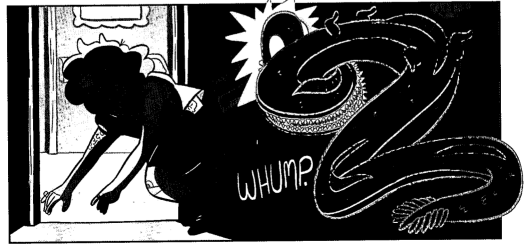

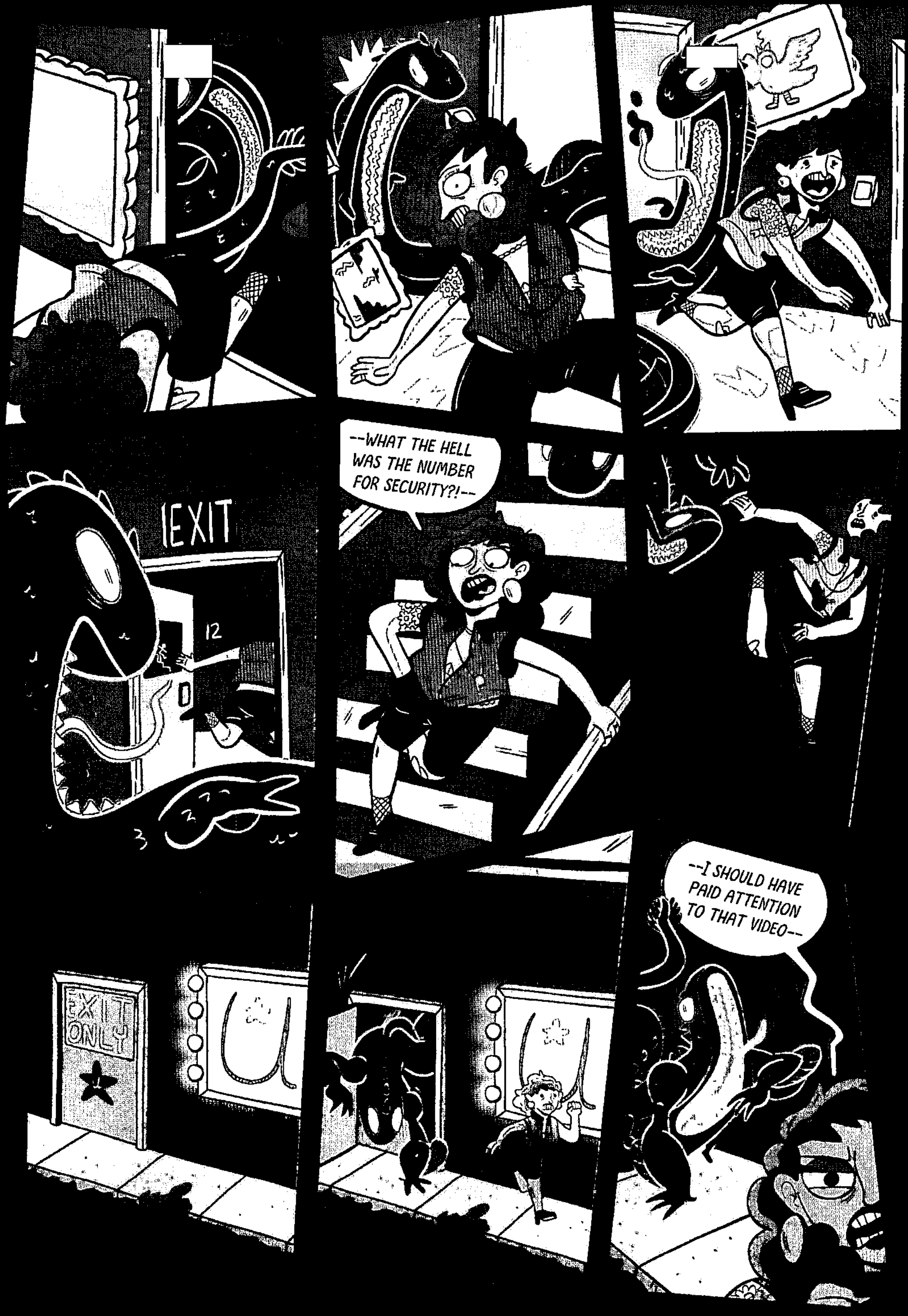
EXIT
12
--WHAT THE HELL WAS THE NUMBER FOR SECURITY?!--
EXIT ONLY
--I SHOULD HAVE PAID ATTENTION TO THAT VIDEO--

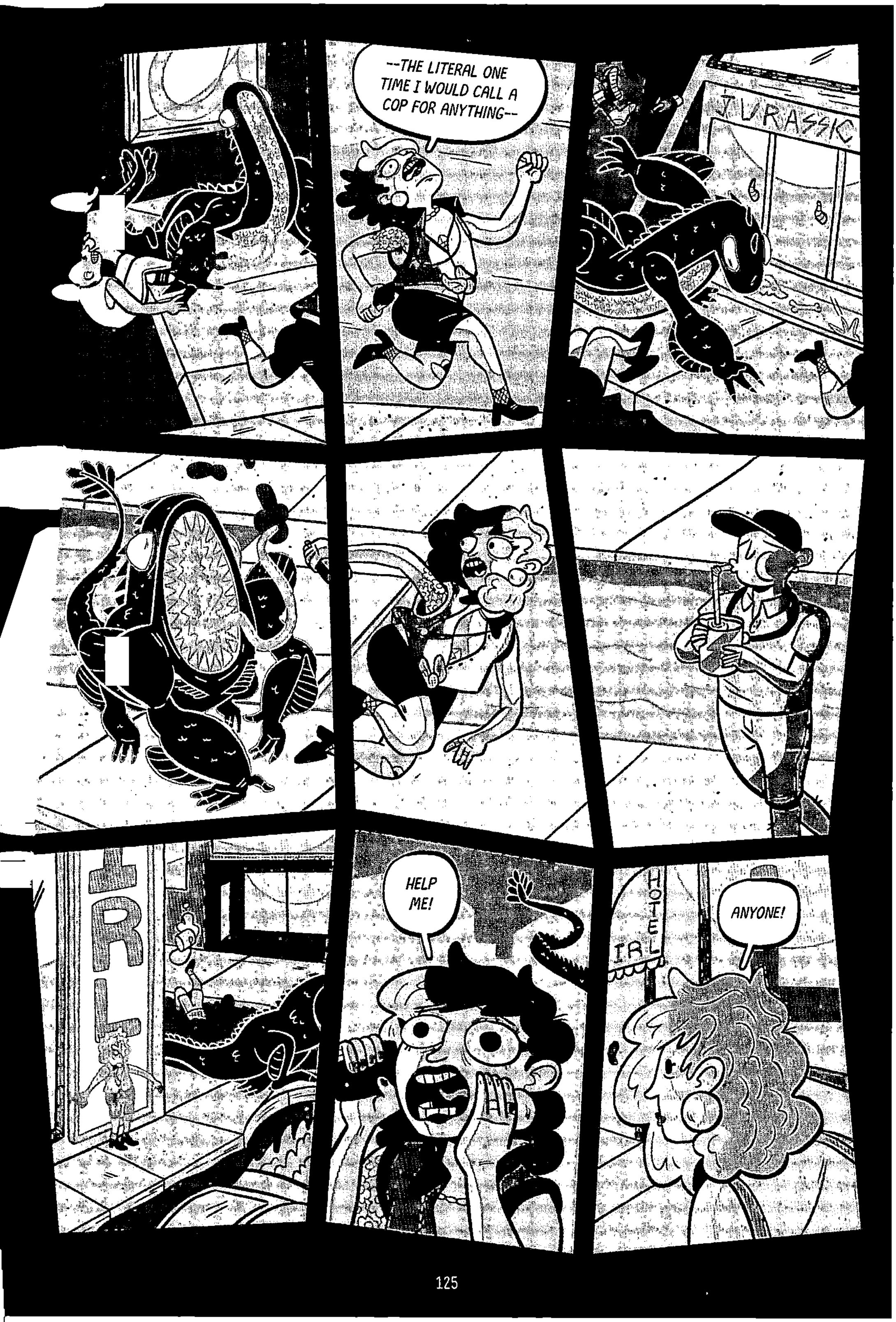

--THE LITERAL ONE TIME I WOULD CALL A COP FOR ANYTHING--
JURASSIC
IRL
HELP ME!
HOTEL
IRL
ANYONE!

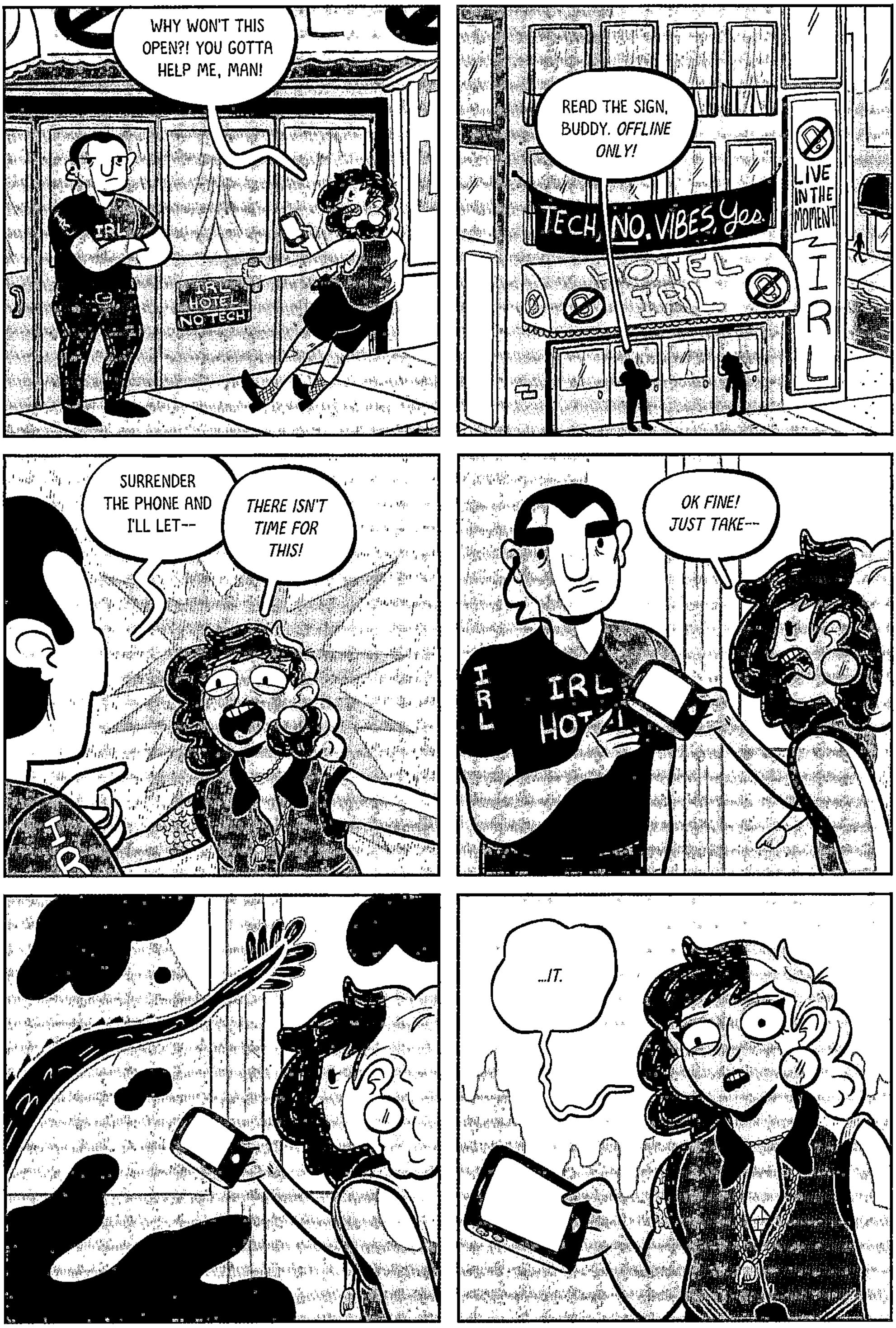
WHY WON'T THIS OPEN?! YOU GOTTA HELP ME, MAN!
IRL
IRL HOTEL NO TECH
READ THE SIGN, BUDDY. *OFFLINE ONLY!*
TECH, NO. VIBES, Yes.
HOTEL IRL
LIVE IN THE MOMENT
IRL
SURRENDER THE PHONE AND I'LL LET--
THERE ISN'T TIME FOR THIS!
OK FINE! JUST TAKE--
IRL
IRL HOTEL
...IT.

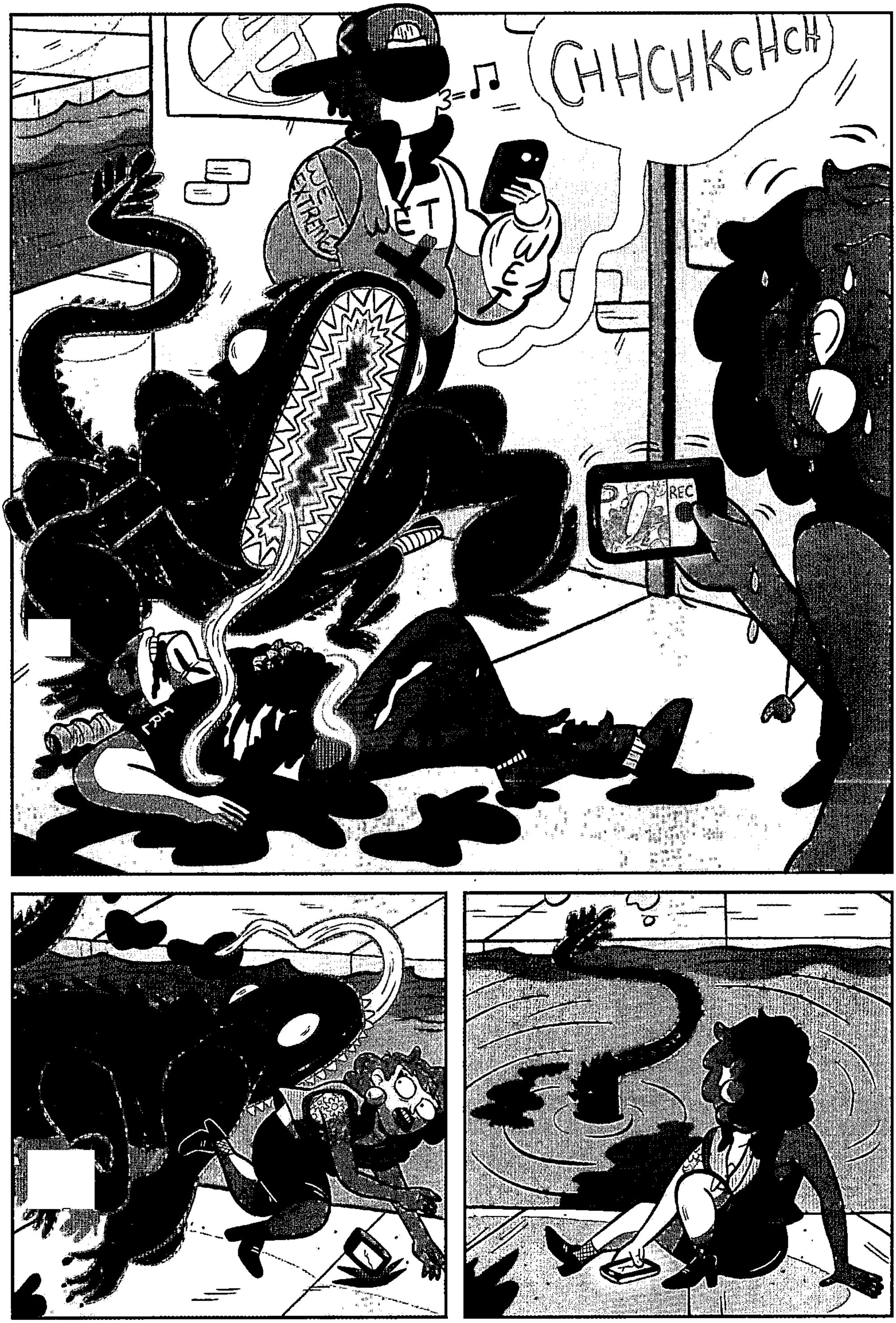
CHHCHKCHCH
JET
WET
REC

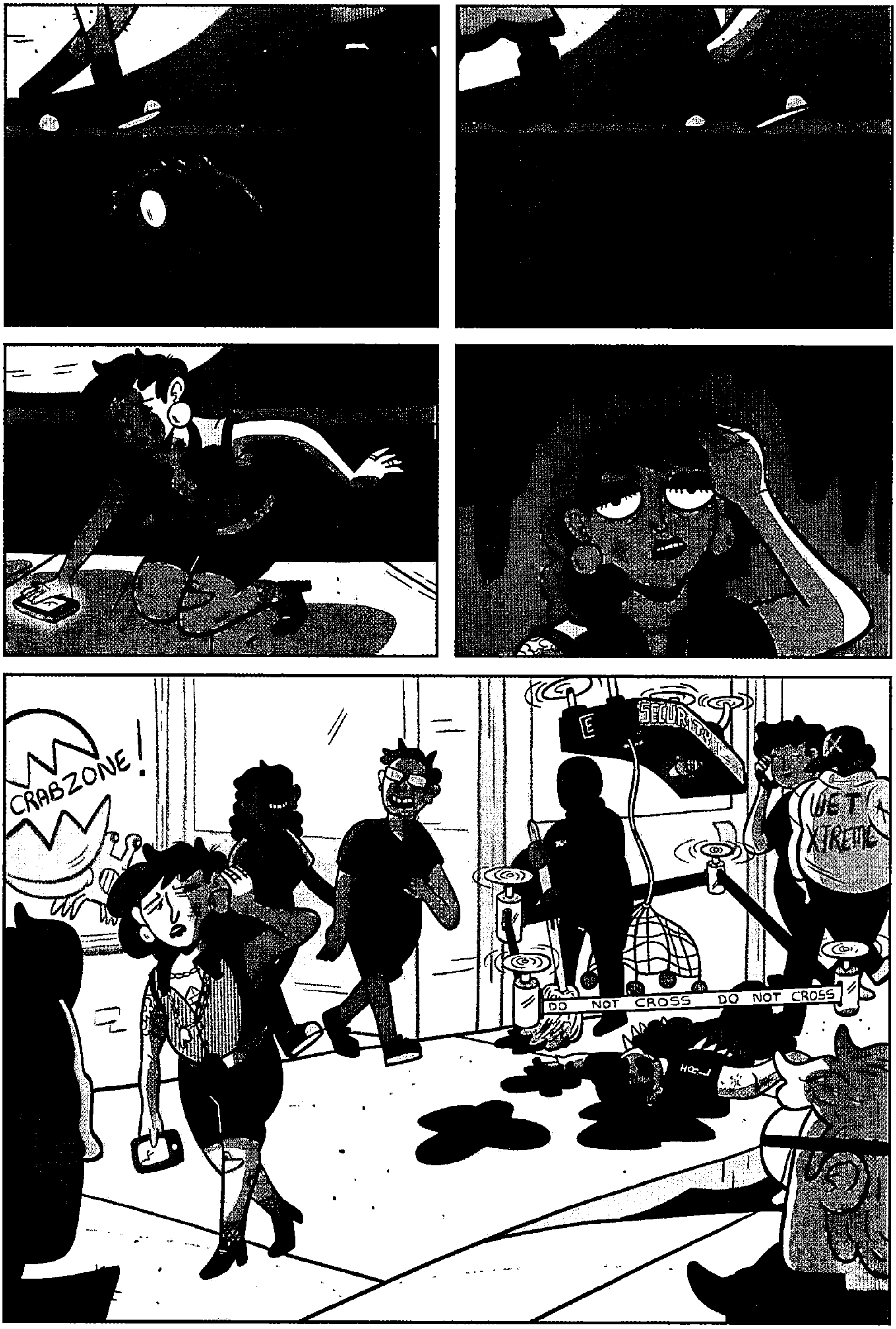
CRABZONE!
SECURITY
WET XTREME
DO NOT CROSS DO NOT CROSS

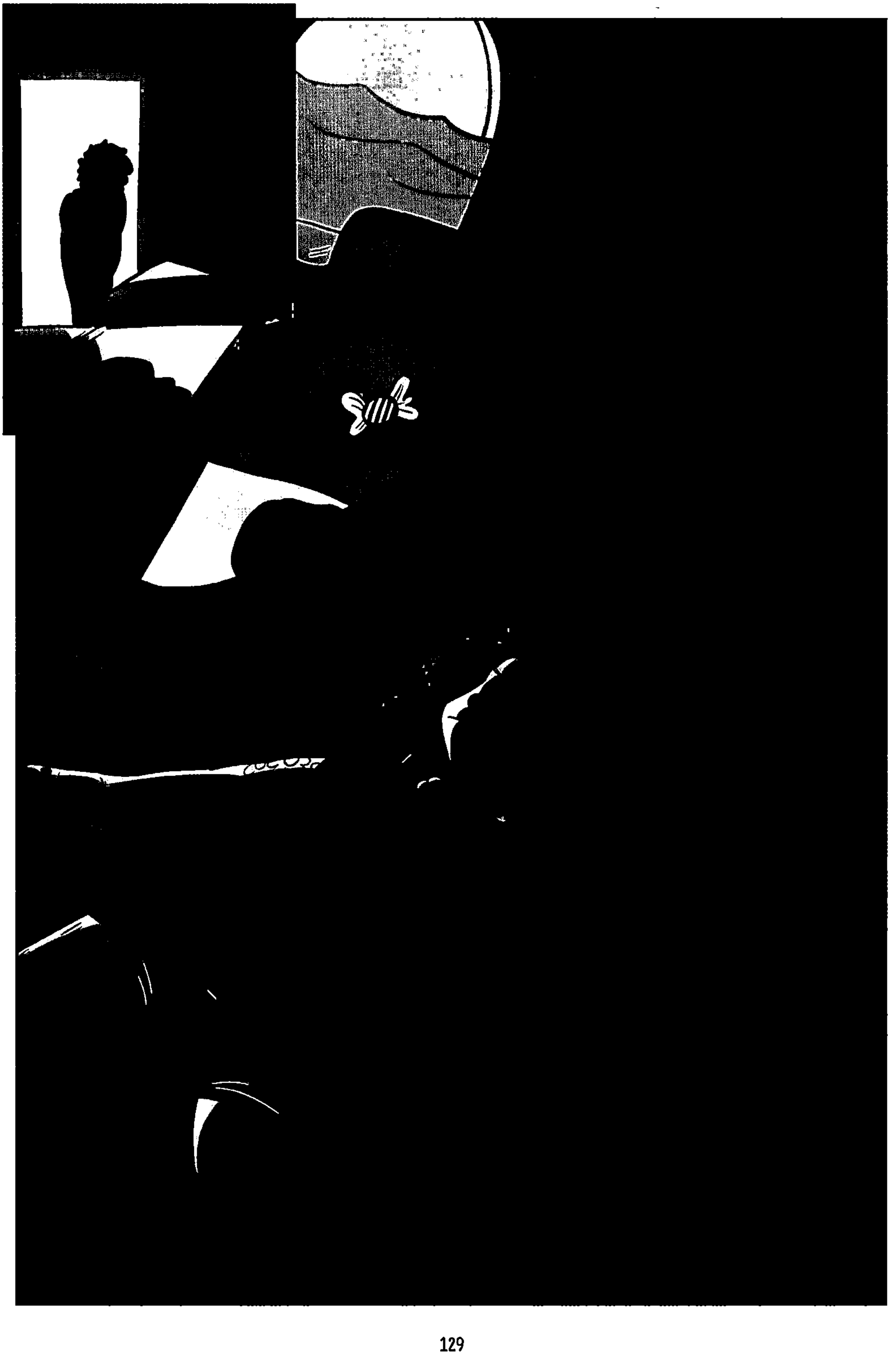

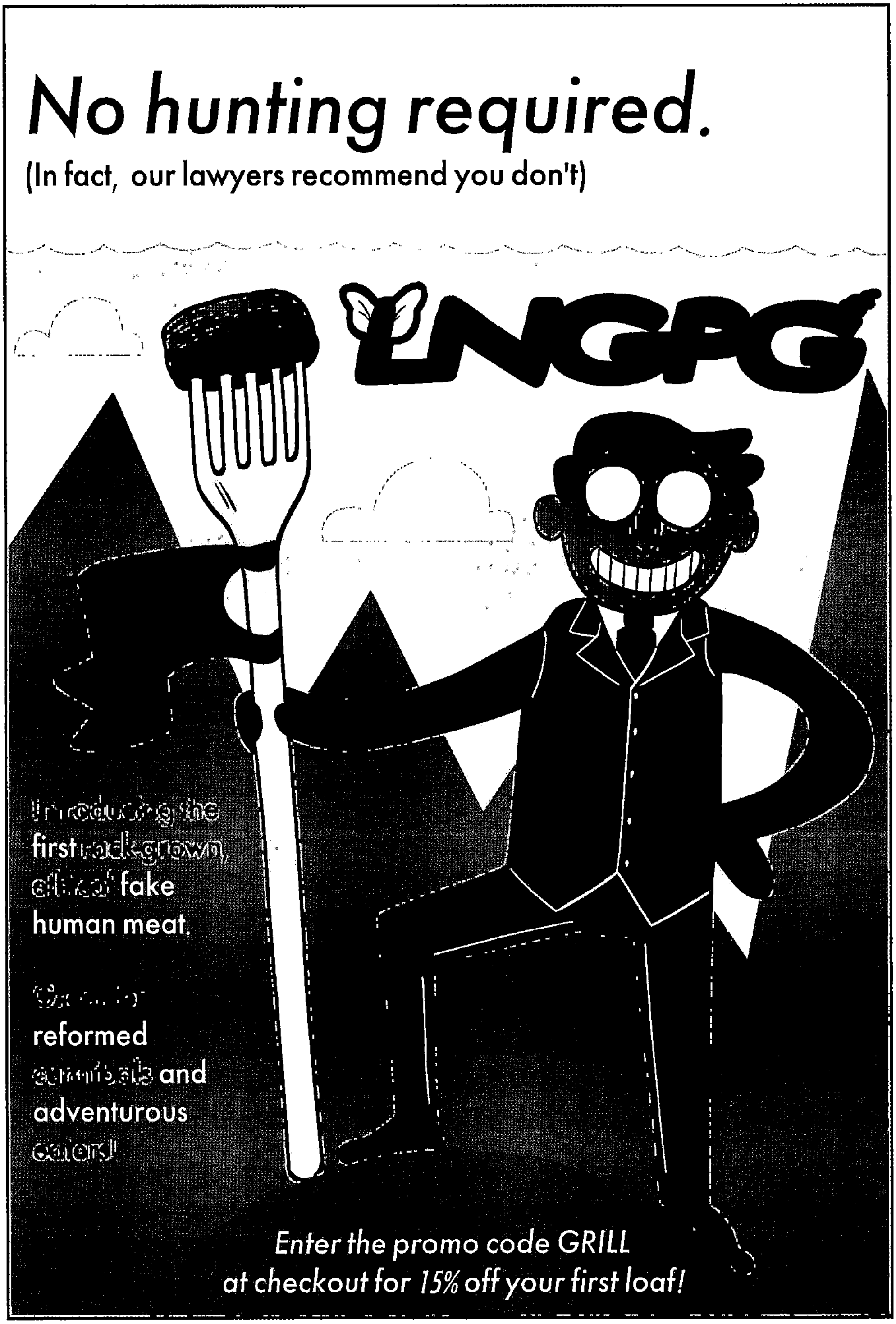

No hunting required.
(In fact, our lawyers recommend you don't)
LNGPG
Introducing the
first rack-grown,
ethical fake
human meat.
reformed
cannibals and
adventurous
eaters!
Enter the promo code GRILL
at checkout for 15% off your first loaf!

SATURDAY MORNING

Catch the 10:30 Courtesy Skimmer to Landing 88A for DANGERGAME MAXX! (If you haven't settled up for this $$$ email me ASAP)

 Mia

I'm glad you left - setting boundaries is good!

call me when you get back to hotel?

everything ok?

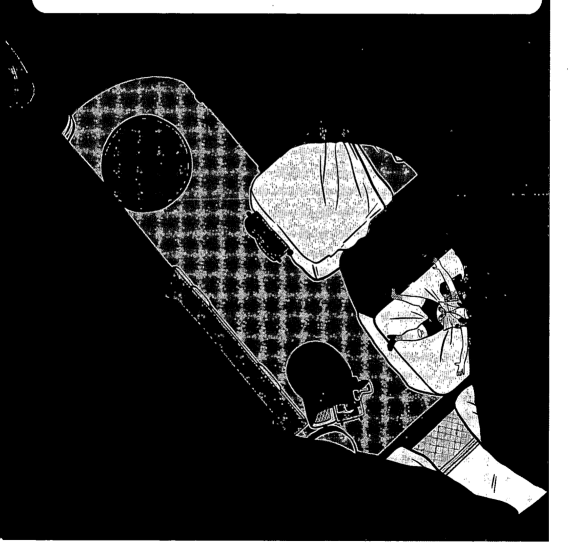

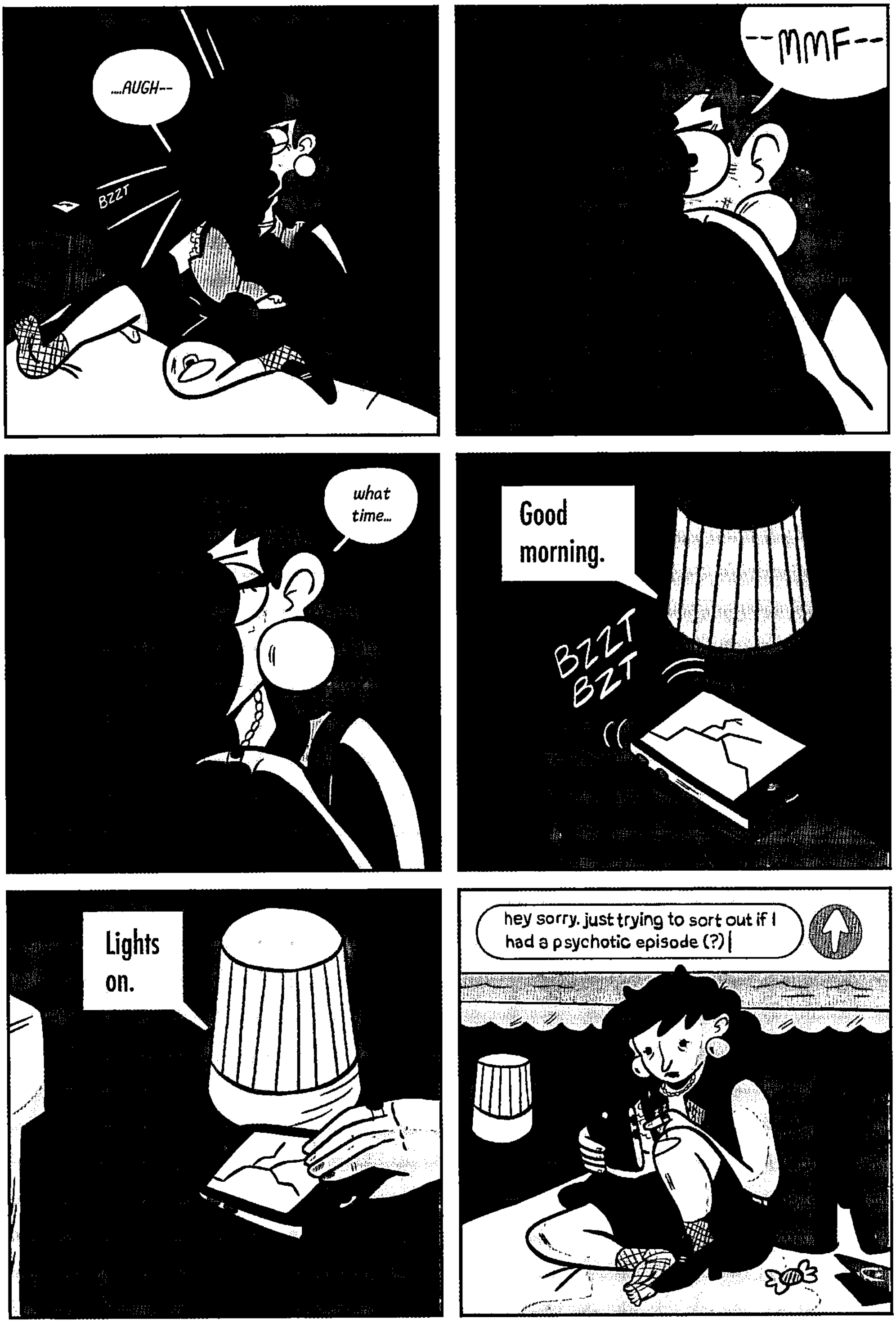
...AUGH--
BZZT
--MMF--
what time...
Good morning.
BZZT BZT
Lights on.
hey sorry. just trying to sort out if I had a psychotic episode (?)

de(?)
CLIK
VIDEO
SHHKS-THNK-
SHF HFHSHHSH
0:7
46

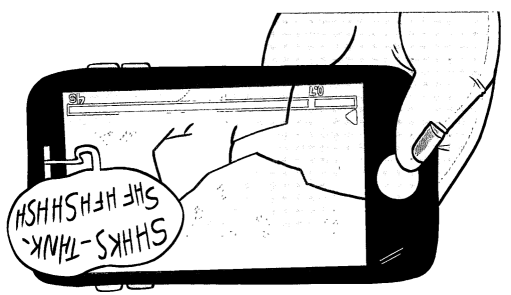

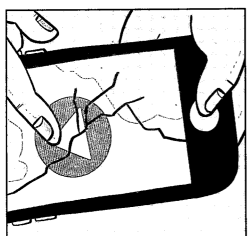

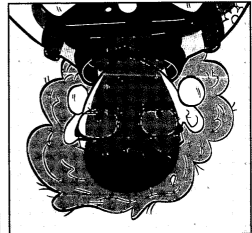

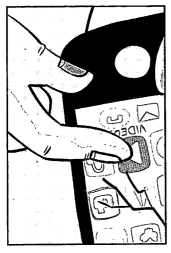

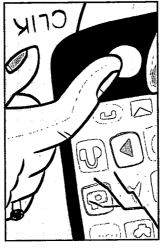

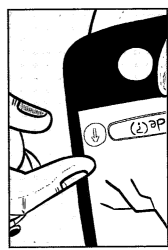

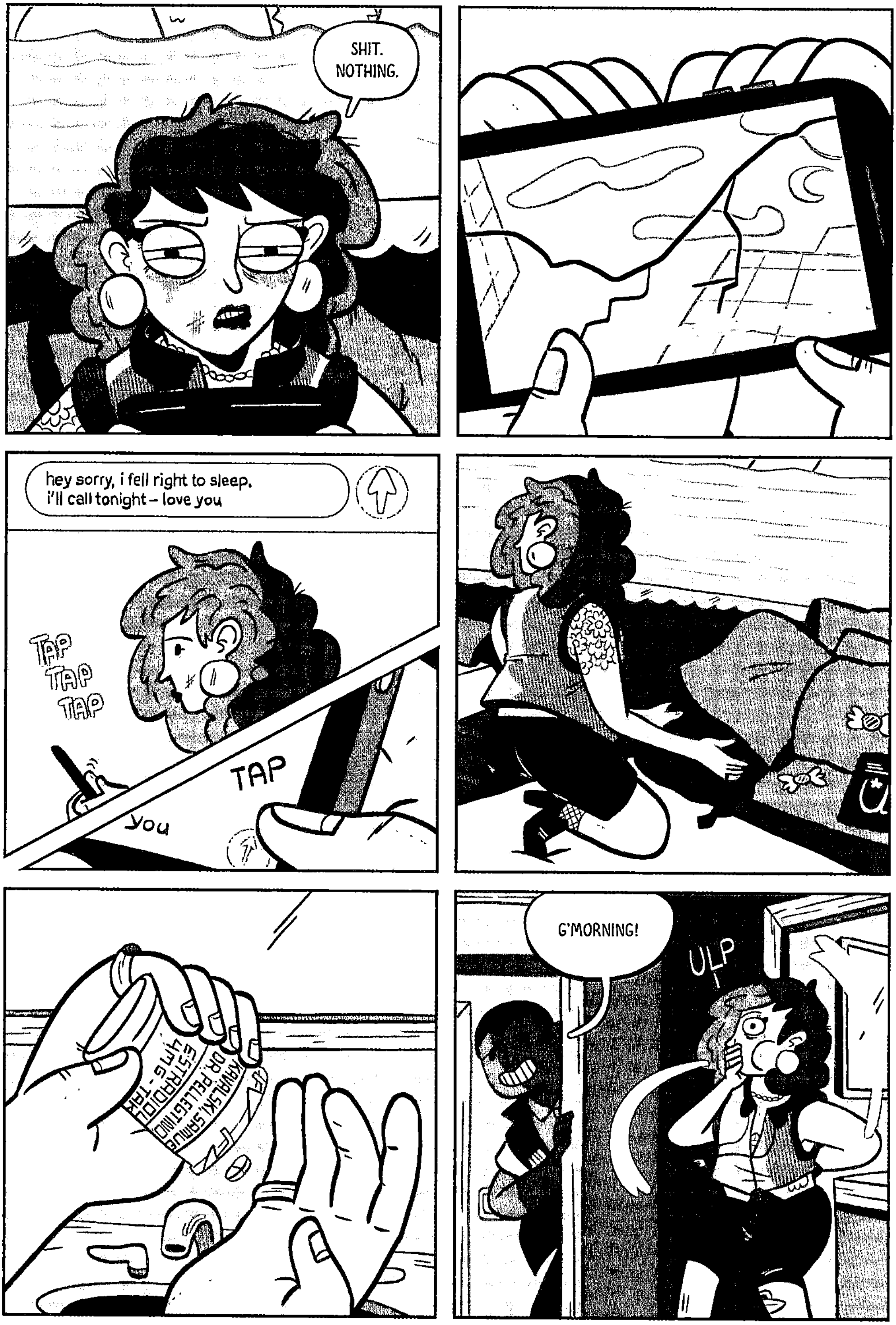
SHIT. NOTHING.
hey sorry, i fell right to sleep. i'll call tonight – love you
TAP TAP TAP
TAP
you
KAWALSKI, SAMUEL
DR. PELLEGRINO
ESTRADIOL
4MG - TAK
G'MORNING!
ULP

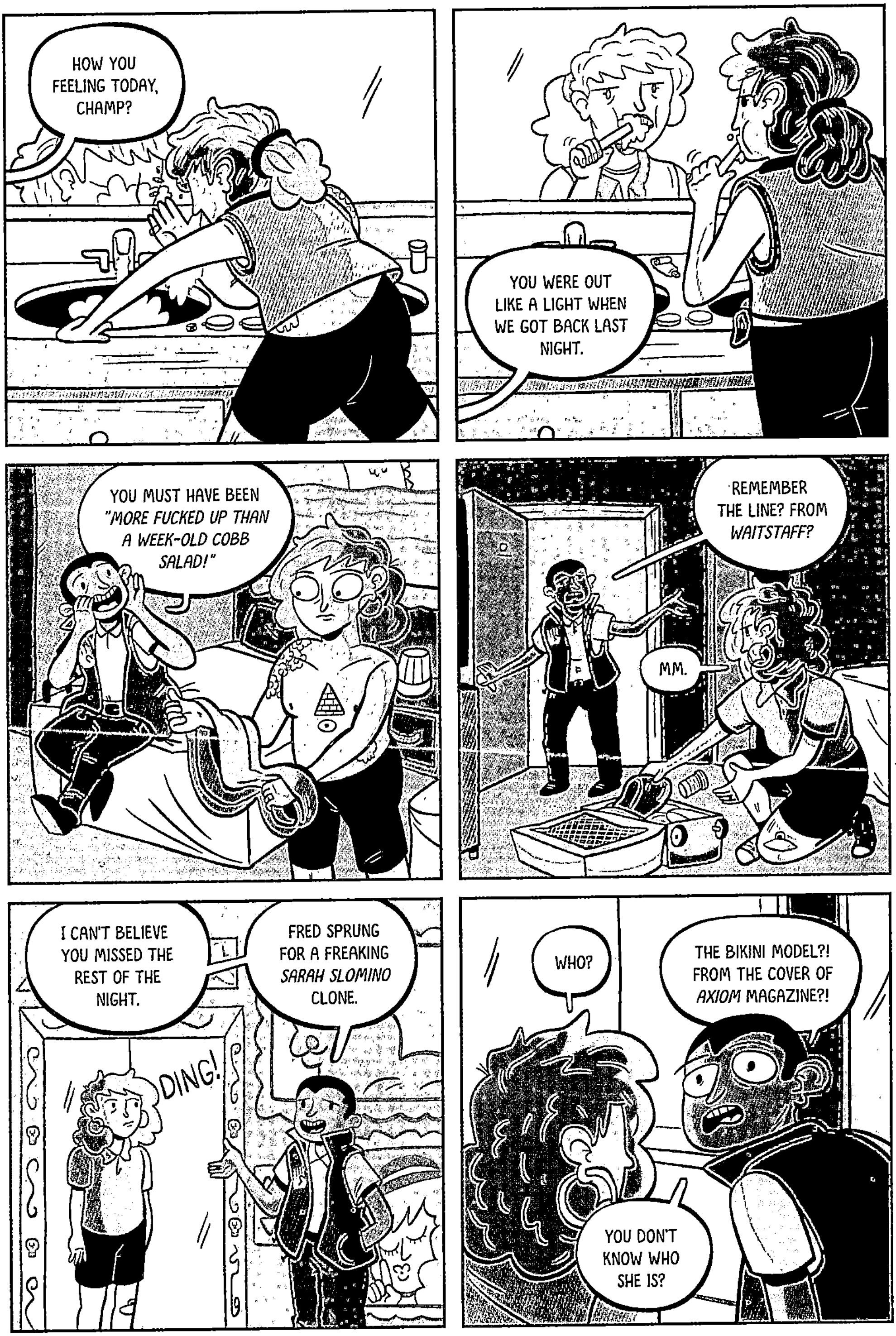
HOW YOU FEELING TODAY, CHAMP?
YOU WERE OUT LIKE A LIGHT WHEN WE GOT BACK LAST NIGHT.
YOU MUST HAVE BEEN "MORE FUCKED UP THAN A WEEK-OLD COBB SALAD!"
REMEMBER THE LINE? FROM WAITSTAFF?
MM.
I CAN'T BELIEVE YOU MISSED THE REST OF THE NIGHT.
FRED SPRUNG FOR A FREAKING SARAH SLOMINO CLONE.
DING!
WHO?
THE BIKINI MODEL?! FROM THE COVER OF AXIOM MAGAZINE?!
YOU DON'T KNOW WHO SHE IS?

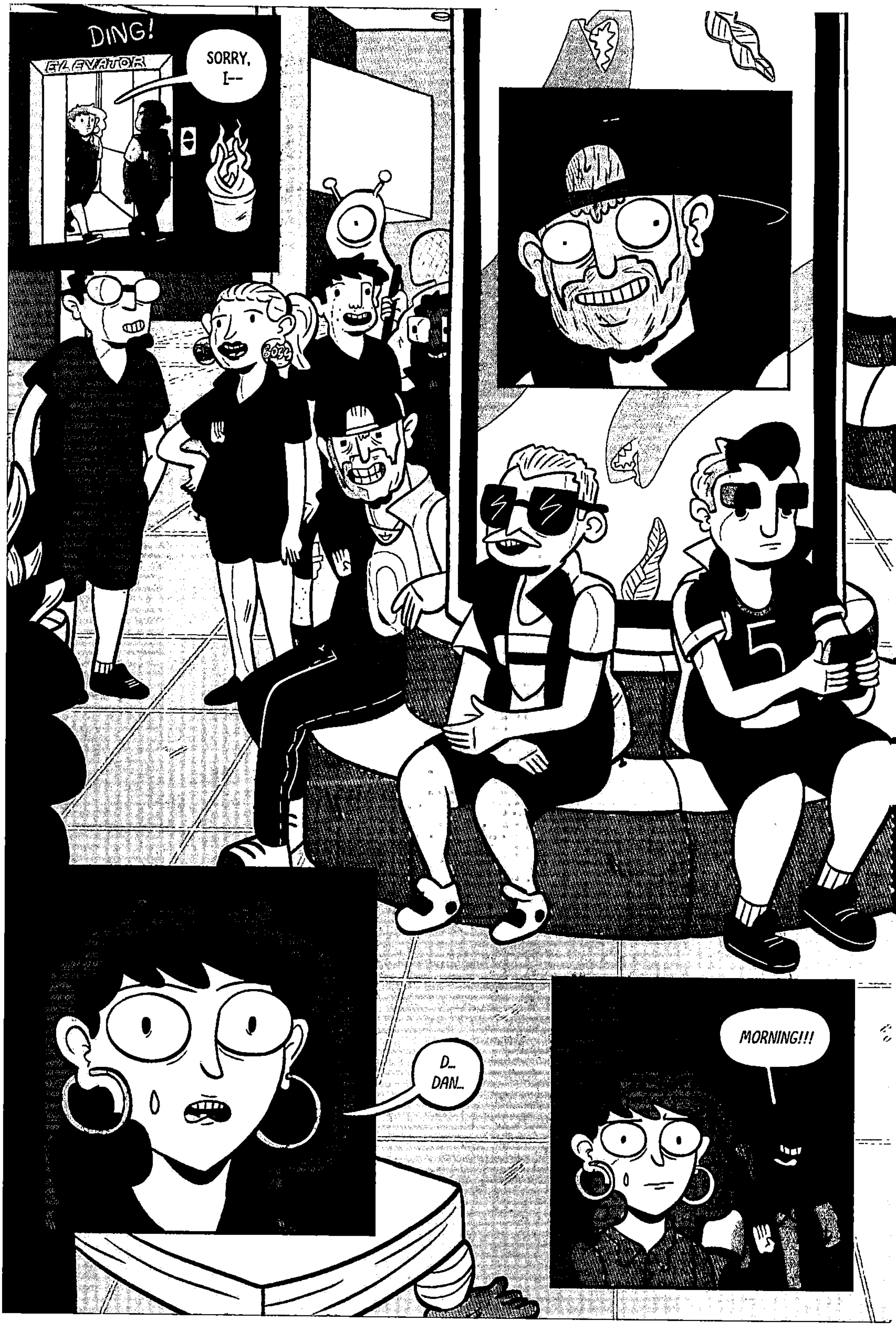
DING!
ELEVATOR
SORRY, I--
D... DAN...
MORNING!!!

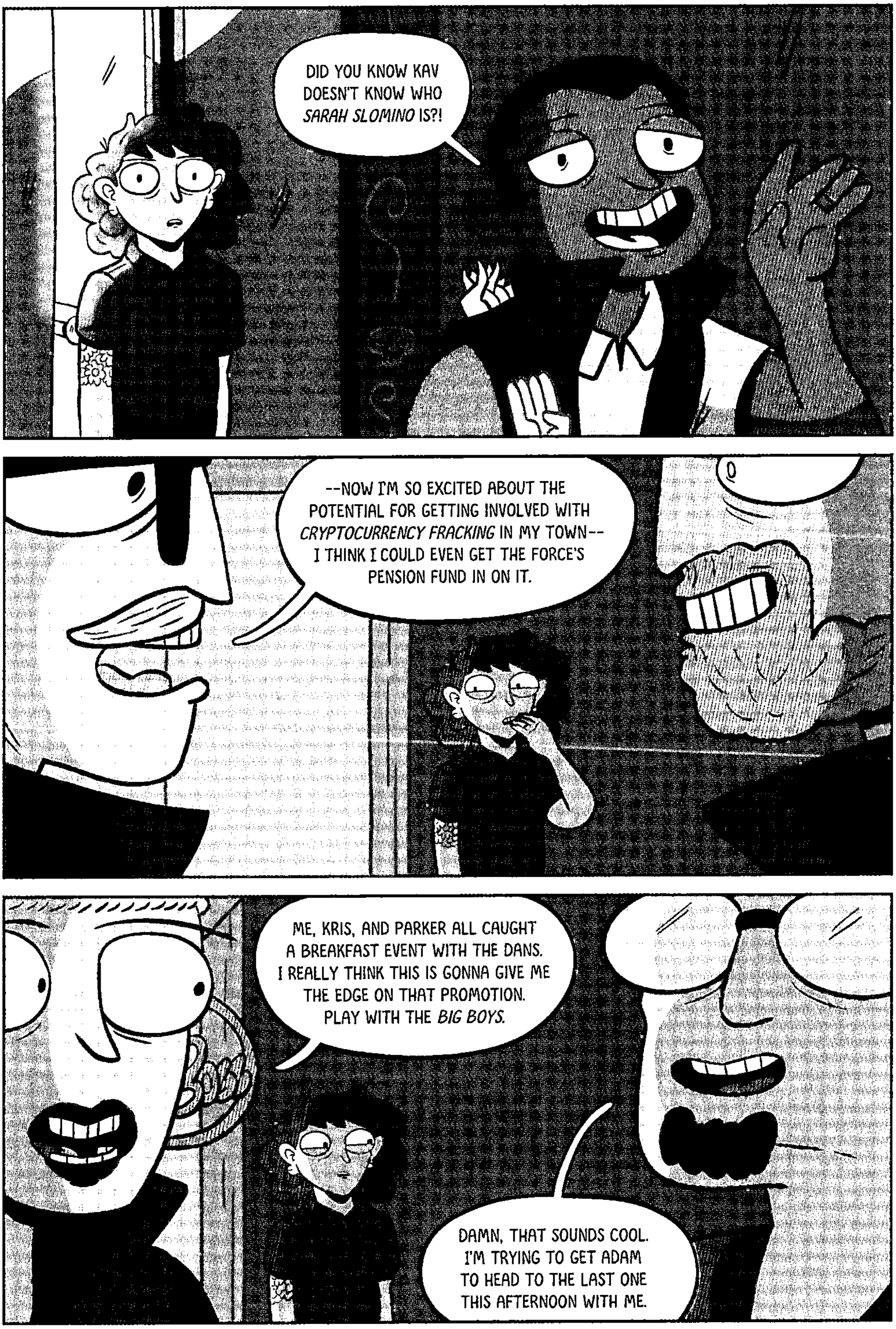
DID YOU KNOW KAV DOESN'T KNOW WHO *SARAH SLOMINO* IS?!
--NOW I'M SO EXCITED ABOUT THE POTENTIAL FOR GETTING INVOLVED WITH *CRYPTOCURRENCY FRACKING* IN MY TOWN--I THINK I COULD EVEN GET THE FORCE'S PENSION FUND IN ON IT.
ME, KRIS, AND PARKER ALL CAUGHT A BREAKFAST EVENT WITH THE DANS. I REALLY THINK THIS IS GONNA GIVE ME THE EDGE ON THAT PROMOTION. PLAY WITH THE *BIG BOYS.*
DAMN, THAT SOUNDS COOL. I'M TRYING TO GET ADAM TO HEAD TO THE LAST ONE THIS AFTERNOON WITH ME.

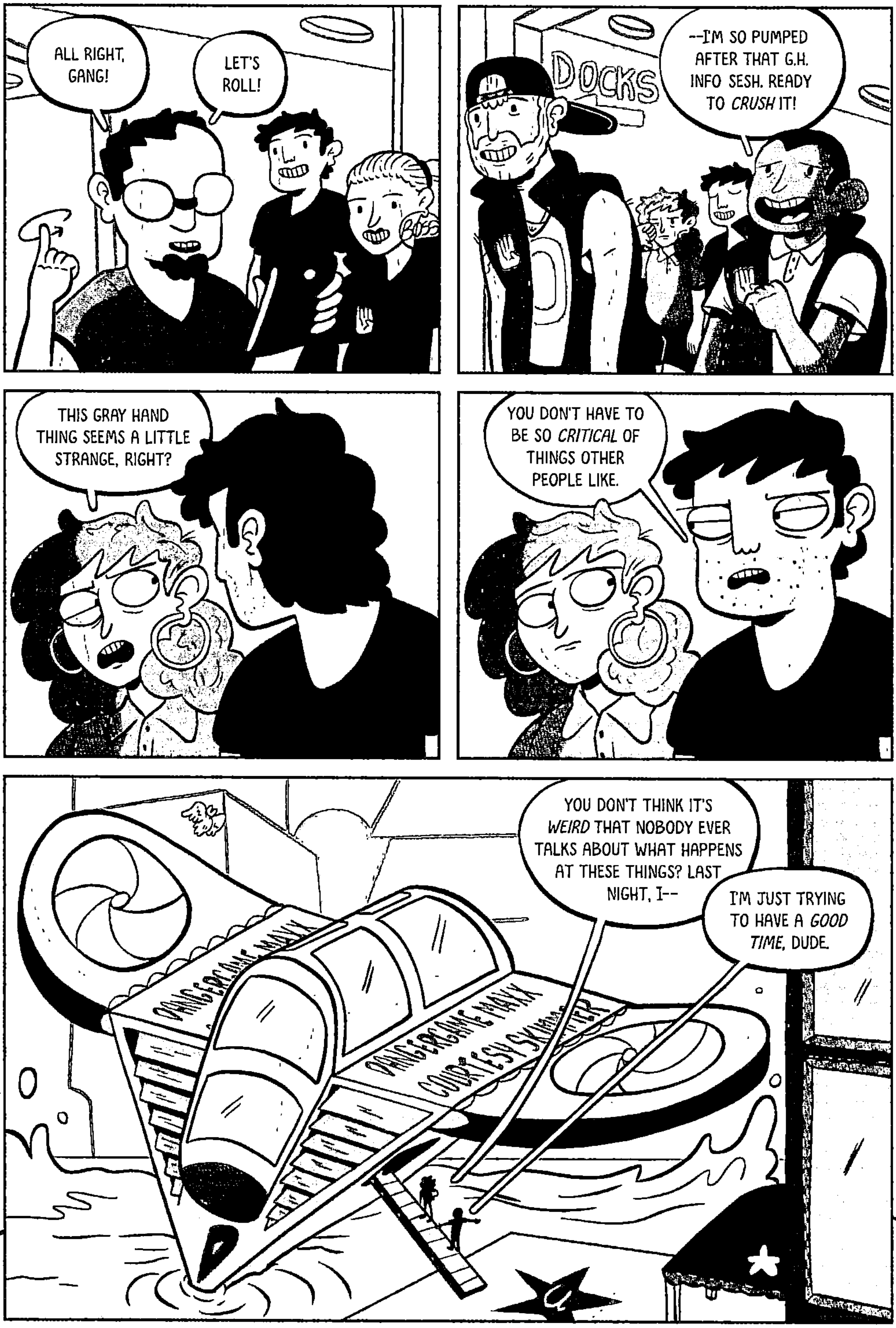

ALL RIGHT, GANG!
LET'S ROLL!
DOCKS
--I'M SO PUMPED AFTER THAT G.H. INFO SESH. READY TO *CRUSH* IT!
THIS GRAY HAND THING SEEMS A LITTLE STRANGE, RIGHT?
YOU DON'T HAVE TO BE SO *CRITICAL* OF THINGS OTHER PEOPLE LIKE.
DANGERGAME MAXX
DANGERGAME MAXX
COURTESY SKIMMER
YOU DON'T THINK IT'S *WEIRD* THAT NOBODY EVER TALKS ABOUT WHAT HAPPENS AT THESE THINGS? LAST NIGHT, I--
I'M JUST TRYING TO HAVE A *GOOD TIME*, DUDE.

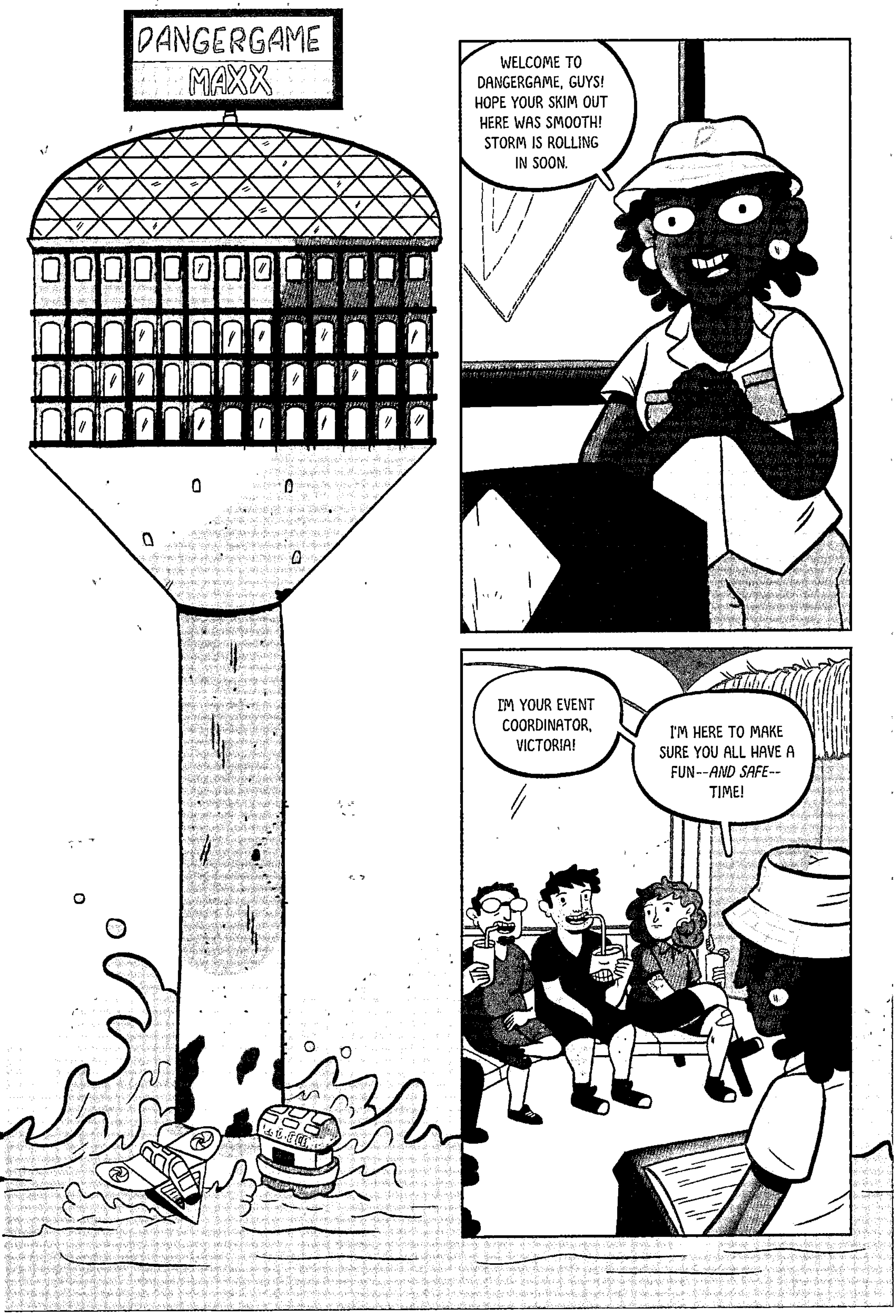
DANGERGAME MAXX
WELCOME TO DANGERGAME, GUYS! HOPE YOUR SKIM OUT HERE WAS SMOOTH! STORM IS ROLLING IN SOON.
I'M YOUR EVENT COORDINATOR, VICTORIA!
I'M HERE TO MAKE SURE YOU ALL HAVE A FUN--*AND SAFE*--TIME!

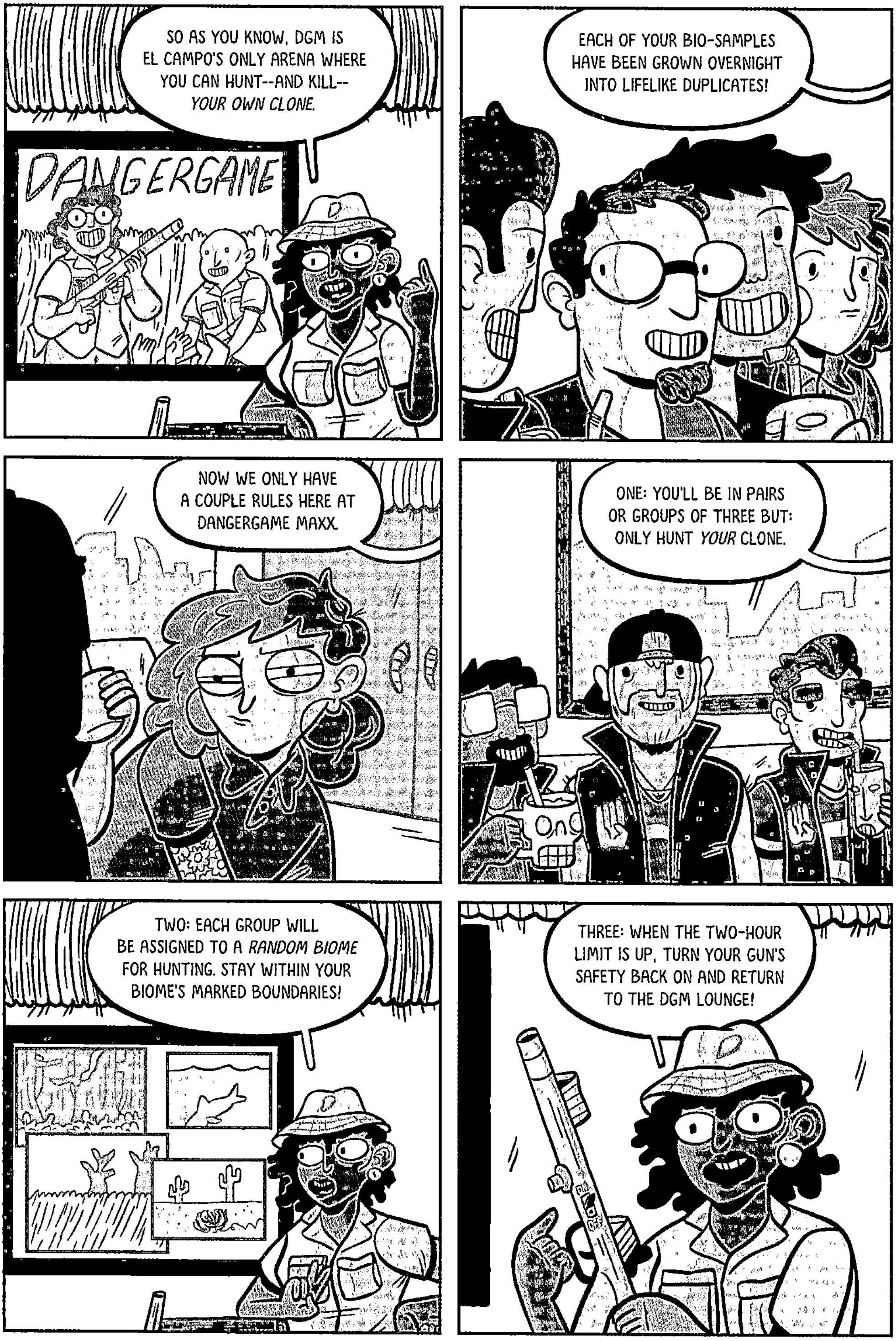
SO AS YOU KNOW, DGM IS EL CAMPO'S ONLY ARENA WHERE YOU CAN HUNT--AND KILL-- *YOUR OWN CLONE.*
DANGERGAME
EACH OF YOUR BIO-SAMPLES HAVE BEEN GROWN OVERNIGHT INTO LIFELIKE DUPLICATES!
NOW WE ONLY HAVE A COUPLE RULES HERE AT DANGERGAME MAXX.
ONE: YOU'LL BE IN PAIRS OR GROUPS OF THREE BUT: ONLY HUNT *YOUR* CLONE.
TWO: EACH GROUP WILL BE ASSIGNED TO A *RANDOM BIOME* FOR HUNTING. STAY WITHIN YOUR BIOME'S MARKED BOUNDARIES!
THREE: WHEN THE TWO-HOUR LIMIT IS UP, TURN YOUR GUN'S SAFETY BACK ON AND RETURN TO THE DGM LOUNGE!

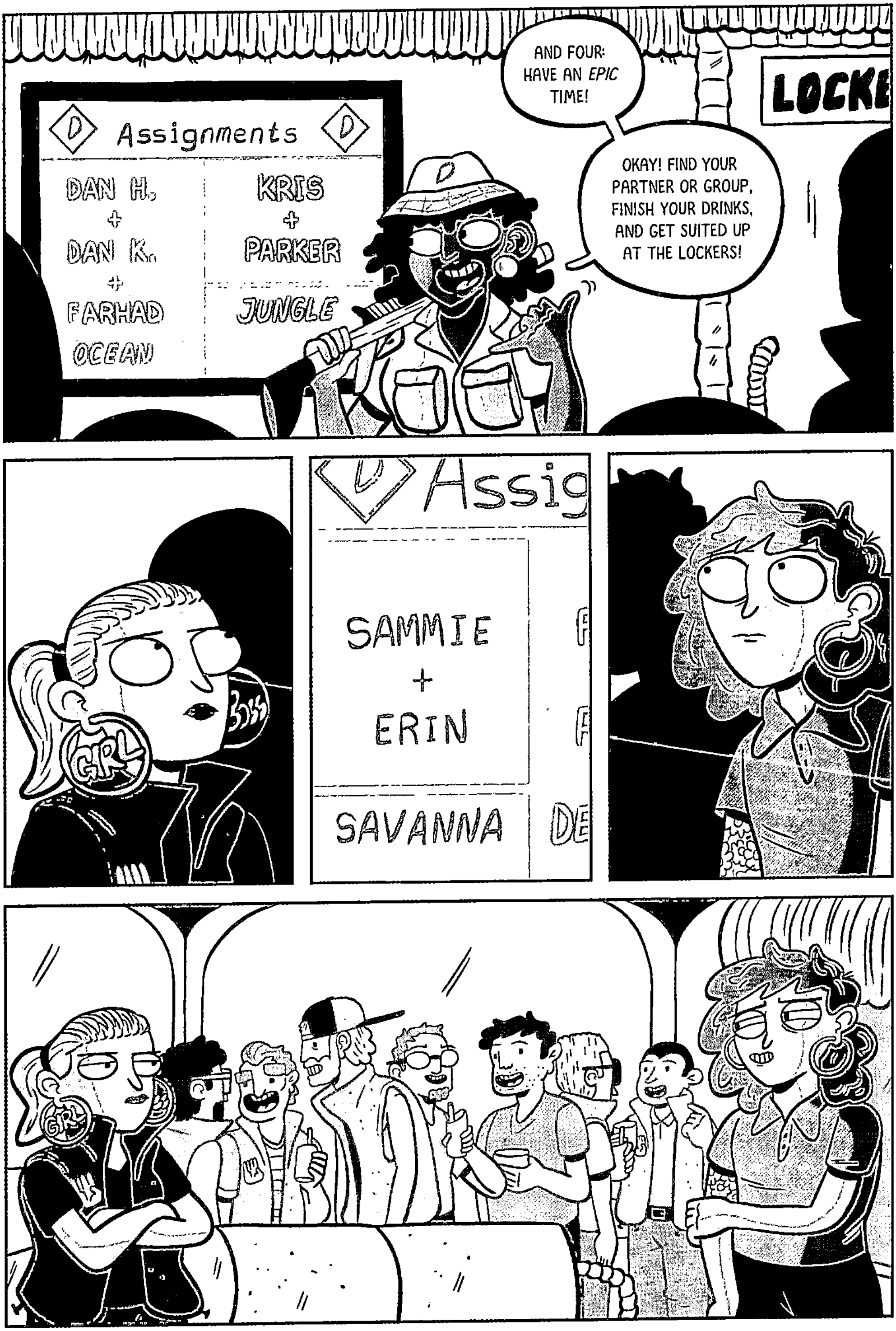
AND FOUR: HAVE AN *EPIC* TIME!
OKAY! FIND YOUR PARTNER OR GROUP, FINISH YOUR DRINKS, AND GET SUITED UP AT THE LOCKERS!
Assignments
DAN H. + DAN K. + FARHAD
OCEAN
KRIS + PARKER
JUNGLE
LOCKE
SAMMIE + ERIN
SAVANNA
GRL
BOSS

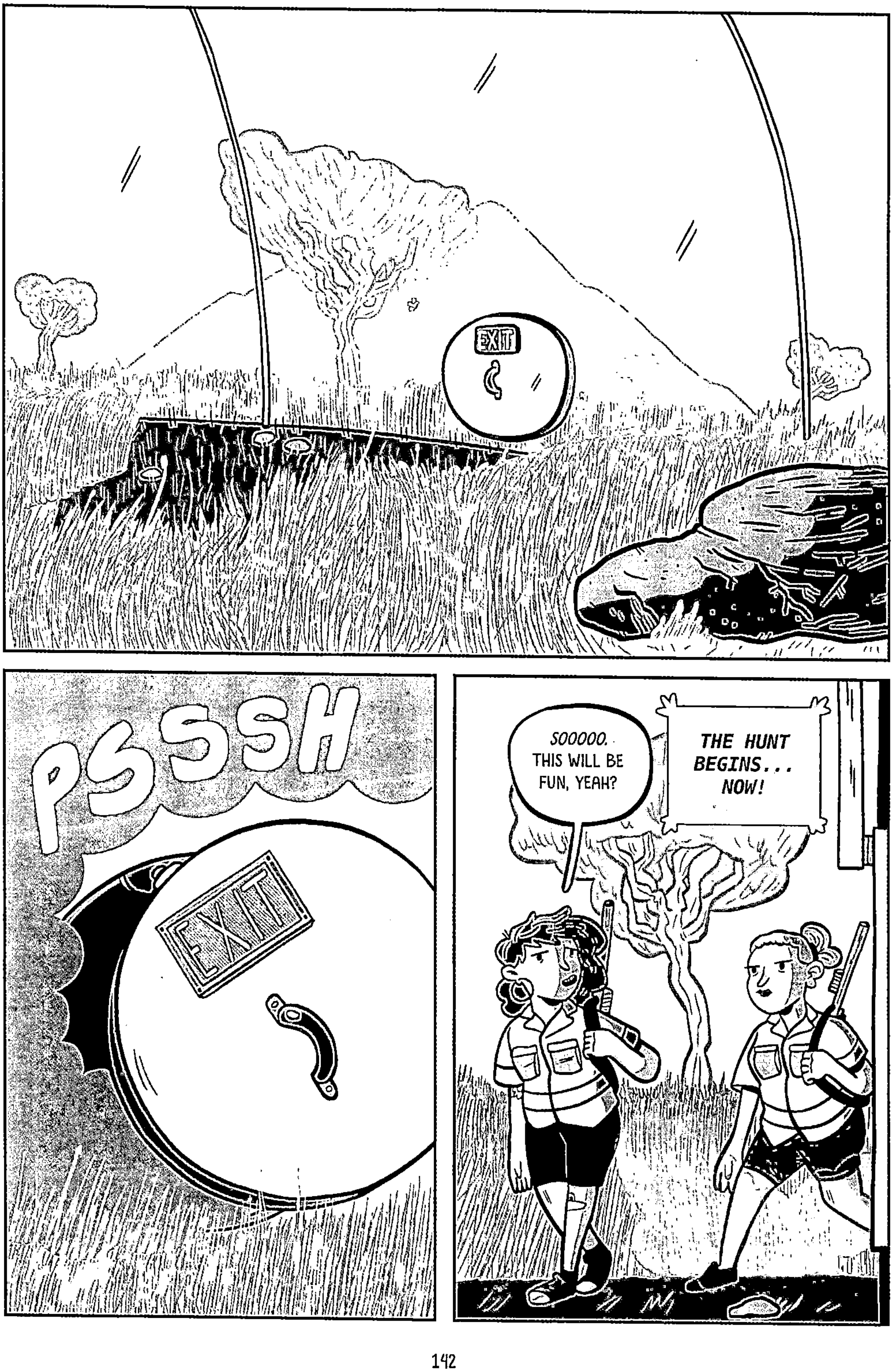
EXIT
EXIT
PSSSH
SOOOOO. THIS WILL BE FUN, YEAH?
THE HUNT BEGINS... NOW!

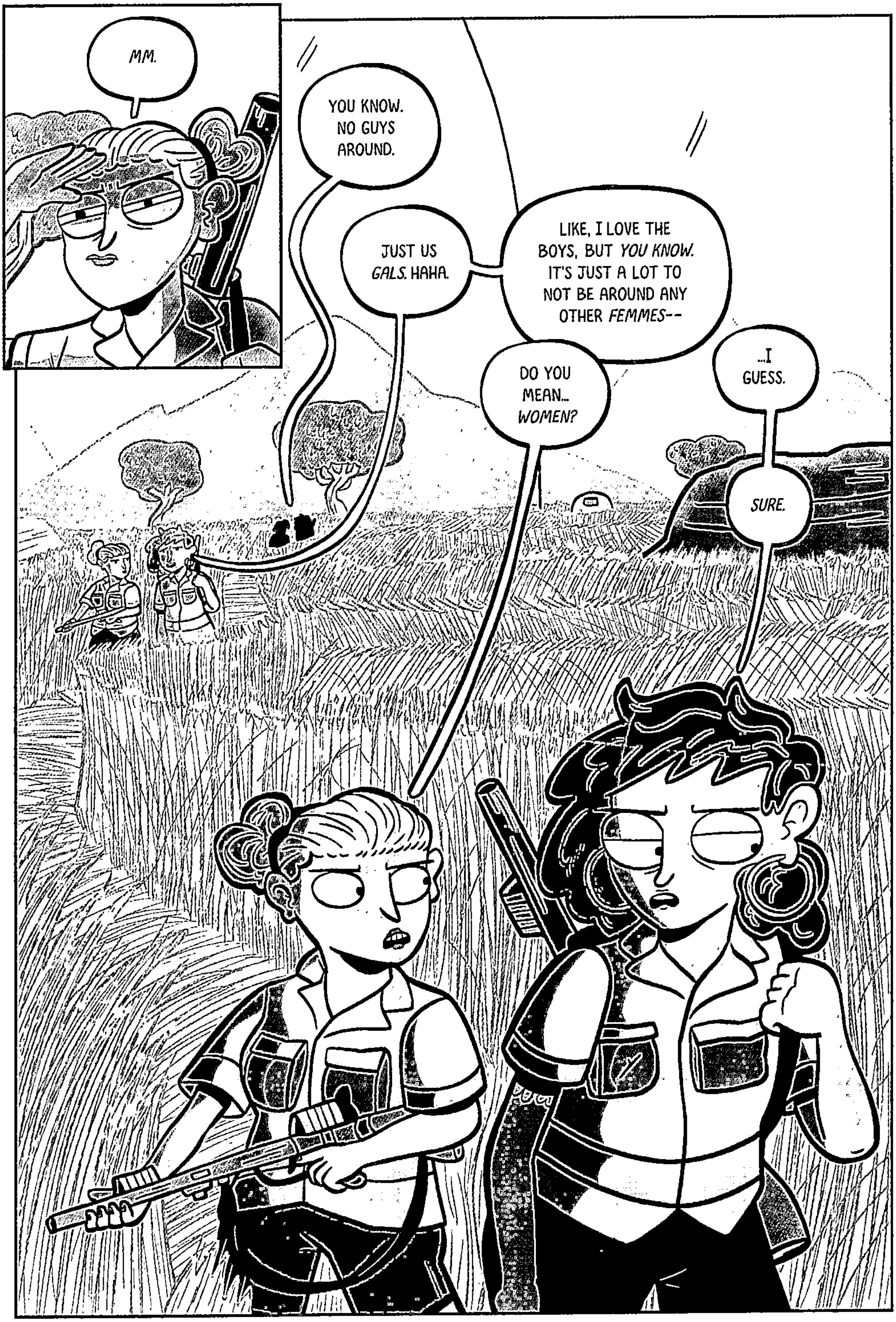
MM.
YOU KNOW. NO GUYS AROUND.
JUST US *GALS.* HAHA.
LIKE, I LOVE THE BOYS, BUT *YOU KNOW.* IT'S JUST A LOT TO NOT BE AROUND ANY OTHER *FEMMES*--
DO YOU MEAN... *WOMEN?*
...I GUESS.
SURE.

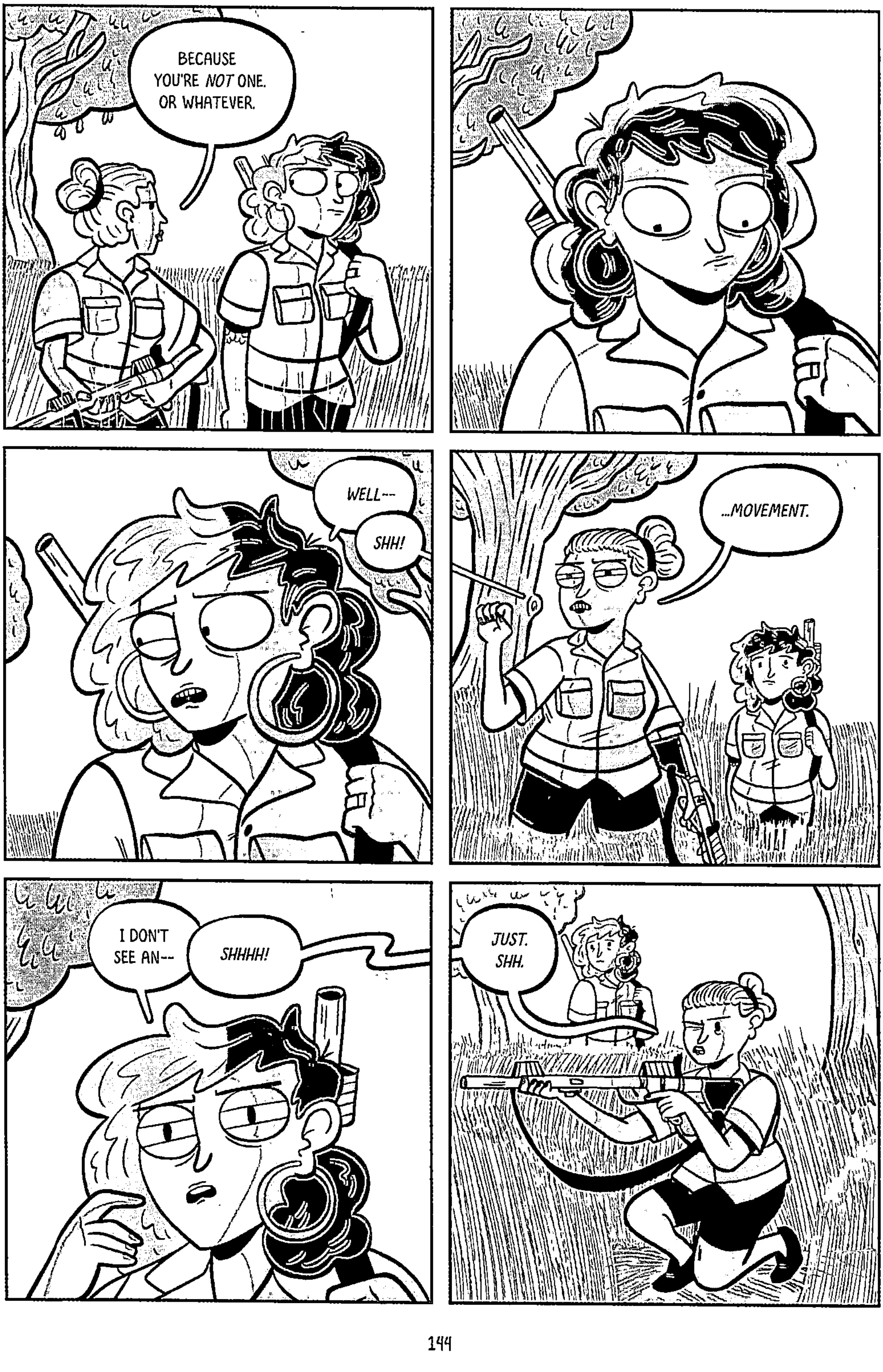
BECAUSE YOU'RE *NOT* ONE. OR WHATEVER.
WELL--
SHH!
...MOVEMENT.
I DON'T SEE AN--
SHHHH!
JUST. SHH.

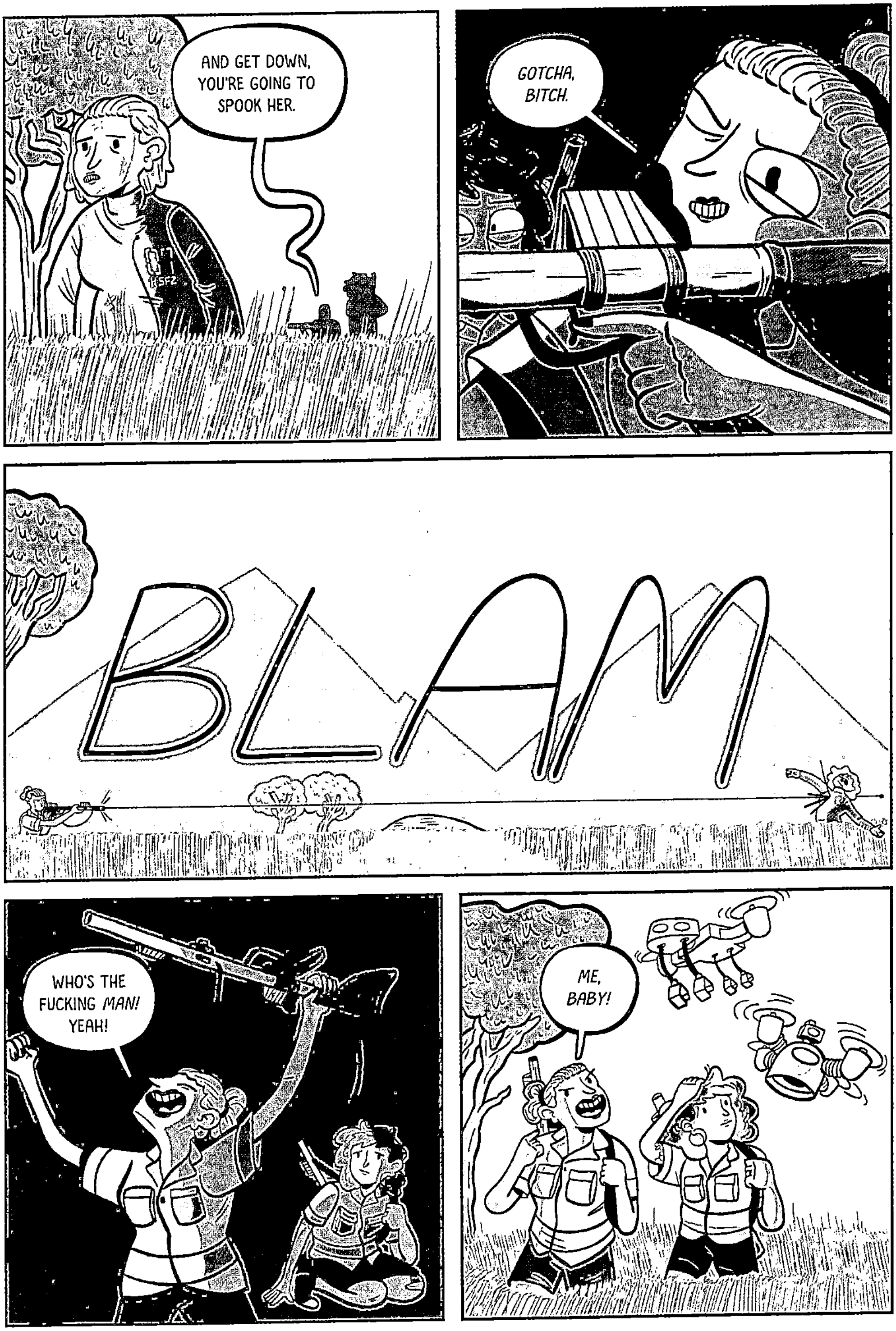
AND GET DOWN, YOU'RE GOING TO SPOOK HER.
GOTCHA, BITCH.
BLAM
WHO'S THE FUCKING MAN! YEAH!
ME, BABY!

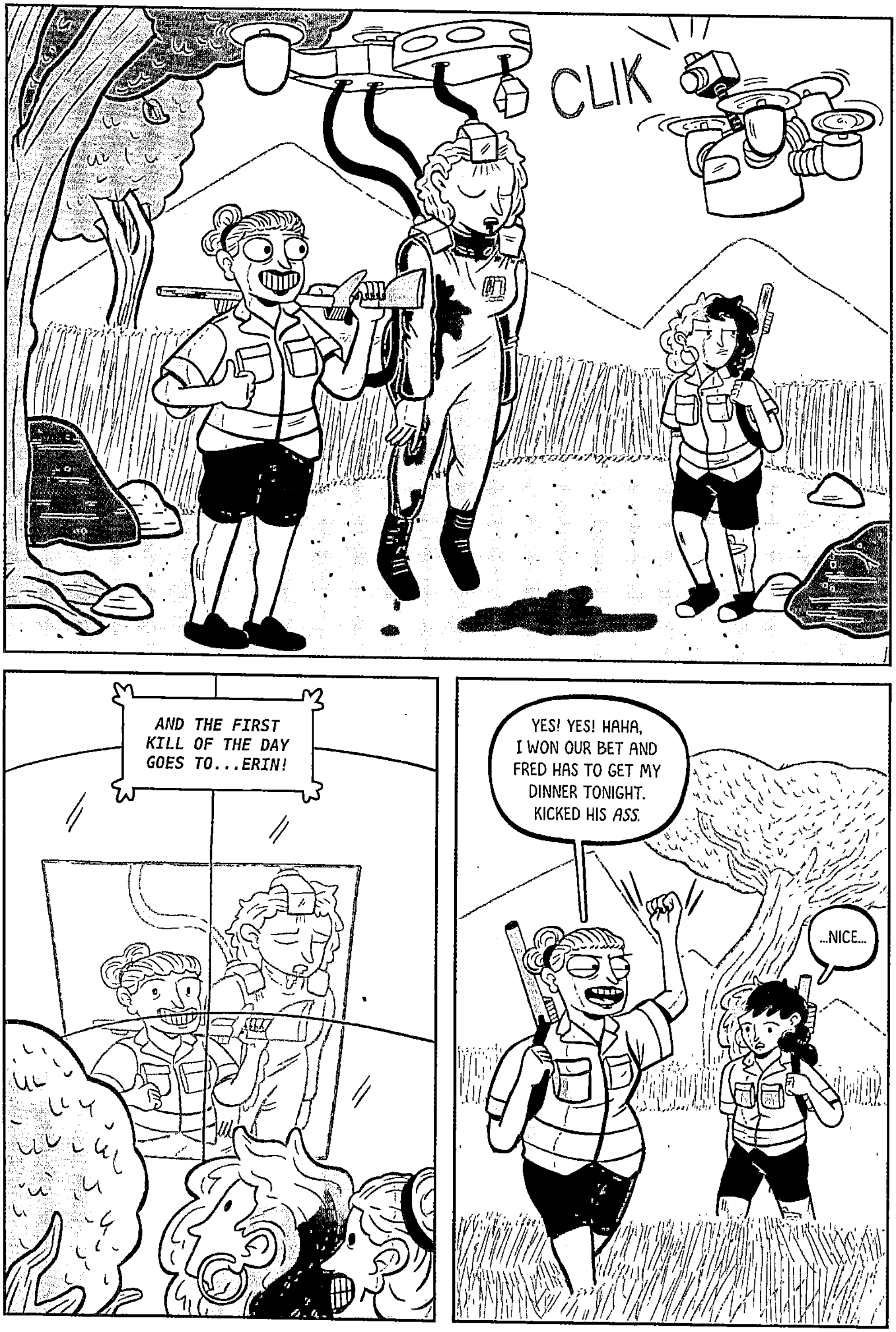
CLIK
AND THE FIRST KILL OF THE DAY GOES TO...ERIN!
YES! YES! HAHA, I WON OUR BET AND FRED HAS TO GET MY DINNER TONIGHT. KICKED HIS *ASS.*
...NICE...

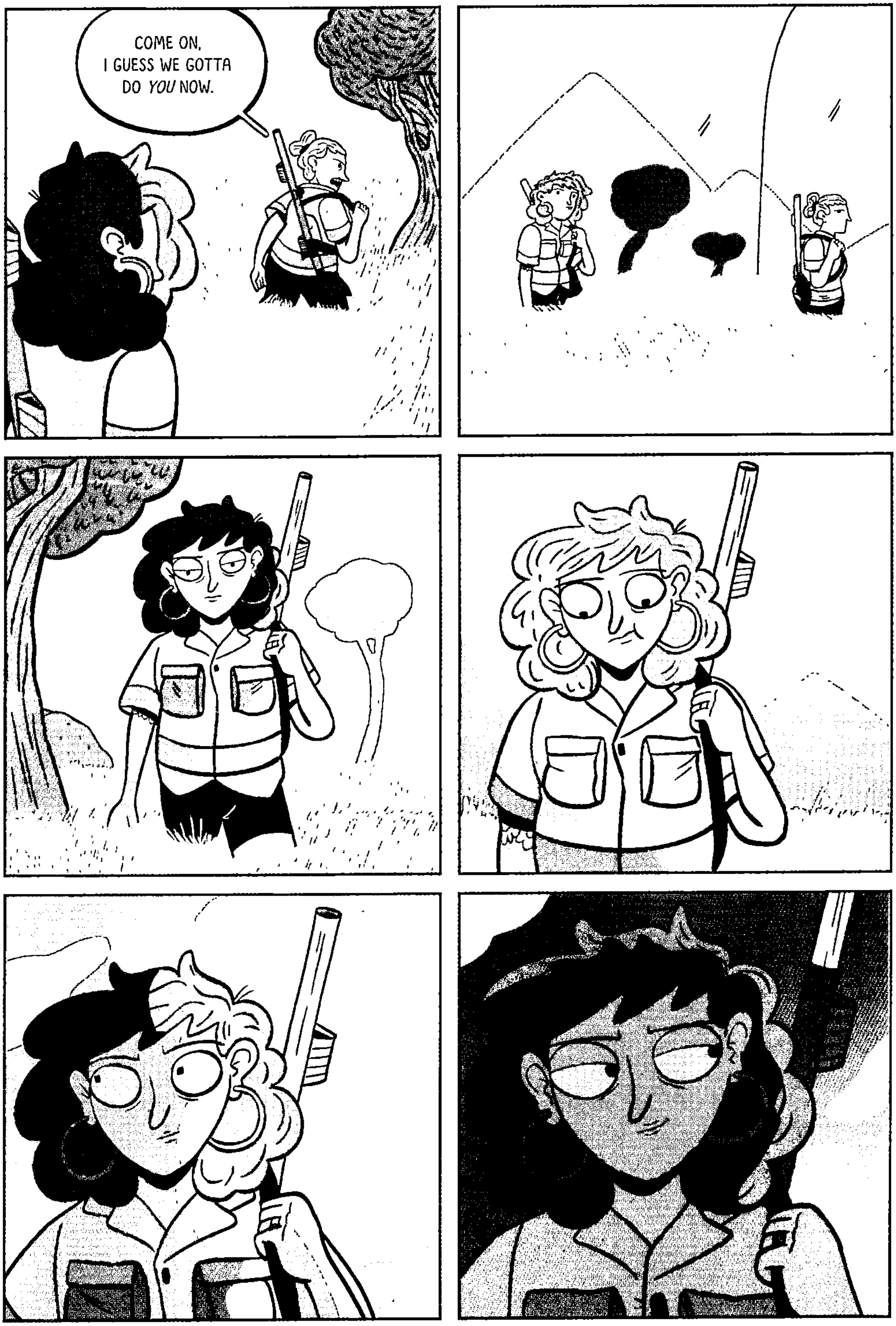
COME ON, I GUESS WE GOTTA DO *YOU* NOW.

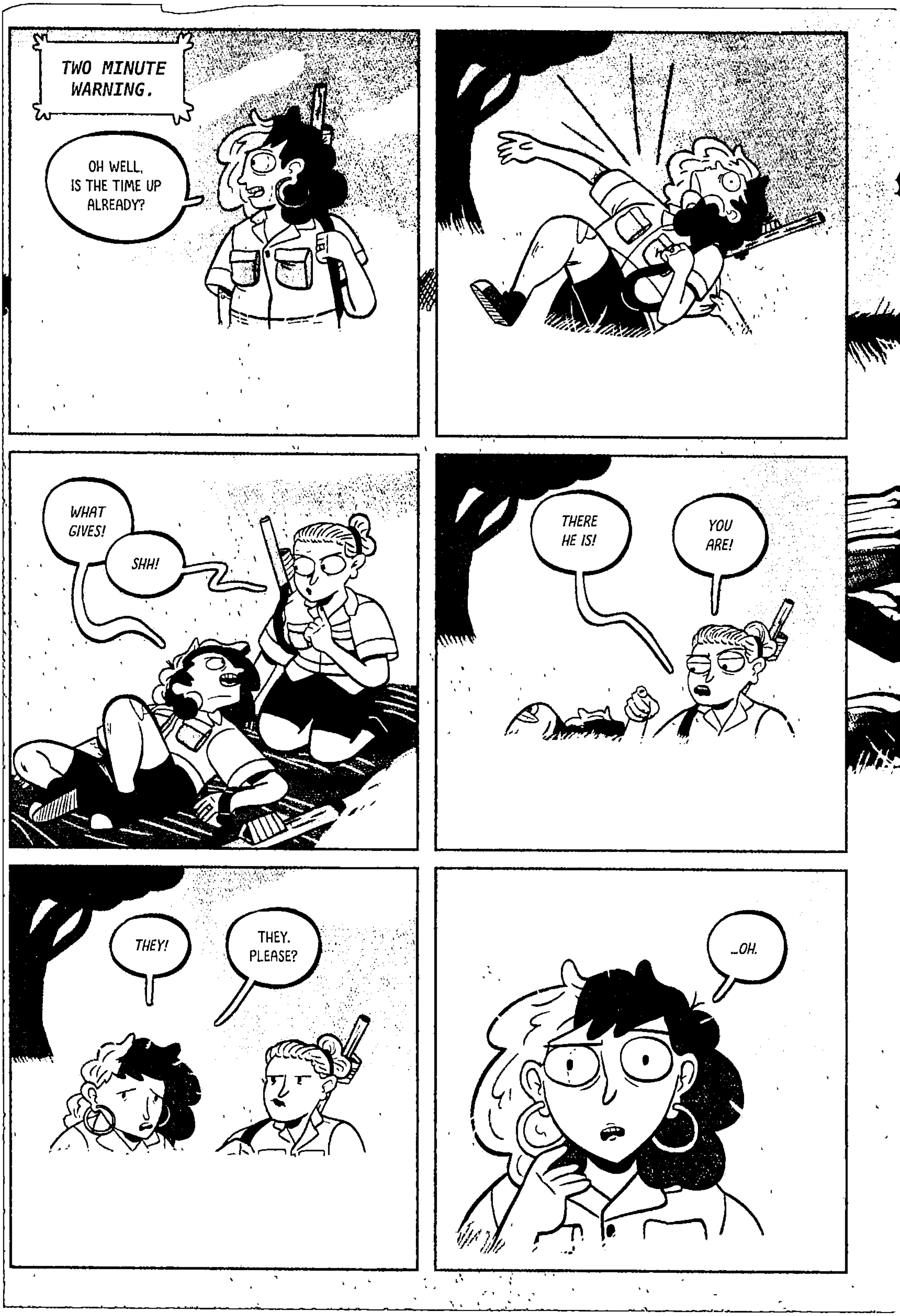
TWO MINUTE WARNING.
OH WELL, IS THE TIME UP ALREADY?
WHAT GIVES!
SHH!
THERE HE IS!
YOU ARE!
THEY!
THEY. PLEASE?
...OH.

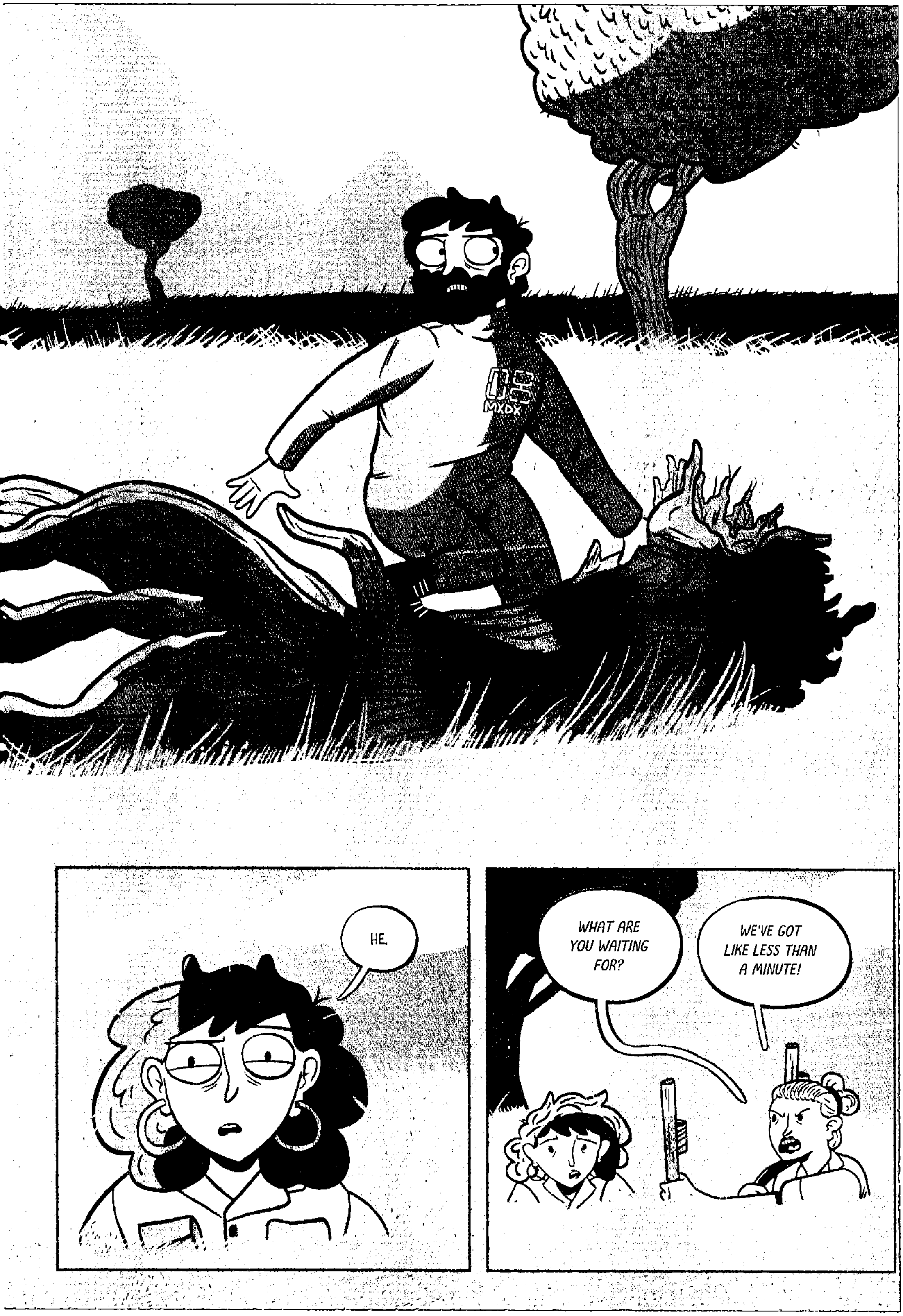
MXDX
HE.
WHAT ARE YOU WAITING FOR?
WE'VE GOT LIKE LESS THAN A MINUTE!

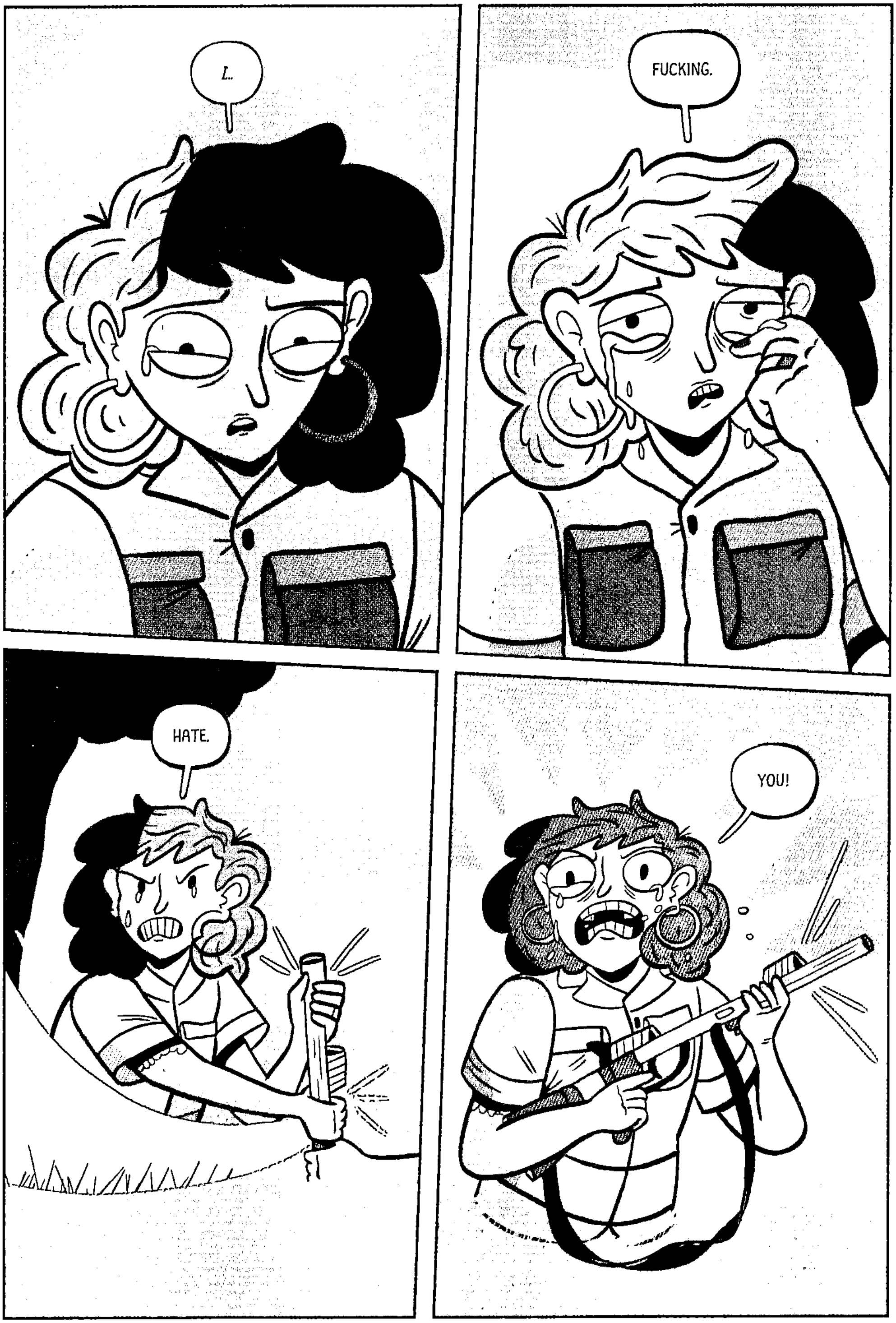
I..
FUCKING.
HATE.
YOU!

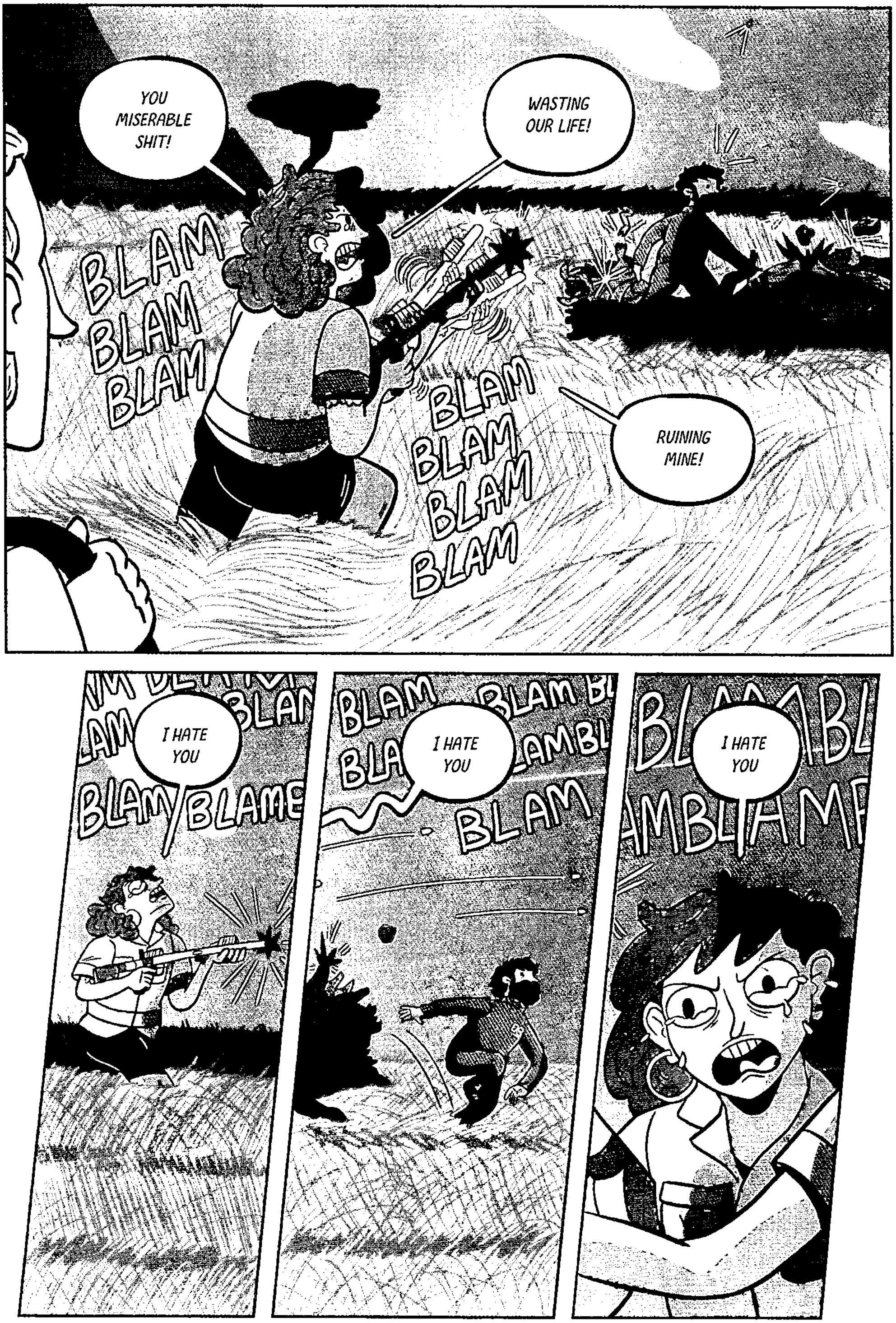
YOU MISERABLE SHIT!
WASTING OUR LIFE!
BLAM BLAM BLAM
BLAM BLAM BLAM BLAM
RUINING MINE!
I HATE YOU
BLAM
I HATE YOU
BLAM
I HATE YOU

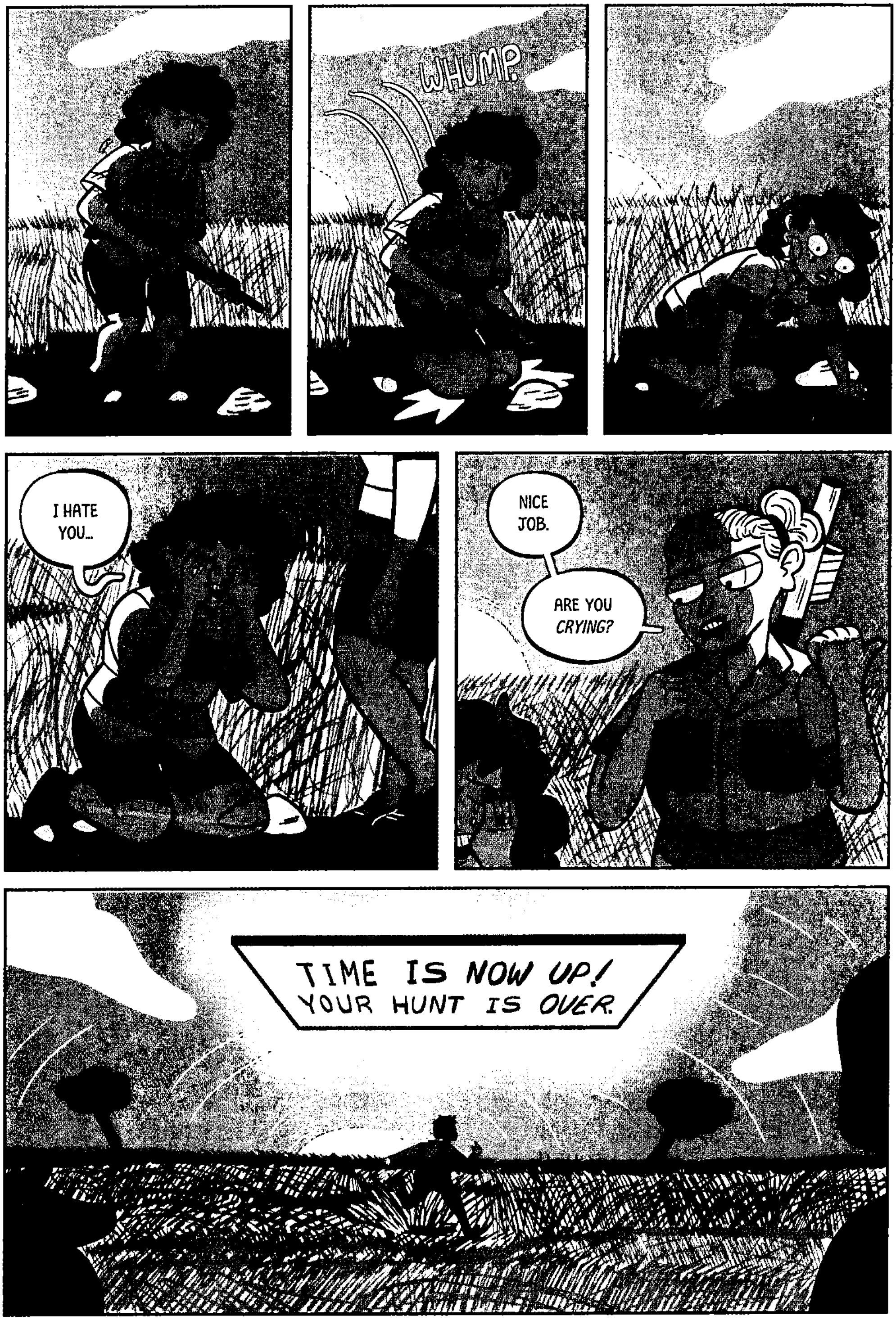
WHUMP
I HATE YOU...
NICE JOB.
ARE YOU *CRYING?*
TIME IS *NOW UP!*
YOUR HUNT IS *OVER.*

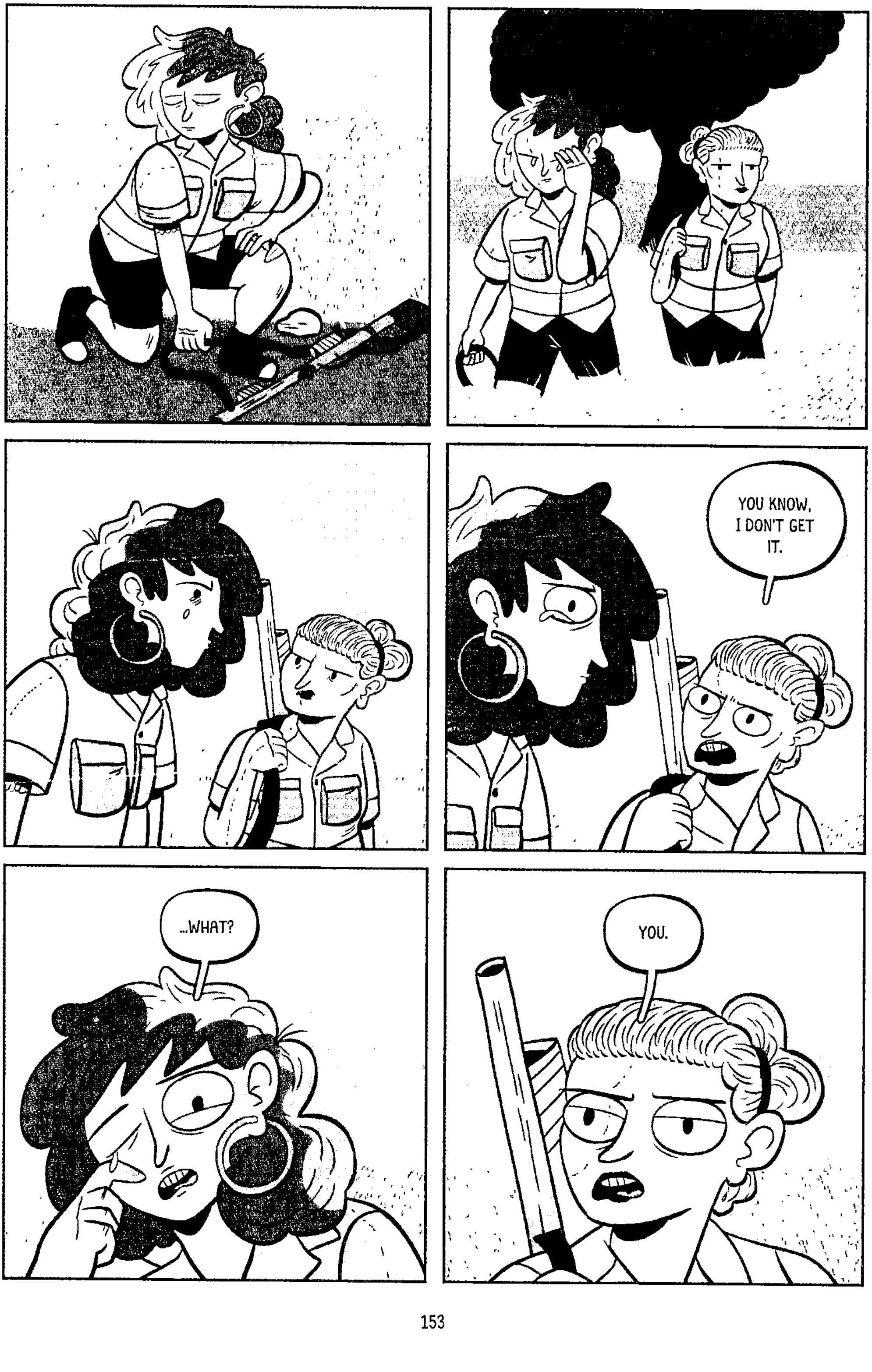
YOU KNOW, I DON'T GET IT.
...WHAT?
YOU.

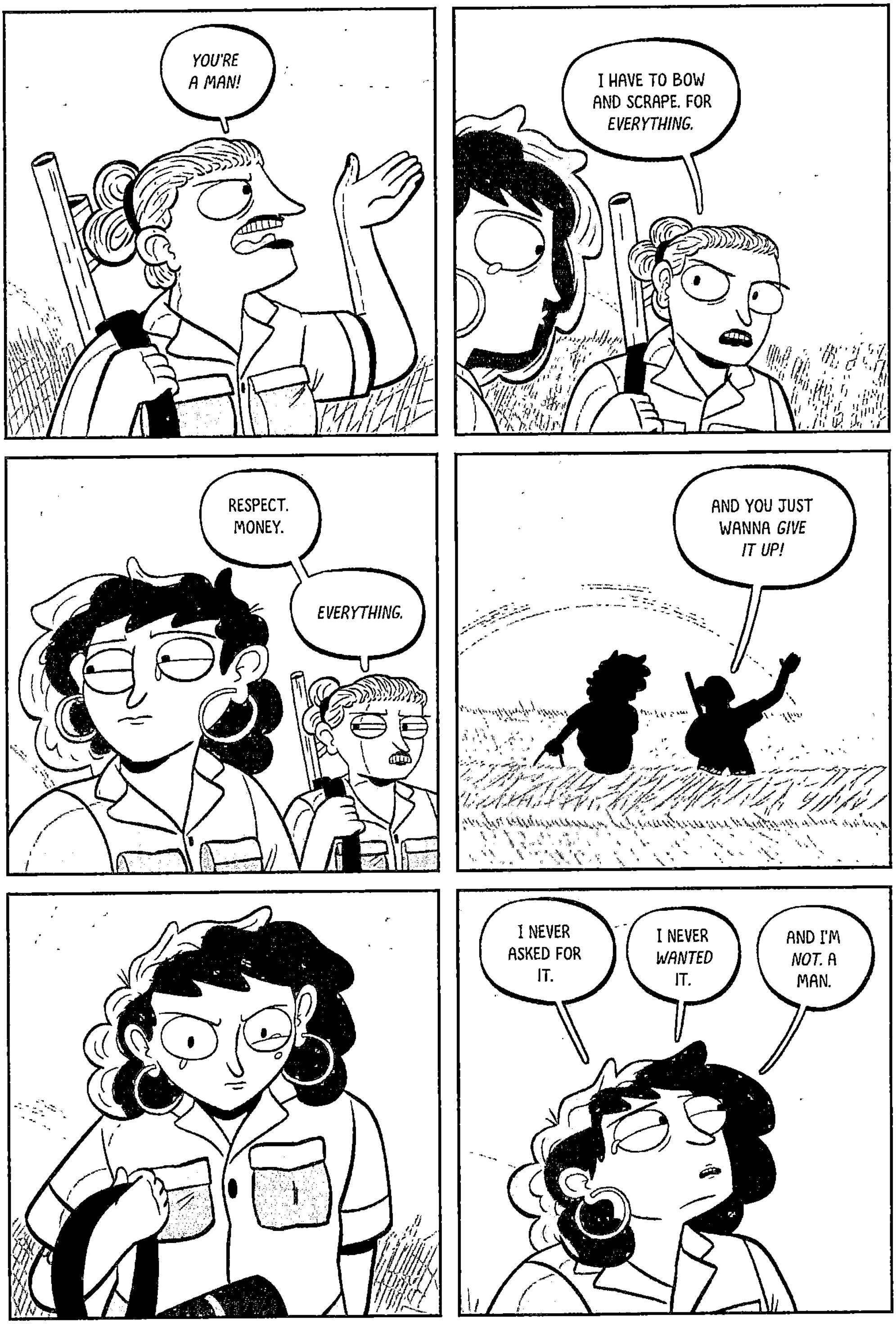
YOU'RE A MAN!
I HAVE TO BOW AND SCRAPE. FOR *EVERYTHING.*
RESPECT. MONEY.
EVERYTHING.
AND YOU JUST WANNA *GIVE IT UP!*
I NEVER ASKED FOR IT.
I NEVER *WANTED* IT.
AND I'M *NOT.* A MAN.

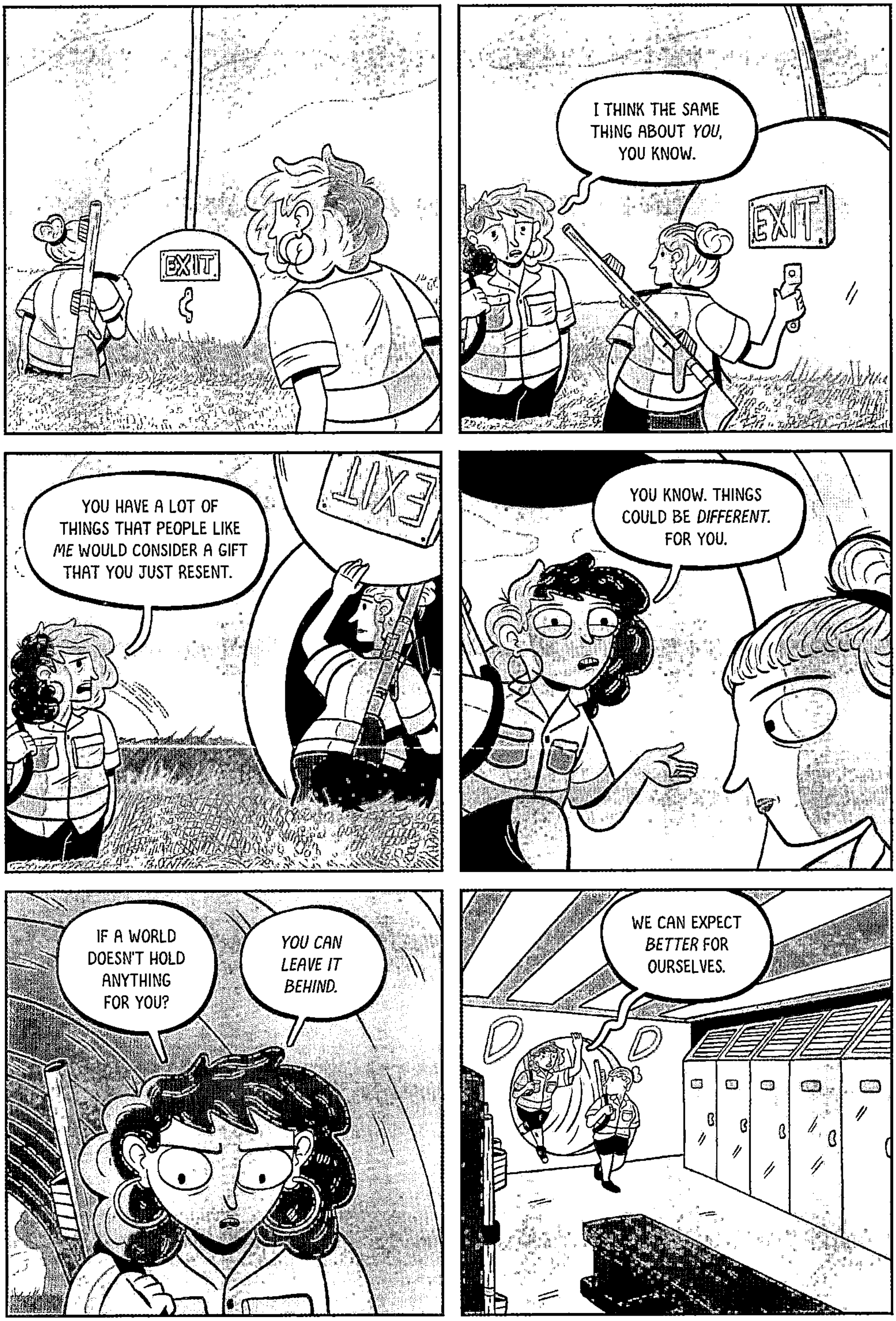
EXIT
I THINK THE SAME THING ABOUT *YOU,* YOU KNOW.
EXIT
YOU HAVE A LOT OF THINGS THAT PEOPLE LIKE *ME* WOULD CONSIDER A GIFT THAT YOU JUST RESENT.
YOU KNOW. THINGS COULD BE *DIFFERENT.* FOR YOU.
IF A WORLD DOESN'T HOLD ANYTHING FOR YOU?
YOU CAN LEAVE IT BEHIND.
WE CAN EXPECT *BETTER* FOR OURSELVES.

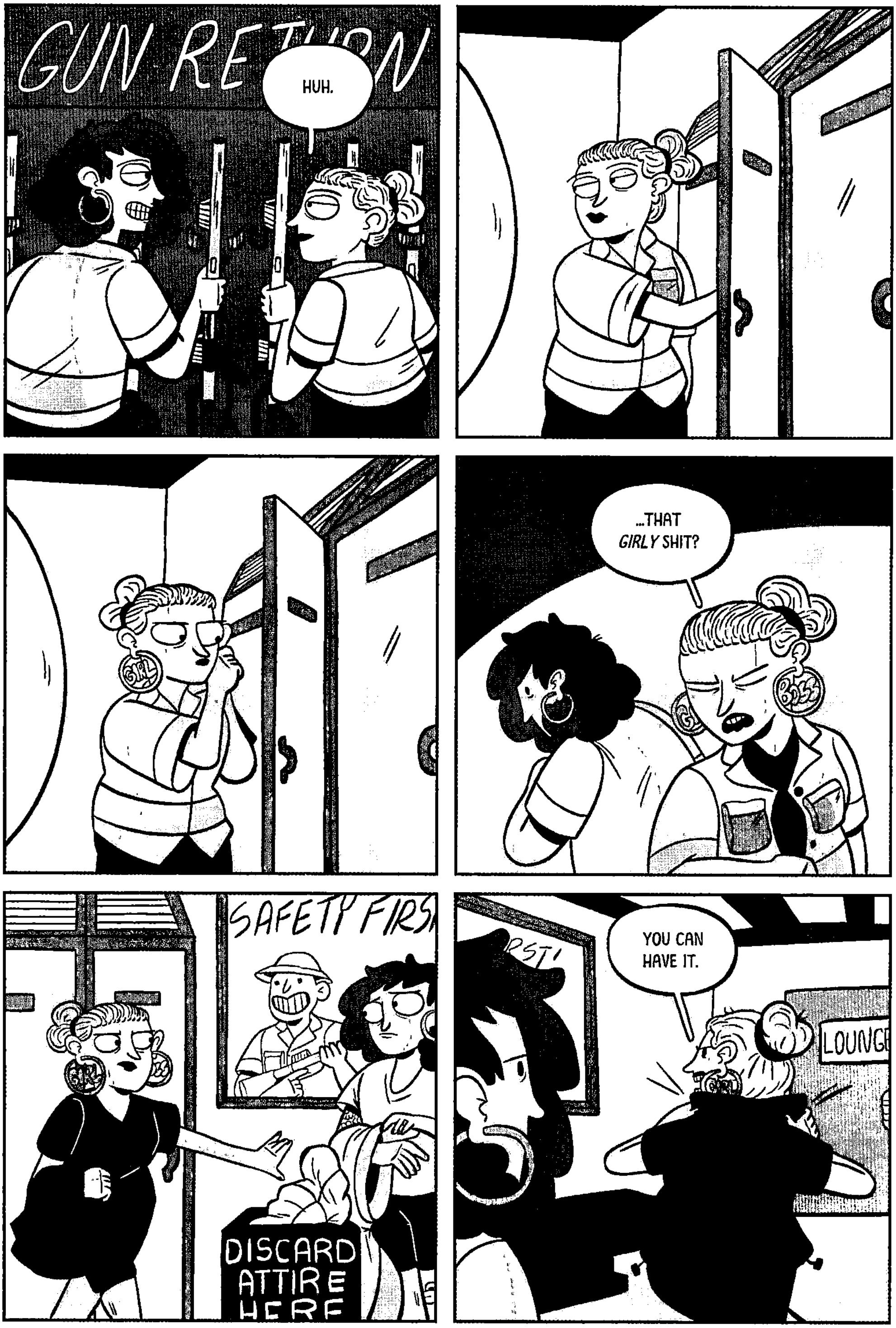
HUH.
...THAT GIRLY SHIT?
DISCARD ATTIRE HERE
YOU CAN HAVE IT.

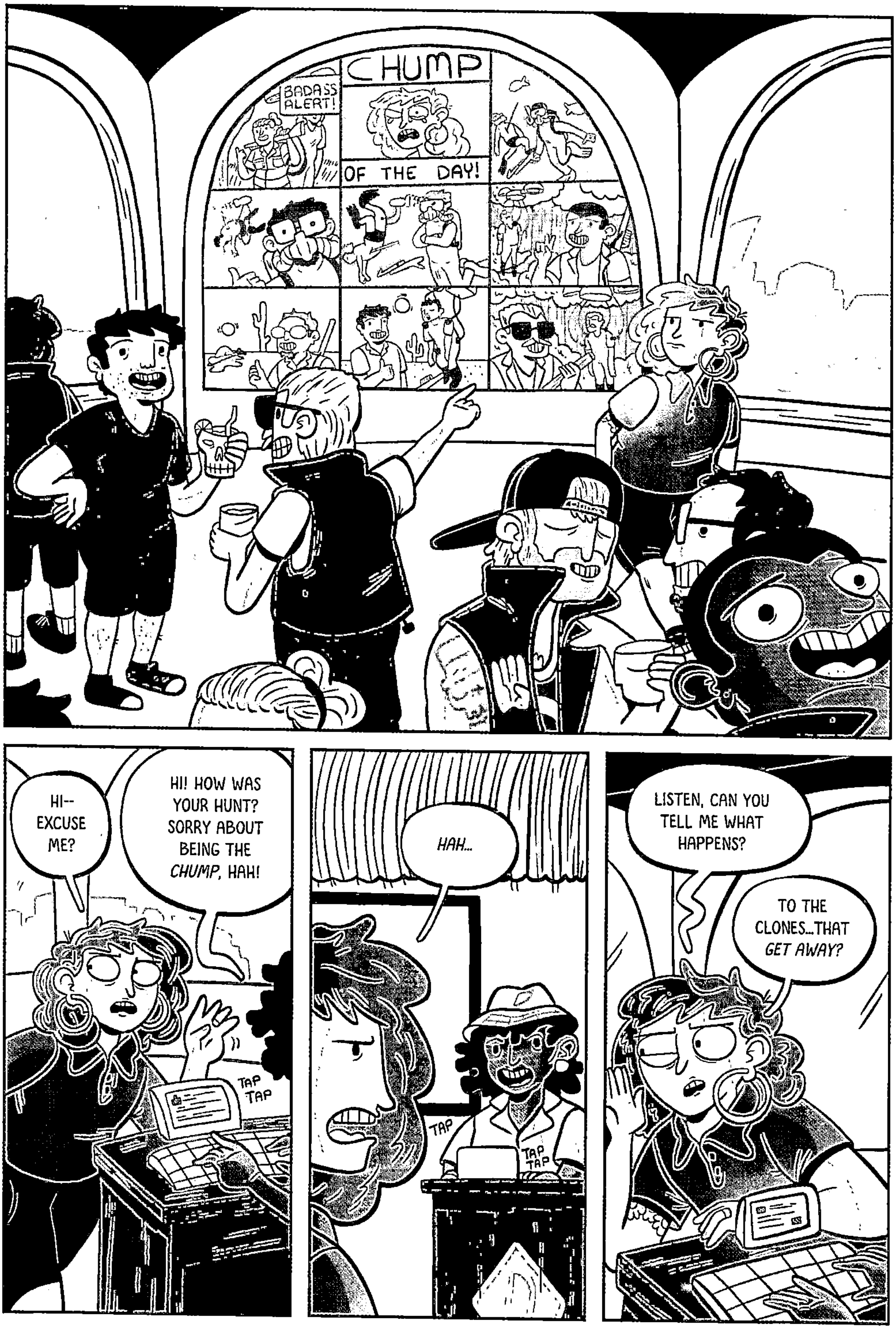
CHUMP
BADASS ALERT!
OF THE DAY!
HI-- EXCUSE ME?
HI! HOW WAS YOUR HUNT? SORRY ABOUT BEING THE *CHUMP*, HAH!
TAP TAP
HAH...
TAP
TAP TAP
LISTEN, CAN YOU TELL ME WHAT HAPPENS?
TO THE CLONES...THAT *GET AWAY?*

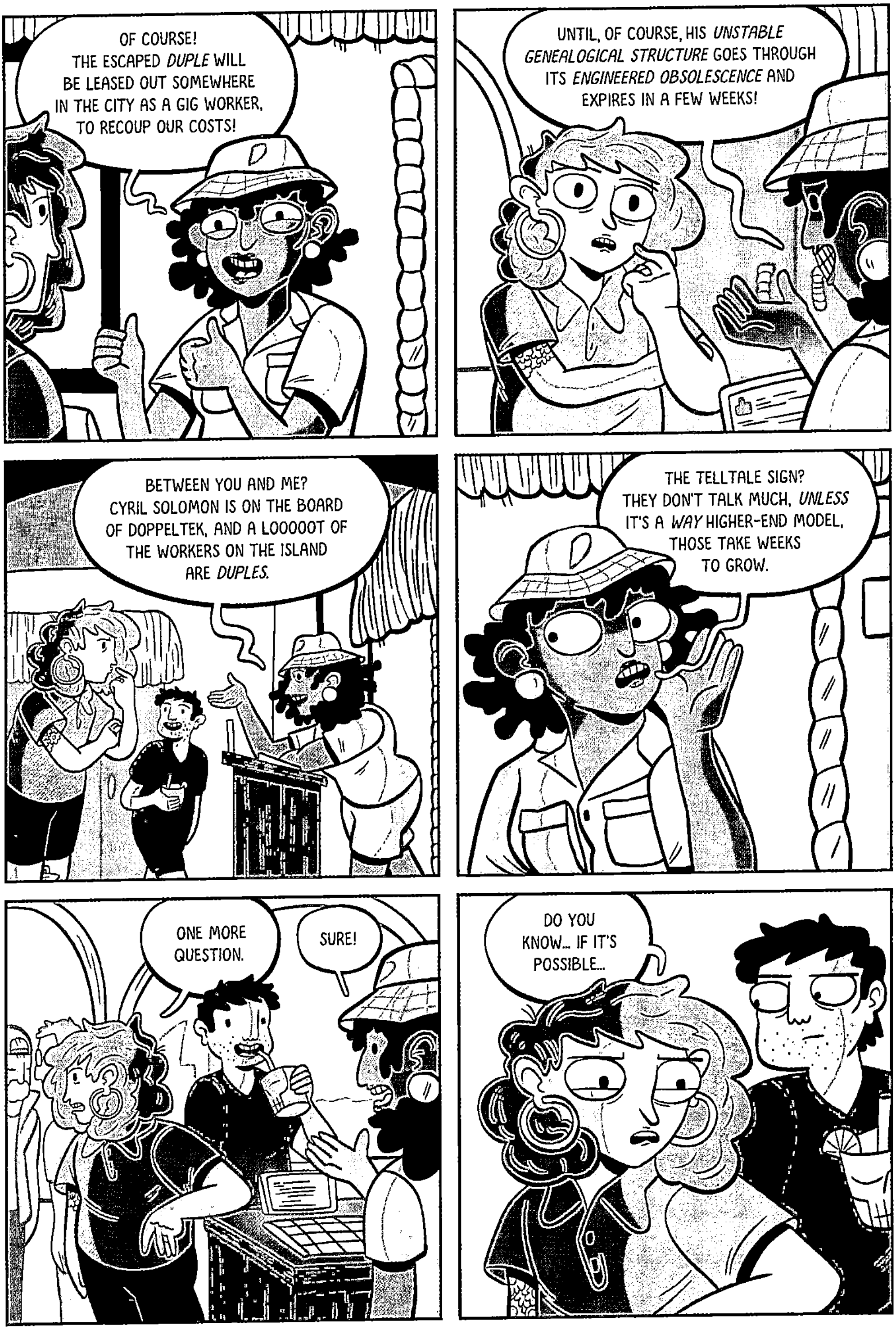
OF COURSE! THE ESCAPED *DUPLE* WILL BE LEASED OUT SOMEWHERE IN THE CITY AS A GIG WORKER, TO RECOUP OUR COSTS!
UNTIL, OF COURSE, HIS *UNSTABLE GENEALOGICAL STRUCTURE* GOES THROUGH ITS *ENGINEERED OBSOLESCENCE* AND EXPIRES IN A FEW WEEKS!
BETWEEN YOU AND ME? CYRIL SOLOMON IS ON THE BOARD OF DOPPELTEK, AND A LOOOOOT OF THE WORKERS ON THE ISLAND ARE *DUPLES.*
THE TELLTALE SIGN? THEY DON'T TALK MUCH, *UNLESS* IT'S A *WAY* HIGHER-END MODEL. THOSE TAKE WEEKS TO GROW.
ONE MORE QUESTION.
SURE!
DO YOU KNOW... IF IT'S POSSIBLE...

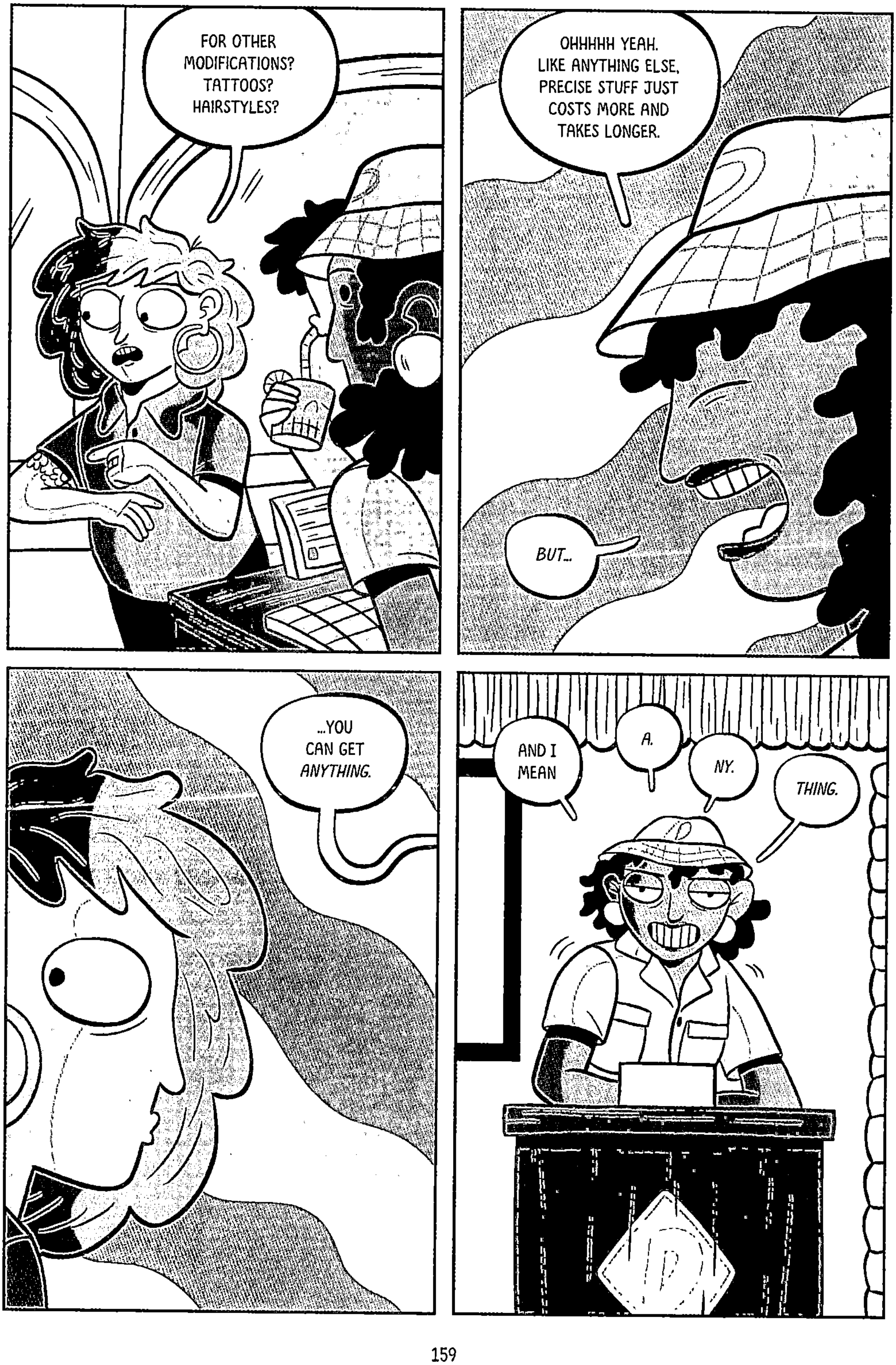
FOR OTHER MODIFICATIONS? TATTOOS? HAIRSTYLES?
OHHHHH YEAH. LIKE ANYTHING ELSE, PRECISE STUFF JUST COSTS MORE AND TAKES LONGER.
BUT...
...YOU CAN GET ANYTHING.
AND I MEAN
A.
NY.
THING.

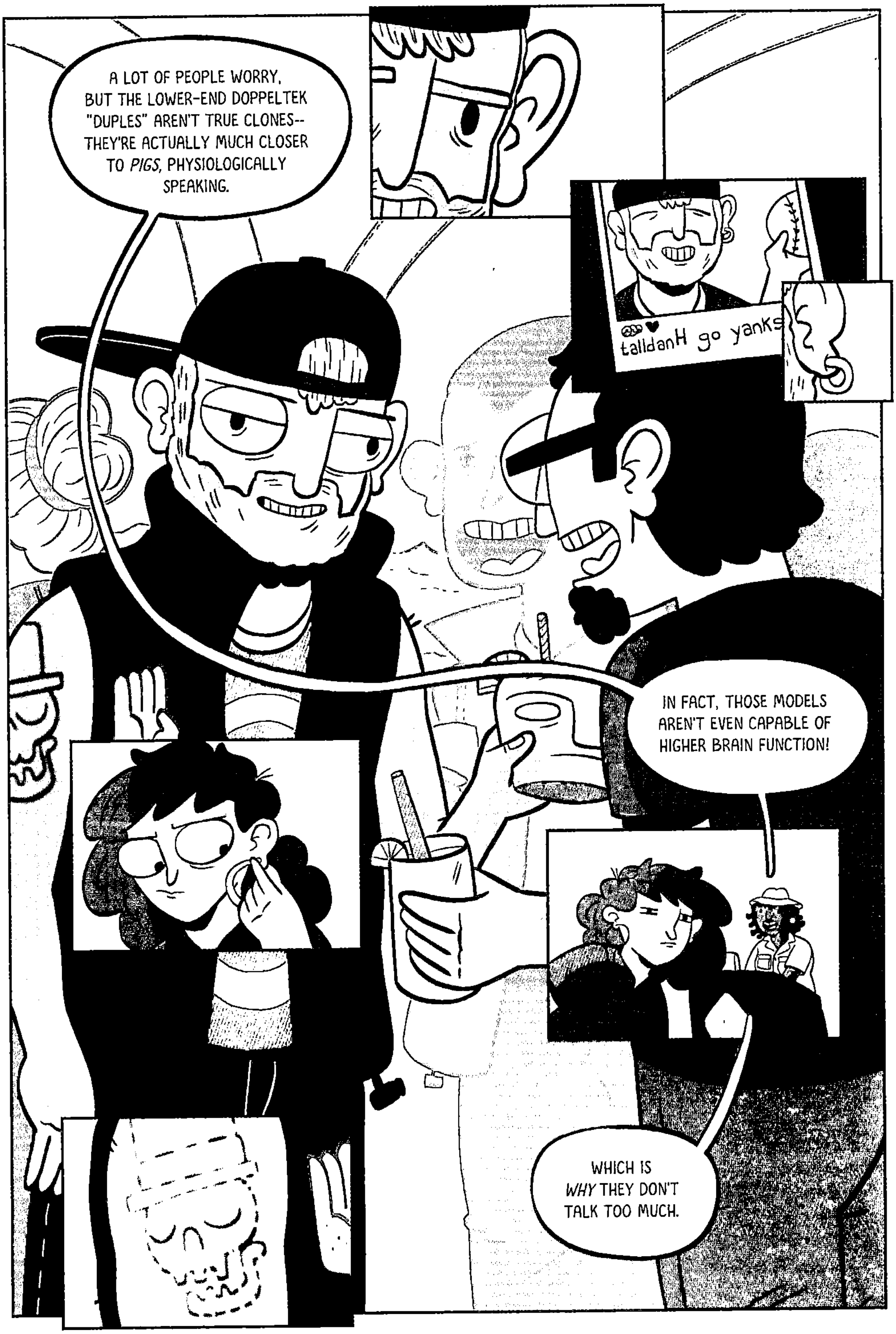
A LOT OF PEOPLE WORRY, BUT THE LOWER-END DOPPELTEK "DUPLES" AREN'T TRUE CLONES-- THEY'RE ACTUALLY MUCH CLOSER TO *PIGS*, PHYSIOLOGICALLY SPEAKING.
talldanH go yanks
IN FACT, THOSE MODELS AREN'T EVEN CAPABLE OF HIGHER BRAIN FUNCTION!
WHICH IS *WHY* THEY DON'T TALK TOO MUCH.

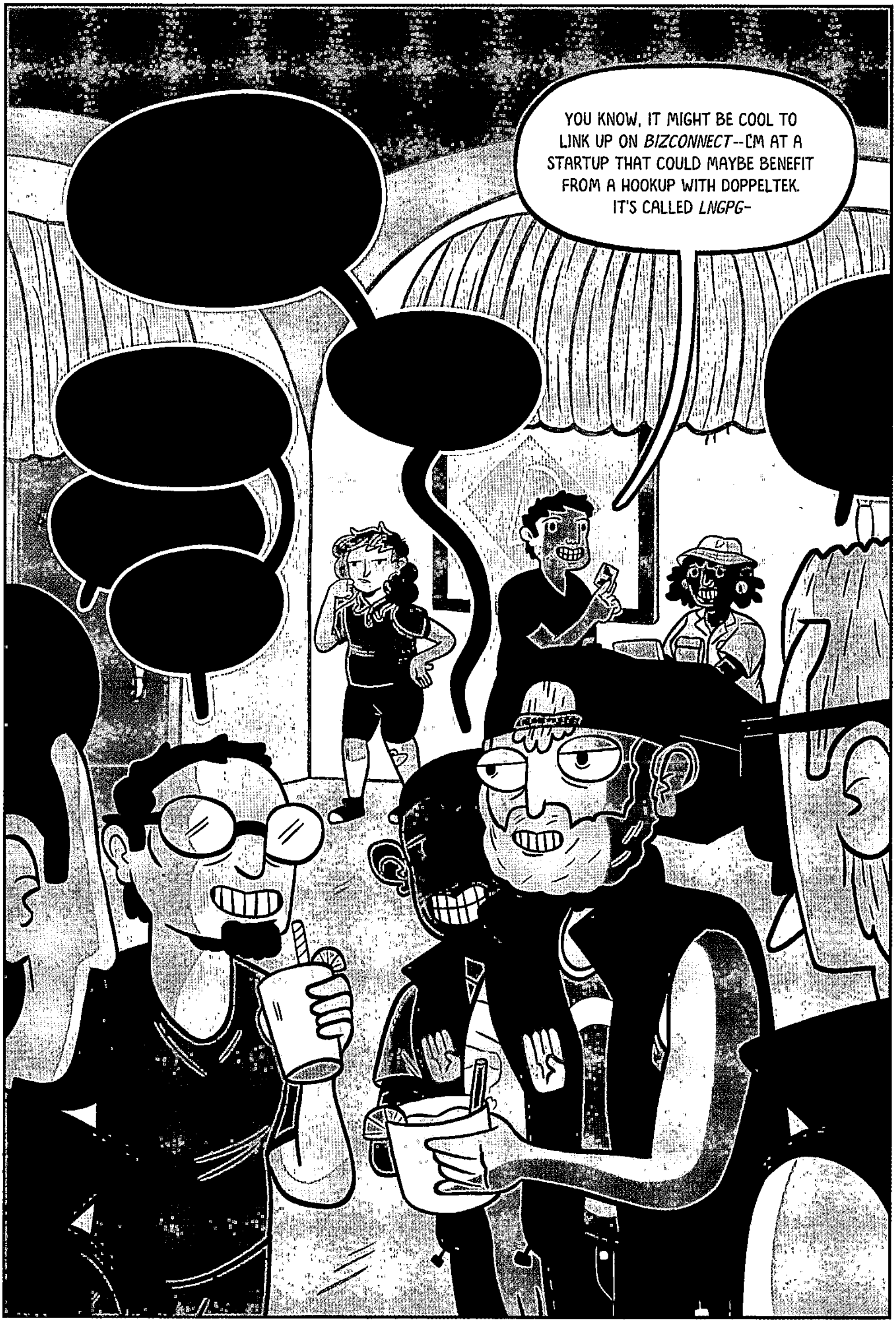
YOU KNOW, IT MIGHT BE COOL TO LINK UP ON *BIZCONNECT*--I'M AT A STARTUP THAT COULD MAYBE BENEFIT FROM A HOOKUP WITH DOPPELTEK. IT'S CALLED *LNGPG*-

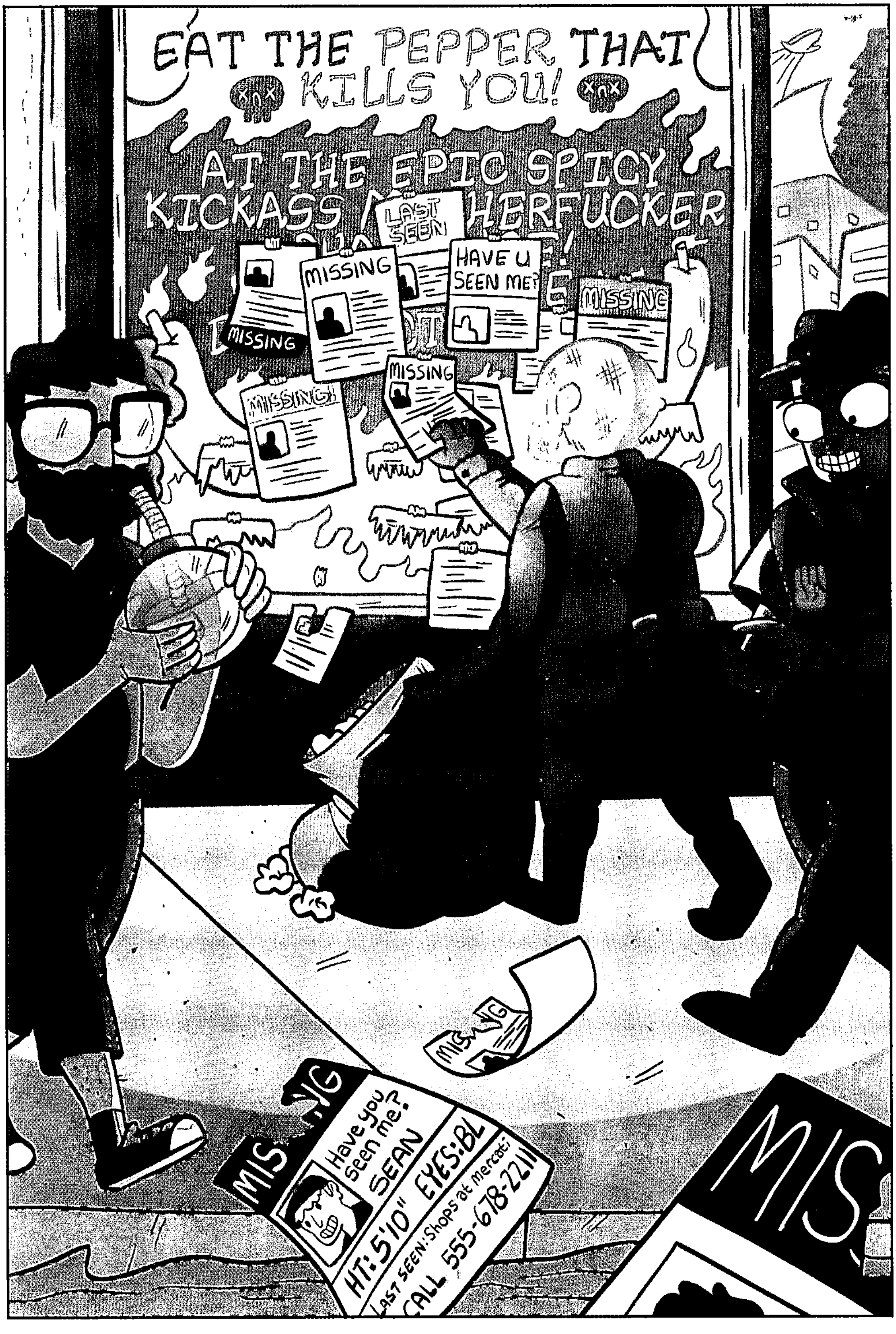
EAT THE PEPPER THAT KILLS YOU!
AT THE EPIC SPICY KICKASS
HERFUCKER
LAST SEEN
MISSING
HAVE U SEEN ME?
MISSING
MISSING
MISSING
MISSING
Have you seen me?
SEAN
HT: 5'10" EYES: BL
LAST SEEN: Shops at mercat
CALL 555-678-2211
MIS

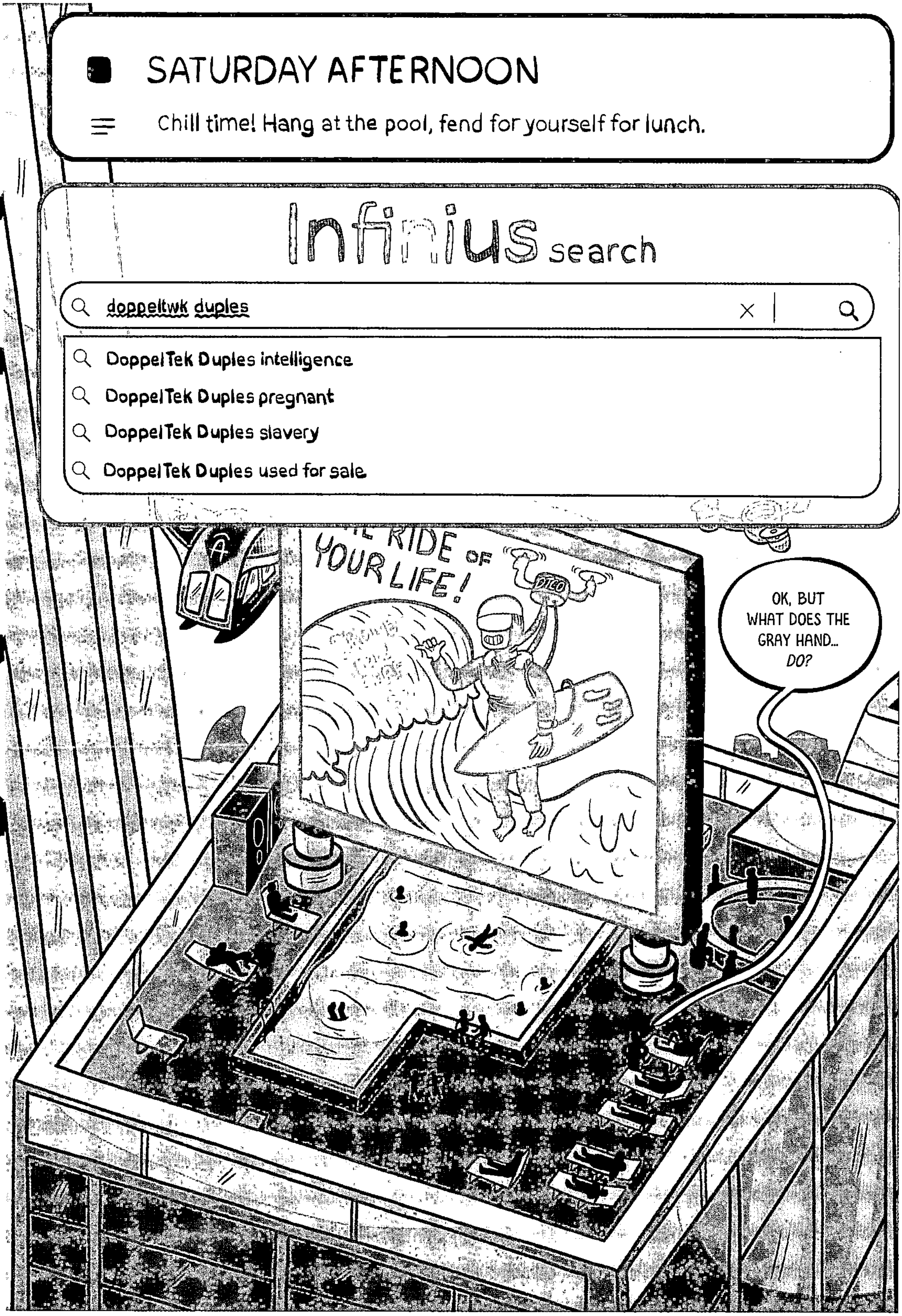
SATURDAY AFTERNOON
Chill time! Hang at the pool, fend for yourself for lunch.
Infinius search
doppeltwk duples
DoppelTek Duples intelligence
DoppelTek Duples pregnant
DoppelTek Duples slavery
DoppelTek Duples used for sale
RIDE OF YOUR LIFE!
OK, BUT WHAT DOES THE GRAY HAND... *DO?*

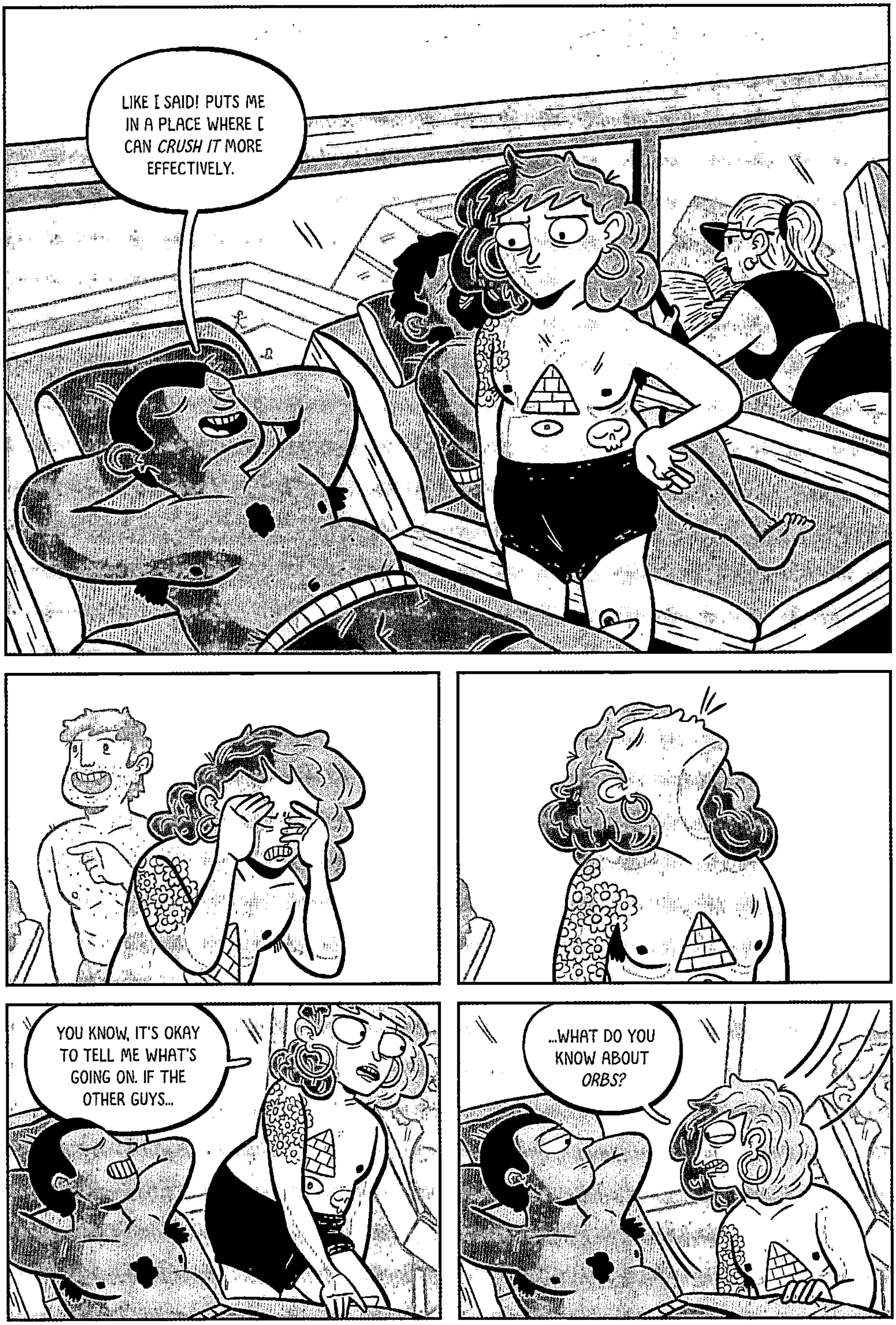
LIKE I SAID! PUTS ME IN A PLACE WHERE I CAN *CRUSH IT* MORE EFFECTIVELY.
YOU KNOW, IT'S OKAY TO TELL ME WHAT'S GOING ON. IF THE OTHER GUYS...
...WHAT DO YOU KNOW ABOUT *ORBS?*

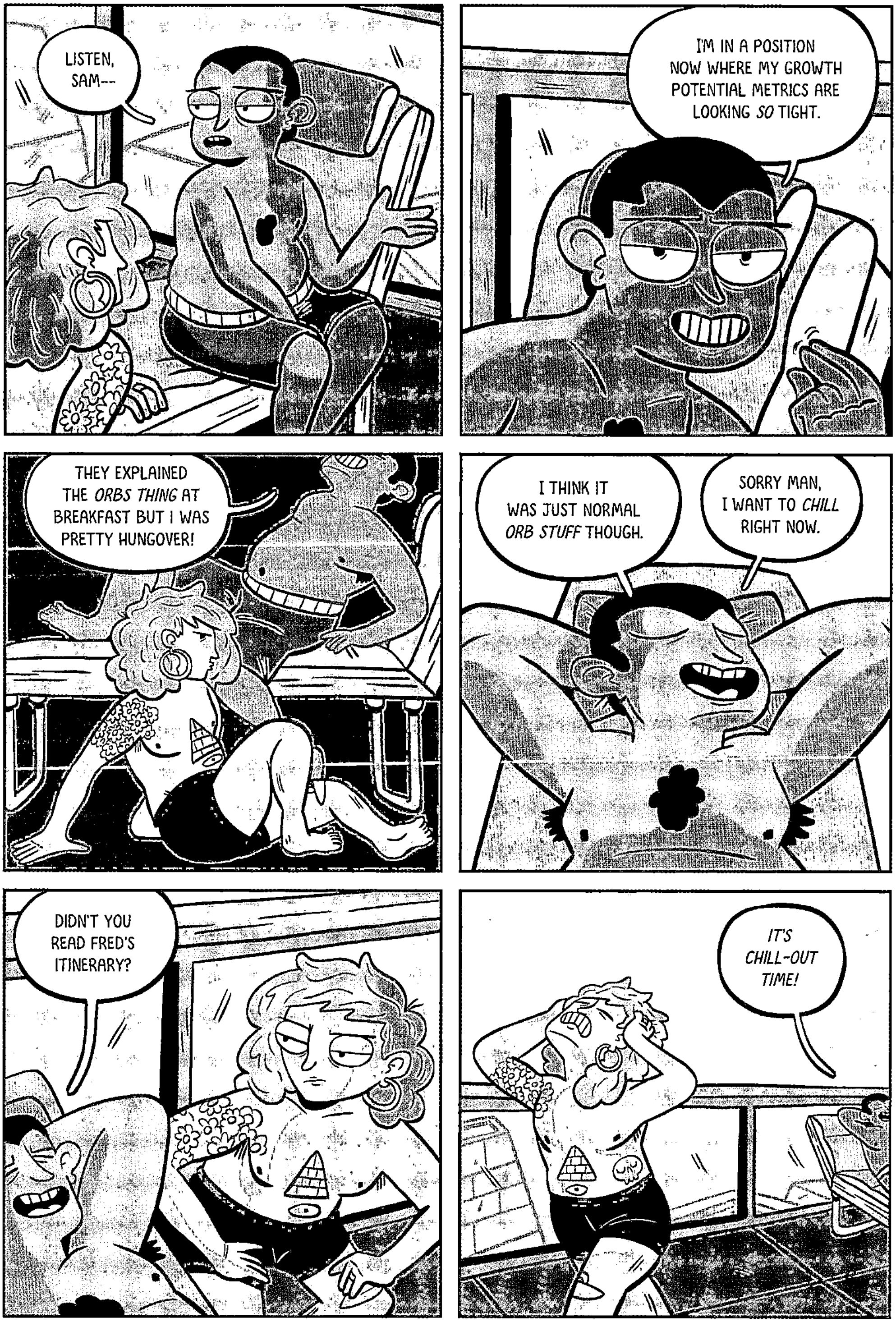
LISTEN, SAM--
I'M IN A POSITION NOW WHERE MY GROWTH POTENTIAL METRICS ARE LOOKING *SO* TIGHT.
THEY EXPLAINED THE *ORBS THING* AT BREAKFAST BUT I WAS PRETTY HUNGOVER!
I THINK IT WAS JUST NORMAL *ORB STUFF* THOUGH.
SORRY MAN, I WANT TO *CHILL* RIGHT NOW.
DIDN'T YOU READ FRED'S ITINERARY?
IT'S CHILL-OUT TIME!

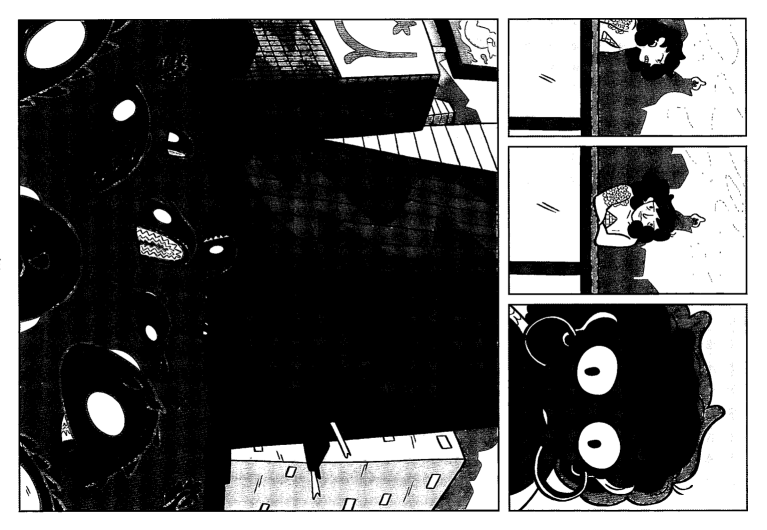

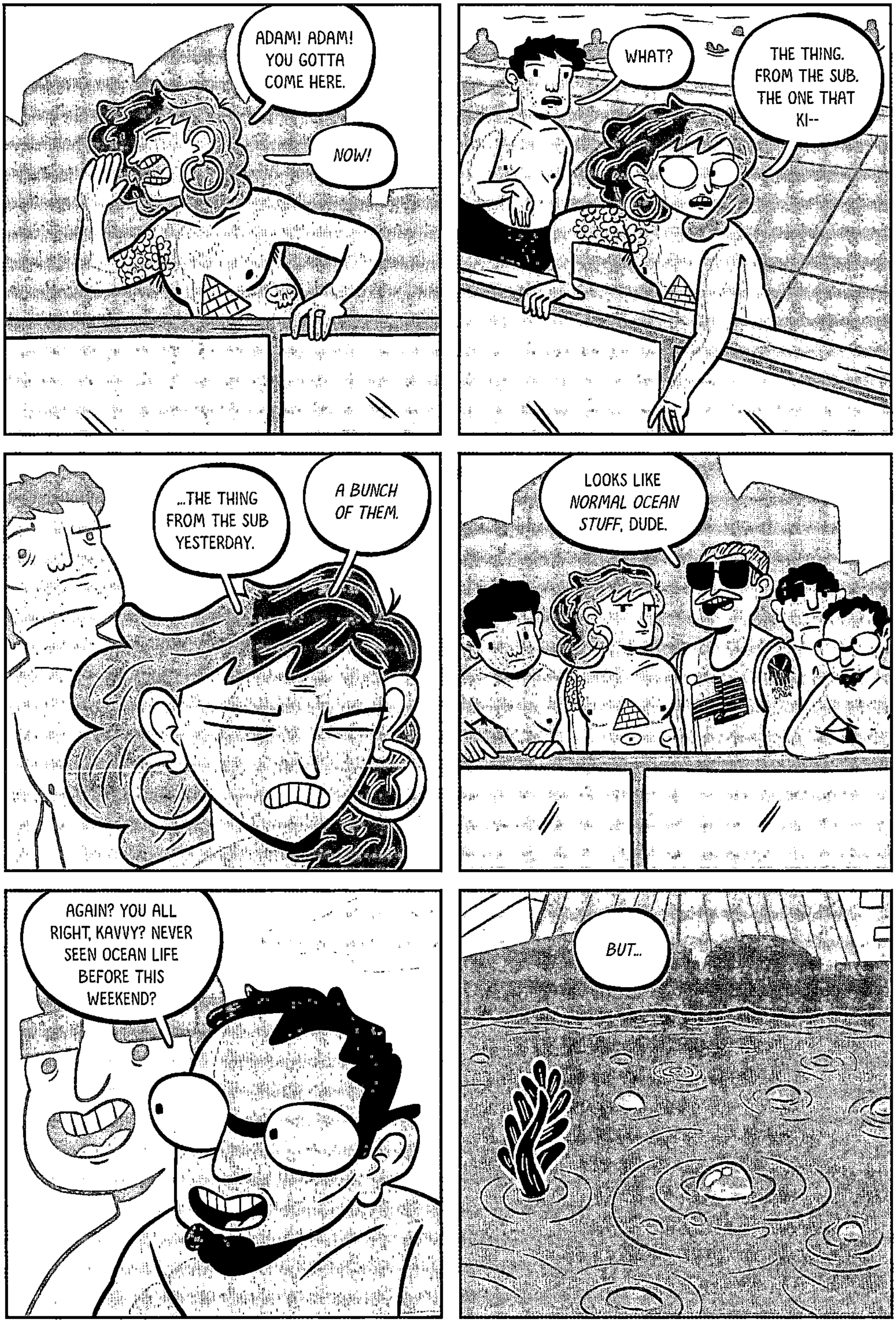
ADAM! ADAM! YOU GOTTA COME HERE.
NOW!
WHAT?
THE THING. FROM THE SUB. THE ONE THAT KI--
...THE THING FROM THE SUB YESTERDAY.
A BUNCH OF THEM.
LOOKS LIKE *NORMAL OCEAN STUFF*, DUDE.
AGAIN? YOU ALL RIGHT, KAVVY? NEVER SEEN OCEAN LIFE BEFORE THIS WEEKEND?
BUT...

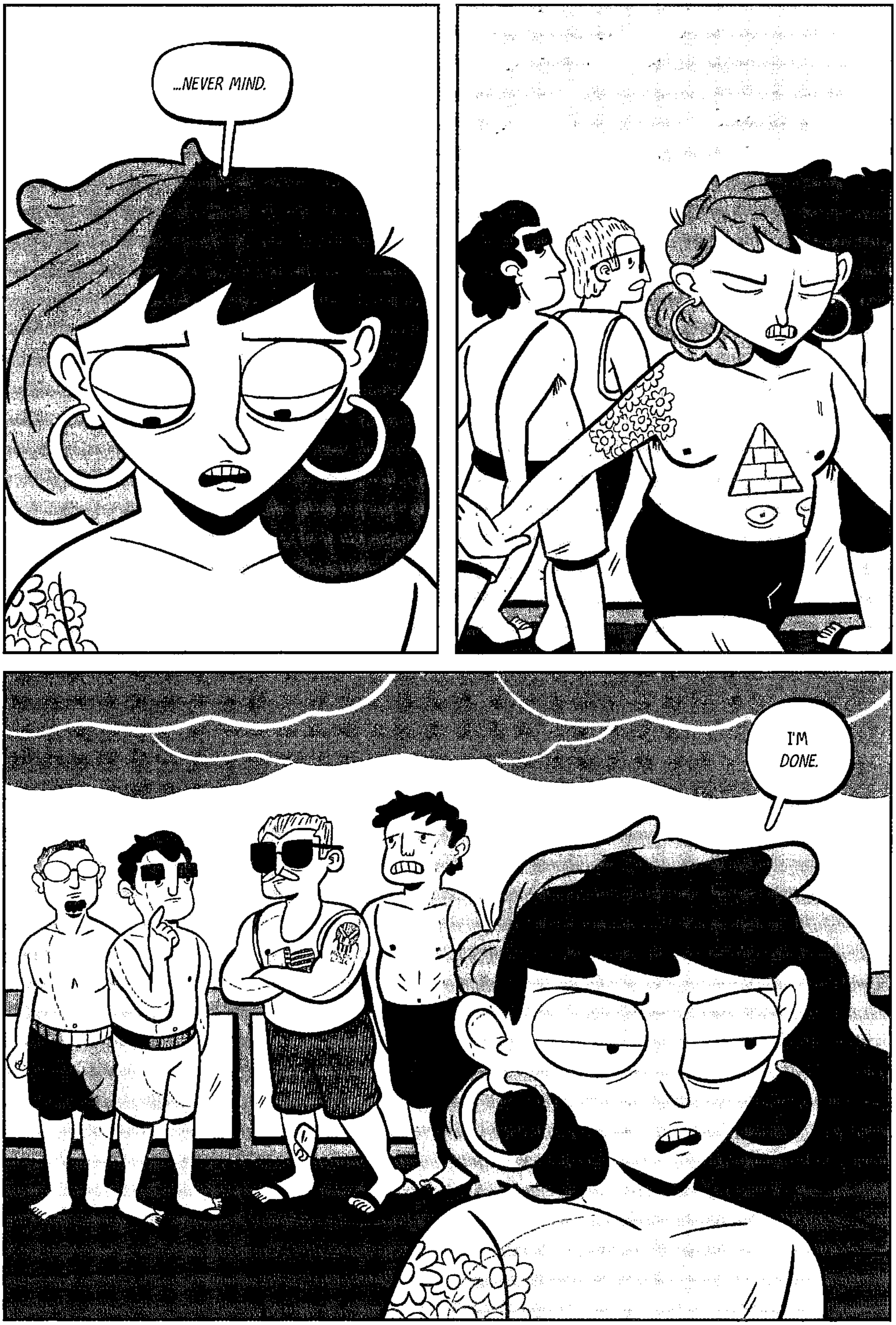
...NEVER MIND.
I'M DONE.

I'M DONE.
SLAM!
DONE!
YOUR BED MADE BY:
...AH, FUCK IT.

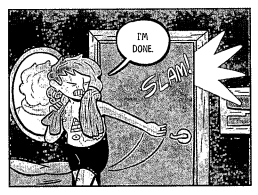

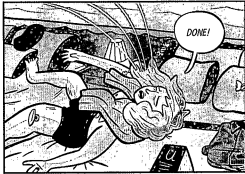

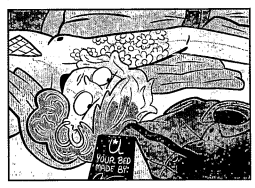

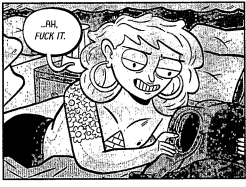

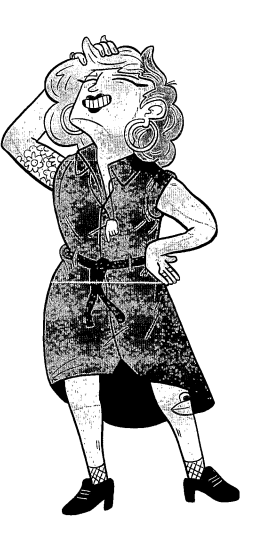

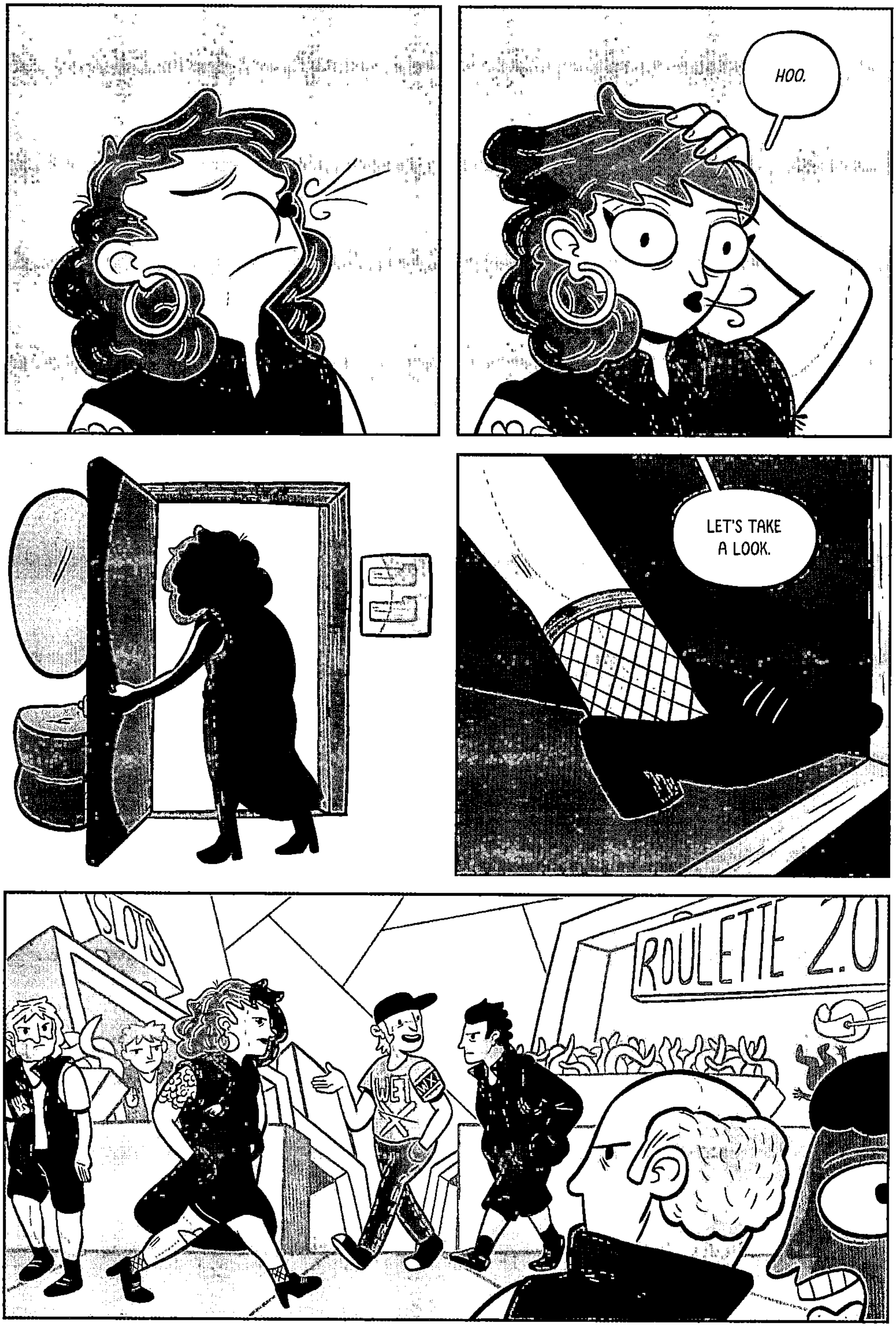
HOO.
LET'S TAKE A LOOK.
SLOTS
ROULETTE 2.0
WET

3:00 PM	FRIEDMANN ROOM: *CROSS-INDUSTRY SUCCESS SECRETS*
4:00 PM	FRIEDMANN ROOM: *SHED YOUR OBSTACLES FOR UNLIMITED GROWTH!*
5:00 PM	ALEXANDRIAS ROOM + VEERMAN ROOM: *BREAKOUT SESSIONS: FORGING A NETWORK IN THE WORLD TO COME*
6:00 PM	MOLOCH ROOM: *BANQUET DINNER NEW MEMBERS WELCOME!*

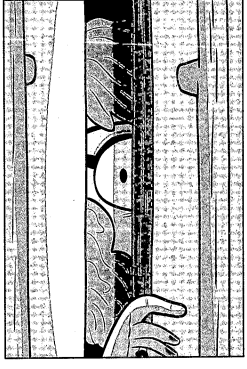

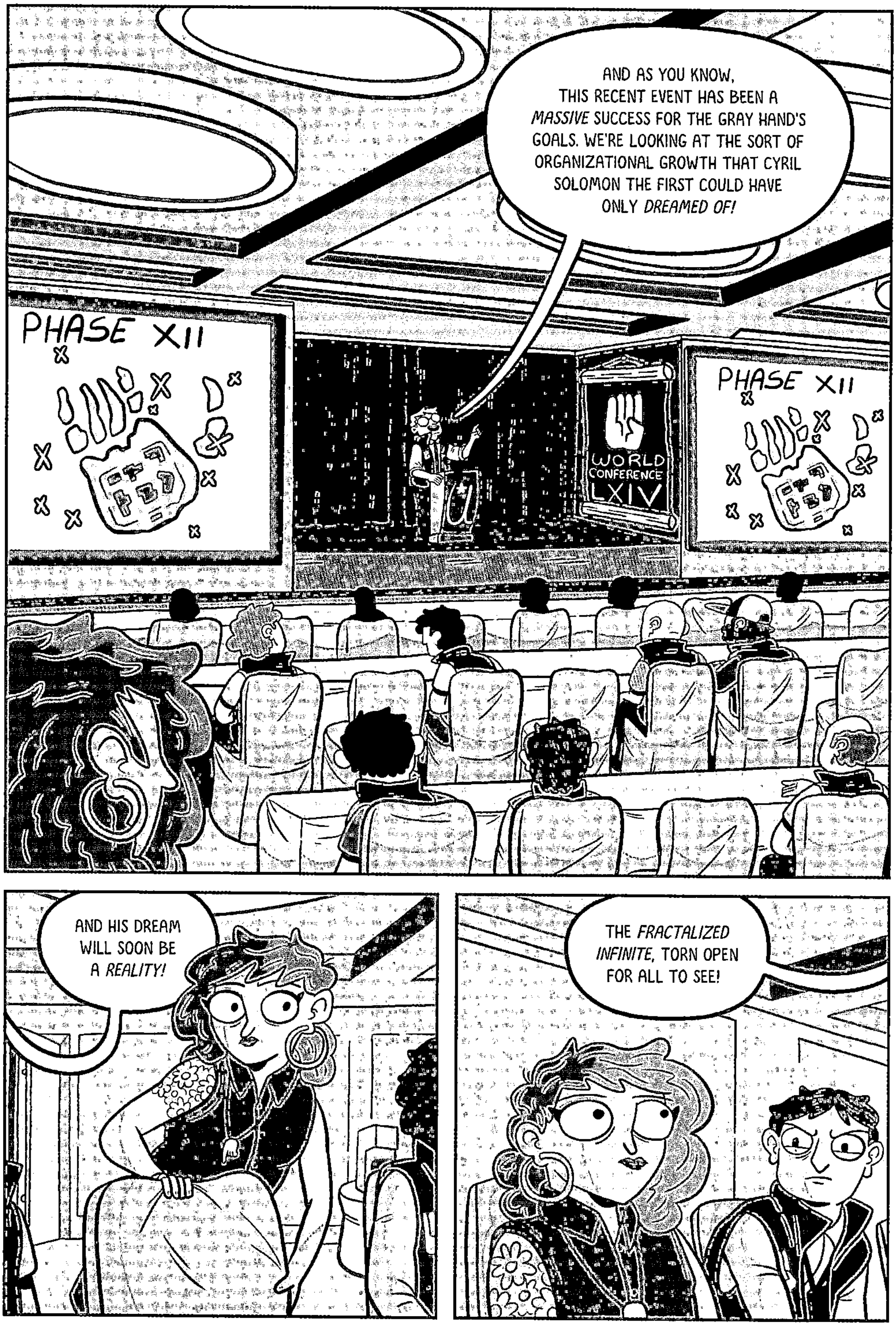
AND AS YOU KNOW, THIS RECENT EVENT HAS BEEN A *MASSIVE* SUCCESS FOR THE GRAY HAND'S GOALS. WE'RE LOOKING AT THE SORT OF ORGANIZATIONAL GROWTH THAT CYRIL SOLOMON THE FIRST COULD HAVE ONLY *DREAMED OF!*
PHASE XII
WORLD CONFERENCE LXIV
PHASE XII
AND HIS DREAM WILL SOON BE A *REALITY!*
THE *FRACTALIZED INFINITE*, TORN OPEN FOR ALL TO SEE!

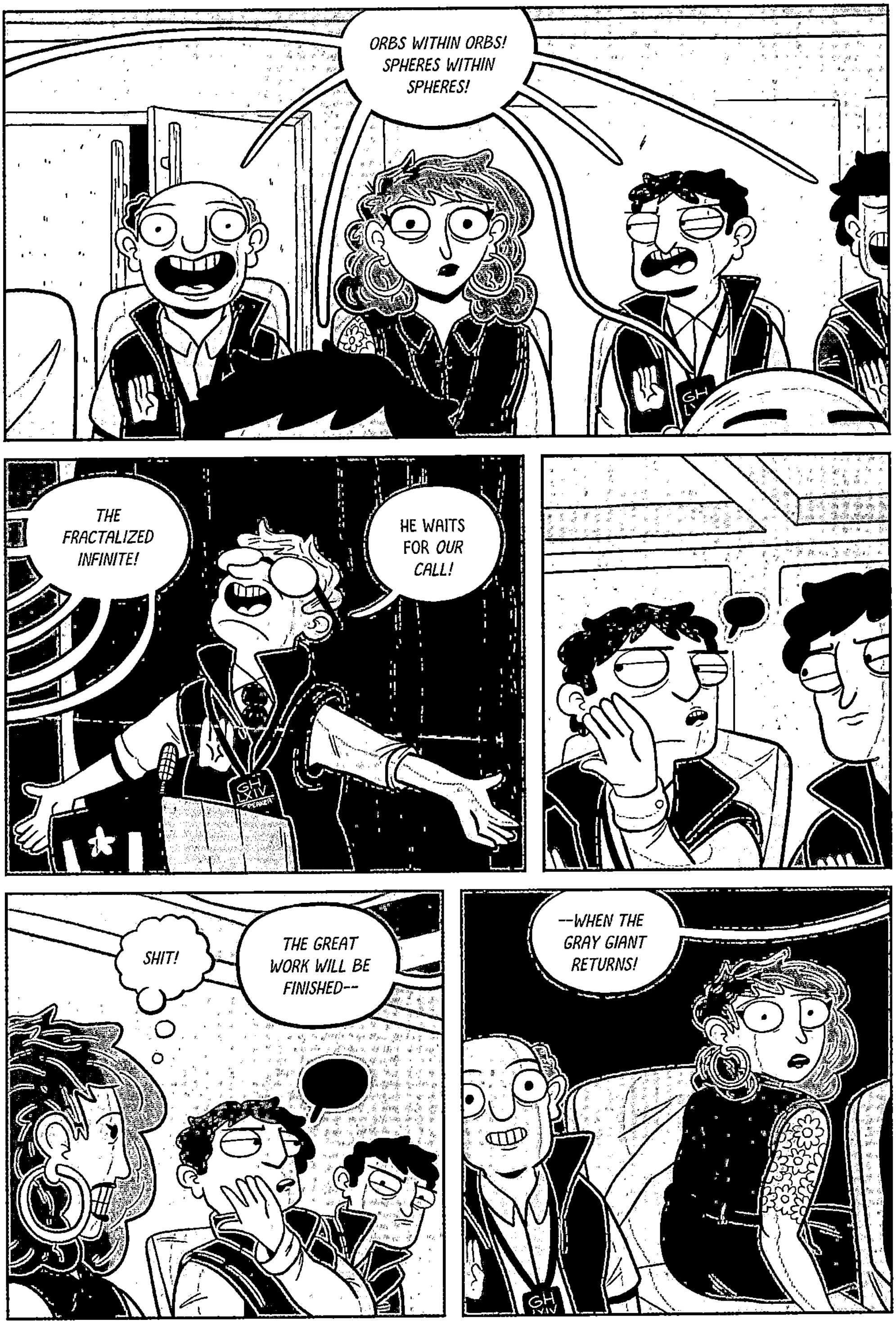
ORBS WITHIN ORBS! SPHERES WITHIN SPHERES!
THE FRACTALIZED INFINITE!
HE WAITS FOR OUR CALL!
SHIT!
THE GREAT WORK WILL BE FINISHED--
--WHEN THE GRAY GIANT RETURNS!

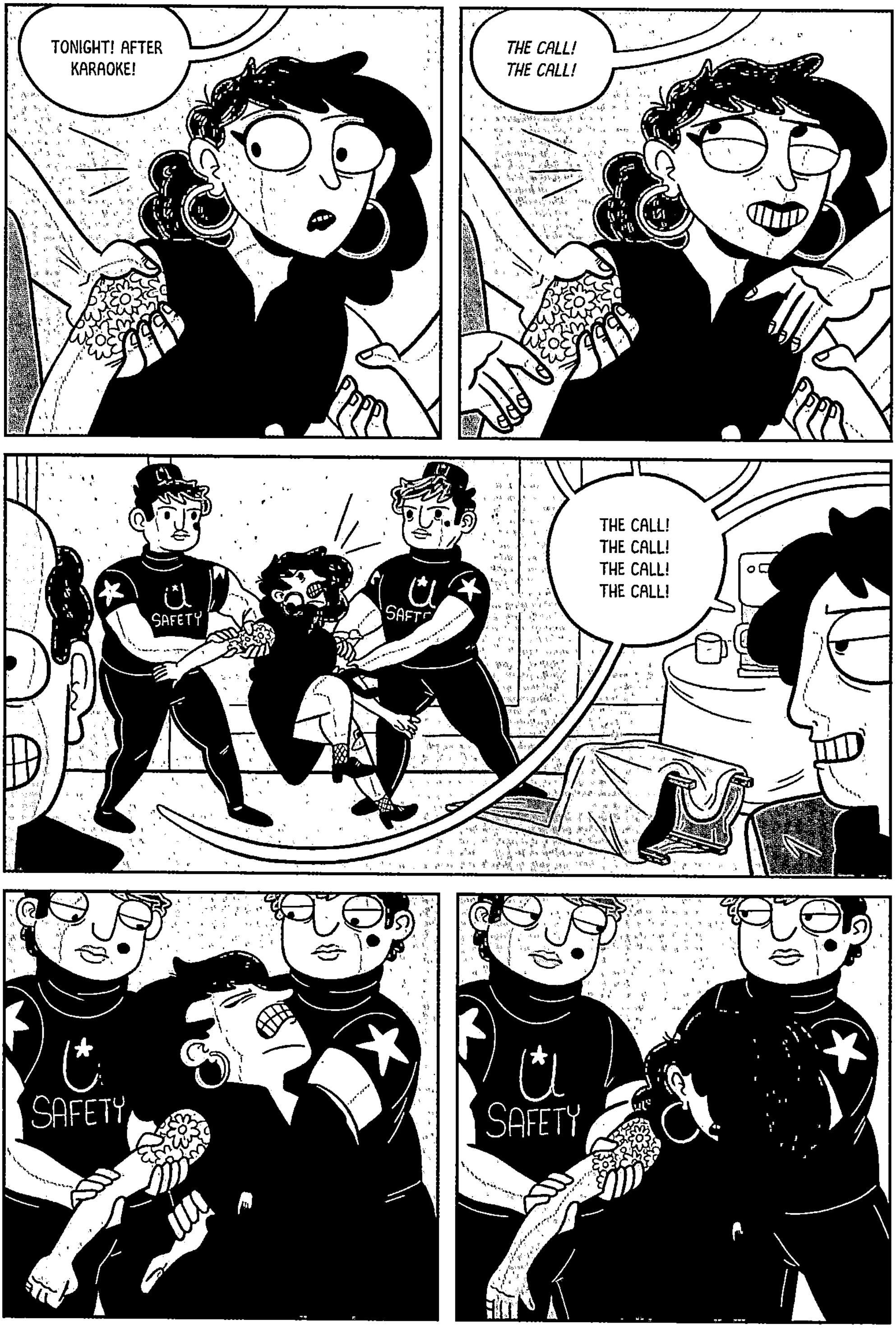
TONIGHT! AFTER KARAOKE!
THE CALL! THE CALL!
THE CALL! THE CALL! THE CALL! THE CALL!
SAFETY
SAFETY
SAFETY
SAFETY

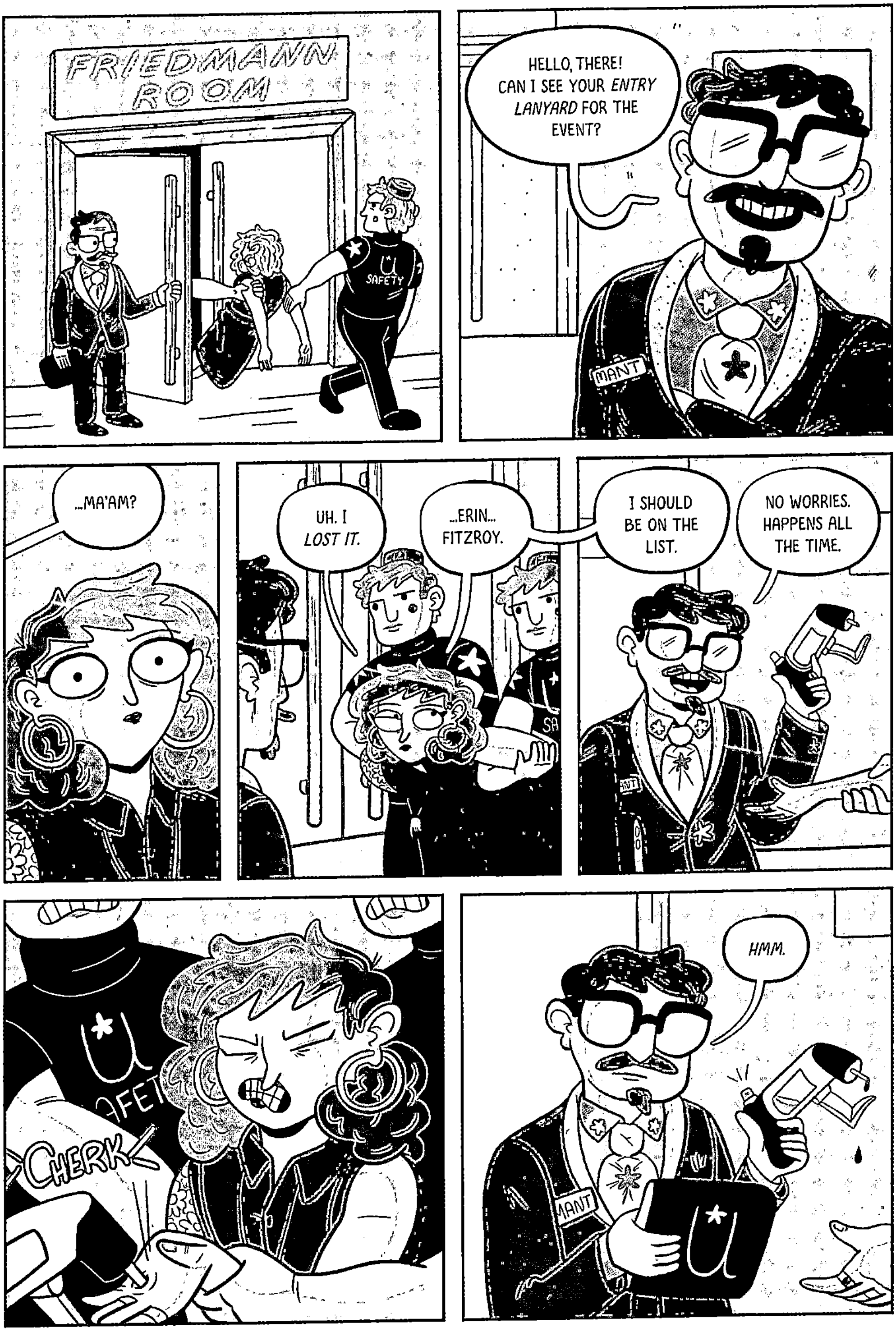
FRIEDMANN ROOM
SAFETY
HELLO, THERE! CAN I SEE YOUR *ENTRY LANYARD* FOR THE EVENT?
MANT
...MA'AM?
UH. I *LOST IT.*
...ERIN... FITZROY.
I SHOULD BE ON THE LIST.
NO WORRIES. HAPPENS ALL THE TIME.
CHERK
HMM.
MANT

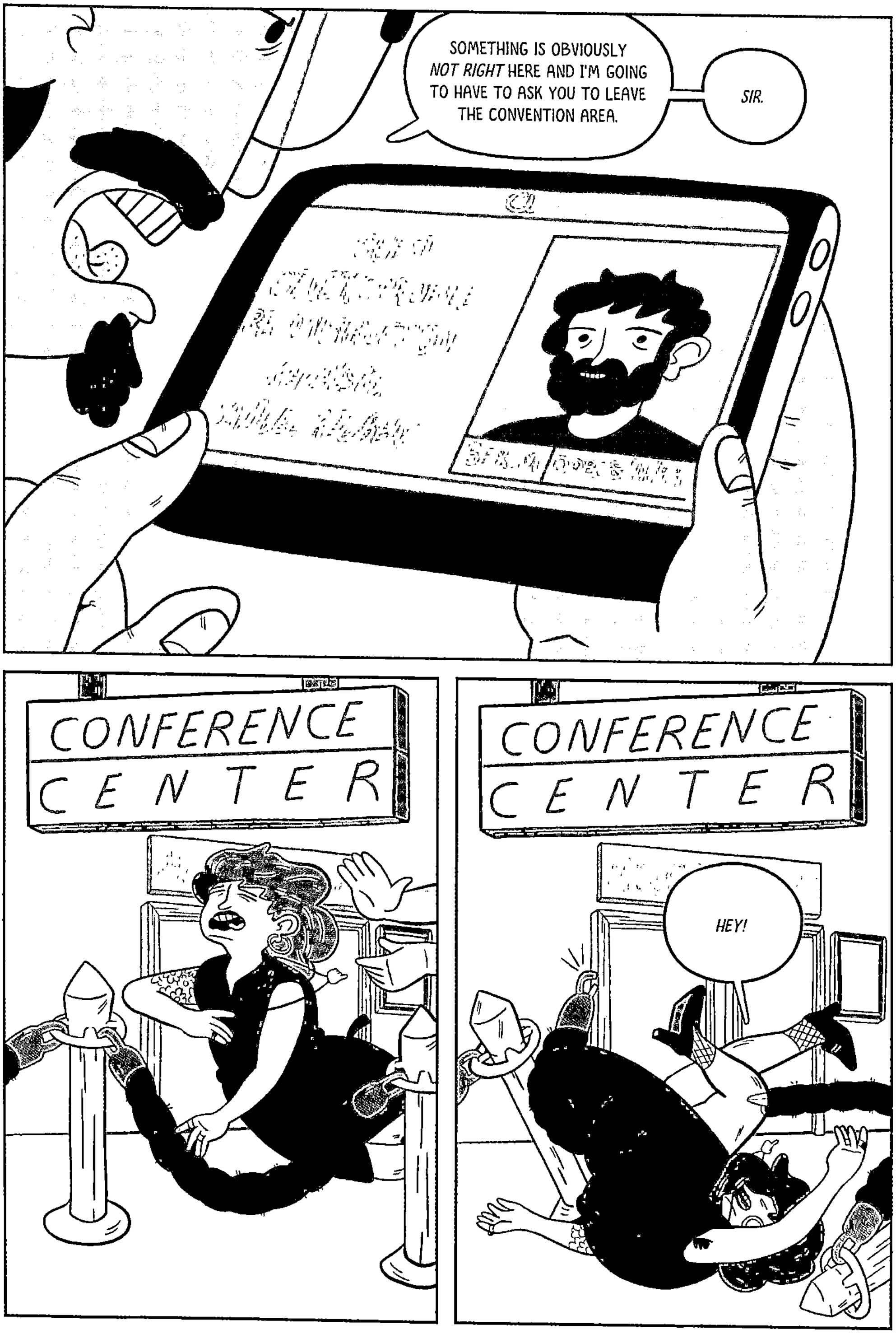
SOMETHING IS OBVIOUSLY *NOT RIGHT* HERE AND I'M GOING TO HAVE TO ASK YOU TO LEAVE THE CONVENTION AREA.
SIR.
CONFERENCE CENTER
CONFERENCE CENTER
HEY!

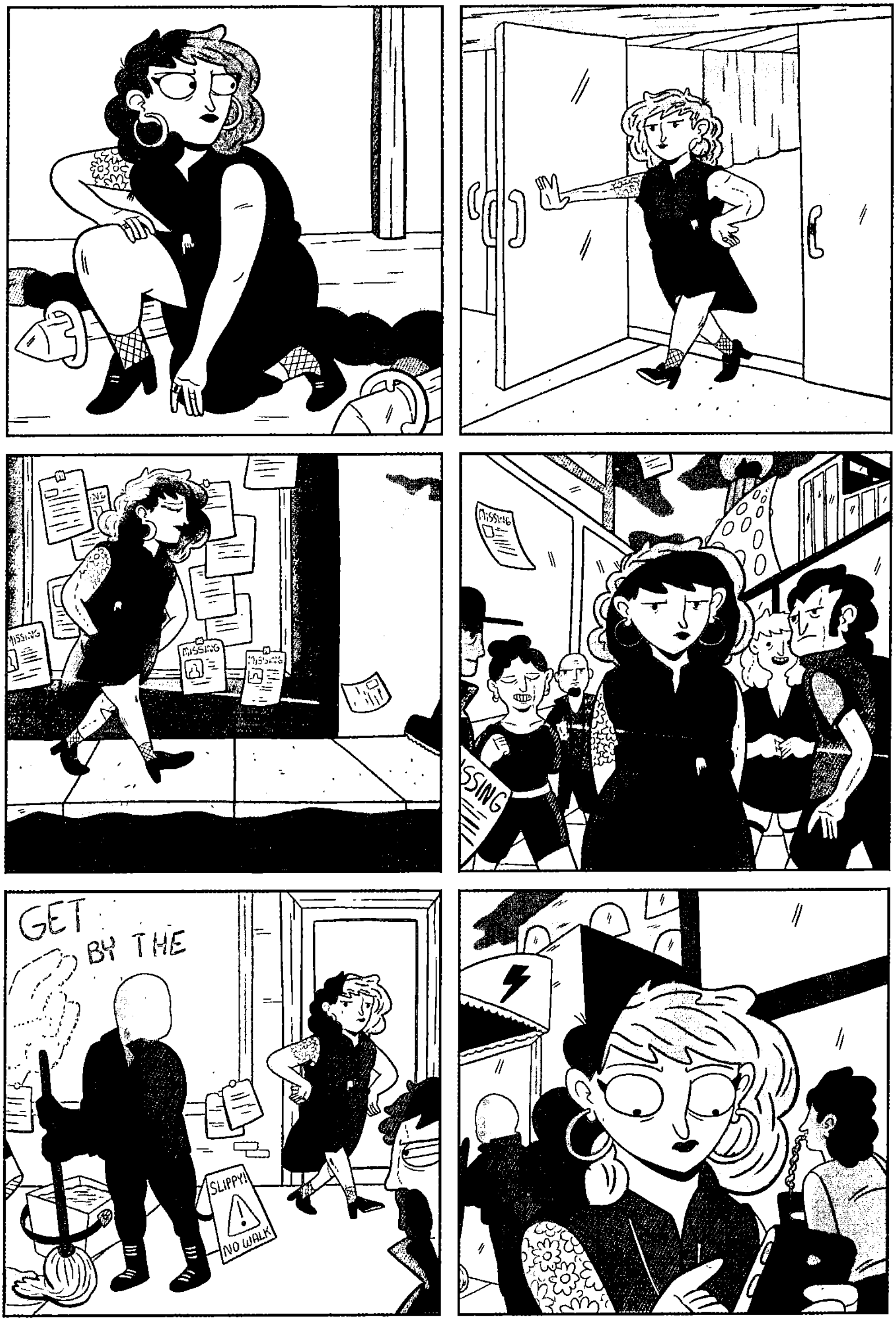
MISSING
MISSING
MISSING
MISSING
SSING
GET
BY THE
SLIPPY!
NO WALK

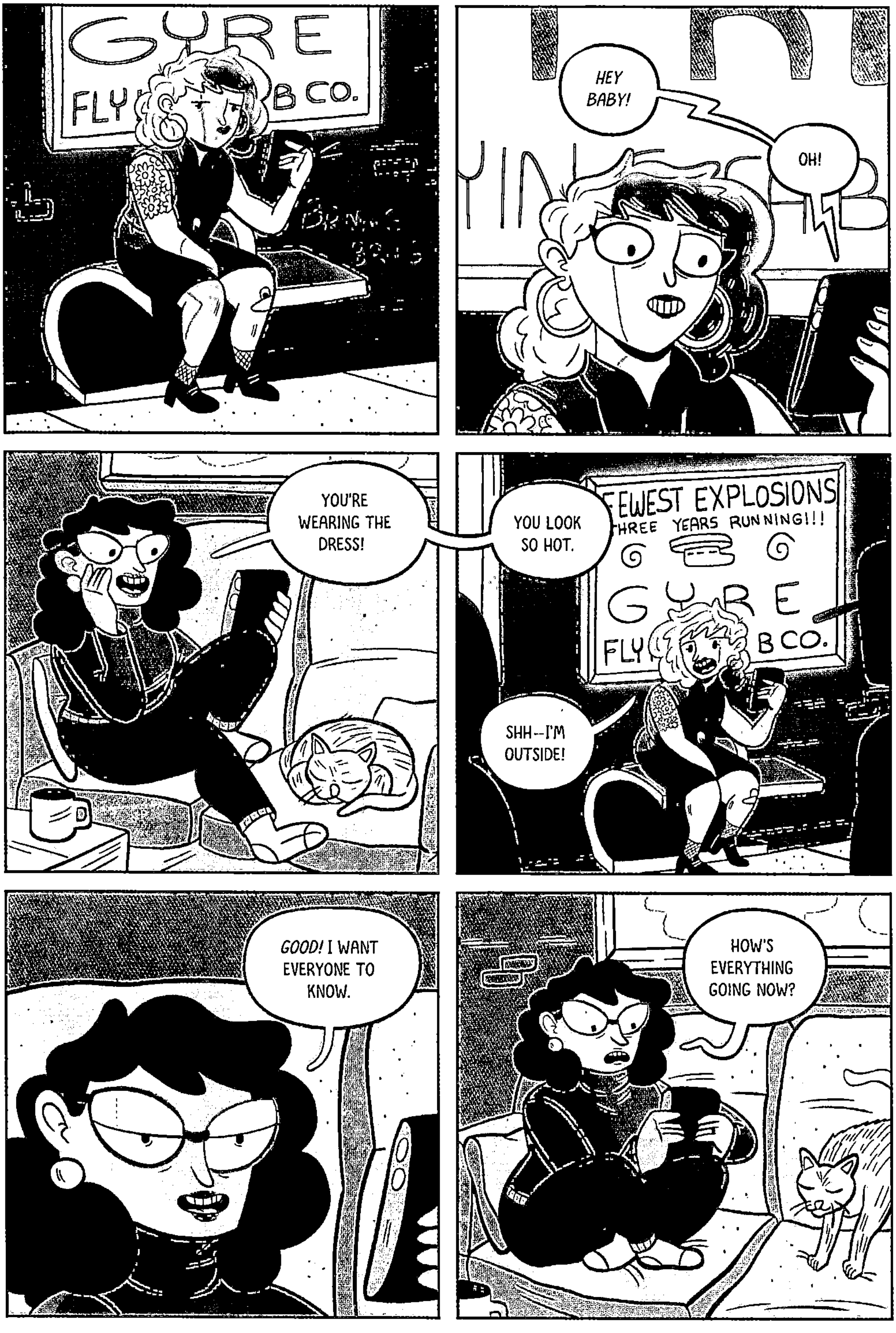
GYRE
FLY
B CO.
HEY BABY!
OH!
YOU'RE WEARING THE DRESS!
YOU LOOK SO HOT.
FEWEST EXPLOSIONS
THREE YEARS RUNNING!!!
GYRE
FLY
B CO.
SHH--I'M OUTSIDE!
GOOD! I WANT EVERYONE TO KNOW.
HOW'S EVERYTHING GOING NOW?

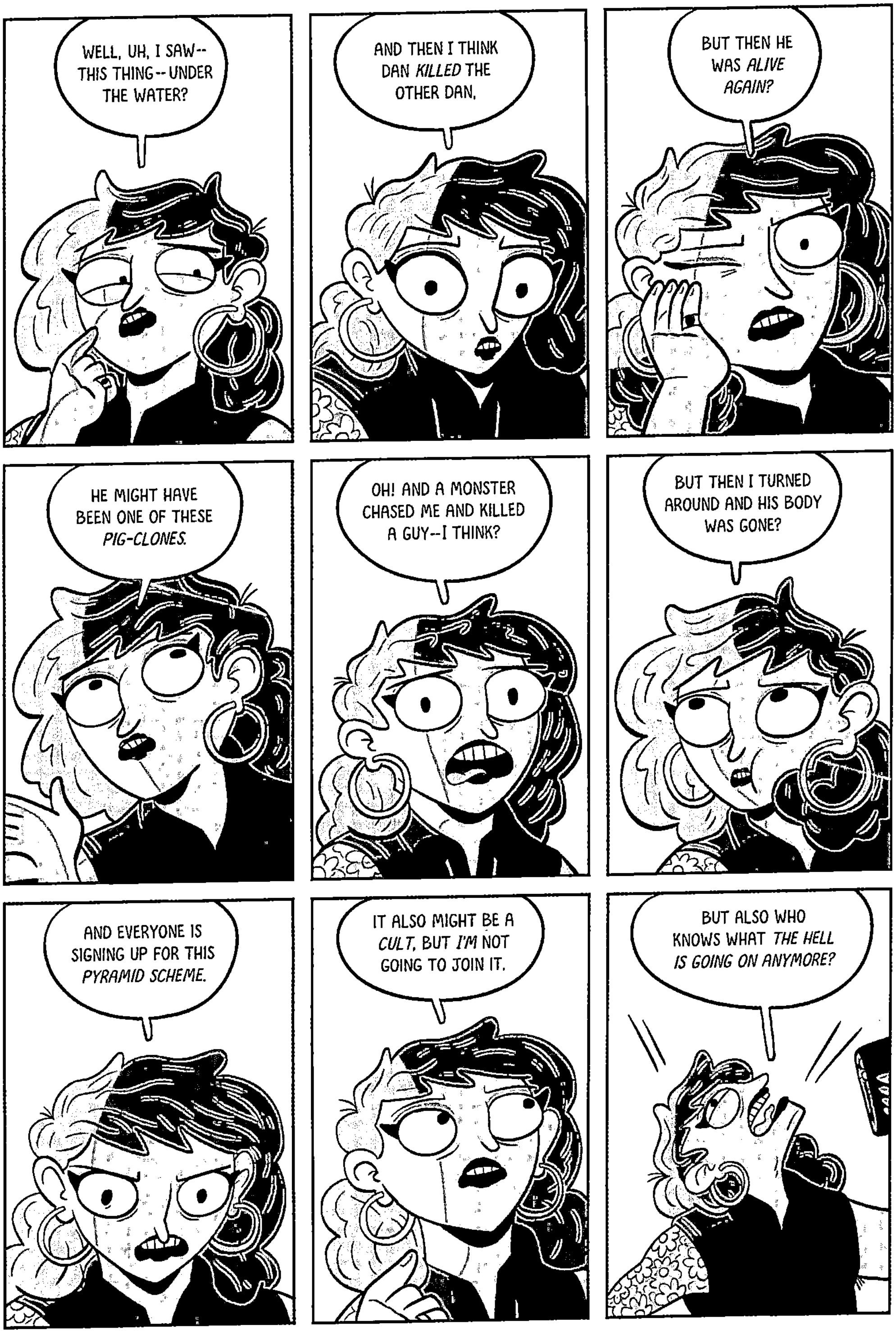
WELL, UH, I SAW--THIS THING--UNDER THE WATER?
AND THEN I THINK DAN *KILLED* THE OTHER DAN.
BUT THEN HE WAS *ALIVE AGAIN?*
HE MIGHT HAVE BEEN ONE OF THESE *PIG-CLONES.*
OH! AND A MONSTER CHASED ME AND KILLED A GUY--I THINK?
BUT THEN I TURNED AROUND AND HIS BODY WAS GONE?
AND EVERYONE IS SIGNING UP FOR THIS *PYRAMID SCHEME.*
IT ALSO MIGHT BE A *CULT,* BUT *I'M* NOT GOING TO JOIN IT.
BUT ALSO WHO KNOWS WHAT *THE HELL IS GOING ON ANYMORE?*

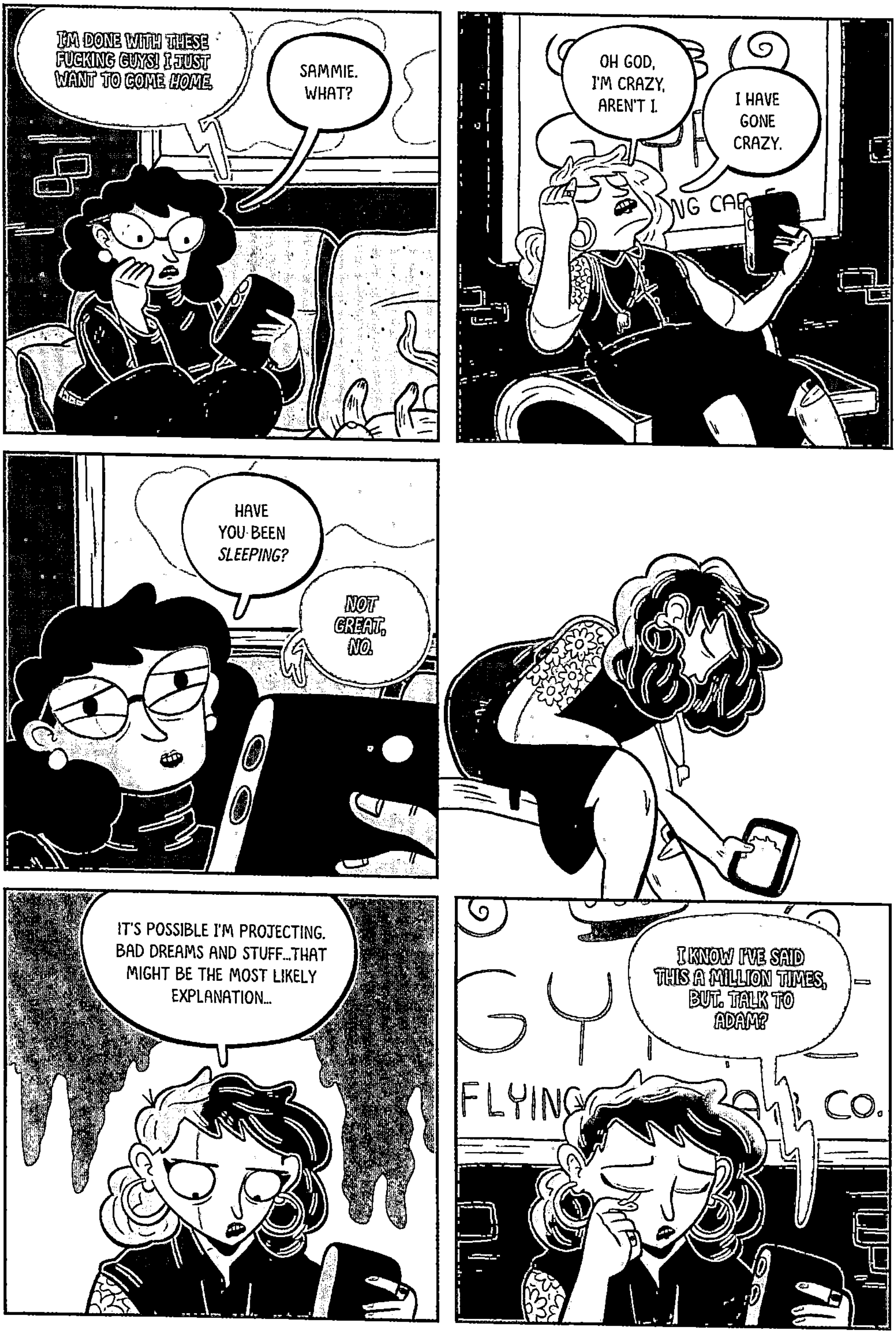

I'M DONE WITH THESE FUCKING GUYS! I JUST WANT TO COME HOME.
SAMMIE. WHAT?
OH GOD, I'M CRAZY, AREN'T I.
I HAVE GONE CRAZY.
NG CAF
HAVE YOU BEEN SLEEPING?
NOT GREAT, NO.
IT'S POSSIBLE I'M PROJECTING. BAD DREAMS AND STUFF...THAT MIGHT BE THE MOST LIKELY EXPLANATION...
I KNOW I'VE SAID THIS A MILLION TIMES, BUT. TALK TO ADAM?
FLYIN CO.

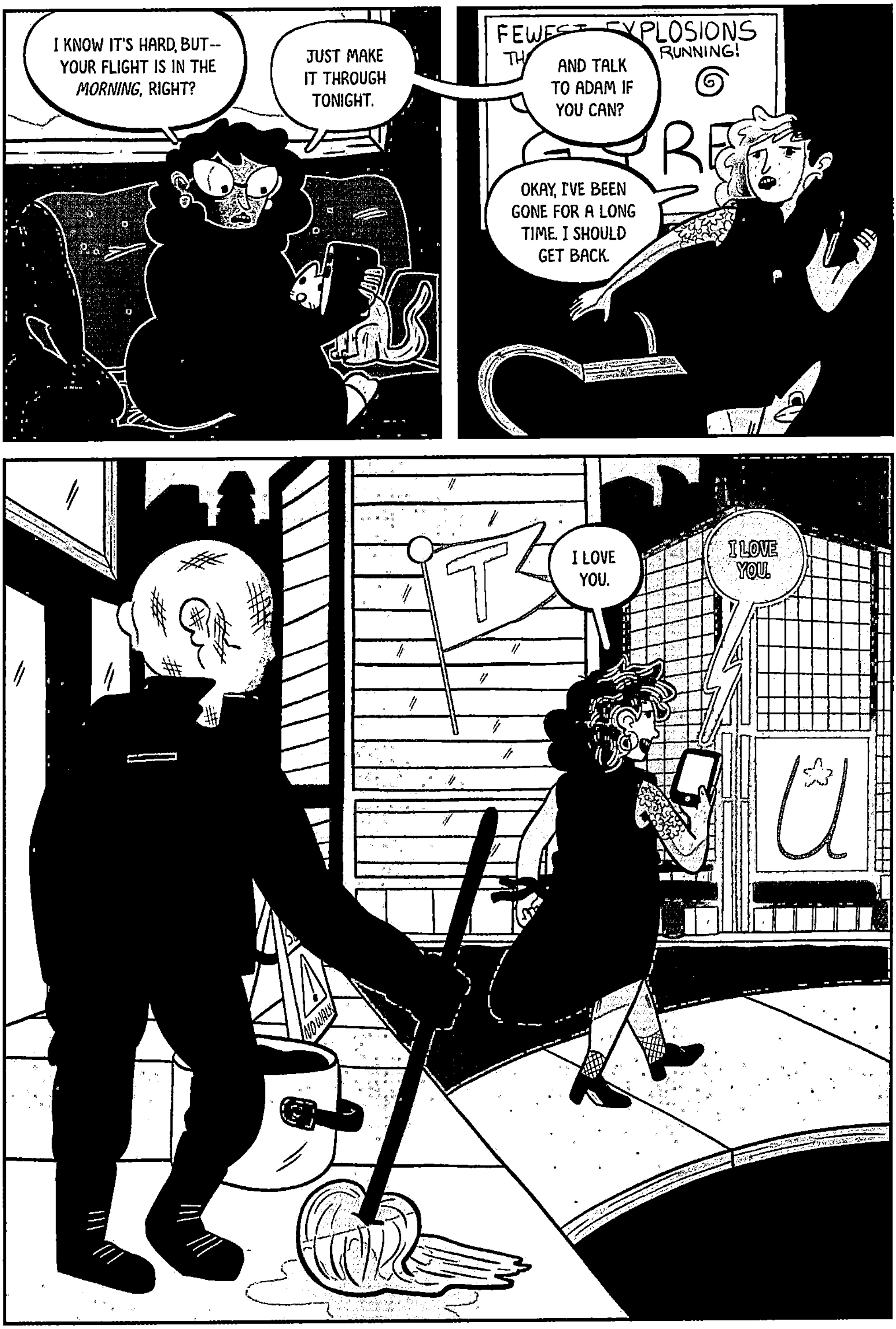
I KNOW IT'S HARD, BUT--
YOUR FLIGHT IS IN THE *MORNING,* RIGHT?
JUST MAKE IT THROUGH TONIGHT.
AND TALK TO ADAM IF YOU CAN?
FEWEST EXPLOSIONS
RUNNING!
OKAY, I'VE BEEN GONE FOR A LONG TIME. I SHOULD GET BACK.
I LOVE YOU.
I LOVE YOU.
T
U

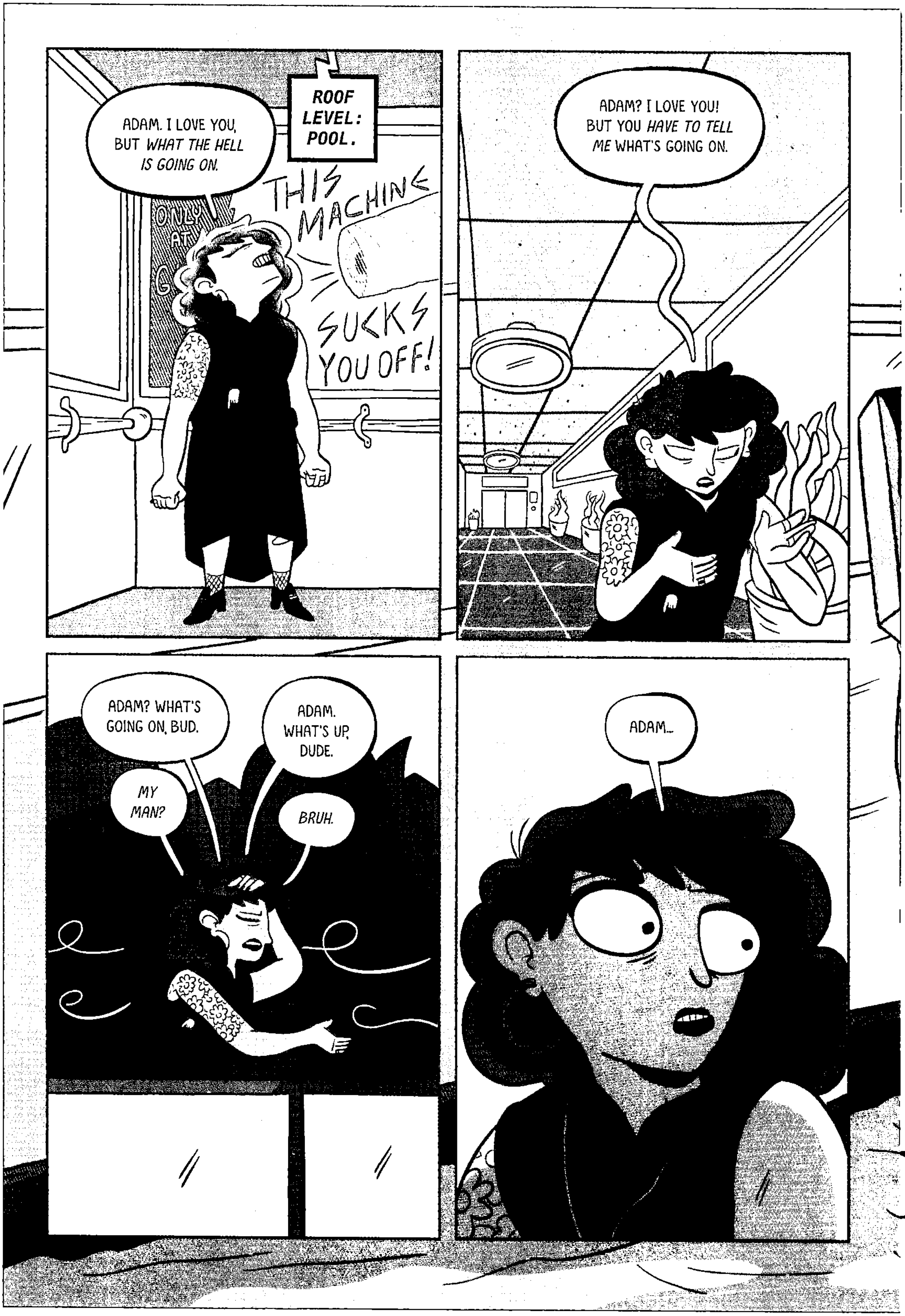
ROOF LEVEL: POOL.
ADAM. I LOVE YOU, BUT WHAT THE HELL IS GOING ON.
ONLY AT
THIS MACHINE SUCKS YOU OFF!
ADAM? I LOVE YOU! BUT YOU HAVE TO TELL ME WHAT'S GOING ON.
ADAM? WHAT'S GOING ON, BUD.
ADAM. WHAT'S UP, DUDE.
MY MAN?
BRUH.
ADAM...

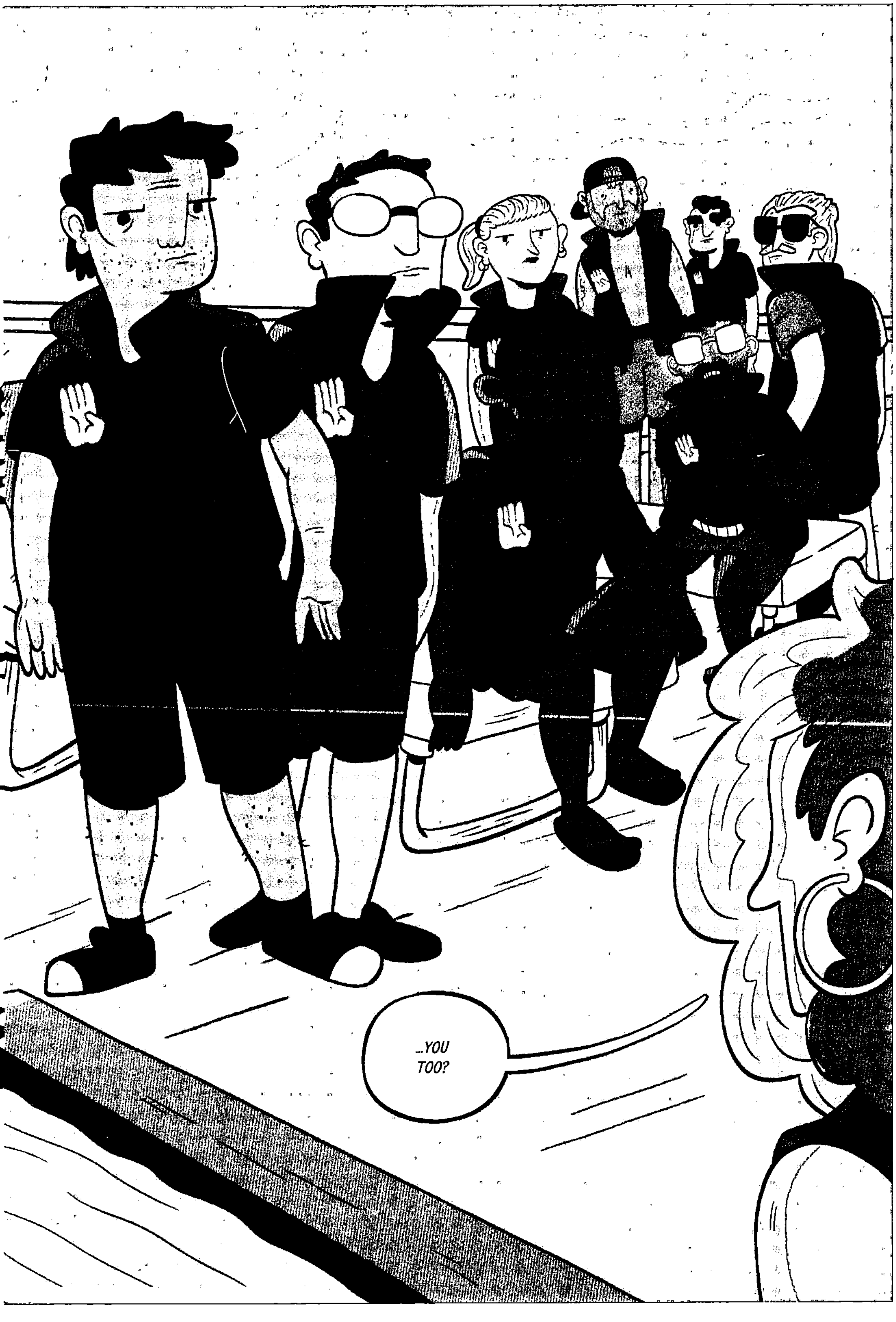
...YOU TOO?

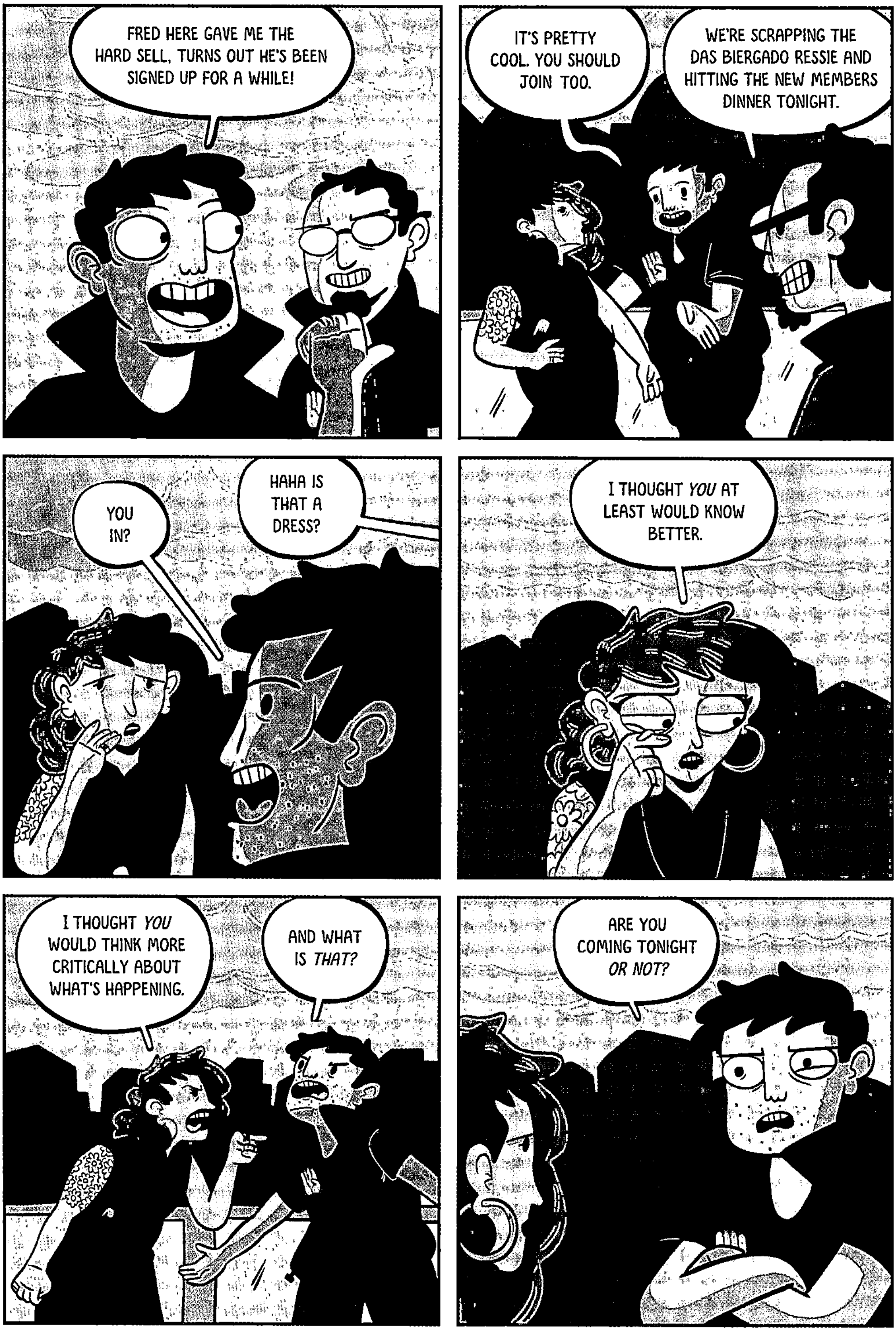

FRED HERE GAVE ME THE HARD SELL, TURNS OUT HE'S BEEN SIGNED UP FOR A WHILE!
IT'S PRETTY COOL. YOU SHOULD JOIN TOO.
WE'RE SCRAPPING THE DAS BIERGADO RESSIE AND HITTING THE NEW MEMBERS DINNER TONIGHT.
YOU IN?
HAHA IS THAT A DRESS?
I THOUGHT *YOU* AT LEAST WOULD KNOW BETTER.
I THOUGHT *YOU* WOULD THINK MORE CRITICALLY ABOUT WHAT'S HAPPENING.
AND WHAT IS *THAT?*
ARE YOU COMING TONIGHT *OR NOT?*

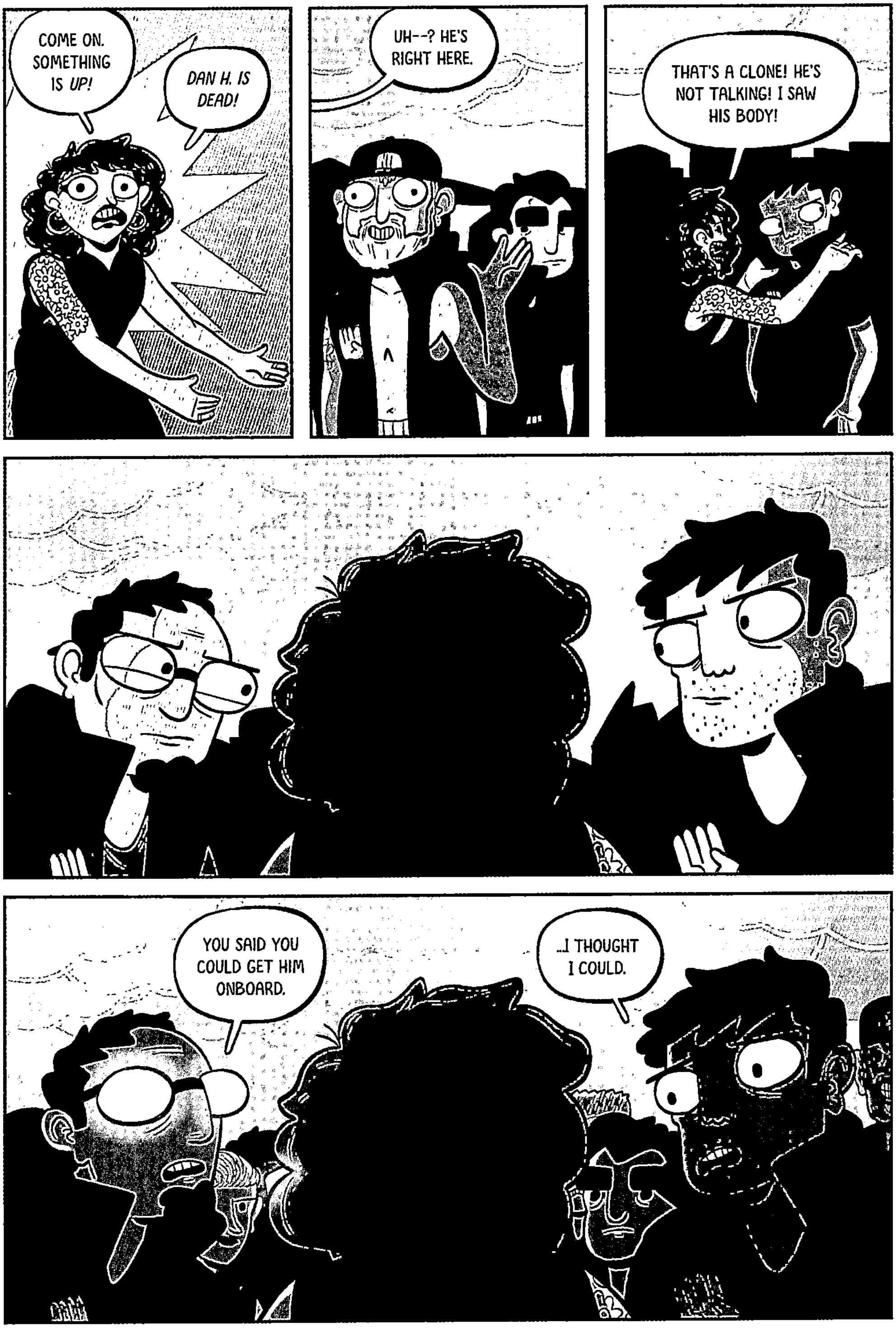
COME ON. SOMETHING IS *UP!*
DAN H. IS DEAD!
UH--? HE'S RIGHT HERE.
THAT'S A CLONE! HE'S NOT TALKING! I SAW HIS BODY!
YOU SAID YOU COULD GET HIM ONBOARD.
..I THOUGHT I COULD.

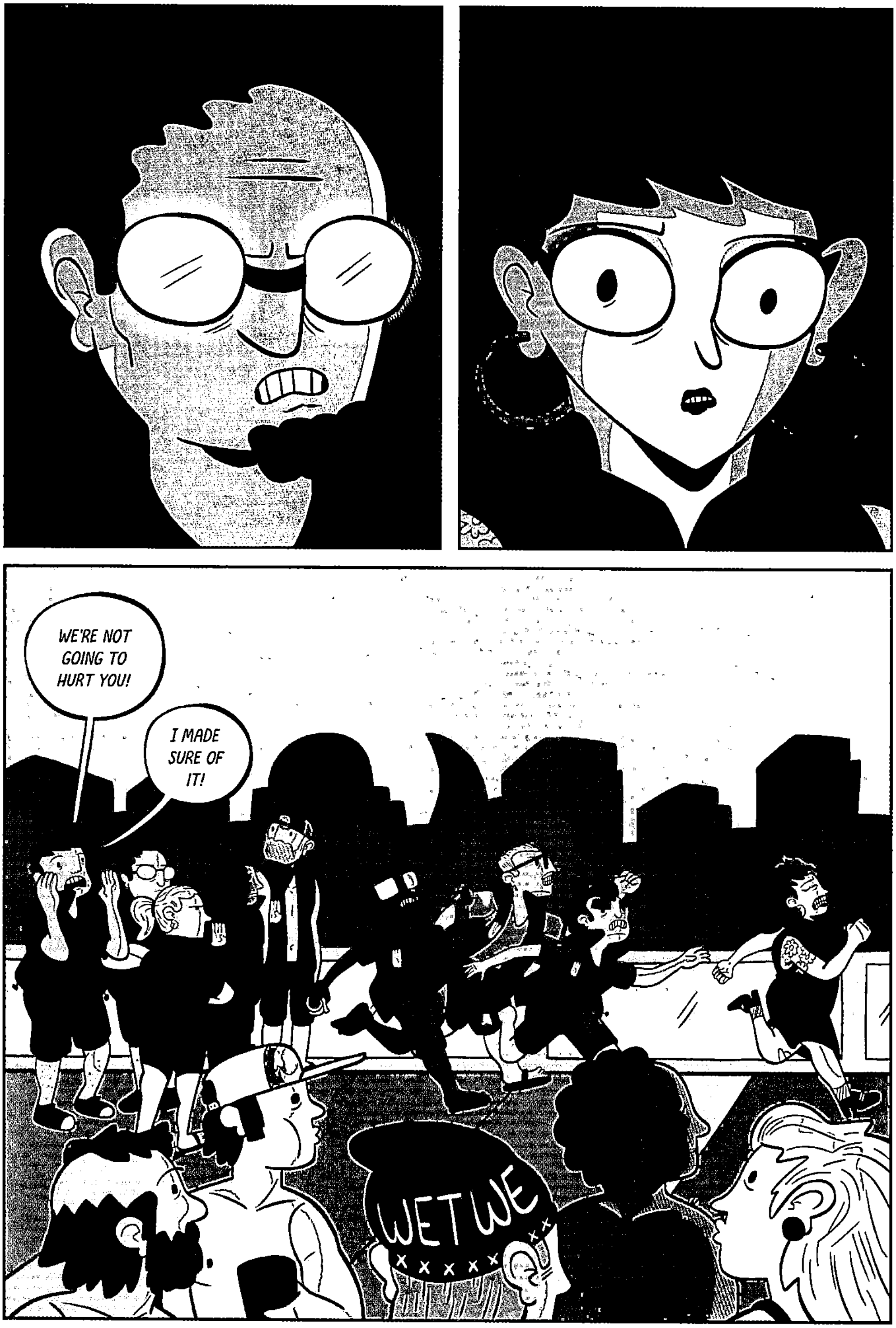
WE'RE NOT GOING TO HURT YOU!
I MADE SURE OF IT!
WETWE

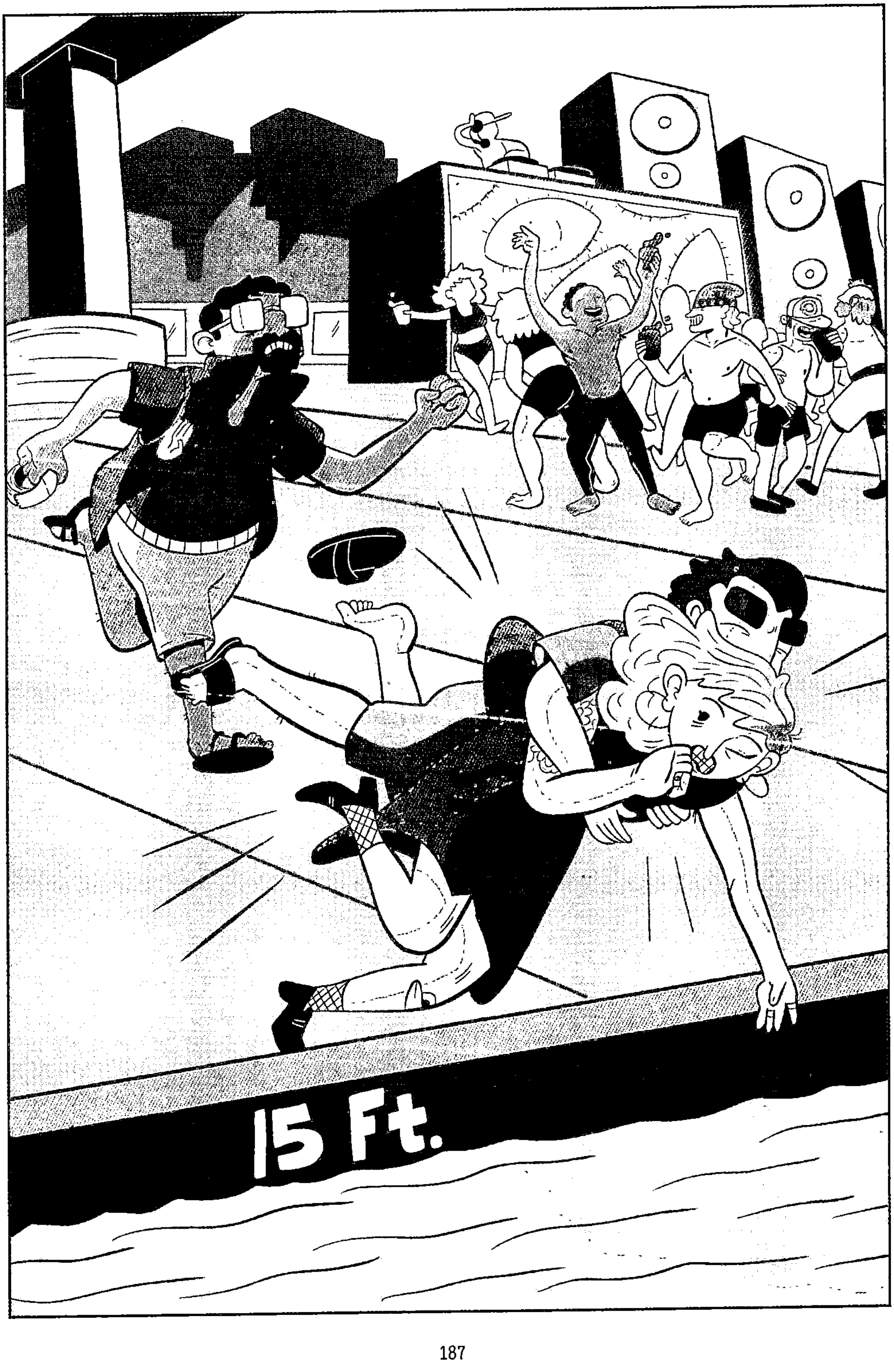
15 Ft.

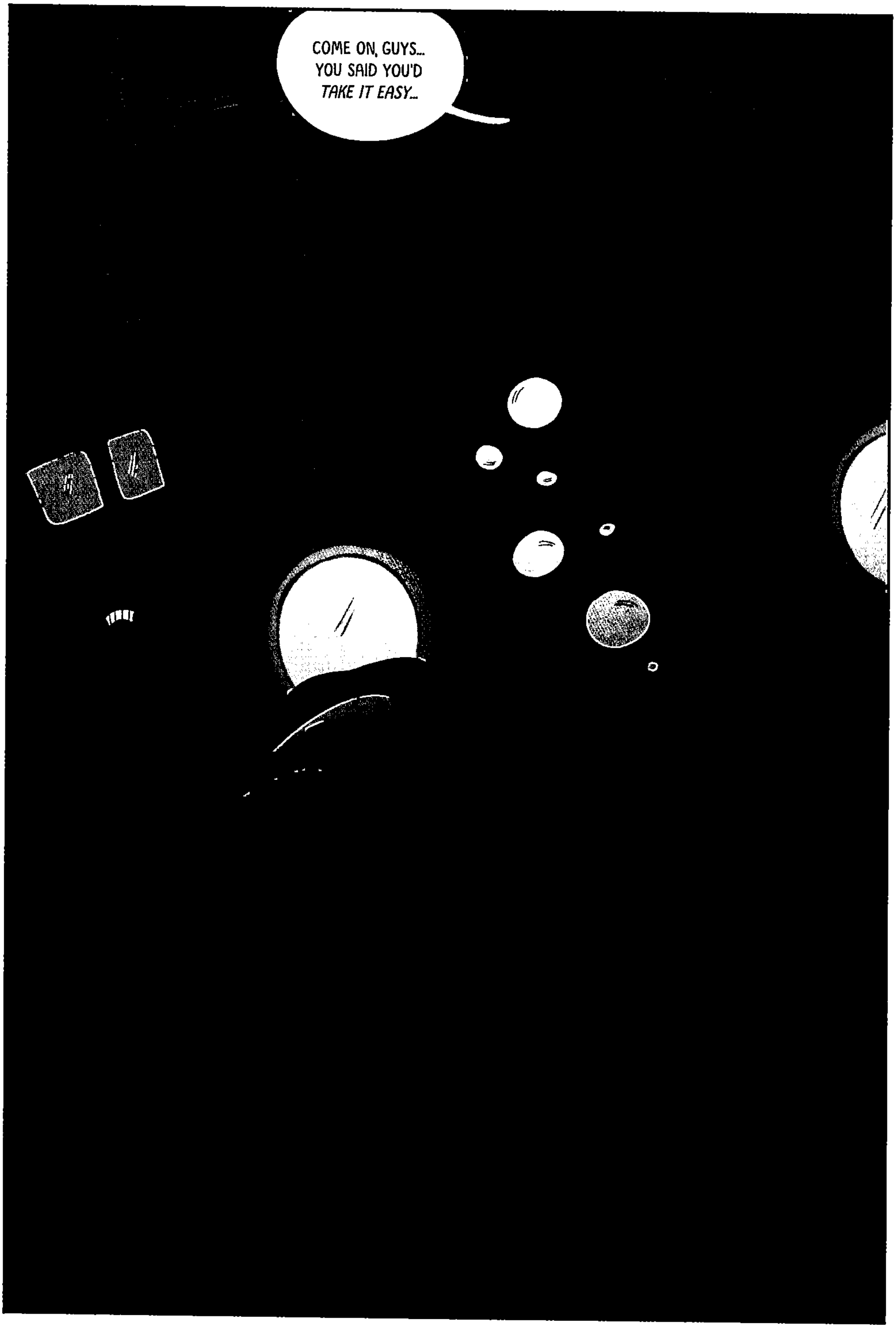
COME ON, GUYS... YOU SAID YOU'D *TAKE IT EASY*...

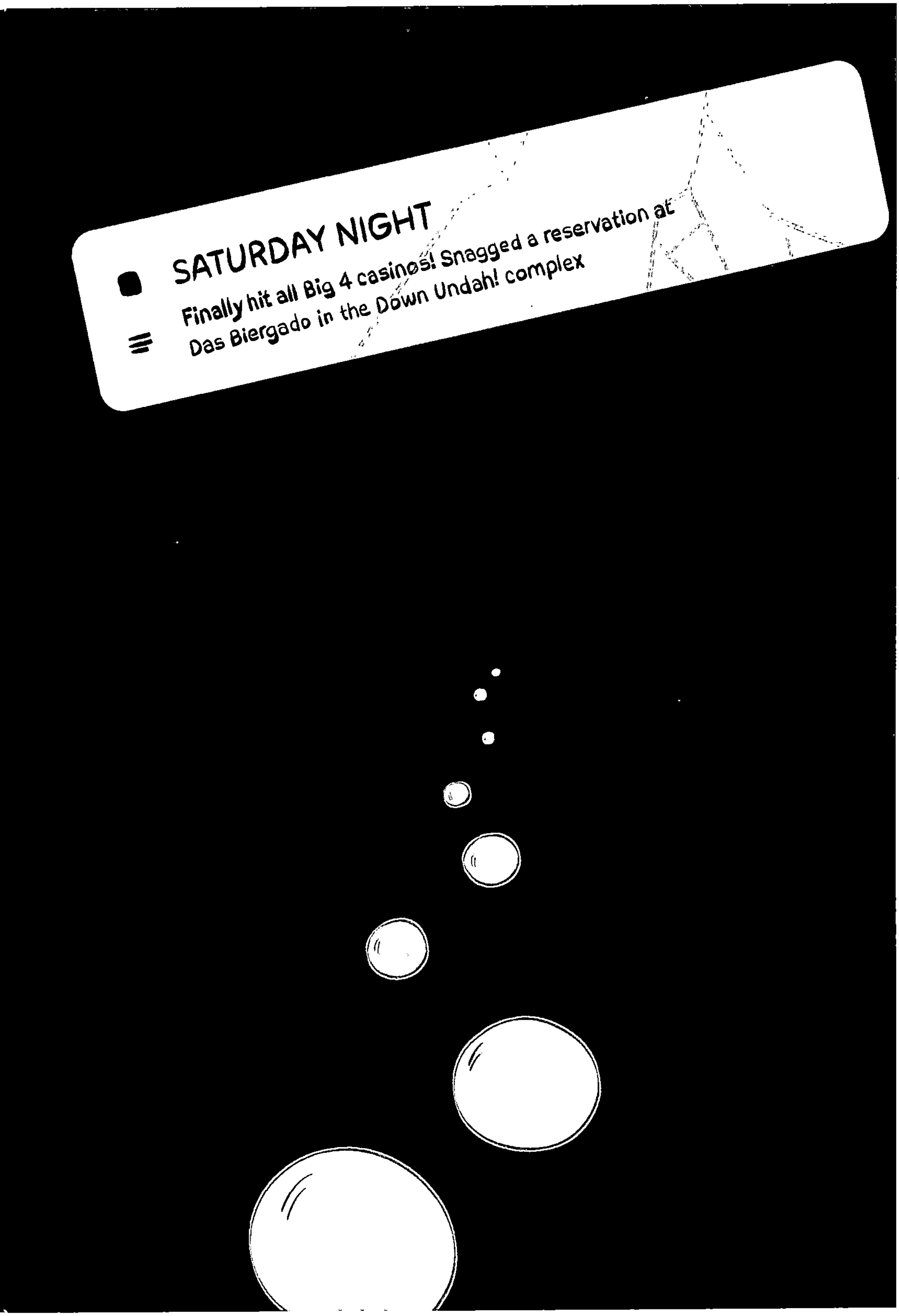
SATURDAY NIGHT
Finally hit all Big 4 casinos! Snagged a reservation at
Das Biergado in the Down Undah! complex

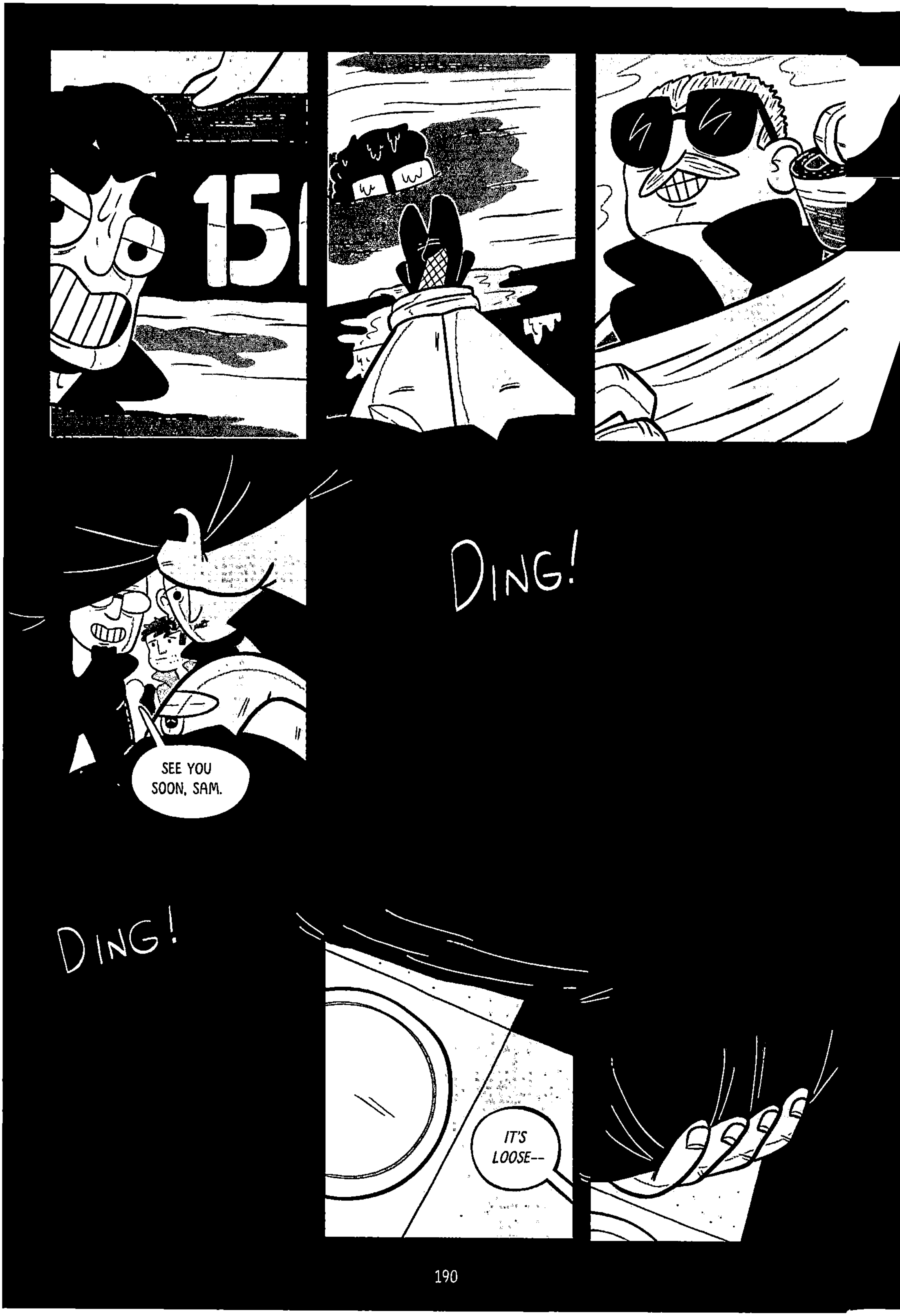
15
DING!
SEE YOU SOON, SAM.
DING!
IT'S LOOSE--

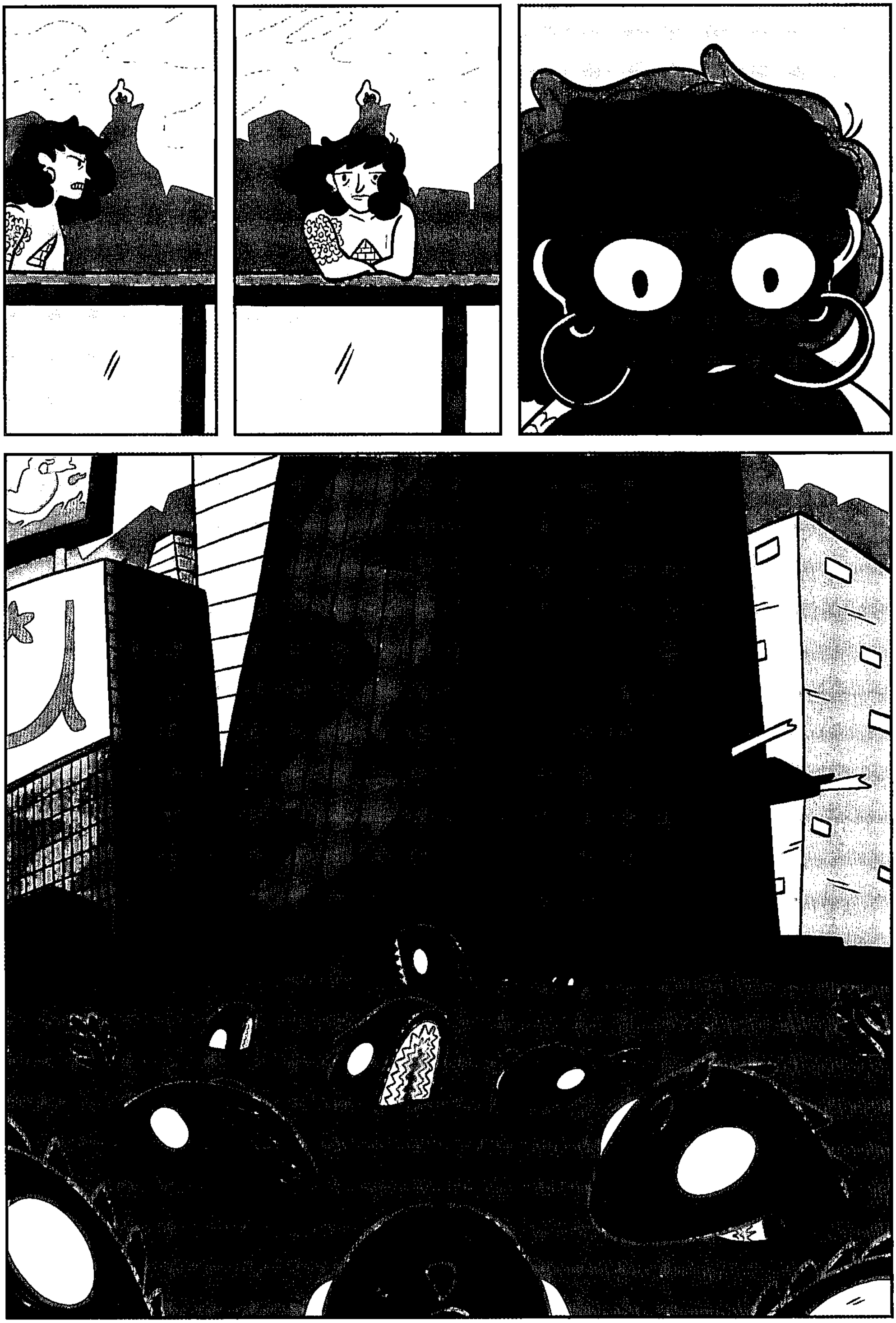

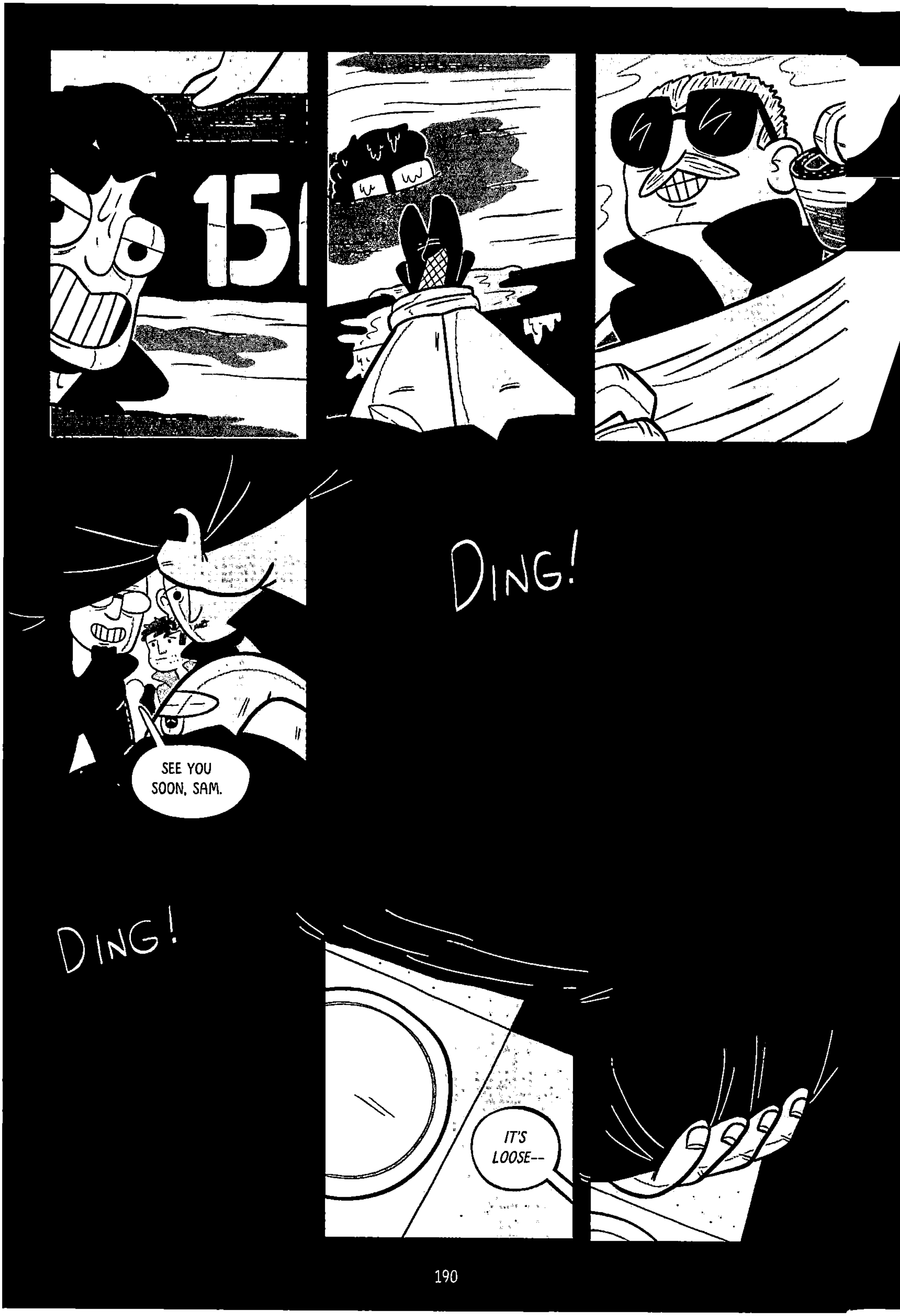
15
DING!
SEE YOU SOON, SAM.
DING!
IT'S LOOSE--

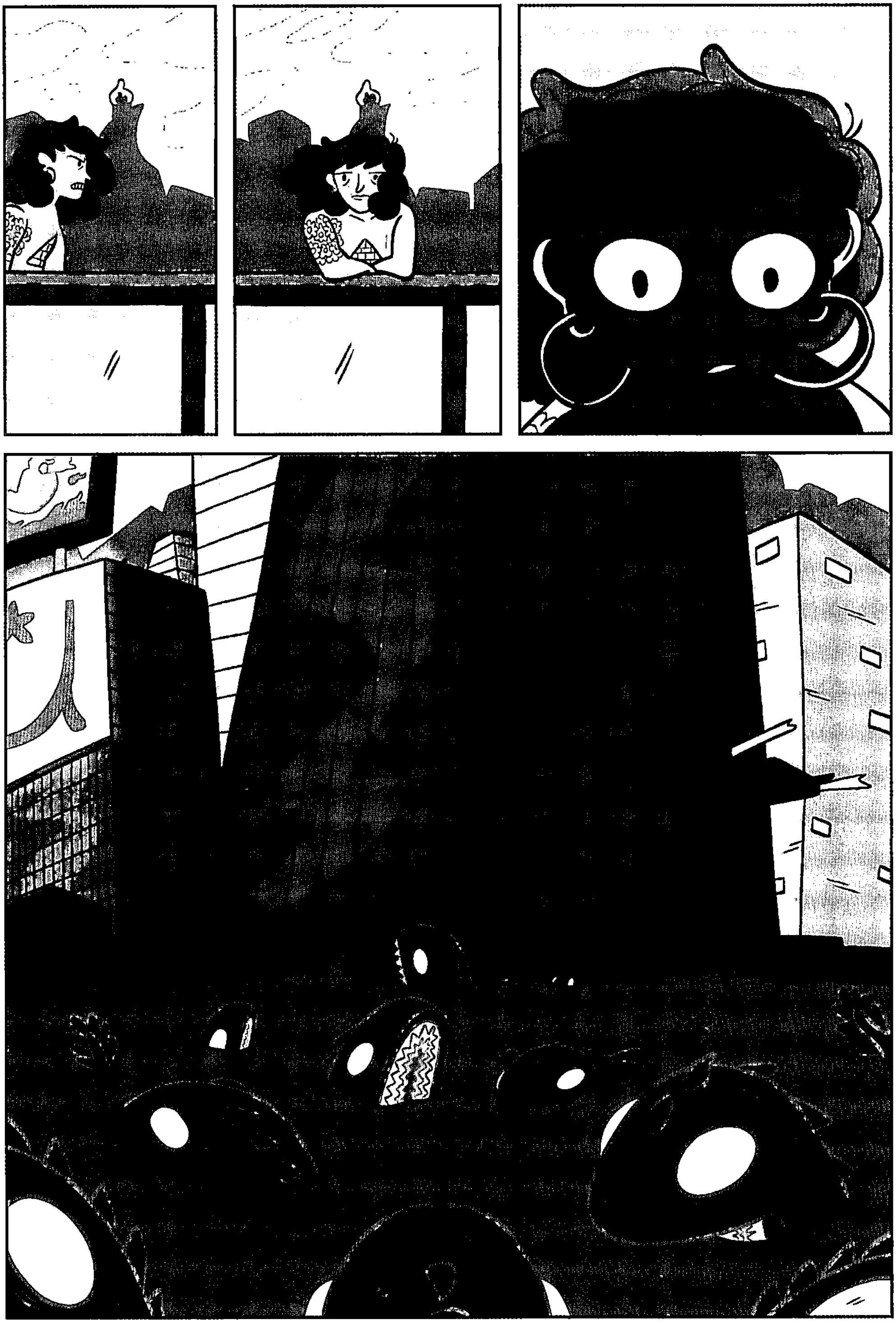

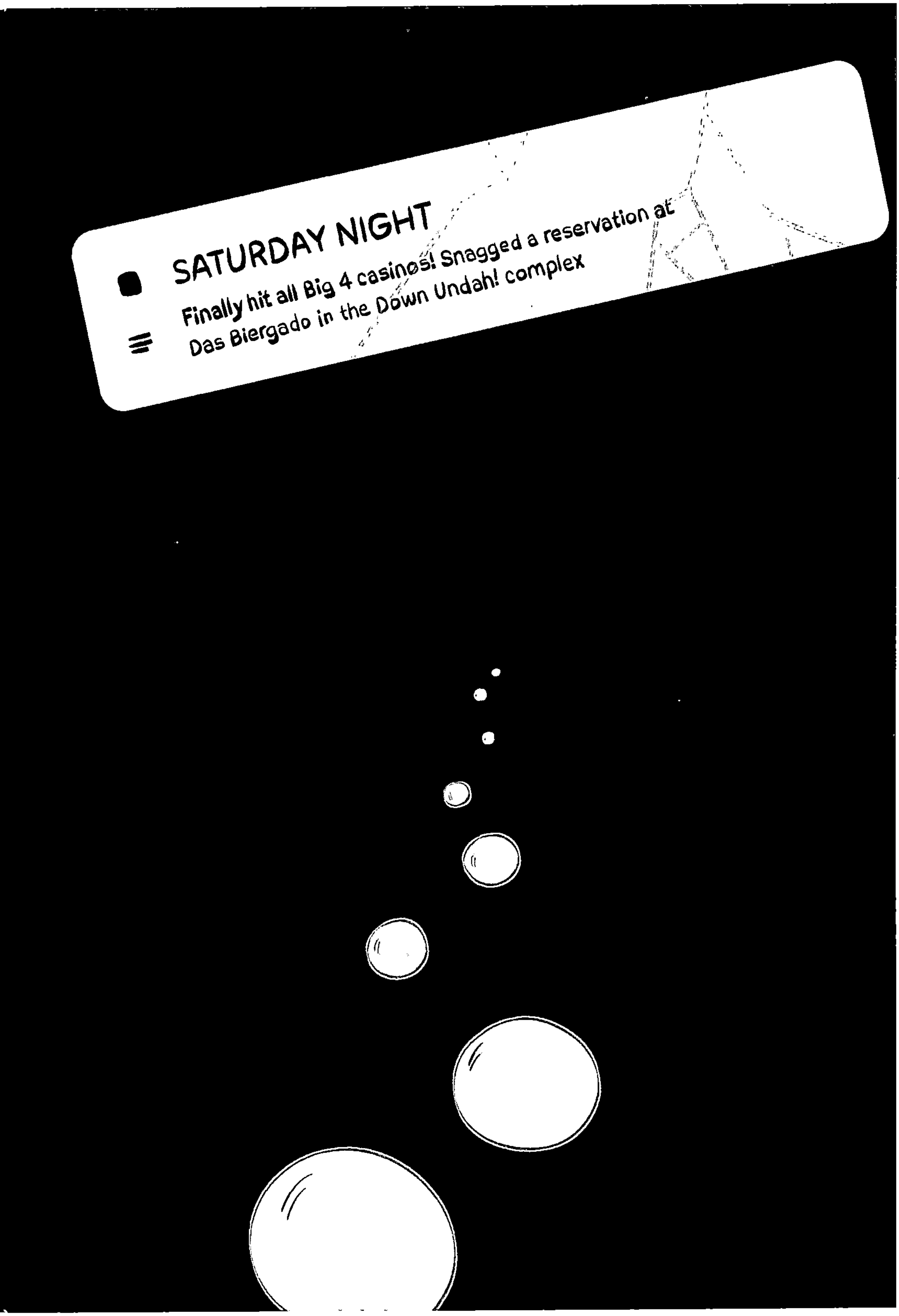
SATURDAY NIGHT
Finally hit all Big 4 casinos! Snagged a reservation at Das Biergado in the Down Undah! complex

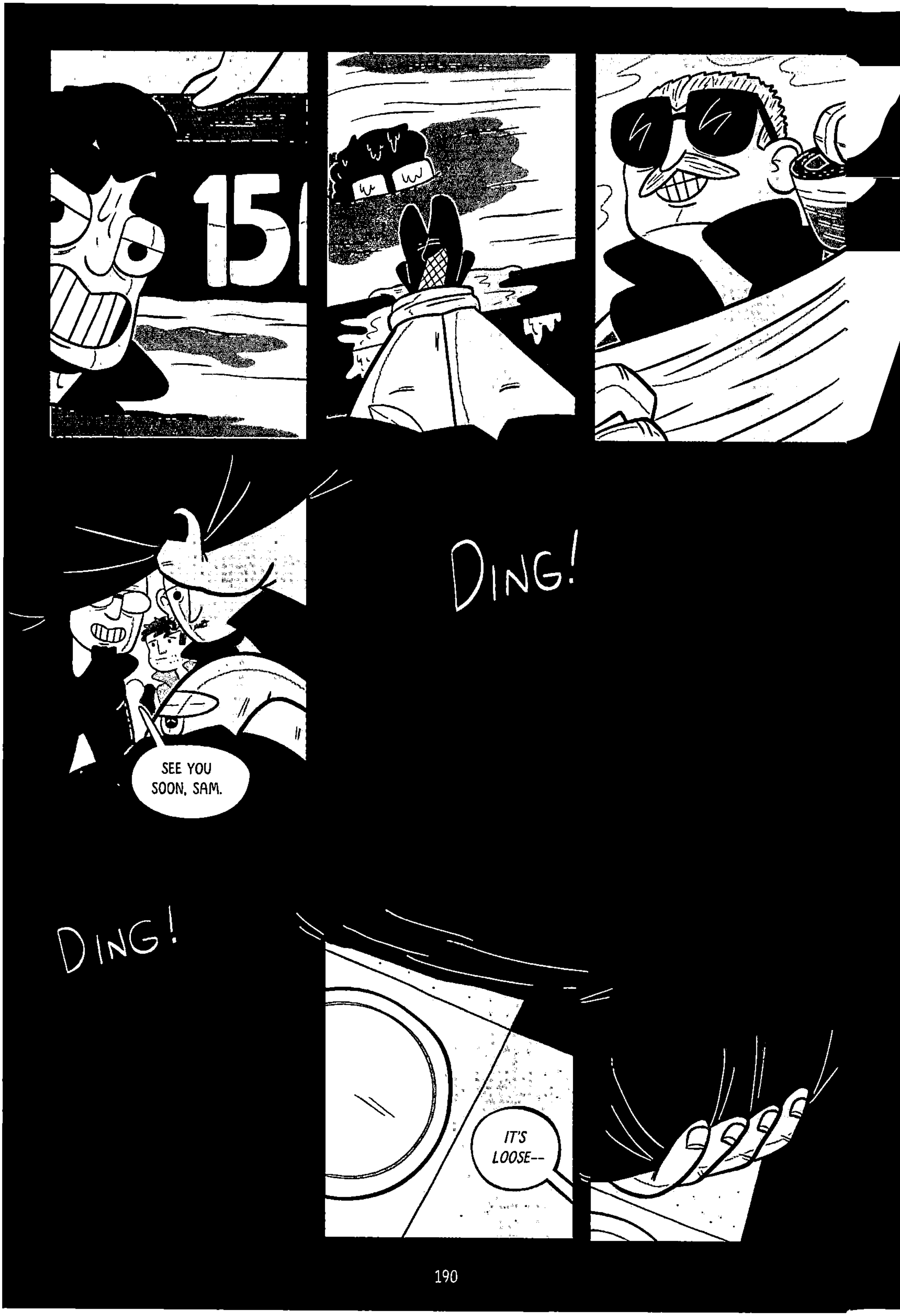
15
DING!
SEE YOU SOON, SAM.
DING!
IT'S LOOSE--

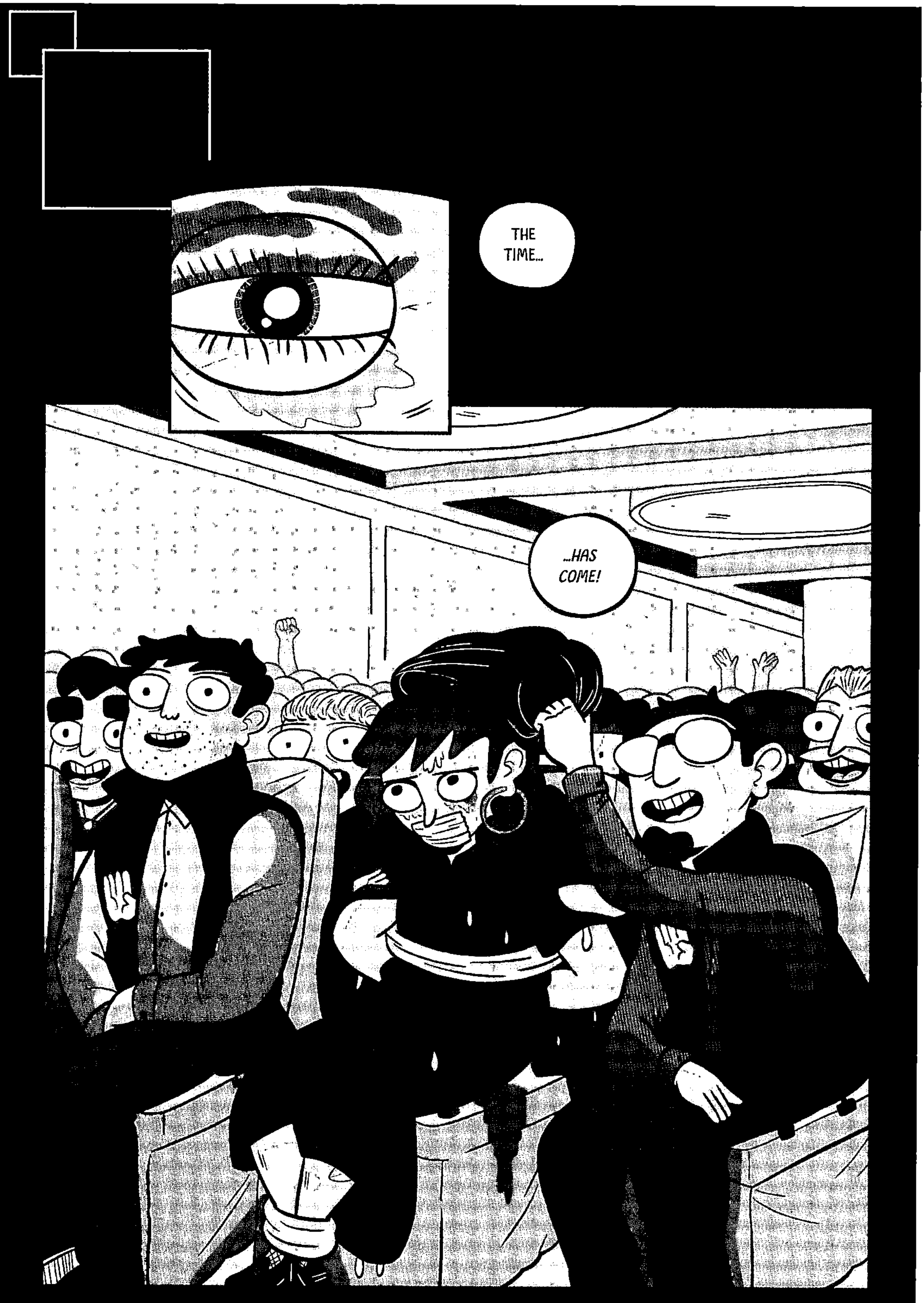
THE TIME...
...HAS COME!

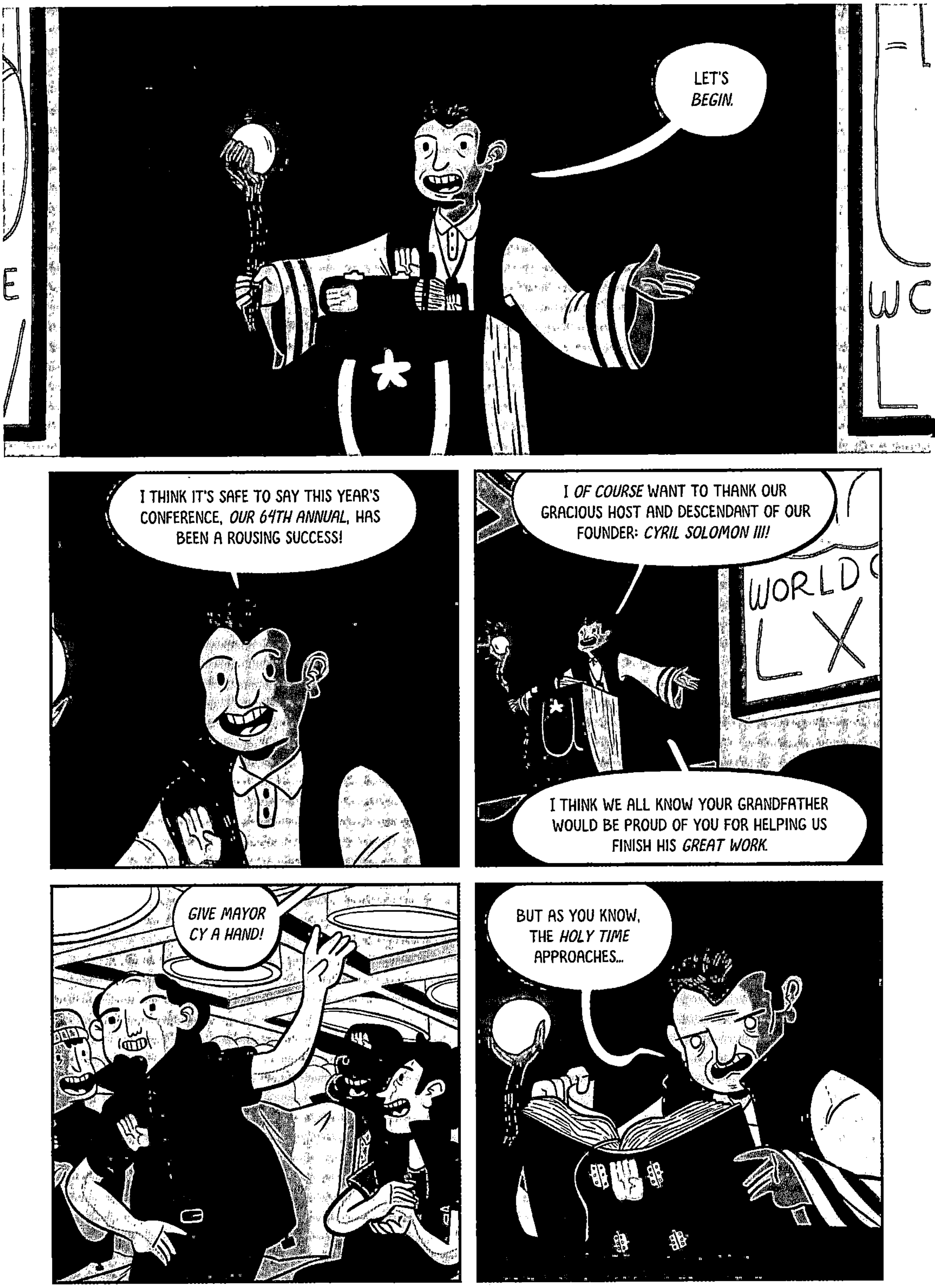
LET'S *BEGIN.*
I THINK IT'S SAFE TO SAY THIS YEAR'S CONFERENCE, *OUR 64TH ANNUAL*, HAS BEEN A ROUSING SUCCESS!
I *OF COURSE* WANT TO THANK OUR GRACIOUS HOST AND DESCENDANT OF OUR FOUNDER: *CYRIL SOLOMON III!*
WORLD
LX
I THINK WE ALL KNOW YOUR GRANDFATHER WOULD BE PROUD OF YOU FOR HELPING US FINISH HIS *GREAT WORK.*
GIVE MAYOR CY A HAND!
BUT AS YOU KNOW, THE *HOLY TIME* APPROACHES...

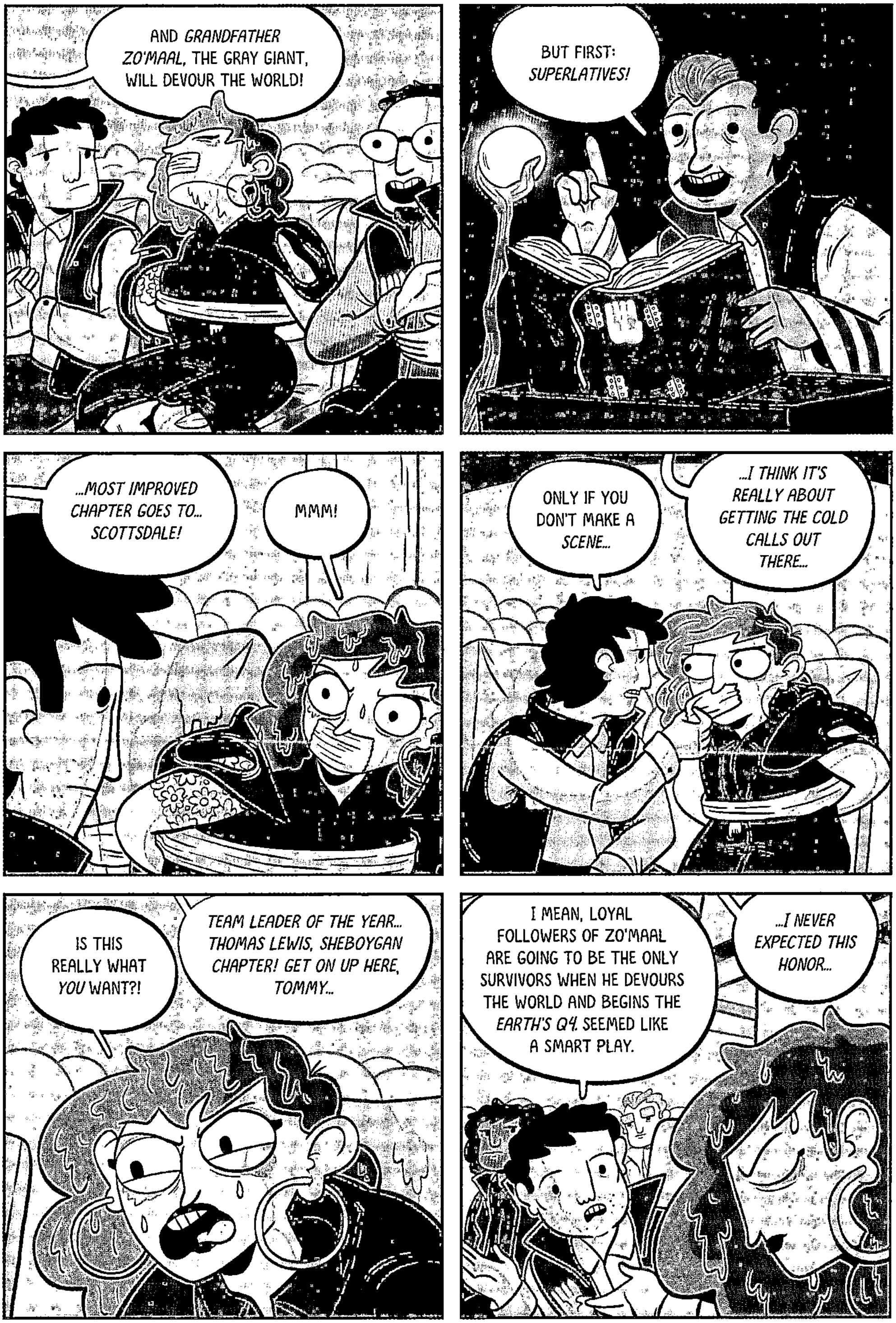
AND *GRANDFATHER ZO'MAAL*, THE GRAY GIANT, WILL DEVOUR THE WORLD!
BUT FIRST: *SUPERLATIVES!*
...MOST IMPROVED CHAPTER GOES TO... SCOTTSDALE!
MMM!
ONLY IF YOU DON'T MAKE A *SCENE...*
...I THINK IT'S REALLY ABOUT GETTING THE COLD CALLS OUT THERE...
TEAM LEADER OF THE YEAR... THOMAS LEWIS, SHEBOYGAN CHAPTER! GET ON UP HERE, TOMMY...
IS THIS REALLY WHAT *YOU* WANT?!
I MEAN, LOYAL FOLLOWERS OF ZO'MAAL ARE GOING TO BE THE ONLY SURVIVORS WHEN HE DEVOURS THE WORLD AND BEGINS THE *EARTH'S Q4.* SEEMED LIKE A SMART PLAY.
...I NEVER EXPECTED THIS HONOR...

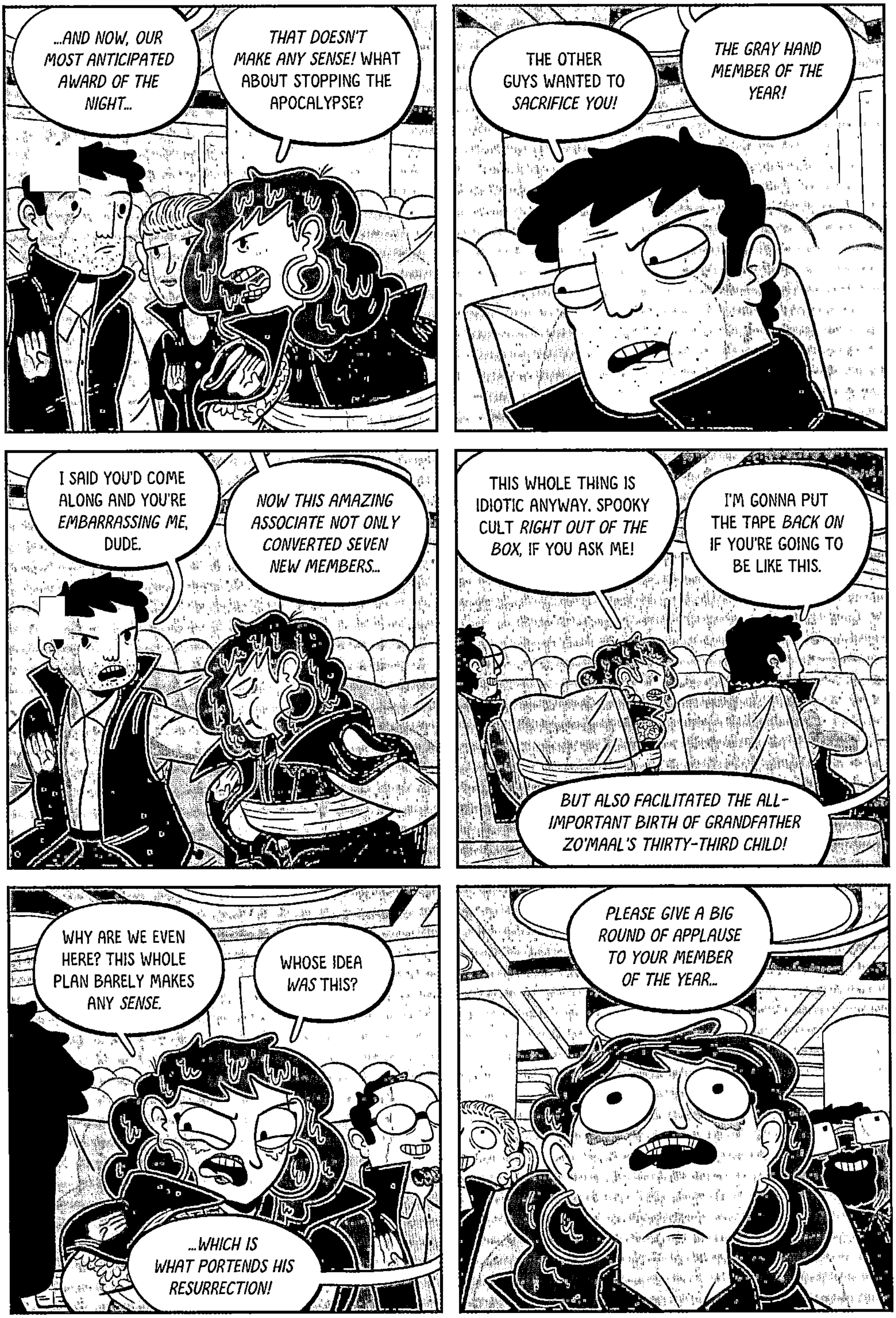

...AND NOW, OUR MOST ANTICIPATED AWARD OF THE NIGHT...
THAT DOESN'T MAKE ANY SENSE! WHAT ABOUT STOPPING THE APOCALYPSE?
THE OTHER GUYS WANTED TO SACRIFICE YOU!
THE GRAY HAND MEMBER OF THE YEAR!
I SAID YOU'D COME ALONG AND YOU'RE EMBARRASSING ME, DUDE.
NOW THIS AMAZING ASSOCIATE NOT ONLY CONVERTED SEVEN NEW MEMBERS...
THIS WHOLE THING IS IDIOTIC ANYWAY. SPOOKY CULT RIGHT OUT OF THE BOX, IF YOU ASK ME!
I'M GONNA PUT THE TAPE BACK ON IF YOU'RE GOING TO BE LIKE THIS.
BUT ALSO FACILITATED THE ALL-IMPORTANT BIRTH OF GRANDFATHER ZO'MAAL'S THIRTY-THIRD CHILD!
WHY ARE WE EVEN HERE? THIS WHOLE PLAN BARELY MAKES ANY SENSE.
WHOSE IDEA WAS THIS?
...WHICH IS WHAT PORTENDS HIS RESURRECTION!
PLEASE GIVE A BIG ROUND OF APPLAUSE TO YOUR MEMBER OF THE YEAR...

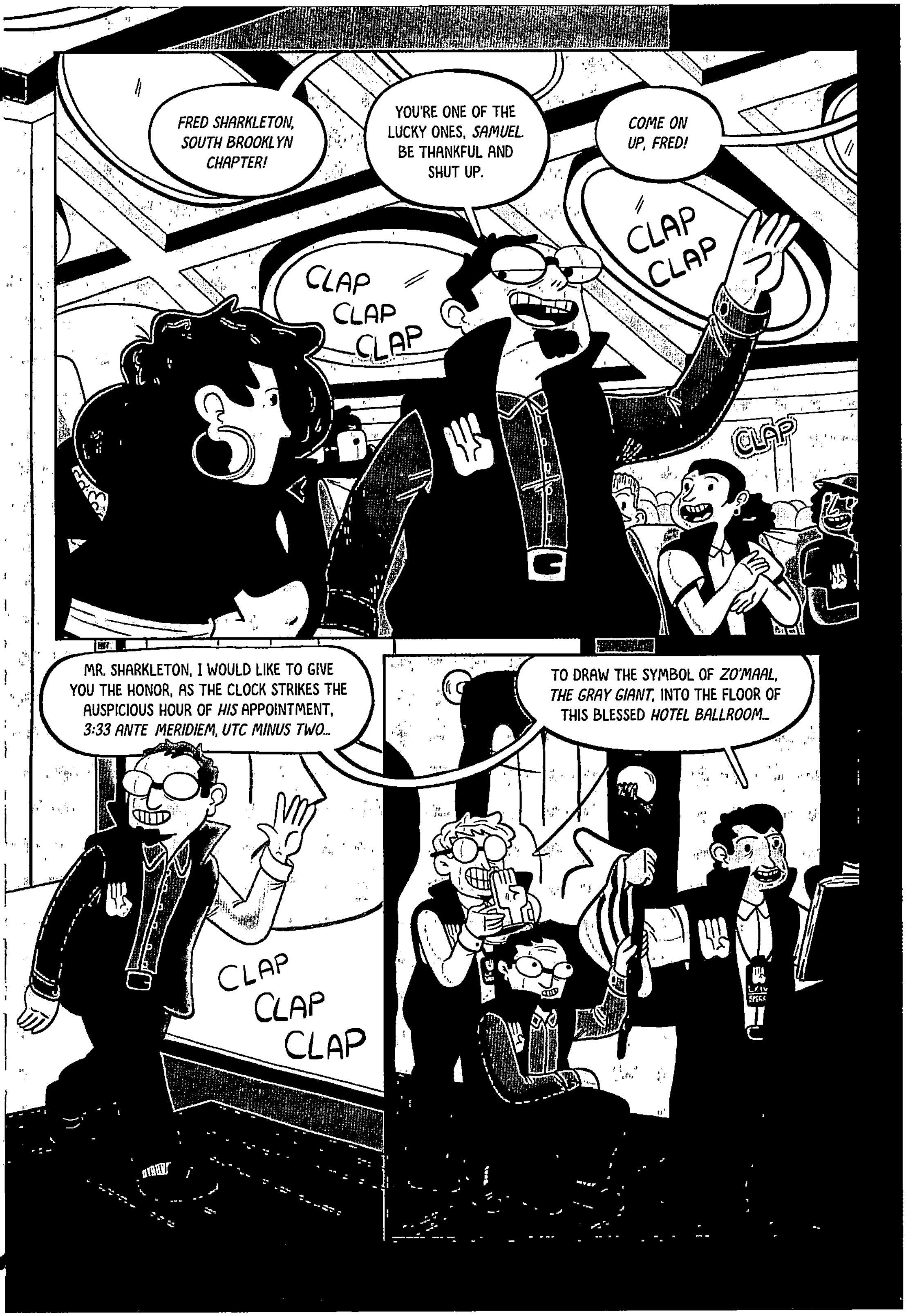
FRED SHARKLETON, SOUTH BROOKLYN CHAPTER!
YOU'RE ONE OF THE LUCKY ONES, SAMUEL. BE THANKFUL AND SHUT UP.
COME ON UP, FRED!
CLAP CLAP CLAP
CLAP CLAP
CLAP
MR. SHARKLETON, I WOULD LIKE TO GIVE YOU THE HONOR, AS THE CLOCK STRIKES THE AUSPICIOUS HOUR OF HIS APPOINTMENT, 3:33 ANTE MERIDIEM, UTC MINUS TWO...
CLAP CLAP CLAP
TO DRAW THE SYMBOL OF ZO'MAAL, THE GRAY GIANT, INTO THE FLOOR OF THIS BLESSED HOTEL BALLROOM...

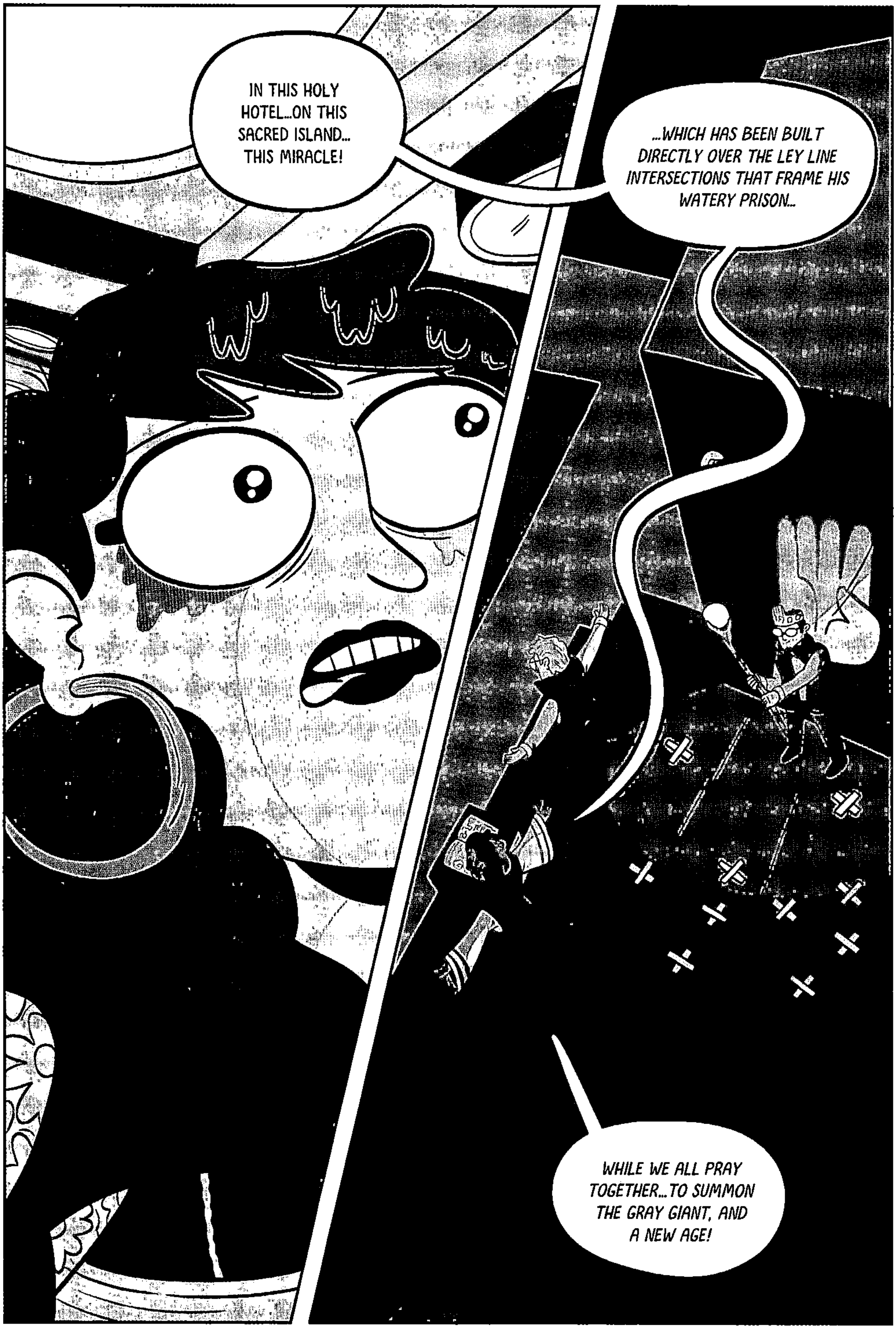
IN THIS HOLY HOTEL...ON THIS SACRED ISLAND... THIS MIRACLE!
...WHICH HAS BEEN BUILT DIRECTLY OVER THE LEY LINE INTERSECTIONS THAT FRAME HIS WATERY PRISON...
WHILE WE ALL PRAY TOGETHER...TO SUMMON THE GRAY GIANT, AND A NEW AGE!

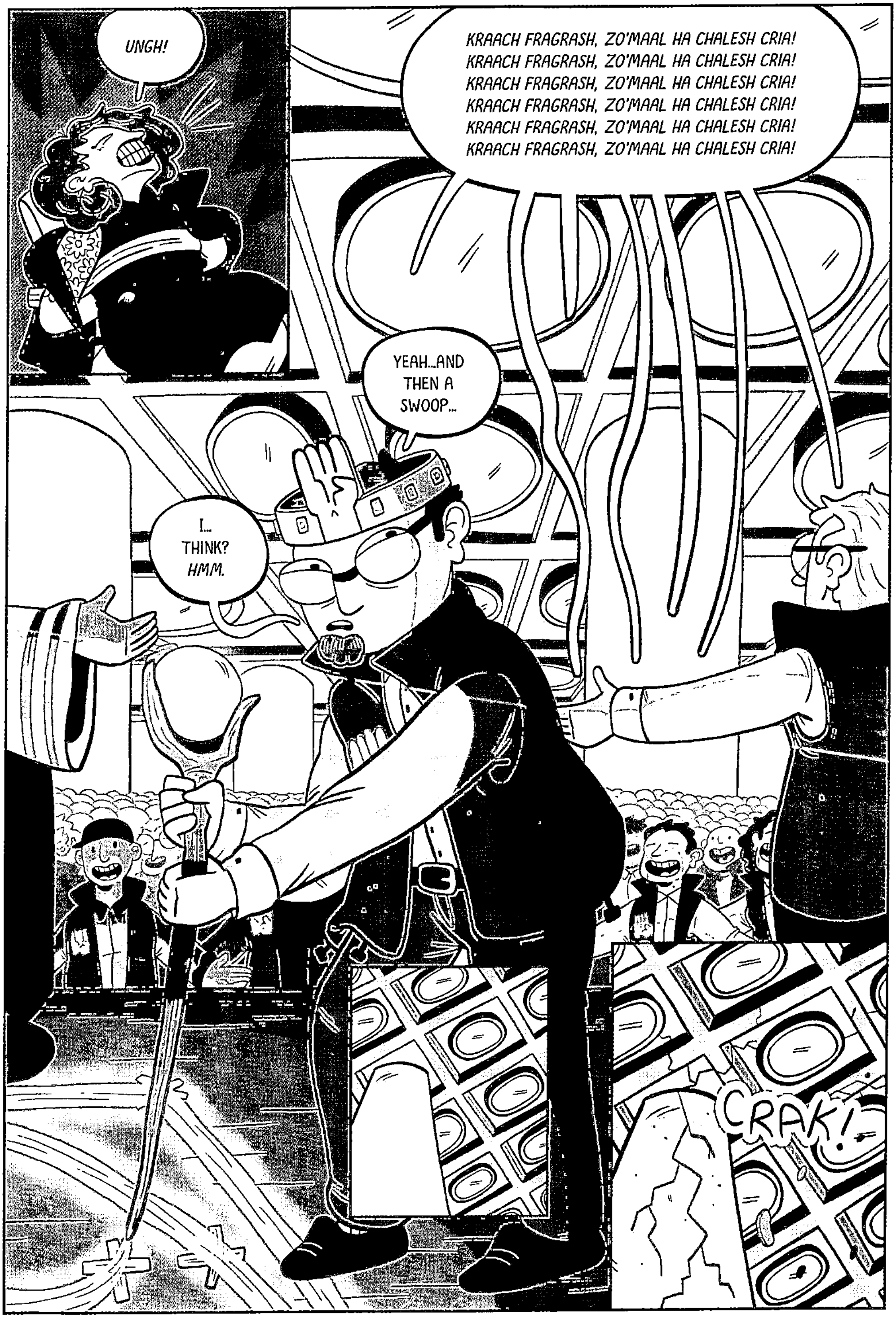
UNGH!
KRAACH FRAGRASH, ZO'MAAL HA CHALESH CRIA!
KRAACH FRAGRASH, ZO'MAAL HA CHALESH CRIA!
KRAACH FRAGRASH, ZO'MAAL HA CHALESH CRIA!
KRAACH FRAGRASH, ZO'MAAL HA CHALESH CRIA!
KRAACH FRAGRASH, ZO'MAAL HA CHALESH CRIA!
KRAACH FRAGRASH, ZO'MAAL HA CHALESH CRIA!
YEAH...AND THEN A SWOOP...
I... THINK? HMM.
CRAK!

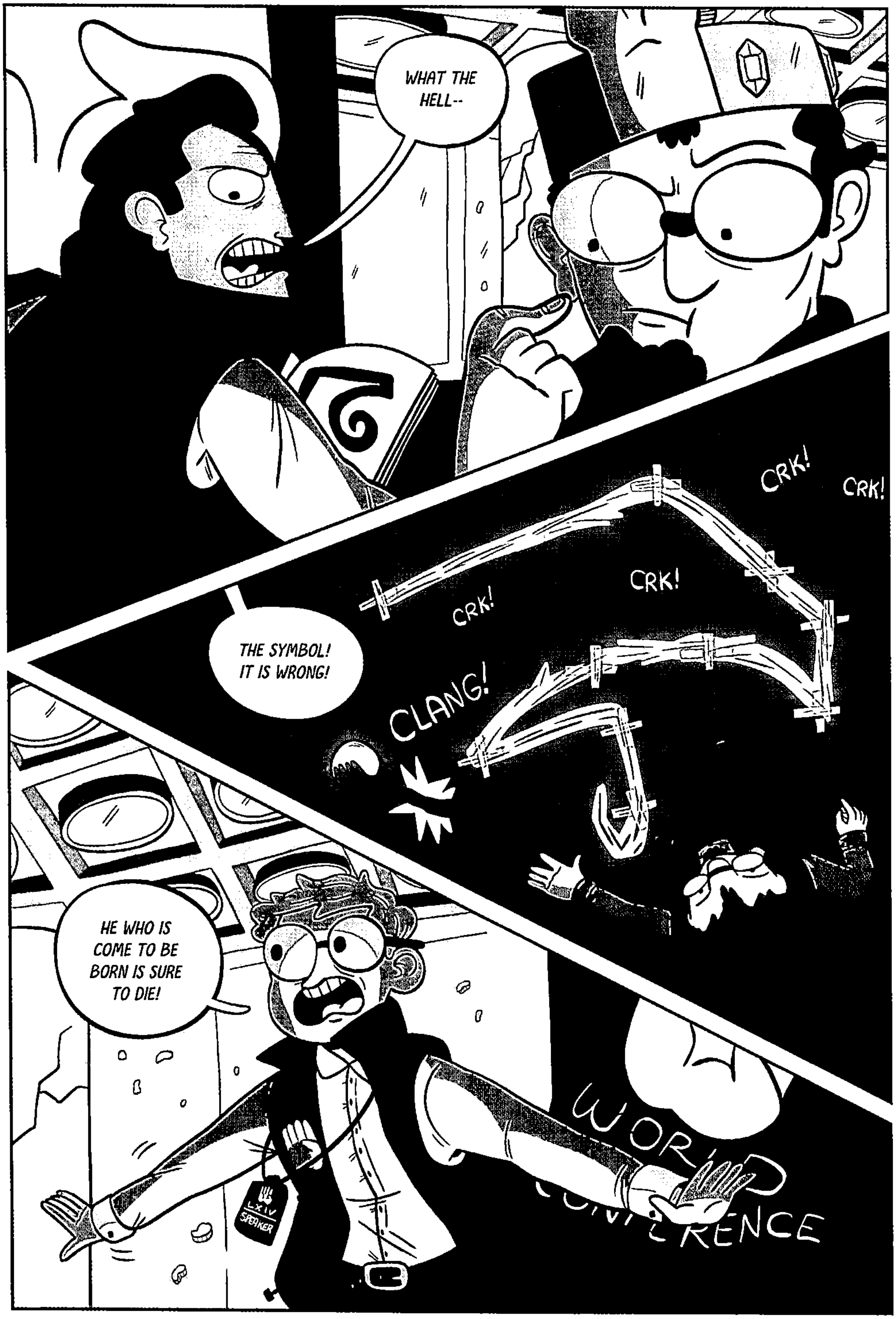
WHAT THE HELL--
THE SYMBOL! IT IS WRONG!
CRK!
CRK!
CRK!
CRK!
CLANG!
HE WHO IS COME TO BE BORN IS SURE TO DIE!
LXIV SPEAKER
WORLD CONFERENCE

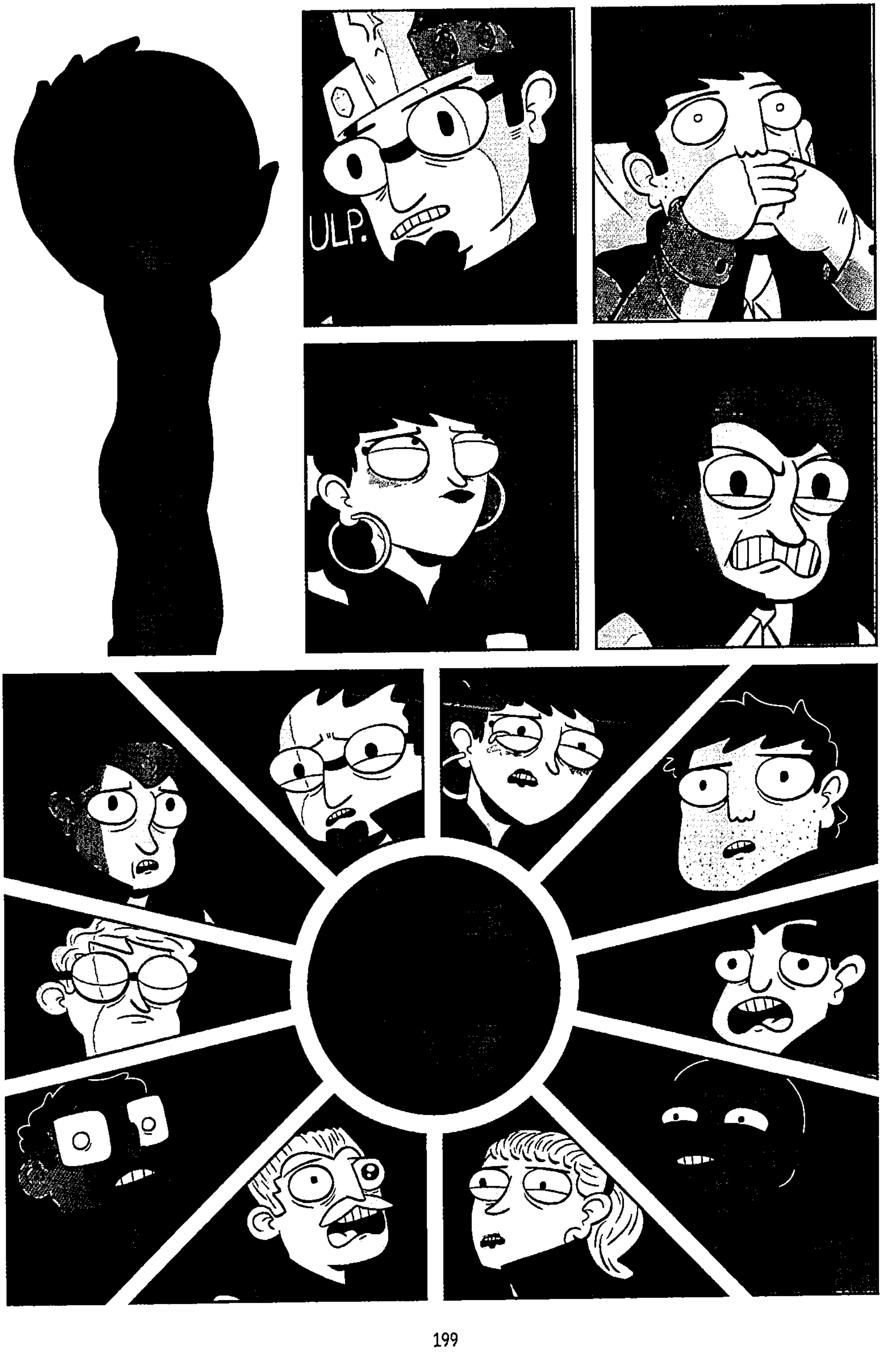
ULP.

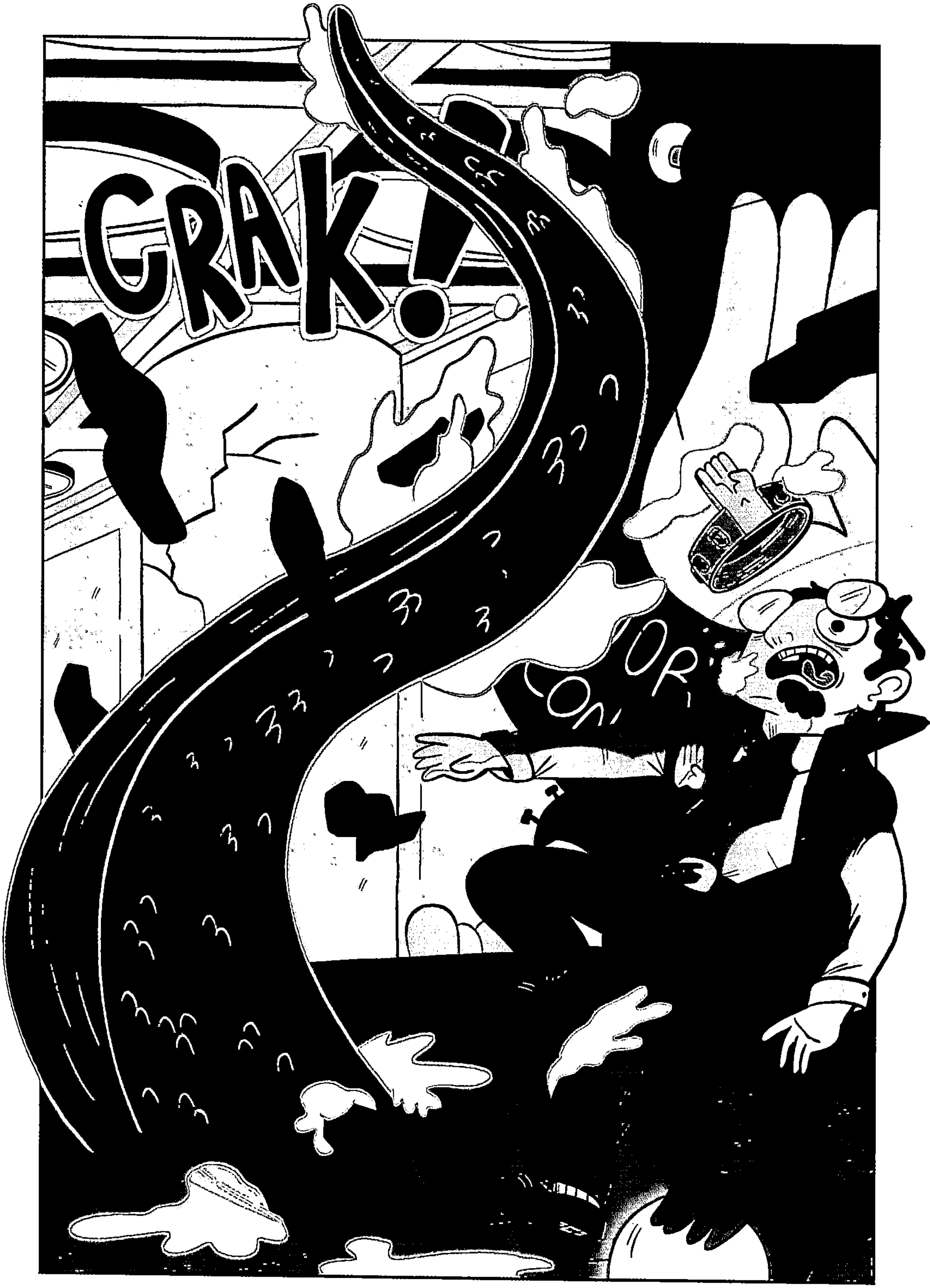
GRAK!

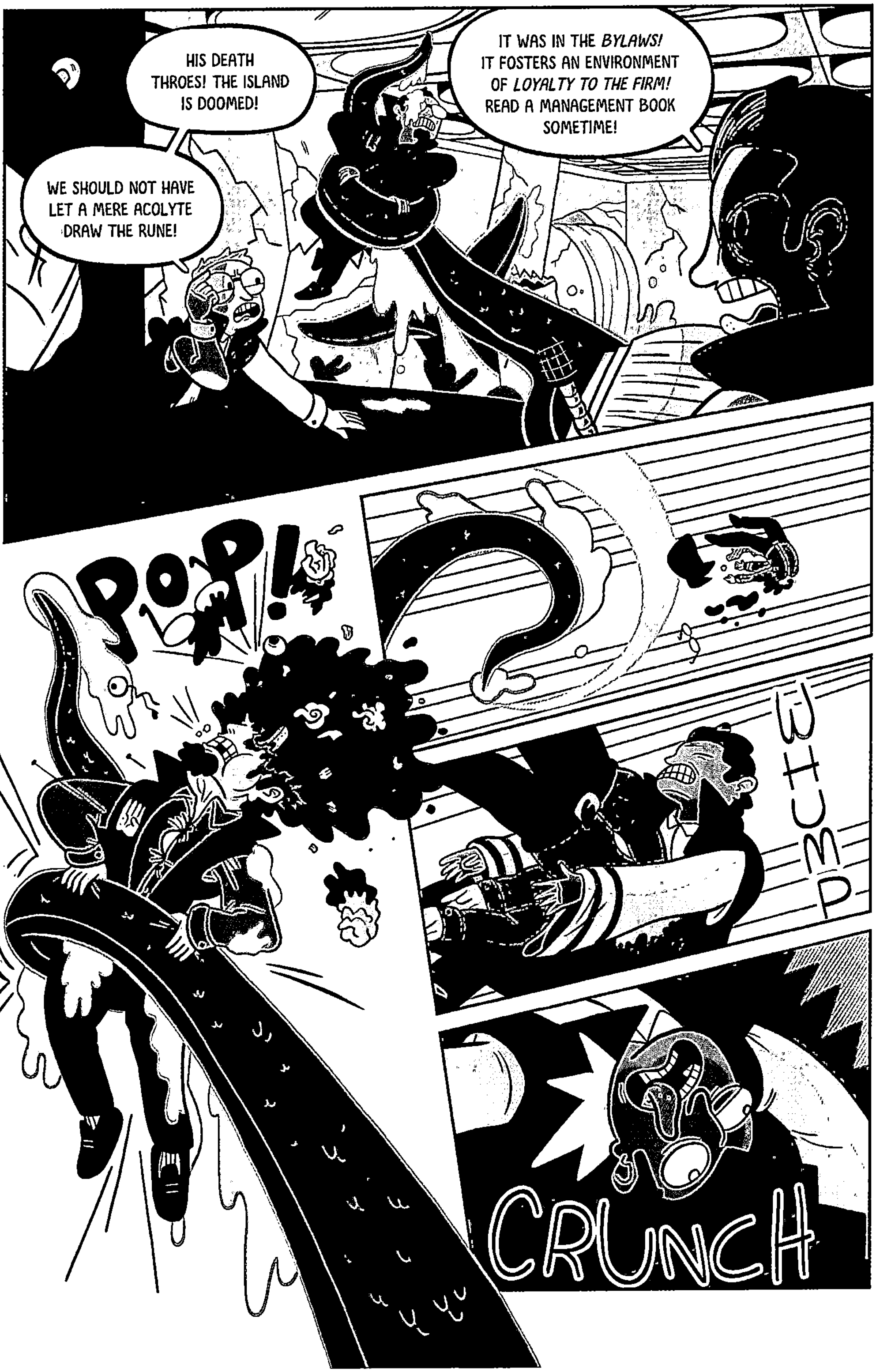
WE SHOULD NOT HAVE LET A MERE ACOLYTE DRAW THE RUNE!
HIS DEATH THROES! THE ISLAND IS DOOMED!
IT WAS IN THE *BYLAWS!* IT FOSTERS AN ENVIRONMENT OF *LOYALTY TO THE FIRM!* READ A MANAGEMENT BOOK SOMETIME!
POP!
THUMP
CRUNCH

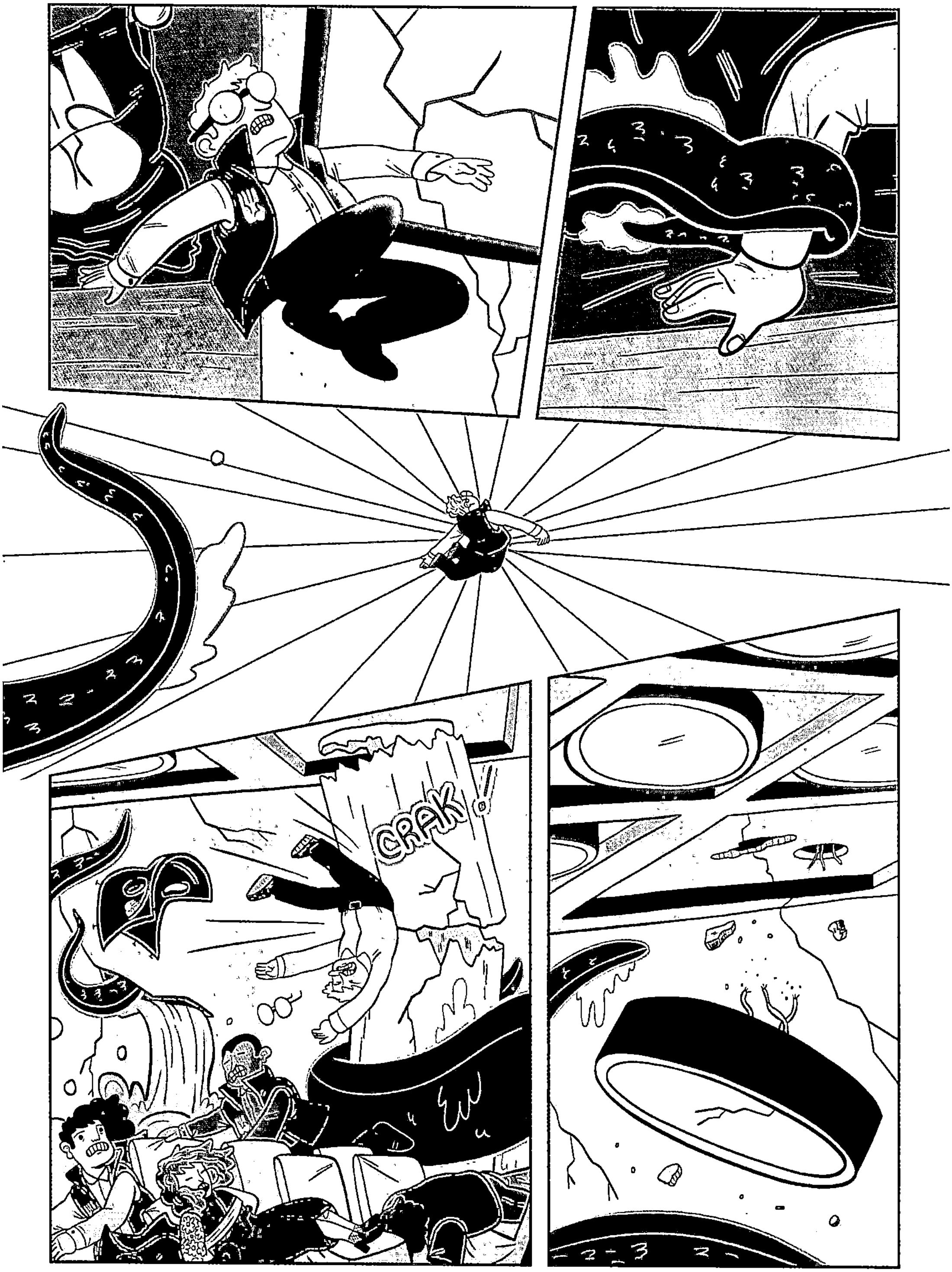
CRAK!

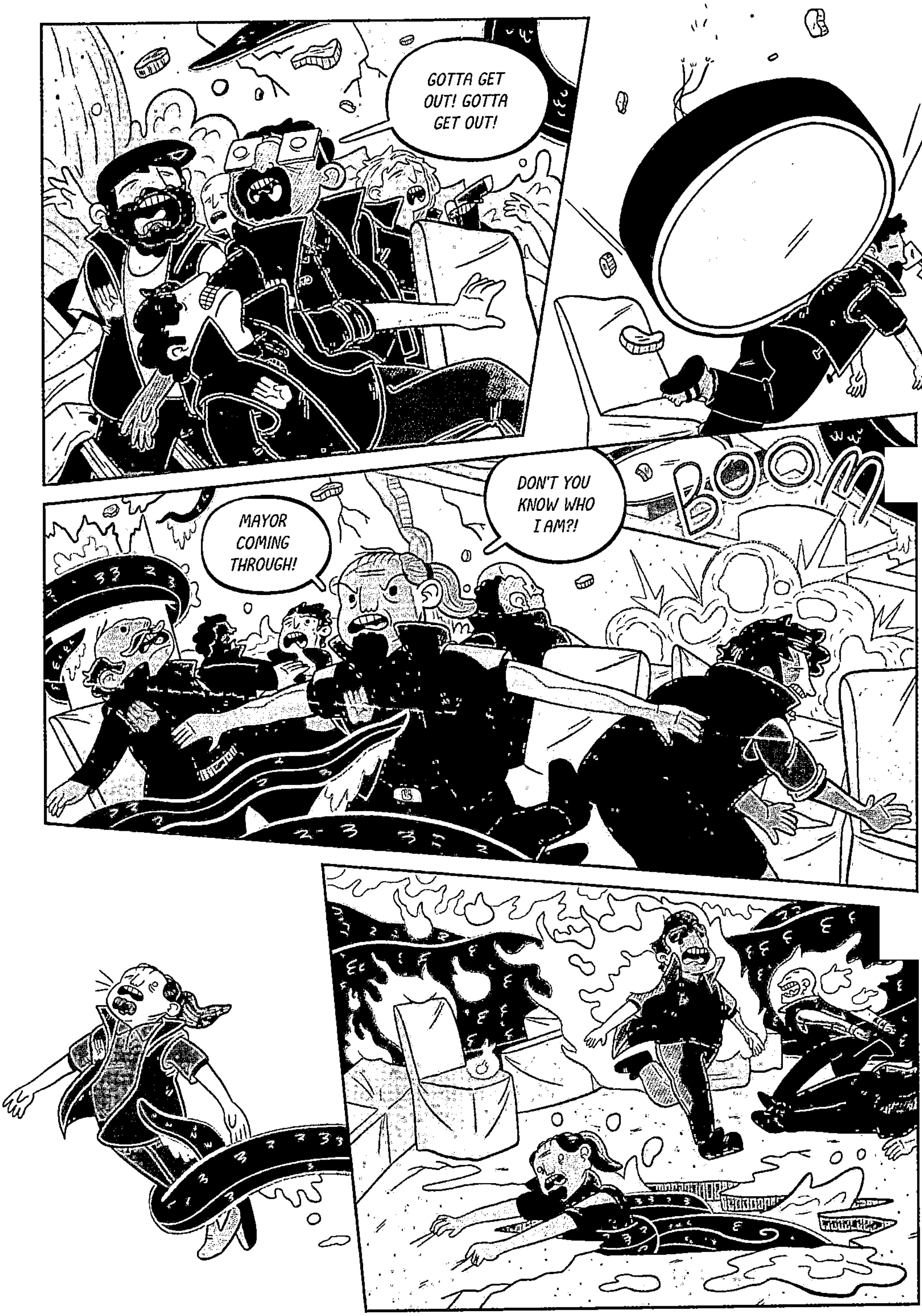
GOTTA GET OUT! GOTTA GET OUT!
MAYOR COMING THROUGH!
DON'T YOU KNOW WHO I AM?!
BOOM

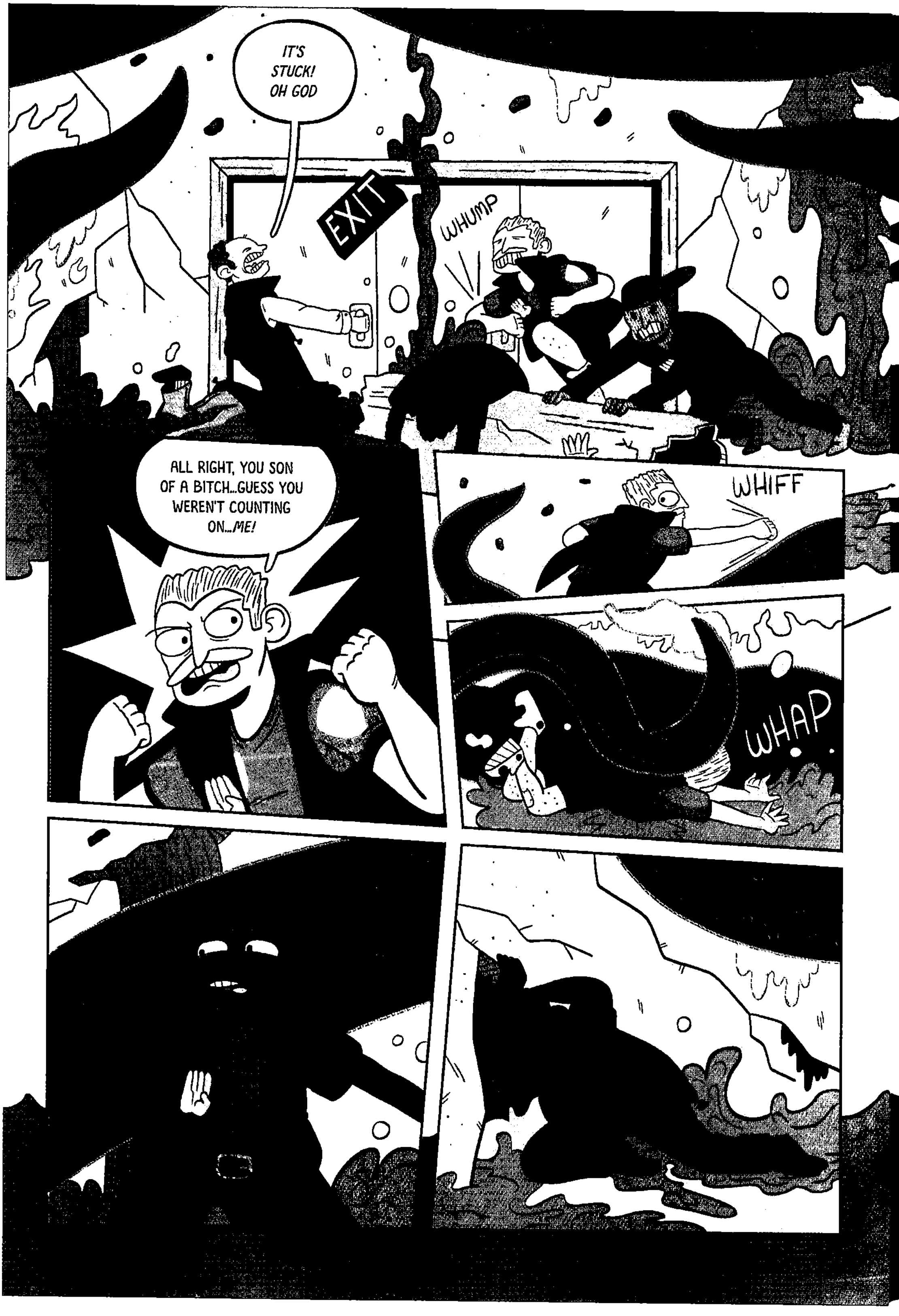
IT'S STUCK! OH GOD
WHUMP
ALL RIGHT, YOU SON OF A BITCH...GUESS YOU WEREN'T COUNTING ON...*ME!*
WHIFF
WHAP

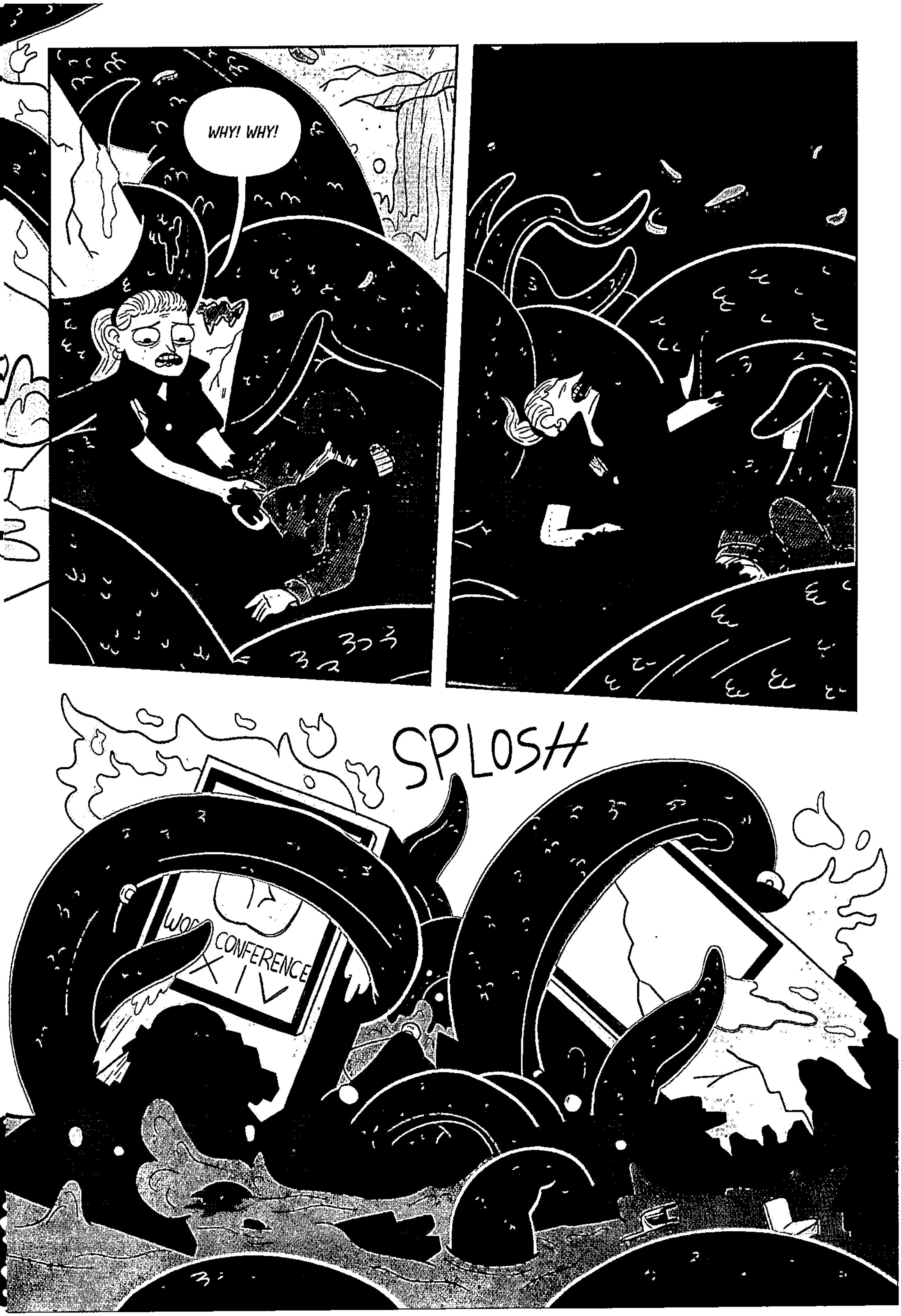
WHY! WHY!
SPLOSH
CONFERENCE
XIV

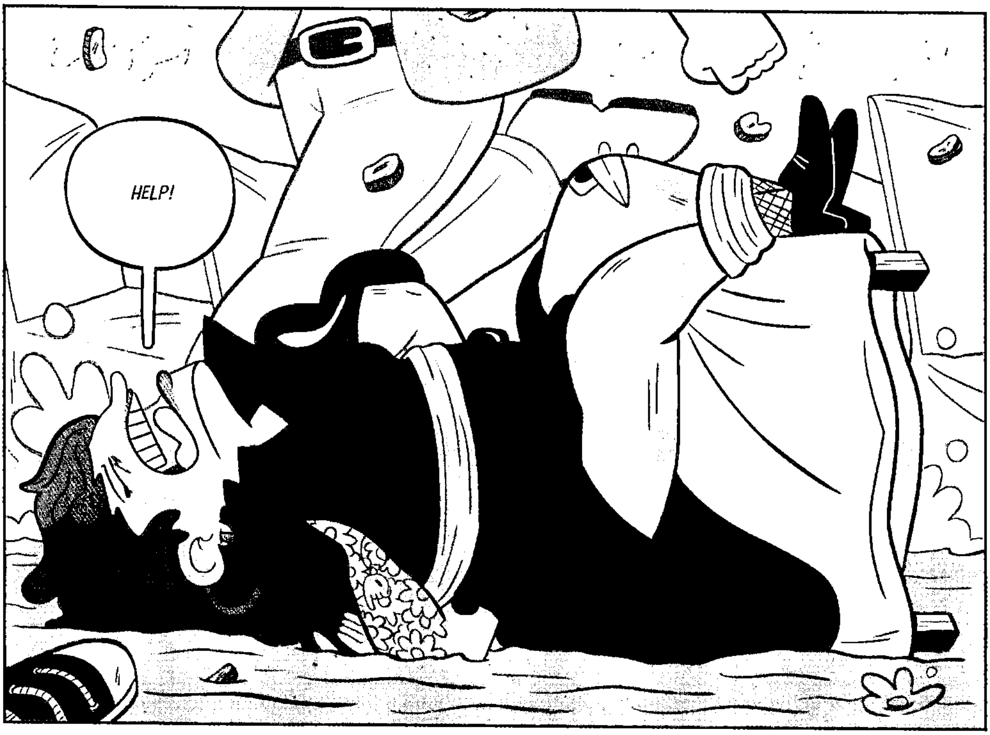
HELP!

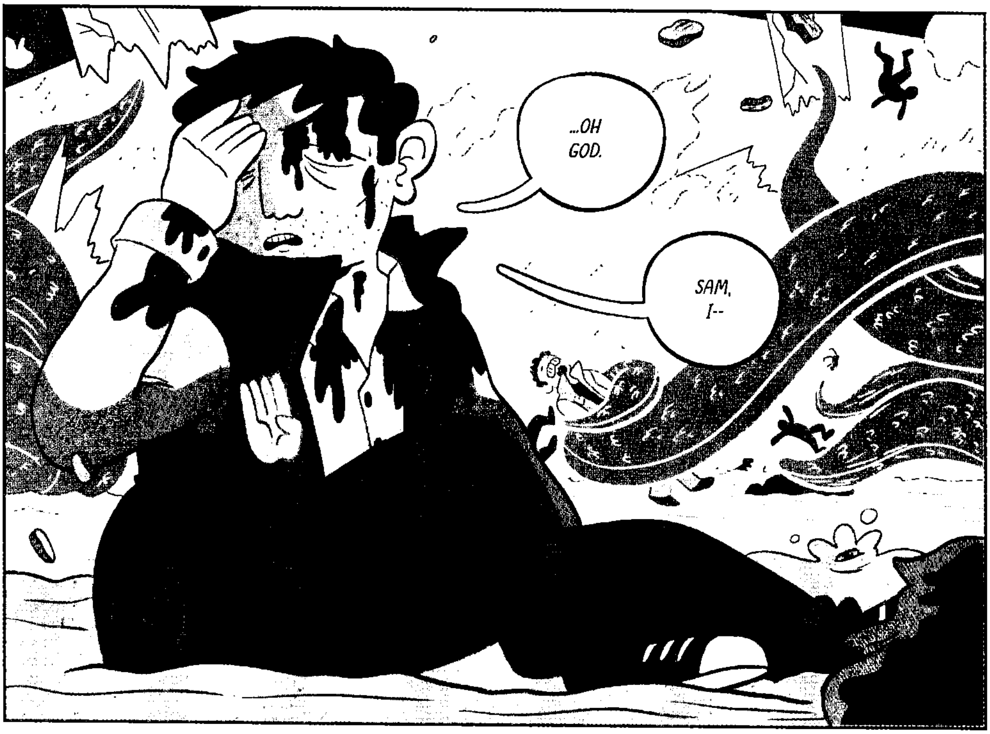
...OH GOD.
SAM, I--

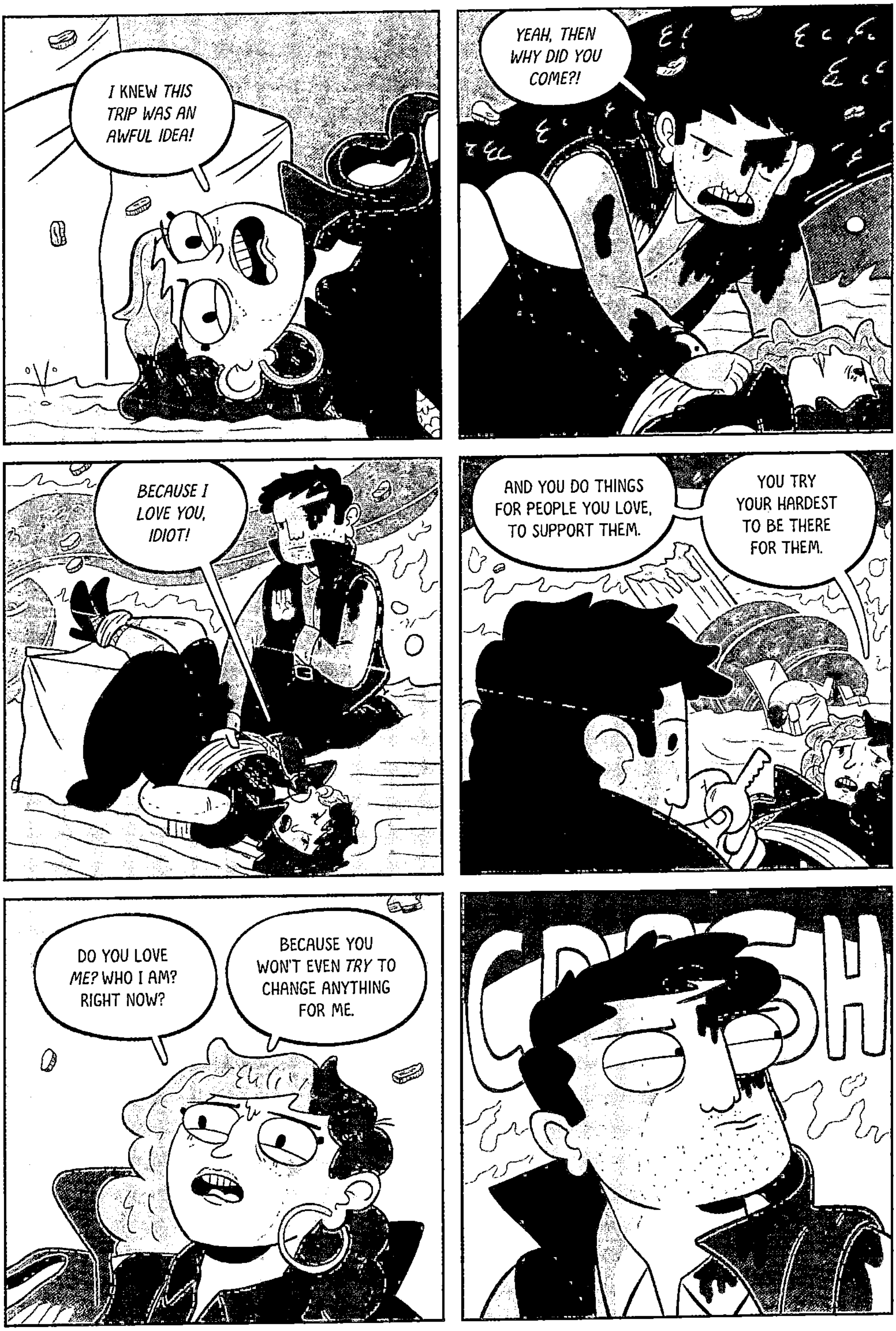
I KNEW THIS TRIP WAS AN AWFUL IDEA!
YEAH, THEN WHY DID YOU COME?!
BECAUSE I LOVE YOU, IDIOT!
AND YOU DO THINGS FOR PEOPLE YOU LOVE, TO SUPPORT THEM.
YOU TRY YOUR HARDEST TO BE THERE FOR THEM.
DO YOU LOVE ME? WHO I AM? RIGHT NOW?
BECAUSE YOU WON'T EVEN TRY TO CHANGE ANYTHING FOR ME.

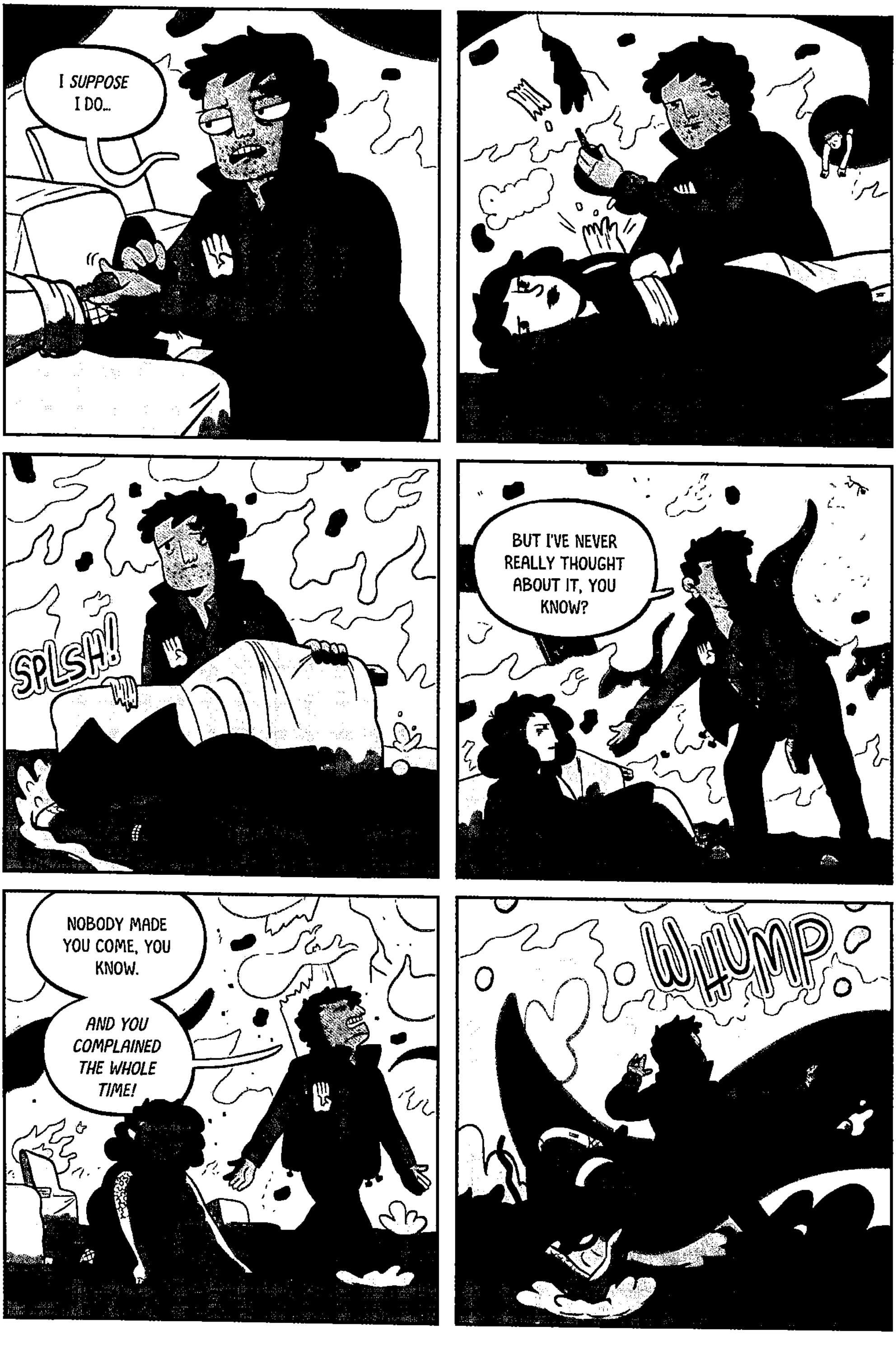
I SUPPOSE I DO...
SPLSH!
BUT I'VE NEVER REALLY THOUGHT ABOUT IT, YOU KNOW?
NOBODY MADE YOU COME, YOU KNOW.
AND YOU COMPLAINED THE WHOLE TIME!
WHUMP

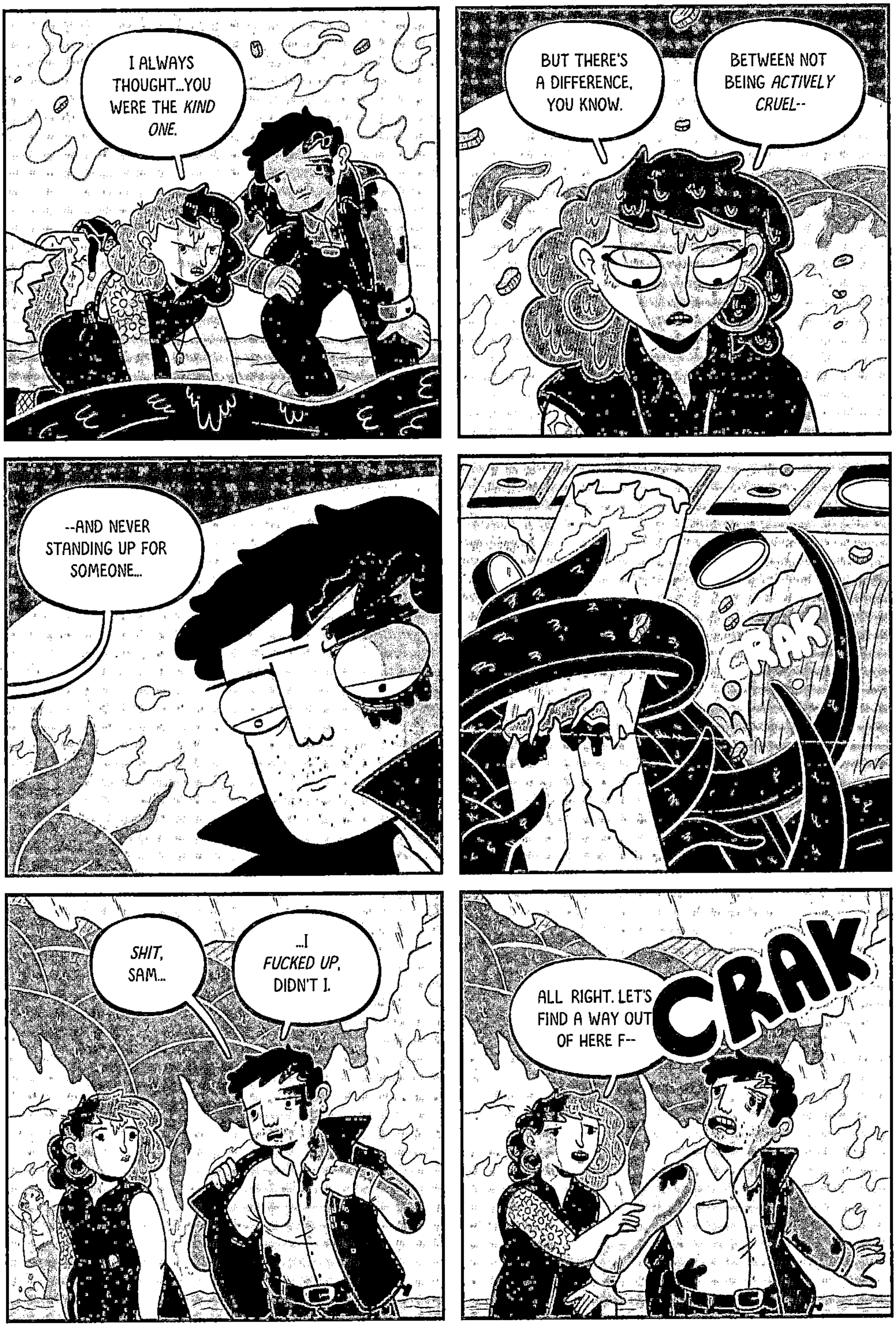
I ALWAYS THOUGHT...YOU WERE THE *KIND ONE*.
BUT THERE'S A DIFFERENCE, YOU KNOW.
BETWEEN NOT BEING *ACTIVELY CRUEL*--
--AND NEVER STANDING UP FOR SOMEONE...
CRAK
SHIT, SAM...
...I *FUCKED UP*, DIDN'T I.
ALL RIGHT. LET'S FIND A WAY OUT OF HERE F--
CRAK

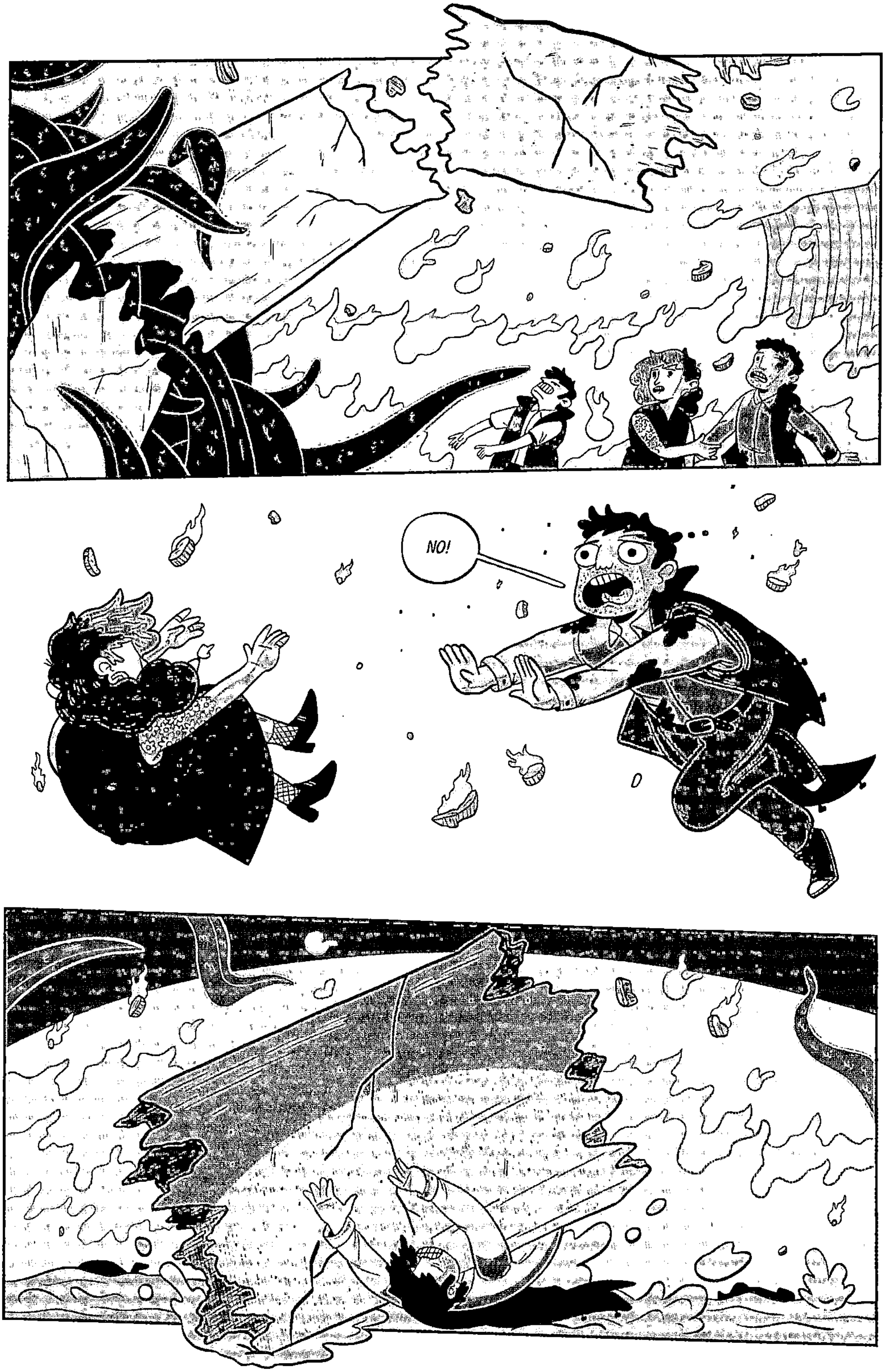
NO!

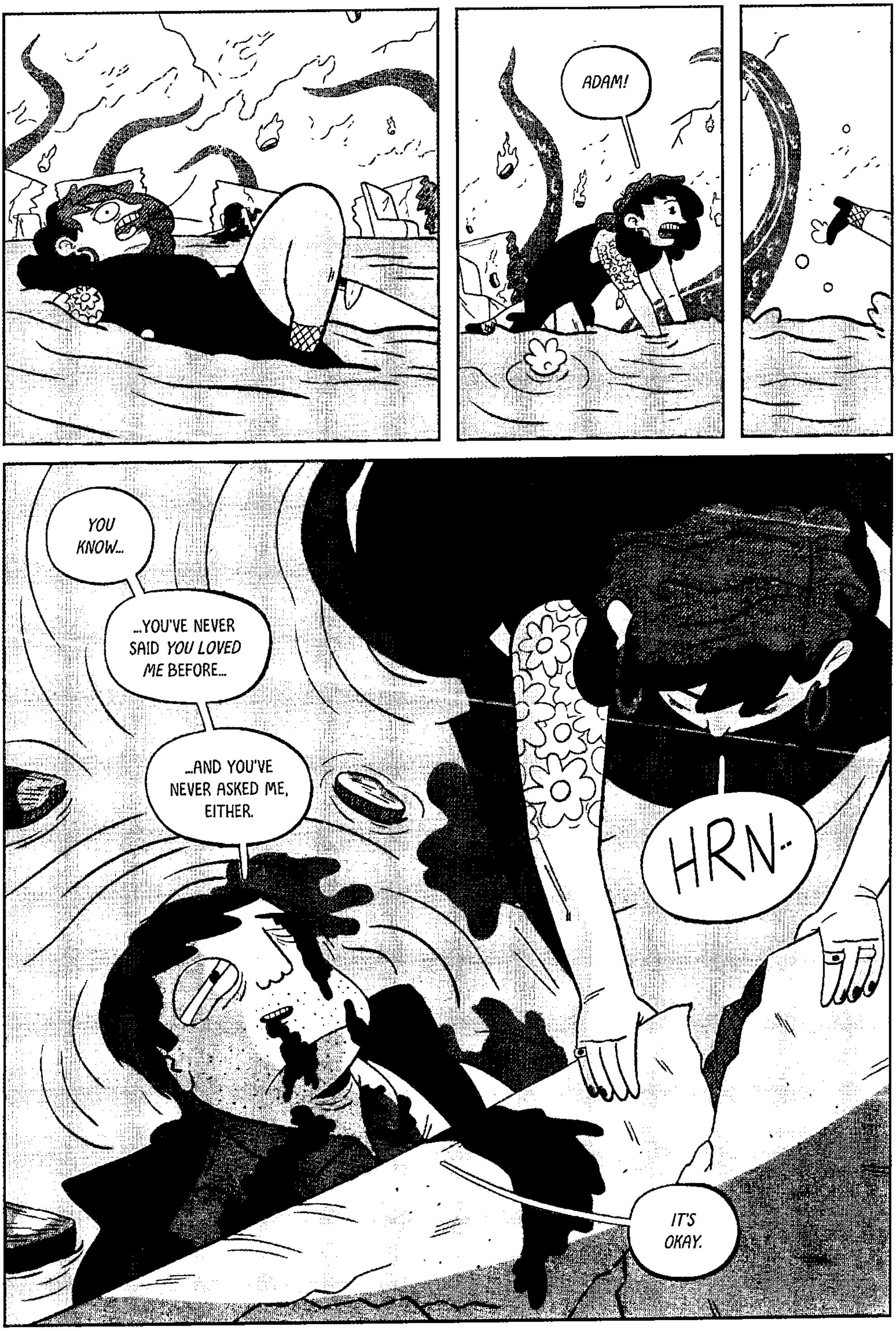
ADAM!
YOU KNOW...
...YOU'VE NEVER SAID YOU LOVED ME BEFORE...
...AND YOU'VE NEVER ASKED ME, EITHER.
HRN-
IT'S OKAY.

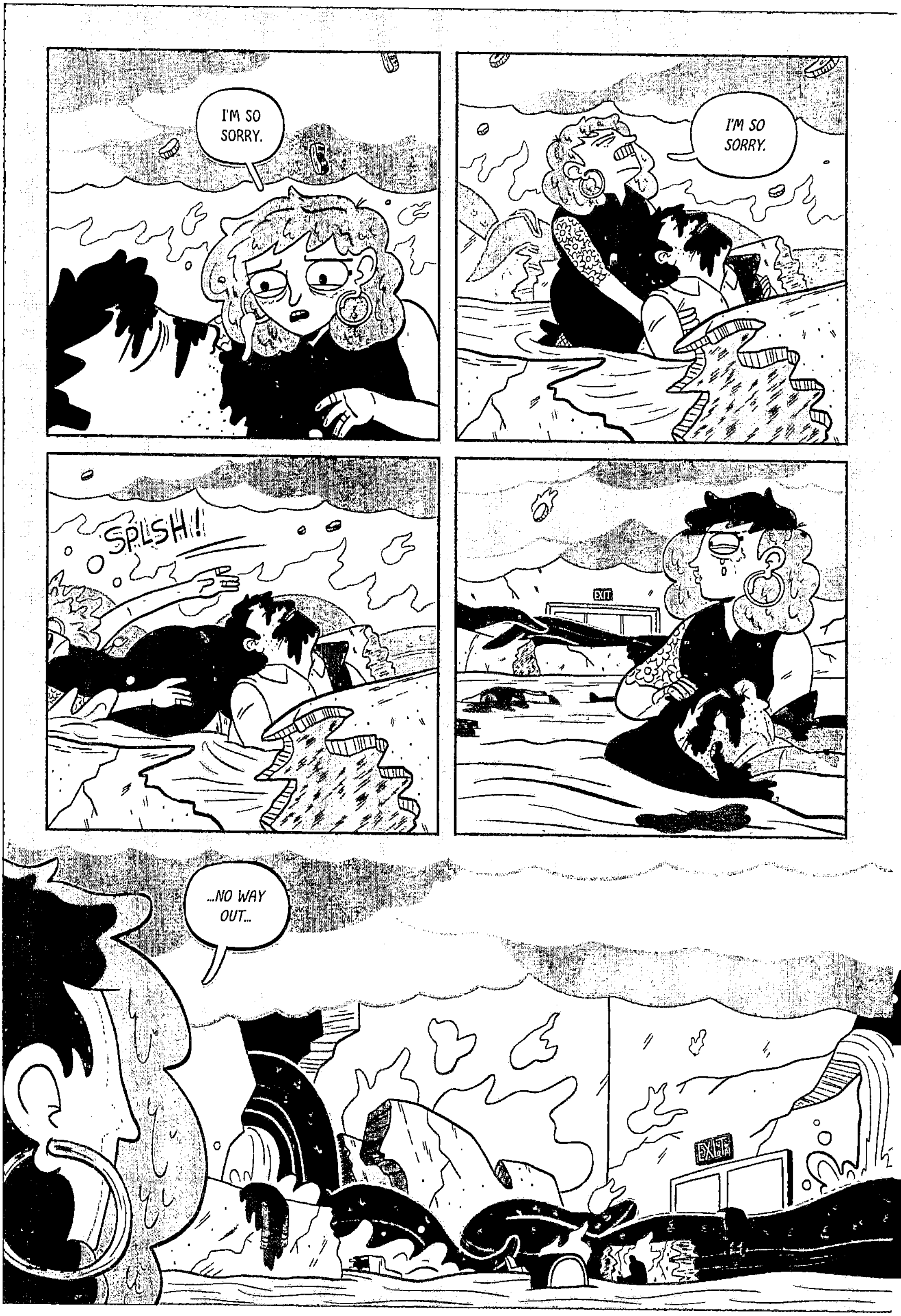
I'M SO SORRY.
I'M SO SORRY.
SPLSH!!
EXIT
...NO WAY OUT...
EXIT

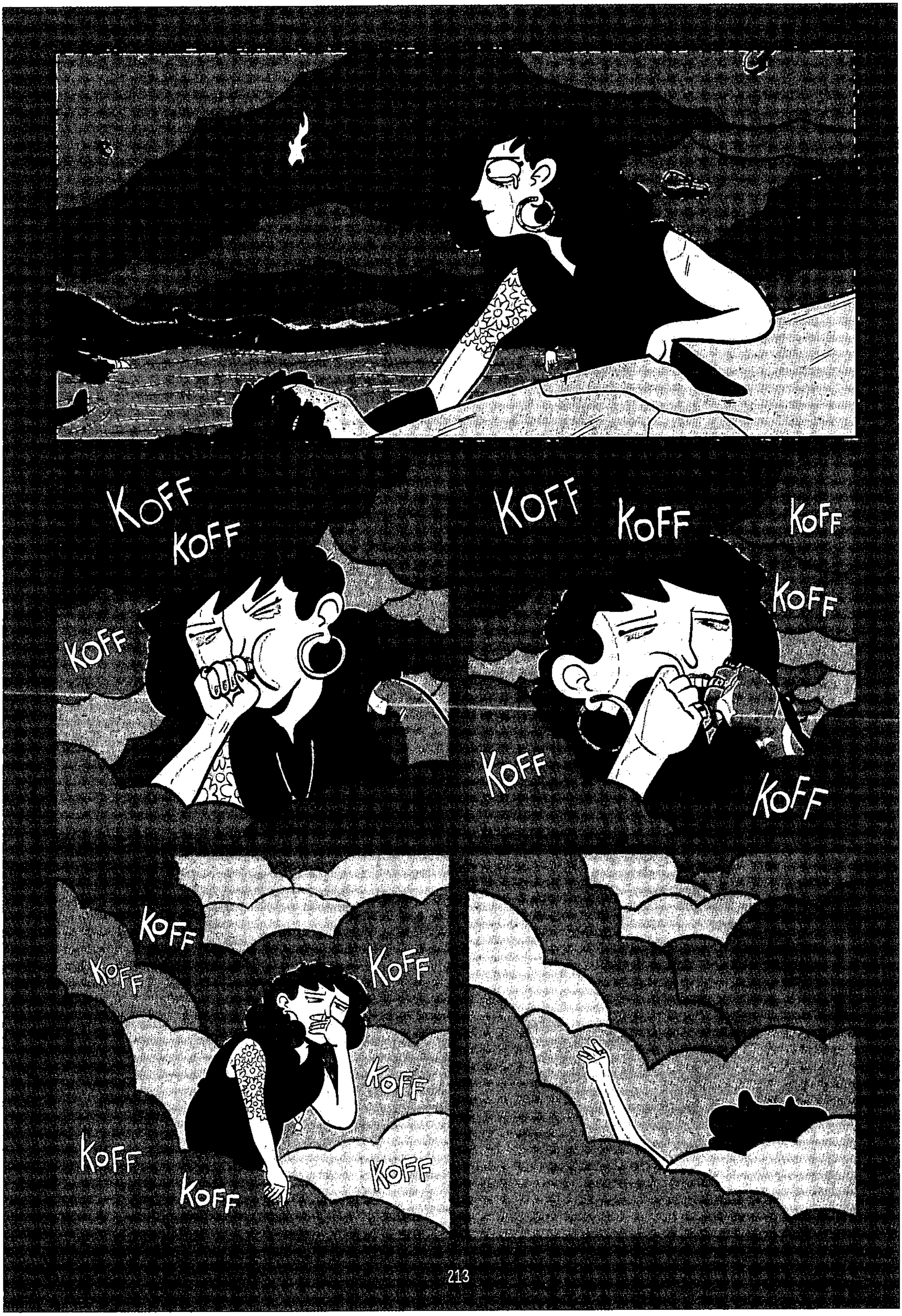
KOFF
KOFF
KOFF
KOFF
KOFF
KOFF
KOFF
KOFF
KOFF
KOFF
KOFF
KOFF
KOFF
KOFF
KOFF

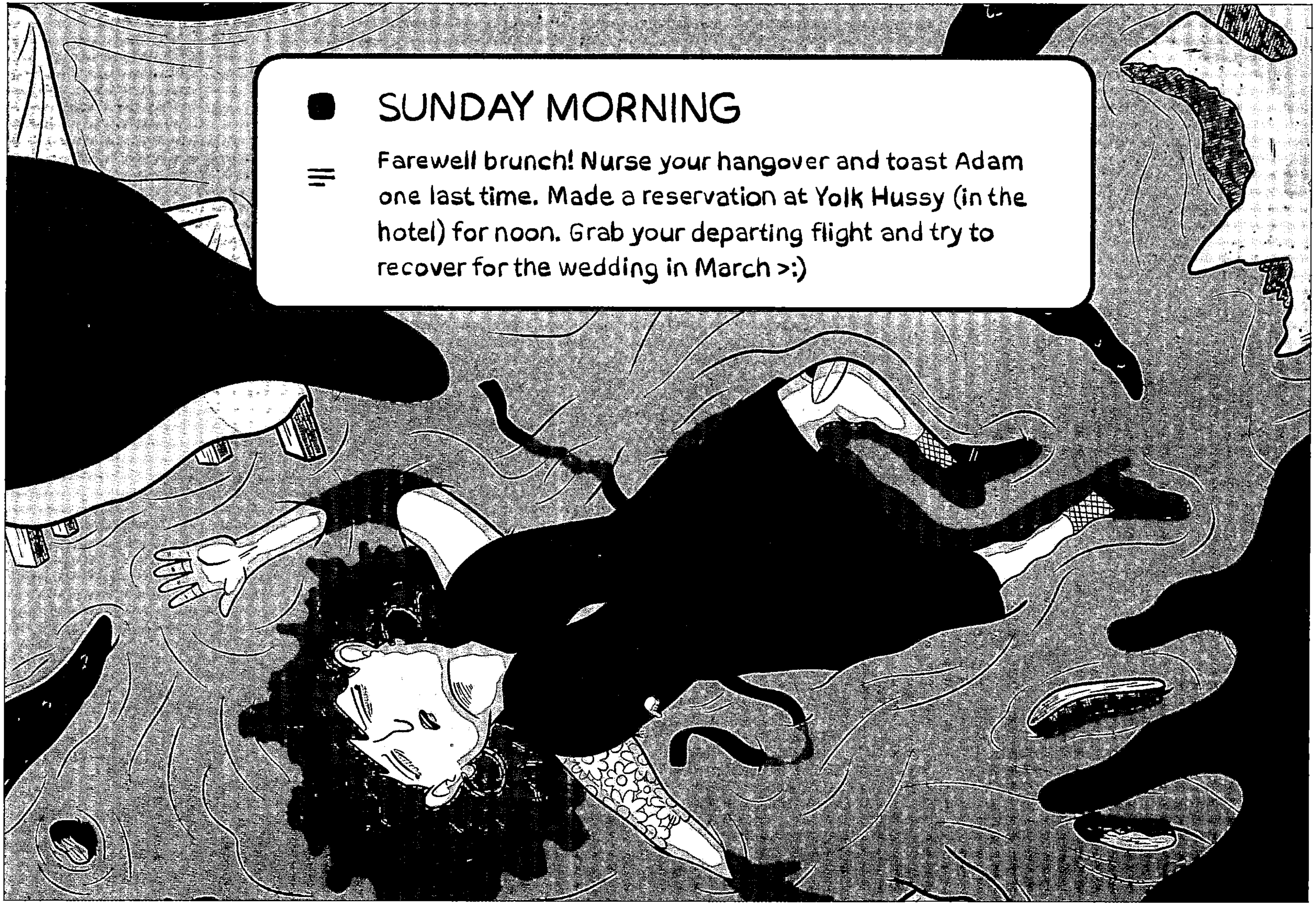
SUNDAY MORNING
Farewell brunch! Nurse your hangover and toast Adam one last time. Made a reservation at Yolk Hussy (in the hotel) for noon. Grab your departing flight and try to recover for the wedding in March >:)

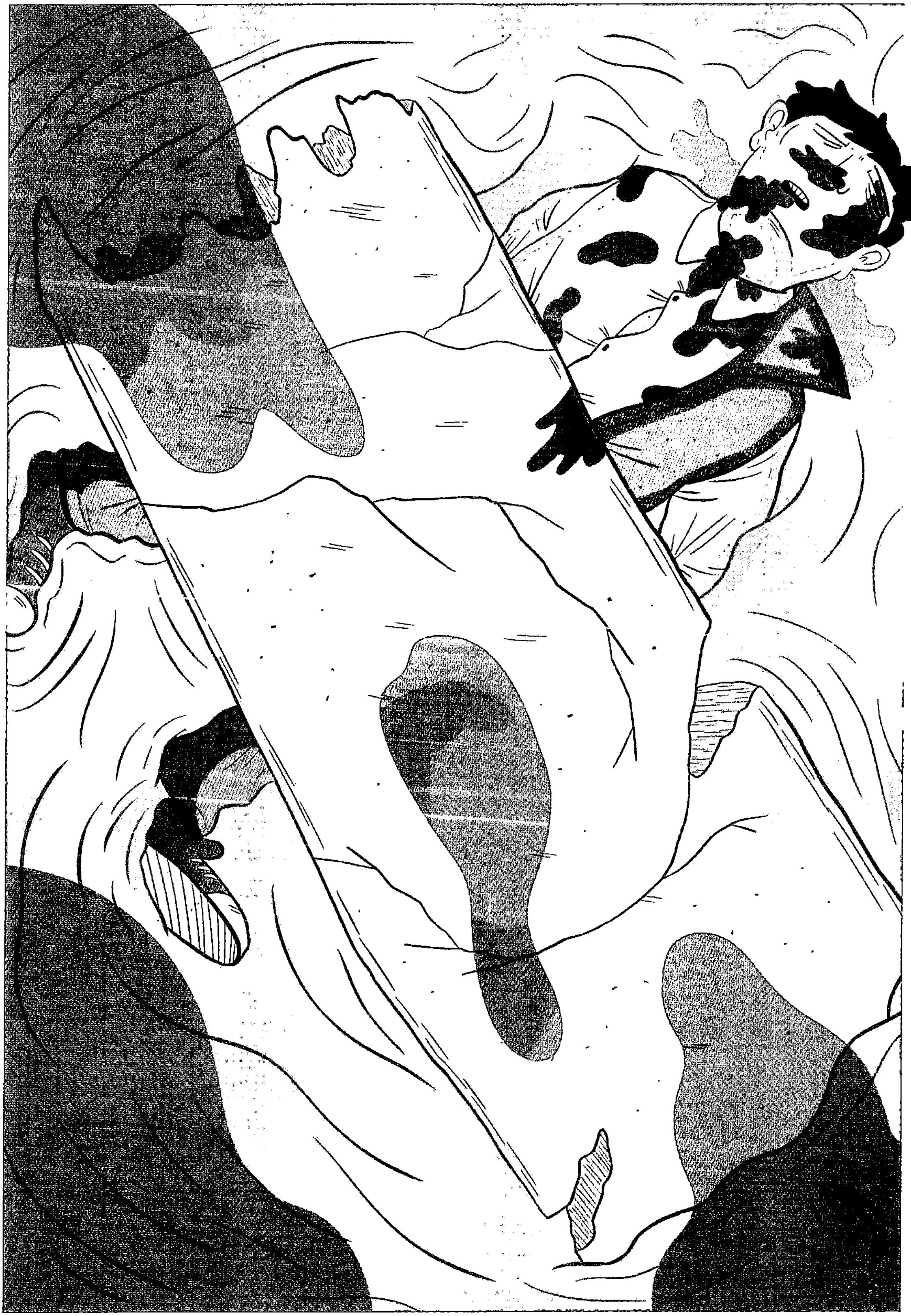

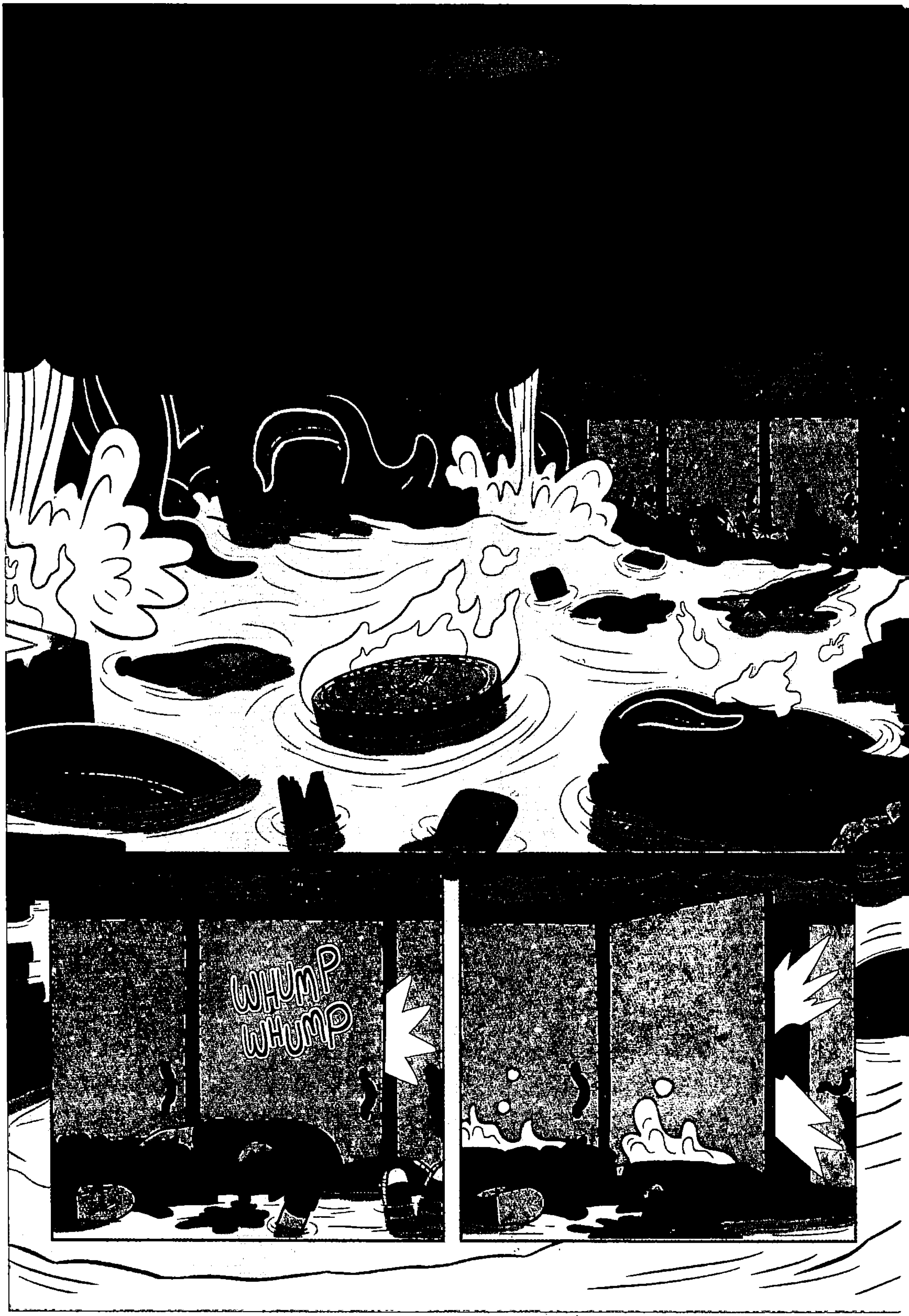
WHUMP
WHUMP

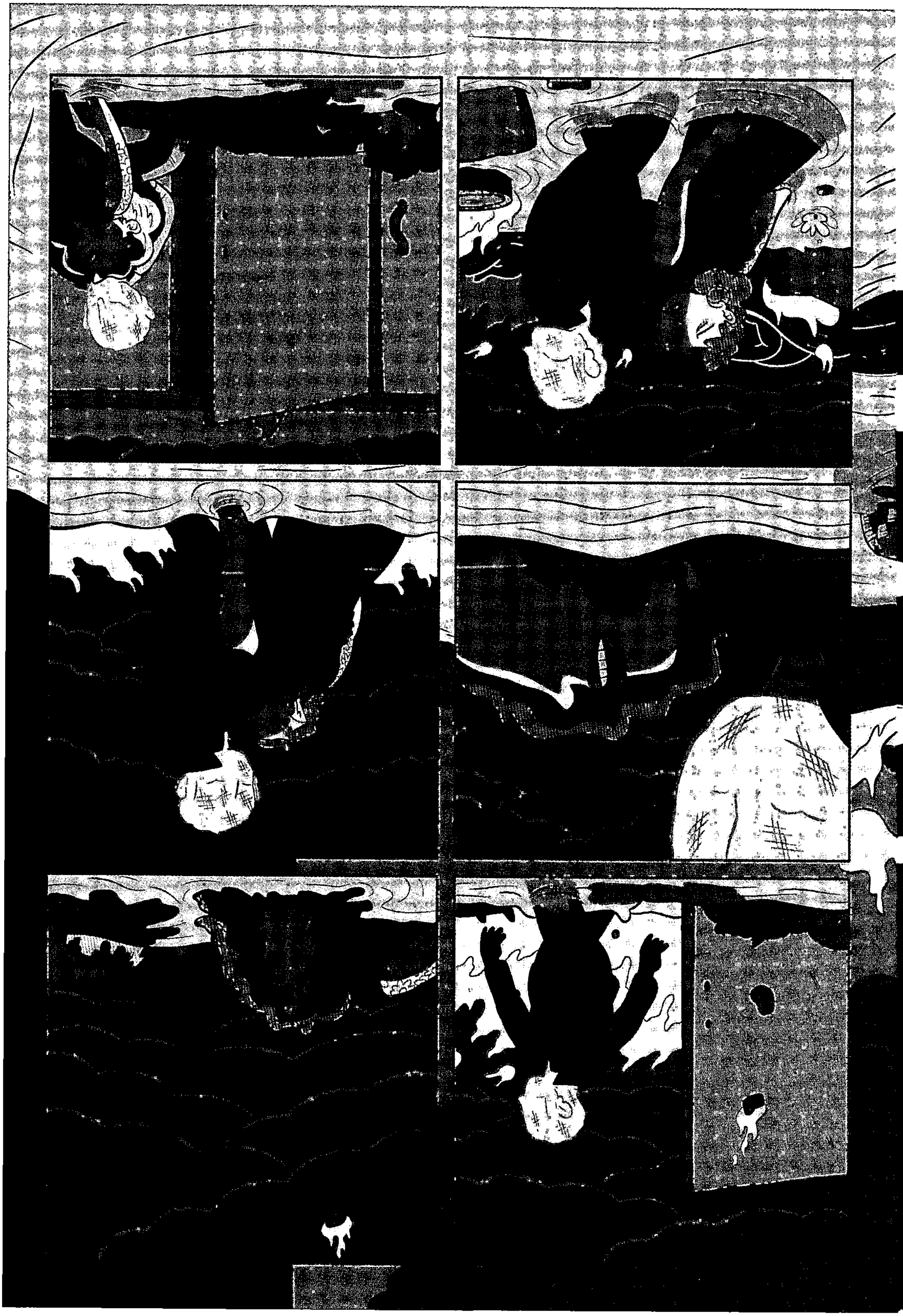

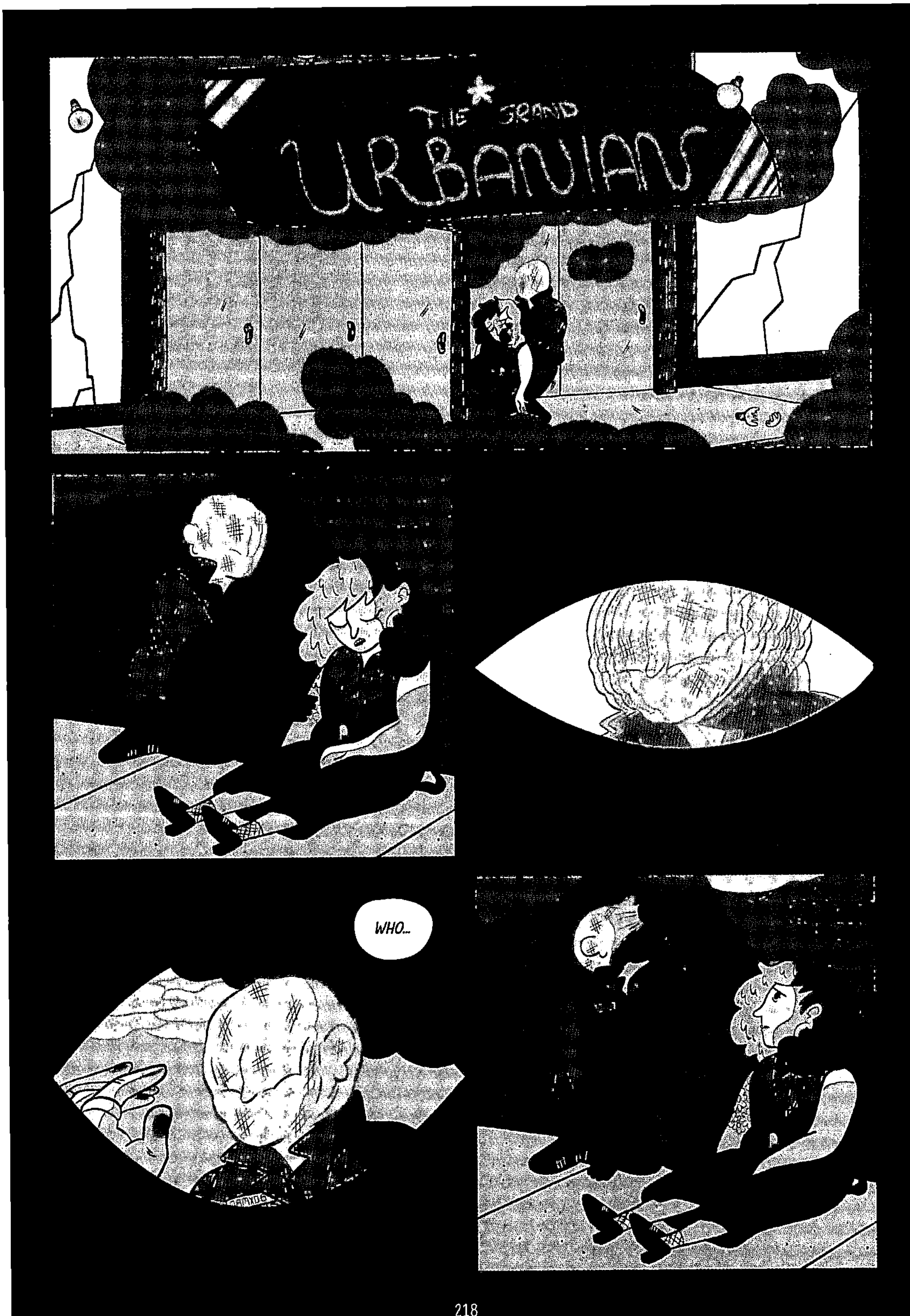
THE GRAND
URBANIANS
WHO...

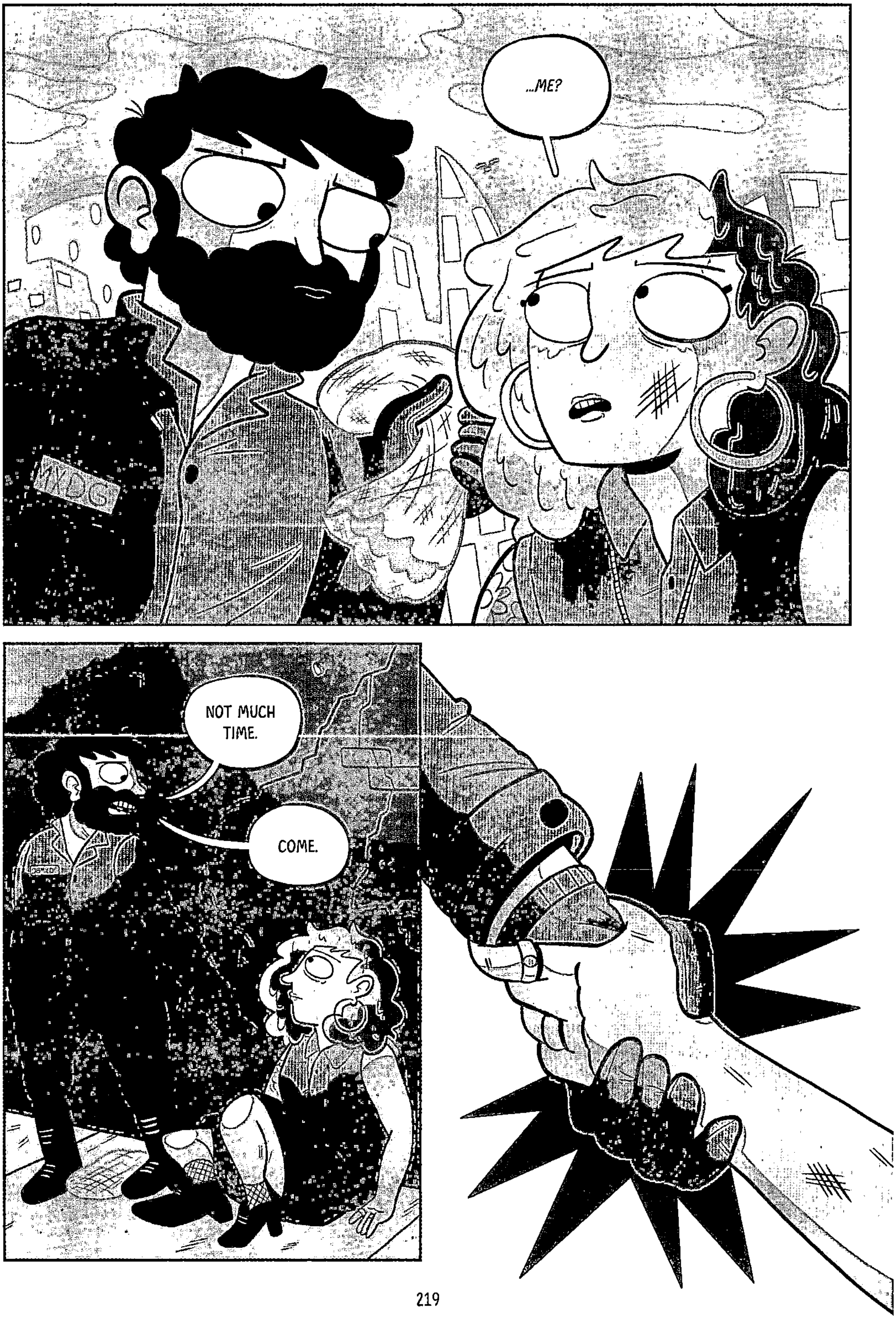
...ME?
MYDG
NOT MUCH TIME.
COME.

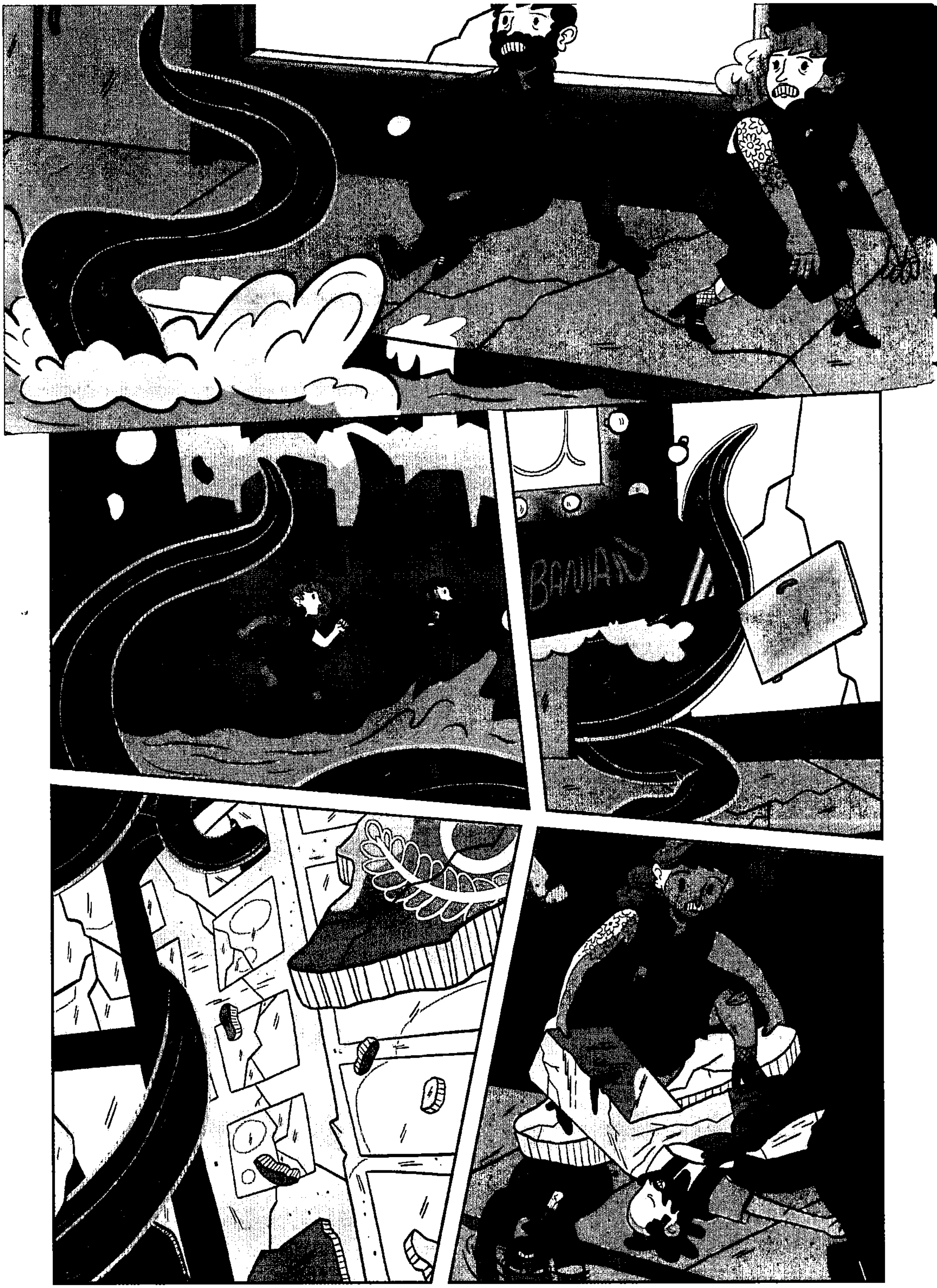

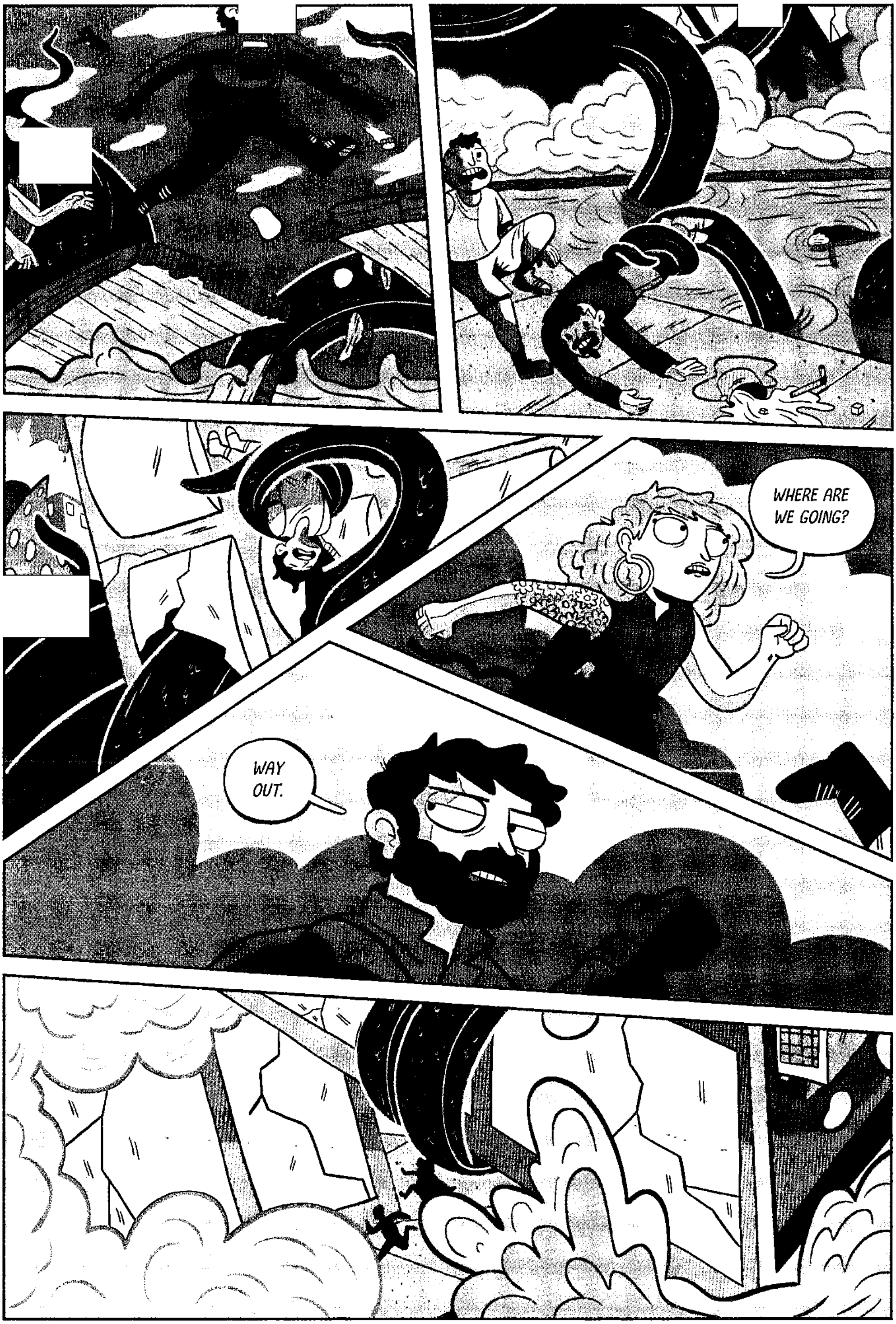
WHERE ARE WE GOING?
WAY OUT.

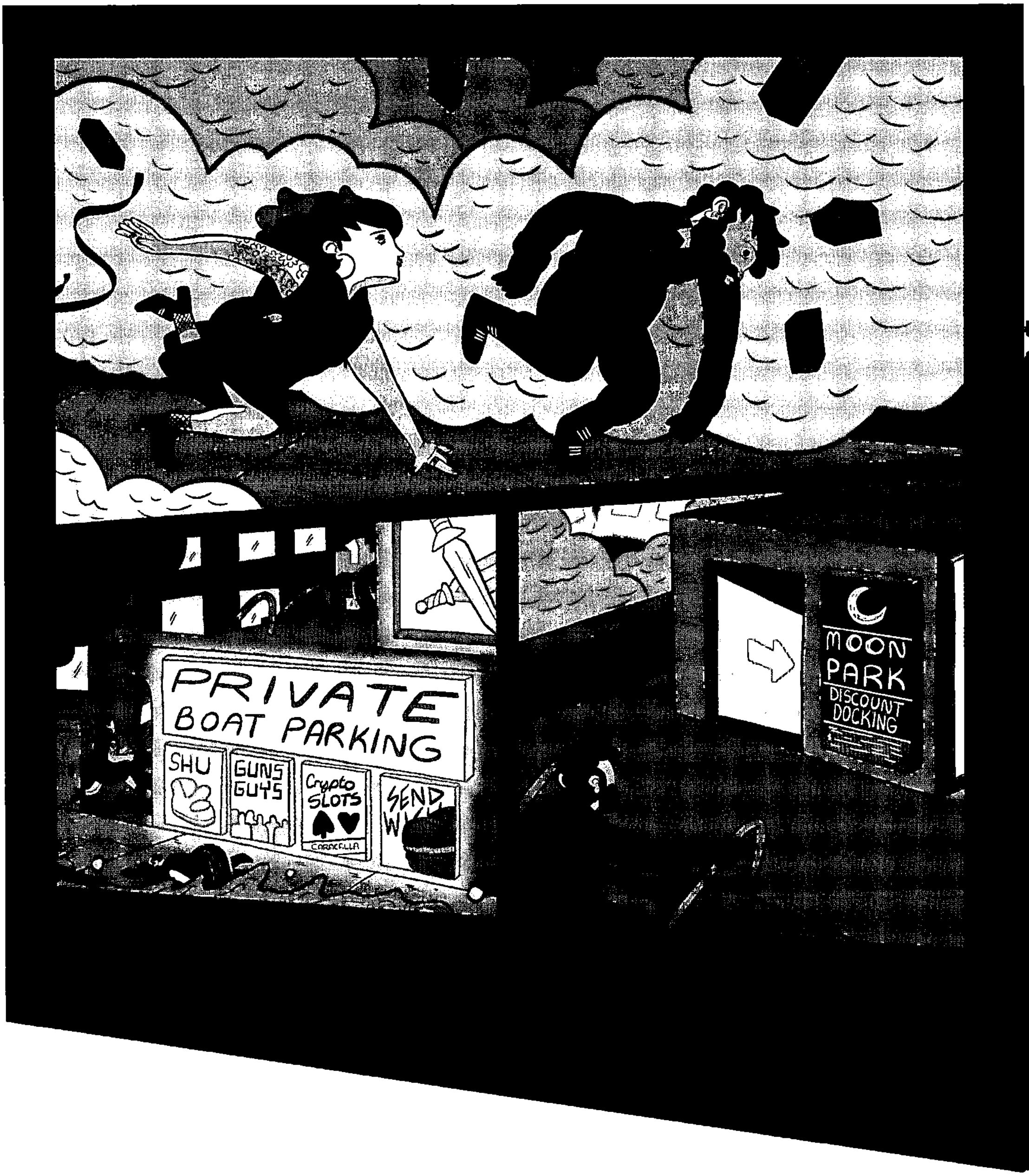
PRIVATE
BOAT PARKING
SHU
GUNS GUYS
Crypto SLOTS
SEND
MOON PARK
DISCOUNT DOCKING

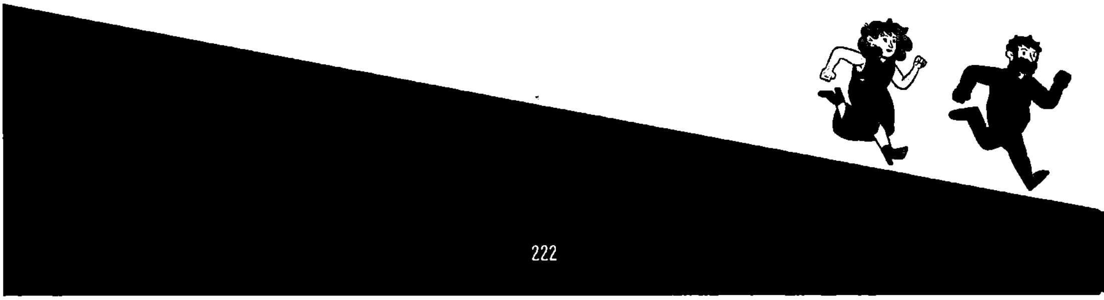

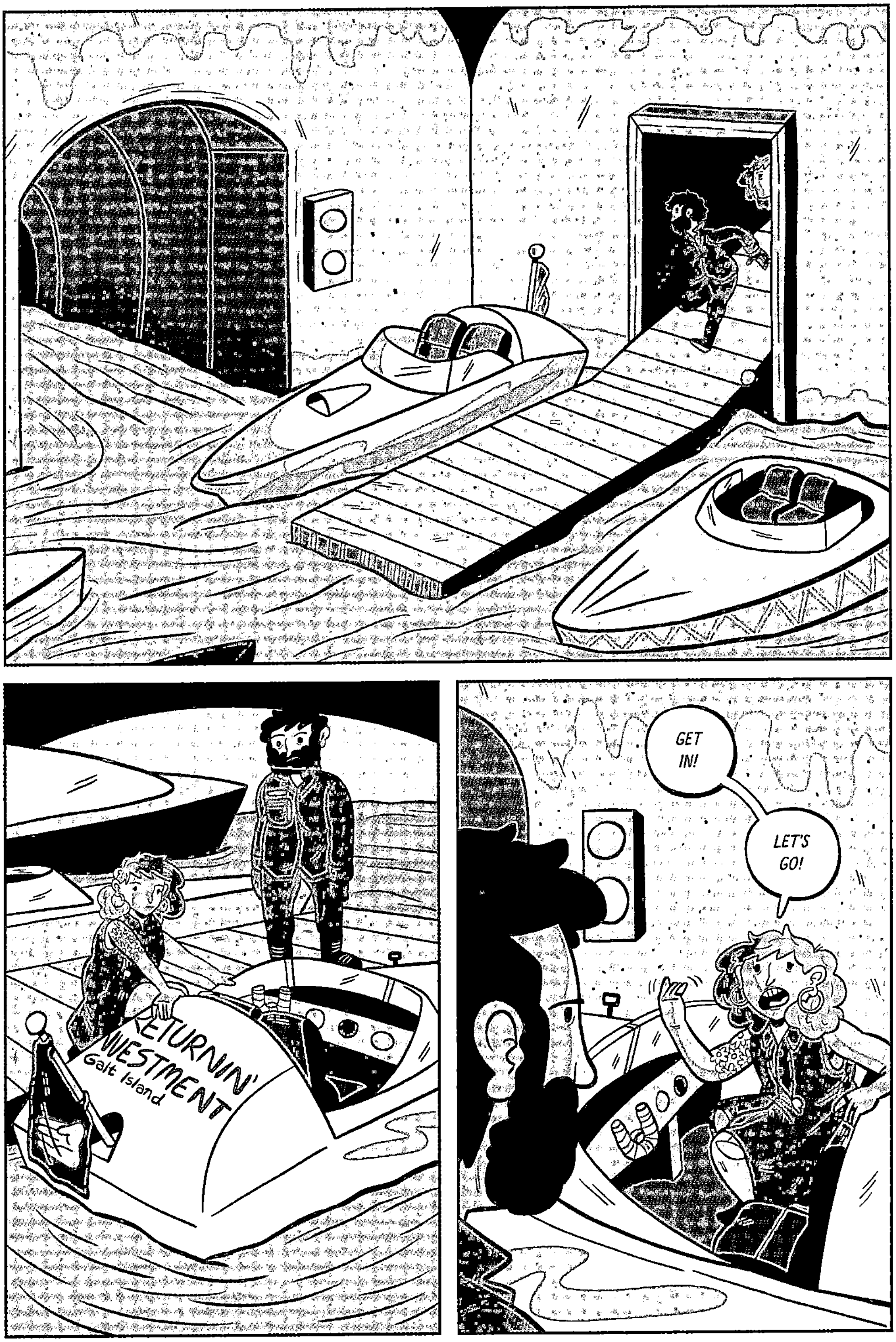

RETURNIN' INVESTMENT
Galt Island
GET IN!
LET'S GO!

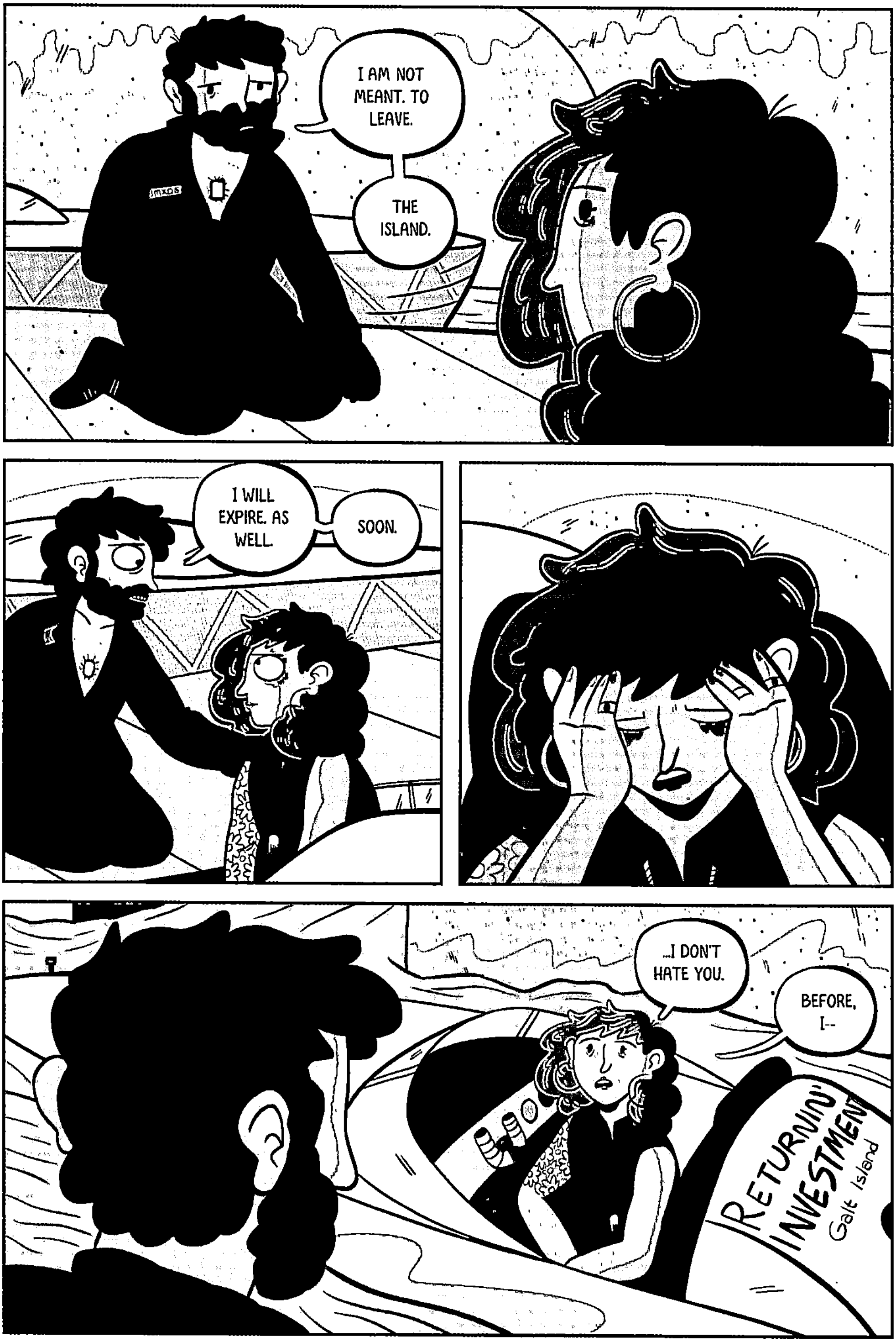
I AM NOT MEANT. TO LEAVE.
THE ISLAND.
I WILL EXPIRE. AS WELL.
SOON.
...I DON'T HATE YOU.
BEFORE, I--
RETURNIN' INVESTMENT
Galt Island

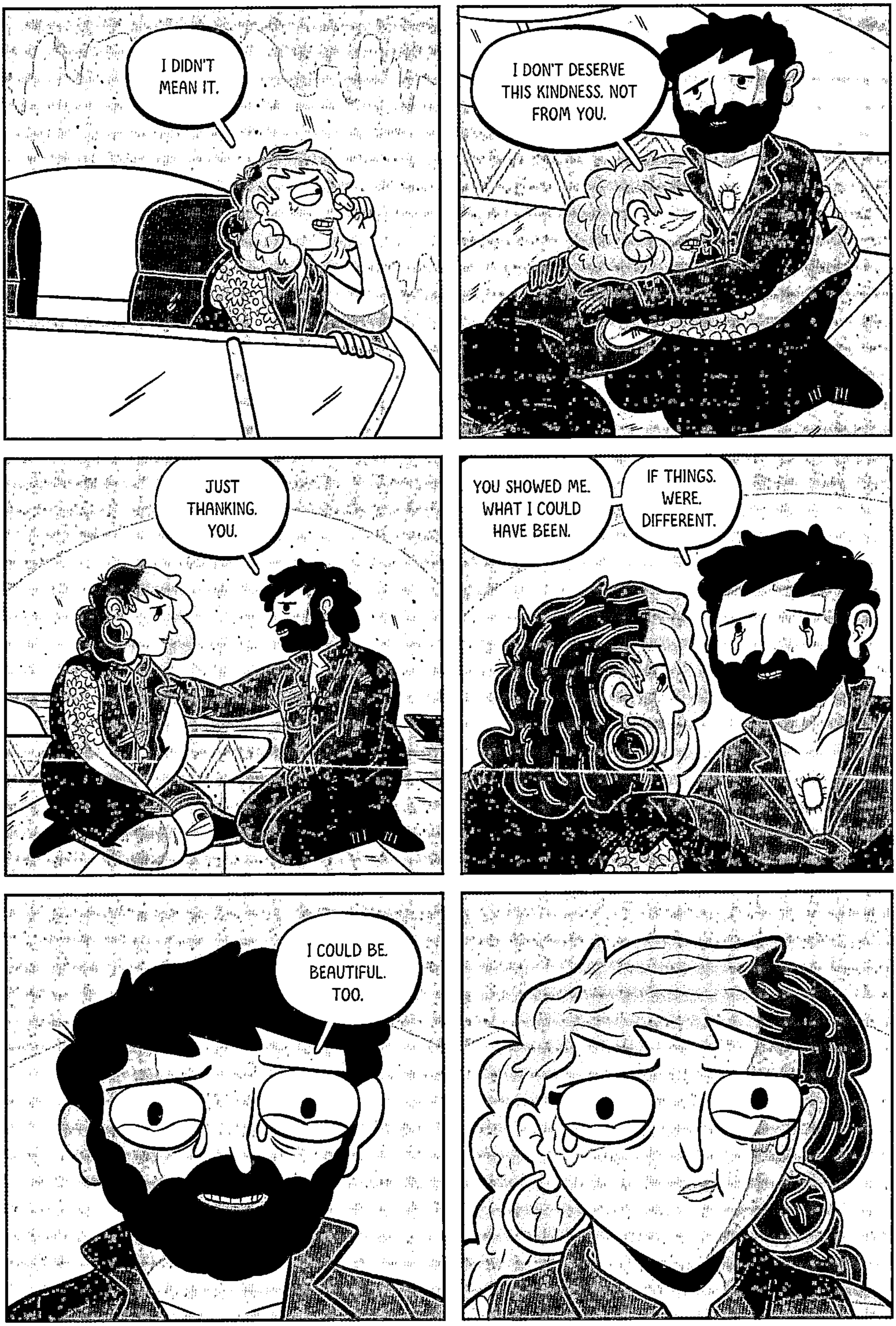
I DIDN'T MEAN IT.
I DON'T DESERVE THIS KINDNESS. NOT FROM YOU.
JUST THANKING. YOU.
YOU SHOWED ME. WHAT I COULD HAVE BEEN.
IF THINGS. WERE. DIFFERENT.
I COULD BE. BEAUTIFUL. TOO.

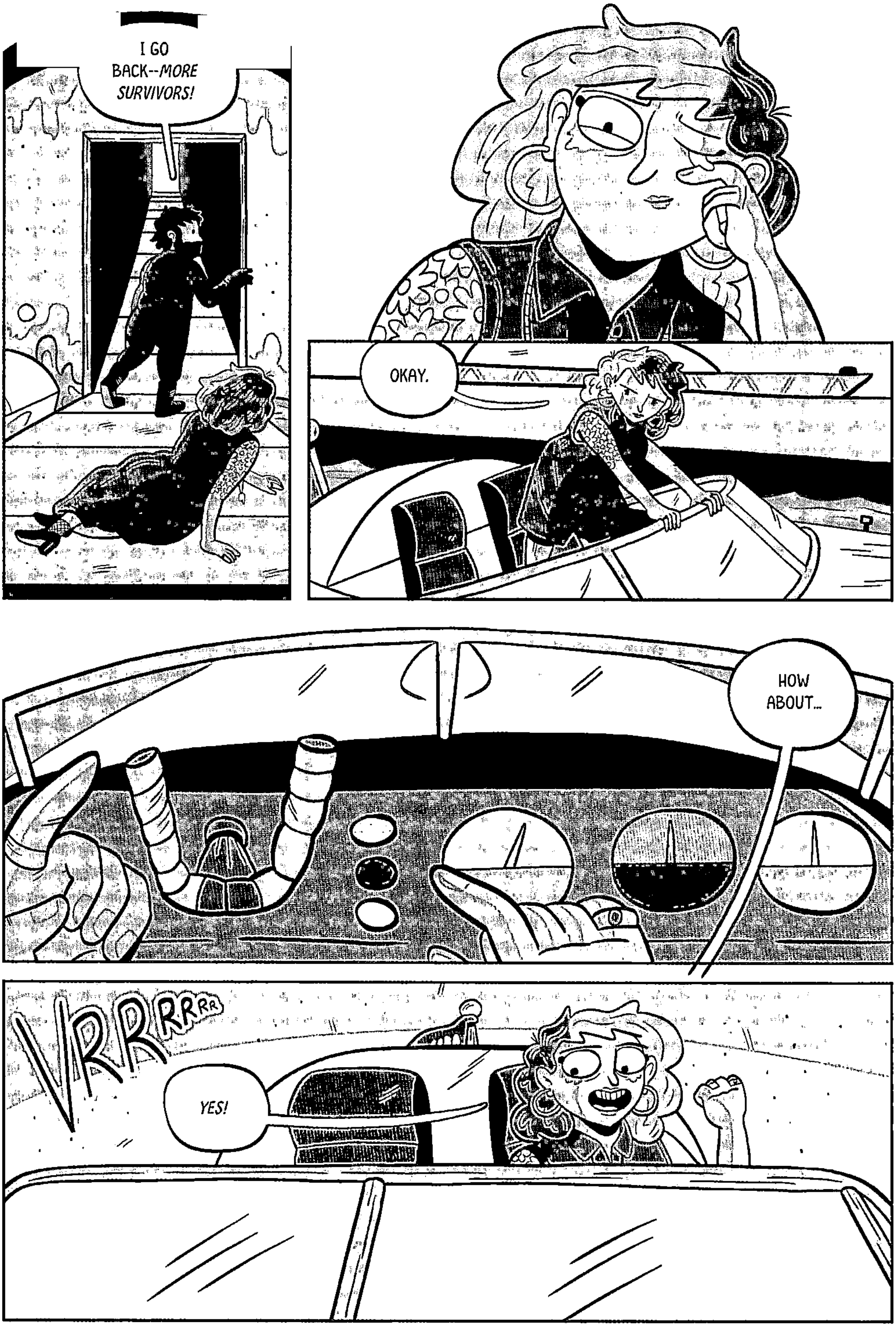

I GO BACK--*MORE SURVIVORS!*
OKAY.
HOW ABOUT...
VRRRRRR
YES!

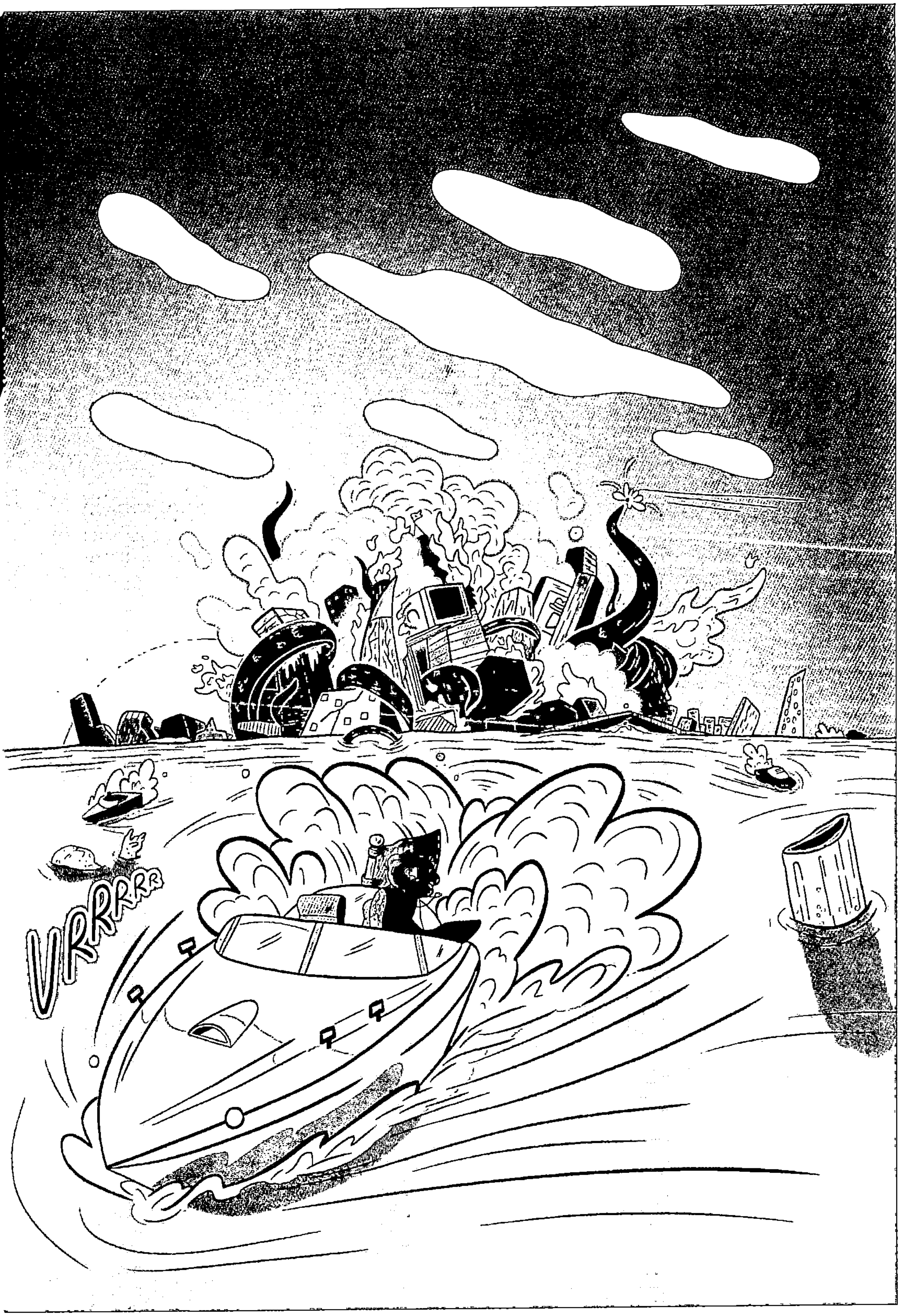
VRRRRRR

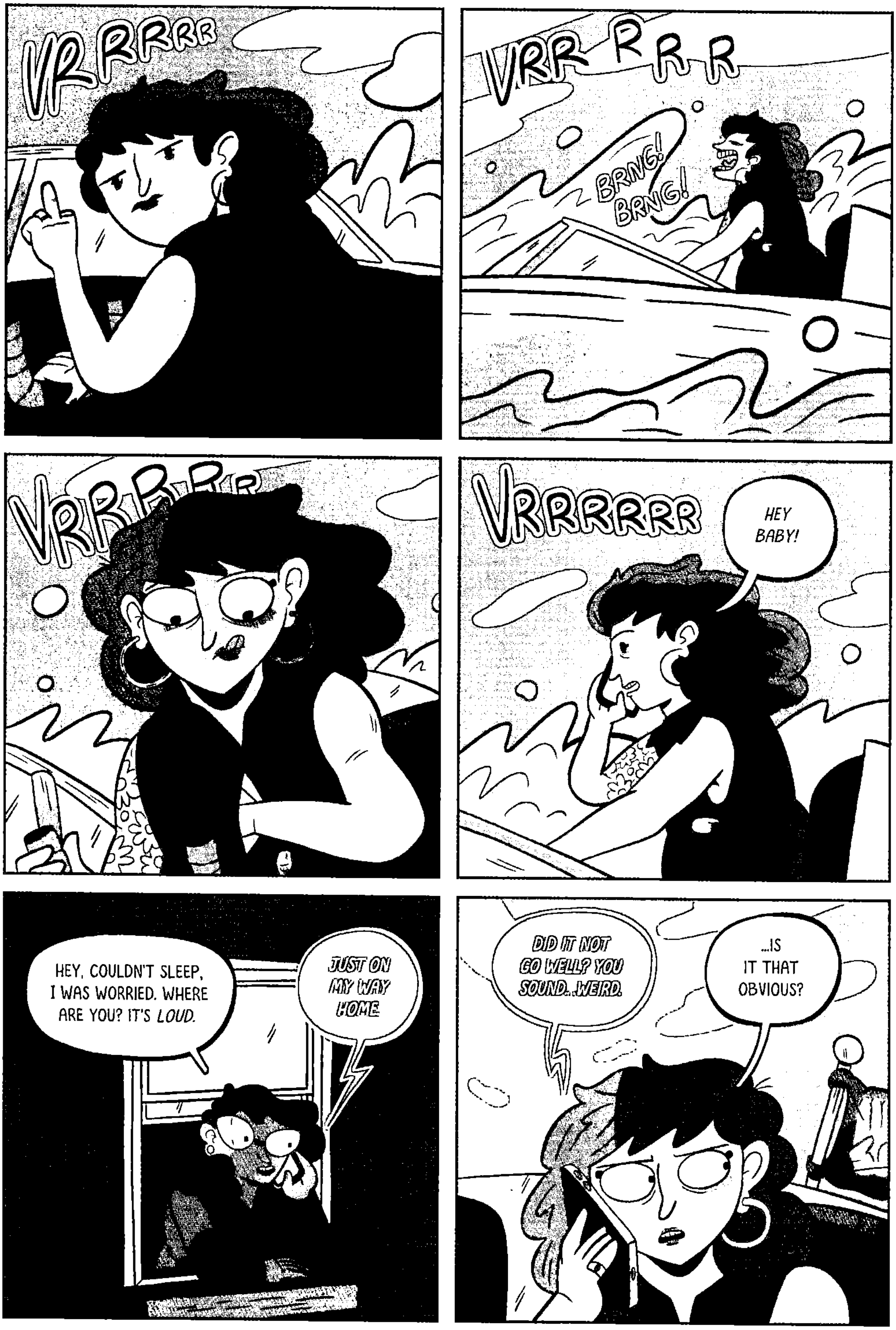
VRRRRR
VRR R R R
BRNG! BRNG!
VRRRRR
VRRRRRR
HEY BABY!
HEY, COULDN'T SLEEP, I WAS WORRIED. WHERE ARE YOU? IT'S *LOUD.*
JUST ON MY WAY HOME
DID IT NOT GO WELL? YOU SOUND...WEIRD.
...IS IT THAT OBVIOUS?

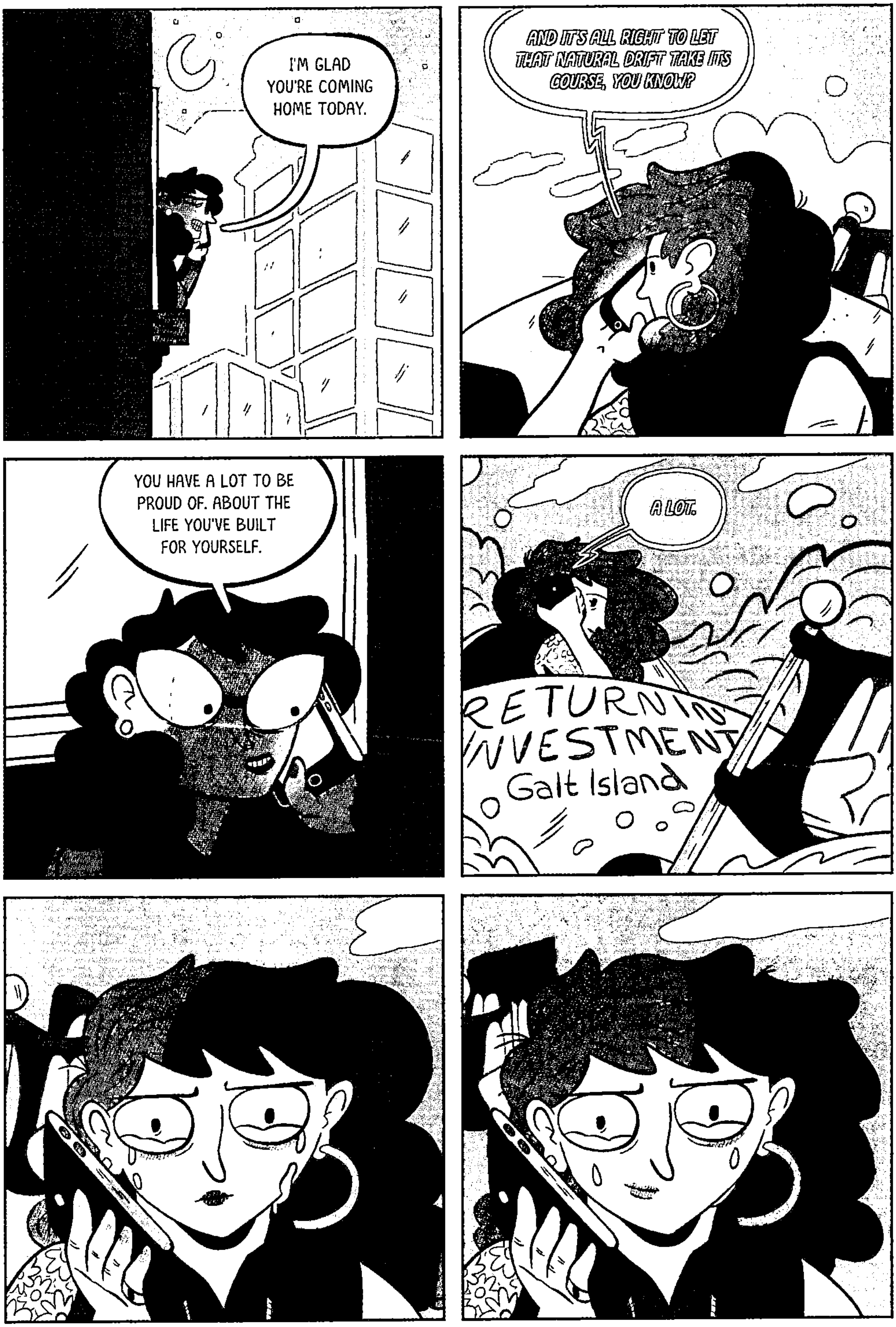
I'M GLAD YOU'RE COMING HOME TODAY.
AND IT'S ALL RIGHT TO LET THAT NATURAL DRIFT TAKE ITS COURSE, YOU KNOW?
YOU HAVE A LOT TO BE PROUD OF. ABOUT THE LIFE YOU'VE BUILT FOR YOURSELF.
A LOT.
RETURN INVESTMENT
Galt Island

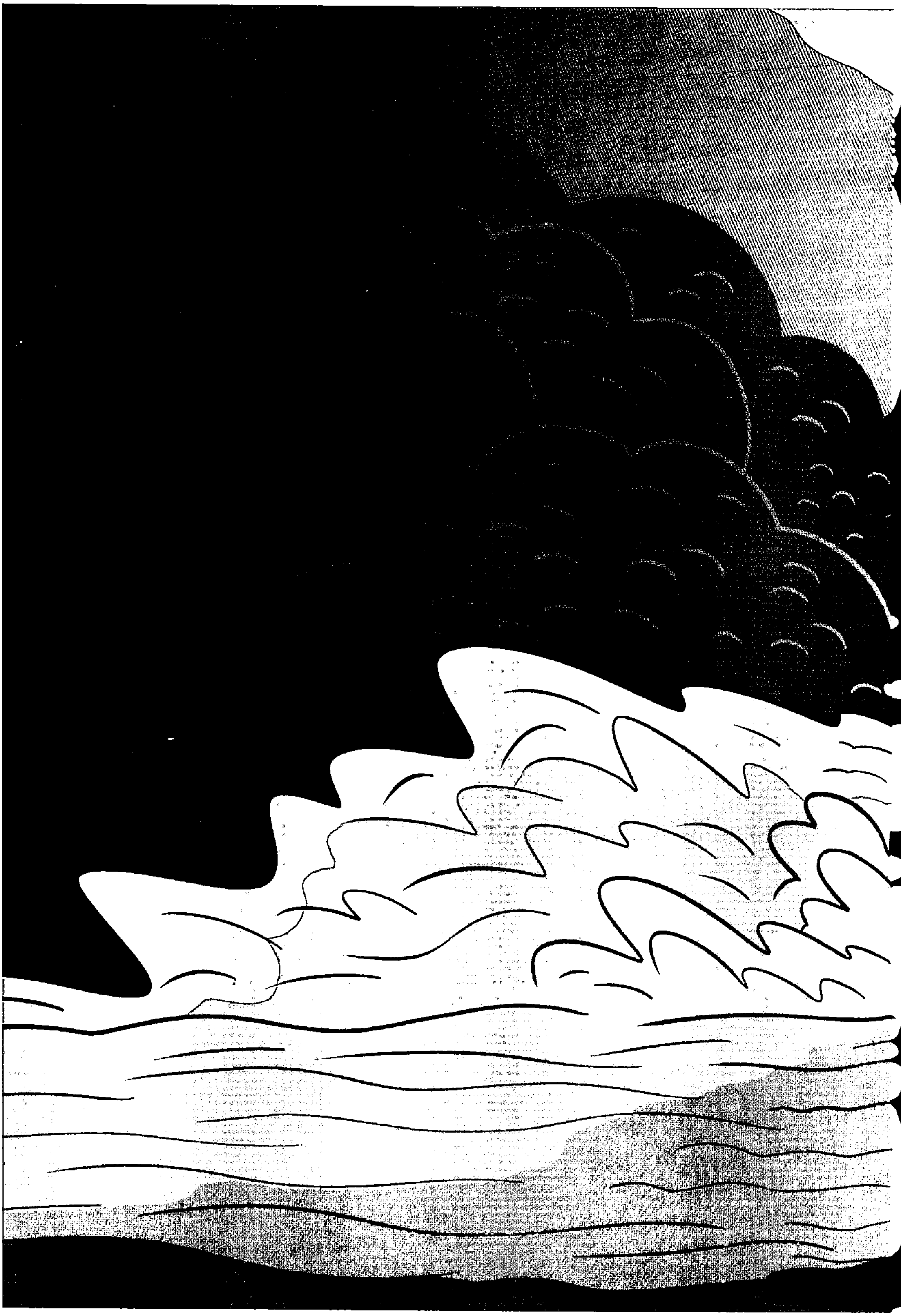

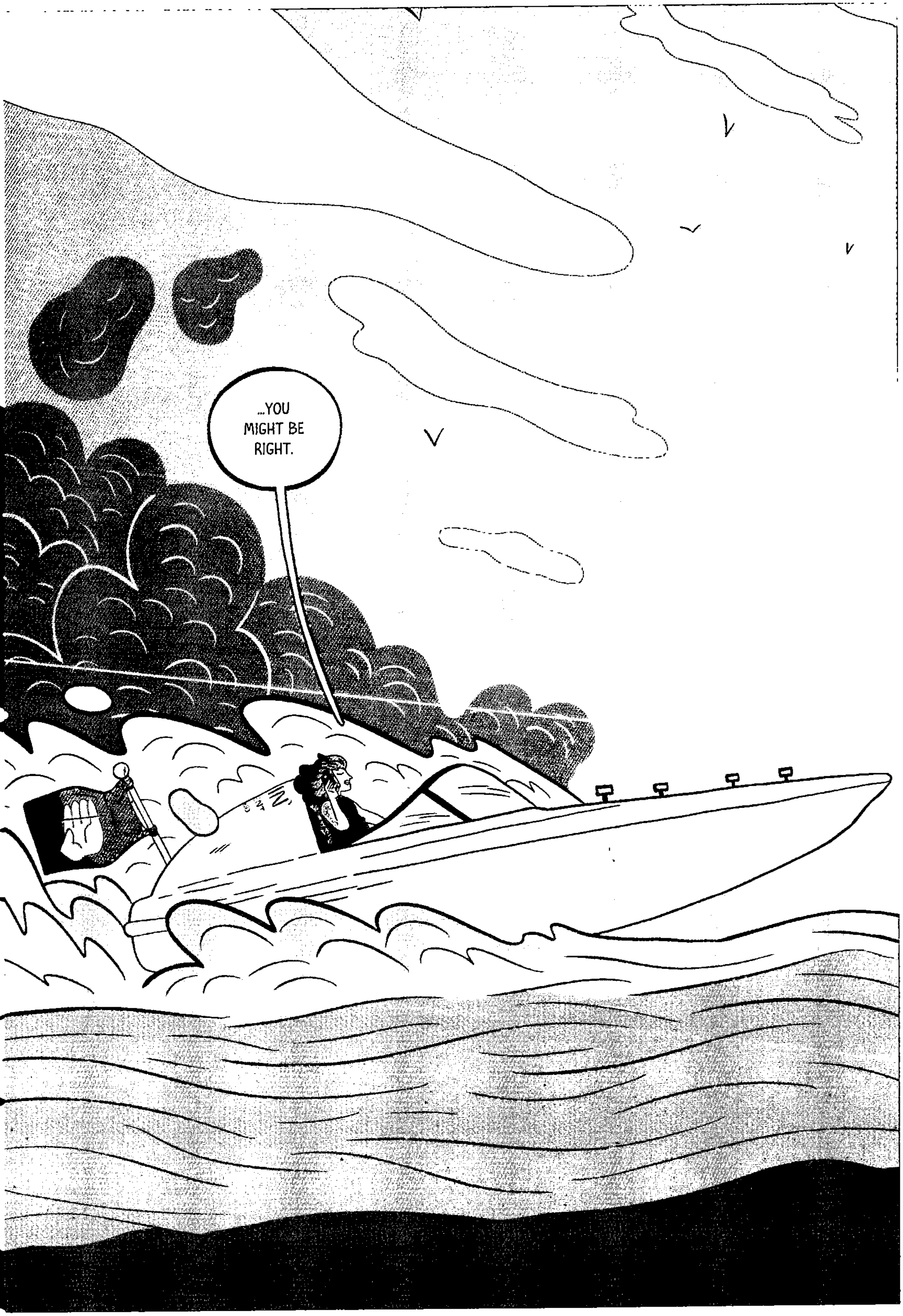
...YOU MIGHT BE RIGHT.

Mattie Lubchansky is a cartoonist and illustrator. They are an Ignatz winner, a Herblock Prize finalist, and the author of *The Antifa Super-Soldier Cookbook.* They live in beautiful Queens, NEW YORK, with their spouse.

Photo credit: Sylvie Rosokoff

This is a book about recognizing the community that's right under your nose. As such, I have too many people to thank for where I am today, but I'll have to try. My spouse, Jaya, most of all, for her truly endless love, support, and devotion, for always being my first reader, and for building the life I've always wanted to live alongside me. Nothing would exist without you--not this book, not even me.

My parents, Steve and Gale, for getting me a drafting table instead of making me go outside. Danny Lavery and Nicole Cliffe, my kindred spirits--for letting me do whatever the hell I wanted to in front of a nurturing audience. Matt Bors, for his assistance in my growth as an artist and writer. The rest of the Nib team--Eleri, Sarah, Andy, and Whit--for being constantly inspiring people to work alongside. Jon Rosenberg, for being my first comics mentor, which I will never forget. My actual college friends--Josh, Chris, Dave, and Dave--lovely and caring men all. All my comrades at the People's Bodega and the Rolling Library, whose work makes my life more worthwhile. My FAITH/VOID bandmates Tim and Brad, who provide a creative outlet that means the world to me. The people whose early reads and story notes proved invaluable: Jess Zimmerman, Mike Anton, Mark Popham, Emily Hughes, Calvin Kasulke, Brandy Jensen, James Frankie Thomas, and Benjamin Alison Wilgus. My incredible agent of eight years, Kate McKean, who I wouldn't have done this without. The entire team at Pantheon, who, inadvisably, took on this preposterous book to add to their intimidating library: Lisa Lucas, Altie Karper, Cat Courtade, Andy Hughes, Peggy Samedi, production editor Kathleen Fridella, copy editor Amy Brosey, proofreader Chuck Thompson, publicist Amy Hagedorn, marketer Sarah Pannenberg, Zuleima Ugalde, and especially my gracious editor, Anna Kaufman. Thank you as well to Beth Fileti, who made the handwriting font used in this book.

And last, to every trans person in my life--every queer, every degenerate--who showed me what it could be like: that I could be beautiful too.

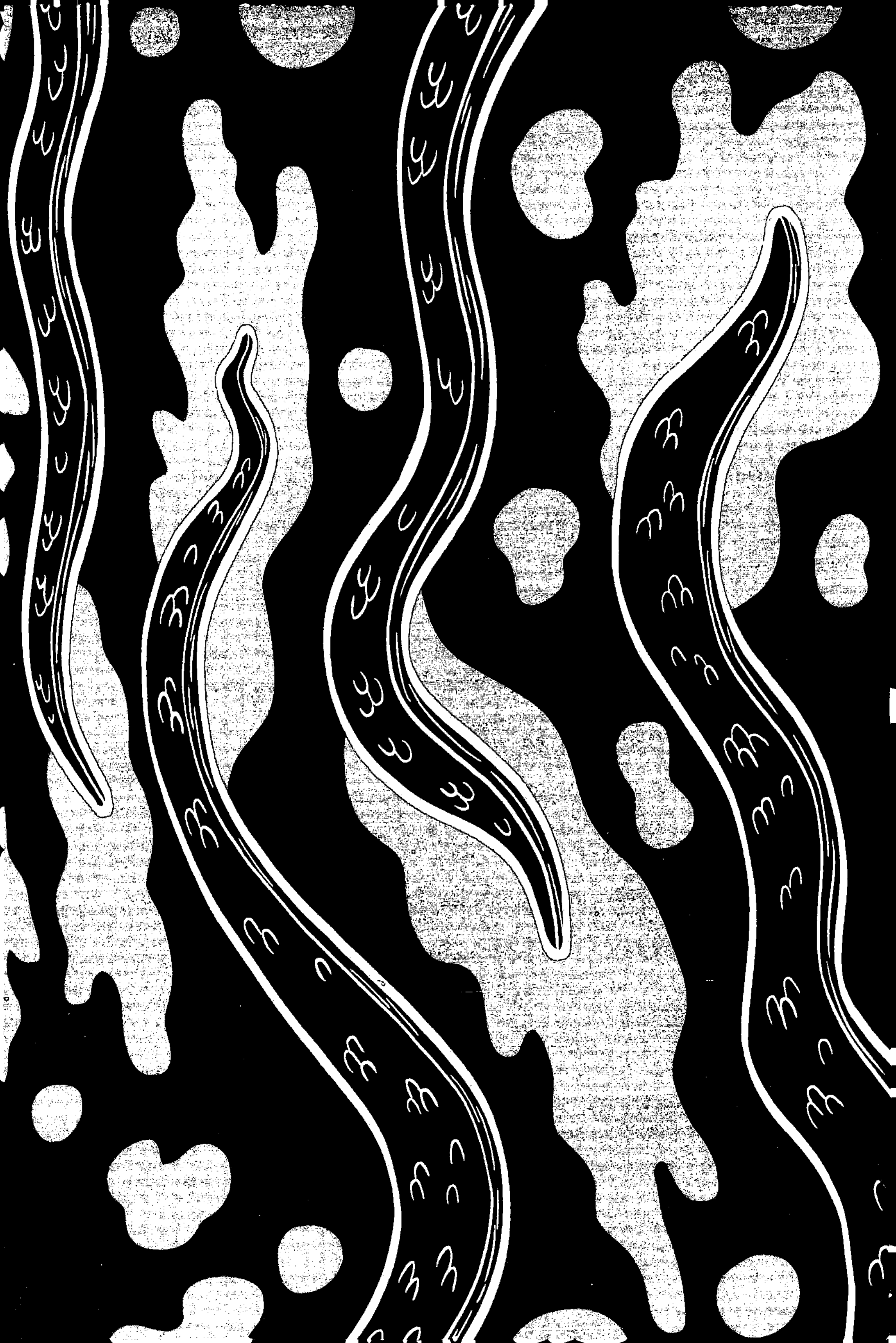